# ALONE IN THE WILD

# ALONE IN THE WILD

## A ROCKTON NOVEL

## KELLEY ARMSTRONG

MINOTAUR BOOKS
NEW YORK

First published in the United States by Minotaur Books, an imprint of St. Martin's Publishing Group

ALONE IN THE WILD. Copyright © 2020 by KLA Fricke Inc. All rights reserved. Printed in the United States of America. For information, address St. Martin's Publishing Group, 120 Broadway, New York, NY 10271.

www.minotaurbooks.com

Library of Congress Cataloging-in-Publication Data

Names: Armstrong, Kelley, author.
Title: Alone in the wild: a Rockton novel / Kelley Armstrong.
Description: First edition. | New York: Minotaur Books, 2020. | Series:
    Casey Duncan novels; 5
Identifiers: LCCN 2019038492 | ISBN 9781250254283 (hardcover) | ISBN
    9781250254290 (ebook)
Subjects: GSAFD: Suspense fiction. | Mystery fiction.
Classification: LCC PR9199.4.A8777 A79 2020 | DDC 813/.6—dc23
LC record available at https://lccn.loc.gov/2019038492

Our books may be purchased in bulk for promotional, educational, or business use. Please contact your local bookseller or the Macmillan Corporate and Premium Sales Department at 1-800-221-7945, extension 5442, or by email at MacmillanSpecialMarkets@macmillan.com.

First Edition: February 2020

10  9  8  7  6  5  4  3  2  1

For Jeff

# ALONE IN THE WILD

# ONE

I wake buried under a hundred and forty pounds of dog. Storm knows she's not allowed on the bed, so I lie there, brain slowly churning, until I remember I'm not *in* bed. I'm on the ground. Cold, hard winter ground—the floor of a tent that is definitely not big enough for two adults and a Newfoundland dog. Which tells me one adult is gone.

I lift my head. Sure enough, there's no sign of Dalton. I peer at the glow of sunrise seeping through the canvas. I've slept in. It's December in the Yukon, when dawn means it's about . . . I lift my watch. Yep, 10 A.M.

I groan. Storm echoes it as she tries to stand, an impossible feat within the confines of this tent.

"Where's Eric?" I ask.

Shockingly, the dog doesn't answer. I blink back the fog of a night that started with tequila and ended with . . . Well, it ended strenuously enough to explain why I'm still in bed at ten, though apparently my partner had no trouble rising early.

We'd left Storm outside last night. That wasn't cruel. It's hovering around the freezing mark, positively balmy for this time of year. Storm has her thick coat and her companion, a wolf-dog named Raoul. We'd brought them on our weekend getaway both for company and for training, Storm as a tracker and Raoul as hunter. Raoul's master doesn't hunt. Not animals, at least.

If Storm is in the tent with the flap closed, that means Dalton let her in. It also means he's taken Raoul. I rub my eyes and spot a note pinned to the tent flap.

When I push Storm, she grunts and shifts enough for me to scrabble over her and pluck off the note.

Hunting. Back for lunch. Coffee in thermos. Don't wander.

The note is the model of reticent efficiency, and I would say that fits our sheriff to a tee, but I've also read his near-poetic academic and philosophical musings, ones that shouldn't come from anyone without a Ph.D., much less a guy with zero formal schooling. That is also our sheriff. Two sides to the same coin. Only I get to see the second one.

I find not only coffee but breakfast in a dog-proof pouch at the end of the bed. Scrambled eggs with venison sausage, and bannock with . . . I lift the hard bread, still warm from the fire, oozing gooey brown dots. Bannock with chocolate chips. I laugh and take a bite. I won't say I'm a bannock fan, but chocolate makes everything better.

I happily munch the bannock and wash it down with coffee. I don't toss any scraps to Storm. Honestly, at her size, she'd never even taste them. Instead, she gets one of my sausages. As for the "don't wander" part of Dalton's note, I'm interpreting that as a suggestion rather than the imperative it seems. Oh, naturally he hopes I'll take it as a command, but he knows better than to expect that. He means for me to stay close, and I will. I'm not about to stay in the tent for two more hours, though.

When I finish breakfast, I open the flap, and Storm clambers out to romp in the snow. She's fourteen months old, which means she's outwardly a full-grown dog, but inside she's still a pup. At thirty-two, I understand the feeling. Or, I should say, I've regained the feeling after sixteen months in Rockton. Before that, while I remember a girl endlessly on the move, endlessly into mischief, that girl vanished when I was eighteen, shoved into hiding by the kind of mistake that banishes one's carefree inner child. Out here, I've found her again . . . at least, when I'm not on duty as Detective Casey Butler.

Dalton and I are on vacation, which means we're taking an entire two days off. Down south, we'd call that a weekend. Up here, with a police force of three, we take time off where we can find it.

Things have been slow in Rockton. The holidays are approaching, and it's as if people decided to cut us slack as a seasonal gift. No assaults. No robberies. No murders. In a town of under two hundred people, the last should be obvious, but this is Rockton. Murder capital of the world, someone used to say. That someone knew exactly what she was talking about, having turned out to be a killer herself.

Rockton is special. For better or worse. Mostly better, but the crime rate is one of those "worse" parts. We can't expect otherwise, really. We are a town of fugitives. Everyone here is running from something. Some are victims, on the run from ex-partners, stalkers, anyone who might want them dead through no fault of their own. This is the true purpose of Rockton—a refuge for those fleeing persecution. It's also home to white-collar criminals, whose misdeeds pay our bills. Then there are those whose mistakes—often violent ones—brought them to Rockton under expensively bought cover stories given even to Dalton. So it's no surprise that we have a murder rate.

For now, it's quiet, and has been for six months. Which means Dalton and I can take an actual weekend off.

Storm and I play in the snow for about an hour before I realize that I should have stoked the fire first. While Dalton had left it blazing for me, he's obviously been gone awhile, and by the time Storm and I collapse, exhausted, the fire is down to embers. I add another log, but it's not going to take. We need kindling.

That's life up here. Constant work just to survive. Heat doesn't come at the flick of a switch. Food isn't the nearest fast-food joint away. Water isn't a simple matter of turning on a faucet. In Rockton, we simulate modern living as best we can—there are restaurants in town, and water does come from taps through a pump system—but everyone needs to work to put food in that grocery, to fill the water tanks when the stream runs low. One quickly develops a healthy respect for our pioneer ancestors.

Storm and I head out to gather kindling. Soon, though, I realize that new-fallen snow is going to complicate the task. Even if I unearth sticks, they won't be dry. That's fine—the best source of winter kindling is dead trees. I'm maybe a few hundred feet from the camp when I find a brown-needled pine that's been crowded out by sturdier siblings.

I start breaking off twigs. Storm dances about, her second wind gale-force strong. When I throw a stick, she chases it, only to notice I'm still snapping off branches. She shoots me a sullen scowl.

"I'm not Eric," I say. "I play fetch properly."

More scowling. Then she flings herself to the ground with a flounce and a sigh.

"Fine," I say with a laugh. "Once and only once."

I take another branch and hold it over my head. She stays where she is, watching me, refusing to fall for this again. I throw it, and she doesn't move until I take off after the branch. Then she bolts up and runs for it.

I'm one pace ahead, Storm right on my heels. She veers to

pass me, and I throw myself down in a home-plate slide. I grab the stick, flip onto my back, and fist-pump it in the air . . . giving me two seconds of victory before I have a Newfoundland on my face for the second time this morning.

Sputtering and laughing, I shove her off. Then, punctuating my own noise, I hear something that makes me go still. Storm lumbers off with the stick as I rise slowly, listening.

It wasn't what it sounded like. Couldn't be.

The noise comes again, a plaintive wail, like a baby's cry.

Storm catches it. She stops and pivots, ears perking. She glances at me as if to say, *What* is *that?*

"I don't know," I answer, as much for myself.

The morning has gone quiet again, and I'm straining to listen and figure out what it really was. I mentally run through my list of "animals that aren't hibernating right now." I've heard a similar sound from a bear cub, but it's the wrong season for that. We have cougars—a female who wandered north of their usual territory and now has grown cubs. The cry didn't sound right for a big cat. Not a wolf or a feral dog, either.

Bird? That seems most likely, and I've decided that must have been what it was when the noise comes again, and it is not like a bird at all.

A fox? They make some truly bloodcurdling sounds. There's a vixen who lives near our house in Rockton, and I've heard her scream and bolted upright, certain someone was being murdered horribly right outside our window.

I'm still standing there pondering when I catch a glimpse of running black fur and realize it's my dog.

"Storm!" I shout as I bolt after her.

She stops, and I exhale in relief. This spring, I had to shoot a young cougar she chased. Thus ensued six months of special training to be sure no wild animal would ever lead her off again.

I jog to catch up.

"We'll go check it out," I say, and she may not understand the words, but I only need to take a step toward the sound for her to bark with joy.

I motion for her to heel, and she does. Dalton and I have spent countless hours training her, and it's paid off. She's not only blossoming into a first-rate tracker, but she's more obedient than I'd dared hope. That's a necessity when your dog is bigger than you.

Storm stays at my side. When a tree prevents that, she falls behind me, as she's been taught.

The wail comes again. It's weak enough that if the forest weren't winter-quiet, I'd miss it. It sounds so much like a baby that I have to pause and ask myself "Why couldn't it be?"

There are people living out here besides us. Rockton has been around since the fifties, and over the years, residents have relocated into the wilderness for various reasons. Their term ran out in Rockton, and they didn't want to go home. Or they disagreed with the politics—as the town became less an asylum for the innocent and more a pay-to-play escape for the desperate—but they still needed the refuge of the forest. Most of these are what we call settlers. True pioneers of the north, some in communities and some living independently, as Dalton's parents did. Then there are the hostiles, and that is . . . a complicated subject that becomes more complicated the longer I'm here and the deeper I dig.

When I arrived, I was told that hostiles were residents who'd left and reverted to something primitive and dangerous. I'm no longer convinced that all of them chose that reversion. But that's a topic for another time. What matters now is that people do live out here, so I might very well be hearing a human infant.

I slow to a walk, straining for the sounds of others. If I hear any, I will retreat posthaste. Even settlers can be aggressive if we wander into their campsites.

Yet I hear only the occasional cry of what, increasingly, I can't imagine as anything except a baby. Then Storm whines. I glance down at her, and she stops. Parks her butt in the snow and gives me a look that asks if we must continue. She follows it with a glance over her shoulder, in the direction of our camp, in case I don't understand what she wants.

She senses danger ahead. No, I suppose that's melodramatic. To be precise, she smells strangers, and she has learned, unfortunately, that not all strangers are kind. Something in the scent of whatever lies ahead worries her.

I motion for her to sit and stay, and she glowers at me. With a grunt, she lifts and then lowers her hindquarters. I'm as trained in Storm's language as she is in mine, and this odd movement tells me that she will sit and stay, but she'd rather come with me.

I hesitate. I've learned the hard way that my dog might be the most valuable commodity I own out here. Never mind how well she's trained; one look at her size gets a settler's mind turning, considering how she could be used, as protection or as a beast of burden.

Taking her with me is a risk. So is leaving her here, commanded to stay, prey for any human or beast who happens upon her.

I nod and motion for her to stay behind me. She doesn't like that but communicates her disapproval only with a chuff. Then she's right on my heels.

After another half dozen steps, there is no doubt that I am hearing a baby. The weak and plaintive cry comes from right in front of me. Yet I see nothing.

I blink hard. I'm in an open area scattered with saplings, not big enough to hide someone clutching a child. The cry comes from right in the middle of an empty clearing, where I see nothing.

Storm whines. When I motion for her to stay behind me, she whines louder, taking on a note of irritation now. She's asking nicely, but she really, really wants the release command. I won't give it. This could be a trap, someone . . .

Someone what? Hiding a recording of a crying child under the snow?

Under the . . .

I tear into the clearing. The heap ahead looks like a buried log, and it's too large to be a baby, but that's definitely where the sound comes from. As I run, the snow deepens, with no tree canopy to block it, and I'm staggering forward in snow to my knees. I plow through, and I'm almost at the heap when my leg strikes something, and I stumble. In righting myself, I uncover a boot.

In two more steps, I'm beside the heap. The cries have stopped, and my heart stops with them. I claw at the snow. My fingers hit fabric. A woman's body. I can see that in a glance, and again, I don't stop for a better look. She is still and she is cold, and I cannot help her.

I keep digging, but there's just the woman, and for a horrible moment, I imagine the baby trapped beneath her. Then, at a whimper, I realize the sound comes from under her jacket. I tear at it, the fabric frozen and stiff.

Blood. I see blood under the snow. I wrestle the jacket open, and there is the baby, clutched to the dead woman's chest.

# TWO

I yank the child free so fast that the momentum knocks me backward. I land on Storm, and my arms reflexively tighten around the baby.

Crushing it.

No, no, no . . .

I struggle upright as I loosen my grip . . . so much I almost drop the baby. I squeeze my eyes shut and shudder. I'm not easily rattled. I've hung off a cliff, fingers slipping, and only thought *Damn, this isn't good.* But here I am freaked out. I know nothing about babies—*nothing*—and I've just dug one out from under the snow, from the arms of the child's dead mother, and . . . and . . .

Focus, damn it! Focus!

Deep hyperventilating breaths. Then I gasp. I'm holding a baby that has been exposed to subzero temperatures. Buried under the snow with its dead mother. There is no *time* to catch my breath.

Clutching the baby, I look around. I spot the nearest object—a fallen tree. I race over, sit, make as much of a lap as I can, and settle the baby on it.

Baby. It's a baby. Not a toddler. Not even a child old enough to crawl. This is an infant so tiny . . .

I suck in a breath. Focus, focus, focus.

It's so small. I don't have nieces or nephews. Don't have close friends with children. I cannot even guess how young this baby might be. I only know that it is tiny and it is fragile, and for once in my life, I feel huge. Massive and clumsy. Even with my gloves off, my fingers fumble with the swaddling.

I'm not sure what "swaddling" should look like, but it's the word that pops to mind. The baby has been wrapped tight in a cocooning cloth. Animal hide, tanned to butter softness.

As I'm unwrapping the baby, I stop. It's freezing out here, and I'm *un*wrapping it? But I have to, don't I? To check for frostbite? Warm it up?

The panic surges on a wave of indecision. Run the baby back to our tent and unwrap it there. No, unwrap it here, quickly, and make sure it's fine.

The baby makes a noise, too weak now to be called a cry. The child's eyes are screwed shut. They haven't opened since I picked it up.

A bitter wind whips past, and I instinctively clutch the baby to my chest. That wind—and my reaction—answer my question. Get to the tent, to shelter. It's only a few hundred feet away.

I open my jacket, and as I do, I curse myself for being a spoiled brat. Last winter, I'd fumbled around in oversize outerwear, and I'd grumbled about it, and the next time Dalton did a supply run, he returned with a new jacket and snowsuit for me. Naturally, he bought me a sleek, down-filled parka that fits perfectly, meaning I have to hold the baby against my sweater, jacket stretched only partway across. A quick second thought, and I turn my coat around, leaving an air pocket at the top.

The whole time I'm fussing, Storm whines, which only fuels my panic. Her anxiety feels like a lack of trust. That's only me projecting, but I snap at her to be quiet. Guilt surges as she ducks her head, and I pat it quickly, murmuring an apology, knowing this is what she really wants: reassurance. I'm freaking out, and that's freaking her out, and she needs to know everything is okay.

Once the baby is secured, I start from the clearing. Storm woofs, and I turn to see her staring at the woman's body.

*Shouldn't we do something about that?*

Yes. Yes, I should. I am a homicide detective, and that woman is dead, blood soaking the snow. I should at least see what killed her. But I have this baby, and it needs me more than she does. I look up, noting treetop patterns and the sun's position and distant landmarks so I can find this spot again.

Then I take off.

There is a fresh surge of panic as I leave the clearing and realize that, having been lured by the baby's cries, I'd paid no attention to my surroundings. Why the hell didn't I pay attention—

*Snow, you idiot. You walked through fresh snow.*

The path back to our campsite is as clear as a bread-crumb trail. It might meander, and yes, a voice inside screams that I need a direct route, but this is the safe one. I take off at a lope . . . until I stumble and realize, with horror, that if I fall, I'll land on the baby. Slower then. Step by step. The baby is breathing—*was* breathing . . .

No, none of that. There isn't time to stop and check. I've left room for it to breathe, and if it managed to survive under a blanket of snow, swaddled beneath its mother's jacket, then it will live through this. As long as it wasn't already too far gone—

Enough of *that.*

I tramp through the snow for what seems like miles. Finally,

I see our campsite marker high above my head, and I divert to a more direct route. The closer I get, the faster I go. When I jog across big boot prints and smaller paw prints, I stop short.

Dalton. I've been in such a blind rush that I've completely forgotten I'm not alone out here, and I nearly collapse with relief at the reminder. I don't care whether Dalton knows the first thing about babies. He's here. I am not alone.

"Eric?"

No answer. I call louder as I continue toward the campsite. I shout for Dalton. I call for Raoul. I whistle, and Storm bounds ahead, as if this means her co-parent and pack mate are back. They aren't. The camp is still and silent, and I realize the boot and paw prints are from earlier.

I check my watch to see it's not yet noon. I curse under my breath and keep going into the tent. When Storm tries to follow, a sharp "no" stops her. She whines, but only once, token protest before she collapses outside, the tent swaying as she leans against it.

I left this morning without rolling up our sleeping blankets. I brush the hides flat as quickly as I can. Then I lay the baby on them.

The infant lies there, eyes shut, body still. It hasn't moved since I left the clearing. I knew that, but I'd ignored the warning, telling myself it'd fallen asleep in relief at being found. As little as I know about babies, I realize this is ridiculous. This is a cold, frightened, hungry infant. When someone came, it should have been screaming, making its needs known now that someone finally arrived to fill them.

I lay a trembling hand on the baby's still-swaddled chest. I don't feel anything, but I'm not sure I would with the way my fingers are shaking. I check the side of its neck, and as soon as my cold fingers touch warm skin, the baby gives the faintest start.

Alive.

I fumble to unwrap the swaddling hides. The tiny body gives a convulsive shudder, and I resist the urge to re-swaddle it. The tent isn't warm, but it's sheltered, and I need to get a better look at the child.

It is naked under the cloths. A baby girl with black fuzz for hair, her face scrunched up as tight as her fists. I take a deep breath, push aside emotion, and begin an assessment of her condition. That isn't easy. I realize how cold her hands and feet are, and I panic. I notice her shallow breathing and shivering, and I panic. I see her sunken eyes, and I panic. But I keep assessing.

Dehydration. Mild hypothermia. Possible frostbite.

Her breathing is clear and steady. Heartbeat is strong and steady. Body is plump and well nourished. These findings calm and reassure me, and then I can turn my attention to the problems.

Triage. Frostbite, then hypothermia, then dehydration.

I wrap her loosely in her blankets and add a thick hide one. Then I systematically warm her hands and feet, first against my bare skin and then under my armpits. Warm, do not rub. My hands against her button nose and tiny ears as my breath warms those.

Now to replenish body fluids. I can tell she is dehydrated, but I can't determine severity.

She needs liquid. That's the main thing. I don't have any food for her. I tamp down panic at the thought that I have nothing even resembling milk. Water. Focus on getting her water.

I hurry out to grab the canteen. Then I stop. Dalton will have it, because I won't need it at camp, where I can melt snow.

Melt snow.

I snatch up the pot and stuff it to overflowing with snow and spin to the fire . . .

The fire is dead.

Of course it is. That's why I'd left in the first place: to gather kindling, which I abandoned back in the clearing where I found the baby. I've been gone long enough that the fire is reduced to ash. It'll take forever to get it going enough to melt water.

Stay calm. Stay focused. I am surrounded by water in partly frozen form. I can do this.

I empty the pot. Grab a handful of snow. Squeeze it in my fist, and watch the water run into the pot. Grab another . . . and see black streaks on my hand. It's probably soot, but it looks like dirt, and that reminds me that my hands are not clean.

Sterilize. That comes from deep memory, a single baby-sitting class taken with friends, before I realized I was not baby-sitter material.

*Then how are you going to look after an infant?*

I can do this. Clean my hands first.

With what? I showered before I came. It's one weekend with backpacks—we have no room for anything we don't absolutely need.

And this is an emergency. Am I going to let a baby die of dehydration rather than risk letting her ingest a few specks of dirt?

I wash my hands in the snow as best I can. Then I'm squeezing out water when Storm, sticking close and anxious, gives a happy bark. At a whistle, she takes off, and I nearly collapse with relief.

"Eric!" I shout. "I need help!"

He comes running so fast the poor dogs race to keep up. He bursts into the camp, as if expecting to see me wrestling a newly woken grizzly. He has a rifle over his shoulder, and he's carrying a brace of spruce grouse, which he throws into the snow as he runs toward me.

"Fire," I say. "I need the fire going. Now. I have to boil water."

"You're hurt? Or Storm?" He wheels to look at the dog bounding up behind him.

"Baby," I say, barely able to get the word out, my heart thumps so fast. "I found a baby."

"A baby what?"

The infant lets out a weak cry, and Dalton goes still.

His head turns toward the tent as he asks in a low voice, "What is that?" and I realize he doesn't recognize the sound. Or if he does, it only sparks a very old memory. His younger brother, Jacob, might very well be the only infant he's ever seen. Dalton was raised in Rockton, where there are no children.

Before I can answer, he's crouched and opening the un-zipped tent flap.

# THREE

Dalton gingerly peels back the tent flap. He peers inside.

Then he jerks back. "It's a baby."

"That's what I said."

He rises, looking stunned. "Where . . . ?"

"I found her with her mother, under the snow. Both of them—the mother and her child. The mother's dead, and I don't know how long the baby was out there, and I've warmed her up, but she's dehydrated, and I let the fire go out, and now I can't boil water to make it sterile and—"

He cuts off my babble with a kiss, gloved hands on either side of my face. Not what I expect, and it startles me, which I suppose is the point. His lips press against mine, warm, the ice on his beard melting against my chin, and it's like slapping someone who is hysterical. Well, no, it's a much nicer way to do it.

I'm startled at first, and then all I feel and smell and see is him, and the panic evaporates. Tears spring to my eyes. As he breaks the kiss, he brushes the tears away and says, "Every-thing's okay. You've got this."

I nod. "I-I don't know much . . . anything really about . . ."

"It's more than I do." He smiles, and then that vanishes, as if he realizes that might not be what I need to hear right now.

"We have this," he says. "We can hold off on sterilizing the water. If she's dehydrated, just use what you have."

He returns to the tent, and I follow with my bit of melted snow. When the dogs crowd in, he waves them back. Storm herds Raoul off, like a big older sister taking charge. He's seven months old, a wolf and Australian shepherd cross, heavier on the wolf, which means he understands pack hierarchy.

After the dogs move, Dalton reopens the tent. Then he stops, and his breath catches.

"Fuck," he whispers. "Are they supposed to be that . . . small?" There's an odd note in his voice, part wonder and part terror, and when I nudge, he moves aside, letting me go in. Then he stays there, holding the flap open.

"I'm going to need your help with this," I say.

He nods, rubbing a hand over his mouth as he eases into the tent. He's still a meter away from the baby, but he moves as if he might somehow crush her from a distance.

"Pick her up, please," I say. "I have to get this water into her."

He inches closer. His arms move toward the baby. Then he stops. Repositions his arms, mentally trying to figure out how to do this.

"You won't break her," I say.

"Are you sure?" He gives me a smile, but worry lurks behind it. He looks back at her. "How do I . . . ?"

"One hand behind her back. The other supporting her head. She's too young to hold it up on her own. She's also too young to escape."

"Got it."

He still makes a few pantomime attempts, reconfiguring his

hands in the air before he actually touches the baby. It's an awkward lift, and when she wriggles, he freezes. I lunge before he drops her. He doesn't, of course. He just tightens his grip a little and looks down at her and . . .

There are experiences I've heard women talk about that I have never had. Never even imagined, to be honest. Hearing about them, I'd inwardly roll my eyes, because if I never felt a thing, then clearly this thing does not exist. Or, as I've learned, I just never experienced it until I met Dalton. That thing they write poetry and songs and cheesy Valentine's cards about. Being in love. Being with someone that you can no longer imagine being without.

When Dalton holds that baby, I get another of those experiences. My insides just . . . I don't even know what. I feel things that I don't particularly want to feel at this moment, may not *ever* want to feel, considering this might be the one thing I can't give him.

I see Dalton holding the baby, and then he looks over at me with this little smile that . . .

Nope, not thinking about that. Tuck it away. Lock it up tight.

"Am I doing it right?" he asks.

"Yep," I say, a little brusquely. "Now I need to get the water into her. I don't know how old she is, but she definitely isn't weaned yet. She'll want something to suck on, but unless you have a clean rubber glove hidden in our packs . . ."

"Yeah, no."

I inhale. "It probably wouldn't do any good. Suckling requires strength, and she's weak. And I need to stop talking." I take a deep breath. "From wild panic to overanalyzing."

"The situation isn't critical. We're only an hour's fast walk from town. We just need to get a little water into her."

He shifts her, getting more confident in his hold. Then he stops. "She's so . . ."

"Small?"

He laughs, but it holds a touch of nervousness. "Yeah, we covered that, didn't we. I just can't believe . . ." He swallows. "All right. I'm going to try to open her mouth so you can drip water in. Just a few drops into the back of her throat, and I'll make sure she swallows it."

"Done this before, have you?"

Another laugh, still nervous. "With a two-hundred-pound man. Years ago. Guy who ran away and passed out from de-hydration. I had to get fluids into him before I hauled him to town for a saline drip. This is a little trickier. She won't need as much water, though."

"True."

He puts a finger to the baby's lips. Dalton isn't a huge guy. About six feet tall. Maybe one-seventy, lean and fit, as he needs to be for life out here. That fingertip, though, seems like a giant's, bigger than the baby's pursed lips. He prods, and her mouth opens.

"Now let's just hope I don't get bit." He wriggles his finger in and then stops. "Though I guess that would require teeth. How young do you think she is?"

"Babies can be born with teeth, but they usually fall out. They don't get more until they're at least six months. She's well below that. Maybe a month?"

"Fuck." He takes a deep breath. "Okay, here goes, I'll prop—"

Her eyes fly open, and he freezes, as if he's been caught doing something he shouldn't. She looks up at him, and it is indeed a picture-perfect scene, as she stares up at Dalton, and his expression goes from frozen shock to wonder.

I want to capture it . . . and I want to forget it. I want to pretend I don't see that look in his eyes, don't see his smile.

"Hey, there," he says, and the baby doesn't cry, doesn't even look concerned. She just stares at him.

"Water," I say, and I feel like a selfish bitch for spoiling the moment, but I can't help it. I need to shatter it, and I hate myself a little for that.

"Right." He wriggles his finger into the baby's mouth. She starts to suck on it, and he laughs again, no nerves now, just a rumbling laugh that comes from deep in his chest.

"Reminds me of a marten I found, when I was a kid," he says.

"A baby marten?"

He shrugs. "I had a bad habit of bringing home orphaned animals. My mom . . ." He trails off, and I realize it's the first time I've heard him use that word. When he speaks of Katherine Dalton, he says "my mother." That isn't who he means here. He means Amy O'Keefe, his birth mother. The parents he never talks about. The ones he can't talk about without a hitch in his words, a trailing-off, a sudden switch of subject. He lived with his parents and his brother out here until he was nine and the Daltons "rescued" him, from a situation he did not need rescuing from.

"Your mom . . ." I prod, because I must. Every time this door creaks open, I grab for it before it slams shut again.

"Water," he says, and I try not to deflate.

I lift the pot, and then realize there's no way in hell I can "drip" it from this suddenly huge pot into her tiny mouth.

"Take out one of our shirts," he says. "Dip a corner in and squeeze it into her mouth."

I'm not sure that's sanitary, but I settle for taking a clean shirt of mine, one fresh from the laundry. As I dip it in, I say, "Is this how you fed the marten?"

"Nah, it's how I fed birds. For the marten, I'd put food on my finger and hope she didn't chew it off." He looks at the baby. "You gonna chew it off, kid?"

"No teeth, remember?"

"These gums feel hard enough to do the job."

I've relaxed now. He's talking about rescuing orphaned animals, comparing them to the baby, and that eases tension from my shoulders. That's what he sees this as—the rescue of an orphaned creature. Not picking up a baby and being over-whelmed with some deeper instinct that says "I want this."

That would be silly, I guess. But we all have our sensitive spots, and this is one of mine: the fact that I cannot provide a child should he decide that's what he wants. It's an issue I never had to worry about because I did not foresee myself in a rela-tionship where the question might arise. Now I do.

I wet the shirt and trickle water in the baby's mouth. I'm being careful to have it close enough, so we can see how much she gets, and suddenly she clamps down on the fabric itself. She sucks hard and then makes such a face that we both laugh.

"Not what you expected, huh?" I say.

Her gaze turns my way. I seem to recall that, at this age, babies can't see more than shapes, but she's definitely looking. Processing. I swear I can see that in her dark blue eyes. Every move, every noise, every passing blurry shape is a cause for deep consideration, her brain analyzing and trying to interpret.

I dip the fabric into the pot and press it to her lips. She opens them and sucks. Makes that same face, distaste and dis-pleasure, like a rich old lady expecting champagne and being served ginger ale. She fusses. Bleats. But when nothing better comes, she takes the shirt again and sucks on it.

When she's finished, she fixes us with a look of bitter ac-cusation.

"Sorry," I say. "We'll do better next time."

We aren't what she wants, though. Not what she needs.

I think of the woman in the clearing, the woman under the snow.

"We should get her back to Rockton," I say. "Can you do that by yourself?"

"What?"

"Her mother. I have to . . ." I look at the baby. "I need to get what I can from the scene."

"Scene?" He adjusts his position, making the baby comfortable in the crook of his arm. "You think she was murdered."

"Possibly. I know that isn't my crime to solve, but this baby didn't come from nowhere. She has family. She needs to go back to them."

I know that, better than anyone, because of the man sitting beside me. The Daltons found a boy in the forest, and they ignored the fact that he was well fed and properly clothed and healthy. Ignored the fact that he already knew how to read and write. They decided he was a savage in need of rescue. There is no gentle way to put it. They stole Dalton from his parents, from his brother, from the forest.

"She needs to get back to them," I repeat, and Dalton's hand finds mine, his fingers squeezing as he says, "She does."

"So to do that—" I begin.

"We have to check out the body."

"I have to check it. You need to take her."

He passes me the baby and starts rolling the sleeping blankets.

"I'm not leaving you out here alone," he says, and before I can protest, he continues. "Yes, you can find the way back. Yes, you have a gun. Yes, I could leave you with both dogs. But an hour or two will make no difference if she's wrapped well. She survived for longer under the snow."

"Yes but—"

"Maybe I should stay and check the body," he says, tying the blankets under his backpack. "I know what to look for, and I'm better than you at tracking, especially with the snowfall. I might also be able to tell if she's from a settlement or she's a lone settler or even where she comes from." He settles onto his haunches. "Yeah, that makes sense. I'll check the body. You take the baby."

I only glower at him. He grins, leans forward, and smacks a kiss on my cheek. "Yep, I'm not sure which is the scarier prospect. We'll both go check the scene first. Wrap her up properly, and I'll break camp."

# FOUR

We're heading back to the clearing. Dalton has the baby snuggled under his parka, left undone just enough to be sure she's breathing. I'm in the lead, the dogs trotting along beside me, confused but calm, sensing we have this under control.

When we reach the deeper snow, it's slow going with the heavy pack on my back. It's not as bad as it sounds, though. On a trip into Whitehorse, I made an amazing discovery: backpacks are not unisex.

I had always worn a regular backpack, and if someone had offered me a "girl" one, I'd have been offended and amused, like when I saw an ad for a women's pen. Except, as I discovered, a women's backpack is a perfectly logical invention. The normal ones distribute the load across the shoulders, but women carry weight better at their hips. My new backpack utilized that, and I no longer felt like the ninety-pound weakling struggling to carry a backpack half the size of Dalton's.

We follow my boot prints into the clearing. A woman died here, and we need to disturb the scene as little as possible. At the clearing edge, I tie Raoul to a tree and command Storm to stay with him.

I return to the spot where I unwrapped the baby, and I set my backpack in the depression I'd already created. Then I unzip Dalton's jacket and carefully remove the baby. She fusses at being pulled away from her warm cocoon. I check her, and then put her back with Dalton, and she promptly quiets.

"The body's over here," I say.

Dalton follows, staying in my footsteps. The woman lies where I left her, untouched, which is a relief. I'd realized too late that I should have re-covered her with snow to stifle the smell from scavengers. But I suppose being frozen muffled her scent well enough.

I was so panicked earlier that I hadn't taken more than a cursory glance at the woman. Now I hunker onto my haunches for a closer examination. She's older than I thought, my initial observation tainted by the expectation that this would be a young mother.

I might be wrong on the age, too. This is a hard life for those who've chosen it. Still, the woman's hair is liberally streaked with gray, and I can't imagine she's younger than mid-thirties. Still young enough to have a child, of course.

She's a settler, not a hostile. In my experience so far, it's been easy to tell the difference. A settler looks like someone who stepped from a magazine article on the Klondike Gold Rush. Sometimes it's the classic version, circa 1898, complete with shabby clothing and beards to their belly buttons. Other times, they resemble modern miners, people who choose to spend part of their year here because there is indeed gold in these hills and streams.

Hostiles look as if they stepped from an entirely different magazine article, one about a newly discovered tribe. At least, that's the first impression. On closer inspection, it's more like they've compiled the most cringeworthy and stereotypical "savage" cosplay outfit imaginable. Filed teeth. Primitive tattoos.

Ritual scarring. Painted faces. Tattered clothing. Zero sanitation.

This woman might be in need of a long shower, a good haircut, and a visit to the dentist, but she isn't a hostile. Her clothing is well crafted. Her hair is gathered into a rough braid. And she has only a smear of dirt on her face, otherwise as clean as I'd be if we spent a week in this winter-frozen forest, with no easy access to bathing.

She lies on her side, legs drawn up as if she'd gone fetal to protect the baby. Blood soaks the snow around her head and legs, hidden under a cleansing fresh layer. I can't estimate quantity of blood loss by quantity of red snow. I mentally add that to my research list, also known as "the list of things I never thought I'd have to know because I'm a homicide cop, damn it."

That's not a complaint. Just a wry admission that my job down south had been very limited, with experts for everything beyond my immediate scope. Up here, I'm not just a homicide detective. Not just a general detective. Not even detective plus basic law enforcement. I am all that . . . and a crime-scene tech, ballistics expert, forensic anthropologist, arson investigator, cold-case expert, even assistant coroner. If it touches on any area of crime solving, it's mine.

Down south, I'd been known as a keener, using my vacation time to attend conferences for areas of crime-scene investigation usually handled by experts. I'd been proud of my extracurricular expertise. Then I came to Rockton, and it was like studying French for two semesters and taking a job in northern Quebec.

Finding the woman's wounds is tricky. Her chest is clean, and there hadn't been any blood on the baby or her blanket. I clear snow from the woman's legs, but she's wearing light tan trousers, and they're only splattered with dark spots that might or might not be blood.

"I'm going to roll her over," I say. "How's the baby?"

"Sound asleep."

I glance up sharply at that, and he says, "I can feel her heartbeat, Casey. She's only sleeping. Keep going."

I ease the woman onto her stomach. I still don't see any sign that bullets or blades pierced her thick parka. I peel the coat off . . . and there's still no blood. Her shirt is tan, light enough that I would notice blood. I don't.

As I ease back, I see a smear of blood on her neck. My gaze moves up to her hat. It's reminiscent of a Russian *ushanka,* with a tanned-hide exterior, fur lining, and ear flaps. I untie the straps. When I try to pull it off, it resists. I have to peel it from the back and her hair sticks to it. Wet hair that froze solid. I run a strand through my fingertips and see red. A blow to the base of the skull.

I shine my flashlight to see her hair is plastered over an ugly cut. I palpate the spot. Her skull doesn't feel dented or damaged. A scalp wound bleeds a lot, and that's what soaked the ground around her head.

I look at the imprint her body has left. When I picture the body lying not in snow but on pavement, I envision a blood pool radiating from thigh level.

Checking her legs more carefully, I find what I'm looking for: a dark patch on her inner thigh. I picture her position again and see her lying on her side, legs pulled up but parted.

I finger the dark patch and find a hole the size of a bullet. Shot in the leg. Did she fall then? Or run a little more? Not far before the bullet lodged in the femoral artery. She dropped, lying on her side, cradling the baby as blood ran into the snow.

Hit in the head. *Then* shot?

I check the scalp again, thinking it might be a bullet graze. No, it's a tear, as if from a tool. Yes, she was indeed hit in the head and then shot.

I'm contemplating this puzzle when the baby fusses. That slams home the reminder that this dead body is not simply a puzzle. It's the child's mother. Her dead mother.

As cops, we catch a lot of flak for what seems like dispassionate disinterest in the human aspect of our work. That's unfair and untrue. We learn to distance ourselves so we *can* view a corpse as a mystery. Otherwise, we remember that we're looking at a life snuffed out, and we get stuck there.

I take a moment to think about this woman, because that helps, too. Place her in context. Mother of an infant. Baby wrapped under her jacket when she's attacked. Her killer leaving them both to die. I can't tell if she bled out or died of hypothermia. Either way, she'd been abandoned by a killer heartless enough to let an infant die a slow and horrible death.

I carefully remove the dead woman's shirt. Two shirts, actually. Layering for the weather. She's naked under that. No bra, obviously—brassieres are hardly a priority out here. That does make me stop to consider. Something seems wrong, but I'm no expert on this, and I won't jump to any conclusion, won't even suggest the possibility I see. There's also something else that pulls my attention away from that.

Scars.

At first, they look like regular scars. Old ones. I have more than my share, the permanent reminders of the attack that changed my life. When you are accustomed to seeing scars across your entire body, they become like freckles for those who have them—you're slow to notice them on others.

These aren't the sort of scars I bear. There's a pattern here. Raised bumps of scars form a mantle across her chest and shoulders. That's the best way I can describe it. A mantle. Three chains of parallel scars that start on one shoulder, swoop down just over her breasts, and then cross to the other shoulder.

Ritualized scarring.

"There's a tattoo, too," Dalton says.

I see it then, on her upper arm. What seems at first a modern circlet tattoo around her biceps, but on closer inspection is rough and primitive. Another one encircles her other arm.

I remember something and move to the smear of dirt on her chin. Under it, I see three raised, round scars. The dirt seems deliberately smeared on. Not painting herself with it, but covering those scars with the only kind of makeup the wilderness allows.

"A hostile?" I murmur. Then I look at the dirt compared to her tidy clothing and general state of cleanliness. "*Former* hostile."

A hostile turned settler. A former hostile with an infant baby. Murdered in the snow. Both of them left to die.

I turn to Dalton. "Should I take her back to Rockton?"

"If it'll help, sure. I can make a stretcher. Get Storm to pull it."

"I mean *should* I. I'd like to. I need to take a closer look, and I need April's help. But is it right to take her?"

He nods, understanding. "I'd say so. If she has people, they wouldn't have found her under that snow. Taking her back will help you find the baby's family. Seems proper to me."

# FIVE

We have the woman on a stretcher, which is really just poles with our sleeping blankets between them. We've crafted a makeshift harness for Storm. She's fine with that. We've been training her to pull because, well, it's the Yukon. That's what dogs do up here.

Storm finds the pulling easy, the stretcher gliding along the snow. If the dead body bothers her, she's gotten over it. Or maybe because we're moving the woman, she feels as if we're helping her. Our biggest problem is Raoul, who wants to pull . . . using his teeth. What seems like strong wolf blood in him might also be husky. Plenty of those up here, and they were one breed Rockton had back when they allowed pets. We'll have to get him in a harness this winter for some early training.

We're nearing the town when Will Anders comes running, and I tense. Our deputy running to intercept us is never a good sign.

"What's wrong?" I call.

"You're back early, that's what's wrong. Is everything . . . ?" He spots the stretcher and slows.

Raoul trots along at Anders's side as our deputy walks over for a closer look. Raoul isn't the most sociable canine, but he has his favorites, which for him means "people he allows to touch him." Anders absently pats the young dog as he walks to the stretcher.

"Wounded settler?" he asks. "April's off today, but I can run and get her to the clinic."

"This one is beyond my sister's help," I say.

"Dead?" There's a long moment of silence before he says, "Not enough murders for you lately, Case, so you're bringing home dead bodies?"

"Ha ha."

Anders bends beside the stopped stretcher. In college, he'd been premed before he decided to serve his country as an army medic. They soon switched him to military police—he has a knack for conflict resolution—but he still has the basic medical training, and his gaze sweeps over the woman, assessing.

"Hostile markings. I'm guessing that's your interest—a subject to study." He rises and undoes Storm's harness, giving her a rub as he sets her free. Then he looks at Dalton. "Making the pup work, boss? Guess you need to hit the gym a little more, huh?"

Anders flexes a biceps . . . which would be far more impressive if he weren't wearing a thick parka. Will Anders is a big guy, a couple of inches taller than Dalton and wider, too, the quarterback to Dalton's running-back build.

Anders is grabbing the harness when the baby fusses under Dalton's jacket.

"What . . . ?" Anders says, staring at the moving lump under Dalton's coat. "Please tell me that's another puppy, because I'm still stinging from being overlooked for that one." He hooks a gloved thumb at Raoul. "I call dibs."

"I don't think you want dibs this time," I say.

Dalton undoes his jacket just as the baby lets out a wail.

"Holy shit." Anders turns to me. "Either you guys have seriously graduated from orphaned wolf pups, or you are a *master* at pregnancy-hiding."

"She was hers," I say, motioning at the dead woman. "She's dehydrated and starving."

Anders looks at the woman. "Uh, not to question your medical expertise . . ."

"I mean the baby," I say with a roll of my eyes. "She needs food and medical attention, so we really need to stop talking and get to town."

Dalton conceals the baby again and cuts along the back path to the clinic while I accompany Anders and the dogs into town. When we enter, a few people run over. Then they see the body and relax, as they realize I haven't brought our sheriff home on a stretcher.

There are plenty of people in Rockton who'll mutter, after a few beers, about how much better life would be without the hard-ass sheriff breathing down their necks. They're like teens whining about strict parents, though. They might complain, but they sure as hell don't want to wake up one day and find Mom and Dad gone. God knows who they'd get in their place.

I field questions, of course. We live in an isolated town of less than two hundred people. Everyone's eager for news, for any change to routine, especially in the middle of winter. That would explain the holiday decorations, too. This is my second Christmas here, and as I learned from last year, this place goes a little nuts at the holidays, to stave off going a little nuts in general as the days get darker and the temperature plummets.

While Anders pulls the stretcher, we pass residents adding to the decorations. Heaven forbid a single wooden porch should lack evergreen boughs woven through each railing baluster. Or any door should lack an intricately crafted wreath. Or any lintel should lack ivy with bright red cranberries. Every tree has been decorated, and that's saying something in a town filled with evergreens. That's still not enough, and people have decorated all the perimeter trees, too. Making holiday ornaments is an all-year craft for some.

I can grumble, but that's more eye-rolling than actual complaint, and even the eye-rolling covers the fact that I secretly love the way Rockton embraces the holidays. My parents celebrated Christmas—my mother wanted her daughters fully assimilated, and any of her own Chinese or Filipino family traditions were ignored. We were Canadians, and we would act Canadian, which apparently meant "Christian" at the holidays, even if we never attended church of any kind.

Neither of my parents was all that keen on Christmas, though. It seemed like more chore than delight for them. An unwanted distraction from their careers. We did all the basics: set up a tree, put out stockings for Santa, exchanged gifts and then had a holiday meal. But the tree went up Christmas Eve and was taken down Boxing Day. There were no concerts or parties. My parents didn't have time for that. Well, no, *they* attended holiday parties—I remember them dressed up, April babysitting me—but only because the social events were necessary evils for career networking.

In Rockton we celebrate all the winter traditions, and that sounds very inclusive of us, but honestly, I think it's just an excuse for more parties. If that leads to a greater understanding of different traditions and faiths, it's a bonus. There are no churches in Rockton, but only because we don't have space for buildings that'll be used once a week. Services are held at the community center, with the various groups agreeing to a schedule.

If there's an overriding theme to our winter celebrations, it's solstice. That makes sense up here, where we are enslaved by sun and season. Next week is winter solstice, the longest night of the year. The party will last for every minute of it, as we celebrate the return of the sun, knowing each day following will be longer, until summer solstice, when the town will party from 4 A.M. sunrise to midnight sundown. When you live without TV and social media, you exploit every excuse for a celebration.

My mood lifts on seeing the decorations. With Rockton's wooden buildings and Wild West flair, there's nostalgia there, too, even for someone who doesn't consider herself particularly nostalgic. Squint past the modern clothing, and you can imagine a town from times past, bedecked in its holiday finest, everyone's step lighter, their smiles wider.

Those smiles dim when they see the dead body on the stretcher, but even then, it's simple curiosity. We are indeed, in so many ways, the Wild West town we resemble, where violence and death are as much a part of life as decorating for the holidays.

I head to April's house, beside the clinic. Like Dalton, Anders, and myself, she gets a small one-and-a-half-story chalet to herself. That's the perk of being essential services. Rockton could build one for each resident—we certainly have the land—but the larger the town is, the more likely it is to be spotted by planes. We use both structural and technological camouflage to prevent that, but we still need to keep our footprint as small as possible.

Anders takes both dogs to Raoul's owner, Mathias, who'll look after Storm while we're busy with this problem. I rap on my sister's door. I almost hope that she doesn't answer. Or that, if she does, she has company. It's her day off, and it'd be nice if she wasn't spending it home alone, but with April, that's like saying it'd be nice if the temperature hit thirty Celsius today. It just ain't happening.

No, that isn't entirely true. It would have been when she first arrived. Now, there is a chance she'll be out, not exactly socializing but at least interacting. Inviting someone into her home is too much. She's been known to haul the toilet tank onto her back porch for pickup to avoid having anyone come inside.

April opens the door as I'm reaching for a second knock.

"What are you doing back?" she says.

"Nice to see you, too, April."

Her brows crease, as if she's trying to figure out why it would be nice to see her. Isabel—a former psychologist—believes my sister is on the autism spectrum, undiagnosed because my parents refused to see anything "wrong" with their brilliant older daughter. They had enough trouble dealing with their rebellious younger one. To them, a diagnosis of even mild autism would have meant April was intellectually imperfect, and so they instead let her struggle through life, a gifted neurosurgeon and neuroscientist unable to form all but the most tenuous of personal relationships, lonely and alone and never knowing why. My parents screwed up my life in so many ways, but compared to what they did to my sister, I got off easy.

When we raised the possibility of autism with April, I'd been terrified she'd see it as sibling envy—me trying to knock down my brilliant older sister. I'd been convinced otherwise by a joint coalition of Isabel, Kenny, and Dalton . . . and they'd been right, which is humiliating to admit, proving how little I know my sister. Too much familiarity and too little actual understanding, a lifetime of trying to get to know her and, when I couldn't, creating her wholesale.

April was fine with the diagnosis. She treated it the way I would have: like a physical ailment. *Here's the problem, and now that we know what it is, let's tackle that.* Relief, I think, at giving it a name.

"I brought you a body," I say.

Her frown deepens, and she's looking for some alternate meaning in this. A sign that I'm joking.

"I found a murdered woman in the forest," I say.

Now she relaxes, and I get the April I know well, rolling her eyes at her feckless little sister. "Really? You don't have to make the world's problems your own, Casey."

"You know me. Can't relax. Always looking for work. If I don't have it, I make some." I pause. "Which does not mean I *made* this dead body. That would be wrong."

A pause. Then, "That's a joke, isn't it?"

I clap her on the arm as I propel her back into the house. "Yes, April. It's a joke." I pull shut the door before she can protest. "Don't worry—I'm not coming in for tea. I found something else, which I'd rather not broadcast."

# SIX

After I explain, we head out April's back door and across her yard to the clinic's rear entrance. As we do, she says, "I hope you're not thinking of adopting this child, Casey."

I tense so fast my spine crackles. "No, I'm not stealing some-one's baby, April."

"The mother is dead. That is not stealing."

"Presumably the father is alive, and potentially other family, which I'm going to find."

"Good. This isn't a stray puppy."

My teeth barely part enough for me to say, "I'm aware of that," but one of my sister's cognitive challenges is interpreting body language, so she ignores that and continues.

"There is no place in your life for a baby, Casey. I realize you're comfortable here, and you've settled into a long-term relationship with Eric, but this is not a situation for mother-hood."

"I found a baby with a dead mother. Buried under the snow. Alone and in distress. I brought her back to Rockton so she doesn't *die*, not to fill a hole in my life."

"There is no hole in your life. You have Eric, and you have

Storm, and you have Rockton and your job. You are happier and more satisfied than I have ever known you to be."

I answer slowly, keeping my tone even. "I appreciate the fact that you recognize I'm happy, April. And there *isn't* a baby-size hole in my life. I just happened to find a child, whom I intend to return to her family. Just because I'm a woman in a happy romantic relationship doesn't mean my ovaries go into hyperdrive seeing a baby."

"Good."

I push open the back door of the clinic with a little more force than necessary. I tell myself that April isn't being patronizing. I've spent my life dealing with this from her, and I'm trying to understand that she doesn't mean it the way it sounds.

Yet it's also a constant reminder that my sister put me into my box when we were young, and nothing I've done since then has—or possibly ever will—let me escape it. I'm reckless. I'm impulsive. I'm thoughtless, rushing headlong into every bad decision life offers. My sole consolation is that anyone who knows me would laugh at all those descriptors.

Inside, Dalton and Anders have the baby on the examining table. As soon as I see that, I barrel into the room and snatch her up.

"You can't leave her on that," I say. "What if she rolls off?"

"She can't even lift her head, Casey," Anders says.

"Which doesn't mean she can't wriggle. Or slide."

He snickers. "Slide off a flat surface?"

"You are both correct," April says. "It is almost certainly safe, given the child's lack of mobility, but a slippery metal table still doesn't seem like the safest place to set a baby." She aims a look at Anders.

"Hey, I'm not the one who put her there," Anders says. "And Eric literally just unwrapped her as you two came in."

April nods at Dalton, as if to say that if *he* did it, then it's fine. The first time they met, she referred to him as my fuck toy, and I'm not sure what was more shocking, the word coming from my very proper sister or the sentiment coming from my very straitlaced sister. In the last six months, she's done a complete about-face, and now, if Dalton does something, then it's the right thing to do. I'm totally on board with her *not* treating my lover like trash, but I can't help wishing I could get a little of that approval thrown my way.

"Eric?" she says. "It's a bit chilly in here for the baby. Could you . . . ?" She looks over to see he's already starting the fire, and she nods, pleased that her trust is so well placed. Anders and I exchange a look.

I hold the baby until the fire's blazing and the chill is leaving the room. Then I lay her on the exam table.

"Would you take over?" I ask Dalton. "I need to find something for her to eat."

"Yes," April says, not looking up from her examination of the baby. "We'll need formula and bottles. Also diapers, for the inevitable after-products of feeding. Tell the general store to put together a box of all their infant supplies."

Anders, Dalton, and I all look at one another.

"Uh," I say. "We don't carry infant supplies. We don't . . . have any infants."

"In case you haven't noticed that in the past six months," Anders murmurs.

April shoots us both a glare of annoyance. "Yes, I have noticed there are currently no babies, but I'm sure there are supplies in storage for them."

"There aren't," I say. "We don't ever have babies here. Or children. Or even teenagers."

She glances at Dalton.

"Yeah," he says. "I was special. But Casey's right. We don't allow anyone under eighteen, and there's a reason why we have a shitload of condoms and diaphragms and every other method of contraception. We're not equipped to handle childbirth or children."

April flutters a hand at me. "Just get . . . whatever."

As I hurry through town, I'm trying to figure out what I *can* get. Milk is the obvious choice. We have it in powdered form, and I know that's less than ideal, but it's that or nothing.

As I'm racking my brain for alternate foods, I keep thinking, *Oh, I can google that.* For someone raised on modern technology, it's a natural instinct. Well, unless it's a medical question, where even "I have an odd rash on my thumb" will lead to "Cancer! Death! Plague!"

Sixteen months in Rockton have not yet rerouted my neural circuits enough to keep me from reaching toward my pocket every time I have a research question. Now, instead of a cell phone, I carry a notepad, where I can write down all those questions for the next time I'm in Dawson City with internet access. This problem won't wait that long.

I need to find a resident who has had a child. That should be easy enough in a town full of people in their prime child-rearing years. Yet that is exactly what makes this not easy at all. Like Dalton said, we don't allow children. We also don't allow spouses. You come alone. You leave everything—and everyone—behind. That means that if you're deeply devoted to a partner, you won't come to Rockton. If you have kids, you won't come to Rockton. There are exceptions, I'm sure, where the danger is so great that you say goodbye to your family for two years. But single and childless is the normal.

I don't even know who has grown children. Residents reveal only what they want and invent whatever backstory fits who they choose to be while they're here.

That's when I spot the one person I know for certain has had a child.

Petra is coming out of the general store after her shift. Before I can catch up, another resident stops to talk to her. I hear them discussing art that the resident has commissioned as a Hanukkah gift. Down south, Petra had been a comic-book artist. Well, *after* she spent a decade as special ops in the United States. She's also resumed the latter job here, as a spy and—at least in one case—assassin for her grandmother, one of the town's early residents and current board members.

Until six months ago, I'd have said Petra was my closest friend in Rockton. The whole "actually a spy and assassin" part has put a damper on that. Petra and I have resumed some form of cautious relationship. We're not going to sit around braiding each other's hair but we weren't exactly doing that before either. It had been a stable, steady, comfortable friendship, and it no longer is, and I mourn that.

When Petra sees I'm waiting to speak to her, she wraps up her conversation quickly. I motion her over to a gap between the general store and the next building.

"We have a baby," I say.

Before I can explain, she says, "You're having a—?"

"No, we found a baby abandoned in the forest. She's very, very young, and we're . . . We're a little lost. We don't exactly have baby guides in the library, and I could really use some help."

When I'd first hailed Petra, her step had lightened, and she'd smiled as she walked over. Now the remains of that smile freeze before sliding away.

"I . . ." She swallows. "I can't really . . ."

"Was that a lie?" I say. "About your daughter?"

Confusion flashes, and then anger. "Of course not. What kind of person would make up . . ."

She trails off because she realizes the answer to that. A child's death is exactly the kind of tragic backstory anyone with her training *might* give. I have no idea specifically what she used to do. "Special ops" is as much as she'll say, but if she's done any spy or interrogation work, she knows only a stone-cold bitch wouldn't have been affected by the story of her daughter, so I must question it.

"No," she says, quieter now. "I would hope you'd know I wouldn't make up something like that, but yes, I get it. Anything I know about babies, I'll happily pass along, though I'll warn that my ex was the expert parent. I meant that if you're looking for someone to care for this baby?" She manages a wry smile. "I'll stick to dog-sitting."

"I understand. If you can pop by the clinic and give us anything—maybe some sense of how old the baby is—that'd be great. Right now, though, we need food. She's not rolling over or lifting her head yet, and as little as I know about babies, I realize that means she's still on an all-liquid diet."

"Damn, she really is young. Okay, well, I guess milk will have to do until you can get into Dawson for formula. We'll need to rig up something to use as a bottle. Let's go into the store. I have a couple of ideas—"

"You have a baby?" a voice says.

I glance over my shoulder and wince. "Does this look like a private conversation, Jen?"

"Fuck, yeah. Why do you think I'm eavesdropping?"

I used to joke that I always wanted a nemesis. I mean, it sounds cool, and I'm not the type of person who makes enemies easily. Neither friends nor enemies. In Rockton, I have more of the former than ever. I also have my first nemesis, and she's standing right in front of me.

"Jen . . ." I say.

"You know, Detective, everyone keeps talking about how smart you are. Not as smart as your sister, but still fucking brilliant. Yet I really have to wonder sometimes. You brought a baby into town, and you think you can keep that a secret? This entire town is going to *hear* exactly what you're hiding within . . . Oh, I'll bet two hours. Petra, you want in?"

"You know what I want to lay bets on, Jen?" Petra says. "How long you can go without insulting Casey. I'll give *that* two hours, though I might be granting you too much credit."

"Someone has to keep our detective on her toes," Jen says. "And it sure as hell won't be you, Miss Artiste. Go draw some rainbows and flowers, think happy thoughts, and keep polishing your nicest-girl-in-town title. You can keep it."

I look at Petra, and I choke on a laugh.

"What?" Jen said.

I turn to Jen. "Yes, there's a baby. Yes, people will figure it out. But right now, that baby needs to eat, and we have to figure out what to give her and how to feed her."

"Powdered milk with an extra fifty percent water plus sugar."

We both look at Jen.

"That's why I interrupted your conversation," she says. "It was too painful listening to you both flounder. A baby needs formula, but watered down and sugared milk will do in an emergency."

"You have kids?" I say.

"God, no. I was a midwife."

Now Petra and I are staring.

"I thought you were a teacher," I say, and I'm still struggling to reconcile *that* with the woman I know. Jen certainly looks like she could have been a teacher—well groomed, late thirties, pleasant appearance—but I cannot imagine her interacting with children. I don't want to.

"You know how much a primary school teacher makes? I was a midwife on the side. Also did some day care in the summer, and I specialized in babies."

"Whoa," Petra says. "I finally know why you're here. It wasn't a real day care, was it? You were secretly conducting Satanic rituals on children."

"Oh, ha ha. That's actually not bad. You get a point for that one, blondie, but no, my kids were just fine. I like children. It's once they hit puberty that they become assholes. Now let's go get what you need."

# SEVEN

By the time we return to the clinic, April has her report ready. The baby is dehydrated and had mild hypothermia but not frostbite. She appears to be healthy. April estimates she's approximately a month old. All of this is what I expected. Even the negatives—the dehydration and hypothermia—are minor and easily reversed. She does ask one question that makes me smack myself for not considering it before.

Were the blankets soiled when I found her?

The baby had been naked and wrapped in hide blankets. No diaper. My very preliminary exam on her mother's body suggested the woman had been dead for hours when I found the baby. The baby has been wrapped in the same blanket ever since. Yet there are no bowel movements in it, and no obvious sign of urination. When I sniff-test, I do smell uric acid, but only faintly. So even before her mother died, the baby hadn't eaten in a while. Is that significant? Maybe not, but it's something for me to remember. It also means she's very, very hungry now. Hungry enough to gobble down our makeshift formula without complaint.

Dalton feeds her. When he's done and Jen says, "Now you

need to burp her," he hands her to me, and I awkwardly pat her back until Jen says, "Burp her, not jump-start her." She takes the baby. "You really don't have any idea what you're doing, do you?"

"No," April says. "It isn't a skill Casey needs when she cannot have children."

Silence falls. Dalton's opening his mouth when Anders says, "And that's no one's business except Casey's, but thanks for broadcasting it, April. I'm sure your sister appreciates that."

April turns on him in genuine bafflement. "I was stating a medical fact. It's hardly Casey's fault—"

"It's okay," I say. "Yes, these aren't skills I possess, so I appreciate Jen's help."

Anders and Dalton quickly change the subject, but I feel the weight of Jen's gaze, and even if I can't tell what she's thinking, I squirm under that.

April is right. Saying I can't have kids should be no different than saying I'm deaf in one ear or my pancreas doesn't produce insulin. It's a medical issue, beyond my control.

I've heard people admit that being unable to have kids makes them feel less like a woman. That's not me at all. I just feel . . . I feel as if an opportunity has been snatched from me, this thing I wasn't sure I wanted, but I would like to have had the option. I don't, and that stings, and it's stung more in the past few hours than I ever imagined it could.

I let Jen handle the burping while I talk to April about the baby's mother. I might not be able to burp the baby properly, but here's something I *can* do for her. I am a detective, and if her mother holds any clues to tell me where this baby belongs, I'm getting them from her.

———

We've put Jen in charge of the baby. I cannot believe I'm saying that. I'm definitely not comfortable with it, but we don't have a lot of options. Dalton and I need to be with April for the autopsy, and Anders has a town to manage.

Also, whatever my issues with Jen, I wouldn't leave the baby with her if I didn't have to admit she could be trusted, at least in something this important.

Once the baby is out of the exam area, we bring in her mother's body and put it on the same table. I undress her and fold her clothing into paper bags that I write on with a marker. Dalton takes notes as I dictate my initial observations while April waits.

I take pictures, too. We have a digital camera and a laptop for me to download the photographs, blow them up, analyze them . . . Crime solving in Rockton might make me feel like I'm working in Sherlock Holmes's time, but I do have access to some modern tech. We generate a base level of solar power for food storage and the restaurant kitchens, and I can tap into that, but I don't use it more than necessary, especially in winter, when the sun is at a premium.

When I undressed the woman in that clearing, I'd made observations that I need to follow up on before April begins her autopsy. So I tell her what I noticed. She listens and frowns and then nods and checks.

"Your observations are correct," she says when she finishes. "This woman is not the infant's mother."

"Fuck," Dalton exhales.

"Seconded," I murmur.

When I'd first removed the dead woman's shirt, what caught my attention was her breasts. I might not know much about babies, but I've worked alongside breastfeeding mothers, and I understand the basic physiological changes that go along with breastfeeding. This woman . . . well, she looks like I'd expect of a middle-aged woman with a D-cup bosom. In short, her breasts are not buoyed by mother's milk. That could mean she was unable to breastfeed, which is why I hadn't mentioned my suspicion to Dalton. It threw a huge monkey wrench into this scenario, and I wanted to be sure. Now I am.

"This woman has never given birth," April says.

"She could have a child without breastfeeding," I explain to Dalton. "But April is talking about her pubic bones. During pregnancy, they separate. The ligaments tear, which you'd see in a recent birth. There's none of that. Long-term, that heals, but it leaves pitting, which I learned from that forensic anthropology text you got me. That's why April believes this woman has *never* had a child."

"So she isn't the baby's mother," Dalton says. "I don't even know where to go with that."

"I do," I say. "Because I've been considering it since I got a good look at her. Unfortunately, that path goes in a million directions."

"I believe a million is overstating the matter," April says.

"It's rhetorical hyperbole," I say. Before she can argue, I continue. "The woman could be related to the baby. She could be a caretaker. She could have stolen it. Of course, if she'd been caught stealing it, whoever shot her should have taken the baby back. If she's a relative or caretaker, I'd expect the parents to be combing the woods looking for her, and we didn't hear anything."

"Does it matter how this woman obtained the child?" April asks, and her tone makes it sound like an accusation but I'm learning not to jump on the defensive.

"It does," I say. "Because if she knows the baby, then her body may provide clues to the baby's home. If she doesn't know her . . ."

I don't finish. This woman is my only link to the baby's origins. If she has no relationship to the child—if they aren't from the same family or settlement—then I wouldn't even know where to begin. It's like dropping a naked baby on a church doorstep. I need something to work with, and this woman is all I have right now.

I will find my clues here. Pretend I really am living in the nineteenth century and channel my inner Sherlock Holmes to tease out the threads leading to a connection that will, ultimately, take this woman and—I hope—the baby home. For that, my best clues might be contained in the literal threads that surround her: the woman's clothing. I force myself to set that aside for now and focus on what her body tells us instead.

This woman was not born in the wilderness. There are fillings in her teeth and the dents of old ear piercings. She also has a mark that may be a belly button piercing.

I take photos of the ritual scarring and tattooing. Both seem unfinished, and the scars are old. She hasn't been a hostile in a while. My mind automatically seizes on this and wants to start extrapolating potential information on the nature of hostiles. But that's not what this is about. File it for later. Focus on the clues for this woman as an individual, not as a general exemplar.

She's lost the tips of two toes to frostbite. The bottoms of her feet are callused and thick-soled. I also note that one of her wrists is slightly crooked, and April confirms that the bone has been broken and healed poorly. That could have taken place with the hostiles or afterward—medicine outside Rockton is primitive, and the fact that it healed at all shows she had basic medical care.

On to cause of death. April confirms it wasn't the blow to the back of her head. That's ugly, and it left a mark on the bone, but it wouldn't have been incapacitating. The wound on her leg is indeed a bullet hole. A pellet hole, to be exact, from a shotgun. We find a buckshot pellet. There's only one, which suggests the gun was fired from a distance. That's not how you use buckshot—if you're hunting large game with a shotgun at a distance, you'd use a slug and, arguably, you should be using a rifle, but out here, people take the weapons and ammo they can get. At that range, a buckshot pellet isn't usually fatal, but if you hit the right spot—like the femoral artery—it can be.

Struck by a blow to the back of the head. Puts on her hat afterward. No time to treat the injury? Trying to get somewhere first? Then she's shot. I don't see any signs that she'd attempted to treat that or even stop the bleeding.

Mental confusion from the head blow? Shock? Hypothermia? She'd been escaping someone in the forest, possibly at night, snow falling.

I remember her position, fetal on her side, protecting the baby.

*I'm just going to lie down for a minute. Rest.*

That's a classic sign of hypothermia. Someone accustomed to life out here would know better, but add the blow to the head with the baby clutched to her breast, and she had good reason to succumb.

Running. Fleeing. Lost. Exhausted. Drop and curl up . . . and bleed out in the snow, too befuddled from a head injury to tend to your injured leg.

The woman's stomach has food in it. Not much, suggesting she hadn't recently eaten. There's nothing for me to analyze there. I don't know what I'd be looking for anyway—*ah-ha, she ate hare, and from the semi-digested bits, I can tell it was a specific subtype, found only on Bear Skull Mountain.* Yeah, no. She isn't starving, but neither had she just eaten before her death. That's all I need.

Speaking of eating, that makes me realize the dead woman

didn't have any supplies on her. No backpack. Nothing to feed the baby either. Does that suggest she fled unexpectedly? She was properly dressed, so it wasn't as if she grabbed the baby and ran out into the snow.

I check her clothing pockets. Only her parka has them, and I find a knife in an interior one.

Clothing next. The most interesting piece had been around her ankle—her sole jewelry. A braided leather anklet inscribed with "Hope. Dream. Love." The letters have been burned in with painstaking care. The leather edges show faint wear. It's not new, but it isn't old either.

Most of the woman's clothing is basic in its construction. It shows a knowledge of tanning and sewing at a journeyman level. It's sturdy, and it does the job. Her jacket and boots are different. They're serious craftsmanship. The parka is done in the Inuit style—caribou with the fur inside, the hollow hairs adding extra insulation. The hood is framed in ermine. Her boots are also caribou, and her socks are mink. Warm and luxurious. All three have decorative flairs not found on her clothing. The jacket buttons are polished stones. The laces on the boots and jacket end in bone carvings of fox heads—gorgeous work that I didn't even notice until now.

Her outerwear must be trade goods. With that, I have my first solid clue. Someone made her parka and boots. Someone with enough talent that others will recognize the workmanship.

The first person I'd normally ask is Jacob, Dalton's brother, who still lives in the forest. He's away, though, on a hunting expedition with Nicole, a Rockton resident. I'm hoping it's more than a hunting trip, but either way, he's not nearby. My second point of contact would be former Rockton sheriff Tyrone Cypher. Yet his winter camp is a few hours away, and he might not be there.

We'll start with option three: the First Settlement. I'd much rather deal with Jacob or Cypher, but I will admit that someone in the settlement is more likely to recognize the workmanship. It might even come from there—after Rockton, they're the largest community in the area.

Once April finishes the autopsy, I go into the waiting room to check on the baby. Jen starts passing her to me.

I lift my hands. "I can hold her if you have to do something, but I need to go talk to Phil." I take the baby and pull her into a cuddle. Then I stop. "What's that . . ." I sniff again and look at Jen.

"Why do you think I was handing her to you?" she says. "I'm about to teach you a valuable baby-care lesson. You can thank me later."

Dalton walks in. "We need to—"

I hand him the baby. "She wants you."

His brows arch, but he takes her. Then his nose wrinkles.

"Jen's going to teach you how to change a diaper," I say. "I'd love to help, but I need to talk to Phil."

I hurry out the door before he can argue.

# EIGHT

Phil isn't at his house. I'll admit to some relief at discovering that, even if it means I have to go find him. When he arrived— or was exiled here as our new town council rep—he'd stayed in his house as much as April stayed in hers.

Well, no, my sister spends most of her days in the clinic, where she interacts with residents, whether she wants to or not. Phil just stayed in his house. Waiting for a call from the council, I suspect, to tell him all was forgiven and he could come home. To his credit, when he realized that wasn't happening, he stepped out and into his role.

It's in Phil's best interests to take a more active part in town life. Which does not mean he's hanging holiday decorations or mulling cider for the weekly wassailing party. Phil is a corporate man. The kind of guy who was born with a cell phone in one hand, a clipboard in the other, and both eyes on the corporate ladder. He's young—thirty—and ambitious as hell. Which makes Rockton his actual hell.

If there's a ladder here, Dalton is ensconced at the top. With a weak sheriff, Phil might have been able to muscle through and crown himself King of Rockton. Phil knows better than to even try it with Dalton, which proves he has some brains to go with that ego and ambition.

Phil is slowly carving out his place, and it's the one he's most comfortable with. A managerial position in a town that really *could* use a manager. So, if Phil's not home, then I'm most likely to find him managing. In the kitchens, analyzing production. In the shops, checking inventory levels. Or simply walking about town, making note of who is chatting on a porch when they're supposed to be working.

I'm directed to the woodshed, where he was seen an hour ago. He's made some adjustments to the winter-supply system, decreasing free allotments of heating wood while also decreasing the cost for extra. There's been grumbling, but his theory is sound. If people get x logs per week free, then they burn x logs, whether they need them or not. This way, they're encouraged to dress warmer or use extra blankets or even socialize more in the common areas, but if they really do want more home heat, the additional fee is reasonable.

These are the aspects of life in Rockton that Dalton just doesn't have the time—or the inclination—to manage. It's a matter of fine-tuning the overall system to balance conservation, labor, and resident happiness. Phil might see this as a hobby to occupy him while he waits for his release papers, but he really is helping.

"He came, he saw, he left again," Kenny says when I walk into the small carpentry shop next to the lumber shed. Kenny grabs his crutches and leads me outside.

Kenny is our local carpenter. He used to also be our lead militia, and while we haven't taken that title away, he's only recently resumed patrols. Six months ago, he took a bullet for Storm. That bullet didn't paralyze him, but he still needs crutches and leg braces. Will he always need them? That's impossible even for my neurosurgeon sister to say. In six months,

Kenny has graduated from bed to crutches. He's working on regaining full mobility while understanding that may never come.

Outside the carpentry shed, he calls, "Sebastian!" The thump of splitting lumber stops, and a moment later, our youngest—and possibly most dangerous—resident appears. Sebastian is a clinically diagnosed sociopath who murdered his parents at the age of eleven and spent the next seven years locked up. Which probably means we shouldn't be giving him an ax and sending him out to the woodpile alone. But Sebastian is . . . an interesting case.

"Hey, Casey," he says as he jogs over, ax in hand. "You're back early. Everything okay?"

"Pretty much. Mathias give you the day off?"

"Nah, I took it. He's in a mood. I decided to chop wood and stay out of his way before we kill each other." His eyes glint at that, almost self-deprecating recognition that—as we both know—this is an entirely valid concern, given the parties involved. "He'll be glad to have Raoul back, though. He spent all morning snapping about how glad he is not to have that 'mongrel' underfoot, which means he misses him."

"Well, Raoul is home, and I'm looking for Phil. Was he here?"

"Yep, he came to check the woodpiles. He left about twenty minutes ago. Said he was heading to the Roc to go over the alcohol inventory with Isabel. You want me to run grab him?"

"I've got it. Thanks."

As Sebastian jogs back to his chopping, Kenny says, "He's a good kid. Really good."

I make a noncommittal noise. Of course, Kenny has no idea what Sebastian is or why he's here. That's on a need-to-know basis, and the only ones who need to know are myself, Dalton, and Mathias. And Sebastian is, in his way, a good kid. At least he's trying to be, and in Rockton, that's what counts.

Sebastian knows what he is, and he's spent years in therapy for it. He's continuing his rehabilitation here with Mathias, the town butcher who used to be a psychiatrist specializing in psychopathy and sociopathy . . . and who may be an expert on the subject in more than just a professional sense.

It's Rockton. Everyone has a story. Everyone has shadows in their past. It's what they do here that matters. Sebastian is a model citizen. Others are not, and they don't have his excuse of mental illness.

Up here, what you were before—and what you are at heart—is not nearly as important as what you choose to be. At least for now, Sebastian chooses this path, and we'll let him have it, while we stand watch in case that changes.

I head to the Roc. It's one of two bars, which may seem unwise in such a small town. Northern communities often struggle with substance-abuse issues. Long cold winters. Limited entertainment options. The isolation and subsequent cabin fever. Rockton deals with that by regulating alcohol even more tightly than other commodities. Part of regulating it is having two bars. Two places to enjoy a social drink while being monitored by staff who will cut you off fast, because if you start a drunken brawl, both you and your server will spend a week on chopping duty.

There are also two bars because the Roc serves dual purpose as a brothel. Yes, brothel. Right now we have a hundred and forty men and thirty-two women. I'm still not convinced that "brothel" is the way to handle that disparity, but I'm a lot more willing to concede the possibility than I was when I first moved in.

It isn't a perfect solution. It leads to an expectation that, if *some* women take credits for sex, maybe they *all* will, if the price is high enough. I dealt with my share of offers when I first arrived, and in the early days of my relationship with Dalton, plenty of residents suspected I hooked up with him just to put a very big barrier between myself and the male population.

However, I will admit that Isabel regulates the sex trade as tightly as she does the booze. Part of that regulation is making damned sure every woman who does it wants to do it, is safe doing it, and can say no to any client. And woe to the man who asks twice once he's gotten that no.

At this time of day, the Roc is closed. It'll open at five, and Isabel's "girls" won't be on duty until nine. That's a recent development, as Isabel tries to make the Roc more accessible to female patrons. I'd pointed out the unfairness of having half of the bars virtually off-limits to female patrons. Isabel saw my point, and we negotiated the nonbrothel early-bird hours.

I open the doors and walk into the Roc, which looks like a Wild West saloon. I'll admit that part of the "female-friendly" schedule changes are totally selfish on my part. The Red Lion can be stuffy. The Roc is a place where you can grab a drink and park yourself at any table and be welcomed into the conversation.

Right now, the inside is dim and cool and smells of pine shavings. The shavings cover the floor, both for atmosphere and easy cleaning at night's end, shavings swept up in the morning and fed back into that evening's fire as kindling. We are conservation kings in Rockton. Also, the shavings smell nice and add to that old-time saloon atmosphere.

I walk behind the bar to the most secure door in Rockton: the liquor safe. It's closed, and I raise my hand to knock just as a noise sounds from overhead. The very distinctive sound of bedsprings squeaking . . . along with other distinctive sounds that often accompany that one.

I could leave and come back in an hour. That would be the

right thing to do. My business with Phil isn't urgent. Not as urgent as his current business. However . . . Well, really, this is just too much fun to resist.

I take a jug of iced tea from the underfloor cooler, pour a glass, and wait. The sounds subside after just enough time for me to finish my drink. Then I head upstairs, calling, "Isabel?"

I reach the top of the steps. "Isabel? It's Casey. I'm looking for Phil, and I was told he was here—"

The door at the end opens, and a woman steps out dressed in a wrapper. Isabel Radcliffe. Former therapist. Current bar and brothel owner. And while I'd love to claim the title of most powerful woman in Rockton for myself, I have to concede it to her. She controls the booze and the sex, and that makes her the queen.

Isabel is forty-six years old and quite possibly the most glamorous woman I have ever met. She's full-figured and attractive, but it's more than that. It's confidence and style, and she oozes both. Brilliant. Manipulative. A sheer force of nature, one I have butted heads with since I arrived, which doesn't stop me from now considering her one of my closest friends. Nor does it stop the head-butting. We'd hate to lose that.

"I found Phil, didn't I?" I say as she pads barefoot down the hall.

Her smile answers for her. It's wicked, and it's very, very pleased with herself, and I can't help laughing. She's had her eye on Phil since he arrived, which I'd been glad to see. She'd spent the last year in mourning for a lover—claiming she was over him, while not so much as glancing at another man. This is a welcome turn of events.

I'm about to comment when footsteps sound behind me. As Dalton comes up the stairs, I say to Isabel, "So, was he worth the chase?"

"Definitely," she says, leaning against the wall. "I'll admit

I was concerned about that. He's very pretty, and too often, men use that as an excuse for lackluster sex. Women do, too, I presume. So it's a relief to get a partner who is both pretty and proficient." She glances at Dalton. "Am I right, Sheriff?"

Dalton arches his brows.

"Just say yes," I say.

"Considering I don't know what she's talking about, that seems unwise," he says.

Isabel smiles. "Oh, believe me, it's wise. Unless you want to say that Casey here is lovely to look at but terribly dull to bed."

Dalton looks at me and jerks a thumb toward the closed door down the hall. "Phil?"

"Yes," I say. "And Isabel assures us he's both pretty and good in bed."

"Just what I wanted to hear." He strides down the hall and bangs his fist on the door. "Phil? Get your pants on. We need to talk."

"Don't keep him long, please," Isabel says as she heads downstairs. "Twenty minutes would be optimal."

I shake my head and join Dalton as the door opens. Phil is fully dressed, as if he'd just been talking inventory with Isabel because the bedroom is a more comfortable place to do business. His fly is down, though, and the back of his hair stands on end.

"Zip up," Dalton says as he walks past.

Phil does and then spots his glasses on the nightstand and grabs them, which is a shame, because I was going to try confirming my suspicion that the lenses are plain glass. Phil reminds me of those stock-photo pictures of young businessmen, where they stick glasses on a male model and take a picture of him with a stack of files, as if every corporate department is filled with guys who look like this.

"I was just . . ." Phil begins, struggling for an excuse.

"Taking Isabel's inventory?" I say.

He actually blushes. It's kinda cute. He's stammering an excuse when Dalton says, "No one cares if you're sleeping with Isabel."

"Well, yes," I say. "I can think of a few women—and men—who'll be disappointed that you've chosen a partner. But *we* don't care. It's a long cold winter, and Isabel is a good choice to make it a little warmer."

"Yeah," Dalton says. "Up here relationships can get complicated. Expectations start low and soar fast. Isabel's a safe bet. It'll be straight sex. No danger of attachment."

Phil checks his glasses for smudges and then puts them on. "Yes, of course. That was my thought. As much as I admire Isabel, you don't need to worry about me forming any undue attachment."

"I meant there's no danger of *her* forming one."

Phil goes still, and the look on his face . . . I could say something, smooth over Dalton's bluntness. Once upon a time, I would have. Now, well, Phil will get over it, and if this makes him work harder to win Isabel's favor, she'll appreciate that.

"So, we're back early," I say.

"Yes, that's right," Phil says, adjusting his glasses. "You are. What happened?"

"We have a baby."

Phil blinks. "You're having . . ."

"Already have one. She's at the clinic."

More blinking. Dalton's lips twitch as he leans against the wall to enjoy the fun.

"She . . . ?" Phil says. "You had a . . . baby?"

"No, *we* have a baby. Rockton does."

"I . . ." Phil sits on the bed. "I don't . . . understand."

"I found an infant," I say. "She was with a woman who I presumed was her mother. That woman was dead. The baby was buried under the snow with the body. There was no one around, so I had to bring her back. She's at the clinic."

It takes a moment for his brain to assimilate this new information. Then he says, "We are not equipped to handle a baby, Casey."

"No shit," Dalton says. "That's why we're talking to you. We need supplies."

I hold up my hand. "We are well aware that this isn't an abandoned puppy. We aren't adopting her. First thing tomorrow, we're heading out to find her family. Given the vastness of this wilderness—and the fact it's winter—that might take a while. It's not like we can go on TV and announce we found a child. The plan is to go to the First Settlement. If they can't help, we'll need baby supplies while we continue looking for her family. So this visit is partly to ask—"

"Inform," Dalton says.

"Yes, *inform* you that we may be making an unexpected supply run. That's a given. The 'ask' part was me suggesting that we use the run to treat residents to some extras for the holidays, since we'd be going to Dawson and only bringing back diapers, formula, and whatever."

"It's been a shitty year, and they deserve a good holiday," Dalton says. "So we're requisitioning—"

"*Asking* for extra funds to do that. We'll even say you suggested it, if you'd like. You can be Santa this year."

"Thank you," Phil says dryly, but I know I've spun this the right way. Phil is a shrewd businessman, and this is a wise investment toward cementing his local reputation.

I continue, "We also need you to speak to the council. Tell them we have a baby. Explain the situation. Give them no opportunity to later rap our knuckles for covering this up. Even they can't argue that we should have left an infant in the forest."

"Agreed."

"We want that done right away, because we know past situations have fostered an environment of mistrust, and we want to be totally aboveboard with this."

"Uh-huh. Which is an excuse for contacting them quickly, when what you really want is . . ."

I smile at him. "You're a quick study. We appreciate that. Yes, informing them of the baby is the excuse. What I really want is to tell them about the dead woman and see if there's any chance they can identify her. She's almost certainly a former Rockton resident. We can't send them a photo, of course—not until we get to Dawson and have internet access—but we'll give you a full description. If she's in their files, we may be able to figure out which settlement she's associated with. Or which settlement's residents she might know from her time in Rockton. Impress on the council that identifying this woman could return the baby to her parents. Otherwise . . ." I shrug. "Maybe you'd like a tiny roomie?"

"No," he says quickly. "Thank you for asking. I will write up a full description of this woman . . ."

I hand him my notes. He takes the page.

"If you learn anything, let us know," I say. "Otherwise, we'll be off for the First Settlement before dawn."

He grabs his jacket from a chair by the bed.

"It's not that big a rush," I say. "I think Isabel wanted to speak to you first. I'll send her up."

Dalton and I head downstairs, to where Isabel is at the bar, writing something.

"He's all yours," I say. "Better hurry, though. It's almost five."

She holds up what she'd been writing. It's a sign.

*The Roc will open at 6 PM today, so as not to interfere with the wassail party.*

"You're so considerate," I say.

She hands me the sign. "Hang it, and lock the door, please."

# NINE

As much as we'd love to head out again, chasing answers, it's already dark. The investigation will need to wait until morning. I stop by the wassail party long enough to announce that there is a baby in town. Residents will hear her, so they need to know she's here and why. I say that I understand people may want to see her, but she's very young and we don't know the full state of her health and immune system and must restrict contact to caregivers only.

After that, Dalton and I pick up Storm and then have an early dinner, while taking the baby for a couple of hours to give Jen time to eat. Overnight, she'll stay with Jen.

Because the Roc opened late, Isabel extends the pre-brothel hours, and at nine, we're there with Anders and April, with Storm gnawing a bone under the table. It's been a long day. Tomorrow will be another long one. We can afford an hour off to enjoy a mug of mulled alcoholic beverage and kettle corn, the festive snack of the evening.

By the time Dalton is two-thirds done with his cider, I'm on his lap. I did not put myself there. I'm not quite sure how

I arrived there, either, which may suggest I've imbibed more alcohol than I intended.

Isabel stops by to refill the popcorn bowl and smirks at us, Dalton with his arms tight around me, his head on my shoulder, nuzzling my neck. If he's doing that in public . . .

"Exactly how much rum is in this cider?" I ask.

"In general?" Anders says. "Or in ours?" He lifts his mug. "I do believe Iz was feeling generous tonight."

"It does seem . . ." April stares into her barely touched drink. "Strong."

"I owe you for earlier," Isabel says to me. She waves at Dalton. "Enjoy."

"This isn't a gift," I say as I firmly move Dalton's hands to my waist. "It's payback."

"We don't ever get to see our sheriff drunk," Isabel says as she refills his mug before I can stop her. "It's adorable."

"It kinda is," Anders says as she leaves. "However . . ." He looks around the Roc, at residents watching their hard-ass sheriff nuzzling his girlfriend.

"Not a good look?" I say.

"He's fine," April says. "There's nothing wrong with mild acts of public affection."

"Nah," Dalton says, straightening. "There is when it's the sheriff slobbering on his detective. And, yeah, you don't need to talk about me in the third person. I've had more than I should, but I'm not that drunk."

"Also, for the record," I say, "there was no actual slobbering. You're just very cuddly. As Will said, it is adorable but . . ."

I slide off his lap. He lets me go with reluctance and a last squeeze before saying, "Yeah, time to cut me off."

"Unless you want the rest of your cider to-go."

The slow smile that crosses Dalton's face has Anders making

gagging noises. April stops him with a sharp rap on the arm, which proves that her drink is indeed strong. Dalton gets to his feet.

"I'll grab take-out cups," he says.

"I thought we weren't allowed take-out alcohol," April says.

"Eric is special," Anders says.

I give Storm a pat under the table as I watch Dalton cross to the bar. He's walking steadily, no sign of inebriation in his gait or his stance. It's still very obvious that he's tipsy. Normally, even here socially, he carries himself with a certain stiffness. Tenser. Harder. Gaze constantly scanning for trouble, the set of his jaw warning that a wrong move could land the miscreant in the water trough outside.

Tonight he's the guy I see at home. Relaxed. Calm. Happy. A slight bounce in his step and the ghost of a smile on his lips. He looks younger, too, and this is one of the reasons he doesn't drink more than one beer in public. When he relaxes, the walls come down, his guard dropping, and people suddenly remember he's only thirty-two, and they start to wonder why he holds so much power, or why a glare from him can have them straightening in their seat, their hearts beating faster.

Isabel fills two bottles with hot mulled cider, leaving them uncapped, steam rolling out. Someone cracks a joke about Dalton getting special privileges, and there's a moment where I can tell Dalton's ready to joke back, the corners of his eyes crinkling. Then he remembers himself and sobers. "You want my job? Privileges come with that, and I don't think you want this"—he raises the bottles—"that badly."

The resident should leave it at that, but Dalton isn't the only one who's had too much, and this guy is new, not yet accustomed to how things work in Rockton. He grins and hooks a thumb at me. "If she's one of those privileges, I'll take it."

Silence drops so fast it ripples through the entire bar, those too far to hear the exchange noticing the hush and following it. A buzz of anticipation follows. A sense of schadenfreude that tells me that this guy has not made friends, no one even taking pity on him by leaping up to pull him back.

"*She* is our detective," Dalton says, his voice tight with warning.

The man chuckles and thumps Dalton on the shoulder. "No offense, Sheriff. I'm just saying you're a lucky guy. Hot booze. Hot chick. Gotta love a position with perks."

Dalton reaches over and dumps the contents of one bottle down the guy's shirt.

"Huh," Dalton says as the guy lets out a high-pitched shriek. "You're right. It *is* hot." He looks at Isabel. "You heat it up a little extra for me?"

"I wouldn't want your drink getting cold on the walk home."

Dalton grabs the front of the guy's shirt. "Special treatment from the barkeep? *That's* a perk. Detective Butler? *That's* a person. Learn the difference."

"You—you burned—"

"First degree, if that. Lucky for you, the doc's sitting right there."

Anders rises. "I'll get this one, April." He puts an arm around the man's shoulders, and the guy flinches, but Anders only gives him a friendly squeeze. "We'll have a nice chat, too, while I'm looking at that burn."

They nearly bump into Kenny, who's just come into the Roc. He looks from Anders to the burned guy. Then he sees Dalton and nods, as if this is all the explanation he needs.

I wave Kenny to our table. "Perfect timing. We were about to abandon my sister."

If it were anyone else, April would say that she'd been leaving. For Kenny, she'll stick around.

Isabel holds out a fresh bottle of cider. Dalton takes it before I can, and he motions me to the door. Storm follows at our heels.

We're outside and away from the Roc before I snatch one of the bottles and take a long draw from it.

My eyes water, and I gasp. "I think she made these even stronger than the ones we got inside."

I take another gulp, and Dalton laughs at that. His gloves go around my hips, and he hoists me onto the railing of a shop, dark and closed for the day. Then he pushes between my knees, and I get a long, cider-sweet kiss.

Storm sees what's happening, sighs, and plunks down to wait, the model of patience. Dalton sips a far more cautious drink from his bottle. Hesitates. Gulps a larger swig.

I laugh and put my arms around his neck, bottle dangling from one hand.

"Having a good night, Sheriff?" I ask.

"It started off good. It's getting better." Another gulp. Another kiss. He blinks, forcing his eyes to focus, and I have to laugh at that.

"You are such a lightweight," I say.

"I'm not the only one."

"Hey, I shoot tequila. Straight."

"Yeah, Miss Two-Shots Max. You like to look like a badass, but I definitely saw some wobbling as we left the Roc."

"Which is one of the reasons we left." I hoist my bottle. "If I'm having more, I'm having it with just you."

"Ditto."

As he kisses me, his gaze shunts to the side, and he gives a start. Then he chokes on a laugh. I look to see . . .

It looks like a person standing there. It's actually a dummy, sitting on a wooden chair. A very homemade dummy, constructed of stuffed trousers stuck into boots and an equally stuffed red flannel shirt. The head is cotton stuffed into a nylon and painted with a red smile and round eyes. More cotton forms a beard. On the figure's head is an old red knit hat.

"Is that supposed to be Santa Claus?" Dalton asks.

I shudder. "Reminds me of the mall Santas my parents made me sit with. We had to get a duty photo every year to send to family—one of me sitting on the knee of some very sketchy Santas. April got out of it, naturally."

He scoops me up.

"No!" I say. "Don't you dare—"

He turns at the last second and plunks onto Santa's lap, crushing the poor dummy. Then he settles me onto his own lap and tugs the knit cap onto his head.

"So, little girl, what do you want for Christmas?"

"Oh God, now I really am scarred for life." I shudder. "Wrong, wrong, so wrong."

He tosses the hat aside and leans back, arms tightening around me. "I'll ask the question like this, then. What do you want for Christmas this year?"

I twist to look up at him and smile. "I do believe I have everything I want."

He goes as red at the Santa's flannel shirt.

"You're cute when you blush." I lean over to kiss him. "Still true, though. If we make that extra trip to Dawson, I'll come up with a completely frivolous wish list for you, but you'll owe me a list, too. As for what I want tonight—"

The sudden wail of a baby sounds in the distance. We look at each other.

"Not that," I say.

"Definitely not that."

We dissolve into tipsy giggles. Then I say, "Gotta admit, you looked damn good holding a baby. It suited you."

His head tilts, and I know he's catching the note in my voice.

A wistful one that says this isn't a hint that I want a child, but maybe a hint that I'm suddenly feeling the loss of that possibility.

"I might look good in a Speedo bathing suit, too," he says. "Doesn't mean I should have one."

I giggle, making me glad he's the only one here. It's definitely not a homicide-detective-worthy sound.

Dalton continues. "Now, if you said you wanted me in a Speedo, I'd get one in a heartbeat. I'm not opposed to them. Just not sure it'd suit me. Not sure it *wouldn't* suit me either. The truth is that I've never given it much thought one way or another. I could wear one if you wanted me to. Now. Later. Or I could go my entire life without ever wearing one, and that'd be fine, too. Which is exactly how I feel about a baby."

He adjusts me on his lap. "I said the same thing the first time you mentioned the issue, and that hasn't changed. I don't have strong feelings either way. I know you probably can't have a baby. We could try and see what happens. Or we can decide that's too stressful and find a way to adopt. Or we can say we're fine like this, you and me. This ball is one hundred percent in your court, Casey. I'm good with whatever you want."

"And if that changes? If you realize you want—or don't want—kids? Would you tell me?"

"Absolutely," he says, and kisses me.

# TEN

We tumble into the house, having consumed about half our cider on the way. Hey, we wouldn't want it getting cold.

The door isn't even shut yet before we're kissing. Dalton doesn't lock it. He never does. That's a show of trust . . . and also a warning. Just try breaking into his house.

Storm knows what's coming and retreats to the kitchen. Dalton scoops me up and carries me into the living room, where the fire burns low. I have him undressed before we reach the bearskin carpet. I may make a few comments about how good he'd look in a Speedo. Totally true. He has a swimmer's lean muscled body, and I thoroughly admire it while he stokes the fire.

We aren't in any hurry. We can't leave for the First Settlement until close to dawn, so we take our time in the firelight. Afterward, he's lying on his back on the rug, and I'm stretched out on top of him, tracing my finger through a sheen of sweat on his chest.

"Definitely getting you a Speedo for Christmas," I say.

He chuckles. "Good luck with that in Dawson. Not much call for them there. Not much use for one either, at this time of year."

"I'll stoke the fire so you can wear it indoors."

He's about to reply when someone bangs at the door. It's loud and insistent enough that we can't just be quiet and wait for them to go away. Dalton starts reaching for his jeans. Then he stops, muttering, "Fuck it," and grabs a blanket from the pile. He swoops it out, letting it fall over us, and then calls "Come in!" as he adjusts the blanket to cover everything it should cover.

The door opens. Footsteps sound. Then the howl of a baby, followed by Jen's voice. "Yeah, I'd scream, too, kid. No one wants to see that. You guys do have a bed upstairs, don't you?"

"The fact we're not dressing to answer the door suggests we're expecting this to be a short visit," Dalton says.

"Oh, it will be. I'm just dropping off your kid. Hope you were done, because this is going to put a damper on things." She holds out the baby, who obliges with a howl.

"What's wrong with her?" I say, sliding off Dalton, blanket to my chest.

"Huh. I don't know. Maybe . . . the screaming? She won't settle. She's fed. Changed. Ready for bed and furious. She's making it very clear that Auntie Jen isn't who she wants."

"Well, I don't think she's looking for us, either. She wants her parents."

"Close enough." She holds the baby out again.

I motion for her to turn around, and she says, "Neither of you has anything I haven't seen before but fine."

Once she's turned, I yank on my undershirt and panties, and Dalton pulls on his jeans. Then I take the baby, who peers at me, head swaying as if trying to focus. Her lower lip trembles. When she lets out a cry, it's not the howl from before, but she's clearly gearing up for it. I pass her to Dalton.

"Me?" he says. "She doesn't want—"

I move his hands, so the baby is pressed against his chest, as she was on the way to Rockton. She fusses for a moment and then settles against him.

"I think she likes you," Jen says.

"It's my smell," he says. "I carried her back to town."

"Whew. 'Cause otherwise, that kid is already developing a shitty taste in men." She pats the baby's back. "Wait until you're a teenager for that."

Jen off-loads a pack from her back. "All the supplies."

"Whoa, wait," I say. "We need to leave first thing in the morning, which means we need a good night's sleep."

"Didn't look like you were sleeping when I got here."

"Actually, we were just about to."

"And now you can. She'll drift off, for a while at least. Either you take her or *no one* in town gets to sleep tonight. My neighbors were already trooping over, accusing me of beating the poor thing. She's in a strange place, and she's scared, and the people she knows best are you two."

"Fine, but come by at nine and pick her up."

"Take her with you."

"Uh, no. We're heading into the winter forest in search of her family."

"Exactly why she should go along. As for the 'winter forest,' she was born there. You guys brought her back, bundled up and happy. She's a month old. That's all she wants. Food. Warmth. Security. Pack her into Eric's parka again and off you go."

"We're taking the snowmobiles."

"Even better. You know how to get a kid to sleep down south? Take her for a car ride. The vibration and the steady noise are kiddie Ambien."

When I open my mouth to protest, she says, "I'm not trying to get out of looking after your kid, Casey. I have my monthly janitorial shift tomorrow. I would gladly—ecstatically—give that up to babysit. But she's already separated from her family, and you guys rescued her, and her tiny brain may not know much, but it knows she's safe with you. If you do find her parents, what are you going to do? Say 'Wait right here and we'll bring her tomorrow'? Her parents must be going nuts. They'll follow you back. Depending on who they are, that might not be safe for Rockton."

I look at Dalton. She's right, in all of it.

"Fine," Dalton says. "Just stay and help us set her up for bed. Tell us what we need to do. Feeding schedule, whatever."

She agrees, and we set up a fur-lined box for the baby in our bedroom as Storm snuffles her.

"The pup has to stay downstairs," Jen says. "As friendly as she is, this is a very tiny kiddo."

"I know," I say. "'Oh, look, they're cuddling' can become 'Why is the baby turning blue?' in a heartbeat."

Jen snorts a laugh. "Exactly. Also, you need a temporary name for her."

"We—"

She lifts a hand. "I've done that for you, too. It's Abby."

My gaze shunts to Dalton, who has gone still, and anger surges in me.

"That's not—" I begin, but Jen's already leaving.

When she's gone, I turn to Dalton. "We don't need to call her that. We don't need to call her anything."

He tucks the baby in, quiet as the front door closes behind Jen. Then he says, his voice low, "No, Abby is fine," and he pulls a thin blanket up and touches the baby's face before going to settle Storm downstairs.

The baby wakes twice for feeding and once for a soiled diaper and once just because, apparently, she's had enough sleep. By five we give up and start breakfast.

Dalton has not yet referred to her as "Abby," and I won't

until he does. While Sebastian is young at nineteen, he isn't the youngest person to come to Rockton. That would be Abbygail. An eighteen-year-old street kid with a history of drug use and sex-trade work, she'd escaped to Rockton and turned her life around, only to be brutally murdered in the case that brought me here. By the time I arrived, she was missing, presumed dead. Everyone still held out hope until that was shattered with the discovery that her death had been even worse than "lost in the woods, succumbed to the environment." It was the human environment here that killed her.

In suggesting we call the baby Abby, I fear Jen wasn't honoring the memory of the much-loved girl. At worst, it was incredibly cruel, even for Jen, and I'd hope she would never stoop that low.

To Dalton, the death of Abbygail is his greatest failure as a sheriff. She went from hating the sight of him to idolizing him, first as a mentor and then as more. That last part was the problem. When she kissed him after her twenty-first birthday party, he rejected her, horrified. She fled Rockton and died in the forest. Or so it seemed. But her killers had exploited her crush and sent her a note, apparently from Dalton, telling her to meet him in the forest to talk. She went, and she never came back.

Jen had been the one to tell me about the kiss. She made it sound as if Dalton took advantage of Abbygail's hero worship. When I learned the truth, I'd confronted her, and she'd shrugged it off, as if she'd known all along and just been stirring up trouble.

So what was Jen's intention calling the baby Abby? Acknowledging that he'd done all he could for the young woman and that her loss haunted him still? Or rubbing his face in his failure? I hope it's the former, but all that matters now is Dalton's reaction, and the fact that he's even considering it gives me hope. It tells me maybe he's ready to honor Abbygail's memory instead of running from it.

Before we leave, we stop at Phil's. He's spoken to the council. They have nothing to say about the baby. They don't recognize the description of the dead woman, though I'm not sure how hard they'd try. On that count, all they're saying is that, while I am free to investigate her death as a way to reunite the child with her family, please remember that I am Rockton law enforcement, and the key word in that phrase is "Rockton." The death of a settler, while tragic, falls outside my purview.

"I told them that your responsibilities here have been light leading into the holidays," Phil says. "Also, such an investigation helps hone your skills and foster better relations with our neighbors."

*Unless I accuse one of them of murder.*

I don't say that. I know Phil is trying for a head pat by defending me, and I give him one, figuratively at least. Then we're off.

Dalton and I share a snowmobile, leaving the other in case Anders needs it. We take turns driving, the other sitting on the back with the baby bundled in their parka. Jen was right that the baby would sleep most of the time. We stop for feedings and changes and cuddles, because the last seems to complete the trifecta of awake-baby needs. When we can't figure out why she's fussing, we bounce her and talk to her and dance her on our knees. That seems to do the trick.

We can't take the snowmobile all the way to the First Settlement. The trails leading into it aren't wide enough, intentionally. Rockton has horses, ATVs, and snowmobiles. The settlements have none of these, and so for them, wide paths only increase the chance that outsiders will find them . . . or that folks from Rockton will mistake it for a rolled-out welcome mat. So we hide the sled off the path and cover it with a tarp and snow. Then we head in on foot.

Rockton began as a refuge for the persecuted, no criminals permitted. That ideology lasted as long as the accounting books balanced. With each major shift in priorities, a group would leave. The First Settlement was founded in the sixties. Fifty years have passed since, and they're on the third generation, with only two original Rockton residents left, including the town leader, Edwin. As the original settlers die out, their town's connection with ours fades.

The relationship has never been friendly, but it has always been one of mutual disinterest. Live and let live. Dalton fears that will change when Edwin is gone. The younger settlers see Rockton as weak and wealthy. We have those horses and snowmobiles and ATVs, and we are soft, living in relative luxury. We've already seen signs of trouble.

While Edwin lives, we are trying to build bridges. While we might be a handful of shepherds protecting a fat flock, we have all the guns we need to repel an attack . . . and soak the ground with their blood. We don't want that, so we work on building that bridge while making sure the younger settlers see what they are up against.

The problem is that Edwin is an aging lion, well aware of the hungry eyes on his throne. This is not a time he can show weakness by getting chummy with Rockton—the king of the jungle conversing with the gazelle. He must instead play the sly fox who always gets the better end of any deal.

The subtle tug-of-war exhausts Dalton. Our sheriff has no fear of usurpation and no patience for politicking. His personal history with the First Settlement doesn't help. He remembers the men who eyed his mother and talked about her like that new resident spoke about me last night, as if she were a potential trade good. When the male settlers give me the same looks, it doesn't foster good relations. I'm less bothered by it than he is, as I suspect his mother was less bothered than his father. Women expect this. It doesn't mean we tolerate it, but it is a fact of our lives.

As we approach the settlement, Dalton hears someone outside it and hails them with a "Hello!" We know better than to sneak up—or give anyone an excuse to *say* we snuck up. It's one of the men, second generation, maybe in his early forties. He's hauling wood on a toboggan, and when he sees us, he nods and then keeps going, letting us follow him to the village.

I don't try to talk to the man. I've learned my lesson in this. What seems common courtesy is seen as timidity, as if I'm making nervous conversation.

When the man doesn't speak, we don't either, not until we're entering the village and Dalton says, "We'd like to talk to Edwin." The man nods and keeps walking, and we stop there, on the edge of the village.

# ELEVEN

The First Settlement is also the largest. It's still a quarter the size of Rockton, with fifteen cabins. On my first visit, I'd counted ten, but there were five more deeper in, like a suburb to the main village. Even the central cabins are sparsely spaced. Protection isn't really an issue out here, and it helps to have that extra room for gardens and privacy.

As we're waiting, a shriek sounds, deep in the village. Dalton's head jerks up, his eyes following the sound. A moment later, a door opens and a man appears, dragging a child by the arm.

"You want to play outside?" the man booms. "Fine. Go to the woodpile and start hauling logs. Come back in when that"—he points at the small heap beside their cabin—"is as tall as you."

The boy is no more than six. He wails his protest, but the door slams shut. My arms instinctively close around the baby under my parka. Dalton strides forward, and I jog after him, torn between not wanting to cause trouble and seeing the child, shivering and sniveling, barely dressed for the cold.

Dalton crouches beside the boy, who sits in the snow, softly crying. Dalton pulls off his hat and puts it on the boy's head. Then he wraps his scarf around the child and whispers something to him. The boy nods and rises, pointing. Dalton strides off, the boy tagging along behind. They disappear behind trees, only to return a moment later, their arms stacked with wood.

Dalton may have no head for politics, but I give him too little credit if I expected him to go after the boy's father, all fire and fury. This is the boy's life. Crying in the snow will not help. Nor will having strangers fix his problems. I watch Dalton haul logs with the boy, and I cradle the baby under my parka and I think, more than I want to, about things I'd rather not.

Another door opens, and Edwin calls to me. As I walk over, the old man's gaze shunts to Dalton helping the boy. He says nothing. He just ushers me inside and shuts the door behind me.

The cabin is blazing hot, the fire roaring. I unzip my parka and remove the baby from the makeshift papoose.

"You'd better not tell me that's yours," Edwin says. "Or time is passing even faster than I feared."

"I found her in the snow."

His brows rise into his hairline, and he looks at me, as if trying to tell whether I've misused a word. We're speaking in Mandarin. Mine is about the equivalent of a five-year-old's, so it wouldn't be the first time I misspoke. I'd much rather use English, but I know to indulge Edwin in this. My Chinese blood elevates me in his eyes. He's an old man, proud of his heritage, dismissive of those who don't share it.

Edwin settles onto his chair. He isn't large, and age has made him smaller still. He's healthy, though, and his mind is fully functional. He's a former lawyer, which makes this old fox particularly crafty . . . though that might be my own prejudice as a cop.

"Found her in the snow?" he says finally.

I nod.

"Well, she isn't ours," he says. "No one here has had a child in five years. Nor do we want her, if that's what you're asking."

"It isn't."

I hope I don't look relieved when he says she isn't theirs. I keep thinking of that boy and his father, and I do not want her to be a child of this settlement. That's unfair, I know. As I said, it's a harsh life, and there is no room for soft parenting. Still, my hands clutch the baby a little tighter.

A rap sounds at the door.

"Come in, Eric," Edwin calls in English. When Dalton enters, he says, "Done playing with Jamie?"

Dalton grunts.

Edwin continues. "I'll see that you get your hat and scarf back before you go. And I'll speak to his father."

Dalton nods, and at that, the matter is dropped.

"So, Casey tells me you found this baby," Edwin says, "and you're looking for her people. As much as it pains me to say this, if she was found in the snow . . ."

He glances toward the door. "It's the beginning of winter. All signs point toward a long and cold one. Our practice of contraception, if I may be indelicate, is limited to less-than-foolproof methods. We advocate keen attention to monthly cycles, and children must be born before late summer. We would certainly never abandon a winter baby, but in the forest, between the hostiles and the nomads . . ." He shrugs. "There is, I fear, a reason why the child was left alone in the snow."

"Under other circumstances, I'd agree," I say. "However, she wasn't alone. We found her with a dead woman who was not her mother."

His eyes glitter. "That is intriguing."

"Yeah," Dalton says. "I know your English seems perfect, but I think the word you want is 'tragic.'"

Edwin only shoots him a withering look. He turns to me and says, "Explain," in Mandarin, a clear slight to Dalton. When I answer, it's in English.

"The woman had been murdered," I say. "She died holding the infant, but our doctor says she's not the mother. The baby was wrapped only in skins, so I have no clues to her identity. I do have some to the woman's, though, which I hope will lead me in the direction I need to go."

I hand the baby to Dalton, then open my pack and pull out a decorated portion of the woman's parka that I cut off for easy transport.

I pass him the piece. I have the ankle bracelet, too, but I want to show him this first. When I do, he gives a slow nod as he runs the fabric through his fingers.

"You recognize the handiwork?" I say.

He hands it back. "If I say I do not, will you accept that the baby is abandoned?"

"We aren't looking for an excuse to keep a baby, Edwin."

"Perhaps. But I *am* looking for an excuse to stop you from returning this child to her family."

"Why?"

"Because you would make a good mother. You are young, strong, intelligent. Eric would make a good father. He is young and strong."

Dalton snorts, not missing the adjective Edwin has skipped.

Edwin only smiles and looks at me, with a wave at Dalton. "See how happy that baby is with Eric? How easily he holds it? How he helped young Jamie? He is a natural father. That's rare. You should take advantage of it."

"By stealing a baby so Eric will be stuck with me?" I say. "Not exactly my recipe for a happy family."

"Oh, I'm sure he would be very happy to be stuck with you. Wouldn't you, Eric?"

Dalton only rolls his eyes, and I say, "I'm not taking this baby from her family. If you know who they are—"

"I do, which is why I am suggesting you forget them. The child was abandoned. Found with a dead woman, who probably *is* her mother. Your doctor was clearly wrong. The child is motherless and alone. You should take her."

"So which is it? The baby was abandoned? Or orphaned?"

He shrugs. "Both. The mother is dead. The father and any other family are obviously not combing the forest looking for her. The child is better off with you."

Dalton tenses. Edwin looks at him, and it's a keen look, a piercing one. I know what's coming next. I feel the subject shifting, and I open my mouth to stop it, but Edwin says, "You don't think you were better off in Rockton, Eric?"

"No," Dalton says tightly. "I don't."

"But Gene Dalton thought you were. Snatched you up and kept you, and you made no attempt to leave. You must have thought it was better. An easy life for a boy. So much easier than in the forest."

Dalton's holding himself so rigid he barely gets the words out. "I did try to escape."

"Eventually, you gave up, though. Resigned yourself to the easier life. Such a hardship."

"My parents didn't come for me," he says. "They obviously thought I was better where I was."

Edwin's laugh is sharp. "So that's what made you stop. A child's pride. The boy sulking in the corner and telling himself his mother and father had abandoned him? Do you really think they didn't risk their *lives* trying to get you back?"

"So you agree then?" Dalton says, his voice low. "That taking me was wrong, and yet here you are, telling us to take *this* child?"

We stand on a precipice. One where I see the answers to

Dalton's past below. I can get them from Edwin. Dalton can get them, too. Yet to take that step means accepting the plummet that must go with it. His relationship with the Daltons is already precarious. If he learns that they didn't just naively "rescue" him from the forest but deliberately kept his birth parents away, he'd need to sever all ties with them.

In redirecting the conversation, Dalton has stepped back from that precipice. He doesn't want answers beyond what Edwin has already given. He isn't ready for them.

I can't tell whether this retreat from truth diminishes Dalton in Edwin's regard. It doesn't matter. Dalton will do what he needs to protect himself until he's ready for more, and no one can judge a person for those choices. They are what keep us sane. What keep us moving forward.

"This is not the same thing," Edwin says. "Your parents were young and naive, but they were good parents, and their sons came first. You were not mistreated or neglected in any way. In fact, I personally worried whether they were properly preparing you boys for this life. It is one thing to teach hunting and foraging and trading skills. But we need more out here. We need a harshness and a ruthlessness that your parents lacked, and therefore could not pass on to you. If your father saw Jamie tossed out of his warm cabin, he'd have gone after the boy's father. You check that impulse. You make sure he is warm, and you help, but you do not let him shirk his duties. You would never say his parents don't deserve to keep him. This baby is different. Her people . . ." His lips curl. "Her people make Jamie's dad look like father of the year."

My breath catches, but I push it back and force myself to say, "Their worthiness as parents isn't for us to decide."

"Is it not? Down south they have child services. When I was a lawyer, my firm took on many cases of parents fighting to have their children returned. I refused to work on them.

While there were cases of injustice, the children I saw were better off. I'm sure you saw the same in policing."

He isn't looking for a thoughtful, long-winded response, and that's the only one I could give. Yes, I saw children taken from bad situations, who blossomed and thrived in foster care. Those are the success stories, and there were plenty of them, but there were others, too. Parents who screwed up and lost their kids and didn't get a second chance. Kids volleyed from institution to foster care and back, who fled to find their birth parents, because however tough that life had been, it was better than the alternative.

"Tell us where we can find the parents," I say. "We'll take it from there."

His lips tighten. "She would be better off—"

"We will take it from there," I say, enunciating each word, my gaze locked with his. "Either you trust us to do that or you don't."

"You'll have to wait until spring anyway," he says. "They're nomadic. Traders. It's an extended family. The parents aren't from Rockton. I've heard they were criminals who fled to the Yukon ahead of the law. I certainly believe it. While I would prefer not to trade with them, they bring items we cannot get otherwise. They travel all the way to Dawson for them. I don't know where they overwinter, but they'll be back in spring."

The baby starts to fuss in Dalton's arms. I reach for the pack and fill a makeshift bottle with warm milk from a thermos. Dalton takes it, and the baby quiets.

"You *are* a natural mother, Casey," Edwin says. "Like Eric is a natural father. You didn't even stop to think what she might want."

"So this family of traders," I say. "They make goods like this?" I lifted the fabric.

"They do."

"And it was on the dead woman. Not the baby. Which doesn't mean the child comes from them."

"One of their women was pregnant when they were here last. I say 'woman,' but she was barely more than a girl. As for the baby's father, let's just say goods aren't the only thing that family sells."

He motions to the fabric. "This woman who died. My guess is that she stole the baby. She must trade with them regularly, and she knew what kind of life that child would have—particularly a girl—so she stole her." He meets my gaze. "To honor her sacrifice, you should keep the baby."

I snort a laugh. "Yeah, no."

He shrugs. "It was worth a try." The old man rises. "Now, let's get your hat and scarf back, Eric. I'll also have you speak to Jamie's mother, Casey. He's our youngest resident, and she may have advice for the baby."

# TWELVE

Jamie's mother seems like a kind woman, if not the sort who's likely to challenge her spouse. Edwin sends the father on an errand, and we settle into the small cabin, Dalton playing with the boy while I talk to his mother. She cuddles the baby and coos over her, and we discuss the challenges of caring for an infant in the forest. Or it's a challenge for me. For her, it's called "life." She's third generation herself, twenty-two years old, her son already five, which makes me wonder just how old this baby's mother is, if Edwin called *her* "little more than a girl."

Afterward, Dalton and I leave. We don't talk for a while—we want to be farther from the settlement before we do. I'm about to speak when Dalton raises a finger and wraps one arm around the baby-bundle under his jacket as he lifts his gun and scans what seems to be a silent forest. Then I catch the squeak of a boot on snow.

I pull out my weapon.

Dalton calls, "You have five seconds to show yourselves."

He doesn't finish the threat. He could say "Or I start firing" but then he'd need to, and that's a waste of ammo.

"Five, four, three . . ." He wheels, gun aimed, and I hear a sharp intake of breath, though I see nothing in the lengthening shadows.

"You settlers love playing this game, don't you?" he says. "Let's test Eric Dalton. See how good a tracker he really is." He wags the gun toward where it's pointing. "There's one of you." He moves it to the left. "Two." Then back around behind him. "Three. Please tell me there's a prize, 'cause there's never a prize, and I'm starting to feel discouraged."

"The prize is you saw us before we put an arrow in you," a voice says.

Dalton grunts. "Guess so. Still, I'd like an actual prize. Okay, kid, step out where I can see you, and let's have a civil conversation."

"Kid?" There's clear affront in the voice, but the young man who steps out isn't any older than Sebastian.

Dalton shrugs. "Compared to me, you are, though you're older than your two companions."

The young man glances around, seeing no sign of his companions. "How can you tell that?"

"Because they let you speak while they cower behind the trees like children."

That brings the other two out. I can't say for certain whether they are indeed younger. All three are in their late teens. The one already out is dark-haired and sporting a sparse beard. The second is another boy, towheaded and smooth-cheeked. The third is a girl with straight dark hair and skin the same shade as my own. When she says, "What business did you have with my grandfather?" I'm not surprised.

"That would be between Edwin and us," I say.

She shrugs off my nonreply, as if she hadn't expected an answer. "We'd like to trade. We have furs. Caribou, fox, ermine, and mink." She passes me her mitten. It's soft suede lined with ermine. "I can make more. Jackets, too." She looks at mine. "They're prettier than that."

I reach into my pocket and tug out the embroidered piece of leather. "Like this?"

Her nose wrinkles. "Better. That crafter has spent too much time on the decoration, too little on the tanning."

"You know the work?"

She shrugs. "I've seen it. You don't want that. You want mine."

"What if I wanted both? Something from you, and something from this person. Your grandfather said it's from a family of traders, and he doesn't know where they overwinter."

"He knows," she says. "And he does you a favor not sending you to them. Your man"—she nods to Dalton—"is too rich, and you are too pretty. They'd offer to trade, and then kill him for his goods and take you."

She has her grandfather's directness, but with her, it's blunt, no coy calculation. Even when she tells me I'm pretty, it's a simple assessment, devoid of flattery.

At her words, my heart sinks. I'd hoped she'd tell me a story different from her grandfather's.

"What are you looking to trade for?" I ask.

She points at my gun, and Dalton mutters, "Of course." I could drop the conversation here. Maybe I should. But an idea sparks. Something I hadn't asked Edwin, knowing I wouldn't get a straight answer. It's too loaded a question to ask outright. This could be a sideways step into it, though.

"Do you know what this is?" I say, lifting my weapon.

Her face hardens. "I'm not an ignorant savage. It's a gun."

"I meant the type of gun. You have a rifle or two in the settlement, right?"

"We do."

"This isn't a rifle. It a handgun, intended for self-defense.

It'll do a lousy job of taking down a buck—unless it's charging at you and you just want to empty the entire magazine into it. This is a semiautomatic weapon. A nine-millimeter. That means two things. It fires a lot of ammo, and it fires a very specific type. I know that's your biggest challenge up here—getting ammunition. No trader is going to carry this."

I open the weapon and show her the cartridges. Then I nod toward Dalton's weapon.

"That's a revolver. Also for self-defense. An entirely different type of ammo, though."

He opens it and shows her.

I continue. "We have a third handgun in town, for our deputy. It's a forty-five. Again, another kind of ammo. Now, first, we can't give you any of those three because they're the only handguns we have, and we keep them on us at all times." I add the last to be clear they won't find them lying around Rockton. "We can get ammo for them. You can't. Once the magazine is empty, you'd have a lovely paperweight."

Her brow furrows, and I realize "paperweight" wouldn't mean anything to her.

"A deadweight," I amend. "Now, if you wanted to trade for a rifle, we might be able to arrange something. We don't carry ours unless we're hunting. Otherwise, they're secured in a gun safe, and even I can't get at them. We'd be willing to consider trading you a rifle but we'd need to know what caliber you have already and whether we can match it. Otherwise . . ." I shrug. "You're back to the same problem of ammo."

The girl nods. "My grandfather is very careful about that. Our rifles are all three-oh-eights."

Dalton grunts behind me. He's finally figured out where this odd line of conversation was going. I seeded in the information about our gun lockers, as a matter of security, but the main purpose is to find out what type of weapons the First Settlement has, and whether they match the one used to kill the murdered woman. While her death isn't my top priority, I'm a homicide detective; I'm not going to ignore a chance to solve it.

There'd been no way to ask Edwin this without his guessing why I was asking and tailor his response accordingly. While his granddaughter is obviously bright and shrewd, she's also young, and she doesn't sense a trap here. She's focused on her goal of getting a gun.

"I can't promise you a trade," I say, "but we might have an old—"

"We want that gun," the bearded youth says, pointing at Dalton's. These two boys have been silent until now. Dalton had called this one the leader, because he stepped out first, but it's obvious that the girl is in charge. She just wasn't foolish enough to expose herself so quickly. Having stepped out, she's done all the talking, and the boys let her, as if they're accustomed to this.

"We want a handgun, as you call it," he says. "I like his. It has bigger bullets."

The girl rolls her eyes. "Bigger only means it'll put bigger holes in our dinner. The barrels are too short, meant for shooting at close range. That's not what I want."

"I want—"

"And what are you going to trade for it?" she says. "This gun is for me."

"You do not need a gun. I will hunt for you, when you are my wife."

"Which is why I am never going to be your wife, Angus," she says, and Dalton snorts at that, earning a sour look from the bearded boy—Angus.

"If Felicity wants to hunt, she should," says the towheaded boy, who looks a year or so younger than the others. "She is good at it."

"Do you mean that?" Felicity retorts. "Or is it false flattery to win my approval?"

The towheaded boy stammers, searching for a response. Then he says, "You are a good hunter, and if you married me, I would let you help me hunt."

"How kind of you," Felicity says dryly. She turns to me. "The gun is for me. My grandfather says I may only have one if I barter for it myself."

"I can't promise anything, but let me see what we have, and the next time we come by, I'll speak to you."

While I'm not eager to supply the First Settlement with weapons, hers is a reasonable request. We shouldn't refuse them the means of survival for fear they'll turn those hunting tools on us. I also suspect Edwin's granddaughter would be a good ally to have among the younger generation.

The trio starts to leave. Then Felicity says something to them, and they stay where they are while she jogs back to us. When she decides we're out of earshot of the boys, she stops.

"I wanted to say thank you," she says. "For taking Harper away."

"We didn't take her," I say. "She left."

Felicity nods dismissively, as if this is the same thing. "She is Angus's little sister, so he will not appreciate me saying this, but even he would agree. She was . . . not right. Dangerous. We knew it. Angus saw it. She would do things that hurt him, and she would not care, as long as she got what she wanted. The elders never saw it. She was very, very careful."

"She was—" I'm about to say "a good actor," but Felicity won't understand that. "She was very good at being what others wanted to see."

"Yes. Sometimes, living like this, it does things to people. Makes them hard and cruel. I just wanted to say thank you." Her eyes cloud for a second as she glances at the boys. "She is gone, yes? Not coming back?"

"Almost certainly not."

Her lips set, as if that's not as clear an answer as she'd like, but she nods and says, "I hope not. For all our sakes." Then, without another word, she lopes back to the waiting boys.

# THIRTEEN

When the young settlers are gone, I say to Dalton, "Were you okay with that? I didn't promise her a rifle."

"If I wasn't okay with it, I'd have said so. It's worth considering. Those boys might be vying for her hand, but they don't interrupt when she talks. That means Edwin is grooming her for leadership. She seems smart, levelheaded. Wanting to trade for her own hunting rifle is reasonable. I'd make it a hard bargain, but I wouldn't discount it."

He slows to adjust the baby, stirring from sleep. She fusses, but a few pats and rubs on her back quiet her.

Dalton resumes talking. "So, the gun that killed the woman didn't come from the First Settlement. That helps."

"It does.

"As for the baby's family, if they're as bad as Edwin and Felicity say . . ." I inhale. "I don't know what to do about that."

He takes a few more steps, and then says, his voice lower, "Yeah, you do. We both do. We wouldn't find a beaten dog in the forest and return it to abusive owners. It's a tough call, but we have to make the choice we can live with. The problem is judging . . ."

"How bad is too bad?" I say.

"Yeah."

He goes quiet after that, and I think he's going to stay that way until we reach the snowmobile. Then he straightens and says, "Main thing now is finding them. I know Edwin says they don't overwinter around here, but the baby hasn't been away from her mother for long. They must be within a day's walk."

I'm about to say that we'll have time to do that today before being stopped by the immovable obstacle of winter. Night. We can't make it before darkness falls.

Dalton has already figured this out and continues with, "We'll head back to Rockton for the night, and then tomorrow, we'll go find Jacob . . ." He trails off, cursing as he remembers his brother isn't around.

"Tyrone?" I say.

He grumbles but says, "Yeah, we'll find Ty. See what he knows about these traders."

The next morning, we take the baby to Jen's place for the day. We expect to be coming back after talking to Cypher, so there's no reason to cart her along. Instead, we take Storm. We'd considered riding the horses, but snow fell overnight, and it's still falling the next morning. So we strap on snowshoes and head out.

Of all the "mobility tools" in Rockton, snowshoes are my least favorite. Dalton jokes that's because—as opposed to the horses, ATVs, and snowmobiles—snowshoes require actual physical effort. It's not just effort, though, it's *serious* effort, more than walking, which seems to defy the purpose of a mobility tool. Except that . . . well, if we're using snowshoes, it's because walking in boots *wouldn't* be faster or easier.

Our weekend trip had been along groomed paths. This walk will have a lot more backwoods hiking, and each step is like clomping down into knee-high mud. Snowshoes keep you on the surface, even if they're hellishly awkward to use. Or they are for me. Dalton's fine with them. He says I just need more practice. Since that means more trudging around in snowshoes, I'll stick to amateur status.

If I will grudgingly admit to one advantage to snowshoes, it's that they're excellent for hunting. They move nearly as silently as cross-country skis, and yes, I've suggested those to Dalton. He's hesitating because that's a mode of transport *he's* not accustomed to, and God forbid *he* should struggle. Admittedly, he's not sure how well they'll work in this environment. Maybe I'll ask for a cheap pair for Christmas to test them.

I might have been hired as a homicide detective, but my self-assigned secondary role is transportation chief, the chick who will ultimately bring to Rockton every possible—and possibly fun—way to traverse the wilderness. Dirt bike, dogsled, and soon, cross-country skis. Dalton doesn't appreciate my efforts nearly as much as he should, perhaps not surprising given that he's spent his career trying to convince residents that traveling outside of the town is *not* fun, not fun at all.

Since we have the snowshoes and we're heading into a game-rich area, we both carry rifles slung over our shoulders. We've also brought a makeshift harness and canvas "sled bag" for Storm to bring back any larger game.

For now, Storm is free to romp through the snow. We've shot four ptarmigan, but Dalton has those slung over his shoulder.

Down south, I'd known plenty of cops who hunted, and some would invite me. I never accepted. I wasn't rabidly against hunting. As a nonvegetarian, I'd be hypocritical to judge anyone for killing their own meat. I just wasn't always convinced that my colleagues hunted *for* meat. Sure, they'd get some of their kill carved up, but most of that stayed at the bottom of their freezer, an excuse for the sport.

Up here, it's all about utility. Meat, fur, even the feathers to stuff pillows and jackets. Nothing is sport. Nothing is waste. That's the type of hunting I can endorse, though neither of us will pretend there isn't pleasure to be had in the thrill of a well-aimed shot.

We have a good three-hour hike ahead of us. Tyrone Cypher is wintering at a cabin he "inherited" when the former owner was killed by our resident cougar.

Cypher had been sheriff of Rockton before Gene Dalton arrived. The council decided Gene's temperament was more suited to the position, and they'd demoted Cypher to deputy. He'd stuck around for a while, but after one too many clashes with Gene, he'd stomped off into the forest, where he's still sulking. Okay, "sulking" might be a slight exaggeration. Cypher had already intended to retire into the forest when his term in Rockton was up. His temper and his pride just sent him there sooner than he planned.

Cypher is happy in the forest. His former job made him a natural for tracking and hunting game. That "former job" isn't as sheriff of Rockton. It's the career that brought him here. Tyrone Cypher was a hit man. The first time he told me that, I thought he was joking. Then I thought he was exaggerating— maybe he *once* killed a guy for money. Nope. He was a career hit man. I'd say assassin, but that conjures up an image that is 100 percent not Tyrone Cypher.

Cypher had been in Rockton when Dalton first arrived. He knows Dalton's history, which makes for an awkward relationship, especially when Cypher sees nothing wrong with needling Dalton about his "wild boy" past.

We're a couple of kilometers from the cabin when Dalton goes still. As he looks around, I lay a hand on Storm's head. When a growl ripples through her flanks, I slide my hand through her collar. She grumbles at that, offended that I don't trust her.

As Dalton scans the forest, Storm resumes that low growl. She's on high alert, her hackles up, body stiff, which means there's a predator nearby. I slide my gun out. Dalton already has his in hand. His head tilts, as if he's spotted something. He slides forward for a better view. Then he nods, backs up, and takes Storm's collar.

"Go look," he whispers, a hint of a smile on his lips. "Slow and careful. I'll direct you."

I nod at my gun.

"Keep it out," he murmurs.

It *is* a predator, then. A dangerous one. Just not the type he expects to barrel out of the forest and attack. Interesting.

I slide forward where he'd gone. It's clear, no chance of hitting branches and giving myself away. When I reach where he stopped, he motions for me to take it one more step. Then he has me crouch until my eyes are at waist level, and he directs my attention.

At first I see nothing but snow and trees. Then I catch movement. A ghostly figure, gray and white fur camouflaging with the winter forest. Brown eyes fix on me. A gray and white snout swings my way, black nose twitching as it inhales my scent. Ear pricked, swiveling when a noise comes from the side, the soft *whoosh* of snow falling from branches.

It's a wolf. A lone young male. He has his head lowered, watching me, wary but curious. If it were a pack, Dalton would scoot me out of here fast. One wolf, though, is very unlikely to attack a person, not unless the beast is sick or starving. This one is muscular and well fed. His fur ripples in the breeze, and he is one of the most beautiful things I've seen in a forest filled with beauty.

I hear wolves all the time, and I've caught glimpses of them. But this is my first actual sighting, and I stay half-crouched and watching until his own curiosity wanes and he lopes off, a silent ghost vanishing into the snowy forest.

When I return to Dalton, I'm grinning. He smiles, pleased. He's about to say something when Storm whines.

"We should take her to sniff where he was," I say. "Let her learn the scent."

"Good idea."

He keeps his hand firmly around her collar and starts into the forest, to where the wolf had been. Storm doesn't budge.

"Nervous because it's another canine?" I wonder.

"Maybe."

When he tugs her, she whines and her head whips around, gaze fixed behind us. She makes a sound that starts like a growl, but then she swallows it and whines instead.

Something moves in the thicker trees behind us. I freeze. We'd presumed the wolf was alone, but that isn't necessarily so.

Dalton's eyes narrow. I resist the urge to watch him and turn my attention to Storm instead. Her gaze stays fixed on a single point. That's reassuring, suggesting she only smells one threat.

She's uncertain, too, about whether or not it *is* a threat. Her whine slips into a growl and then back to a whine. Her ears prick forward and then relax. Her snout wrinkles, but she doesn't bare her teeth.

I hunker to her height and look where she does. I see snow and trees. Then movement above my crouched head. Moose? Caribou? That would explain Storm's reaction. Ungulates might not be predators, but they're still dangerous. Storm surprised a doe last fall and took a good kick in the ribs as it fled.

Yet the shape has moved behind a tree, and if it were an ungulate, I'd see the hindquarters sticking out. It's at least as tall as me and can hide behind a thick tree trunk, which only describes one beast in this forest.

Human.

# FOURTEEN

I glance at Dalton. He's seen what I have. He grunts, considering, his hand on his gun. Then he motions for me to hold the dog while he circles around. I aim my gun at the tree, but it's a one-handed aim, my other on the dog's collar. I flex my left hand, ready to release the collar and steady my weapon if I need to.

Dalton takes two wide steps, his snowshoes coming down soundlessly. Another flicker of movement. My hand nearly releases Storm's collar. Then the figure steps out and says, "Eric."

I exhale. My gun lowers. Storm whines and dances, not excitement but nerves. She knows who this is, and she still isn't sure what to make of her, isn't convinced she *doesn't* pose a threat. But I know better. Dalton does, too, holstering his gun as he approaches her.

"Maryanne," he says.

I release Storm and move forward as the dog stays close enough to brush my leg. Maryanne is—or was—a hostile. I hesitate to say "was" because I'm honestly not sure of her status with them. I believe she left her group this spring. I cannot say for certain, because our relationship hasn't progressed far enough for me to ask.

Maryanne is a former resident of Rockton. That much I can say for certain. Dalton had been a teenager when she arrived. As a biologist and professor, Maryanne found peace and happiness in the wilderness, and when a group headed into the forest, she joined them.

Gene Dalton had pursued the quartet, and the militia found their camp destroyed, splattered with blood but no bodies. A year later, Dalton ran across Maryanne in the forest. When she'd been in Rockton, they'd been friends, Maryanne teaching him the science of the wilderness while he taught her the reality of it. So she very clearly knew Dalton, trusted him, liked him. And when he found her in the forest, she attacked him. He'd nearly had to kill her to escape.

Earlier this year, we'd encountered Maryanne again, still with the hostiles, but . . . I'm not sure of the analogy to use here. She was like someone buried under an avalanche who had clawed her way up just enough to be heard.

That avalanche was the collapse of her own mind into madness. She'd cleared just enough of a hole in the mental confusion to hear Dalton, yet she was still at the bottom, out of his reach. The encounter, though, had been a tipping point for her. She heard a voice she recognized, and she could make out the sunlight above and start climbing toward it. And here is where the analogy fails, because in such a case, you'd eventually be able to offer the victim a hand to haul them out. Maryanne is not ready to take that hand, because what she's suffered isn't hypothermia and broken bones. Her damage goes deeper.

Some of that damage is physical—teeth filed, ritualized scarring, an ear and a couple of fingers blackened by frostbite. For a brilliant woman to start regaining her self-awareness and realize what she's done to herself? To know it isn't just a bad tattoo that can be covered up with long sleeves? And to know what those physical signs represent, proof of what she had become, the things she had done as a hostile? Maryanne is indeed still buried, under an avalanche of shame and self-loathing now, and we cannot seem to pull her out.

We've seen her a few times over the summer and fall. Her mind has cleared enough to communicate with us . . . when she chooses to. We've tried leaving supplies out for her, but that is too much like leaving food for a stray dog, and she shuns our offerings. What we want is to bring her back to Rockton. Part of that is, of course, selfish—she represents the key to understanding the hostiles. But even without that, we want to help her.

Letting Maryanne stay out here hurts no one but her. And yet, here she is, in the middle of December, with ragged boots and multiple shirts and no jacket, wearing a thin hood tied over her head. On her hands, she's tied more skins, wrapped around like extended sleeves, her fingers bare inside.

This is where my beliefs waver. Where they have always wavered. I struggled with that as a patrol officer seeing the homeless. Yes, if you choose to live on the streets, no one should be able to forcibly remove you. But at what point are you no longer making a sane choice? If I recognize signs of mental illness or drug addiction, how do I know whether you are still capable of making that choice? At what point would I be infringing on your rights if I shuttled you off to a shelter or a hospital? And at what point am I failing as a public servant, as a human *being,* if I do not?

Maryanne is aware of her choices and her options. She stays out of shame and fear, and so, is that enough for me to say "it's her right"?

I see the same war on Dalton's face. As he approaches her, his cheek tics in a way I know well. He's holding in his frustration. What *she* sees, though, is anger in those blazing gray eyes.

She takes a step back. "Eric?"

"Hey, Maryanne," I say, giving him time to cover his reaction. "May I bring the dog over?"

She nods and smiles. It's a tight-lipped smile, as always, just as she barely opens her mouth when she speaks. Hiding her filed teeth.

I lead Storm to her, and she pushes her wrapped hands out to pet her, rubbing her back and sliding her fingers through the thick fur, warming them.

I take off my backpack. "I have extra mittens. Why don't you take—"

"No," Dalton says, so low it's more growl than word. He pulls the backpack from my hands and snaps the zipper shut. "Casey is not giving you her gloves."

Maryanne blinks. "I . . . I don't need . . ."

"Fuck yes, you do. How do you think you got frostbite the last time? Apparently, you kind of like it."

I have to bite back the urge to stop him. I know what he's doing, and I keep silent.

"You don't want help from us, remember?" he says. "So you're not getting Casey's extra mitts or sweater or whatever else she wants to give you. Not unless you're willing to accept real help."

She takes a slow step back.

"Yeah, that's great," Dalton says, tossing my backpack down. "Turn tail and run, like you do every time we say something you don't like. And next time we see you, it'll be your frozen corpse in the snow. Or maybe we won't find that until spring thaw. That'll be fun. Casey will blame me for not letting her give you stuff. She might even dump me for being such an insensitive ass. Imagine how we'll both feel, knowing we couldn't help you. But we can't keep doing this, Maryanne. A pair of mittens isn't going to get you through this winter. You need proper shelter. Like a cave."

Her brows rise at that, and I see a flash of the woman she was. "A cave?"

"It belonged to a friend of ours. He . . ." His voice catches before he pushes on. "He passed away this spring. I sealed it up, so all his stuff is still in there. It's nice, for a cave."

"It really is," I say. "It has a couple of rooms, plenty of skins, a firepit, preserved meat and food, weapons. He was living better than most settlers."

"Yeah," Dalton says. "It's fully stocked, and it's secure. It's not exactly warm when the fire goes out, but it isn't freezing either. The temperature in a cave—"

"—is consistent year-round," she says, her voice scratchy, unaccustomed to more than a word or two at a time. "It's approximately the same as the average temperature in the region."

Dalton allows himself a smile. "You remember. Good girl."

He gets a look for that, definitely the Maryanne she used to be.

"I would like that, Eric." She speaks in that same rusty voice, faltering and hesitant.

"All right then. Let me give you directions—"

I lay my hand on his arm. "I'd like to take her to Rockton to see whether she can identify . . ."

"Shit. Yeah. Okay." We exchange a look that says, *Yes, I really do want to see if she can ID our victim, but I also want April to take a look at her, and this is a good way to go about it.* A solid reason for Maryanne to come to Rockton.

I turn to Maryanne. "We found a dead woman with a baby."

She inhales sharply. "A dead baby."

"No, the baby's fine. But the woman shows signs of having once been . . . what you were."

"A hostile. You can say the word, Casey. I knew it, and it is not wrong. That's what we—I . . ." She swallows. "It's accurate, and yes, I will look at this woman, though I'm not sure I'd be able to identify her."

"Whatever you can give will help. Will you come? Please?"

Maryanne nods.

Dalton reaches to take the dog from me. "You two go back to town. Storm and I can talk to Ty."

When I hesitate, he says, "I have Storm and two guns. I'll be fine."

"Maybe we can walk partway with—"

"We'd be heading off the path soon. I'd rather you went back while we're still on it."

He's right—that's safer, with a straightaway to Rockton. He gives me a one-armed hug and leans over as close as our snow-shoes will allow. His lips press against my forehead, and he murmurs, "I'll be fine."

He will be. Before I came, he spent most of his alone time in the forest. I nod, and he gives me another quick hug and then heads off.

"You're lucky," Maryanne murmurs as he leaves.

"Yep, I am," Dalton calls back, not turning.

I smile. Then I dig in my backpack for the extra mittens and an extra scarf, and hand them to her, and we head out.

# FIFTEEN

I'm not much for initiating conversation. I'm fine with joining it or even sustaining it, but put me in a group and I keep
quiet until I have something to say. One on one, I'll talk, but
even then, I prefer an easy rhythm, with room for comfortable pauses, like I get with Dalton or Petra. I'm also fine with
someone who picks up the slack and keeps me entertained, like
Anders or Diana.

People have called me reserved, even standoffish. They
chalk it up to my Asian ancestry—clearly, I'm playing to type.
That's bullshit. My mother had no problem talking. It was my
Scottish dad who'd been content to listen and let her fill the
silence. I don't tell people that. If they want to cast me into an
"inscrutable Asian" stereotype, then it keeps me from having
to speak to them.

It isn't long into the walk with Maryanne before I'm really
wishing I'd let Dalton walk back with her. He knows Maryanne. All I can think of are the questions I want to ask, and as a
scientist, she'll be the first to realize I'm treating her as a subject
rather than a person.

So I offer her things, like an overexuberant puppy dropping

gifts at a stranger's feet. Would you like to wear the snowshoes? No? Are you warm enough? I've got a hood, so I don't really need my hat. I'm wearing an extra sweater—would that help? Oh, I should have offered food and water. I have both. Okay, well, just let me know if you get hungry or thirsty or you need to stop for a rest . . .

It's a wonder I don't drive her off, screaming into the forest.

I do mention that I'd like our doctor to take a look at Maryanne. She tenses, and I can tell she'd like to flee, but she's a smart woman and she knows a checkup is in her best interests. When she agrees, I seize on a topic of conversation and tell her all about my sister—her name, her specialty—and that gets her interest, as a fellow scientist, but it's still awkward, as if we're both fumbling for common ground.

"Had you ever been up here before Rockton?" she asks finally. "To the Yukon, I mean?"

I shake my head, and I'm about to expand on that, but she takes over, this clearly being more than an idle question.

"I did," she says. "My parents were late-era hippies. I grew up on a tiny island in British Columbia where they taught at the one-room schoolhouse. We raised goats for milk, chickens for eggs. We grew all our own vegetables. Vacations for us meant camping someplace even more remote than our island."

Her speech isn't fluid. It stops and starts, and she struggles for words, and sometimes, her voice cracks from disuse.

"Like the Yukon," I prompt.

She nods. "We came up here a few times. For people who worshiped Mother Nature, this was our mecca. There were jamborees in the seventies, and we piled into VW vans and drove. I remember this one event where they'd hired Native Canadian locals. They showed us how to track animals, how to start fires with flints, led us through rituals that I'm sure were completely fake."

She pauses for breath, and I let the silence go on, not wanting to rush her.

After a moment, she continues, "One day, I overheard two of them. Some people at the jamboree had been talking about going into the bush permanently. Just drive north until their car ran out of gas, walk into the forest and live off the land. These locals laughed about that. Said they wouldn't survive a week. I was about eight at the time, and I told my mother, and she said the idea of running off into the forest was romantic escapism. Those campers wouldn't survive without access to modern amenities, not when the biggest complaint at the jamboree was how far people had to walk to the showers."

The path branches, and I wave her down the left side. After a few more steps, she resumes her story. "People in Rockton are like some of the ones at those jamborees. They're aghast at the portable toilets and lousy showers, but compared to backcountry camping, Rockton is a four-star wilderness resort. When I first heard rumors and whispers about Rockton, I thought it couldn't possibly be real. The chance that I could escape my situation by going to a place where I'd gladly *pay* to vacation? I also needed that escape. My husband . . ." She shakes her head. "It's an old story. I won't bore you with it."

"I wouldn't be bored."

A smile my way. "Another time. This is . . ." A deep breath. "I know you want to know what happened to me, and that's where I'm heading." Another smile. "Eventually. My point was that those Native guides said the jamboree people wouldn't survive a week in the woods, and my mother thought they meant because of the lack of amenities. What they really meant was basic survival. The four of us who left Rockton didn't wander into the forest with pie-eyed visions of Mother Nature providing what we needed. I was a biologist with backwoods experience. One of the men was an engineer turned eco-house builder, specializing in northern living. Another was a doctor who'd hiked the entire Appalachian Trail alone. The woman was a third-generation wilderness guide. We had the skills. We knew where to camp. How to camp. How to secure our food supply. But we had no idea . . ."

She takes a deep breath. "The hostiles came in the night. We didn't stand a chance. We'd heard the rumors, of course, of wild people in the forest. The others scoffed. Personally, I was fascinated by the tales—modern folklore in action, the creation of a monster to shape behavior. Fairy tales to keep us out of the forest. In not believing, we weren't prepared.

"It happened so fast. I know that's what people always say, but you don't really understand the phrase until something like that. One minute, you're sleeping, and the next . . . chaos. Shouting. Screaming. Shadows against the night. That's all they were. Shadows. They put out our fire before they attacked. I woke to Dan—the doctor—screaming like I'd never heard a person scream. They'd sliced open his stomach and . . ."

Her breathing picks up. She scoops snow with a shaking hand. Two mouthfuls. Then, in a calm monotone: "They killed the men. Then they trussed up the other woman—Lora—and me and dragged us off. After that? It's a blur. Mostly."

She starts to shiver, and I take off my jacket, though I know it isn't cold making her shake. I still put my parka around her, and she takes it, gripping it close.

"That's all I can manage for now," she whispers.

"It's enough," I say. "Thank you."

She nods.

"Would you like a story about Rockton?" I say. "I may have a few."

She manages a smile. "I'll take as many as you've got."

# SIXTEEN

We're close to Rockton. I'm listening for signs of activity out-side the town.

"We'll loop around—" I begin, and the bushes explode, a gray canine leaping through.

It looks like a wolf, and my hand drops to my gun. Then Raoul jumps on me with a gleeful yelp . . . and Maryanne attacks. It happens in a blink. I'm relaxing, recognizing our freckle-faced wolf-dog as he plants his forepaws on my stom-ach, but Maryanne sees only a wolf leaping onto me. In a blink, she has her knife out and she's attacking with an inhu-man howl.

I grab Raoul and roll, shielding him. The knife slashes through my doubled-up sweaters and slices my arm. I let out a hiss of pain as Raoul whimpers under me.

"He's ours," I say quickly. "He's okay."

Silence. Gripping Raoul by the collar, I turn over to see Maryanne staring at my arm. Blood drips into the snow. She looks down at the bloody knife in her hand. Then she wheels, and I know she's going to bolt. I let go of Raoul and grab her by the pant leg. The seam rips as she lunges, but I hold tight.

"Please," I say. "I'm all right. It was a mistake. I'm—"

Bushes crash. Raoul ducks and sidles up against me, still lying in the snow. He whines as Jen bursts through.

"You damned mutt," she snarls. "What the hell—"

She sees Maryanne, who is poised there, mouth open.

Jen blinks. "Fuck."

Maryanne's eyes go wide, realizing what she must look like. She lunges away again, and I'm dragged a few feet before I manage to stop, still holding her tight.

"Jen, go," I say. "Please. Maryanne, I'm sorry. It's okay. Everything's okay."

She's pulling, and I have her pant leg in both hands now, pain ripping down my injured arm. Jen's saying something, but I can't make it out. Raoul thinks it's a game and growls, dancing around us. Maryanne gives one big heave, and I'm certain that's it. She's gone, and goddamn it, why the hell is Raoul—

Maryanne stops. "Eric?" she whispers.

I follow her gaze to see a figure loping toward us. It's not Dalton, though. It's Sebastian. He skids to a stop, seeing us.

"Shit, I'm sorry. I was walking him off leash and . . ." He sees Maryanne—gets a good look at her. There's exactly two seconds of silence, and I swear I see his brain whir, lightning fast. Then he smiles and extends a hand. "Sebastian."

She blinks, and when she speaks, it's a near mumble as she tries to keep her teeth covered. "You looked a little like Eric, as a boy."

Sebastian's smile grows. "You knew Sheriff Dalton when he was younger? Cool." His voice is calm, completely unperturbed by this wild-haired woman clad in makeshift clothing.

"I'm sorry," Jen says. "Didn't mean to startle you. This damned mutt and this damned kid . . ." She glowers at Sebastian.

"Thanks for helping me get him," Sebastian says.

Jen rewards his politeness with a raised middle finger. He ignores it and takes Raoul by the collar, scolding him in French.

Sebastian looks at Maryanne. "He's mostly wolf, but he's tame. He's pretty well trained until he wants to run, and then he somehow forgets his own name."

She smiles at that, forgetting her teeth until her hand flies up to cover them, but Sebastian pretends not to notice. He has a way with people. Of course, that has something to do with being a sociopath. He's not the stereotypically suave charmer that Hollywood loves, but there's a disarming charisma to him that's hard to ignore when he switches it on.

"Sebastian?" I say. "On your way through town, could you please find my sister and ask her to meet me at my old house? Tell her to bring a first-aid kit."

"What do you need me to do?" Jen asks.

I hesitate. I want to tell her to just back off and stay out of our way after nearly sending Maryanne fleeing into the forest. But she's been quiet since then and looks almost abashed.

"Bring food and drink and clothing," I say. "Whatever you spend, we'll reimburse. Just do it as discreetly as possible." I pause, realizing who I'm speaking to. Shit. "This is very important. Don't tell anyone—"

I stop suddenly. "Wait. If you're here, where's the baby?"

"In a snowbank over there. Don't worry, she's got plenty to eat. I tied some bacon around her neck. That's okay, right?"

"Jen? Where's—"

"With Will at the station. We were out for a stroll when this kid lost his wolf puppy. I gave the baby to Will and came to help round up the damned mutt."

"Which was very kind of her," Sebastian says. "And has nothing to do with the fact that the reason Raoul took off is because she yelled at him for running to see the baby."

"Fuck you, brat. Keep your damn wolf on a leash or the next time I see it . . ." She catches my eye and grumbles, "Keep him on a leash."

Jen stalks off.

"She's really very nice when you get to know her," Sebastian says, and then shakes his head and mouths to Maryanne, *No, she's not.*

"I heard that!" Jen calls back.

"I didn't say a word."

"Believe me, I still heard it."

Sebastian gives Raoul a pat and says goodbye to Maryanne and they take off, zooming past Jen on their way.

"He seems like a sweet boy," Maryanne says.

I make a noncommittal noise and lead her toward town.

As eager as I am to get Maryanne to the clinic to attempt identification of the dead woman, I know I need to take this slower. Let April examine her first at my house. I want her checked out and I want the rest of her story—whatever can help me understand hostiles, for this case and beyond. Once Maryanne sees the dead woman, though, her obligation is fulfilled and she can flee into the forest. So that will need to wait until post-examination. It's not as if I can leave town chasing new clues anyway, not while Dalton is gone.

The back door to my old house is locked. Increased tensions with both the hostiles and settlers have made it seem unwise to leave buildings with open access to the woods. For my old place, though, there's a key under the back deck, since it is technically still my lodgings, and sometimes, if work's slow, Dalton and I have been known to go on patrol and sneak in the back for an "afternoon nap."

Maryanne has said nothing since Jen and Sebastian left, and I've spent the walk stifling the urge to hold her arm to make sure she doesn't bolt. My own arm is fine. The blade sliced the skin, nothing more. A bandage will fix it up.

I open my door and usher Maryanne through. She steps in and stops. I'm behind her, and she's blocking the entrance, but I pause, waiting. When she doesn't move, I slide past her, and I realize she's crying. She's standing just inside the door, silent tears rolling down her face.

I take off her parka. She doesn't even seem to notice. I bend and unfasten her boots, which really are little more than hides roped around her ankles. I untie the bindings and then head into the living room, saying, "I'll start the fire."

I keep an ear on the kitchen. If the door squeaks, I'll be there in a flash. Instead, tentative footsteps slide across the kitchen. I hurry to get the fire going. It's laid, needing only a match to light—at this time of year, an "afternoon nap" is a whole lot less enticing if it means setting a fire first.

I get it started in seconds; then I feed in more kindling and put the kettle on. When I turn, Maryanne stands in the middle of the room. She looks at the roaring fire, the kettle, the sofa piled with pillows, the bearskin rug, inviting in a way only a fireplace-rug-in-winter truly can be. She stares. Blinks. Then her knees give way. I lunge, but I'm too slow, and she falls onto the rug. Tears stream down her face, silent at first, and then ripping out in racking sobs as she crumples, arms wrapped around her chest.

I should go to her. Hug her. Comfort her. Instead, I manage a few back pats and "It's okay" and "You're safe now," which are as awkward for her as they are for me. So I leave her to cry, and I dart around, getting things to make her comfortable. Put pillows on the floor. Grab more from behind the sofa and blankets from under it—in a place this small, you use every cranny for storage. I build a nest around her, as if she's a toddler who might fall.

Then I go into the kitchen. There's not much there. Instant coffee and tea in the cupboard. Powdered creamer and sugar. A bottle of tequila hidden under the cupboard. I bring it all. Then I check the kettle. It's barely simmering.

I don't ask Maryanne whether she wants tea, coffee, or tequila. She's crying softer now, collapsed on the rug, hugging a pillow. I drape a blanket over her. Then I pour tequila into one mug, put a tea bag in another and coffee in the third. The kettle gives one chirp, and I have it off the hanger. I fill the two mugs. Then I set them on a tray in front of her.

"Food's coming," I say. "But I have tea, coffee, and tequila."

"Tequila?"

She lifts her face from the rug. I hold the mug out.

She shakes her head, shivering. "It'll be a long time before I'll even want painkillers."

I push forward the other mugs. She accepts the coffee and rejects creamer or sugar. She sits up, blanket still over her shoulders as she wraps her hands around the mug. She leans over it, bathing in the steam.

I put the kettle back over the fire, in case she wants more. Then I look around.

"I should have a sweatshirt upstairs," I say. "And socks maybe? I'll run—"

A hard rap at the door. I open it to find Jen with a duffel bag, which she shoves at me.

"Clothing," she says. "It's mine, but it should fit. There are snacks in there, too. I'll drop off a hot meal when I bring the baby."

"Baby? I really can't—"

"If you need me to take her a while longer, I will, but she's fussy and cranky, and she wants her mommy."

"Yes," I say evenly. "Unfortunately, we have no idea where to find her."

She snorts. "Whatever."

"She doesn't want *me*, Jen."

"Well, yeah, she'd probably rather have Daddy. Typical female, already making eyes at the big, bad sheriff. But since he's not here, you'll do."

When I start to protest, she says, "I'm not trying to get rid of her, Casey. Just take her, rock her a bit while April looks after . . . the patient, and she'll fall asleep, and you can call me to take her back. She's unsettled, and she needs sleep, and she's not getting it until she sees temporary Mom or Dad."

I pause and heft the duffel, turning toward the living room.

"And I'm sorry about spooking . . . the patient," Jen says. "She just surprised me, that's all."

When I glance over, she says, "Yeah, I'm apologizing. To her, mostly. It's like when I kicked your damn dog, I didn't think. I just reacted. I'd never have done it otherwise."

I nod. "Go ahead, and bring the baby."

# SEVENTEEN

I'm getting Maryanne into the clothing when my sister arrives. April walks in, sees what we're doing, and says, "You can stop that, or we'll just be taking it all off again."

April glances at Maryanne and nods. It looks like a curt nod, but it's simple efficiency, as she strides past us to set down her bag. Maryanne could be any patient in the clinic, just another job in April's day, no greeting required.

We've fielded complaints about my sister's lack of bedside manner. I direct the residents to Dalton, who reminds them that we spent the last fucking year without a fucking doctor, and now we have a fucking multi-degree neurosurgeon, and they're complaining because she doesn't ask how they're fucking doing—which, considering she's a fucking doctor, she's going to find out anyway, isn't she? That's verbatim, although he may find an opportunity for another profanity that I've missed.

I think we should work on this with April. Dalton says no. Not a "Fuck, no" or even "Hell, no," which means he isn't adamantly opposed to a little gentle guidance, but since it's not a lack of compassion, residents should adjust their expectations instead. As Dalton says, "They want a fucking hug? Talk to Isabel's girls." He has a point. He also said, "Would they complain so much if April was a man?" Ouch.

He's right. I'm not sure I would have advocated for a softer touch if she were a man, and that stings. Especially when, as a cop, I'd been accused of not being "warm" enough, while no one ever said that to my male colleagues. It burns to realize I fell into the same trap, but it's a reminder I need sometimes. Just because I advocate for gender equality doesn't immunize me against promoting stereotypes. Even Dalton, who has never treated me differently than he would a male colleague, had an all-male militia until I arrived, and he'd never considered how that might discourage women from joining.

With Maryanne, though, I am glad of my sister's cool professionalism. As April conducts a preliminary examination, Maryanne visibly relaxes. This is familiar. It's what she would have expected for a routine physical. Check heart, check eyes, check throat, check teeth . . .

April checks the last as perfunctorily as the rest, without even a moment's pause at the filed teeth. But then, after the quick assessment, she says, "Dental work will be required," and Maryanne cringes, just a little.

"There's a cavity at the back," April says. "Possibly two. We have medication to help with those if they cause pain eating. The front teeth will require caps."

"Caps . . ."

"Unless you planned to grow new ones, which I would not advise."

Maryanne snorts a laugh at this, and I relax. My sister has been attempting humor lately. That's one of the biggest hurdles with her condition—she struggles to understand jokes, and her silence marks her as humorless. She's working on that. The problem, of course, is that with her absolute deadpan delivery, people usually aren't sure she *is* kidding.

"I hadn't considered caps," Maryanne says. "That would work, I think."

"It would. I have one on my left upper lateral incisor. Casey chipped off the corner. She threw a baseball for me to catch, and her aim was atrocious."

"What?" I say. "When was this?"

"When you were three. You must remember, Casey."

"Not if I was three, I don't."

"That may explain why you never apologized."

"I'm sure I did at the time."

"No." She pauses. "You did cry. Quite a bit. I suppose that's an apology." Her tone says she's granting me the benefit of the doubt here. A lot of benefit for a lot of doubt.

"Well, I am sorry," I say. "Very sorry."

"I suppose an apology twenty-nine years late is better than none at all."

Maryanne laughs, though this, I know, is not a joke.

"April's right," I say. "Caps will fix your teeth."

"They will cover the damage," April says. "They will not 'fix' them. Nothing can be done about that. They've been filed. Intentionally. Whoever did that to her needs to be arrested, Casey. It's assault, at the very least."

"I did it to myself," Maryanne says, her voice very quiet.

April frowns. "For what purpose?"

"April . . ." I say.

"No, it's all right," Maryanne says. "I know you need to hear my story, Casey. Whether it's to help with this baby or the poor dead woman or the hostiles in general, you need it. I'm just not sure it will make much sense. It's like . . . a fever dream. I'd never done drugs. Well, nothing stronger than marijuana, but we didn't consider that any more a drug than alcohol. I certainly never experienced hallucinations with it."

"You wouldn't," April says. "Marijuana is not a hallucinogenic drug."

Maryanne meets my gaze and the corners of her lips quirk, as if she's figuring out my sister. She just says, calmly, "No, I suppose it isn't. But I had friends who experimented with hallucinogens. Sometimes, what they experienced wasn't so much a hallucination as a waking dream. It was real. Very real. That's what it was like for me. It was real, and I had no sense that it wasn't normal, that this wasn't who I was."

She stops. Squeezes her eyes shut and shakes her head. "No, that's not . . . That's not quite right. In the beginning . . ."

She looks at April. "I'm sorry, Doctor. You were conducting an examination. I'll wait for this."

April looks at me. I'd like Maryanne to continue—I'm afraid if she stops, she won't ever restart.

I'm still hesitating when Jen opens the door, baby in one arm, dinner in a bag over her shoulder. I tell April to continue her examination, and I take the baby, who is indeed fussing, sucking on her lower lip, as if she's a few seconds from crying.

"Is this the baby?" Maryanne says, rising. A smile spreads, a real one, her entire face lighting up as she forgets to cover her teeth. "The one who was with a former hostile?"

I nod. "The woman wasn't her mother, though."

"No, she wouldn't be. There . . ." She swallows. "There are no babies. They do not—"

She rubs her hands over her face, the move agitated, as if she's trying to scrub a memory from her mind. She stops, forcing her hands down. When she speaks, her voice is lecture-impassive. "If we become pregnant, they make sure we do not stay that way."

She catches our expressions and shakes her head. "No, not me. I had a hysterectomy a few years before I came to Rockton. I was spared . . . that."

April and I exchange a glance. Then April says, "I would like to conduct a full physical examination. Given the circumstances you were living under, there could be damage that your hysterectomy would not have prevented."

Maryanne looks at her a moment before realizing what she means. She gives a short laugh. "No, oddly, that is another thing I was spared. Children are forbidden, but so is rape. Sex must be consensual." She pauses. "Or as consensual as it can be under the circumstances." Another pause, and a wan quarter-smile. "From an academic perspective, let's just say it was as consensual as it has historically been for women. We knew the advantage of taking a mate, and we did so, and while I did not meet the love of my life, my relationships were, in some ways, healthier than the one I came here to escape. You may certainly conduct a full exam, Doctor, but rape trauma is the one thing I don't suffer from."

The baby sleeps, and Maryanne relaxes into the examination. I know from experience that bouncing back from the physical ailments is usually the easy part. The human body is a marvel of resiliency. The mind is an entirely different matter. On the surface, it has that same resiliency, yet even after we seem to be back on our mental feet, functioning and happy, the damage lingers, tucked down in the creases, impossible to scour clean.

The body repairs itself, leaving only scars where the skin can't quite smooth away the damage. The mind does the same—it re-forms, it adapts, it builds bridges over the damaged parts. I can hide my physical scars with long sleeves and jeans, but I don't. They're part of who I am. Part of my history, and no cause for shame. I wish I could be as open with the mental scars. I probably never will be.

The physical damages make me look like a survivor. The psychological damage makes me feel like a victim. I know that's wrong; I just can't seem to get past the divide.

Maryanne's scars will not be badges of honor. They do show that she survived trauma that would kill most people. Yet she won't ever feel that way. When she's ready to return to civilization—be that Rockton or Halifax—she'll want help covering those signs.

In her examination, April suggests ways to conceal the rest of the physical damage. It's reassuring for Maryanne, hearing her trauma discussed in the same way a cosmetic surgeon might suggest fixing a crooked nose. April doesn't mean it to be soothing—she's ticking off the boxes that will return her patient to optimal health. Yet Maryanne *is* soothed, and that's what counts. Caps will cover her filed teeth. Plastic surgery will remove blackened tissue and make the frostbite damage less obvious.

Maryanne eats after her physical. As she does, while April makes notes, I say, "May I ask you questions?"

She smiles. "May I hold the baby afterward?"

"Certainly. I have a thousand questions, as you might imagine. But I want to begin with ones that April may be able to help me with."

My sister looks up. She says nothing, though, just resumes her note-making.

"You say that your party was attacked in the night," I begin. "The party who left Rockton with you."

"Yes."

"Were they the same people who took you away? Held you captive?"

She nods. "Yes."

"Is there any chance they weren't? I know you said it was chaotic. Is it possible you were attacked by one group and then given to another?"

I get identical looks of confusion from Maryanne and April.

Maryanne says slowly, "I'm not sure I understand . . ."

"Is there any chance that the people who attacked your camp were not the group you later joined? Or if there were any members you never saw again?"

"It really was a blur of faces, both at the attack and later." She pauses. "Maybe if I had a better idea what you were looking for . . ."

I hesitate. As a cop, I would never share a theory with a witness. Not unless I'm trying to lead them into confessing themselves. Otherwise, it really is "leading." Tainting their testimony. So I have to stop here and analyze. What are the chances that, if I give Maryanne a theory, she'll intentionally or subconsciously shape her testimony to support or refute it, depending on her gut reaction?

She is a scientist. Whatever damage she's suffered, she's made incredible strides toward recovery. Her intelligence and self-awareness have fully returned, and I think I need to trust that.

"I'm not a psychiatrist," I say. "Or a psychologist or an anthropologist or anyone else who might know more about human evolution and behavioral changes. But I struggle with the idea that people who leave Rockton—modern humans—can revert to something that . . . primitive in a few years."

I adjust the baby to my other arm. "The theory in Rockton has always been, simply, that these people left, and because they left, they 'reverted' to a more 'primitive' form. That they were inherently more violent than the settlers, and they embraced that part of themselves when they left. I don't think that's how it works with people. I think there must be some . . . outside influence that at least escalates the process."

"You're completely right," Maryanne says. "What happens out there isn't a natural process of devolution. It's the tea."

# EIGHTEEN

"The . . . tea?" That's all I can manage, and when April asks, "Who provides the tea?" I am grateful. Then I'm immediately shamed by that gratitude, because I'm only glad that *I'm* not the one asking what might be a stupid question.

"No one, right?" I say to Maryanne. "They make it themselves."

She nods. "From a root and plants. I don't know the exact ingredients. The shaman is the only one who can make them."

"Shaman?"

"That's what I'd call her now. They don't have a name for any roles. The shaman conducts rituals and makes the teas."

"Teas?" April says. "More than one?"

Maryanne hesitates. "Maybe? I always thought of it as the same tea, but in two concentrations. One is for everyday drinking and the other is for rituals. They both . . ." Maryanne rubs her face again, this time paired with a convulsive shiver. When she speaks, her voice is lower, professorial detachment evaporating. "They make everything okay."

Neither of us speaks. After a moment, Maryanne says, "May I go back?"

When I tense, she manages a wan smile. "I don't mean go back into the forest. I mean may I go back to my story. That will make this easier, and possibly more comprehensible, if such a thing is possible."

"Of course," I say. "Whatever works for you." I glance at my sister. "You don't need to be here for this."

She starts, as if from sleep. Blinks. Pauses. Then straightens, saying, "If we are discussing the effects of a potential drug, then I do believe I need to stay."

She doesn't actually need to stay, and I realize I have, inadvertently, achieved exactly the thing I'd tried to so many years ago. I have brought April something that catches her interest. Still, I have to ask Maryanne if she's okay with April staying. She is.

Maryanne continues. "I told Casey that the hostiles attacked at night. They killed the men and took the women. Two of us. We were initially separated. A classic technique: Separate, isolate, and disorientate. I woke in a cavern—too small to sit up in. I had a guard. He wouldn't speak to me. Wouldn't even look at me. They'd only bring water. I was in that cave for days, maybe a week. By the time they hauled me out, I was starving and feverish and half mad with fear and confusion. They gave me food and the tea. As soon as I drank the tea, I knew it was drugged. Everything became . . . unreal."

She shifts her position. "That's the best way to describe it. It took away the fear and the dread. When they put me back into the cave, I slept soundly. The next day, they brought me out and offered me food and more tea. I only wanted the food. That wasn't an option. Both or nothing. I refused the tea for three days, until I realized my choices were that or starvation. I drank, and they let me stay outside the cave with the group. It felt like I was in a trance. Doing as I was told earned me food and sleeping blankets and a spot by the fire. The chores were like being at camp. Gather wood. Cook. Clean. Sew. A few of the men paid me extra attention, but they didn't bother me. They were trying to get *my* attention."

"As a potential mate."

"Yes. During my more lucid periods, I'd remember to be afraid. To want to escape. The best plan, however, seemed to be to do exactly what they wanted. Just keep drinking the tea and being a good girl, and I'd get my chance. Then they brought Lora."

"The other woman who'd been taken with you."

She nods. "Lora wouldn't drink the tea. They brought her to show her how well I was doing, how much better shape I was in. I tried to persuade her to drink and bide her time, but to her, I was weak, surrendering when I should be fighting. She was a twenty-five-year-old wilderness guide, tough as nails. I was a middle-aged academic. We . . . we'd never really gotten along. She fought them every waking second and eventually, they fought back. They beat her. They gave her only enough water to survive. Then they took away her clothing. After a week, she escaped."

I raise my brows, and Maryanne nods. "Yes, they *let* her escape. I realized that later. One of the men tracked her. A week later . . ." She swallows and rubs her face. "They took me to see her. To see . . . what was left."

I tell her she doesn't need to continue, but she says, "No, this is part of the story." Another few minutes of silence before she says, "She'd collapsed. Exhaustion. Hypothermia. Starvation. She couldn't go on. The tracker had tied her to a tree. Then he put tea beside her. Drink the tea, and he'd give her food and clothing. She didn't, and so he left her there, and I . . ."

Maryanne swallows. "I hope she just fell asleep. Died quietly. If not . . ." Another swallow, harder. "Something got her. An animal. Either it scavenged her dead body or it killed her.

That's what they brought me to see, and that was a message. Drink your tea and behave, and do not even think of running, or this will happen to you."

"So you stayed?"

"I still planned to escape. I'd give it a month, even two, until they trusted me. I'd be fed and strong, and I'd have clothing and weapons, and I wouldn't end up like Lora when I ran. Then they gave me the other tea. There was no peaceful trance with that."

She looks at me. "I've never been an angry person. No matter what my husband did, I stayed calm and looked for solutions. I *had* anger, though, and that tea brought it out. It induced hallucinations and violent frenzies and . . ."

Her face reddens. "It induced *all* the impulses. It unleashed the id, and it was addictive. Not so much the drug itself as the experience. Cathartic. In my already confused state, it felt as if I'd discovered something I'd been looking for all my life. Like our family friends dreaming of walking into the wilderness and reuniting with Mother Nature. I embraced it, and I'm ashamed of that now, but when it happened . . ."

She looks at me. "Most of the time, we drank the first tea, the same as you'd have your morning Earl Grey. Then there were the rituals with the other one, so you went from a sense of tranquil unreality to those wild, primal frenzies. There wasn't anything else. After a while, it became harder to focus, harder to think straight. All that mattered was surviving. Hunting, finding shelter, protecting territory, satisfying needs and urges."

She shifts position again. "When I met you and Eric in the forest that first time, I was in what you might call a down phase. We all were. In a frenzy, we'd have attacked and taken what we wanted, but in the down phase, they could think it through enough only to threaten you."

"They'd still have killed us, though," I say. "That's why they asked Eric to remove his clothing. So they wouldn't ruin it when they killed him."

She nods. "Yes. They'd have killed him and any other men in your party. They'd have taken you. Young, strong men seem like an asset, but they're also competition for goods and women. A young, strong woman is the truly valuable asset."

She inhales. "I didn't recognize Eric. That's no excuse. I was still watching them do exactly what they'd done to my own party from Rockton, and I wasn't lifting a finger to stop it."

"You couldn't."

"Yes, but I wouldn't have either. In that phase, I would regret what happened, but it would never occur to me to stop it. When I did recognize Eric, though, it was like a light in the darkness. That one tiny pinprick that cut through the fog. Once I started remembering, I couldn't stop. It helped that I didn't go back to the tribe. That wasn't really a choice. Our entire hunting party had been wiped out, including our leader. I'd lost my mate a few months before, and that left me vulnerable. I had enemies, including the shaman, who was the dead leader's mate. Not returning turned out to be my salvation. My mind didn't clear overnight. Even now, sometimes I wake up, and I can't remember how I got where I am. I'm alive, though, so I'm clearly not wandering around in a daze. I think it's more like blackouts, lost memory."

"Effects of long-term drug use," April says. "My doctoral advisor had a subspecialty in hallucinogens. What you are likely looking at is something that produces effects similar to PCP. Long-term use leads to long-term effects, as with most drugs. Blackouts or loss of memory would be one of them."

"Will that stop?" Maryanne asks.

"While I believe that 'long term' implies it isn't permanent, I can't say that without further research."

"Which we will do," I add quickly. "If it isn't likely to clear up on its own, there must be treatments."

April gives me a look. Brain damage isn't something that heals like torn tissue, and she doesn't want me sounding so certain, but thankfully, she doesn't say anything. Maryanne isn't a child needing sunshine and roses, but she is fragile, and if I lean one way, it'll be toward convincing her that a normal life is possible.

It helps that I believe it. I've seen people come back from situations that I'm not sure I could have psychologically survived. Determination and optimism might not solve every issue, but it gets you a good chunk of the way there.

For all my sister's challenges, she understands this. She would never tell Kenny that he won't walk again, and nor will she tell Maryanne her mind might never fully heal. Her glare just warns me to watch my step, because I'm such a sunshine-and-roses person myself that I might blithely lead poor Maryanne down the happy path of delusive hope. Yeah, my sister really needs to get to know me better.

With that we reach the end of what Maryanne can tell me for now. I have more questions—so many more—but she's tiring, and that trip down memory lane wasn't a joyful one. As eager as I am to take her to try identifying the dead woman, she needs a rest first and, again, I'm otherwise stalled until Dalton returns, hopefully with information on where to find the baby's parents.

# NINETEEN

As Maryanne naps, so does the baby, while I make notes on Maryanne's story. As I watch the baby soundly sleeping, I marvel at my maternal skill. All those stories about babies crying constantly and moms never getting a moment to themselves, and here I am, with time to write down all my notes and then make coffee and even leaf through a novel I'd accidentally left under my old sofa. Clearly Edwin is right, and I'm a natural mother.

Yeah . . . I'm not that delusional. The baby deserves all the credit for this. I'm guessing that, at this age, they sleep a lot of the time, like Storm and Raoul did as puppies. Also, having lived in the wilderness, born in winter, the baby wouldn't be accustomed to a cushy life where Mom and Dad can jump to fulfill her every need. She's curled up with Maryanne on the sofa, snuggled deep into a soft source of body heat, and she's happy.

The baby does eventually fuss, and I take her from Maryanne, who is so deeply asleep that if the house caught fire, I'd need to haul her out. Alone in the wilderness she's probably done little more than nap for months now, staying just warm enough to doze without drifting into the endless slumber of hypothermia.

When Maryanne does wake, I summon Jen to take the baby while I finally escort Maryanne to the clinic, where I hope she can identify the dead woman.

We're at the clinic, having come in the back way. April has made sure it's empty, and I ask her to stay in the front room, in case anyone arrives. Maryanne and I walk in to find the dead woman on the examining table. Maryanne takes one look and stops midstep. I resist the urge to jump in with questions. I can see mental wheels turning, and I don't want to do anything to put on the brakes.

Maryanne walks to the table. She looks down and whispers, "I'm Ellen." She looks over at me. "That's what she said. *I'm Ellen.* I met her . . ."

Maryanne looks around, and I push over a chair. She eyes it, this simple object that would once have been so familiar. Then she gingerly lowers herself onto it.

I pull another chair from the next room and sit in front of her.

"'Met' isn't quite the right word," Maryanne says. "I encountered her. It was . . ." She shakes her head. "Time is difficult to judge. I remember it was warm that day. It might have been last summer. It could even have been the one before. I'm sorry I can't be more specific."

"That's fine."

"We were gathering berries. If you need the exact time of year, that could help. They were crowberries. I was with the shaman and the two other women from our group. She"— Maryanne gestures toward the dead woman—"came out of the woods. Carefully. I remember that. She made enough noise so we'd hear her, and she had her hands raised so we could see she wasn't armed. She did everything right."

"And?"

"The shaman tried to kill her. It was like the men with Eric. He'd be an asset as a worker, as a fighter, but all they see is competition. Our power, as with most patriarchal tribes, came from our mates."

"Fewer women means more opportunity to snag a powerful man."

"Yes, and I would strongly suspect that freeing Lora was the shaman's idea. Lora was young and strong and pretty. If she'd survived, she could have taken the best mate, become the most powerful woman, possibly even become shaman. This woman"—she nods at the body—"wasn't young, but she'd still be competition. The shaman ran her off and tried to get us to hunt and kill her, as a supposed threat to the group. We were in a down phase, though, so myself and the other women pretended to give chase but didn't put much effort into it. She got away easily."

"Do you know what she wanted?"

"That's what I'm struggling to remember. She spoke to us, but while I would have understood her at the time, the memory faded quickly. What I remember isn't the conversation but the gist of it. She wanted to help us. I was confused at first, because she said something about help, and I thought *she* needed help, but that wasn't it. She wanted to help us."

"But before that, you didn't know her. She wasn't from your tribe."

Maryanne shakes her head. "She was a settler, not a hostile."

"Could you take a look at this?"

I rise and fold back the sheet to show the woman's—Ellen's—

upper-chest scarring. Before I can say anything, Maryanne sucks in breath.

"Oh!" she says. "That's . . . Yes, that's the other group." She looks at me. "There are two tribes in this area. I don't know if there are more farther afield, but we only had contact with this other one, and as little of that as possible. It was like two wolf packs, equally matched in size, with enough territory that they didn't need to cross paths. My feeling is that the two groups had been linked at some point."

"One initial group that split," I say. "Like Rockton and the settlements."

"Yes, but that's just my presumption. It wasn't as if we sat around talking about our tribal history. I don't know if it was the drugs themselves or the result of living that way, but everything was very focused on the now. Any discussions we had were the simple exchange of information needed in the moment. *The fire is too small. We need more kindling. Hey, that's my meat.* Even things like hunts or gathering expeditions were very in the moment. *We're running low on meat, so we need to hunt. It's blueberry season, so we should pick blueberries.* When someone died, we buried him and divided up his things, and rarely referred to him again."

She takes a deep breath. "And that's the very long way of saying that there were two tribes, but we didn't interact, and if there was any connection between the two, no one ever mentioned it to me."

Maryanne runs her fingertips over the woman's raised scars. "This is definitely their work. When I met her, though, I had no sense she was a hostile. If anyone had suspected she came from the other tribe, that would have been far more worrisome, being so deep into our territory."

"My guess is that she'd been a hostile and left them. She has facial markings, too, which she covered with dirt. The chest ones seem unfinished, but they aren't fresh."

"Left her tribe to become a settler. That would also explain why she'd reached out to us as a party of women. Like an ex–cult member trying to help those still drinking the Kool-Aid." A wry twist of a smile. "Or, in our case, the tea."

She steps back for a broader view of the woman. "If she did leave her tribe and stumbled onto them again, that might have explained how she died. They would have killed her. I see you've shaved part of her head. I'm guessing that was what did it? A blow to the skull?"

"Is that a common attack method for hostiles?"

A humorless chuckle. "Their murder modus operandi is 'whatever gets the job done.' They have knives, but they'd grab a rock if that was closest at hand."

"She did suffer blunt-force trauma," I say. "But cause of death was a shotgun pellet."

"Well, then that's not the hostiles. Some use bows and arrows, but no one would ever get access to a gun, much less ammunition."

So I have a name for the woman. The fact that she'd tried to help Maryanne and the others gave me some small insight into her. While she could have stolen this baby for herself, I'm leaning harder now toward other possibilities.

If the baby's mother belonged to the trading family that Edwin dislikes, then perhaps Ellen thought she was saving the child. With Maryanne and the others, rescue would have been warranted. With the child, though . . .

We were back to the problem Dalton and I discussed yesterday. At what point do you declare parents unfit? The baby is healthy, showing absolutely no signs of neglect or abuse. Yet, according to Edwin, the family prostitutes its daughters. If he's right about that, then looking after a baby girl is little different than treating your sled dogs well.

What if that is the sort of situation we find? A child who will grow up to that sort of life?

For now, I need to focus on finding the baby's parents. I hope Cypher can shed more light on that.

# TWENTY

I talk to Phil about Maryanne. I'm trying to play fair with all parties, especially in light of the "Whoops, guess the council *isn't* responsible for hostiles" revelation. I'm feeling sheepish about that, and in response, I decide to be aboveboard regarding Maryanne's presence.

I explain to Phil. He responds with a shake of his head and zero questions, as if he's beyond surprise when it comes to Rockton. He'll tell the council Maryanne is here and sees no issue with that. It's a humanitarian gesture.

At one time, I'd have thought Phil incapable of understanding that concept. While he doesn't exactly trip over himself to offer her hospitality, he doesn't question giving her a house for the night, food, fresh clothing and supplies come morning.

I've brought the baby back from Jen's, and Maryanne is resting, so I've requisitioned a men's parka from the supply shop, put the baby into the front sling we fashioned yesterday, and tucked her under the jacket. We're both restless, and walking with her seemed like a fine solution, though it might suggest that I have far more experience with puppies than babies.

She doesn't sleep, but she settles in with only the occasional grunt to let me know she's there.

Walking through town means more stopping-and-greeting than actual movement, especially when I have a baby strapped to my chest. It's like walking Storm—even after a year, people still stop me to give her a pat. The baby doesn't want to be patted. She conveys that with a yowl the first time a resident's icy fingers touch her cheek.

So I take her out of town. There's a path that runs just beyond the forest edge, one that residents are allowed to use if they really feel the need to commune with nature. I can go farther, of course—perks of being law enforcement—but with the baby, I'll stick close. It's also dark. Not night yet—not even dinnertime—but dark nonetheless.

I see the glow of Dalton's flashlight first, bobbing along like fairy-fire. Then Storm gives a happy bark and thunders down the path. I drop to one knee before she bowls me over. While I pet her, she dances and whines as if we've been separated for months. Then she sticks her big nose into my parka and licks the baby. The baby's head rolls back, as if trying to see. Storm snuffles the black-fuzzed head, and the baby only grunts in surprise.

Dalton approaches with a guy half a head taller than him, a burly bulk of a man with a snow-crusted beard halfway down his chest.

As I stand, Cypher says, "Either that's a baby under your coat, kitten, or you've taken up serious snacking."

"My snacking habits are none of your concern," I say. "But yes, it is a baby."

Cypher gives me a one-armed hug, which I return. Then he peers down at the baby, who whimpers in alarm.

"Still scaring dogs and small children," Dalton says. "You

might want to trim that beard." He pauses. "No, I guess at her age she can't see more than shapes. It must be the smell."

"Ha!" Cypher jabs a finger into Dalton's chest. "You're getting better at the jokes, boy. They're even close to being funny. Also, you really gotta stop letting this girl of yours wander around the woods. If she's not tripping over dead bodies, she's rescuing wolf pups and throwing bear cubs, and now she's bringing home lost babies. Must be a talent."

"I don't find the dead bodies," I say. "I make them, to liven things up."

"Hey now, that's my line."

"You make any dead bodies lately, Ty?" Dalton asks as we head for home.

"Just the kind I can throw into a stew. And, before you ask, that doesn't include people. My hit-man days are behind me . . . unless you need someone put down, and then I'll make an exception."

"For a lifetime supply of coffee creamer?" I say.

"Hell, no, kitten. I want the coffee, too. I'm a skilled tradesman. I don't come cheap." He looks over at the baby. "Mind if I hold the tyke when we get inside where it's warm?"

Dalton and I exchange a look. Cypher sees it and sputters. "What? You think I'll drop her on her head? My own girl grew up just fine. Twice as smart as her old man."

"You have a daughter?" I say.

"I do indeed. She's a lawyer down in Hawaii. Not the profession I would have chosen, but she isn't fond of mine either, so we agree to disagree. She married a few years back, and she's got herself a pair of twin babies. I haven't broken them yet."

"You've . . . seen them?" I say.

"Only once so far, but I plan to get down again this spring. Fly south with all the other snowbirds, work on my tan on Waikiki."

I stare at him.

"What?" he says. "You've never heard of these big things called airplanes? Sure, first I gotta get to Dawson, and that's a good week's walk, which is why I don't do it in the middle of winter, even if I'd appreciate that sun and sand even more."

"I never knew you had a kid," Dalton says.

"Because you never asked." Cypher throws his hands in the air. "No one asks. I'm just the crazy ex-sheriff who lives in the forest."

We're in Rockton now. People have heard us coming. More accurately, they heard Cypher. He tramps out of the forest like a Norse giant, clad in fur and snow. People clear a path all the way to the police station.

The first time Cypher walked in, they'd scattered even faster, all Dalton's bogeymen-of-the-forest stories springing to life. They've seen him enough now that they don't flee; they just retreat.

I'd lit the fire in the station before I left, and when we walk in, Dalton swings the kettle over the flames. Then he helps me out of the parka and takes the baby.

"She have a name?" Cypher asks.

I glance at Dalton.

"Abby," he says. "Or that's what we're calling her for now."

Cypher takes Abby and dangles her in front of his face, his one hand supporting her neck. "You didn't have your name stitched on your blanket? What kind of foundling are you?"

I settle in by the fire. "How much did Eric explain?"

"Just that we'd discovered a baby and a dead woman—who isn't the mother—and we need help finding the actual mother," Dalton says as he preps the French press. "Tyrone wouldn't let me tell him more. His price for information is a one-night stay in Rockton, with access to food and a shower. I agreed, but he refused to talk to anyone except you. I think he figured if I got his information, I'd renege on the bargain." He shoots Cypher a look.

"I wasn't questioning your integrity, boy. Your voice just isn't nearly as sweet as Casey's. Now, what's going on with this tyke?"

I explain. When I tell him who Edwin fingered as the family, he lets out a string of curses, and then stops short and puts his hands over the baby's ears before finishing.

"You know them," I say.

"Fuck, yeah."

"And they're not actually upstanding citizens."

"Fuck, no."

I rise to take the whistling kettle, but Dalton beats me to it.

"Edwin says they . . . sell their girls," I say. "Prostitute them."

"Yeah, sorry, kitten. I know you were hoping I'd say that's a load of hogwash, but it's not. I don't trade with that family unless I absolutely have to—they have some items I can't get elsewhere. And, yeah, sex might be on that list of rare commodities, but I'm sure as hell not buying it like that."

Cypher settles in, grunting as he shifts his bulk. "I don't have an aversion to such trade in general. If a woman's willing, and it's a clean transaction, well, I figure that's better than going into a bar and ending up with a woman who drank more than you realized. These particular traders offer me a girl every time, and they get the sharp side of my tongue instead. One of the girls even asked me to take her away and marry her."

He scratches his beard. "Shit. I didn't know what to do. Ended up saying no, and then spent a whole lotta time feeling bad about it. It's a complicated situation. I sure as hell don't want some little girl who stays with me because I rescued her. I could take her to Dawson, but what then? Give her a few grand and abandon her? She's never lived outside these woods."

"If that ever happens again, bring her here," Dalton says.

"It's not that simple," Cypher says. "It isn't like those girls are tied to a wagon, beaten and bruised, and I'm trading with their daddy while pretending not to see them because I really need new underwear."

I snort, and he arches his brows. "You think I'm kidding about the underwear, kitten? You try making them from deer hide. Going without ain't an option. I tried that one summer. It was warm enough, but then you got the chafing and the hanging and—"

I hold up my hand. "I get the pict— Nope, sorry. I don't get any picture at all."

He chuckles. "Point is that those girls aren't being held against their will. There's three of them—sisters—and if I tried rescuing two of them, they'd scratch my damned eyes out. The third—the one who asked—wasn't looking for rescue. She just figured I'd be a good provider. If I did walk her to Dawson, she'd turn around and find her way back to her family." He waves at Dalton. "Like you did, when the Daltons brought you to Rockton."

Dalton goes still. I stiffen, looking over. He says, very softly, "I tried to get back to my parents. To my family."

"Exactly," Cypher says, blithely missing Dalton's body language. "You were better off here, but you still wanted to return to your folks out there."

Dalton's storm-gray eyes fix on Cypher. "Better off?"

Cypher waves away Dalton's words—he's ready to move on. I'm trying to decide what to do when I hear myself saying, "Why did you think that?"

Dalton's gone still again, his nostrils flaring as if he's struggling to breathe. I could withdraw the question. Maybe I should. I don't.

"Why do you think Eric was better off in Rockton?" I press.

"Was something wrong with him? Was he sick? Malnourished?"

"Nothing like that. I'm sure his folks were decent kids. But they were already leaving him to fend for himself. That ain't right."

"What?" Dalton says, his face screwing up.

"Your daddy—Gene Dalton—saw you a few times out there, all by yourself. Hunting and fishing. You told him your parents had gone off to trade, and you were old enough to look after yourself. They must have taken Jakey with them. Gone for weeks, they were, leaving you alone."

"That . . . no, that never . . ." Dalton struggles for words. "That did not happen. Yes, I was old enough to go hunting or fishing. But for a morning or an afternoon. If my parents went trading, we all went. I never spoke to anyone from Rockton before Gene Dalton captured me."

Cypher frowns. "Maybe you've forgotten. Anyway, I don't know the details, and I might not have had much use for Gene Dalton, but your momma was a good woman. She wouldn't have kept you if there wasn't a problem with your folks. I wouldn't have let them keep you either."

There's a set to Cypher's jaw, one that says he's not trying to convince Dalton; he's trying to convince himself. He believed whatever tale Gene Dalton spun, and he cannot afford to second-guess now.

"Eric?" I say. "Maybe you want to take Abby home for a nap. You could check on Maryanne, too."

His lips tighten, and my gut seizes. I shouldn't have asked about his parents. I should have respected Dalton's wishes and kept out of it until he was ready. When he sees my face, he squeezes my hand and leans over to whisper, "Nothing I didn't already suspect."

Before I can react, he says, "Let me take Abby and Storm

for a walk. I should check on Maryanne. I'll be back in twenty minutes."

When Dalton's gone, I say to Cypher, "May I ask you a favor?"

"Sure, kitten. What is it?"

"Don't mention his family—either one, really. He has good memories of his birth parents, and what the Daltons did is confusing. I know you didn't mean anything by it, but I'd be very happy if it didn't arise in conversation again."

He looks toward the door Dalton exited. "He's upset."

I could almost laugh at his genuine surprise. He really did miss the clues, even as they'd flashed neon-bright. I remember who I'm talking to and limit my response to, "He's angry about what happened back then."

Cypher looks at me. "You can say he's upset, Casey. I'm not one of those assholes who'll give a guy flak for showing a bit of emotion. If it bothers him, I won't bring it up."

"Thank you. Now, about finding this baby's family . . ."

"Yeah, that was the topic of conversation, wasn't it?" He eyes me. "As for giving the baby back, Edwin's right. Those traders went on a long supply run." He stretches his legs. "Could be spring before they get back."

"Damn. So I guess we'll just need to adopt her."

"Seems like it. I know you and Eric are busy with your jobs, but you've got a town full of folks who'll help babysit, and you'd make good parents."

"People keep telling me that," I murmur. "So this family, they must have left in the last few days. You don't think we could catch up with them?"

"They move fast."

"Huh. Weird, though, don't you think? That they'd decide to do a supply run at this time of year. You said yourself that you wouldn't travel to Dawson in winter. Too hard going."

He shrugs. "That's me."

"Yet they not only chose to leave as soon as the weather got bad . . . but they'll be away all winter, when people would be most in need of trade goods, willing to pay dearly for food and ammo."

"I didn't say they were *good* traders."

"You and Edwin have decided the baby would be better off with us. I get that. Under the circumstances . . ." I exhale. "Well, I don't know what's going to happen under the circumstances, but I'm not about to hand a baby girl back to a family who'll prostitute her when she's old enough."

"They don't really wait until they're old enough."

"And you think I'd return a child to that? All I want is to assess the situation. Maybe they abandoned the baby. Edwin thinks so. Maybe the woman who died found her in the snow. Or maybe the mother is frantically searching for her child and can be convinced to leave her family and raise Abby in a safe place. I have no idea what our next move is, but I'd like you to trust us."

He sighs. "Don't get your back up, kitten. I know you and Eric gotta do the right thing, but sometimes, doing the right thing isn't really doing the right thing, if you know what I mean. You tie yourselves into knots weighing the ethical and moral bullshit, when common sense says 'Fuck that.' If a kid has a choice between growing up with good parents who'll give her the best fucking life they can . . . and parents who'll whore her out before she's old enough for high school? Pretty sure *no one* sees much of a decision there. It just seems best to me if I say the family's long gone, and any fault for a fib falls on me. I won't lose a moment's sleep over it."

"True, but now that I know you're fibbing, I will lose a *ton* of sleep over it, wondering if I should tell Eric my suspicions, wondering if I stole a baby from a young woman needing rescue herself, wondering if—"

"Life would be a whole lot easier if you could just shut off that brain of yours. Same with Eric. Yeah, what happened to him was messy, but he's fine now, and the Daltons are down south, and his parents are dead, and he's still got Jacob, so what good does it do to dig up the past?"

I ignore that and say, "This family of traders didn't go to Dawson. So the question is whether you're going to help us get to them, or we're going to track them down on our own."

He sighs and grumbles and says, "We can talk about that over dinner. I'm hungry, and I want a shower and a proper sitdown meal in your restaurant."

# TWENTY-ONE

Dalton returns with Abby and Storm just before we head out. We're putting Cypher up overnight in one of the empty apartments, and he wants to shower before dinner. He also wants clean clothing and a full line of toiletries, including beard scissors.

"You're going to dinner with us," Dalton says. "It's not a date."

Cypher doesn't respond to that. I glance over, and he's scratching his beard. When he catches my eye, he looks almost sheepish.

"So," he says, clearing his throat. "Earlier, I might have said I don't have any problem with the concept of . . . purchasing the time of . . . ladies . . ." He glances over, clearly hoping to be freed from this conversation with a nod of understanding. I frown, pretending I have no idea what he's talking about.

He clears his throat again. "Last time I was here . . . I overheard a comment that led me to asking your deputy a question, which he confirmed."

Another look my way. Again, I offer Cypher no sign of rescue. Dalton's busy murmuring to Abby, who is awake and trying to look around.

Cypher continues, "It seems you have legalized the, uh, sex trade in Rockton. So I thought, maybe, if I cleaned myself up, one of your, uh, ladies might consider . . ."

Dalton looks over, brows raised, as if he caught just the end of that conversation.

"He's getting himself dolled up because he *is* hoping for a date," I say. "A paid one."

Cypher glowers at me.

"What?" I said. "Did I misinterpret?"

He mutters under his breath.

"You can try," I say. "But we'd need to front you credits. They don't take hides in trade. Probably best if I speak to Isabel, and she can have a word with her girls, and they can get a look at you over dinner and let her know what they think. It's entirely up to them."

"As it should be," he says. "But, well, while I'm open to possibilities, there was one lady in particular who caught my eye. That's what led to the conversation with Deputy Will. She came by to give him shit about something, and he made a comment, and after she left, I confirmed the sex-trade thing. I'm presuming, from his comment, that she's one of the . . . ladies for hire."

"Ah, you already have your date picked out. I'll ask Will who—"

Before I can finish, Jen marches over. "You steal my baby, and you don't bring her back? I said her feeding time was six, and it's already ten after, and I see you just waltzing around with her, while she freezes her tiny ass off."

As she talks, Cypher steps away—quickly. I don't blame him. I'd like to escape, too. But something in the way he quickly sidesteps catches my attention.

Jen sees him. "Oh, it's Grizzly Adams. Come down from the mountain, did you? You don't need to jump. I don't bite."

"I wasn't jumping, miss. I was moving downwind so you don't smell me before I get a shower. Which I was just about to do."

"I've spent the last two days changing shitty diapers. You can't smell any worse than that." Jen reaches for Abby. "Gimme."

I catch the look Cypher is giving her, and I accidentally say "Jen?" aloud, and she turns on me with a snapped, "What?"

I motion to Dalton, whose eyebrows disappear under his hat. He looks from Cypher to Jen.

"What?" Jen repeats.

"I think we'll keep the baby for now," I say. "We'll feed her, and then Petra wanted a visit. We'll leave her and Storm there over dinner. Would you mind doing us a favor, though? Tyrone's going to get cleaned up and grab dinner at the Lion, and I'm not sure we'll be done with the baby in time. It's probably best if he doesn't walk into the Lion unescorted."

"You want me to eat dinner with Grizzly Adams?" She looks over at him and shrugs. "Fine with me, but you'd better make sure he *wants* to have dinner with me. He looks ready to bolt back into the forest."

"Like I said, miss, I just don't smell too good."

"It's Jen. I haven't been a 'miss' for a long time. If you're okay eating with me, then sure, go get your shower. I'll come by in thirty minutes. Just don't make me wait. I'm hungry."

She leaves before he can answer. I call after her, "Thanks, and dinner's on us!"

"It better be," she calls back.

When she's out of earshot, I say, "That's all we're paying for, too."

Dalton watches Jen. "She's the . . . ?"

"Can't even get the rest out, can you?" I murmur.

"She's a little rough around the edges," Cypher says. "But

I'm not exactly smooth myself." He eyes her retreating form. "You think I have a shot? I mean, if I pay, obviously."

"Here's the thing," I say. "When Will said we have sex workers, he didn't mean Jen. Yes, he may have made a smart-ass comment to her. That's because she's been known to moonlight, which is strictly prohibited. As far as I know, she hasn't done that in a while. So my advice is to have a nice dinner, see how it goes, and if she makes you an offer, I'll tell Isabel it's a special case."

"A charity case," Dalton says.

Cypher pokes him in the chest. "How about you just go back to *not* trying to be funny, boy. I don't need charity. I just need a long shower, some good soap, and clean clothing. And beard trimmers."

"Or hedge clippers," I say.

"Oh, you too, huh? I clean up just fine. As you will see."

"Actually, we won't. You get Jen all to yourself. Tell her we decided to eat in with the baby tonight. Go have your date, and try not to spend too much of our money."

We're at home with Abby and Storm. Dalton checked on Maryanne earlier, and she's fine. He sensed she'd had enough company for the day, so he had Anders take her dinner and a few supplies, and she's in for the night. Anders will keep an eye on the place and make sure no one goes nosing around. He'll also let us know if Maryanne gets skittish and bolts.

I feed Storm and then Abby while Dalton makes dinner. He's better at that. It wasn't a skill I developed at home—we had a housekeeper who cooked. That's no excuse, I know. It just always seemed like there were other things to do, and it was easier to buy takeout or cook a pot of pasta or slap together a sandwich. I *can* cook—I'm just not very good at it, and the limited ingredients here frustrate me. Dalton's never known anything else.

Tonight, he's making venison cutlets with a mushroom ragout on a bed of egg noodles. Everything is fresh—the meat hunted, the mushrooms picked and dried, the egg noodles handmade. We may not have a supermarket's worth of variety here, but the food is worthy of a posh Toronto eatery.

I'm putting Abby to bed when Dalton declares dinner ready. We eat in front of the fireplace, Storm at our feet, Dalton stretched out on the sofa, me curled up at the other end, plates on our laps, wineglasses on the side tables.

I plan to find other conversation for the meal, but as soon as we settle and I open my mouth, I hear myself saying, "I'm sorry."

He glances over, brows rising.

"Earlier with Tyrone. When he mentioned your parents, I should have dropped it, and I didn't."

He turns to me, and his head tilts, just a little, eyes piercing with a look I know well, from our earliest days. That keen scrutiny, as if he's trying to peer right into my brain and figure out what I'm thinking.

"Is that what was bothering you?" he says.

I glance over.

He sets his plate down, one knee coming up onto the sofa. "You looked freaked out when Tyrone was talking, and I thought you were just shocked by what he said. Were you honestly worried I'd be mad at you for asking?"

"It's your business, and if you wanted details, you'd ask. I shouldn't do it for you." I put my fork down. "It's not just *for you,* either. I want to know. I want to understand. That isn't right."

His head tilts again. "Being concerned for me isn't right?"

"It's . . ." I flail my hands. "Complicated."

"Yeah, it is. Those relationships are complicated. Ours isn't, and if I'm making it complicated, you gotta tell me so I can stop. I sure as hell don't want you thinking you need to tread lightly or you'll piss me off. You asked the obvious question. One I should have asked myself, but . . ."

He shrugs. "It feels like picking at a scab. That scab's not healing, though. I just . . ." He exhales, a long hiss of breath between his teeth. "I just don't want to get into it."

He stops, lips parting. "Fuck, that sounds bad. It's not that I don't want to get into it with you. I don't want to get into it with myself. Best to stuff it under the bed and tell myself it doesn't matter. Except it does matter. I haven't gone to see the Daltons since you arrived, and part of that's because when we have time off, I want to be with you. But part of it is that you give me an excuse. They're my parents, and I should want to see them. Only they're *not* my parents, and unless they have a damned good excuse for what they did, I'm not eager to spend my free time with them."

He looks over at me. "They don't have a good excuse, do they?"

"I have no way of knowing that, Eric."

"But you think the same thing I do. They lied about my situation. They made shit up to justify bringing me into Rockton."

"Gene did."

He rubs his mouth. "Yeah, and I don't know how to deal with that, because my gut says he lied to my mother, too. He presented her with a situation she wouldn't argue with. Like Edwin trying to tell us the baby had been abandoned. If that's the case, then I'm doing a shitty thing, shutting Katherine Dalton out of my life. But if it's not? If she knew, too?"

He looks at me. "If she knew too, that's gonna hurt. I need those answers. I'm not ready to march down south and get them. But you don't ever need to worry that you're going to upset me by prodding. Fuck knows, I'm the king of pushing people to face shit they don't want to face."

He lifts my plate and holds it out. "Eat."

When I hesitate, he leans in, his forehead touching mine. "I love you. You know that. Sometimes I wish there was something more to say, a higher escalation. I can't find the words to go beyond it, you know?"

I nod, still not speaking. I feel his breath on my lips, close enough to kiss, but he stays there, just breathing.

"I'm still afraid," he says, "of doing something to scare you off. I'm mostly past it, but I worry that if I dive into this, and I can't deal with it, you'll decide I'm just too fucked up to be with."

"Pretty sure my baggage is as heavy as yours."

"Yeah, but what's in your baggage has been sorted and arranged, and you open it up for a look now and then. Mine's stuffed in a suitcase full to bursting, held by triple locks, and I don't even peek inside. You shouldn't feel like I'd go ballistic if you even jangle the lock. Especially when I'm throwing yours open, riffling through it, tossing shit everywhere so I can see what you've got in there."

I laugh softly. "That is an awesome analogy."

"Thank you. Totally true, too. I love you. I don't want to lose you. You're going to need to be patient with me. Right now, my life is fucking awesome, and if there's this one suitcase under the bed that I don't want to touch, I know that isn't healthy, but I'm not ready to rip it open. You may, however, jangle the locks now and then to remind me it's there, and that I need to deal with it eventually."

I press my lips to his. It's meant to be quick, but he bears into it, pulling me against him, the kiss hungry, edged with desperation. I slide my plate onto the table and pull him to me as I fall back onto the couch.

# TWENTY-TWO

I'm on the floor, resting on my stomach, eyeing my plate of half-eaten food.

"You know what we need?" I say. "A microwave."

Dalton snorts and pushes up. "You southerners make everything complicated." He pulls out a tray that hangs over the fire, sets our plates on it, and adjusts it over the flames. Storm lumbers over to lie closer to the fire. She doesn't even eye the plates. She knows better.

"A microwave would be faster," I say.

"But it wouldn't give the meat that nice, smoky taste. And if you were so hungry, maybe you shouldn't have insisted on sex halfway through dinner."

"Insisted?" I sputter. "I don't even remember *asking*."

"Exactly. That only makes it worse."

I pitch a pillow at him. He catches it, scoops me up, and deposits me on the sofa, then drops the pillow on my head. When I go to throw it back at him, he lifts my wineglass, and I stop.

"Thought that'd work," he says, handing me the glass as he takes away the pillow. "Don't wanna spill the wine."

He's about to settle in beside me when the baby wails. He levers up, but I put a hand on his knee.

"I've got this," I say.

I root my panties and bra out of the pile of clothing—somehow, this seems the proper line between acceptable and unacceptable attire in front of an infant who can't see more than blobs. I pull them on as I head upstairs.

By the time Abby is changed, our meal is warmed.

"You eat first," I say. "I'll handle cuddling duty."

I sit on the sofa with Abby, and she snuggles against my bare skin. Storm lies on my feet. I have Abby cradled in my arms, which apparently is the proper position for breastfeeding, because her head turns and her tiny mouth clamps down on my bra. I laugh and shift her away, murmuring "Sorry," as I sweep my hair back over my shoulder.

I look over at Dalton, and I'm about to make a comment when I see he's staring, and the look on his face . . . It's the same look I'm sure I had, watching him cradle the baby that first time, an expression of revelation and a pang of unexpected longing from some instinctive place.

He looks away quickly and says something, too gruff to make out. I slide over and kiss his beard-rough cheek. He turns to meet the kiss, hand slipping into my hair. It's a quick one, and then I'm back in my corner, watching him eat as he sneaks almost guilty glances my way.

We'll have to deal with this. With the questions Abby raises for us. But I'm no longer freaking out at the thought. For now, we have other concerns. I start by telling him Maryanne's story. He stops eating several times as I talk, chewing over my words with his dinner, but he says nothing until I'm done. Then he's done, too, and he wordlessly switches his plate for the baby so I can eat.

"Huh," he says as he bounces Abby, hand behind her head, as if this has become second nature.

"Yep," I say. "Huh, indeed. Thank God I didn't tell anyone else about my 'council is responsible for the hostiles' theory. You should have seen the look I got when I asked Maryanne whether anyone else could be involved. I felt like Brent with his crazy conspiracy theories."

I pull my legs up, sitting sideways and cross-legged as I dangle one hand to pet Storm. "For the record, I knew I was being paranoid suspecting the council."

"Yeah," Dalton says. "Because they are *never* behind the weird shit that happens here. It's not like they're bringing in killers without warning us or setting spies among us or planting a goddamn secret agent to assassinate liabilities."

"Petra will love 'secret agent.' She might want a badge."

He snorts. "Nice job of ignoring my point, Detective. You never blamed the council. You only floated the possibility. Your primary suspicion was simply that the hostiles didn't just devolve into fucking savages after a year or two in the wild. Now we know your main hypothesis is correct. The hostiles aren't residents-gone-wild. They're a cult."

My brows shoot up.

Shades fall over his eyes—the pride of a brilliant man who realizes he can misunderstand concepts those from "down south" take for granted. It only lasts a second, though, before he relaxes as he remembers who he's with.

"Yeah," he says. "That might not be the right word. We had someone up here, a few years back, escaping a cult, so I did some reading. Maybe not as much as I should have."

"The fact that you did *any* research to help understand a resident's situation puts you head and shoulders above most of us, Eric. And my look didn't mean you had the wrong idea. It was surprise that you had the right one."

When he chuckles, I say, "Sorry, that came out wrong. I'm not surprised that *you* had a good idea. I'm surprised because I hadn't thought of it that way. While I never dealt with cults down south, I did attend a seminar on them. Most times, you have a charismatic person recruiting easy targets—people who want to get rich or feel loved and accepted, depending on what your cult is selling. They're always selling something. The hostiles don't fit that."

"Yeah, crappy analogy."

"No, it's not, because the basic idea still works. People who leave Rockton *are* seeking something. A more natural way of life and a stronger community. Most of all, though, they're looking for a new *experience*. That's what Maryanne wanted. The hostiles aren't willing recruits, though. Sure, I suppose it's possible someone could be attracted to that lifestyle, but mostly, they're being brainwashed. That's where the cult analogy works best."

"It starts with the tea," Dalton says. "A group of settlers, maybe with some experience in drugs, looking for *that* kind of back-to-nature experience. Rockton got a lot of that in the early years. People grew their own marijuana, their own mushrooms. Neither was particularly conducive to productivity, though."

I smile. "No, I suppose not. But yes, back to nature can mean plant-based methods of communing with the forest. Early settlers probably did experiment with what they found out there." I turn to him. "What is out there, anyway?"

"Fuck if I know. We still get residents poking around. They end up in the clinic for smoking all kinds of shit."

I laugh.

He shifts Abby to his other arm. "No one's ever found anything that'll send them on a drug trip. My guess is that whoever concocted this tea knew exactly what they were doing. They didn't just randomly throw plants into a pot."

"The inventor and their fellow settlers get into it, and everyone likes how it makes them feel. It makes them more comfortable with violence, more fixated on daily survival and less concerned with everything that gets in the way of it."

"The tea hones their survival instincts and dulls their self-awareness."

"So they don't sit around moaning about wanting a shower." I remember what Maryanne said, about how that was the big concern with her parents' hippie friends. Scarcity of creature comforts is the thing people complain about most in Rockton. I've learned to live without a microwave and internet access, but that doesn't mean I don't feel the lack of them. That's where Dalton has the advantage.

It would be simpler if we could temporarily forget the lack of comforts. That's why we control alcohol so tightly. It's also why Rockton had a hellish problem with a homemade drug when I arrived. Drinking the hostiles' tea would be rewarding in so many ways.

I reach for my wine and sip it, thinking. "I feel like there's more to it, but we have a good starting hypothesis. We know at least some hostiles are there against their will, and we'll need to decide what to do about that. For now, in regard to Abby, we know she isn't a baby hostile, and we know the dead woman—Ellen—was a former hostile. She wasn't shot by one, though, so it seems any connection to the hostiles is only tangential. Our goal is finding Abby's family."

I tell him what Cypher did—and did not—say on that matter.

"Yeah, fucking complicated," Dalton mutters. "Everything always is. He'll tell us where to find these traders, though, especially if he gets laid tonight." He looks at me. "So Jen, huh?"

I sputter a laugh that startles Abby. She cranes her neck, looking toward the source of the noise. Dalton hands her to me, and I expect her to complain. Instead she snuggles, cheek on my bare skin, chubby legs and arms drawing in like a frog's.

I stroke her back. "Yep, Jen. Gotta give him credit for keeping his aspirations reasonable."

Dalton throws back his head and laughs, and Abby makes a chirping noise, but only snuggles more, as if she can burrow into me. I tug up a blanket.

"Isabel and Phil, Cypher and Jen . . ." I say. "Spring must be just around the corner."

"Nah, up here, it's winter that gets them. Long, cold nights." His gaze travels over me, still in my panties and bra. "Speaking of which . . ." He leans toward me. "I was kinda thinking we might spend our evening playing a game." He waggles his brows.

"Uh-huh," I say.

He leans to whisper in my ear. "I swiped Scrabble from the community center. You in?"

I grin. "Totally."

"How about you bring Abby's bed downstairs so she can hang out with us. I'll start coffee and break out the homemade Irish cream."

"And cookies?"

He smiles. "I believe I can find cookies."

It's just after eleven when a familiar pound on the door has Dalton calling, "Come in!"

A moment later, Anders steps around the corner, his hand over his eyes.

"Ha ha," Dalton says. "We're decent."

Anders walks in and looks at the Scrabble board. "You guys know how to rock an evening in, don't you?"

I lift my cookie. "We do indeed."

Anders shakes his head. "It's been, what, a little over a year, and you're already an old married couple, spending your one evening off playing Scrabble and drinking coffee."

"It's spiked coffee."

"Ooooh, living it up. Better be careful. Too much of that might lead to the proper definition of couple's night in." His gaze travels over to my shirt and jeans, crumpled on the floor, and he glances back at me, realizing I'm wearing the shirt that Dalton is not. "Ah, no, Scrabble is the afterglow. Carry on, then."

He reaches down to scoop up Abby. As he does, he gets a look at my tiles. "Boss? Better block 'phone.' Casey's about to change it to 'xylophone' for a gazillion points."

I smack his leg.

"Hey," he says. "Baby on board. Careful."

Dalton alters "phone" to "telephone." I smack Anders again.

"I like you just fine, Case," Anders says. "But he's the boss. Now he owes me at least two days off for helping him win."

"He was already winning." I wave at the board. "House rules allow profanity, and he's really, really good at it."

Anders laughs. Then he hunkers down. "So, as much as I'd love to share one of those spiked coffees, I'm not interrupting your evening merely to be annoying."

"Merely," Dalton murmurs.

"Disrupting your sappy domestic bliss is always a valid side goal. However, my main purpose is to tell you that someone was skulking around your old house, where Maryanne is spending the night."

I shoot upright. "What?"

He motions me down. "It's okay. It was just Phil, who already knows she's there."

"You said 'skulking.' That implies he wasn't popping by to see if she needed extra pillows."

"Yeah, it was weird, which is why I'm here. And before you freak out, Casey, I confirmed that the doors were locked and ordered one of the guys to keep a watch on the house while I ran over here. I didn't tell him that anyone is in it—just that a resident was poking around your old place."

"Okay. So explain the skulking weirdness," I say.

"I'm getting to that. Just fending off 'Oh my god, you saw criminal activity and just walked away!'"

"I never—"

"The point?" Dalton says. "Or do I need to go investigate myself while you two squabble?"

Anders continues. "Phil was definitely skulking. Dressed in dark colors, no flashlight, hood pulled up. He was wearing one of the militia parkas instead of his completely inappropriate for the weather but terribly stylish ski jacket."

"Was he doing anything besides skulking?" I ask.

"Yep, which made it extra weird. So, I'm on patrol, and on each round, I pass the house twice. I'm literally walking by the front when he darts from behind a tree. I'm, like, seriously? Could you not wait ten seconds for the guy with the flashlight to move on? I turn off the flashlight and take it slow, but I'm not Eric Cloud-Foot. You can hear my boots crunching snow. I slip around the house, and Phil's trying the back door. Like he expects it to be open. I yell 'Hey!' and he takes off." Anders shakes his head. "The guy would starve to death as a cat burglar."

"You're sure it was Phil? You saw his face?"

"No, he had the sense to turn that away from me. But, like I said, world's worst cat burglar. He might have found new clothes and tied a scarf around his face, but he still wore the boots he had the council ship up."

That was one concession the council made, likely to counter Phil's sense that he'd been exiled here. *What? No, that'd be illegal.*

*You're being held there as an emergency measure to fill an essential position, for which you will be well compensated. I know it was unexpected, so just tell us what you need from your condo.*

Phil's winter wear was what you'd expect from a Toronto exec whose subzero excursions were limited to the half-kilometer walk between his condo and the subway station. Phil has never confirmed his actual city of origin, but I'd lay serious money on Toronto. He has that New York Lite vibe. His boots are definitely not the bulky, rubber-soled footwear that keeps us warm and upright out here.

"What the hell is he up to?" Dalton mutters. He looks at Anders. "You okay watching the baby for an hour or so?"

"If I get a spiked coffee and one of those cookies."

"One coffee," I say. "And don't go inviting all your friends over for a party as soon as we leave."

# TWENTY-THREE

Dalton pounds on Phil's door. He has to do it twice before Phil pulls it open, robe tied over his bare chest and sweatpants, feet equally bare, one hand holding his glasses as he blinks at us, as if bleary-eyed with sleep.

"Eric? Casey?" He lifts his wrist to check the time, and blinks again, as if struggling to process the fact that he's not wearing his watch.

Phil may be a shitty cat burglar, but his acting skills aren't half bad, if a little community theater.

"Why were you at Casey's old place tonight?" Dalton asks.

"What? When? I haven't been out since dinner."

"No?"

Phil finds the expression he wants, somewhere between annoyance and condescension. "No, Sheriff. I don't socialize in the evenings."

"Just the afternoons," I murmur, and his cheeks color at that. He opens his mouth, but I cut him off with, "So you haven't been out in the last few hours?"

"That's what I said."

Dalton steps forward, and Phil backs up with a snarky, "Please come in. Two A.M. is a perfectly fine time for a visit."

"It's not even midnight," Dalton says.

I ease by them and lift one of Phil's boots from the mat. It's still caked with snow.

"You thought you could put that one past a fucking detective?" Dalton says, pointing at the boot.

"I meant that I hadn't been out and walking around. Not that I hadn't stepped beyond my door. One of the shutters was banging. I couldn't see anything, though I'd like Kenny to check in the morning. I'm sure I heard a clatter."

"On the rooftop maybe?" I say. "Santa making a practice run?"

I get a cool look for that. Then his lips purse. "Are you saying someone was at the house where you're keeping Maryanne? Perhaps *that's* what I heard—someone went to the wrong perimeter house searching for her."

I'm about to call his bluff. Then I reconsider and nod. "Someone who spotted her when I brought her in. They got curious and snuck in for a closer look."

"Perhaps, but I wouldn't be so quick to write off a potential threat as mere curiosity."

"Threat?"

"She's a hostile. She makes people nervous. Remember how they tried to lynch Oliver Brady. If they know you have a hostile here, they might decide to do something about that."

"Most residents don't even know what hostiles are," Dalton says. "Hell, they see Tyrone Cypher and think that's what I mean. And Ty's in town tonight, so if they decide to form another mob, they'll just go after him. Which is fine. He can look after himself. Give his rusty occupational skills a workout."

"Tyrone Cypher has no legal authority here."

"I don't mean his skills as a former sheriff. I mean from when he was a hit man."

Phil looks at Dalton. "I realize I'm still relatively new, but I believe we may dispense with the hazing jokes. Whatever Rockton's issues, the council would not put a killer on the police force."

"Uh . . ." I say. "I know you've read my file."

"You're an exception." He pauses. "Like Deputy Anders."

"Given the track record of Rockton law enforcement, I suspect 'killing someone in cold blood' is actually a prerequisite. Except for Eric. Eric's special."

"In so many ways," Phil murmurs under his breath. "My point—"

"Your point was that you think Maryanne is in danger," Dalton says. "And it's interesting that you jump to that rather than the more mundane explanation of a bored resident. Also interesting considering *you're* the person who was trying to break into her house. Ever been diagnosed with multiple personalities?"

"Don't give him any ideas," I say.

"I wasn't. Dissociative identity disorder is exceptionally rare and experts disagree on whether it exists at all." Dalton catches my look. "We had a resident who said she had it. So I did my research. She was wrong. Had a helluva time convincing her of that, though."

"Cultists, psychopaths, multiple personalities, hit men . . . Is there anyone you haven't had here? Oh, wait. No zombies. At least not yet, right?"

"Actually . . ."

I arch my brows.

Dalton says, "Well, he wasn't *really* a zombie. But he hated it here. Wanted to go home before his two years were up. He was looking for a loophole, and he knew we can't handle residents with serious mental illnesses. Seems he'd seen a TV special raising money for . . ." His eyes roll up, accessing his files. "Collard's syndrome? Cotard's delusion? Something like that. Anyway, it's a real illness where people think they're dead and rotting. He faked that. I convinced him he was wrong, which was much easier than convincing the multiple-personality lady."

"Do I dare ask what you did?"

He shrugs. "We can't have rotting residents. That's unsanitary. So I dug a hole, cuffed him, and tossed him in."

"Whereupon he had a miraculous recovery."

"I'm a man of many talents. Especially when it comes to sniffing out bullshit." He turns to Phil. "You don't have dissociative identity disorder. And you're not a zombie. But you were spotted trying to break into Casey's old place tonight."

"No, I was not. If someone was, then I would suggest you reconsider Maryanne's stay in Rockton."

I eye him. "Would you?"

"Yes. Personally, I have no problem with it, and neither does the council. But, if she's in danger, then I would suggest you give her supplies and turn her out."

"In the middle of the night?"

He hesitates.

"How about first thing in the morning?" I say. "Before dawn."

Phil nods. "That should be acceptable."

"Really?" Dalton says. "'Cause if you're worried about a resident attacking her, that would happen at night."

I hold up a hand against Phil's protest. "You're not half bad at this game, Phil. However, the next time you decide to play dress-up, I'd suggest changing your boots. They're very recognizable. Let's go sit down and chat, shall we?"

When he doesn't answer, Dalton and I pull off our outerwear and proceed into the living room.

Phil lowers himself to the sofa. "I don't see the point of this. Someone spotted a resident attempting to break into your old house, and that resident mistakenly identified my boots."

I sigh. "I just took off my stuff. Please don't make me go outside and find the fresh trail you made through the forest to my old house."

He goes still.

"It's winter," Dalton says. "You walked through snow and made a trail that we don't need Storm to follow. Now, if you need us to prove this, I'll go out myself while Casey warms up, but if I find that trail, you've just undone every iota of goodwill you might have built since you got here. Trust is—"

"Fine," Phil says. "It was me. I was curious about Maryanne, and I will admit I went about it the wrong way."

"Yeah, no," Dalton says. "You weren't sneaking in the back door to watch her while she sleeps."

"You weren't actually trying to break in at all," I say. "You knew that door would be locked. You stepped out from behind a tree right when Will passed by. You waited for him, so he'd see you try breaking in. You wanted us to think Maryanne was in danger. You want us to get her out of here before dawn. Why?"

I think I know the answer, but I'm still smarting from my mistake with the hostiles, and so I will hold back here.

"I . . . I just feel it's unsafe," Phil says. "Volatile elements and all that. It seems unwise. I wanted to alert you to the possibility of trouble."

Dalton leans back on the sofa. "Well, then, next time, just come and tell us. We're the local law. We'll decide whether there's a credible threat. I say there isn't, so Maryanne stays. In fact, I'm going to encourage her to stick around an extra day and night. Casey and I have a baby's family to locate, and Maryanne really should get more medical treatment—"

"No," Phil says. "I'm sorry, but we are not a rehabilitation facility. We can provide emergency aid, and of course we aren't going to send her into the wilderness without supplies, but she must go by dawn."

"Why don't we ask the council about that?" Dalton says. "Dawn is midmorning. We'll call them at nine and relay your concerns—"

"No, you can't . . ."

When Phil trails off, Dalton leans forward. "Can't what? Can't tell them that you spoke to us about this? You've dug yourself into a hole here, and you're still grasping at roots, trying to yank yourself out. But you're grabbing the ones that are going to snap and send you falling back into that hole with a busted leg. Slow down and think."

Phil does. Then his lips form an unspoken curse.

"Yeah," Dalton says. "You just advised us to get Maryanne out, and even if we do that, there's nothing to stop us from innocently mentioning it when we talk to the council next. Telling them that you insisted."

"The council didn't say they were fine with having Maryanne here, did they?" I say, finally working up the courage to voice the suspicions Dalton is obviously suggesting. "*They're* the threat, not random residents."

Phil's mouth opens. Then he thinks better of whatever he'd been about to say and withdraws.

I push on. "You dressed up and pretended to try breaking into Maryanne's place in hopes we'd worry and shuffle her out before . . . before what?"

He still doesn't speak. He's not denying it either, though.

"Oh, for fuck's sake," Dalton says. "Would charades help?

You act out the situation, and we can guess what the problem is?"

Phil glowers . . . and says nothing.

"He wants us to guess," I say. "By now, Phil, you've realized that there are a lot of little moments during your stay here when you make a decision that sets your feet on a certain path. Like those old Choose Your Own Adventure books. Constant choices, and for some there's no turning back. This is one of those forks. If the council told you to do something about Maryanne, and you did, that would be your quicksand fate. There's no convincing us later that you were still on our side. Instead, you warned us. That's another of those paths, because if the council finds out, you've walked into more quicksand. Now you're into the smaller choices. They're subtler. They're you choosing where you're going to stand on that line between the two sides. If you decide to stop here, I understand."

Dalton grumbles under his breath.

I shoot him a look. "The main thing is that we've been warned. Of course we want more. But I understand the position you're in and the dangers of telling us more. I also hope that you understand, Phil, that by *not* telling us more, you leave us to imagine the worst. I do believe some elements of the council are working toward our common goal. But some of them are very clearly not."

He's quiet for another few moments. Then he says, "What if I don't necessarily agree? If I believe the council is indeed acting in Rockton's best interests, but that they overestimate the danger and . . ."

He trails off, and we wait. When he speaks again, his tone is slow, measured. "Being in Rockton, my vantage point has changed, yet I still try to balance the needs of the individuals with the needs of the whole. Ultimately, any choice must favor the whole—keeping Rockton safe and self-sufficient. However, living here, I think you two sometimes fail to see the larger picture."

"That if the town loses money, we shut down?" Dalton says. "Fuck no, we don't see that at all. That shit grows on trees, doesn't it?"

"Rockton isn't a nonprofit," I say. "No one expects that. We do think it should be a not-*for*-profit, though."

"This isn't the time for that discussion," Phil says. "My original point wasn't financial. By big picture, I mean security as well. We make choices to protect the whole. You both do, and the council does, and some of them are choices you'd rather not make. The difference is . . ."

Phil searches for something and then blurts, "Zombies."

I lift my brows.

He continues. "Let's say one person in your city becomes a zombie. There's a chance of treating her, but an even greater chance that she'll infect others and it'll spread. The obvious solution is to kill her. But what if this zombie is Casey? That will affect your decision. Likewise, living here, you can never be completely unbiased. Imagine you have a resident who is at high risk of going south and telling the world about Rockton. Imagine she's also a friend. If you fear the council might take drastic measures to stop her, will you inform them? What if you don't and she tells her story to the world, and Rockton ceases to exist? She lives and others don't because there's no Rockton to escape to?"

"Fine," Dalton says. "You're saying we might not be the best judge of threats because we live among the residents as individuals. Not arguing. But Maryanne isn't going to lose her mind, revert to being a hostile, and start murdering residents."

"Does the council know that? I *am* trusting your judgment, but I also see their point of view. They asked—" He takes a deep breath. "They *ordered* me to bring her to Dawson City. After you two left pursuing the baby's parents, I was to sedate her and enlist the help of residents who have a working relationship with the council."

"So the council planned to take Maryanne," I say. "And then what?"

"Get her appropriate medical and psychological treatment. I believe them when they say that. However, it's still removing her against her will. Also, I know you've taken an interest in the hostiles, Casey, and having lived here, I fully support any research that might eventually lead to the end of that particular threat. However, if I challenge the council, they'll recall me, fire me, and replace me."

"But you *want* to be recalled," I say.

"If I stay a year, I earn a quarter million on top of my salary. If I defy them, I might as well tell future employers that I spent the last eight years in Tibet with monks. That's lovely for personal growth, but on Bay Street, no one cares about your self-actualization."

He looks at us. "I'm never going to see the beauty of the north and fall in love. However, I am committed to Rockton for my own reasons. I can be an ally, but I need your protection in return."

"In other words, this meeting never happened," I say. "We get Maryanne out before dawn, so you can say we left with her before you could."

He shakes his head. "What you do with Maryanne is your own concern. However, come morning, you must report to me that she's left of her own accord, and you have no idea where she went. You cannot track her because you have a lead on the baby's parents, which is your priority." He pauses. "I trust that Tyrone Cypher's presence here means you have a lead?"

"We do."

"Then follow it."

# TWENTY-FOUR

We veer past the place we gave Cypher for the night, in case we can talk to him now and save a step in the morning. But there are signs he's not alone. I stick a note under the door warning we'll return at six.

Back home, I update Anders while Dalton changes and feeds Abby. We set the alarm for five, which gives us four hours of sleep. Abby allows us almost that much, rising at four thirty, and I'll forgive her for that.

After breakfast, I take Abby so I can talk to Cypher while Dalton takes Storm to the storerooms, where he'll pack supplies for Maryanne.

When I rap on Cypher's door, it takes a while for it to open, and then Jen's there with her foot on the note.

"It's five in the fucking morning," she says.

"Five forty-five. And that note you're standing on says we'll be by at six, so I can come back in fifteen minutes if it makes a difference."

She lets out a string of profanity. I wait it out.

She glances at the bedroom. "You taking him?"

"Undetermined. However, I do need to give you this little

one." I gesture at Abby, tucked under my jacket. "But, like I said, I can give you fifteen minutes."

She eyes that direction again, and I hear Cypher rising with a bleary, "Jennifer?" Then a few profanities of his own, in obvious disappointment at finding himself alone.

"Make it twenty," she says.

I leave just as Dalton passes with Storm. I tell him I'll swing by my old house and wake Maryanne.

Once she's up, I tell her there's some concern over the council's interest in her, and we're not overly worried, but it seems wise to head out before dawn. She decides on another shower as I make breakfast, and I ask if there's anything in particular she'd like us to pack, after I run through the list of what we have.

"I do have one request that you probably can't fill," she says. "I know you said there are books at the cave, and I see you're grabbing some more for me but . . . I don't suppose there are any reading glasses. I had laser surgery before I came to Rockton."

That's one of the prearrival suggestions, because we can't supply contacts or easily replace glasses.

"However," she says, "I've aged since then, and I've had trouble with my sewing lately. I tried a book last night, and I can manage it, but yes, evidently, I'm getting old."

"Considering the median age here is late thirties, reading glasses are a must," I say. "There's a stash of them in the library. I'll grab a few for you to try. Also, let me know if you want a specific type of fiction or nonfiction. If Eric grabs books, you'll end up with everything from historical romance to archaeology to biographies of obscure ancient warlords."

She smiles. "Not because he'll randomly grab a handful, but because he's read them all himself. I remember that. Especially the romance. One of the militia razzed him for reading one, and Eric said he was learning skills that guys obviously hadn't, considering he was always complaining about his three ex-wives." Her smile deepens. "Guess he did develop those relationship skills."

I return the smile. "He did indeed."

"Well, presuming you have historical romances and weren't just teasing me, I'll take some of those. Maybe fantasy, too. And mystery. Oh, and nonfiction, textbooks or whatever . . ." She waves a hand. "Honestly, you can do exactly what Eric would. Just get me a random selection of everything. I'll be like a kid in a candy store."

Despite his presumably good night, Cypher isn't any easier to deal with than he was yesterday. He does not want to tell us where to find Abby's mother, and Jen isn't helping. She hovers with the baby until she overhears the situation, and then it's "What kind of monster are you, Casey?" in far more profane language. And also "If you don't want the baby yourself, at least give her to someone who does," until I snap.

"Come on, kitten," Cypher says when I tell them off. "We're only trying to help."

"By accusing me of wanting to turn this baby over to a family who'll whore her out when she's twelve?"

"Jen didn't mean it like that."

"Yeah, actually, she did. You might want to get to know someone before you sleep with her, Ty. We're on a schedule here. I'll take Abby with us, and we'll see if we can track down Jacob and get his help finding this family. Because I will find them. I will evaluate the situation. If there is no way to resolve it, then I *will* keep this baby."

Both of them look over my shoulder. I turn to see Dalton standing there.

My cheeks heat. "I didn't mean— Obviously, I wouldn't decide on my own to . . ." I swallow. "I was only reassuring them that I wasn't trying to get rid of Abby."

Dalton glares at Cypher and Jen. "What the fuck?"

"Yes," Jen says. "We upset your princess."

"Hey," Cypher rumbles, turning a look on Jen. "I figured you were just sounding off. If you were really accusing Casey of wanting to get rid of this baby, maybe you oughta head on home, 'cause that's some world-class bullshit right there."

I expect Jen to tell him to go screw himself and storm off. Her mouth does set in a firm line. Then she says, still glowering, "Casey knows I didn't mean it. She's a bit sensitive."

"Yeah, I'd be sensitive too if you accused me of that." He turns to me. "I will take you to this trader family, kitten. I'm trying to make the situation easy for you, but that's not my place." He turns to Jen. "We'll be back before dinner. Can I ask you to join me? Or did I just blow my chances?"

Jen's eyes widen, as if she'd figured *she'd* blown *her* chances. Then she shrugs and says gruffly, "I guess so. Better be back by seven, though. I need to eat." She hesitates, considers. "If you're late, we can grab a drink."

"If I'm not late, then we'll do both. Now, you mind taking the tyke from Casey? I think we're best leaving her behind for now."

I agree. Unlike with the First Settlement, I will definitely want time to evaluate the situation before I hand Abby over.

We are gone before dawn . . . if not quite as early as we anticipated. As we're slipping into the forest, I swear I see Phil standing at his bedroom window, watching us with disapproval, as if we're teens who promised to leave the house quietly and did everything short of setting it on fire as we went.

I walk up ahead with Storm and Cypher. That gives Dalton time to talk to Maryanne. Cypher regales me with tales of life in the wilderness. He goes overboard being entertaining, as if that's an apology for earlier.

Usually Jen's insults slide past, but sometimes they cut a little too close to truth. I'm not trying to get rid of Abby, but I'm susceptible to the charge because I want to believe Jen's right—that the proper and humane thing to do is keep Abby here and give her the kind of life every child deserves.

But isn't that what Gene Dalton thought when he saw Eric? *That child deserves better . . . and I can provide it.* Classic white-savior syndrome. I see this child who comes from a place I deem less "civilized," and I will save her, and the world will throw laurels around my neck for my selflessness.

Pimping your child goes way beyond "less civilized." Few people would say, in that situation, that I should mind my own business. But if I don't confirm the situation, how different am I from Gene Dalton? Yet if I do evaluate, where do I draw my line? That I will return her if her mother agrees to come to Rockton? That I will return her if they promise—cross their fingers, hope to die—never to prostitute her?

It's not as if I haven't considered this. The problem is that I can't stop considering it. My brain is a gerbil in a wheel, squeaking endlessly and getting nowhere. Having Jen act as if I'm blithely going to hand Abby off is like slamming a sliver deeper into a festering infection.

As we walk, I watch Storm explore and let Cypher's tall tales clear my mind. Then we near Brent's . . . and my mood stumbles as I realize I'm going to a place where I lost a dear friend, where I held his hand as he died.

Dalton catches up then. He gives Maryanne's supply pack to Cypher with, "You can carry it uphill." He leans in to whisper to Cypher. "Maryanne's getting tired. She won't say it, so tell her you need a rest. Casey and I will go in first."

Cypher heads back to Maryanne as Dalton and I carry on. After a few steps, I glance over my shoulder.

"Maryanne's fine," Dalton says. "I just figured we might want to go up alone."

I squeeze his hand. "Thank you."

His hand moves around my waist. "You doing okay?" He pauses. "That's a rhetorical question—I know you're not okay, and I know you'll tell me you are. Not sure why I bother asking."

I lean my head against his shoulder. "I'll be fine. It's tough coming up here, but it's amazing that we have this place for Maryanne. I like knowing Brent's cave and his things will help someone."

"Yeah, I was thinking that, too. I also meant, though, that this morning's bullshit is bugging you. But I get the feeling you don't want to hash that through with me."

"I didn't mean—"

He bumps my shoulder. "It's fine. I get it. We're stuck in a loop we can't escape until we have additional information, which we'll get soon, I hope."

"Yes." I move behind him as we start the ascent. "Also, about earlier, when you walked in on me with Jen and Cypher."

He chokes on a laugh.

I slug him in the ass. "Not like . . . Damn it, don't put that in my head."

"I didn't say a word."

I grumble under my breath. "You knew what I meant. But what you heard me say, that I'd take Abby myself, I wasn't making a statement. I wouldn't do that without talking to you."

"I know. You were just telling Jen that she's full of shit. Which, personally, I think we should tattoo on her forehead."

"True. But I know it sounded bad, when that isn't something we've discussed."

He shrugs. "It is, though. I said the baby ball is in your court."

"I'd rather it wasn't. If it comes to that, I'd like us to discuss it. I honestly don't know what I want. I'm not considering the options because I don't want that to influence my decision about giving her back."

"We need more information."

"We do. So let's get Maryanne settled, and then we'll go get it."

# TWENTY-FIVE

Maryanne is thrilled with her new lodgings. It's a cave. Literally a cave, and not the kind we see in depictions of Neolithic humans, some massive cavern that opens on ground level. This is up a mountainside, where we need to crawl through an opening that Storm no longer fits. From there, we climb down into a cavern the size of a small room. There's an even smaller one for sleeping. The main room has a natural chimney, which is what made Brent choose the spot.

It's the sort of place I'd consider a wonderful weekend adventure. A truly unique experience. But, well, it's a cave. There's a limit to how comfortable and well-appointed it can be. For Maryanne, though, it's ten times better than where she's lived for the past decade. So we settle her in and leave her happy.

We put on our snowshoes after that. Cypher wore his own homemade ones on the way to Rockton, so all three of us are outfitted. He's as proficient as Dalton and finds much amusement in me toddling after them like a two-year-old.

Cypher knows where the trading family winter camps. When the weather turns bad, they switch from traveling salespeople to pop-up store.

It is not an easy walk. I've always kept myself in good shape—it helps combat the muscle aches of my old injuries. I have never, though, been as physically fit as I've become up here. Amazing what an outdoorsman lover, an energetic dog, and a lack of couch-suitable entertainment will do for your fitness level. Yet despite all that, by the time we near the spot, I'm ready to collapse. Fortunately for my ego, Cypher is the first to say, "Now *this* is a workout," as he starts lagging behind with me, huffing and peeling off his parka.

Storm feels it, too, giving me her are-we-there-yet look. I don't suggest a rest. We'll barely make it by midday, and we already got a brief rest at Brent's. We stop to give Storm water breaks—and take long pulls at our own canteens—but nothing more.

"You don't feel this at all, do you?" I say as I move up beside Dalton.

"Feel what?" he says.

At my scowl, he grins and says, "Nah, I feel it, and I'll feel it a helluva lot more tomorrow."

"You'll be wishing you installed that hot tub," I say.

He laughs. "Fuck, yeah."

Last year, a group of residents had written a request for a hot tub. It had been posted, along with Dalton's creatively profane response. Then, a couple of months ago, we went to the hot springs outside Whitehorse, and Dalton discovered the appeal, particularly after a long day of winter work. Curious, I'd gone online and found a radio clip about a guy with a hot tub who lived off-the-grid in the Yukon wilderness. His was modeled after a hot spring—a big barrel of hot water, rather than the modern Jacuzzi-style tub with jets. So, while I may have said earlier that I wanted gift ideas from Dalton, I was totally lying. Kenny's working on a hot tub for our backyard. If other residents want one, they can commission their own. This one's ours.

Cypher tramps up to tell us we're getting close. We'd guessed that from the faint smell of smoke. When I crane my neck, I see it spiraling up a few hundred feet away.

"You'll stay back here with your pup, kitten," Cypher says.

My back must rise at that, because he lifts a hand. "Let me and Eric make the approach. Eric can put his scarf on and pull up his hood, and we'll let them think it's Jakey. They don't have much trade with him. Bad blood."

I arch my brows. "You're going to let them think Eric is the guy they don't like?"

"The bad blood is on Jacob's side. They thought he'd make a fine son-in-law, so they kept bugging him to take a free-bie, and when he didn't, they sent one of the girls to follow him and climb into his sleeping blankets. From what I hear, he didn't just refuse nicely. Got himself into a right temper over it, which isn't like our Jakey at all."

True—Dalton is the brother with the temper—but I can imagine how that would have set Jacob off. After their parents died, Jacob had been on his own. As a teenager, he'd had an encounter where he'd been taken captive and sexually assaulted. Dalton doesn't know that. I'm not sure anyone does besides myself and maybe Nicole. If someone crawled into Jacob's bed after he'd made his refusal clear, he would not respond with a gentle rejection. I don't blame him.

Cypher continues. "Jacob stays away as much as he can. I haven't seen them myself much since I've opened trade with Rockton. They're a nasty bunch. Not fit to raise dogs much less . . ." He trails off and shoots me a sheepish look. "Sorry."

"I've gotten the message loud and clear," I say.

"And she doesn't need it on constant repeat," Dalton adds. "Casey's going to need to talk to these people herself. We both want to evaluate the situation."

"I understand that," Cypher says. "But if all three of us tramp in there, we'll put them on the defensive. Especially once they realize you two are from Rockton. I can pull a little sleight of hand with you, Eric. When they find out you aren't Jakey, they'll be pissy, but I am not responsible for a misunderstanding. With Casey, though, you could only pretend she's Edwin's granddaughter, and believe me, that'd be worse."

The plan seems overly complicated and makes me wonder exactly what we're dealing with here. But if it is a delicate situation, Cypher is right that all three of us shouldn't go marching in. There's also an advantage to having me and Storm hang back where we can come to their aid in case of trouble.

They continue on, and I take Storm off the path. I know not to wander far, but that rising smoke is an easy landmark. In a small clearing that's been intentionally clear-cut, I take off my snowshoes and perch on a tree trunk. I expect Storm to drop at my feet in exhaustion, but she sits, looking up at me. Looking up . . . looking down . . . looking up.

"Fine," I say with a sigh, toss my pack down and then drop onto the ground.

Storm grunts in satisfaction and curls up with me. From puppyhood, we taught her that she can't sit on laps and sofas and beds, and we'd congratulated ourselves on our forethought. While it was difficult to keep her on the floor when she was a tiny bundle of fur who only wanted to cuddle, we knew that one day she'd take up the entire sofa. The problem is that, to indulge her need for puppy cuddles, we'd get down on the ground with her. Perfectly reasonable . . . except that she came to expect that, and while she'll curl up at our feet, if she's tired and cold, she wants us to cuddle with her . . . on the snow-covered ground.

We curl up together, resting and snacking on venison jerky. I listen for trouble from the direction of the camp, but the murmured voices stay low and calm.

Once Storm has had her cuddles and her food and water, she's ready to play. I pick up a stick and say, "I am not chasing this. Just so you know."

She dances in place. I throw it. She hesitates, looking my way, then chuffs a look of disappointment at my old-lady frailties before taking off after the stick. We do that a couple of times, but it's clear I'm being judged, so I switch to hide-and-seek. This is one of her favorite games. She sits, looking the other way, while I run a twisting trail before hiding downwind.

I make this one as tricky as I can. I hop on a couple of stumps and leap off them to interrupt the trail. I even climb a tree and slip into the branches of another. When I finally hide, I pick a spot behind a bush where some small beast has crawled under and died, masking my scent. I crouch behind it, mitts over my nose, hoping Storm appreciates this.

Peering through the bush, I watch her untangle my trail. My stump jump doesn't stump *her* at all. The tree leap does, but only for a moment before she's tearing through the snow following my trail and—

Metal glints in the midday sun. I'm not even sure what I see—some instinct processes the sight before my brain fully comprehends, and I charge from my hiding spot with a "No!" as I race toward Storm. As I do, I see the long barrel of a rifle pointing through the trees. Pointing at my dog.

I slam into Storm's side, and we skid across the snow, me sprawled over her. There is no shot. Just a grunt of surprise, and then footsteps approaching and a man's voice saying, "What the hell is that?"

I lift my head. As I do, I see his face and . . . There is still a gut instinct women have, an inner alert system that says, "Do not go home with this charming guy you met in a bar." One glance at the man with the gun makes me decide I will not tell him who I am. Maybe it's the set of his thin lips. Maybe it's a glitter in his dark eyes. Maybe it's merely a sixth sense that says beware.

"It's . . . it's a dog," I stammer, pitching my voice low. "My dog."

I stay on the ground, over Storm, my face turned down just enough to let my hood shadow my face.

The man tilts his head. "Where'd you come from, boy?"

I mentally nod in satisfaction as he makes the mistake I hoped he would when I changed my voice. I remembered the first time I met Cypher, when he mistook me for a boy. It's easy to do, with my size and build, especially if I'm wrapped in my winter wear.

Cypher also mistook me for Indigenous. I could roll my eyes at that, but it happened even down south. I am a racial puzzle that strangers want to solve, even when I'd rather they looked at me and only saw a person.

"I'm with my dad, trapping." I lift my chin a little. "I have a right to be here. My mother's family is Tr'ondëk Hwëch'in."

His snort suggests he isn't the type to respect territorial rights.

"Get up, boy."

When I hesitate, he points the gun and growls, "I said get up. This ain't your land. Hasn't been in five hundred years, so don't pull that shit on me. You know who this land belongs to? Whoever has these." He taps his gun. "So get on up and let me see that so-called dog of yours."

I rise slowly, my hand on Storm's collar. I pat her head and murmur words of reassurance.

"That's a dog, huh?" he says, eyeing Storm.

"Yes, sir."

"Never seen one like that."

I shrug. "Dad got her for me in Dawson. He didn't know how big she'd get."

He eyes Storm. "Good for pulling sleds, I bet."

I laugh softly. "No, sir, she's no sled dog. No hunter either. Dad calls her a waste of good food, especially in the winter, but I hunt for her, so he lets me keep her."

His hand snatches my jaw. I don't see it coming until his icy fingers clamp on my chin. Storm growls, but I twist her collar, a warning for silence.

"I need to get back to my dad, sir," I say, as calmly as I can.

"Do you?" He turns my face. "You're a pretty boy, aren't you? Pretty little half-breed."

My eyes narrow at the slur, and he laughs. "Got some fire, huh?" He strokes my cheek with his callused thumb. "Such soft skin. Makes me wonder . . ."

He yanks down my hood. My hand flies up to stop him, but again he moves too fast. Then he grins, and there is no humor in that grin, no lasciviousness either. There's something deeper, hungrier, uglier. His hand vise-grips my chin, fingers digging in.

"Look at this," he says with a low whistle. His other hand rakes through my ponytail hard enough to pull out hair along with my elastic. I still don't fight. I just breathe through my mouth, keeping my temper down so I don't alarm Storm.

"Not a boy after all," he says.

He reaches for my parka zipper. I beat him to it, yanking it down as I glower up.

"Sorry to disappoint," I say as his gaze moves to my breasts, nearly invisible under my double layers.

"Nothing wrong with that," he says. "You might not be a boy, but some men like to close their eyes and pretend." He winks. "Not my style, but I don't judge. And I can see the appeal of a woman who can pass for younger, if you know what I mean."

My stomach churns at that. I've only unzipped my parka to

my waist, so he can't see my shoulder holster, but the weight of the gun reassures me.

"I'm going to take my dog and go now," I say.

He throws back his head and laughs. "You really do have some spark. What part of this conversation made you think leaving was an option?"

"I would suggest you might want it to be," I say.

He reaches for me. I see that one coming, but it's too dangerous to fight. He grabs my hair. His fist wraps in it, and he throws me to the ground.

Storm lunges. I'm still gripping her collar, and she yanks me up as she lunges for the man, snarling. He raises his rifle.

"Get your dog under control, girl," he says.

I pull her to me and stay down, sitting on the ground. Storm positions herself over me.

"I said get your damned dog under—"

"What you have got there, Owen?" a woman's voice says.

# TWENTY-SIX

I twist as a figure emerges from the trees. She's wrapped tight in a parka, hood pulled up, bulky boots on her feet. In her hands, she holds another rifle. When she turns to me, I see a face even harder than the man's.

She pulls down her hood to get a better look at me. She's younger than me, maybe mid-twenties. Blond hair. Wide-set blue eyes. High cheekbones. A mouth that looks like it should be pouting in some sultry ad for fifty-dollar lipstick. Pretty, in a chilly Nordic way.

I glance at the man, having not paid close attention to what he looks like until now. He's closer to my age, dark-haired, sporting a solid build with a scar cutting across his nose.

As she approaches, he gestures at me, grinning like a child showing off newfound treasure.

"Huh," the woman says. Her gaze is as coldly assessing as his. "Where'd she come from?"

"She says she's with trappers, but I ain't seen no trappers. I think she's all by her lonesome. Just her and that thing." He motions to Storm. "She claims it's a dog."

"Huh," the woman says again. She turns that assessing look on Storm and then back to me.

"You think she'll fetch much?" the man says.

I shrug. "Not really. She expects *you* to fetch *with* her."

The man snorts a laugh.

"I don't get it," the woman says, in a low tone that warns me she doesn't appreciate being excluded. She doesn't know what playing fetch is, meaning she's from these woods, like Dalton. The man is not.

"You're asking how much you can get for me," I say. "Thank you for your interest, but I'm not for sale. Now, I'm going to take my dog—"

The woman swings behind me, lightning fast. My hand clenches, itching to feel the gun in my hand, but I've missed my chance to do that easily. As my heart picks up speed, Storm growls. I pet her and murmur that it's all right, even if I'm no longer sure it is.

"How do you feel about getting yourself a husband, girl?" the man says.

"I've got one. Also, I'm not a girl. I'm older than either of you."

"She's got a smart mouth, doesn't she?" the man says. "That'll bring the value down."

The woman snorts. "Did it bring *my* value down, Owen?"

He grins at her. "That's a different story."

"It's just a matter of finding the right buyer. Like with any goods, you turn the flaws into assets. You're not going to sell that mound of fur to someone who wants a hunting dog. And you're not going to sell this girl to a man who wants a quiet little mouse. Well, unless you cut out her tongue. Which is always an option."

I want to say they're trying to spook me. That's what Dalton and I would do, the sort of repartee that, afterward, we'd laugh about and say "Can you believe they actually took us seriously?" That could be what's happening here. They'll talk about selling me like a side of venison, and then, when they demand my coat and my snowshoes and whatever else I have of value, I'll gladly hand them over, scamper off into the woods, and consider myself lucky.

And yet . . .

Those words aren't directed at me. They pass right over my head to her partner, said in the same way she might suggest cutting my hair.

Cold nestles in my gut. I knew the man was trouble. Manageable trouble, though, like an asshole who might hassle me in the city. The woman is the bigger threat, and I realize I should have pulled my gun earlier.

Pull my gun when she was nearby? When she was close enough to run in and shoot me?

No, trying to end it sooner might very well have made it worse.

Storm keeps growling. The woman says to her partner, "Take the dog."

"And shoot it?" he says.

"If you need to," she says. "Otherwise, someone will want it, if only as dinner."

My hands wrap tight in Storm's fur. "She's fine. I can control her."

"You keep thinking you've got options here," the man says. "Like this is a business negotiation. Now hand over that dog—"

"Why not make it a business transaction?" I say. "Wouldn't that be easier? Yes, you have me dead to rights, but I'm going to be trouble. You see that already. So let's negotiate. I accept my capture. You find a . . ."

I'm struggling to say "buyer," but my lips won't form the

word. "A man who wants me. I play the scared mouse, and you get your money, and then . . . Well, then it's up to me. If he relaxes his guard, I can escape, and you've still made your money. You didn't sell false goods. He just failed to protect his purchase. You keep the money. I get the chance to escape. I'm willing to take that risk, if we can do this in a civil manner."

Owen's lips curve in a slow smile, his eyes glinting in a way that is no longer mercenary interest. "Clever girl. What do you think, Cherise?" He must be addressing his partner, but his gaze never rises from me. "I do believe we have some room to negotiate."

Storm wrenches from my hand. I'd loosened my grip, relaxing as I talked, and now she rips free and I spin, to stop her from going after Owen. But it isn't Owen she's leaping at. Cherise is raising her rifle . . . straight at me.

Storm slams into Cherise just as I hit the ground. I roll up and grab the barrel. As I do, the gun fires and I glance over at Owen because I do not forget he's holding a gun of his own. But he has it lowered, and he's leaning back, watching with amusement.

Cherise struggles with Storm, who's snapping and snarling. Not biting, though. Never biting. The sheer weight of her is enough to put Cherise on the ground.

Cherise's hand drops to a pocket on her thigh. I grab her wrist, pin it, yank out the knife, and throw it as far as I can. Then my hand goes to Cherise's throat, as I take Storm's place.

I glance over at Owen. I'm awkwardly positioned, with him behind me. He could attack, and I'd never see it coming. Yet he's still leaning against a tree, not the least bit concerned that his partner is pinned. When he catches my eye, he winks and my stomach clenches.

I've made a mistake here. A very dangerous one. I *did* think I was being clever, offering a solution that would make them relax their guard so I could escape. But in doing so, I've sparked Owen's interest . . . and could have earned a bullet from Cherise.

I should feel shocked and sickened. Instead, rage washes over me. White-hot, all-consuming rage.

I slide the gun from under my jacket, keeping it close to my body so Owen won't see. When Cherise spots it, her eyes only narrow and meet mine in defiance.

I jam the barrel under her throat. "You didn't like my offer? Then say so. You don't need to be a bitch about it."

I'm speaking low, my words only for her, but Owen hears and his laugh rings out behind us.

"Cherise didn't like your offer because she's the clever one here," he says. "And no one takes that away from her."

"No," Cherise says, her teeth gritted. "I didn't like her offer because you were fool enough to consider it, Owen. A pretty girl shows a bit of spirit and intelligence, and you fall over yourself."

"So you were jealous? That's new. I like it."

"'Cause you're a fucking idiot. I don't give a shit if you want to screw her. I do give a shit if your dick stops your brain from working. She wasn't going to negotiate with us. She was just buying time and keeping you from hurting her damned dog. Now, since you haven't noticed, she's got a—"

My free hand chops down on her throat, cutting her off in a strangled gurgle. I wrap my hand tight around her throat and twist toward Owen, my gun swinging on him. His eyes widen. Then he laughs. Throws back his head and laughs.

"Gun on the ground!" a voice snarls as someone crashes through the forest. "Fucking gun on the fucking ground, now!"

I do not for one second think the newcomer is talking to me. I recognize the voice, the words, even the crashing of brush.

Storm lets out a bark and races to meet Dalton.

"Back to Casey," he says after a pat on the head, and she returns to me, tossing Cherise a growl for good measure.

"Jacob?" Cherise says, and it's clear from her voice that she's trying to come up with another explanation. This man might look like Jacob, but he certainly doesn't sound like him.

"Nah," Owen says. "This is his big bro. Hey, Eric, long time."

"Not long enough," Dalton mutters. "You remember the position, Owen? I put you in it often enough. I'm sure you must remember."

"Fuck you." Spots of color touch Owen's cheeks. "This isn't Rockton."

"Yeah, it's not. But I still have the gun, and you're still a fucking idiot."

Cherise lets out a cackling laugh at that, but Dalton ignores her, his attention on Owen.

"On your hands and feet," Dalton says. "Ass in the air. I know you remember it."

"Eric?" I murmur. His gaze shoots my way, and I subtly shake my head. I've already made an enemy here in Cherise, and I don't want to make the situation worse by humiliating Owen in front of her. Dalton's gaze goes from Owen to Cherise, and he grunts, and I know he understands.

"Just put the rifle on the ground," Dalton says.

Owen does. Dalton walks over and picks it up.

"Hers is over there," I say, gesturing. Dalton nods and collects it.

Then he looks at me. "You okay?"

I don't answer, but he must see something on my face and his goes rock hard.

"What happened?" he says.

"I was playing hide-and-seek with Storm," I say. "These two are the ones who found me."

"And . . ."

I shrug. "They said something about selling me as a wilderness wife, blah, blah, blah."

A laugh sounds. It's not Dalton, who—despite my light tone—looks ready to spit bullets. Cypher strolls from the forest.

"That's your own fault, kitten," he says. "You are such a sweet and docile little thing. Can't blame them for thinking you're in need of a big, strong husband. They were just taking care of you."

"Evidently," I say.

I rise off Cherise, keeping one eye on her in case she attacks. Dalton walks over and lowers his lips to my ear. "You okay?"

"I will be," I murmur as softly as I can. "But I'd like to ease out of this."

He nods. There's nothing to be gained by getting into a pissing match with these two.

Dalton kisses the top of my head and tugs my hood back up.

"Are you shitting me?" Owen says. "The cowboy? Really?" He shakes his head. "You can do so much better, girl."

"Girl?" Dalton's brows shoot up. "She's a woman, and her name is Casey."

Owen ignores him. "What the hell do you see in Deputy Dawg here?"

Now my brows are rising, as I say, "Deputy?"

"Owen left Rockton right before my father retired."

"Eric's the sheriff now," Cypher says. "Casey here is a homicide detective. Or is that homicidal detective?"

"Depends on the situation," I say, smiling my thanks at him for continuing to lighten the mood.

"You're . . . a detective?" Owen says. "Like, a cop detective?"

"That's usually what 'homicide detective' means," Cypher says. "You picked this boy for his looks, didn't you, Cherise?"

Cherise doesn't reply. She hasn't spoken, and in that silence, I feel her assessing, evaluating, and I suppress a shudder. A keen intelligence always catches my attention, but this isn't the kind that promises a challenging game of Scrabble. This promises a knife through your back when you least expect it.

Owen says, "I thought cops had laws about height and what-not. She's such a tiny thing."

"And yet she had you and Cherise at her mercy, both of you armed, too. Size isn't everything. I'm sure Cherise tells you that all the time."

Owen only throws off the insult with a laugh. He's *not* the bright one. Nor is he particularly dangerous, much slower to take offense than his partner. I don't want to be alone with Owen, but he isn't the type to pull a knife over what's obviously just ribbing between men.

Cypher continues, "If we're done chitchatting and waving guns and trying to sell human beings, I'd suggest we go back to camp. We were just chatting with your family, Cherise. I think you'll want to be part of the conversation."

Family?

Oh, shit.

This pair didn't just happen to stumble on me close to the traders' camp. If I hadn't jumped to that conclusion sooner, it's because when I thought of this family's poor daughters forced to prostitute themselves, I had *not* pictured the woman standing in front of me.

At first, I only deliver a mental kick in the ass for my pre-conceptions. Then it sinks in.

These two people—this *couple*—are part of the trading family we've come to see about Abby.

I look from Cherise to Owen, and my insides freeze.

No. Please, no.

The same thoughts connect in Dalton's mind. His eyes

widen, just a little. Then they harden to cold steel, and when he looks at me, his jaw is set so tight every muscle stands rigid.

I want to tell him we can stop here. Cypher's right. Jen's right, too, God help me. We need to retreat and forget this madness, and keep Abby, because if these two are her parents . . . ?

My breath comes fast and hard, and I swallow. Then I squeeze my eyes shut and push down the panic. Nothing will change if I stick around for a definitive answer. It'll just save me from second-guessing later.

Cherise and Owen never need to know we found a baby— possibly *their* baby. I don't care if that isn't my decision to make. I will make it.

As we head out, Dalton falls in beside me, leans to my ear, and says, "Yes," and my eyes mist. I squeeze his hand. "Thank you."

"No question," he murmurs. "No question at all."

# TWENTY-SEVEN

We enter the traders' camp. It's more of an encampment. I'm not sure if there's actually a difference between the terms, but to me, a camp is a small and temporary arrangement. An encampment is bigger and more permanent.

They have three tents plus two igloo-like snow structures. There are sled dogs, too, which confuses Storm, who's never seen so many canines in one place. She sticks close to us, like a child hiding behind her parents on the first day of kindergarten. I let her stay there. The dogs seem friendly enough, but unless we're told she can visit, it's unwise to presume. And we aren't told anything of the sort.

Near the fire sits two young women and a man in his fifties. I don't see the matriarch, and when I look around, Cypher says, "The girls lost their ma about six months ago. We were just talking about that when Eric heard the shot and took off like one."

"I'm sorry for your loss," I say to the man.

The patriarch—I haven't been given names—shrugs and says, "Cancer. It got bad, and she decided she was done."

I hope I don't blink at that. I can't tell if he's saying she committed suicide or they helped her. I've known people who died of cancer, and I cannot imagine what it'd be like out here, with no access to doctors or painkillers. What shocks me is the way he says it, so matter-of-fact. It's like saying one of the sled dogs had to be put down . . . and not even a favorite dog at that.

None of the three daughters give any other reaction. They just wait for us to get on with the conversation. Or so it seems until I notice the youngest daughter's eyes glistening. When Cherise shoots her a sneer, the girl blinks fast and straightens. They are very clearly sisters. All blond and pretty with a similar look—tall and thin and a little bit distant.

If I'd peg Cherise at mid-twenties, I'd put the middle sister a few years younger and the youngest at maybe nineteen. When the youngest glances Cypher's way, there's trepidation and anxiety in the look. I remember what he'd said about one of the girls asking him to take her. Those looks say she's worried that he might say something and get her in trouble.

As I'm thinking this, the middle girl says to Dalton, "I knew you weren't Jacob."

Dalton turns to her. "Never said I was."

"You're nothing like him," she says. "He's . . ." She wrinkles her nose. "Skittish. Weak. I don't know how he survives out here."

"I would suggest that you don't know my brother very well. And you don't know *me* at all."

She smiles. "We could fix that."

"I'm married," he says.

She shrugs. "I don't care."

"His wife might," Cypher says. "You can ask her. She's sitting right there."

The middle sister's gaze trips over me, and she shrugs again. Then she turns to Dalton. "Offer stands." She smiles at me. "Unless you have a problem with that."

"Don't worry, Leila," Cherise purrs. "His wife is just as helpless as she seems. She'll be fine with it."

Leila's brow furrows as Owen laughs, and she scowls at him. "What's so funny?"

"Not a damn thing." He waves at Dalton. "Go for it. Please."

"It's not Casey you need to worry about," Dalton drawls. "If I'm stupid enough to fuck up what I have with her, that's my problem. And I'm neither stupid nor remotely interested."

"So you say, in front of her."

"I'll say it behind her back, too. You come sneaking into *my* bed, and you'll find my brother really *is* the nice one."

Cherise and Owen laugh and the girls' father joins in. Even the youngest smiles, though she tries to hide it.

Family? Hell, no. This is a pit of vipers.

"Are we done with this bullshit?" Cypher says. "These two need to get back to Rockton, and we have trading to do. First, though, I think Casey was hoping to see the baby."

My gaze shoots to him. He pretends not to notice.

"Baby?" Cherise says.

"The new family addition. I heard one of you girls is a momma, and Casey was hoping for the chance to bounce a baby on her knee." He looks around. "You hiding the little tyke?"

The family's expressions . . . I hesitate, worried that I'm seeing what I want to see. But there isn't a single look of comprehension among them. The youngest sister frowns, as if she's misheard. The father scowls, as if Cypher is making some kind of joke. Cherise peers at Cypher, as if there's some hidden meaning to his words. Owen and Leila just look confused.

"Baby . . ." Cherise says carefully.

"Right. You know, miniature human. Demanding little critters that expect everyone to wait on them hand and foot. Are you the proud new momma?"

Cherise looks nothing short of horrified, and I restrain a shuddering sigh of relief.

"There's no baby here," the father snaps. "You think we're fool enough to have one in winter?"

"Or fool enough to have one at all," Leila says.

"I'd like a baby someday," the youngest says, her voice soft. "But not now."

I want to drop the matter here. See? There's been a terrible mistake, and these are not the parents. Yet I hear the father's words and wonder what would happen if one of the girls did give birth in winter. Edwin mentioned abandonment. That's what people used to do, whether it was a baby or an infirm relative, when winter came with no extra rations to sustain the weak.

If that is the case, then I need to know that I can stop searching. *Fine, you abandoned your baby, and now we have it and may proceed with whatever option we choose.* However, if Abby's mother is still out there, I need to keep looking.

I'm struggling for a way to get a definitive answer when Cypher says, "See, that's what I was wondering. I told Casey and Eric that if you folks did have a winter baby, you might be willing to part with it. But since you don't . . ."

When I realize what he's saying, I flinch. The words have barely left his mouth before Cherise pounces.

"You want a baby?" she says to me.

"We're not—" I begin.

"If you had one, she might be willing to pay," Cypher says. "But since you don't—"

"We can fix that," she says. "Make us an offer, and me and Owen will consider giving you a baby."

"Unless the problem is the cowboy," Owen says. "Which I'm sure it is. In that case, I can fix it for you." He winks at me, and I tense, my gaze shooting to Cherise. But she only says, "For a *price* he will. I'm not giving you free access to my man."

"Unless the problem's yours," Leila says, "in which case, I'll help. For the right price, of course."

"Jesus," Cypher mutters. "You want to get in here, Missy? Offer to rent out your baby-making body parts, too?"

The youngest shakes her head, her gaze lowered, and I shoot Cypher a look to back off her. He frowns, as if genuinely baffled.

"We aren't in the market for a baby," I say. "Ty's beating around the bush here, and I appreciate his discretion, but it's leading to a serious misunderstanding. We found a baby. A little boy, left in the woods. He seems to have been abandoned, but we want to be absolutely certain there isn't a family frantically looking for him before we send him down south for adoption."

Leila's mouth opens, and I know she's about to claim that, whoops, yes, she totally forgot about that baby she left in the forest. Cherise beats her to it with a more measured, "All right. It is . . . possible that we had a winter-born child. If we didn't say so, it's because we don't need your judgment. You have no concept of a life where horrible choices must be made."

"Like leaving a baby to die of cold?" Dalton says. "Or be ripped apart by predators? Instead of just suffocating him mercifully? Also . . ." A pointed glance around their well-stocked camp, complete with storage facilities. "I can tell you folks are hard up for supplies. I have no idea how you'll get through the winter."

Cherise glares at him. "Don't presume to understand our choices. I thought I had suffocated the child, but clearly, I was too distraught to do it properly."

Dalton's mouth opens, and I know he's going to tell her to cut the crap, but a look from me stops him. I must admit, I'm impressed by Cherise's performance. But dragging this out isn't going to help anyone.

"So you bore a son?" I say.

I'm sure I say it with complete calm, and certainly the others don't react. But by now, I've realized their father is patriarch in name only. I sense that the real power lies in a nearby grave, her position taken over by Cherise, who sees the trap in my words.

"Did you say son?" she says carefully. "A boy?"

She's gauging my reaction as carefully as I'm gauging hers, like prizefighters in the ring trying to anticipate the next blow and react accordingly.

I could gamble here. I don't need to, though. I shrug and say, "Okay, you got me. It's a girl."

She leans back. "Of course it is. I know my own child."

I take my backpack, dump the water from my canteen and hold it out. "I'll need proof."

Her face screws up.

"Proof that she's yours," I say. "Proof that you're a nursing mother."

Leila bursts out laughing. Cherise swings on her so fast, the next thing I see is blood in the snow and then Leila cupping her nose. She didn't make a sound, only glares at Cherise before dropping her eyes in submission. Cherise's gaze turns on Missy. I expect the youngest to look away fast, but she holds her sister's gaze with a level, open stare. Not challenging her, but not backing down either. Cherise snorts, and it's an animal sound, the alpha accepting that no threat is forthcoming and leaving the younger one be.

"That's enough, girls," their father says, and it is the voice of every parent who doesn't want to seem as if he's lost control of his children. The girls ignore him—they're already settling in after their scuffle.

"So the baby isn't from here," I say. "That's all I wanted to know. However, if you have any idea who she does belong to, and you're correct, we'll pay for that information."

"Two hundred dollars' worth of goods," Dalton says. "Tell us what you want, and I'll get it in Dawson or Whitehorse."

The patriarch's eyes glitter. "Alcohol. That's liquid gold out here, especially this time of year."

"We'll take *some* alcohol," Cherise says. "Among other things. And we want a thousand dollars' worth."

"First you need to get us the information," Dalton says. "Then we need to confirm it. Then you can choose between two hundred dollars from your shopping list or four hundred from ours."

"Five hundred."

Dalton looks at me. He's not verifying the amount. With my bank account, that's pocket change. He's seeing if I have any restrictions or limitations to add.

I pet Storm and casually say, "We have a doctor in town who will examine the mother, to be sure she gave birth at the time the baby was born." Of course, there's no way to be quite that specific, but these aren't medical professionals.

I continue. "So if someone claims to be the mother in hopes of getting a reward, it'll be a waste of everyone's time. The mother must come to Rockton for the child."

In other words, I don't want this family taking the mother captive and then calling us to deliver the cash.

I add, "And if the child was abandoned, we're fine with that. We won't judge the mother's choice, and we will make sure the baby goes to a good home."

"How much will you get for that?" Cherise says.

"Paid adoptions are illegal in Canada."

She snorts. "Their laws are not our laws. If you sell the baby—"

"We won't," Dalton says. "We may keep it or we may find a suitable home, but no cash will exchange hands. People aren't trade goods."

She rolls her eyes at our ridiculous scruples. This is a woman who was sold herself, from a very young age, probably—as I realize now—by her own mother. That practice hasn't stopped since their mother died. Cherise certainly was ready to see what she could get for me. I would like to say I can't wrap my head around that—how could you be sold yourself and then do the same to others? The truth is much more complex. Just ask anyone who was abused as a child and does the same to their own offspring.

As we finish the negotiations—which is mostly closing any loopholes for Cherise to exploit—we're preparing to leave when the father says, "I'm glad we reached an agreement here. I've always said that trade relations are important."

Dalton slowly turns but says nothing, waiting for what we both know is coming.

"We'd be a valuable trade partner for Rockton," the man says.

He means that we'd be valuable to them. I see Dalton getting ready to make some sarcastic comment, but then he tightens his jaw and slides a look my way, tossing this grenade to me.

"That's an interesting proposition," I say. "If this goes well, we could discuss it." I take off my pack and open it. "We don't have a lot of need for trade supplies in Rockton, but there's always an interest in craftsmanship. We'd love work like this."

I pull out the piece I'd cut from the dead woman's jacket. I'm not eager to open trade with this family, but if I were to hazard a guess on the artisan, I'd point at Missy. If she can create items that Rockton considers valuable, it might help her position here.

But when I show the piece, I get only blank expressions.

Then Cherise says, "I don't have time for pretty sewing, but Missy might be able to do something like that."

Missy nods. "They say I do fine work, with my tanning and my crafting." She takes off her coat and passes it to me. It is indeed excellent, and I say so, but when I ask if she does anything decorative, she considers and then says, "Those we trade with are looking for practical pieces. Long lasting and warm and pleasant to wear—soft furs and smooth leathers. They aren't interested in work such as that, so I haven't tried it, but I could, if you left that with me."

I say I will, though I assure her that Rockton is interested in general craftsmanship, too, and while a little decoration would be appreciated, what she's already doing would also be valuable. Far more so than the meat or hides her family would otherwise provide.

"As for this work . . ." I lift the piece, and I'm ready to ask if they recognize the workmanship, but Cypher catches my eye and I stop before linking it to the baby. We'll deal with this family if that's our only way of finding Abby's mother, but I shouldn't provide clues to set them on her trail.

I cut the piece in two and leave half with Missy, and we say our goodbyes. Storm and I walk in front, the guys behind, all of us quiet. Once we're far enough from the encampment, Cypher says, "That piece you were showing. You didn't just happen to be carrying that in your pack, did you?"

"It's from the dead woman. Edwin identified it as that family's work, and he said one of the girls was pregnant, so it all lined up."

"He lied," Dalton mutters. "Lied and sent us on a wild-goose chase."

"I think he was hoping to send us into a dead end," I say. "Tell us what we needed to conclude it was the baby of a family who shouldn't be raising one. We'd decide to keep

Abby. Everyone's happy. Well, you know, except the actual *mother.*" I shake my head. "Sure, I get that he thinks we'd make good parents, but what about *her?*"

"He lied because he knows where that comes from," Cypher says. "And he doesn't want you and Eric going there." He glances at Dalton. "It's from the Second Settlement."

# TWENTY-EIGHT

There are two major settlements out here, both originating from Rockton. The first and, yes, the second. No reason to get fancy with names. The first is an actual settlement. It's been in the same place since Edwin led a group from Rockton. The second is more nomadic. They build semipermanent residences, which they abandon when the food supply shifts. They'll also move if they feel at all threatened by trappers, miners, settlers, or hostiles. The Second Settlement does minimal outside trading, and that's a two-way street of paranoia. They don't like mingling with others, and others don't like mingling with them. Secretive and eccentric. That's what I'd call them. As for Cypher's opinion:

"Batshit fucking crazy," he says as we walk. "You were telling me you think the hostiles are some kind of cult. If they are, they might have come from the Second Settlement, 'cause those fuckers *are* a cult. Except they aren't the kind that recruits in shopping malls. Their doors are closed."

"But you know them?" I say.

"Once upon a time, I was an exception to the rule. And the rule itself wasn't so much a rule as a general guideline. While they didn't throw open their doors to traders, they did business with a very select number of settlers. They picked me because I was sheriff when a group of them left Rockton. I let them go and sold the council a line of bullshit about how hard I looked for them. So, when I left Rockton, they invited me to trade. But then, about five years back, they had a change in leadership, and the doors swung shut."

"Why did Edwin lie?" I say. "If they don't trade, he can't be worried about us opening a line of exchange with them."

"You know Edwin," Cypher says. "He's a crafty old bastard. He's hedging his bets here, protecting what's his. The Second Settlement doesn't hold a grudge against Rockton. If you go sniffing around . . . ?"

He shrugs. "You and Eric make a good team. That's why Edwin's reopened that connection. He might talk shit about Eric, but he trusts him. Eric's a strong leader. Tough and fair. He can be a pain in the ass to deal with, but you're not. You're the diplomat. If Edwin's opened that door for you two, the Second Settlement might, too. Edwin doesn't want that. Also, the old man's got a nasty streak. Giving you their baby would warm the cockles of his heart all winter."

I'm not sure that last part's true. Edwin might really have presumed the winter-born baby had been abandoned. It's still a shitty thing to do.

"So where do we find them?" I ask.

Dalton jerks his chin east. "That way, almost a full day's walk. Yeah, I keep tabs on them. Never talked to them. I was raised not to. They made my birth parents nervous, so we steered clear. Gene Dalton wanted nothing to do with either settlement and advised me to do the same. But I always know where to find them. They've been over there for the last few years."

"So back to town for the snowmobiles?" I ask.

Dalton shakes his head. "There aren't any trails out there. We gotta walk. Which means going back to town and gearing up for a full-on camping trip."

"Why don't I head on back to Rockton and you kids overnight at my place," Cypher says. "It's a helluva lot closer than Rockton. If you strike out from there in the morning, you'll reach the Second Settlement by afternoon. You'll need to grab a tent to overnight on the way back, but I've got one and plenty of blankets. Take what you need from my supplies." He smiles. "That gives me permission to take what I need from yours."

Cypher leaves for Rockton, and by nightfall we're made it to his winter cabin. It used to be owned by a settler named Silas Cox. Come winter, Cypher would rent a sleeping bag in the corner. Then Cox fell victim to the local cougar, and Cypher took over the lease. When spring arrives, he'll be on the move, following game and trading, like Jacob. In winter, though, everyone wants a place to hunker down, and this is Cypher's.

Since taking possession, he's made repairs. Cox had been the kind of guy who builds a half-assed structure and stays until it rots. Cypher has filled cracks between the logs, fixed the roof, and added a sturdy food-storage compartment around back. When we get inside, we find as cozy a cabin as you could want. It's only about ten by fifteen feet, but out here, extra room means extra heating. The interior has a fireplace, an underfloor icebox, a low bed, and a table with one chair.

Before we split from Cypher, he'd asked us to check his snares. Trapping is his preferred hunting method—he doesn't use guns and has never mastered a bow. We leave Storm inside with some dried meat and head out in the dark, flashlights in hand. The snares haven't been checked in two days, and we find two snowshoe hares, a marten, and a mink. Dalton skins the marten and mink for Cypher. The meat is only eaten late in a cold, hard winter, and we presume Cypher won't want it, so we cook it up for Storm. What she doesn't eat, I'll dry in strips overnight in the fireplace and we'll take it with us for her.

I cook one of the hares for our dinner. We don't eat anything else with it. Cypher isn't a gardener, and 90 percent of his food stores are meat, so we won't raid his meager supply of dried greens, berries, nuts, and roots. We have a half dozen chocolate-peanut-butter protein bars in our packs and split one for dessert.

We're in bed by eight. That's what can happen when night falls by late afternoon, and you haven't slept more than a few hours in days. We don't sleep, though. No sex either. It's been a long and unsettling day, and even after we crawl into bed, we don't talk about it right away. We've let Storm stay in the cabin—there's plenty of room.

I curl up with Dalton, my cheek resting on his bare chest, listening to his slow breathing. Feeling the tension, too, strumming through him, and waiting for him to speak.

"What happened today . . ." he says finally. "With Owen and Cherise . . ."

"Trying to sell me?" I say, my voice light. He's on his back, and I roll on top of him, my arms crossed on his chest. "Owen came out first, and I had that situation under control, so I tried to defuse it rather than fight. I didn't expect Cherise."

I purse my lips. "Pretty sure no one expects Cherise. She is a piece of work. But I still wasn't in danger of being carted off like a side of venison. I was trying to keep things cool until . . ."

I remember, and I shiver. I don't mean to. I can't help it. Under me, Dalton goes rigid.

"What happened?" he says.

"Cherise happened," I say, again keeping my voice light. "I got a bit of a scare, but . . ."

I want to fluff it off. But after a moment, I say, "We'll need to keep an eye on her. She's smart as hell, and twice as vicious."

He nods. Says nothing, his nod tight as he holds in whatever he's thinking, whatever he wants to say.

"Eric?" I say.

"I'm concerned about Owen," he says. "That's not underestimating Cherise. She's a fucking cobra. She's smart, though, like you said, so I get the sense she can be managed. Very, very carefully managed. With any luck, she'll decide she doesn't want to lose Rockton as a prospective trade partner. But Owen . . ."

He exhales, breath hissing through his teeth. "The way he was looking at you . . ." Dalton makes a face. "I don't mean I'm jealous. None of that territorial bullshit. Men notice you. They pay attention. You don't pay attention back. If anyone tries anything, you take care of it—you don't need me to protect you. But Owen . . . Fuck."

"You know him."

"Yeah."

"What was he in Rockton for?"

Another exhale. "That's what I want to talk to you about. If I'm hesitating, it's just . . ." He waves his hands, gesturing, and I start to roll off, but he holds my hips. "It's the usual bullshit, this part of me that wants to smooth it over, pretend it's not that bad, so I don't scare you off. I wouldn't do that. You need to know. I just . . ."

Another helpless wave. "You were in the forest, playing with our dog, and a couple of psychos threatened to kidnap and *sell* you. That's fucking nuts, and it's just another day out here, and it shouldn't be. Biggest thing you should need to worry about is the wildlife. But no, it's the crazy people who want to kill you or, now apparently, sell you."

I laugh. I can't help it. It starts as a snicker, and then I'm sputtering, choking on laughter.

"It's not funny, Casey," he says.

"Oh, but it has to be, doesn't it? Otherwise, *we'll* become the crazy people." I settle in and look down at him. "We're in the Yukon wilderness. There are people here for this lifestyle, like you and me and most settlers. But there are also people with a certain level of eccentricity and, yes, crazy, who come here *because* of that. They're here to escape the norms and rules of life down south. That can be a positive thing—they want something less rigid and more natural. Or their disregard for the rules of law is the *reason* they're happier here, where they can do whatever they want. That's going to mean, overall, a high quotient of . . ."

"Batshit crazy, as Ty said?"

"In every possible way, the good and the bad. It's a world of extremes. It's like walking down a city street and winnowing out all the average people, the people who are happy enough going about their lives. The people who don't yearn for more, yearn for change, yearn for *different*. That's who we have here, long-term. The dissatisfied and the dreamers and the doers and, unfortunately, the dangerous—those who want to box up their superego and let their id run free. You get that down south, too. It's not as if people like Petra and Sebastian and Cherise and Mathias are some new species I never knew existed. I've met variations on all of them before. There's just a significantly higher concentration here."

"Yeah."

"As for Owen . . ." I prompt.

Dalton sighs and reaches for his canteen, taking a slug and then offering me some, which I accept.

"Owen came to Rockton five years ago. I was deputy, and it was a little more than a year before Gene retired. Owen and I are about the same age, and that caused problems. He saw me as competition."

Dalton rolls his eyes. "By that time, I'd had my bad experience with a woman, so he was welcome to them. It's not like he'd have had a problem anyway. When he showed up, they paid attention. He screwed around a bit, and then he set his sights on Isabel, which I couldn't figure out."

I sputter a laugh. "Don't let her hear you say that."

"Nah, she said it herself. I don't mean any insult. But she was fifteen years older, and he had his pick of women, and it wasn't as if he knew her well enough to fall for her. He acted like a new stallion in a herd of mares, making his way through them, and when he came to Isabel, he figured he'd have a go and then move on. I mean, *obviously* she'd be all over that, right?"

"She wasn't, was she?"

"Hell, no. Isabel might have an eye for younger men, but she's never been hard up for attention, and she's a helluva lot pickier than 'young and good-looking.' When Isabel rejected him, she figured he'd sweep up his wounded pride and stalk off. He didn't. The more she said no, the more he wanted her. Pretty soon, she complained to Gene."

"How'd that go?"

He shifts and makes a face. "I said this was shortly after my 'bad experience.'"

I know what he's talking about. When Dalton was young, he had plenty of women happy to introduce him to the joys of sex. He'd been in his late teens, and they'd been five to ten years older, so everyone knew it was just fun. Then he reached his early twenties and relationships became a possibility. He wasn't interested, and if the women were, he stepped away. Then he hit the one who didn't give up so easily.

"It wasn't even one of my usual casual-but-committed relationships," he continues. "We hooked up a couple of times, and she hinted at wanting more. Seeing the warning signs, I backed out, as gently as I could."

"She didn't take 'no' for an answer."

He nods. "At first, it was like she was just trying to change my mind. But then . . . I'd come home, and she'd be in my kitchen, making dinner in her underwear. I'd be sleeping, and she'd slip into my bed. Hell, she walked into my *shower* once. Fucking scared the life out of me. First time I ever locked my doors."

"Shit."

"Yeah. It was bad. If another woman even talked to me, she'd get in their face, and it wasn't like I was trying to pick anyone up. We're talking conversations with women. Normal conversations."

"What'd you do?"

"Tried to handle it myself. When I couldn't, I asked other guys for advice. They laughed. Told me I should take advantage. So I went to Gene. He didn't laugh, but he didn't see the problem either. Even my mother wasn't much better. She felt sorry for the woman, who'd obviously fallen hard for me, and said I should be more understanding. Maybe I should give her another chance. This woman is fucking up my life because she wants me back . . . so I should give in? Because, fuck yeah, that's the kind of woman I want." He shakes his head, and in his eyes, there's old hurt, old pain, old anger.

"That's bullshit," I say.

"Yep, but it happens to women all the time, doesn't it? That's what I realized. Gene was telling me that this woman wasn't a threat, wasn't actually *hurting* anyone—including me. She just liked me a lot, as if . . ." He waves his hands. "As if that's my fault, because I'm so irresistible."

I smile. "I think you are. But yes, it's bullshit, and yes,

women hear that all the time. *He just likes you. You should give him a chance.*"

"Exactly. I pulled my head out of my ass and realized that when women came to us with the same problem, we didn't do jack shit. If it wasn't assault, then it was just a guy trying to get sex."

"Boys will be boys."

"Right. And this is my very long way of explaining what happened with Owen and Isabel. Iz came to Gene with her complaint. Gene told her to be firmer with her refusals."

I snort a laugh.

"Yeah," Dalton says. "No one is firmer with her refusals than Isabel. So I tried to handle Owen and made an even bigger enemy in the process. I also realized this wasn't some guy being atypically aggressive with a woman. He had a past. He must. So I started digging. It was the first time I'd done that."

"And?"

"First, I checked his reason for being here. As deputy, I didn't have access to that, but I knew where to get it. I discovered that he'd come here after an attempt on his life. He'd had a fling with a married woman, and the husband went after Owen, who narrowly escaped. The man vowed to finish the job. So Owen came to Rockton."

"Uh-huh. Not exactly how it happened, is it?"

"No, and Gene should have looked at Isabel's complaint and at least wondered if there was more to Owen's story. He didn't. So I did some research when I went to Dawson. Turned out there was no fling, but not for lack of trying on Owen's part. He was stalking this woman, and her husband went after him because the police wouldn't. I also dug up his name as the defendant in a rape case. What they used to call date rape."

"He wanted sex, and the women didn't, so he took it."

"I'm not even sure if he asked. It was a college thing. A frat party. She said he put something in her drink. He denied it and said the sex was consensual. It never went to court. She dropped the case and dropped out of college, claiming harassment from Owen and his buddies."

"I wish I could say I've never heard that story before."

"Yeah, so the fact this asshole has turned his eye on you has me worried. Just because Cherise has the upper hand in the relationship doesn't mean Owen is harmless."

"Thank you for telling me."

"I'd never *not* tell you. As much as I hate making this place any scarier than it is."

I hug him, and he pulls me into his arms as we curl up for sleep.

# TWENTY-NINE

We're asleep, and I'm dreaming of Abby. Dreaming that she's lost in the woods, and I hear her crying, and I can't find her. I'm running through the forest, bottle in hand, thinking she's hungry and I need to feed her. I'm following her cries . . . and then she stops. Just stops.

I startle awake. Storm whines, and I realize she was already up. She's still lying on the floor beside me, but she has her head raised, and she's whining deep in her throat. She smells or hears something.

The cabin is silent and nearly dark, with just enough moonlight streaming in for me to see the outline of Storm's massive head. She glances my way, and I catch the gleam of her eyes. Another whine, sharper now. She rises with the huff of propelling her big body off the floor. Her nose nudges me, and I run my hand over her head as I listen for what woke her.

A whisper of movement. That's what I catch. The soft sound of a foot in snow. Then another. A noise follows. A grunt? I think of bears, but even if one woke from hibernation, the sounds are too soft for that. They're too *careful* for that. Something is outside, and it is staying as quiet as it can.

A bump startles me. It's a soft thud. Someone bracing against the wall? Trying to peer in a window?

I glance at Dalton, but he's sound asleep. If I rouse him, however gently, he'll startle awake with enough noise to scare off whoever is out there.

We're several hours' walk from Cherise's camp, and I can't imagine she'd have let Owen follow us. But they may have tracked us after sundown.

Another bump against the wall, and I peer at the window. Storm whines again. She's rigid, staring at that wall, her tail sweeping the floor. It's not a happy wag. It's cautious, uncertain.

I slide out of bed and keep bent over beneath window level. I tug on jeans, a sweatshirt that turns out to be Dalton's, and my parka. Then I retrieve my gun.

I glance at the bed again, in hopes my moving around has brought Dalton closer to waking, but he's still dead to the world.

I head for the door. Storm follows, nails clicking. I back up and tell her to stay, adding reassuring pats. She is not reassured. When I pull on my boots, her butt bobs off the floor.

I consider. When Owen and Cherise first caught me, I'd wished Storm hadn't been there. She was a weakness they could use against me. Yet she may have saved my life. It's like Dalton with me. He'd love to tuck me away in a safe spot when danger strikes, but he knows I belong at his side, where we can look after each other. I need to start thinking the same with Storm. We trained her for work, and I have to let her do it, not play overprotective mom and tuck her away.

I give the release sign, and when she comes over, I tell her to stay close and stay quiet. As I ease open the door, she's right beside me.

We slip outside, and I pull the door shut behind us. There's a flashlight in my pocket, but I keep it there for now. I have my gun in hand instead, as I look over the snow-covered field. It's a three-quarter moon on a cloudless night, and the light reflects off the snow, lifting the glade to soft daylight.

I adjust my gun and glance at Storm. Her nose works madly, but she's still processing the danger, not ready to commit to a decision.

We start along the wall, toward the spot where I'd heard the thumps. The squeak and crunch of snow announces our approach, and there's little I can do about that except keep my gun trained and my ears tuned for the sound of flight. Nothing comes.

I reach the corner and duck before peering around with my face at a height any intruder won't expect. There's no one in sight.

I ease around the side and check the back, in case the person ducked there. Nothing.

Backing up, I look at the snow. It's trampled in a path from Cypher walking to his storage shed. I don't see any other trail.

I bend to examine the prints. They all look to be from the same set of boots, which suggests they're Cypher's, but even as a prank he'd never sneak around a cabin with two armed cops sleeping inside. I'm still bent when I see smaller prints leading from the forest and back again, and I'm leaning in for a closer look when Storm growls. I turn to find myself looking at a pale figure poised at the forest's edge.

I'm on eye level with it, and our gazes lock. I tighten my grip on the gun and rise as slowly as I can, while giving Storm the signal to stay where she is. She does, but she's growling, her hackles raised. The intruder isn't watching me now. He's looking straight at her. He takes a step our way. Then another.

Storm feints, obeying the order to stay while surging forward in warning. He stops, tilts his head, considers, and then cannot resist another careful step.

It's the lone wolf from the other day.

He's paying me no attention. I'm not the one he's here for, not the one he's curious about. He takes another step as he watches Storm. She makes a noise that starts as a growl, then switches to a whine before ending with a growl. She is curious, too, as she was with the sled dogs. Curious yet wary. She is no longer the pup who tore after a young cougar. She bears the scar from that encounter, and it has carved a path in her neural network, straight to her memories, as my scars do to mine.

I lower my hand to pet her head as I murmur reassurances. The wolf is as tall as Storm, but she's significantly heavier, all thick muscle to his wiry frame. Between her size and my gun, she is safe. If she becomes distressed, we'll withdraw into the cabin. But it is safe to satisfy her curiosity.

When I pet her, she is indeed reassured, and she relaxes. Both the whines and the growls subside, and she eyes the wolf, taking his measure. Then she puffs up in a way that makes me smile. She pulls herself straight and tall, displaying her full size. Her tail stays high, indicating welcome but not submission. Her head lifts, and her ears relax. If she is nervous, she doesn't show it. She has assessed the wolf, declared him to be a lesser beast, and stands before him as a haughty queen, giving him permission to approach.

With Raoul, Storm is the "alpha." She's bigger and older, and so she is in charge. This wolf looks like a larger version of her pack mate, and so she will not bow to him.

The wolf continues his slow approach. When he's within a couple of feet, he stops and the silence is broken by two canines sniffing the air madly. Then he stretches his muzzle, and their noses touch. As adorable as it is, I'm tensed for trouble, the mom assessing another child, still not convinced he doesn't pose a danger to her baby.

While I have my gun, I'm also ready with my foot. I do not

want to shoot a wolf for a show of dominance. I've dealt with enough stray dogs to know that a well-placed kick will allow us to retreat into the cabin.

The wolf circles Storm, sniffing her. I instruct her to stay standing. Her head turns, though, following his progress. When he reaches her rear, he sticks his nose under her tail, and she jumps. He backs up only a second before returning, determinedly sniffing her there as he begins to whine and quake with obvious excitement. That's when I realize why this wolf has conquered his fear of humans to make his way here.

"Oh," I say, the word coming on a laugh.

They both startle.

"Sorry," I murmur.

The wolf tries sniffing under Storm's tail again, but she keeps it firmly down, and I have to chuckle at that. I also give her the release word. I'm not going to make her stand there, suffering the unwanted interest of this wolf.

She turns to sniff him. He keeps trying for her tail, but she shoulders him aside and huffs. I tense. He accepts her annoyance, though, and lets her sniff him. Greetings over, she hunkers down, an invitation to play. He races around her, and she spins, ready to give chase, but he's only trying to get behind her again.

Storm snaps and growls, and she issues the play invitation again. He seems to accept . . . and then swings behind and tries to mount her. I don't need to intercede. Storm yanks away, grabs him by the foreleg and throws him down with a growl that very clearly says there will be none of that.

Two more invitations to play only result in two more aborted mountings. Finally she huffs her disgust at me, and I have to laugh.

"I know," I say. "You want to be friends, and he's just looking to get laid. Some guys, huh?"

It's clear that the wolf really is only interested in one thing, and he's not getting it—Storm won't let him, and I wouldn't either. She retreats behind me, and I shoo him off with a "Hie! Hie!" as I lunge in his direction.

As the wolf flees into the night, the cabin door bangs open and I hear, "Shit! Casey!"

I look around the corner to see Dalton, staring at the retreating wolf.

"Uh . . ." I say. "Did you forget something?"

He looks down.

"Yep, clothing for one thing. Please get back inside before you lose any body parts I'd really rather you kept. I was, however, referring to . . ."

I lift my gun. "What were you going to do? Punch the wolf in the nose?"

He blinks, obviously still waking up. Then he says, "Wouldn't be the first time. The last one was a feral dog, though."

"Back inside," I say.

Storm and I follow Dalton. He's shivering, not surprisingly.

"Was that the same wolf?" he says.

"Yep, remember how we were talking earlier about unwanted advances and guys who don't take no for an answer? It seems Storm has a suitor."

He blinks, still bleary-eyed. "What?"

"She must be coming into estrus," I say. "I haven't seen signs, but she's old enough, and that wolf picked up a scent that said, if his advances weren't accepted right now, they might be soon."

"Shit."

"Yep. I know when we took her for her annual shots, the vet mentioned spaying, and we hadn't made a decision on that. We're going to need to."

I crouch and hug Storm, running my hands over her as she trembles in lingering excitement from the encounter.

As I pet her, I say, "Down south, spaying would be a no-brainer. No one needs more dogs. Here, though? I don't know. There could be some advantage to breeding her once. If we do want more working dogs in Rockton, we know she has good genes. On the other hand, we don't want every wolf and feral dog volunteering as puppy daddies."

"Is there some way to control her cycles?"

"Doggie birth control? I have no idea. More research for our next trip to Dawson." I give her one last pat as I stand. "At least one of us might be able to have babies, huh?"

I say it lightly, but I feel Dalton's gaze on me.

"I was kidding," I say.

"Kidding . . . and not kidding." He checks his watch. "It's after five, so I think we're up for good. If I put on the kettle for coffee, can we talk about this?"

I shrug. "Nothing to talk about, really. Yes, it's on my mind lately, for obvious reasons, but talking is just treading the same ground over and over. It doesn't get me anywhere."

He fixes me with that look, trying to extract from my brain the answers I'm not giving. Then he puts the blackened kettle directly on the fire.

"You need to teach Ty how to set that up properly," I say.

"Guy drinks instant coffee with powdered creamer. I don't think he cares whether he's heating the water right."

He backs from the fire and pulls on his sweatpants. He's still adjusting them, not looking at me, when he says, "You had so much other shit to deal with after the beating. Just getting up and around again. Then getting your strength back. Getting on the police force. All the things they said you couldn't do, and you did. This other thing was . . ."

He struggles for words. "It's an injury to a muscle you weren't sure you'd ever want to use. Except it's more than just a muscle that doesn't work. It's something they took from you, on top of all the rest, something you can't fix through sheer determination and hard work."

Tears roll down my cheeks. I don't even realize it until he reaches for me. He has put into words everything I've been feeling these last few days, and it's as if I've said them myself, but better, because I didn't have to.

Fourteen years ago, four men beat me and left me for dead. They took my mobility, leaving me with a leg injury that doctors said meant I'd never run again. They left me with scars—physical and psychological—that people said meant I'd never become a cop. They took my pride, too, and my dignity and my self-confidence.

But I triumphed because I fought back in the way that really counted. I *can* run. I *am* a cop. And while there's still psychological damage, in regaining my mobility and achieving my career goal, I won back my pride and my dignity and my self-confidence. Wherever those four thugs are now, I have a better life than they do. I'm sure of it. So I won.

Except now, as Dalton says, there's this one thing they took that I cannot regain. It didn't matter before because I never saw myself as a mother. I had an all-consuming career and no interest in long-term relationships. Being with Dalton changed both those things and nudged that old scab. Then came Abby, and seeing Dalton with her and feeling my own reaction to her has ripped that scab clear off, and it hurts. It hurts so much.

Tied up in that pain is rage. Those men *did* take something from me, something I cannot get back, and here is this life choice that I'm not even sure I want, but I should damned well have that option. I don't, and it is their fault.

I say all this to Dalton. The kettle boils and it boils, and I'm still talking, the words rushing out. Finally, there's nothing more to say, and I take the kettle and pour the coffees, brushing him off when he tries to help. I measure in the creamer with such care you'd think it was powdered gold. Then I stir, slowly and deliberately, giving myself time to recover.

"There are options," he says. "If that's what you want."

"I'm not sure it is. I have no idea right now, and no time to sit and think about it. There's no point either. If we don't find Abby's family, then she's one option, and I'd do that before I'd even try carrying a baby to term myself. If we do find her family, then I need to figure out whether what I'm feeling is just a surge of maternal instinct. Then you and I need to talk about it, either way, and . . ."

I wave my hands. "Part of me wants to consider options, and another part says that's like deciding which university to send your kid to before she's even born."

Dalton settles onto the bed with his coffee and motions for me to sit beside him. I do, and Storm moves to lie across our feet.

"So," Dalton says. "You know that the council has threatened to kick me out of Rockton. Even when they don't say it, I feel the weight of that hammer over my head. This woman, who is very smart, once told me that the best way to cope with that is to figure out a game plan. What I'd do if it happened."

"I never said it was the *best* way. Just one way."

He waves off the distinction. "The point is that my brain works like hers does. We need solid footing. I need to know that if I get kicked out, I have a plan. So I'm going to suggest that she needs the same thing. A plan for what we'd do if we ever decide we want one of those wrinkly things that screams for us to feed her and screams for us to change her shitty diaper and won't let us sleep more than three hours at a stretch."

"You make it sound so enticing."

"I know. But in spite of their unbelievably selfish behavior, I will admit that I do see an appeal to babies that I never did before. Which is not to say that I want one. If we don't find Abby's parents, then I would seriously consider it and lean toward yes. Otherwise, I'd back up to just seriously considering it, for some point in the future."

"Agreed."

"So, let's jump past Abby and jump past the soul-searching and decide on a plan of action, should the answer be yes, we want kids. How would we do that?"

I exhale. "Okay. Well, the problem, according to the doctors, isn't whether I could get pregnant but whether I could carry to term. I would try, but it's not like taking endless shots on a basketball net, waiting to sink one. Trying and failing would be . . ."

"Traumatic."

When I make a face, he shakes his head and says, "My mom—my birth mother—lost a couple of pregnancies after Jacob, and I might have been young, but I remember it was really hard on them. So that's an option, but with a limited number of trials."

I nod.

"And if those trials put you in danger, would I have the right to say stop?" he asks.

"You would."

"Good. Next option."

I go quiet for a moment. Then I say, "Adoption is the most obvious. Maybe even the best to start with, but it's not easy getting a baby. Even if we could . . ."

"You'd prefer your own. Our biological child."

I'm about to shake my head. Then I pause to consider it more. "All other things being equal, yes, I suppose I would, as selfish as that is. But I'd take another baby in a heartbeat. Having our biological child isn't that important. It's just . . ."

I squirm, and his arm slides around my waist.

I continue, "I would worry that, given your situation, even

if you felt okay with adoption, you might have misgivings later. What if it's a very young mother who later regretted her decision? What if the child grew up wanting answers, wanting his or her biological family? That's probably natural at some point, but I think it would be . . . difficult for you."

He opens his mouth, and I can tell he's ready to deny it. Then he pauses, like me, to consider before he says, "I would like to think I'd be fine. I do see your point, though, and it wouldn't be fair to a kid if I brought my baggage into parenthood. However, if adoption is the best option, I'd be fine. I'd make sure I was."

"The other is surrogacy," I say.

He frowns, and I explain.

"So, we rent a womb?" he says.

I sputter a laugh. "It's a little more complicated, but yes, that's the basic idea."

"Okay," he says, nodding. "So that's the plan, then, if we ever reach that stage. Try ourselves, and if that doesn't work or it endangers you, then option two is surrogacy. Option three is adoption." He looks at me. "Does that help?"

"It feels a little silly, coming up with a course of action for something we may never want, but . . ."

"It's never silly if it makes you feel better."

I lean over to kiss him. "It does. Thank you."

# THIRTY

We set off after a world-class breakfast of instant coffee, protein bars, and venison jerky. Then we walk all morning in snowshoes, carrying provisions on our backs, stopping only to dine on . . . water, half a protein bar, and a slab of venison jerky. I can grumble about the menu, but by lunch, I'm like a starving cartoon character, spotting shy Arctic hares and seeing only their plump bodies roasting on a spit.

Off again, and it's midafternoon before Dalton slows to examine landmarks, like reaching the right neighborhood and slowing the car to read street signs. Storm whines, and we go still, listening. When we hear the crunch of snow he calls, "Hello!"

The footsteps stop.

"I'm letting you know we're here," Dalton says. "We're armed, and we have a dog. That's not a threat—again, just letting you know so we don't give you a scare. We're restraining the dog and lowering our weapons. We'd like to speak to you, please."

Silence.

Dalton grunts, as if to say he hoped it'd be that easy but

knew better. Still, he tries again with, "My name is Eric Dalton. I know the Second Settlement is out here, and we found something in the forest that we're told might belong to you. We only want to return it."

More silence. Dalton grumbles now, but I catch the faintest whisper of fabric. I touch Dalton's arm and direct his attention left, where a figure stands in shadow, watching us as cautiously as any wild beast. It's a young man, late teens, maybe twenty. He carries a bow, but it's lowered, and he's just watching, reminding me of that wolf the day before.

"Hello." I resist the urge to say we come in peace, though I doubt this young man would get the reference. "We just need to speak to someone from the Second Settlement. My name's Casey. This is Eric."

He keeps watching us with wary curiosity.

"And this is Storm," I say, nodding down. "She's a dog, not a bear." I smile. "She gets that mistake a lot."

No reaction.

"I'm holding her by the collar," I say. "She's big, but she's friendly, if you want to come closer."

He doesn't move.

"May we speak to you from there?" I ask.

When he stays silent, I'm beginning to wonder if he understands English. Then he says, "Yes."

"Before we do," Dalton drawls, "I'd appreciate knowing if we need to watch for anyone jumping at our backs. I'm sure you aren't out here alone."

Silence, and even from here, I swear I see the boy considering.

Finally he says, "The others are close. They'll come if I call them."

"Fair enough," Dalton says.

"I'm going to remove my pack," I say. "I'm getting something out that I want to show you."

I take the remaining piece of Ellen's parka from my bag and hold it out. "We're told this was made by someone in the Second Settlement."

He squints. Then he eases forward, until he's about five feet away. He reaches out, and I pass him the material. He peers at it and then shakes his head as he returns it.

"It's not ours."

"You sure?" Dalton asks.

The young man's eyes flash. "I know the work of my people. I don't know what you've found, but if that was what led you to think it is ours, then someone has made a mistake. Or someone is trying to cause trouble for us. We don't want the kind of trouble that comes with you."

"Me?" Dalton says. "Who am I?"

"It's not who you are. It's where you're from." His gaze travels meaningfully over Dalton's clothing. "Rockton. My people separated from yours, and we ask only to be left alone."

"And you're not missing anything?" I ask. "Missing any*one*?"

"No, we are not."

"You sure?" Dalton says again.

He gets that same flash of annoyance, stronger now. "If we were missing a person, I'd be out here hunting for him."

"Maybe you are," Dalton says.

"Then I'd be more interested when you said you found something of ours, wouldn't I? We have no quarrel with Rockton. If we had someone missing, we'd be grateful for your help. If we found one of yours, we would return him."

Despite those flashing eyes, the young man keeps his voice calm. He's well-spoken. Polite. I get a distinctly different vibe from him than I do from the First Settlement. There's no challenge here. We're just two groups occupying the same region, and this one would rather keep those lines of separation clear. Like an introvert neighbor who thinks it's very nice that you're throwing a BBQ and hopes it goes well, but doesn't want to attend, and would politely request that you stop asking.

"You have any idea where this came from?" Dalton says, pointing at the fabric.

"No, and if I did, I would tell you."

"All right. We'll keep looking then."

The young man nods and withdraws without another word.

We watch him go. Then Dalton says, "You buy that?"

"He seems sincere, but Ty was certain he knew where it came from. That kid really doesn't want us getting closer to their settlement. I'm not ready to drop this on his say-so."

"Agreed."

We follow the young man at a distance. According to Dalton, he's heading toward the settlement. Moving quickly, too.

We start closing the gap between us. It's better to catch up with him on the outskirts, where it's too late to blow us off again, yet it's clear we aren't trying to ambush his settlement. I spot smoke rising over the trees ahead when Dalton grasps my arm. His hand drops to his gun, and I pull mine.

Dalton pivots. "Step out. There's a gun trained on each of you."

His gaze flicks in the other direction, and I turn that way, my gun rising.

Silence.

"Look," Dalton says. "I don't want to pull this shit. We're walking to your village. We talked to a kid from it, but we need more information, and he didn't seem the right person to give it. We appreciate your caution, but our guns do a helluva lot more damage than your bows, and they work a helluva lot faster. Also, you're making our dog nervous."

As if on cue, Storm growls.

"Just step out please," Dalton says. "Then we'll all lower our weapons and talk."

No answer.

"Fuck," Dalton grumbles. He turns to me and says, loud enough for them to hear, "Don't you just get tired of this shit?"

"I do."

"Do people pull this crap down south?"

"No, but we have cell phones. We can call before we show up."

"Well, that's what we need. Cell phones. Can we get a few of those?"

"Sure. First, you need a cell tower."

"Fuck."

"Or we could do it the old-fashioned way," I say. "Ring their doorbell."

"Hell, yeah." He raises his voice more. "You guys got a doorbell? No? How's this?" He raps his knuckles on the nearest tree. "Sheriff Eric Dalton, of Rockton, calling with my wife, Detective Casey Butler, also of Rockton. May we come in?"

A man appears from Dalton's direction, shaking his head. "I suppose you're trying to be funny," he says, no rancor in his voice.

"Yeah," Dalton says. "I make a better asshole than a comedian, but I'm trying a new tactic."

The man's lips quirk as he walks over. "Might want to keep working at it, but I appreciate the effort."

He's in his mid-forties, a tall, rangy man with weathered skin. He's dark-haired and round-faced, and his countenance reminds me of the young man's. A relative, I'd guess.

The other man comes into view but stops short as he sees me. "Tomas?"

"Yes?" the older man replies.

"You get a look at the girl? She's not from Rockton. She's Edwin's."

Tomas turns his gaze on me and frowns. He takes in my clothing. Then he looks at the other man. "Just because she's partly Asian does not mean she's related to the only Asian person you've met."

"I'm not," I say. "I know Edwin, but I'm no more likely to share ancestry with him than with you." I glance at Dalton. "Or with him, which would be really awkward."

Tomas chuckles. The other man's eyes stay narrowed in suspicion.

Tomas stretches his hand to me and then to Dalton. We shake it. The other man stays where he is.

"We met a young man a few minutes ago," I say to Tomas. "Maybe late teens? He bore a resemblance to you. Your son?"

"Nephew," Tomas says. "But my wife and I have been raising him the last few years. We saw you tracking him and got concerned."

"I apologize for that," I say. "We have some questions. We found a . . ." I hesitate. "A body. A woman dressed in clothing that we were told came from the Second Settlement. But your nephew didn't recognize it. He said no one's missing, and he obviously wanted to leave it at that but . . . We need to find out where she belonged. Even if she's not yours, any help would be appreciated. I understand you prefer not to have contact with Rockton."

"Eh," Tomas says with a shrug. "We're not exactly hiding behind a wall with archers and a moat. We do keep to ourselves, but we'd like to help you find this poor woman's people. That's only right."

The other man snorts and stalks off. Tomas shakes his head with a wry smile. "While not everyone here will be so helpful, they won't object to me speaking to you."

"Thank you." I take the scrap from my pocket. "The person who sent us to you had a long-standing trade relationship with your settlement, and he was convinced someone there—maybe someone who used to live there—did the craftsmanship."

"How is Tyrone?" Tomas asks, and I must look surprised, because he laughs. "Not many people have had that 'long-standing trade relationship' you mentioned. Tyrone was sheriff when my brother and I left Rockton, and I advocated for trade with him when he left himself. We had a change in leadership a few years ago and . . ." He shrugs. "Tyrone Cypher is an unusual man. He made our current leader nervous, and she decided to cut ties."

"Ty's fine, thank you," I say. "And yes, he's the only one who recognized this."

I hold out the piece. The man frowns. He takes it and examines it, his frown growing.

"You don't recognize it?" I ask.

"No, I certainly do. I was just wondering why Lane—my nephew—told you otherwise. But I shouldn't wonder really. People here can be very secretive, and my brother always had a touch of paranoia, which is how the two of us ended up in Rockton in the first place. I apologize for Lane. He didn't mean any harm. Yes, I definitely recognize this, because it's my work. Well, the leatherwork is mine. The decorating is my wife's."

He smiles, his eyes warming. "She's the artist. I just try to provide a canvas halfway worthy of her art."

"It is gorgeous work," I say.

"But you mentioned that you found it on a dead woman. No one's missing from our village. While we do trade with former members, no one has left in years and the only woman we actually trade with—"

He trails off, and he blinks. When he speaks, his throat dries up, and he has to try twice before he says, "Could you . . . describe this woman?"

"Are you familiar with the hostiles?"

He pales. Then he forces a ragged laugh. "Haven't heard that word in a very long time. We call them the wild people. But yes, it's hard to live out here and *not* know them, as much as we might wish otherwise. This woman . . ." He swallows. "You asked that for a reason, didn't you?"

"I did."

"Ellen," he murmurs.

I nod. "That was apparently her name." I take out the leather anklet she'd worn. When I pass it over, he stares at it and sways, just a little. His eyes squeeze shut, and he nods, as if to himself, and says, in a small voice, "How did it happen?"

"She was shot," I say.

He flinches. Then he says, slowly, "And this, Sheriff, is the truth of your earlier words. Why your guns are so much more dangerous than our bows. Yes, it is possible to accidentally shoot someone while hunting, but the chances of killing them are slight. We always hope that the scarcity of ammunition will decrease the use of firearms in these woods, but . . ."

His gaze rises to Dalton's, meeting it. "That will not happen while Rockton has guns and ammunition, and the willingness to trade both."

My brows rise.

Dalton says to me, "Yeah, under Tyrone, Rockton traded ammunition to help those who chose to leave. Giving them a higher chance of survival. Of course, another philosophy is that if you *don't* trade, maybe they'll see the light and come back. That's what Gene thought. By the time he left, people had found other sources of ammo, and I'm sure as hell not giving them extra."

He looks at Tomas. "I'd supply it in a matter of life or death.

I'm not going to let anyone starve. But personally, I'm on your side. I'd like to see a lot fewer guns. Fuck, I'd make our own residents use bows if that didn't mean we'd be facing settlers and traders and miners with guns. Rockton hasn't supplied weapons or ammunition in years. And, though you haven't suggested it outright, we didn't kill this woman. We found her on a camping trip."

Tomas nods. "I wasn't accusing you, but thank you for clarifying. I'm guessing that's how it happened? A hunting accident?"

"It's . . . difficult to tell," I say. "The reason we're pursuing it is that she had something . . . with her. Something that may be important to someone."

I still want the chance to evaluate Abby's parents before I return her. I know I may not have that right. Yet after meeting Owen and Cherise, I will place myself in this role, judging who does and does not deserve their child back.

If I need to justify *that,* I'll do it with the reminder that Ellen could have rescued Abby from abandonment. If her parents were from the Second Settlement and hid the pregnancy, they won't want their fellow settlers knowing what they did. If the Second Settlement was complicit in the abandonment, they won't want her back. Either way, the settlement might lie and take the child to save face.

When I say this, being cagey, Tomas's gaze drops to the bracelet, still in his hands.

"Not that," I say. "If anyone in the settlement knew Ellen well, we'd love the chance to speak to them. I'm trying to piece together her final days."

The corners of his lips rise in a strained smile. "You really are a detective then."

"I am."

"Well . . ." He trails off, and I can see him thinking. Considering his options.

Finally, he says, "My wife was close to Ellen. They were friends. I would appreciate the chance to speak to Nancy—my wife—first, if you don't mind. I'd like this news to come from me."

"We understand."

"I'll go into the settlement and tell people what has happened. They won't be thrilled at you being here, but with a death involved, they will understand. Many were fond of Ellen. This will be difficult."

I nod. He starts to leave. Then he looks down at the bracelet. He stares at it a moment before clearing his throat, his expression unreadable as he says, "May I ask . . ." Another glance at the bracelet. "I'd rather not show this to anyone yet. It was . . . very personal."

Dalton and I exchange a glance. I agree, and Tomas pockets the bracelet before heading toward the village.

# THIRTY-ONE

It takes a while for Tomas to return, but we expect that. We take off our snowshoes and packs, drink some water, share another protein bar, and play with Storm. Or Dalton plays with her. I lie on my back in the snow. Just making snow angels, really. Not collapsed from the exhaustion of snowshoeing all day.

When Tomas returns, he's alone, and I'm braced for "Sorry, but you can't come in," but he waves for us to follow. After a few steps, he says, "Nancy is . . . taking it hard, as you might expect. She'll speak to you, but she asks for a few minutes to gather her thoughts."

"Of course."

As we approach the village, I expect a loose cluster of buildings, like the First Settlement. Instead, there are a few small outbuildings clustered around two large ones that remind me of Indigenous longhouses.

"Communal living," I murmur. I think I've said it low enough, but Tomas hears and smiles.

"Yes. It's more economical for heating and food. Everyone works together, whether it's cooking or child-rearing." He glances to the side and his smile grows. "Speaking of child-rearing . . ."

A little girl, maybe five or six, comes racing over and throws herself into Tomas's arms. He swoops her up and swings her about as she squeals. I notice a boy a year or two older eyeing us. Tomas waves him over.

"These are my children," he says. "Becky and Miles."

"Eric," Dalton says. He shakes the boy's hand. The girl just giggles, but when I introduce myself, she shakes mine. They aren't really interested in us, though. Both pairs of eyes are fixed on our furry companion. I introduce Storm and have her sit while the children pet her.

"Can you guys do me a favor?" Tomas asks. "Your mom is busy right now, so I'd like you to stay with us. We're going to speak to the elders."

"And if you can keep Storm company while we do that, we'd appreciate it," I say. Then to Tomas, I add, "She's very well trained, and we'll be close by."

He nods and charges the children with "watching" the dog, which really means just walking along beside her and petting her while we all enter the first longhouse.

A campfire within is the main source of light, and it takes a minute for my eyes to adjust. As I look around, I remember once going to a park with re-created Iroquois longhouses. That really is what this reminds me of. Down the center is a workspace, where women sew and children play and men whittle. Bunks line the walls, three high. Drying herbs and vegetables hang from the ceiling.

At the back sits a group that I'm guessing are the "elders," since they're talking, rather than working. The eldest is in her sixties. That makes sense, given that the Second Settlement launched in the seventies.

At the First Settlement, we're always met with a combination of curiosity and hostility, emphasis on the latter. It's saber-rattling. They want us to know how strong they are, how well defended. A pissing match that we must engage in, or we're the submissive wolf rolling over to show our unprotected belly.

In the Second Settlement, we get curiosity tempered by caution. While Tomas's daughter ran out to see us, her brother held back, and that's what many of the adults do. They withdraw, physically and emotionally, stepping backward to let us pass, their faces blank. Even in their caution, though, there is politeness rather than aggression. *You are welcome enough here, but please don't stay long.*

Others are more like Tomas and his daughter, the friendliness outweighing any reserve. They smile, and they nod as we pass, and I do the same in return. Storm's presence lures a few of the children closer, especially when they see Tomas's kids petting her. I get her to sit a few feet from where the elders wait, and the children surge in, with adults supervising.

There is another thing I notice as we walk. Signs of . . . well, the words I consider and reject are "religion," "faith," "ritual," "belief." It's not as if I'm seeing crucifixes or dharma wheels or anything I recognize, yet my brain still identifies them as signs of a ritualized faith. There is what appears to be an altar built of stones and filled with dried grasses that add a sweet, pleasant scent to the campfire smoke. Other stones line the walls, each carved with an unfamiliar symbol. I see ones that look like stylized versions of wind and rain and snow. I also spot animal carvings, too many to be mere toys. And the sleeping berths bear more carvings, some symbols and some animals.

I struggle not to draw conclusions from what I'm seeing. Take in the data and store it for processing once I have more information.

I don't get more information on this by speaking to the elders. Well, I do . . . and I don't. It's not as if they extend a ritual greeting or ask that we all bow our heads in prayer before we speak. But there is a calm here that reminds me of a church, a hush and a peaceful contentment, and a reverence in the way Tomas addresses the elders. I may not see religion and ritual, but I feel it.

The conversation itself is a ritual I know very well. We have been presented to the leader—Myra—and she welcomes us, and we extend our greetings and explain our purpose. She expresses sadness at our news, gratitude for our attempts to find this woman's people, and promises of cooperation. It's like when I'd dealt with crimes involving an organization of any kind, social or political or business. "Yes, this is a terrible crime, and of course, we're here for anything the police need to solve it." Honest intent or empty promises? That's always the question, and if I was to hazard a guess, based on my experiences, I'd say that the Second Settlement isn't going to actively block my investigation, but they're not going out of their way to help it either. Ellen isn't theirs, and since she'd been shot— and they forbid guns—her death isn't theirs either.

The meeting lasts about fifteen minutes, and it's nothing more than a formal exchange of information and promises. As we leave the longhouse, the women at the cooking pit press food into our hands, fresh stew in beautifully carved wooden bowls and hunks of warm bread. They give some to Tomas, too, for himself and his wife, and we all thank them as we depart.

When we're out of the longhouse, Tomas quietly offers to switch bowls with us.

"In case you're at all concerned about the contents," he says. "I spent a lifetime with my paranoid brother. I would understand if you'd prefer to eat what they gave me."

We assure him we're not worried, and he passes his bread to the kids, who trail along after us with Storm.

"I'm going to ask you two to go back into the big house," he says to the kids. He looks at us. "May they take the dog?"

"Of course," I say.

The girl starts to give Storm her bread, but Tomas pulls her hand back. "Never feed an animal anything that she might not normally eat. It can upset her stomach. Ask Josie if they have bones instead. Big bones, from caribou or moose. The dog will like those better."

I motion for Storm to go with the kids, and she gives me a careful look, as if to be sure she's understanding. Then she lets them lead her back into the longhouse.

Tomas takes us to what seemed like a storage building, small and round. As we approach, I see smoke rising from it.

"As much as we believe in communal living, we also understand that sometimes, privacy is required, and in the winter, we can't just head into the forest to find it. This is our alone-hut, for individuals and"—he winks—"couples. Nancy will meet us in here."

It's a hide-covered structure, and he pulls back the flap. We have to duck to go inside. It's brighter than the longhouse, though. There's a fire and a hanging lantern. A woman sits on the floor. She's about my age. Tears streak her face, but as soon as the flap opens, she jumps up to greet us. Tomas waves her back inside. We enter, and he hangs back, as if uncertain. She tugs him in, and his face relaxes with relief. She takes one bowl from him and sets it down on the ground, and they sit, her hand entwined with his.

We introduce ourselves.

"I'm sorry for your loss," I say, and down south, that would be a cliché, but it really does say what needs to be said, *all* that can be said when talking to a stranger.

Nancy's eyes fill. Tomas grips her hand tighter, both hands wrapping around it. She sees we aren't touching our food, and says, "Eat, please. I won't, but you should. It's good stew, and the bread is even better."

We take a few mouthfuls, and both are indeed excellent. Once I've had enough to be sure my belly won't rumble, I say, "I'm not sure how much Tomas told you. I was a homicide detective down south."

She frowns and glances at Tomas.

"Nancy hasn't been down south," he says. "She was born in the Second Settlement." He quickly explains what a homicide detective is, and her brows furrow, as if she's struggling to understand the need for such a job.

I say as much, lightly joking.

She nods and says, "I know it's different down there. There are so many more people. It's good that they have people to do that job. But Tomas said Ellen was killed by accident."

"We hope so," I say. "Right now, I'm trying to piece together her final days. She had something with her. Something I need to return. I'm sorry I can't say more than that."

Her lips curve in a wry smile. "Because whatever this thing is, it's valuable, and if you say what it is, people here might falsely claim it."

"Probably not," I say. "But we need to be extra cautious."

"We understand," Tomas says. "We'd like to do whatever we can to help Ellen."

Nancy hesitates at that, and her gaze drops, just a little, but then she nods and squeezes her husband's hand. "Yes. Anything you need. She was a dear friend."

"She didn't live here, though?"

Nancy shakes her head. "We asked her to. We . . ." She looks up at me. "I know nothing of how a detective works down south. I realize it is a job, and therefore, you might want only the details that will help you."

"Just the facts, ma'am," Tomas says, and we exchange a smile for a joke the other two won't get.

"Down south, we're on a schedule," I say. "People's taxes

pay our salaries, so we need to be efficient. Brutally efficient even. Up here, it's different. Eric and I can't get home tonight anyway. As long as the settlement doesn't mind us setting up our tent nearby, we're in no rush. Here, I have the luxury of time, and I appreciate that. It gives me a chance to get a better understanding of the victim. In other words, take your time. Anything you want to explain, I'd like to hear."

"All right. If I go too far off topic, please stop me, but I . . . I would like you to understand more about us, too. It isn't as if we saw Ellen struggling to survive and closed our doors to her. We don't do that."

"I understand."

"We've helped a few of the wild people. Some in our community disagree with that. We believe in harmony with nature—the spirits of the forest and all that live in it. We hunt, of course. But we don't interfere with other predators, which includes the wild people. The question we disagree on is whether 'interference' includes helping them escape their situation."

She shifts, getting comfortable, and Tomas pushes blankets forward to let her lean on them. She smiles at him, and it is the smile of a long-married couple, instinctively understanding what the other needs and still able to appreciate these small acts of kindness.

"Ellen and I spoke often of her past," Nancy says. "I've taken her story to the elders, in hopes of convincing those who say we shouldn't interfere with the wild people. Ellen herself, though, would not speak to the elders. She was . . . conflicted on this. I'm not sure how much you know about the wild people."

"We're helping a woman who left them recently," I say. "She's a former Rockton resident. Eric knew her. He grew up there."

"Oh." Her eyes widen as she looks at Dalton. "You're the boy. The one Tyrone spoke of."

Dalton nods, his jaw set, and Nancy sees that, murmuring, "I'm sorry. I didn't mean to pry. I just remember Tyrone's stories."

"Ty has plenty of those," Dalton says. "Not all of them true, but yeah, I was born out here and . . . taken to Rockton."

She rocks back, as if stopping herself from comment. She reaches for her bowl instead and takes a spoonful of stew. Then she stops, frowns, and pulls a shotgun pellet from her mouth.

"Thought you folks didn't use guns," Dalton says.

"We don't," she says. "But sometimes we still find pellets in the meat. When other settlers injure large game without killing them, those end up in our food."

"It's been happening more and more recently," Tomas mutters. "Someone cracked a tooth just last month."

I reach to take the pellet, but Nancy tucks it aside, as if she didn't see me reaching. I hesitate and then withdraw my hand wordlessly.

I resume our conversation. "So we know this woman, Maryanne, and her situation. She left Rockton with a party of would-be settlers, and they were set upon by the hos—wild people. The men were killed. The women were taken."

"Oh!" Nancy's hand flies to her mouth, her eyes rounding. "I'm—I'm sorry."

"That isn't how they 'recruit' around here?" I ask.

"Not Ellen's group. The wild people actually rescued her. Ellen and her husband were up here mining. They were new at it—it was only their second season. They were crossing a river swollen with spring runoff when they fell. He drowned. She made it to shore, but all their supplies were gone. She was nearly dead when the wild people took her in."

"And she stayed with them."

Nancy looks at her husband, as if unsure how much to say.

Tomas makes a face. "That's the problem. They have these teas. They're . . . like ours, but not like ours."

"I've heard about the teas. They— Wait, you said they're like yours?"

He nods. "We have two. There's the peace tea. It's . . ." He looks at me. "Have you ever smoked weed?"

"Once." I quirk a smile. "It wasn't quite my thing. Slowed me down too much."

"Right. That's what it does. Relaxes you, makes you happy and peaceful. We have a tea like that for relaxing. The same way someone might have wine with dinner. Then there's the ritual tea. There's this root that grows wild here. I have no idea what the real name is, but we call it the dream-root."

"A hallucinogen."

"Yes. We use it for ceremonies. To bridge the gap between us and nature." He lifts his hands, as if warding off comment. "Yes, I know. Between that and the peace tea, it sounds very nineteen sixties. But we have our ways here, and they don't harm anyone."

"I wasn't going to question," I say.

Tomas chuckles. "Tyrone sure did. He thought we were all a bunch of loony hippies, dancing naked in the woods. Our ways were definitely not his."

"These teas, though," I say. "I'm told the wild people have two as well. One that makes them calm and one that causes hallucinations. Are they the same?"

"I'm no scientist—I was a truck driver down south—but from what Ellen said, I think theirs are stronger versions of ours. Much stronger. Ever tried peyote?"

I shake my head.

"I have," he says. "That's what our ritual tea is like. We drift into a dreamlike state, hence the name. What the wild people take makes them, well, wild. Increased violence. Increased sex drive. Their version of the peace tea is also stronger. Between the two brews, they seem to make the wild people stay with the group. Ellen had family down south. Parents, siblings, friends, a job. She only came to the Yukon for an adventure that was her husband's dream. She had no interest in staying long-term, let alone permanently."

Nancy nods. "But the tea made her forget the rest. Her family, her job, her life. At first, she stayed with the intention of getting well enough to travel back to the city. Then she just . . . forgot all that."

"How did she come out of it?" I ask.

Nancy glances at Tomas, uncomfortable again. This time, he isn't quite so quick to answer but rubs his beard, and looks back at his wife.

"There are . . . rules," Tomas says. "Every community has them. Ours is no different. There are laws meant to protect us, and there are laws meant to protect our way of life, to put our belief into deed."

"Religious prohibitions," I say.

He makes a face. "I wouldn't call what we practice a religion. I guess it is, but I was raised Catholic and . . ." He exhales. "Call it what you will. A friend with far more education than me said it's a belief system rather than a religion. Part of that belief system is noninterference. We don't interfere with Rockton or the First Settlement. We don't interfere with nature, either, any more than is needed for survival."

"And you don't interfere with the wild people," I say. "Or you're not supposed to. But there's some differing opinion on whether they've actually *chosen* that lifestyle. The woman we know was clearly a hostage, at least at first, and after a while, she was still hostage—to those teas. Her free will was being held hostage."

"Yes," Nancy says. "Ellen stayed by choice, but at what point was it no longer a choice? If she chose to drink the tea, and it caused her to stay, does that mean she *chose* to stay? Some here would say yes. But drinking the tea is a requirement for staying in that group. And it isn't as if she realized she was losing her free will and *chose* to keep losing it."

Tomas chuckles. "Nancy's better at explaining this. It makes my head hurt. All I know is that it doesn't seem right, leaving them out there like that, if they don't have the . . . what do we call it down south? The mental capacity to choose."

"Like seeing an addict on the street and not getting them to a shelter because they initially chose the drugs."

"Exactly."

"So, what you're trying to say . . ." I hesitate, consider their situation, and reword it. "In a case like that, someone might choose to help a person when their community says they shouldn't. If their community learned of it, they would be in trouble."

Neither speaks, but both give me a look that says I've guessed correctly.

"Okay," I say. "How Ellen extricated herself from the wild people is unimportant. You say your community has helped some of them. I'm guessing that means they've offered assistance to wild people who have voluntarily left their tribe. That is allowed. That's not interference."

Nancy nods. "If they leave on their own, we can offer food, trade goods, even shelter. Two of our members were former wild people. Ellen wanted to live on her own and, when she was ready, travel back home. She left her group the summer before last, and she hoped to return home in the spring. She was so excited . . ."

Nancy's voice catches. Tomas puts his arm around her shoulders, and she leans against it. I eat more of my now-cold stew and glance at Dalton. He's been silent, letting me handle this. When he catches my eye, he nods, and I'm not aware that I'm communicating anything to him, but after a moment, he speaks.

"When's the last time you saw her?" he asks.

Nancy starts, and it might be surprise at Dalton talking, but it's more, too. She's sinking into her grief, and we've finally reached the heart of what I really must ask her. We can't let her drift now. That's the message Dalton read in my look.

*This is going to be tough, and I need help.*

*I need someone to push. Someone to play bad cop.*

When Nancy hesitates, Dalton says, "This is important."

"I know," she says. "It was eight—" Another catch. "Eight days ago. She needed supplies."

"Like what?"

Dalton grills Nancy on specifics. It isn't easy. Speaking of Ellen in the abstract had been fine, but now Nancy must dissect what she realizes is the last time she'd ever see her friend. Tomas glances at her, concerned, but he doesn't interfere and Nancy gives no sign she needs to stop.

Ellen had came by on a supply run. She did that weekly. As a lone settler, without the time to build a permanent residence, she lived light, with only a tent and a pack. It was easier for her to trade weekly with the settlement, giving them her extra meat and furs in return for dried vegetables and other foodstuffs.

Her last visit, however, had been unscheduled. She usually stopped by on what they called "the sixth day"—Saturdays. This visit came on a Tuesday, and she'd brought an entire caribou plus three hares, hoping to trade for winter blankets and scraps of leather.

Dalton frowns. "She lived alone last winter, and this one isn't any colder."

"She said she used last year's blankets to sew summer clothing."

"Why now? It's been fucking freezing for two months."

They both flinch at the profanity, and it takes him a moment to realize it. He nods, understanding. There are people in Rockton who take exception to his language. If they're troublemakers or chronic complainers, he might even pile on a few "fucks" to annoy them. But if they are good people, like these, he holds back.

Nancy admits she doesn't know why Ellen suddenly wanted extra warm blankets. There's hesitation, suggesting she found this odd herself, but Dalton only nods, as if accepting her explanation. Then he says, his voice casual, "A caribou and three hares. She must be a really good hunter."

They say nothing, but their discomfort is palpable.

"That normal for her? Bringing so much meat, three days after her last visit?"

Silence. Dalton's gaze cuts my way, bouncing the ball over.

"I know you trade with a very limited number of people," I say. "I'm guessing Ellen was an exception because she's a former wild person. In need of help."

They both nod, as if grateful for the easy answer.

"What about others?" I say. "Regular settlers who need assistance?"

"It would depend," Tomas says. "We'd never turn away someone who was in desperate need, of course. We make exceptions. But only in emergencies, and then we direct them to other sources, such as the First Settlement."

"What if an accepted trade partner, like Ellen, brought you goods from someone else?"

They exchange a look.

"That would be . . . prohibited," Nancy says. "By our laws."

"Which Ellen knows. She'd never risk your friendship by openly trading on someone else's behalf. But if she says nothing . . ."

They don't answer.

Dalton surges forward, clearly ready to press the matter, but I shake my head. I consider for a minute, and then I say, "Ellen was a good friend, yes? And also a good person, it seems. If she knew of someone in need, she would trade for them and not tell you. I respect that. However, given that she is dead—possibly murdered—I need to pursue this. I'm not asking you to confirm that she was trading for a third party. But did she give you any idea what she needed those leather scraps for?"

"She said she was going to try her hand at sewing."

"Did she need a specific size of scrap?"

Nancy shakes her head. "I had scraps no bigger than my hand, and I said they were useless but she took them."

"Did she request anything else? Anything unusual?"

"Salve," she says. "For her lips, she said."

"Were they chapped?"

Nancy shakes her head.

Scraps of leather, any size. When we were diapering Abby, we used fabric scraps for extra padding. That could suggest Ellen was caring for the baby herself, but she hadn't requested anything she'd need to feed Abby. The mention of salve, however, reminds me of a colleague joking about his wife putting lip balm on her nipples during nursing. That would suggest Ellen wasn't caring for the baby herself; she was helping Abby's parents get supplies they needed.

"About that caribou," Dalton says. "Did she usually bring in game that large?"

"She said she got lucky," Tomas explains. "We didn't question."

"How did she usually hunt? With a gun?"

"Oh, no," Nancy says. "The wild people don't have guns. They're like us. And we allowed her to hunt on our territory, which means she isn't allowed to use guns. She wouldn't anyway. She only traps and fishes." She hesitates, as if seeing the problem with that, given that Ellen brought in a caribou.

"Had the caribou been shot?" I ask, trying not to glance at where Nancy tucked away the pellet.

"She brought it partly slaughtered," Tomas says. "She kept the head. She said she wanted the antlers, but I suppose, if someone gave her the animal, it could have been shot in the head. That's what I figured. That someone traded the caribou to her, and she was trading it to us, which wouldn't break our laws. I hadn't thought of it being shot, but I suspect that's the caribou they used for the stew today."

The stew with shotgun pellets.

We run out of questions shortly after that. We know Ellen had made an unscheduled stop in the Second Settlement, trading for unusual items and using unusual payment. That supported the idea she'd been helping Abby's mother. That might also suggest Abby's parents were responsible for the caribou Ellen brought in.

They'd shot it and removed the head, so it wouldn't be obvious that someone else killed the beast. From what Tomas said, though, it wasn't the first time they discovered pellets in their meat, and that's been more common lately. Had Ellen been working with Abby's parents for a while? If so, wouldn't someone have realized the pellet-shot meat all came from her?

I might get more answers by tracking the source of the stew meat, confirming it came from that caribou. But when I ask if I can personally thank the cooks for the meal, Nancy shuts me down. Oh, she's polite about it, saying she'll pass on my appreciation, but I know when I'm being blocked. She doesn't want me speaking to them. Just like she didn't want me having that pellet. I get the latter, though—I surreptitiously scoop it up while the children bring Storm to show their mother.

We wait outside as the children say their goodbyes to the dog. While they do that, I pull the pellet from my pocket for a discreet closer look.

It's a buckshot pellet—the same kind that killed Ellen.

# THIRTY-TWO

Tomas takes us to a place where we can camp for the night. As expected, there's no invitation to stay in the settlement, but we wouldn't have accepted one anyway. We do take the food they offer, along with Tomas's help locating a well-situated campsite.

The site has obviously been used before and recently, with only the lightest layer of snow over a campfire circle, log seats, and a spot cleared for tents. Tomas says it's for the teens and unmarried adults who need an escape from the close quarters of the longhouses.

As I watch Tomas leave, Dalton says, "You want to go after him," before I can ask.

"Something's up," I say, "and it's not just that shotgun pellet. I think Tomas had an affair with Ellen."

Dalton's brows shoot up. Then his face falls with, "The bracelet. Fuck." He mutters a few more curses, and I understand his disappointment. Nancy and Tomas seem like a deeply committed, loving couple, and no one wants to think a guy who has that at home will betray his wife. But I suspected it from the moment his eyes lit on that bracelet, the flash of grief as he realized who'd died. Asking us not to mention the bracelet cemented my suspicions—this isn't a polyamorous relationship, where Nancy knows what he's doing and approves.

"I'd just like to follow him," I say. "See if he takes a moment to find his game face before he heads back to his wife. You and Storm can come along, but I'd appreciate it if you hang back."

He nods, and we set out. I leave the snowshoes. The forest here is dense enough that I can jog through the light snow.

Soon I see Tomas trudging along ahead. I slow to keep out of sight and follow him for about a hundred feet. After a glance, he makes a left off the trodden path. I slip after him, tracking his jacket in the fast-falling twilight. Finally, he comes to a clearing, where he sits on a fallen tree.

Tomas pulls the bracelet from his pocket and runs his fingers over the leather. Then he clears the snow, digs a shallow hole, and lays the bracelet in it. His hand touches the discarded dirt, ready to refill the hole. After a pause he takes the bracelet out and runs his thumb over it. His head drops and his shoulders shake, racked with silent sobs.

I glance over my shoulder but see no sign of Dalton and Storm. They're there—just giving me room. I look at Tomas again. As a person, I want to leave him to his grief. As a detective, I cannot. I have a murdered woman, and now I'm looking at her secret lover . . . whose wife tried to hide a shotgun pellet that may have come from the murder weapon.

I step from the trees and say, "I'm going to need that bracelet back."

Tomas jumps. I have my gun lowered, but his gaze still goes to it and his eyes widen.

"We're alone in the forest," I say. "I'm not about to demand murder evidence without a gun in my hand." I put my hand out. "How about you give me that instead of burying it?"

"Burying?" Another widening of the eyes. Then he winces.

"Burying the evidence. No, that wasn't what I was doing. It's just . . ."

"Maybe not evidence of a crime, but evidence of a secret. A lover's gift."

He nods, his gaze still down, shoulders hunched as he sits with the bracelet in his hand. "I wanted to bury it. Pretend it never happened. But that isn't fair. It isn't right. This was . . ." His hand closes around it. "Important."

"So what were you going to do with it?"

He exhales. "I don't know. I should talk to Nancy. That's the right thing to do, and maybe I'm a coward, but I just . . ." He opens his hand again. "I shouldn't pretend it didn't happen. Nancy and I need to discuss *why* it happened. I just . . . I want to protect my family. Down south, I had girlfriends and lovers, and that's all I thought there was, for a guy like me. Then I met Nancy, and she's so much more. A friend, a partner, a lover. And now . . ." He takes a deep breath. "I just don't want Nancy to think I blame her."

"Blame your wife for you screwing around? I should hope not."

He looks up in genuine confusion. "Screwing . . . ?" A short laugh. "Of course that's what you thought. That's how these things normally go, isn't it? I wasn't having an affair with Ellen."

"But you wanted to," I say. "You gave her that."

He shakes his head. "I'm not the one who gave it to her."

There's a moment where I don't understand. As soon as I do, I feel stupid. I also feel very close-minded. My brain drew what seemed like the obvious conclusion, because it's the one that fit the norms I was raised with, and even if I'm long past that, my mind still follows that long-carved path.

I remember Tomas's pain on seeing the bracelet. I remember how he'd hesitated, coming into the tent with Nancy, how he'd hung back and made sure of his welcome before comforting her.

It was behavior consistent with a man who'd cheated on his wife. It wasn't, however, what I'd expect from a man who'd *just* discovered his wife had been cheating on him.

"You knew," I say. "About Nancy and Ellen."

He forces a wry smile. "I might have barely gotten my high school diploma, but I can figure some things out just fine. I knew they were more than friends. I just . . ." He takes a deep breath. "I thought it was a fling. That bracelet means it was more. Nancy loved her and . . . I didn't expect that."

"Finding out your wife was having a fling with a woman must have come as a shock."

That twist of a smile again. "Such a shock that I went crazy and shot Ellen? The redneck trucker so horrified by the thought that his wife prefers women that he destroys the evidence? No. I knew what Nancy was when I married her and . . ."

His face screws up in pain as he rubs his hands over it. "Growing up, my friends called gay people fags and homos. Did I stop them? Hell, no. I chimed in, because that's what we were taught—that homosexuality was wrong. When I was twenty, a bunch of us were at a bar, and my friends went after a gay guy. We beat the shit out of him, just because we were drunk and spoiling for a fight and he seemed a perfectly fine target. After I sobered up, I realized what I'd done, and I was sick. I didn't exactly start joining gay-pride parades, though. I just stopped caring about other people's sexual orientation. Then along came Nancy, and I still didn't care, but in the wrong way, you know?"

"You married her knowing she preferred women."

He nods. "That's not acceptable here. We might be all about nature and kindness and love thy neighbor, but we must procreate, and for Nancy to say 'Sure, I'll have babies, but I'd rather be married to a woman' was not an acceptable work-around. Her parents caught her with a settler girl, and they offered her in marriage to this other guy. Nancy said she'd rather marry me. I was . . ."

He flails his hand. "I was a twenty-five-year-old man who figured he wasn't ever getting a wife because he wasn't born here. Then this eighteen-year-old girl is in trouble, and she wants to marry me, and I like her, and I know this other guy's a jerk, so I say sure. Look at me. A damn hero stepping up like that. A hero, though, would have taken her out of here. Taken her back to Rockton and let her go down south to be with someone she wanted."

The tears start again, and he looks away, bracelet still in his hands. I remember their obvious love and affection for one another, and I know they've made the best of a difficult situation. Nancy just needed more, and she'd tried to get it without hurting her husband. I don't see wrongdoing on either side. I see tragedy. The question I must ask, though, is whether one tragedy led to another. Led to murder.

I don't question Tomas further. There's no point. He knows he's a suspect. He may even realize Nancy is, and something tells me he'll protect her even more than he'll protect himself.

I tell Dalton about Nancy and Ellen. He says, "Fuck, that's a mess all around."

He's right. Everyone loses here. And for what? As Tomas said, marrying a woman wouldn't have stopped Nancy from procreating, if that was so important to the settlement. They never gave her that option, though, which means that, like most of those objections, the justifications are just excuses to backfill a decision rising from ignorance rather than rational thought.

However "enlightened" the Second Settlement is, they'd

still brought their prejudices with them, because those who made this law had grown up in the same world as Tomas, where it was fine to insult and beat homosexuals because they needed to be "scared" onto the right track.

The settlement elders had given Nancy an ultimatum, and she made the best of it, choosing her own husband. Tomas knew he wasn't her actual "choice," but he went along with it, driven by those old prejudices, too, the ones that doubtless whispered that if he was a good enough husband, Nancy wouldn't miss anything. Only she did. Ellen comes along, they become friends, and then more than friends . . . and Ellen winds up dead.

Tomas might have said he understood—maybe *wanted* to understand—but when he first found out, had he seen red, grabbed his forbidden shotgun, and hunted down his rival? Or did Nancy do it in a lover's quarrel? Perhaps she expected to go south with Ellen in the spring, and Ellen told her no. Or Nancy didn't *want* to go south, so Ellen threatened to tell Tomas about them.

Where does Abby fit into this? Nowhere, I realize. Nor does she need to. Ellen was helping Abby's parents. She might have been looking after the baby when she'd been shot, and with Abby hidden under Ellen's coat, her killer never realized they'd almost claimed a second life. Solving Ellen's murder may not find Abby's parents, but it is still justice for one victim I found in the snow.

The big clue here is the shotgun. I suspect that someone in the Second Settlement is cheating on the "no firearms" rule. They've gotten hold of a shotgun and been shooting their prey and then jabbing in an arrow making it look as if the beast was brought down with a bow.

Does the entire settlement know someone's breaking the law? Are they turning a blind eye because it's winter and meat equals survival?

Nancy knows what's going on, though. I'm certain of that. She knows who has a shotgun, and that's why she tucked away the pellet.

Is it Tomas's shotgun, and she's covering for him? Or has she only figured out that *someone* in the village is using a gun, and she's protecting whoever it is?

I need to find out who has that gun.

# THIRTY-THREE

Dalton and I are talking around the fire when we hear running footfalls. We shine our flashlight and a voice huffs, "It's Tomas," sounding out of breath, before he appears. He bursts in and stops, panting, "Nancy's gone. I got back to the village, and went to speak to her. When I couldn't find her, I thought she was avoiding me. Miles said she'd told the kids to stay with the other women, that she needed to find Lane."

"Lane?" I say, and it takes a moment for me to remember that's his nephew. "Where is he?"

"Hunting. Lane . . . struggles with village life. His mother died when he was a boy, his father passed five years ago, and he lost his best friend the summer before last. Lane's had a rough go of it lately. He spends most of his time hunting. Nancy and I worry about him, but the elders tell us not to interfere. He's the best hunter we have."

"Because he's not using a fucking bow," Dalton mutters.

"What?" Tomas says, sounding genuinely surprised.

"Someone has been hunting with a shotgun," I say, "while pretending to use a bow. That's why you've found so many pellets in the meat. Nancy figured out it was Lane, and now that Ellen has been killed with a firearm . . ."

Tomas's eyes widen. "You think Nancy's gone after Lane. I thought . . ." He swallows. "I thought that was just an excuse to get away, that she was distraught over Ellen. Lane would never hurt Nancy, but we still need to find her. It hasn't snowed in three days, and there are too many prints for me to track. You'd mentioned your dog can do that."

"She can," I say. "But she'll need—"

He's already pulling a shirt from his pack. He manages an anxious smile. "I used to watch a lot of cop shows."

"All right then. Let's go."

Storm picks up the trail easily. According to Tomas, Nancy rarely leaves the settlement in winter. The rest of the year, she loves to walk and gather berries and nuts and greens, but in winter, she hunkers down with her needlework. It's been days since she's been beyond the perimeter, so her trail is easily followed.

It's only 10 P.M., but it's been dark for hours. All around us, the forest slumbers, and every step we take seems to echo. It also means that every noise Nancy or Lane makes will do the same, and we've been out less than twenty minutes before we hear their voices on the night breeze.

"You made a mistake," Nancy is saying, her voice low and urgent. "I understand that. This is why we don't use guns, Lane, and when we do, we make mistakes even more easily because we're unaccustomed to handling them."

"I *still* don't know what you're talking about," Lane replies.

"The gun. The one you got in a trade from those . . . those people. You've been using it to hunt. I told you that you needed to be more careful. If you wanted to do that, then you couldn't hunt on our territory, where someone could get hurt."

"And I told you I don't have a gun."

"I found pellets in the hares you brought us last week. I showed them to you."

"And I said they weren't mine. It's like the elders say— sometimes they get into our game from other hunters."

Nancy's voice rises in frustration. "I'm trying to help you, Lane. You tell me you don't have a gun? All right. Then take that gun that I'm clearly imagining and get rid of it, please. Hide it somewhere."

"I don't have—"

"Stop, Lane. Just listen to me and protect yourself. This woman from Rockton, her entire *job* is finding people who kill others. Your uncle told me all about it. She's trained to find murderers by studying blood and bullets and dead bodies. If your gun killed Ellen, she won't understand that it was a hunting accident. She'll find the gun and know it's the one that killed Ellen. Then she'll read your fingerprints on it. But if there's no gun, you're safe."

"I don't have a gun."

"Then who does?" I say as I step into the clearing, gun in hand. "Besides me."

Nancy staggers back, Tomas rushing in to catch her. His arms go around her, and he tugs her out of the way. Storm growls beside me. Through the woods, I see Dalton soundlessly slipping behind Lane.

"If this was a hunting accident, then I *will* understand that," I say. "Like your aunt said, you lack experience with firearms. But, like she also said, I can indeed connect your shotgun to you and to the pellet that killed Ellen. There's no point in arguing it wasn't you. Just explain what happened. If you made a mistake, then it was only a tragic accident."

It wasn't. I'm certain of that. I might not be a forensics expert, but I know Ellen died at night. The only thing Lane had been hunting at that time was Ellen herself. Step one, though, is getting a confession to the killing.

"I don't have a gun," he says.

"Then who does? Has someone you know been giving you their game? Trading it?"

This makes no sense, but I'm giving him an out here. Dalton's behind Lane, still tucked into the dark forest, his gun drawn. I have mine out, too. Lane's face says he's two seconds from bolting, and I need to give him an explanation that will allow him to relax. Then I can get the truth.

Still, he shakes his head and says, "I don't know what you're talking about."

Nancy breaks from Tomas's arms and steps toward her nephew.

"Lane, please," she says. "I know you're scared—"

"I'm not scared," he says, jaw setting. "I don't like being accused of things I didn't do."

"Nobody is accusing you," I say. "We just want to know what happened. Give us that, and this will be over."

"Listen to her," Nancy says, taking another step toward him.

"Nancy?" I say. "Move back, please."

She shakes her head, her gaze still on her nephew. "I know you'd never hurt me, Lane. You are a son to me, and I trust you completely."

I don't like her tone or her words. They're too much, her gaze fixed on him, her voice low and soothing, and it's exactly what I've done with dangerous suspects.

*I know you don't want to hurt me. You don't want to hurt anyone. You're not that kind of person.*

Words I'd said when I knew my suspect *was* that kind of person, but I was trying to defuse the situation, while my colleagues kept their guns trained on the suspect.

Half the time, the suspect called me on my bullshit. Yet I continued doing it for those where my words did nudge something deep in them, did convince them to surrender.

That is what Nancy is doing here. Except she's not a trained officer. And the fact that she's doing it tells me Lane *isn't* a sweet, harmless young man. I sneak a glance at Tomas. His face is taut, gaze fixed on his wife as he rocks forward, torn between pulling her back and not wanting to set his nephew off. His gaze cuts my way, communicating exactly what I expect—a warning and a plea.

"Nancy?" I say. "I know you're trying to help, and I know Lane would never hurt you, but I have a gun, and my dog is trained to attack. Any wrong move, however unintentional, could get both of you hurt. Just step back, and let us handle this. Lane isn't armed. He's not going to hurt himself. He's listening to us. I just need you to—"

Lane lunges, and there's nothing I can do about it except bark at him to get back, get the hell away from Nancy. He grabs Nancy and yanks her to him, and Tomas lunges toward them, but Lane already has his arm around Nancy's neck, a hunting knife in his hand.

"Why?!" Lane screams at his uncle, spittle flying.

Tomas falls back with the force of that scream, the venom in it. Even Dalton startles. Storm growls, hackles rising.

"Why do you care?" Lane screams at Tomas.

"Do you mean why do I care about you?" Tomas says. "You're my nephew, my brother's child, you're a son—"

"I mean her." Lane shakes Nancy. "Why do you care what I do to her? You knew what she was doing."

"I . . ." Tomas swallows, and when he says, "I'm not sure what you mean," it's obviously a lie.

"That wild woman. Your wife was . . . was . . ." He can't finish, his face choked with rage. "She betrayed you with a *woman*."

Nancy's gaze shunts to her husband, but Tomas straightens, voice calm as he says, "That would be between my wife and myself, Lane. Yes, I knew, and I've done nothing about it, which means it is none of your concern."

"She betrayed you."

"I don't see it like that."

Lane snarls, "My father always said you were a fool. He told me about her." He shakes Nancy again. "How you married her even after she was found with another girl. You were a fool then, and you're a fool now, but you're still my uncle. You were good to me. Better than my father ever was. You were good to her, too, and we don't deserve it, but at least I appreciate it. I care about you. I won't stand by and watch you be *humiliated* by your wife."

Tomas goes still, drawing in ragged breaths. "Lane, let her go. Please. If you really do care about me, you will let her go. I love you. I'll help you, no matter what you might have done."

"What I *might* have done?" Lane's face contorts in a sneer. "You know what I did. I did what you couldn't."

"Lane?" I say. "Stop right there. Whatever you are about to say, consider it before you do. Let Nancy go, and we can talk."

I'm not giving him a free pass. Once he speaks those words, though, he tumbles over a precipice. Admit to one murder, and it'll seem easy to commit a second.

"I don't want to stop," Lane says. "Why should I? I'm not ashamed of what I did. I—"

"Lane?" I say. "That's enough. Let Nancy go—"

"Yes, I killed that woman. Shot her and left her to die. She deserved it, and so does this filthy excuse of a—"

Dalton grabs Lane's knife arm. He'd been sneaking up from behind, Lane so intent on his confession that he never realized Dalton was with us. Now Dalton yanks Lane's arm back, the knife dropping. I run for the weapon. Tomas runs for Nancy and pulls her from the scuffle.

Dalton wrestles with Lane. I can't do more than stand back, my gun aimed. I could threaten to shoot Lane, but he's in such a frenzy, I doubt he'd hear. I could hardly follow through either, with Dalton lost in that blur of blows.

Dalton goes down, his knee buckling under a savage kick. Lane wheels and runs, and I lunge after him, but I'm too slow—my bad leg will never let me keep up with a fit young man. I see Storm. Lane is running across the clearing, past where Storm's huge black form blends into the night. Her gaze swings on me, a question in it.

I instinctively raise my hand for her to hold her stay. Then I remember my thoughts from earlier. Storm is a working dog, and I need to use her.

"Go!" I say, pairing the command with a wave that releases her.

She's off like a shot. She isn't built for speed, though, and she has to give chase, the two of us running after Lane, oblivious to whatever is happening behind us. Storm closes her gap, as I fall behind, my bobbing flashlight beam allowing me only glimpses of them ahead.

Storm catches up, and she's right behind him, and I think she'll have no idea what to do next. Which proves, I suppose, that I really am a fretful parent, worrying about what I haven't prepared my "child" for. My "child" is a dog. A predator. No one needed to show her what to do when Cherise posed a threat to me. And no one needs to tell her what to do when she catches up to Lane. One powerful lunge, and she's on him, knocking him facedown in the snow.

It's the next part that confuses her, as it did with Cherise. She's been taught not to hurt people. Even in play, she can never snap or snarl or growl, even grab an arm with the intention of clamping down. She's *too* well trained here, those teachings overcoming instinct. She takes Lane down and then just stands on him, and looks back at me, but I'm fifty feet away. Lane flips over, shoving at her even as I shout a warning.

Lane scrambles up, and Storm knocks him down again. He slams a fist into her chest, and a snarl of rage behind us tells me Dalton is coming. Yet he's too far back, and so am I, and Storm's trying to figure out what to do, butting at Lane while he hits her.

I have to clamp my jaw shut not to call her back. I'm almost there. Lane's unarmed and—

A flash of silver.

He has a knife.

"Storm!" I scream, which is not a command, not a goddamn command at all. "Come! Storm, come!"

The knife slashes. Blood sprays onto snow, and I scream again. Then something bursts from the forest. A blur of gray. I'm only ten feet away, close enough to see what it is. The wolf.

He grabs Lane's arm. His teeth clamp down, but the young man's wearing a thick parka, and the wolf only hangs there. He bites hard enough to startle Lane into dropping the knife, though. Lane realizes there's a hundred-pound wolf hanging off his shoulder, and he screams, kicking and punching.

I'm there. Finally there. I ram the flashlight into my pocket, holster my gun, and grab Storm's collar to drag her back. I ignore Lane. I know he's my target, but there's blood in the snow, and it belongs to my dog, and that's what matters. The wolf can take Lane for all I care.

Lane and the wolf fight, battling with growls and grunts and gasps of pain. Storm whines, her body trembling as I run my hands along it. She flinches when I find the spot where the knife went in, but she doesn't stop straining to see the fight, nudging me out of the way when I block her view.

The blade sliced her left shoulder. Her fur is wet and sticky with blood, and I tug out the flashlight for a look. It's a slice, not a stab, and as I palpate the wound, she huffs in annoyance more than pain, Mom fussing over a scraped knee when her child just wants to run back onto the playground. That reassures me even before I get a good look at what is indeed a flesh wound, a shallow slice maybe two inches long. It'll need stitches, and I'm sure as hell not letting her jump into the fight, but she's all right.

I see Dalton then. He's circling Lane and the wolf, looking for an opening. His knee gives a little when he feints too fast, telling me Lane really did give it a solid kick. The wolf and Lane are squaring off, circling each other, Dalton outside looking for a way in.

Looking for a way to get between Lane and the wolf.

Oh, hell, no.

I pull my gun. "Lane! Get on the fucking ground, and we'll take care of the wolf."

Lane's gaze darts my way.

"You heard me!" I bark. "On the ground now."

He spins and kicks at Dalton, aiming for his wounded knee, and rage fills me, the kind of rage that let me shoot Blaine Saratori, the kind that had me put a bullet through Val's head. But I learn. Each time, I learn because I can never pull this trigger and *not* question afterward. With Blaine, I have every reason to question. I made a mistake. With Val, I did not, but I still suffer for it, wonder if there'd been a way to protect Dalton without killing her.

This time, there is no question. Dalton isn't in lethal danger—Lane is just really, really pissing me off, trying to literally throw Dalton to the wolves.

So I shoot, but it's aimed over them. The gunfire startles Lane, and it warns Dalton, and between the two, Lane's kick is aborted as Dalton dodges. Lane comes out running as he tears into the forest. The wolf starts to go after him, and my idiot lover leaps between them.

"No!" Dalton shouts, startling the wolf, which skids to a halt.

Dalton's bigger than Lane, and he's making himself bigger still, puffed up, gun out, shouting at the wolf. Personally, I'd let the damned beast go after the bastard, but this is why, no matter which roles we play best, the "good cop" is the guy in front of me.

The canine stands his ground but shows no sign of attacking. Storm is fine, and her attacker is gone, and the wolf himself seems all right. He approaches Storm, stiff-legged, and we let them do the sniff-greeting again. Of course, he's hoping for a reward from his rescued damsel, but this time, as soon as he sniffs behind her, she snarls and spins away, and after one more halfhearted try, he lopes into the forest.

"Sorry!" I say. "No reward sex for you." I turn to Dalton. "And definitely none for you. What the hell was that? Coming between a confessed killer and a wolf?"

He pauses and then says, "I was worried about the wolf."

"Right answer." I lift up to peck his cheek. "Even if it's utter bullshit, and you just saw a dangerous situation and decided to play hero by leaping into the middle of it."

"I didn't actually leap in. I was looking for a way to break it up."

"Refereeing a wolf fight?" I shake my head. "I don't think the wolf would have listened. Hell, I don't think either of them would have." I look in the direction Lane went. "So I guess we're stuck tracking him."

"Is Storm okay?"

He bends to pet the dog, and I hand him the flashlight and point out the damage.

"I should stitch her," I say, "but we have surgical strips in our packs at camp. That'll do. We just need some way to mark this spot so we can pick up Lane's trail after."

Dalton digs into his pocket, and I'm about to point out that tying a marker to a tree won't work at night. Instead he pulls out a package of surgical strips.

"The man comes prepared," I say as I take them.

"Do I get reward sex for *that*?"

"You just might. Now hold her steady while I clean the wound and plaster it shut."

# THIRTY-FOUR

Once Storm's fine, we track Lane. It's easy at first. He doesn't have a flashlight or a lantern. In winter, under a three-quarter moon, the reflection off the snow is enough. However, that leads to a quandary for Lane. More open land means better light but deeper snow. His choices are clear sight or easy movement. He tries both, racing through thicker woods, and probably tripping over an obstacle or two until he veers to less dense forest, and then staggers through knee-deep snow. Eventually he finds a happy medium. He's still walking through snow, though, meaning we barely need Storm to track him.

At some point, he must realize that and he heads for the foothills. There he finds windswept rock to run across, and Storm earns her keep then. Ultimately, though, we lose him. Storm is wounded, and she's been up since her wolf suitor came to call yesterday morning. She isn't the only one flagging either. When Lane plays one too many tricks on us, we run out of the patience needed to keep Storm on target. We also run out of the will to push her when she's so obviously exhausted.

Lane has confessed to killing Ellen. He's a threat to Nancy, but . . . While I won't say that's the Second Settlement's problem, I have no jurisdiction here. The dead woman was their friend. The killer is their resident. I have no right to keep investigating. I will, if they ask for help, but I have a baby momma to find, and solving this crime doesn't get me any closer to resolving that one.

When Dalton came after me, he'd told Tomas to take Nancy home. That's where we go, and it's seven in the morning by the time we get there. It'd have been longer if we backtracked, but I'm blessed to be with a guy who doesn't need to follow his own footprints to find his way in the forest.

Tomas and Nancy haven't told the elders anything. They're waiting to talk to us, and I fear that means they want us to cover for Lane. They don't. He didn't kill Ellen in self-defense. He has no excuse and no remorse, and he followed up one cold-blooded murder by attempting another, this time against the woman who raised him.

I can blame a twisted sense of loyalty to his uncle or the homophobic teachings of his settlement, but neither is an excuse for murder. Whatever his father and the settlement taught him, Tomas and Nancy raised him in a loving and open-minded home.

We speak to the elders with Tomas and Nancy. Lane will face their judgment. They'll wait for him to return, protecting Nancy and the children, and if Lane doesn't come back, then yes, they would appreciate our help finding him.

Afterward, Tomas and Nancy ask us to join them for breakfast before we leave. The children feed Storm, who is doing an excellent impression of a fur rug, sprawled on the snow, refusing to move. Apparently, she's getting breakfast in bed, and I have no doubt she'll rouse enough to eat it. I wouldn't mind an hour of sleep myself before the long walk home, but I can also rouse myself to eat, and I know Tomas and Nancy want to talk to us.

We're barely settled into the small alone-hut when Tomas says, "I would like to ask for transportation down south. For my family."

"What?" Nancy says, startling enough that she nearly drops her breakfast bowl.

Tomas doesn't look at her. "We'll go to Whitehorse. I should still have money in an old account. It'll be enough to get us started. I'll set up Nancy and the kids someplace outside the city, where they'll be more comfortable, and I'll rent an apartment and find work in Whitehorse."

"Did I miss our discussion on this?" Nancy says. "Because I'm quite certain I'd have remembered it."

Tomas folds his hands in his lap. "I should have done this twelve years ago. Taken you away instead of marrying you and tying you down with—"

"With our *children*?" Her voice rises. "If I have ever—ever—given the impression that I consider our children anything but blessings—"

"I don't mean it like that," he says quickly. "I just . . . I made a mistake, and I want to fix it now." He looks at her. "I want to set you free."

"Set me free? Or be rid of me?"

Dalton says, "Maybe Casey and I should wait out—"

Nancy doesn't seem to hear him. "I made a mistake. Not a mistake in what happened with Ellen. Maybe I should say that was wrong, but it was something I needed. The mistake was not telling you that I needed it and working out a solution together. If you want to leave, then I understand, but as for setting me free?" She meets his gaze. "You never held me captive. I could have left anytime I wanted. I didn't want to."

I slide toward the exit, Dalton following, but Nancy stops us.

"Yes, we apologize for making you bear witness to a very personal conversation," she says, "but I have a feeling if you aren't here, this won't be resolved. You are our passage south. We need to decide this before you go."

That isn't true. We'll be back. But I understand what she's saying. They've avoided this conversation for over a decade, and if we're awaiting an answer, they can't push it aside again.

"Do you want this?" Nancy asks Tomas. "If you do, then yes, we'll go south and start over in separate lives sharing our children. Because that last part is the most important. I'd never give them up, and I'd never ask you to. They are ours, whether we are together or not. But if you're offering me a way out of this marriage, the answer is no. I don't want that. If you're saying I can stay on the condition this never happens again . . ."

She meets his gaze. "I cannot promise you that. I have no idea if it will or won't, and that is a very long conversation we need to have if we want to make this work. But I would *like* to make it work. You are my partner. You are my friend. You are my lover. Nothing has changed for me. With Ellen, I was answering a question about myself that I should have answered twelve years ago. And I don't know if I did. I found something I needed, but it didn't change what I already have, and I'm not sure what to make of that. I need time to work it through, if you can give me that."

Tomas nods. That's all he does. Wordlessly nods, his eyes glistening.

"You want me to stay?" she says.

Another nod, and a quiet, "Please."

"Then the question is 'do *we* stay.' And the answer . . ." She exhales. "The answer is no. Not here. Not after all this. It will be too hard for the children, and really, that's just the excuse I think we needed to go. We'll remain for the winter and then we'll decide our next step."

And now, in the midst of tragedy, I need to ask them a question unrelated to any of this. I kick myself for not doing it earlier, but it isn't as if I'd forgotten the reason we were here: to find Abby's parents.

Earlier, it'd been clear that Nancy didn't realize Ellen had been trading goods to help Abby's mother, so I didn't see a lead there. Also, I'd suspected one of them might have murdered Ellen, so I hadn't been about to expose Abby's existence. Now, though, with Ellen's death unrelated to Abby, there's no reason not to ask.

I ask with extreme care, hoping I won't seem too callous.

*Sorry your nephew murdered your friend and lover, but while I'm here, maybe you could help with this other case?*

It helps, of course, that the "other case" is a lost baby. It's hard to begrudge help with that. They are both horrified and relieved. Horrified that Lane almost accidentally killed an infant . . . and relieved that the child is safely in Rockton.

"We had no idea," Nancy says. "It makes sense, now that you've told us. Yes, she'd have wanted those scraps for diapers and the balm for breastfeeding. There were other items, too, and they all fit. She was helping a woman who'd borne a winter baby."

"As she would," Tomas says softly.

Nancy's eyes glitter with tears. "Yes, she would. Absolutely. I only wish she'd told us, if only so we could help you get that baby back to her mother. She must be going mad with worry. When we find Lane, he may be able to tell us what Ellen was doing or where she was coming from when he . . . when he . . ."

She breaks off, her voice catching. Tomas reaches for her, hesitating a little, but she falls into his arms. We slip out after that, followed by Tomas's promise that they'll help us in any way they can. In return, we promise that we'll be back in a week or so, to see whether they need help finding Lane. Then we're gone.

We rest back at our campsite. We must, considering how far we need to walk. A four-hour nap before we break camp and walk until the sun starts to drop. I want to push on after that, but Dalton says no. We're less than halfway home, with no chance of making it back without more sleep. Better to find a spot and get our shelter up before it's fully dark.

We're in bed by six, asleep 1.5 seconds later. As exhausted as we are, though, we don't need twelve hours of sleep, so we're on our way again by three in the morning, our flashlights leading us through the darkness.

It's nearly noon when we reach Rockton, and I can say with absolute certainty that these were the most physically strenuous three days of my entire life. Dalton's promise of an entire batch of fresh-baked cookies may be the only thing that gets me through the last ten kilometers. I'm holding him to that, too, and washing them down with multiple mugs of spiked coffee, followed by an afternoon nap that may last until morning.

I reach the town perimeter and topple face-first into the snow. Or I try to, but my feet tangle in the snowshoes and Dalton grabs me before I snap my ankle with my drama-queen gesture. He lifts me over his arms, and I struggle to get out, saying, "I'm fine. Just being a brat."

"Too late. I'm carrying you."

I start to settle in. Then he flips me over his shoulder, firefighter style, which is a whole lot less flattering.

"No, no, no," I say, renewing my struggles. "Just let me—"

"Too late."

"You can't—"

"—embarrass you by carrying you over my shoulder through town? Yep, I believe I can."

Storm starts dancing around us, barking, finding her second

wind. I grab the back of Dalton's parka and yank, and I'm just goofing around, but it's hard enough to make him stagger, and apparently Storm chooses that moment to cut in front of him, and we all go down in a heap of curses and yelps and giggles.

As we untangle ourselves, a voice says, "First, you disappear for three days. Now you are napping at noon. I understand the holidays are coming, but as a taxpayer, I object."

I twist to see Mathias standing there. "Since when do you pay taxes?"

"I treat each and every person in this community with marginal respect. It is very taxing."

We untangle, and Dalton and Storm rise as I snap off my snowshoes. "What are you doing out and about?"

"There is caroling. It began at ten in the morning. After two hours, my choices were to walk in the forest or begin a quiet but relentless slaughter of the offenders. Knowing the latter would force you to work through the holidays, I chose the former. It is my gift to you."

"Thanks."

We start for the town.

Mathias falls in beside me. "Also, speaking of relentless, we must discuss this constant flow of visitors you have unleashed on our peaceful village, Casey."

"Peaceful?" Dalton says. "Where have you been living?"

"In a town where people do not wander in from the forest and make themselves at home. Your detective is the Pied Piper of the Yukon, leading people to our town with her charming manner and sunny disposition."

I look at Dalton. "You have another detective?"

"Compared to me, you *are* pretty damned charming. Not sure about sunny, but people definitely find you less intimidating than me, which just means they don't know you very well."

Dalton turns to Mathias. "Yeah, we've been doing more outreach since Casey's been here. Building relationships with the community really wasn't my strength, apparently. If you're talking about Tyrone—"

"I'd rather not really. Mr. Cypher has chosen his alias well. I do not know what to make of him, and I have decided he is a puzzle I do not care to solve. The problem is that the procession of strays does not end. I discovered only today that you had a hostile in town. A live hostile, which you promised me for study, and you whisked her in and out without a word to me."

"You requested a hostile," I say. "I chose to deny that request."

"Instead, you give me other strays. A wolf and a feral boy."

"First, you *asked* for Raoul. Plenty of people wanted him, and you got him, and therefore you owed me a favor, which you repaid by taking Sebastian, who is a resident, not a stray. Also not feral."

"He spent half his life being raised by narcissists who treated him as a fashion accessory. Then he spent the other half imprisoned for their murders. He may have learned very pretty manners, but Sebastian is as feral as that half-breed dog, and I have spent six months sleeping with one eye open, wondering which will kill me first."

I could point out that Sebastian doesn't live with Mathias, but instead I shrug as we enter town. "Fine. Give me the dog. Our deputy will be thrilled to have—"

"It is too late. Raoul is accustomed to me."

"Then I'll take Sebastian back and—"

"He is accustomed to me as well. And it is my duty to monitor him, for the sake of the town. No one else is equipped or trained for such a task."

"You're just bitching for the sake of bitching, aren't you?"

"I do not *bitch*. I simply point out that you need to stem

this flow of strays. You have barely removed one when another takes her place."

I stop and look at him. "What?"

"You have a visitor. She is in the town square. William attempted to show her the hospitality of the police station, but she is another of your wild things and refuses to go indoors. She is with Raoul and Sebastian. Raoul is guarding her. Sebastian is . . ." He purses his lips. "I am not certain what he is doing. Perhaps drinking in the rare beauty of this wilderness flower. Perhaps considering the myriad ways he could kill her with maximum efficiency, should she prove a threat. He may be doing both simultaneously. It is Sebastian."

I pick up my pace, breaking into a jog as I shout back, "Next time, Mathias? Cut the preamble and get to the damned point."

"That would be no fun at all," he calls after me.

# THIRTY-FIVE

When Mathias says we've attracted another woman from the woods, hinting she's young and attractive, my first thought is Cherise. Yet when I draw close, I spot a small dark-haired figure, one who is younger and significantly more welcome than Cherise. It's Edwin's granddaughter, Felicity.

Sebastian is neither gaping at her nor plotting her demise. He's playing host, pulling out his charm and his manners and his high-society upbringing, telling Felicity a story complete with blazing smiles and dramatic gestures. There's no flirtation there. Yes, she's his age and pretty, but if he's noticed that, he's tucked it aside, as if it would be rude to see her as anything but a guest in need of hospitality.

As for Felicity . . .

I remember when I was thirteen, and my mother sent me to finishing school. Okay, it wasn't called "finishing school." I'm not sure those exist anymore, and I sure as hell wouldn't have attended. It was billed as weekly classes for teen girls to learn teen-girl stuff, everything from putting on makeup to protecting yourself online.

I might never have been the most feminine girl, but I was not opposed to learning the secret language of stiletto heels and smoky eyeliner. While the class offered that, it was more like a finishing school, with lessons for privileged young ladies to learn to act like privileged young ladies.

I *was* privileged. I took private lessons and flew business class—well, unless there weren't enough seats, and then my parents put April and me in economy, supposedly as a lesson so we'd grow up vowing to get the kind of careers that meant we never needed to fly coach again.

The point is that those girls should have been my people. Except I was a half-Asian tomboy from the suburbs, and they were all white, elegant, and city-bred. I felt like a gawky country girl stumbling into a debutante ball.

That's how Felicity looks sitting beside Sebastian. She follows his story stone-faced, her gaze locked on him in a look of barely concealed panic. Not so much transfixed as held captive, fearing if she moves a single muscle she'll reveal herself as a teenager from a very different planet than the one this self-assured and animated boy clearly inhabits.

When Sebastian sees me, he smiles and stands with "Hey, Casey," and I swear Felicity deflates in relief.

"I was keeping Felicity company while she waited," he says. "Talking her ear off with my boring stories." He flashes a smile her way. "Sorry."

"Yes." Color rises on her cheeks. "I mean, yes, you were keeping me company. No, your stories were not boring." She flails a moment, as if struggling to find the girl I met the other day, the one who'd been equally self-assured in her natural environment. "I came to talk to you, Casey."

"And now you can," Sebastian says. "You're free of my awkward hospitality."

"Yes." Another mortified flush. "I mean, yes, she's here, and yes, you do not need to stay with me any longer. Thank you for keeping me company. It was very kind."

He grins. "My pleasure. I will leave you in Casey's capable hands."

He jogs off, and Felicity watches him go.

"How . . . old is he?" she asks tentatively.

"Nineteen. He's our youngest resident."

"Oh. I am eighteen. Angus is twenty, and that boy seems . . . older, but he didn't look it, so I thought . . . I suppose that is how boys are, down south."

"Not exactly," I say. "Sebastian is a special case, but I'm glad he kept you company."

"He was very entertaining. His stories were funny." She takes a deep breath, throwing off any lingering discomfiture, and turns to me. "I have information you want. I would like to trade for it."

I glance around. Dalton's taken Storm to get her stitched up at the clinic, and he's left me to this.

"All right," I say. "Let's go into the police station—"

"I would prefer to stay outside."

"May we at least leave the town square? Everyone can hear our conversation here."

She nods, and we begin walking.

"You found a baby," she says. "That's why you came to my grandfather. You didn't tell me that. You should have."

"Edwin had already told us where to find the baby's parents."

"He lied."

"So we discovered," I mutter. "The clothing came from the Second Settlement, not the trading family he sent us to."

"Did you speak to the traders?"

I nod.

"And what did you think?"

"You were right. Not the sort of people I care to do business with."

"They *can* trade fairly. The problem is that we only use them when we must, and then they know how badly we need their supplies, so we pay far too much. Grandfather would prefer not to do business with them. He'd rather do business with you."

"Understandable. We'd rather do business with him."

"Good."

She slows to look up at a decorated pine towering over us. I imagine her assessing not the beauty of the object, but the relative wealth that it requires—the expenditure of both time and goods.

"It's the holidays," I say. "Time to celebrate the solstice."

She nods. "We do that as well. We do not string berries in trees, though."

"The birds will appreciate them."

She snorts. "The birds that come for those will not be good eating."

Apparently she thinks our decorated trees are luring dinner. I'm about to say not everything is about food, but fortunately, I do nothing so thoughtless. For settlers, everything *is* about food—or shelter or basic survival.

"People enjoy seeing the birds," I say simply.

"You sound like those from the Second Settlement."

I glance over at her. "I thought you didn't have contact with them."

She shrugs. "That is my grandfather's way. It is their elders' way. It is not our way." She pauses to watch a few residents race by, sliding on the packed snow and laughing like children. She shakes her head. "It is different here."

"They're just on lunch break before their afternoon shift."

"So you met the Second Settlement," she says. "What did you think of *them*?"

"Interesting."

A snort. "That is one way to put it. They have ideas. Odd ideas. They won't trade with you, though. Not the way we will."

"I got that impression."

She nods, satisfied. "My grandfather should have let you go to them. There's nothing to fear. He just worries." She looks at me. "I would like a gun."

"So you've said. But right now we're still busy trying to find this baby's parents."

"That is why I'm here. To trade. It is also why you should have told me about the baby. I know who it belongs to."

"Do you?" I say, keeping my voice calm. "Oddly, your grandfather said the same thing. Those traders also tried to claim her."

"Is it a her?" Something flickers in her eyes, gone before I can chase it. She nods. "You have been fed many lies, but I tell the truth."

"In return for a gun?"

"Yes."

I face her. "Yeah, here's the problem with that. Edwin told us the baby was from these traders, in hopes we'd keep her and avoid contact with the Second Settlement. The traders told us she was theirs, in hopes we'd pay them for her. Now you're telling us you know where she belongs, in hopes of getting a gun. See the pattern? We've spent a damned week tramping through the forest, trying to give a family back their lost baby. This doesn't benefit us at all, and everyone *else* is trying to benefit from our good deed, and I'm getting really pissed off. If you don't actually know who this baby's parents are, then I'd suggest you turn around right now and go back to the First Settlement or you are never going to see a gun from me."

She eyes me, much the way she might eye a wolf in the forest, trying to decide exactly how dangerous it is. "You're frustrated."

"How very astute of you."

Her lips quirk. I won't call it a smile, but it's something. She might be appreciating my directness. Or she might be amused at my show of weakness, allowing my temper to get the better of me.

"No one out here will reward you for your good deeds," she says.

"I'm not looking for—"

"A reward, I know. You want us to help or stay out of your way. Instead, we're making your task unnecessarily difficult."

"Yes."

She eyes me again, head tilting as if considering. Then she says, "It is a test. Not intentionally or overtly, but in the end, you are being tested. Do you see through the lies? How easily are you manipulated? How much can you be used? That's what everyone out here is thinking. How useful can you be to them? And you are thinking the same thing. Can the First Settlement be useful? The Second? The traders? Tyrone? Jacob?"

She lifts a hand against my protest. "Yes, Jacob is Eric's brother, and you are not trying to use him, but it is still a reciprocal relationship. Your goal is not to take advantage but to establish mutually beneficial relationships. Everyone else is doing the same. They're just less concerned about making those relationships fair. Everyone wants the best deal. You would not take advantage of Jacob. You might not even take advantage of me, because I am young. But if you could take advantage of those traders? Of course you would. Everyone wants something. No one wants to be cheated."

She's right, of course. That isn't only life up here; it's life in general. It's just more obvious here, everyone angling for an advantage over the limited resources we share.

"They are testing you," she says. "You're a good person. The question is *how* good, and can it be used against you? You ask whether I'm lying. I'd be a fool to do that, wouldn't I? It would be cheating you on our first trade. Foolish and shortsighted, like a bear trampling an entire berry patch for one meal. Better to cultivate the patch."

"And you're cultivating me."

"You know I am. There's no point in lying. Also, I don't do it. That's my grandfather's way, and it works for him. It does not work for me. If I don't want to tell you the truth, I won't answer. When I say I know where to find this baby's parents, I'm negotiating in good faith. I'll take you to them, and then you owe me a gun."

"You'll hold this child hostage for a gun."

Something flashes behind her eyes. Then her jaw sets, and she says simply, "I would like a gun. I believe finding this baby's parents is important to you, and therefore worth the price I'm asking."

*If I don't want to tell you the truth, I won't answer.*

I remember her expression when I said the baby was a girl. That flicker of emotion.

"You know her parents," I say.

"Did I not say that?" she snaps, annoyed at being more transparent than she intended.

"I will pay you for this information." I say. "Five hundred dollars' worth of our goods or two hundred and fifty of your choice, to be purchased in Dawson."

Her eyes harden. "That means nothing to me."

I wince. Of course. Unlike Cherise, who travels to Dawson, Felicity has never used money. "Right, sorry. Five hundred dollars would buy you five good pairs of boots or five decent parkas or five hundred cans of soup."

She tries to cover her shock, and says nonchalantly, "How many guns?"

I smile. "Nice try, but if the council caught us buying guns for you, they'd kick us out. Later, I can try to negotiate to get you *one,* but I can't promise that now. It's the five hundred in random goods or two-fifty in goods of your choice, same as I offered Cherise."

She blinks. "You offered Cherise so much for finding this baby's parents? That was . . . unwise." She says it carefully, an adult gently admonishing a child too young to know better.

"In retrospect, it probably was. Fortunately, it seems I'll be paying you instead."

"I will take your goods minus the price of a gun, which you will get me before spring or pay me double its value in additional goods."

That's fair, but I pretend to consider it before agreeing.

"The baby's mother is from the First Settlement," she says. "She is—was—a companion of mine. We'd meet up with a couple of the Second settlers around our age. My grandfather doesn't know this, and I would appreciate you not telling him."

"I won't. I'm sure he's seen it with others, though. You're two small communities with a limited number of people your own age. Down south, that'd been like the kids from neighboring small-town schools hanging out together." I smile. "It widens the dating pool."

She frowns, and I'm about to explain when she figures it out, deciphering unfamiliar words from the context.

"You mean our choices for marriage prospects," she says.

"Or just romantic relationships."

A wave of one hand, dismissing the concept. I suppose, to them, dating would be similar to wooing a hundred years ago. There's always an end goal, and that goal is finding a marriage partner.

"I sought out their young settlers for an exchange of ideas," she says. "I see advantage in that where my grandfather does not. We hunted together. We camped together. We grew close."

"You became friends."

A twist of her lips. This is a girl who sees friendship—like romance—as a frivolity for those who can afford to be frivolous, and she cannot.

"You became allies," I say, and she nods, clearly more comfortable with that. "But your friend—your *companion*—found more. She found a marriage partner."

Felicity's face darkens. "That was not supposed to happen. Intermarriage between the communities is forbidden."

I chuckle. "When it comes to romance, nothing tastes as sweet as the forbidden fruit. People have written a thousand stories about it."

"*Romeo and Juliet*," she says, her lip curling. I must look surprised because she gives me just the faintest hint of an eye roll. "We are not savages. The first generation brought their stories, and my grandfather brought books. We all know *Romeo and Juliet*. A ridiculous tale of two foolish dolts."

I have to smile at that. "They were very young."

"I heard the story when I was younger than the characters, and my reaction was no different. Romeo is madly in love with some other girl, sees Juliet, and falls madly in love with *her*. The boy wanted to be madly in love, nothing more."

"I'm not disagreeing."

"Even Sidra said Romeo and Juliet were dolts. And then what does she do? Falls madly in love with a boy from the Second Settlement and runs away with him." Felicity harrumphs. "They might as well have committed suicide. For all I know, she died in childbirth, with no one to help her." Felicity's face stays dark, scowling, but I see the fear in her eyes. Fear and worry and hurt.

"The baby has been well fed," I say. "She'd need her mother alive for that."

She nods, the relief seeping out. Then she snaps, "Then Sidra was lucky. But what about next time? Is she going to continue breeding with him? Without any help? I could have—" Her teeth shut with a click, and she retreats into a deeper scowl. "Dolts."

"You didn't know she was pregnant," I say softly.

"How could I? She left the summer before last, and I warned her that if she went, I wouldn't . . ." Felicity swallows and doesn't finish.

"You said you wouldn't help her, but you didn't really mean that. She took you seriously and stayed away."

"I was angry. I begged her to stay. Not to give him up. I knew better than to ask that. But if she'd given me time, I could have brought Grandfather around to the idea. She didn't even give me time to *ask* him. She staged her own death, like Juliet. Can you believe that? They both did, the fools. They left bloodied clothing, and I was supposed to grieve as if she'd died." Her jaw tightens. "I didn't. That would feel like a lie. So I pretended I didn't believe she'd died, and everyone thinks I just can't handle the truth."

"She put you in a very awkward position."

"Yes, she did. Grandfather listens to me, but she didn't trust me. She thought if she asked, they'd marry her off to Angus. I've known her since we were babies, and she is . . . She was very important to me, and I was not so important to . . ."

A deep breath as she blinks back tears and straightens. "She chose him. She met him, and she chose him, and she forgot me."

It's an old story. Diana accused me of shunning her when I fell for Dalton. Of course, that ignores the fact that she dumped me with every new boyfriend since we were in high school together. Also, the entire reason I'm in Rockton is because she and her ex conspired to convince me I'd been found out for Blaine's murder.

This has, I suspect, been the complaint of friends since time immemorial. A romantic partner shouldn't replace a best friend, but they are competition for that role. In circumstances like mine, your lover is also your friend, yet it's not like simply adding a new friend to the mix, because you want plenty of alone time with this one. That leaves your best friends to the timeworn wail of "you're always with them," devolving into the desperate battle cries of "bros before hos" and "chicks before dicks."

I doubt Sidra forgot Felicity. It just feels that way.

As much as I value my friendships, no one can ever be as close to me as Dalton. We work together, play together, live together, plan our futures together. That doesn't mean I fail to understand Felicity's hurt. I felt it myself every time Diana swanned off with a new lover, forgetting me until a hole in her social calendar needed filling.

I could give Felicity advice. But she won't want it. She needs to work this out for herself. Instead, I ask if she has any idea where to find Sidra and her partner. She doesn't know exactly where they're camping, but she has a rough idea. The region is about a half day's walk from here . . . in the direction of where we found Abby.

"May I see the baby?" she asks.

"Of course."

# THIRTY-SIX

Petra has Abby while Jen naps. We pass Dalton, who strides by with a gesture that I think means he'll catch up with us, but he's moving too fast for me to be sure. I call after him that we'll be at Petra's, and he lifts a hand in acknowledgment without slowing.

When Petra opens the door to Felicity, she does a subtle shift into the young woman's line of sight, as if blocking her from seeing Abby.

"This is Felicity," I say. "She's Edwin's granddaughter. She's a friend of the baby's mom."

Petra nods, but she's still wary as she escorts us in. We find Abby in a wooden cradle that someone has painted with a carousel of wild animals.

"We're gone three days, and you guys have built her a cradle and decorated it."

"She was in a box," Petra says. "A cardboard box."

I lift a fur teddy bear from the floor and sigh, shaking my head. Abby's eyes open, and her head rolls as her lips purse in what threatens to be a wail if I don't pick her up in the next two seconds. I scoop her out of the cradle and hug her, crooning under my breath. She snuggles in and then stops, head rolling again.

"No, Eric isn't here," I say. "You have to make do with me."

"Daddy's little—" Petra begins, and then her gaze shunts to Felicity and she stops herself. This isn't our baby. She has parents, and unless they abandoned her, she's going back to them. Still, Petra's lips tighten as she assesses Felicity again.

I turn to Felicity, who hasn't said a word. I hold out Abby, and she just stands there, looking at her. Then she touches one finger to the baby's cheek.

"Does she look like your friend?" Petra asks, and there's challenge in that, as if she's going to make damned sure we aren't being misled.

"She looks like a baby," Felicity says. "My friend does not."

I smile at that. "True."

"Sidra has skin the color of mine," she says. "Her grandmother was Arab. That's what Grandfather called her. Sidra has dark hair and blue eyes. The boy—Baptiste—is French. He also has dark hair, but lighter skin and brown eyes. I see nothing that says this baby is not theirs, but they will need to confirm that, of course."

I explain the full situation, and Petra only says, "So you don't even know if your friends had a baby?"

"We'll confirm it, like Felicity says," I counter. "Now—"

Two sharp knocks at the door, and I see Dalton through the front window, something in his hands. Petra calls a welcome, and the door clicks open and then smacks into the wall, as if he has his hands full.

"You breaking down my door, Sheriff?" Petra calls as she walks into the front hall. "Ah, you come bearing gifts. You're forgiven. You will have to pay the toll, though."

"Better ask Casey. I promised her a whole batch."

He walks in with an insulated box and a thermos. Abby has her head up again, wobbling toward him.

"Someone hears you," I say. "Trade?"

He takes the baby, and I get the treats. The thermos holds spiked coffee, and the box is stuffed with chocolate chip cookies, warm from the oven.

"Oh my God," I say. "I love you."

"I keep my promises." He hefts Abby, talking to her. While I know it's gas, I swear she smiles up at him. "How about you, kiddo? You want a cookie? Irish coffee? Make you sleep really well tonight and let us get some rest?"

Abby coos at him.

"She has parents," Felicity says.

"Everyone does. I'm hoping that means you can help us get her back to them?"

Felicity hesitates. There's annoyance in her gaze, offended on her friend's behalf at this man who's playing with Abby as if she's his. Not unlike Petra eyeing Felicity, ready to defend my claim on the baby.

I tell Dalton about Sidra and Baptiste as I pass out cookies. Felicity examines hers and then takes a tiny bite, startling at the taste and pulling back as if poisoned.

"What is this?" she says, touching her fingertip to a gooey chocolate chip. "Fruit gone bad?"

"Does it taste bad?" I say.

"Don't say yes," Dalton says. "Or she won't let you finish that cookie. Casey is very protective of her chocolate chips."

"This is chocolate?" Felicity touches it again. "I've heard of it in books." She puts her fingertip in her mouth, tasting it and then nodding. "It's good. I just didn't know what it was." She lifts the cookie. "And this is a cookie?"

"Yep." I take a mug from Petra as she brings them. "This is coffee. Spiked with brandy. Alcohol. Which you are, by Yukon law, one year too young to drink."

"We don't drink it anyway," she says. "It is forbidden."

"Well, you can try it or we can brew you a regular cup."

She considers and then accepts a quarter cup. We sit and make plans for tracking Abby's parents. It's too late to head out today, so we'll start before dawn. Felicity will come with us. She insists before I can offer. She's making sure *her* tip is the one that leads us to Abby's parents and there's no wiggle room to claim otherwise. Or that's what she says. The truth, I suspect, is that she wants the excuse to reunite with her friend.

Stubborn pride. The kind that only hurts yourself, that stops you from having something you really want because God forbid anyone should think you want anything.

I understand that. I understand it all too well.

"You can stay in my old place," I say.

Felicity shakes her head. "I have a tent and blankets. I will camp outside your town."

"Yeah, no," Dalton says. "First, you don't trust us to play fair with your lead, and we don't trust you not to send us on a wild-goose chase like your granddaddy did."

"I would not—"

"Second, I cannot allow anyone to camp outside our town. You are a guest here, but you're also an intruder. You'll sleep where I tell you to sleep."

"She can stay here," Petra says.

Dalton and Petra exchange a look. Petra isn't being hospitable; she wants Felicity under watch. When Dalton's gaze slips my way, I hesitate. Petra is the council's tool. She has killed for them. She has also vowed that her loyalties lie with Rockton itself over the council and even her grandmother.

At what point is a lack of trust simply caution? And at what point does it tip into pride?

*You hurt me. I feel betrayed. I understand that it wasn't about me, but I want to stand my ground. Keep that door shut so you can't hurt me again.*

That's what I feel, and it is exactly what I suspect Felicity does, with Sidra.

"I'll go with you tomorrow, too," Petra says when I finally agree.

"We shouldn't take the baby," Felicity says. "So we won't need you to look after her."

Petra looks at Felicity and bursts out laughing. "Yeah, kid, I'm offering to go along as the babysitter. You just keep thinking that." She turns to me. "I'm guessing you'll take Abby tonight and—"

"Her name is Abby?" Felicity says. "How do you know that?" Her expression says she's guessed the answer, and she'd better be wrong.

"We don't know what Sidra and Baptiste named her," I say. "But we needed something to call her. It doesn't mean anything."

Felicity's gaze moves to the painted cradle and the toys. Then she looks back at me.

"Yes," I say, "we have too much free time here. People wanted to do something for Ab—the baby. Sidra will be welcome to take anything they've made. Now, I think we should—"

"I'd like to go along tomorrow," Petra repeats, as if I've forgotten the request. Technically, she should ask Dalton, but her gaze is on me.

When I don't answer, she says, "Will has to stay in town. Tyrone is still here, but you'd need to pry him away from Jen. Also, with you both being gone for a few days, it's been easier on Will having Tyrone around playing backup deputy."

"We've already found Ellen's killer," I say. "This is a simple tracking mission. I'm not even sure both Eric and I need to go."

Dalton's grunt tells me I am mistaken in this.

"I have tomorrow off," Petra says. "And I'm requesting permission to accompany you. Who knows, maybe you'll find another baby along the way and need someone to look after it." She shoots an amused glance at Felicity.

She's really saying that she doesn't trust this girl. Doesn't trust we aren't being led into a trap. If I refuse the request, I'm being stubborn . . . and maybe a little petty.

"All right," I say.

"Good," Dalton says. "Now, Felicity, I'm guessing no one has given you a tour of the town?"

"No, but I don't need—"

"We insist. It's only polite. Get your stuff on, and we'll show you around."

Dalton doesn't insist on the tour to be hospitable. It's a message, one Felicity can take home to the First Settlement, like when I told her how we store our guns and how tightly they're controlled. He also shows her that, as part of the "tour."

*We have guns. More than you do. And they're locked up so tight even our residents can't get at them, so don't even think about stealing any.*

We introduce her to the militia and explain the twenty-four-hour armed-guard patrols. We show her the storehouses, windowless and well secured. Of course Felicity realizes what's happening. But we don't need to point out the security features—she's already looking and calculating.

At first, I'm surprised she initially declined the tour. She's Edwin's granddaughter, and this is a rare opportunity to assess our wealth and defenses. She must be curious, too. That, I realize, is where I'm mistaken. Yes, she's curious, but she's also wary, and this is why she didn't want to come inside—because she didn't want to see more.

I had a friend in elementary school who was from a less affluent part of the city. I know that private and charter schools are popular in the States, speaking to the quality of the public school system in some areas. In Canada, private schools are for the rich. My parents used to say they were for parental bragging rights. That's not entirely true, but our public school system is good enough that parents like mine rightly declared a private education unnecessary. But there are still differences between schools themselves, and this girl's parents drove her to ours.

We became friends, and one day, I got permission to bring her home. I'd been so excited to show her my house, with my big bedroom and private bath and huge yard. That wasn't showing off—I was too young to understand such a thing. I just wanted her to see my domain, the places that were uniquely mine.

When I invited her back, she refused, and an invitation to her home never came. It's only now, as an adult, that I understand. My house was a glimpse into a world of privilege. A world where you don't share your bedroom with two sisters and your bathroom with your entire family. Where you don't bother with the neighborhood playground because your yard is bigger. Where you can open the fridge and eat whatever you want because it'll be replaced as soon as it's gone.

In my house, she saw what she lacked through sheer happenstance of birth. Had I gone to her place, I'd have seen the same—except for me, it'd have been spending time with her tight-knit, loving family. If I'd experienced that, would I have stayed away, too, avoiding a very different reminder of what could be?

Felicity looks around Rockton and compares it to what she has, and it makes her uncomfortable. Ambition is healthy. Envy is pointless and potentially destructive. It leads to the dissatisfied cry of "Why?"

*Why do they have this, and I do not? It isn't fair. They don't deserve it. They haven't earned it.*

But Felicity quickly finds the solution to her problem. The only healthy solution to envy: What can I learn from this that will make my own life better? She begins to examine our building construction and asks questions about our sanitary system. We answer, and we continue with the tour.

Afterward, we don't invite Felicity to join us at home. Petra will take care of her. We need time to rest and be alone. We indulge in a long dinner for two. Then Dalton goes to the station for a bit of work while I take Abby. By eight, we're asleep.

# THIRTY-SEVEN

The next morning, we're off by seven, walking with flashlights into the darkness. Felicity and Petra are with us. Neither says much, and I get the impression that was the state of things last night.

When we meet up with Dalton, he says to Petra, "You got that gun I dropped by?"

She hesitates only a second before nodding and opening her jacket to reveal her personal handgun. If we get into trouble and Petra pulls out an unauthorized weapon, it'll tell Felicity we're lying about our gun regulations. Petra understands this and plays along.

We take Storm with us. Abby stays behind. I do not expect that we're going to find unfit parents at the end of this journey. At worst, it might be a young couple who, with great reluctance, abandoned a winter-born child. That's horrifying to us, but it's the way Sidra was raised, and possibly Baptiste, too, and it's been the way of hunting societies since time immemorial.

If this is the situation, I'll struggle to see them as good parents for making that choice, but I must put that aside and ask instead "What if you could keep her?" *What if we gave you what you needed to make it through the winter with an infant?* If the answer is still no—that they are not ready for a child—then we'll take her.

If they want Abby, I'll still bring Sidra back to Rockton to ensure she is her mother. How much of that is healthy caution and how much is a secret hope that we can keep Abby? I don't know, and I'm afraid to analyze. I do know that I will not stand between these parents and their child.

It's late morning by the time we reach the area, about five kilometers past where we found Abby. Before Sidra left, she told Felicity that this would be a good area to live, where they had camped and hunted and fished with Baptiste and others from both settlements. Sidra framed it as an offhand conversation.

*Hey, you know that spot where we all camped last summer? That'd be a good place to live, don't you think? Not that I'm planning to run away and fake my own death so I can be with my beloved or anything like that . . .*

Clearly it'd been a hint. A plea even. Like giving an estranged friend your new phone number, in case they find that jacket you left at their apartment once.

*If you want me, you know where to find me.*

The place is a river valley with abundant game and fresh water and mountain shelter. While that sounds like a settler's paradise—and therefore, it should already be occupied—it is only one spot in a thousand just like it out here. It's just a matter of picking the one that suits you best. Like pioneers heading west and choosing their plot of land. The possibilities stretch to the horizon.

When the pioneers headed west, they each got a hundred and sixty acres. Out here, a settler can "claim" even more. There is no actual claim, of course. Anyone can hunt or fish or walk through your territory, and challenging them on it would be pointless. The territory this couple have staked out is huge, so they won't rush to find exactly the right spot to build a permanent home—perhaps one for summer and one for winter. The upshot is that we're talking a general area at least couple of kilometers, and that's not easy to search.

We split up. Dalton assigns me Storm and Petra, and he sends us to check flat and open areas along the river. Meanwhile Felicity knows a half dozen spots where they camped over the years, and she'll show those to Dalton.

We've been searching for over an hour when our paths cross and Dalton asks to take Storm. While he wanted her with me for protection, she's better sniffing those old campsites to see if she can pick up a scent.

Petra and I continue hunting along the river. She's been quiet, but now she says, "I heard you brought Maryanne to town."

I grunt a nonreply.

"Did you get any answers from her?" she asks. "About what the hostiles are, how they came to be?"

I bend and check what looks like a boot print in well-trampled snow.

"I know you thought the council was responsible for them," she says. "Did you find anything to support that?"

If she said it with even a hint of mockery, I wouldn't answer. But her tone sounds genuinely curious . . . with a hint of trepidation. Is that fear I'll uncover the truth? Or fear that there *is* a connection?

Her gaze shutters, giving me nothing.

I consider. Then I say, "Tea."

Her brow furrows. "What?"

I twist, still hunkered down. "The hostiles consume a narcotic and a hallucinogenic tea. Same as the Second Settlement, who seem to use the latter for something that seems almost like prehistoric rituals."

"Prehistoric people consumed ritual hallucinogens, probably because the altered state made them feel as if they were seeing and communicating with their gods."

I nod. "Whatever the hostiles have added to the Second Settlement's brew makes theirs far more potent. And more dangerous. Theirs is addictive, and it affects free will—they're happy and content, and they stop thinking about their other life, eventually stop remembering they had one."

She listens, saying nothing.

I continue. "In high doses—or maybe with an added ingredient—it induces frenzies. Heightened id, lowered super-ego, if you took Psych 101."

A strained smile. "I did. Does that explain the violence, then?"

"Apparently." I rise. "I believe it's a natural evolution of something that began in the Second Settlement. They discover this root that makes a ritualistic tea. Someone from the settlement experiments and creates a new version and then breaks away from the group—or is kicked out—and starts their own community, which devolves into what we have today."

I wait for her to jump on the fact that I'm absolving the council, but she still seems to be processing, so I say it for her. "A natural evolution based on natural substances, with no outside influence. I still, however, hold the council responsible for allowing the devolution. Rockton has been reporting hostiles since Tyrone was sheriff. Yet the council dismissed the claims as . . ." I throw up my hands. "I don't even know what they thought people were seeing. Bears? Settlers?"

"I was told it was both," she says, unexpectedly. "That some settlers were more violent than others, and some had 'reverted' more than others—not being as 'civilized' in their dress and their mannerisms. The more extreme accounts were thought to be wild animals mistaken for humans, probably bears."

I wait for her to add a justification, a defense. Being a thousand miles away, the council understandably questioned the wild stories, like the tales of ancient sailors spotting manatees and somehow mistaking the ugly sea mammals for beautiful women. Isolation plays tricks on the mind, heightens fears and desires. To the council, Rockton's hostile sightings were no different from Bigfoot sightings. Even I will grant them that, and I expect Petra to point this out. Maybe she thinks it's obvious. Maybe now that I've acknowledged my mistake, she doesn't want to rub my face in it.

When she says nothing, I continue. "The point is that with so many sightings and encounters, they should have encouraged investigation. Better yet, they should have sent a team to investigate. What they'd have found isn't a tribe of happy former Rockton residents gone native. It was a drug-enslaved cult where at least some of the members, like Maryanne, didn't sign up voluntarily. She was from Rockton. Her whole party was—the two men the hostiles brutally murdered and the two women they took hostage. Maryanne played along, expecting the chance to escape, and instead fell under the influence of the tea. The other woman did escape—and was hunted down, tied up naked, and left to the elements and the predators and the scavengers. This is what the council allowed."

Petra looks as if she's going to be sick. I don't expect that either. She takes a deep breath before straightening with, "All right."

"All right what?" I say, a little sharply.

Silence. Then, "All right, I understand, and I agree this has been handled badly."

I wait for more. When it doesn't come, I'm annoyed, and I don't like that. Am I spoiling for a fight? My mistake with the hostiles and the council has bruised my ego, so now I want Petra to say "I told you so" so I can light into her?

Today's hunt has me on edge, and Petra's not giving me the response I want so I'm being cranky.

Forget hostiles and the council and Petra. None of them have anything to do with returning Abby to her parents.

I find a footprint, and I focus on that. It's near the riverbank, pointing inland.

The river is mostly frozen, but temperatures haven't dropped enough for it to be a solid sheet of ice, and we're near an inlet that's running too fast to freeze. That's why the snow is so trampled—animals finding this spot and drinking. I definitely saw a boot print, though, and when I search, I locate more. Humans have used this spot for water. Possibly also for hunting. Drops of blood and scattered white fur suggest an Arctic hare was killed as it came to drink.

It's been two days since the last snowfall. These prints are even more recent, layered on top of animal ones. When I get about three meters from the river, the prints fan out, the animals and the humans going their separate ways. I can get a better view of the human ones here. Two sets, one about a men's size ten, and one a little bigger than mine. A man and a woman, both dressed in boots like what Ellen wore, thick and heavy, with no tread.

The human prints lead to the remains of a camp. A year ago, I'd have walked right through it. Now I notice the rectangle where a tent stood. I see irregular patterns in the snow where items were set down. I spot blood under a tree nearby, where game was hung and slaughtered. And there's the firepit. It's only a circular patch of packed snow, but I dig down to find embers still warm.

"A camp," Petra says, as if just realizing this.

I nod.

"What's that over there?" she says.

I twist, still crouched, as she heads toward whatever she's spotted. When I catch movement in the trees, I start to call a warning. Then I see a dark parka-like jacket on a man Dalton's size.

She's looking at something else, and as she bends for a better study, the figure moves from the trees, and it is not Dalton.

"Petra!" I call, my own gun out, rising.

She spins to her feet . . . and the figure raises a rifle.

"Stop!" I shout. "There is a gun pointed at your head, and there are two more people walking up behind you right now." I'm hoping I'm loud enough for Dalton to hear if he's nearby. "We are all armed. Lower your weapon—"

"Lower yours," the man says. He's young, and his voice is deep and seems steady, but I've dealt with enough situations like this to recognize that tremor, the one that says he's in a situation he's not equipped to handle. It's too easy to pull that trigger when you're afraid and angry and trying to pretend you are willing to do it. I know that better than anyone.

"Baptiste?" I say.

His shoulders jerk just enough for me to know I've guessed right.

"Where's Sidra?" I ask.

"That's my question to you," he says, in a voice that carries the accent of those raised in the Second Settlement. "What have you done with my wife?"

"Nothing," I say. "We came looking for you. We're with Felicity."

"Felicity?" Baptiste spits, and his gaze turns on me. "*She* took Sidra, didn't she? Dragging her back to that grandfather of hers. If I—"

Petra flies at him. She dives at his legs, knocking him back. The gun fires. Not a rifle but a shotgun blast.

"Casey!" Dalton's voice slams through the forest.

"Gun down!" I shout, as much for Dalton as for them, to let him know I'm fine. "Put the goddamn gun—"

"I've got it," Petra says. "We're both fine, no thanks to this idiot."

"And no thanks to the idiot who jumped a kid with a shotgun," I say as I walk over.

"I didn't expect him to have his finger on the trigger."

"In the real world, people often do. We aren't all government-trained secret agents."

"I'm not . . ." Petra trails off, shaking her head.

"Not government trained?" I say.

She only rolls her eyes and holds out the shotgun. I walk past her to where pellets peppered a tree. I dig one out.

A buckshot pellet.

Just like the one that killed Ellen.

# THIRTY-EIGHT

I turn to Baptiste. He's about eighteen. Brown eyes. Dark curls cut in a mop that makes him look like the puppy-cute guy in a boy band. He's trying very hard to play this cool, setting his jaw and hardening his eyes, but those eyes don't have the life experience to harden. He reminds me of every kid I questioned who got caught up in a petty crime with his friends, struggling to play it tough while two seconds from breaking down and admitting he's made a huge mistake, but he'll take the punishment, just please don't call his parents.

Dalton comes at a run, calling a warning before he bursts through, as if we wouldn't hear him. Baptiste gives a start as Storm races past.

"She's a dog," I say, patting her head. "Eric, this is—"

"You!" Baptiste spins on Felicity, who's trailing Dalton. "What did you do with Sidra? Did you take Summer, too? I swear if you hurt either of them . . ."

Summer.

The baby's name is Summer.

That throws me enough that it takes a moment for me to react, and Dalton beats me to it, grabbing Baptiste's shoulder as he advances on Felicity. Even then, my brain throws up excuses. Maybe Summer is a friend. Or a pet.

*Yes, Casey, they have a pet dog named Summer, and this isn't Abby's father. It's pure coincidence that their dog is also, apparently, missing.*

Dalton's hand tightens on Baptiste's shoulder. "You see those guns pointed at you, kid? Those mean 'Don't move.'"

"Just like the one you had pointed at me," Petra says.

"You moved," he says.

"And could have gotten you both shot up with those pellets," I say.

Those pellets.

He was carrying a gun loaded with buckshot.

Like the weapon used to kill Ellen.

The weapon Lane swore he didn't have.

Yet Lane also swore he murdered Ellen.

A flash of Tomas saying Lane had a friend who died last year. Then Felicity saying she and Sidra hung out with two kids from the Second Settlement.

Shit.

Questions and theories ping through my brain, and I squeeze my eyes shut and push them back. Gather more data. Work this through.

"Where is Sidra?" Felicity says.

"That's what I'm asking you," Baptiste says, as they lock glowers. "You took her back to your grandfather, didn't you?"

"She's missing?" Felicity's eyes snap. "You lost your baby, and now you've lost Sidra?"

"I didn't lose—"

"Enough," Dalton says. "Felicity, go sit over there with Petra. Baptiste, you and Sidra have a baby?"

"Had," Felicity says. "Had and lost—"

Baptiste swings on her, and Dalton and I both raise our

weapons, ready to order him back, but it's only a warning lunge, accompanied by a snarl.

"Felicity?" I say. "Sit and be quiet, please. Even if he provokes you."

"I'm not the one—" Baptiste begins.

"You don't get along," I say. "That appears to be an understatement. But we need answers, and we aren't getting them with you two spitting at each other like bobcats."

That is really what they look like, backing up, glaring at one another. It reminds me of Diana and Dalton, Diana convinced he's keeping her from me, and Dalton hating the way she's treated me. The lover and the friend as rivals. It doesn't need to be that way, but sometimes it is, and as with Dalton and Diana, it goes deeper, to a fundamental personality clash that the competition only exacerbates. I suspect that's the same here—that even without Sidra in the middle, these two never got along.

I walk to Baptiste's other side, forcing him to turn away from Felicity.

"You have a baby," I say.

He nods, and I see the struggle to remain calm, not to shout that his child is missing and his wife, too, and he doesn't have time to stand around answering my questions. The fact that he's trying suggests I was right—he's not usually a hothead who threatens strangers with shotguns. He's backed into a wall and acting out of character.

Is he? If he killed Ellen, then shooting Petra *wouldn't* be "out of character."

Tuck that aside. Focus.

"A girl or a boy?" I ask.

"A girl. Summer."

"How old is she?"

"Thirty-eight days," he says, so quickly that I suspect, if given a moment, he could tell me the number of hours, too.

"What happened to Summer?" I ask.

"The wild people took her."

Petra snorts. "Is that the Yukon equivalent of 'dingoes ate my baby'?"

I give her a hard look, but she meets my gaze, her expression saying she's already decided these aren't suitable parents, based on nothing more than the fact that she doesn't want them to be.

"Evidence suggests dingoes may actually have eaten that woman's baby," Dalton says.

When I look at him, he shrugs. "I read about the case. The problem with her story was that dingoes weren't known to take children. The problem with your story, kid, is that the same applies to those you call the wild people. They don't have kids. It's against their rules. So they sure as hell aren't going to steal one."

This isn't entirely true. We know Maryanne's group prohibited children, but that doesn't mean others followed the same laws. Dalton's just putting Baptiste on the offensive, trying to break his story.

"We found evidence," Baptiste says. "The wild people came, and they took her."

"They snuck into your tent in the night?" Petra says. "Plucked her from your arms while you slept?"

"We did not sleep with her in our arms. Sidra's mother lost a child by accidentally suffocating her in the night, so Summer slept in a box that I built. It was evening. I was hunting, and Sidra was with the baby. She was making dinner while Summer slept in her box, right near the fire. Someone grabbed Sidra from behind. Put a sack over her head. She fought, but she was overpowered. She heard grunts of communication, like the wild people. She smelled wild people. While she was bound and blinded, they took our baby. In her place, they left one of their skulls, the sort they use to mark territory. They told Sidra not to come for Summer. The voice was low, guttural, like the wild people. They said Summer was theirs. Sidra screamed and screamed, and finally I heard her and came running. We found tracks. We tried to follow them, but they went on the ice and we could not."

"When did this happen?"

"Ten days ago. We have been searching ever since. A friend is searching, too. She used to be one of the wild people. She said she would find Summer, but we have not seen her since she left, and then, last night, Sidra disappeared."

"This friend," I say. "You said she's a wild person? Are you sure she didn't take Summer herself? That'd be a nice trick—steal your child, blame it on the others, and then offer to get the baby back herself."

Baptiste hesitates. I'm watching for some sign of calculation in his gaze. There are possibilities here that lay the blame for Summer's fate at his feet. Maybe he exposed her himself, pretending hostiles took her. Maybe Ellen *did* take her—rescuing her from unfit parents. If so, he'll see an opportunity here to blame Ellen, especially if he knows she's dead and can't defend herself.

I'm watching for the look that says he's considering his options. Yet when he hesitates, he only seems to be thinking through what I've said, wondering if it's possible that Ellen took their baby. Then he shakes his head.

"No," he says. "When Sidra told her the wild people took Summer, Ellen was confused. Like you said, she claimed they don't have babies. She knows of two groups in the area. Tribes, she calls them. Neither allows babies. She thought we were mistaken. Then we showed her the skull, and she said it was definitely the wild people. Her own tribe, judging by the markings. After thinking about it for a while, she said she remembered one woman who wanted a baby. Ellen wondered whether this woman might take Summer, in hopes that the tribe would let her keep her. Or maybe she wanted a baby more than she wanted to be in the tribe."

"Take Summer and flee with her," I say.

He nods. "There wouldn't be any reason for Ellen to steal Summer."

"Down south, plenty of people can't have babies and would happily pay for one."

His brow furrows. "How would Ellen get Summer down south?"

"Maybe she didn't think you should keep Summer. You and Sidra have only been on your own for a year. Adding a winter baby seems . . . unwise."

His cheeks color. "It was an accident. Ellen used to be a nurse. She said if we didn't want the baby, she'd have helped us end the pregnancy. If we did want the baby, she'd help us with that, too. It was completely up to us. We decided to have the child. The birth was easy, and Sidra's milk came in, and Summer was healthy."

All true. Abby—Summer—was indeed healthy and well cared for, and from what I learned from Tomas and Nancy, Ellen had been helping the young couple, just as she promised.

So why was Baptiste carrying the gun that might have killed Ellen? I'm not seeing an easy answer here, and I need to set that aside. There's a bigger issue to deal with.

"Tell me about Sidra," I say. "She disappeared last night?"

Baptiste nods. "When I woke, she was gone. I didn't worry at first. She isn't sleeping well, with Summer gone. Neither of us is. She also needs to rid herself of the milk a few times a day. Ellen said that was important. She has to . . ." He struggles for the words. "Express, Ellen said. Express the milk, even if it goes to waste, so she'll keep producing it for when Summer comes back to us. It's painful—the milk—so Sidra often gets up in the night. I've told her to just do it in the tent, where it's warm, but I think she liked the excuse to . . ."

Baptiste looks away. "It hasn't been easy for us, with Summer gone. Sidra thinks I blame her because she was with Summer when it happened."

"Do you?" That's Petra, challenge in her voice.

Baptiste snaps, "Of course not. Sidra was ambushed. Maybe it's my fault. I ran as soon as I heard her screaming, but it wasn't fast enough to catch whoever took Summer. Sidra says she doesn't blame me, and I say I don't blame *her*, but . . . It's been difficult. I think she's found excuses to spend time away from me, and that hasn't made things easier. When I woke and found her gone, I didn't want to run after her. I . . ." He trails off.

"You wanted time away, too," Petra says. "You did blame her."

He spins on her, and I cut in with, "Petra? This isn't about you."

Her eyes spark, but her cheeks color, too, even as she turns a glare on me. I meet it evenly. She knows what I mean, just as I know why she's saying this. She lost her daughter in a car accident. At the time she'd been divorced, but she'd had a good relationship with her ex . . . until the accident. Petra had been called to pick up her daughter unexpectedly after having a couple of glasses of wine. While that impairment didn't contribute to the accident—it was the other driver's fault Petra blew under the legal limit—her ex couldn't forgive her and drove her to the brink of suicide.

Now she's looking at Baptiste—whose baby was lost on her mother's watch—and she sees her ex, and I need her to back the hell down. We lock gazes, and after a moment, she nods.

"Continue," I say to Baptiste.

"I knew Sidra needed time away from me, like she does after an argument. I wanted to give her that, but I wanted her to know I care, too. If I left her alone too long, she might think I don't want *her* around either. I got up and made her breakfast, and then I went looking for her. I discovered she hadn't been out expressing milk. She'd been emptying her bladder. I found the spot. I also found her night-torch there, extinguished, and signs of a struggle."

"Hostiles stole my wife?" Petra says.

I let her have that one, and I watch Baptiste as he snaps, "No. I understand you're blaming me, but it doesn't appear to be wild people. One person took her. One pair of tracks. They didn't leave behind anything as they did with Summer. I followed the tracks, but whoever took her knows how to cover a trail."

"Of course they do," Petra mutters.

"So first you lose your baby," Felicity says, "and then you lose your wife."

Dalton rolls his eyes my way. I know exactly what he's thinking: *Well, at least neither of us needs to play bad cop here.* We have Petra *and* Felicity for that.

Felicity keeps going. "And you didn't even lose them to the same people. *That* would make sense, if the hostiles kidnapped Sidra to feed the baby. But no, it was different attackers." She meets his gaze. "Or was it the same attacker? You wanted Sidra, and the only way you could have her was to run away with her. The next thing you know you're stuck with a wife and a baby—"

"Stuck?" His voice rises. "Stuck? I would happily be *stuck* with Sidra for the rest of my life. I'd happily be stuck with her and twenty children if that's what she wanted. And before you accuse me of not wanting Summer, I did. It was our decision to keep her, and I never regretted it. I want my baby and my wife back, and I'm trying to be patient here, but the longer you keep accusing me of hurting them, the longer someone is actually hurting them."

"We have Summer," I say.

"What?" He turns on me, blinking as if he's misheard.

"Summer is in Rockton, and she's safe."

He teeters, eyes shut, relief shuddering through him. Then his eyes snap open. "You took her? Someone from Rockton stole—"

"No, you dolt," Felicity says. "Why would they be here if they stole your baby? I brought them to you."

"I'm not a dolt," he says slowly, as if restraining his temper. "I had to ask. The same as you had to ask whether I hurt Sidra, when you know how much I love her."

"And I had to ask that because I know you have experience faking deaths. Also experience behaving like utter fools, reenacting Romeo and Juliet."

He sputters for a moment before facing me and saying, evenly, "If you suspect me because of that, let me assure you that Sidra and I are not children who thought faking our deaths would be romantic. Has Felicity told you why we did that?"

"Because the settlements would have forbidden your marriage," I say.

"Yes, but we had a plan for dealing with it, one that wouldn't have left our families grieving for us. We planned to leave together, with notes to explain, and then we'd return in a few years, after we had a child so they could not separate us. Sidra wanted to ask Felicity for help. I argued, but she trusted her friend. She didn't even get a chance to explain the plan. As soon as she said she wanted to leave with me, Felicity threatened to tie her up and keep her from making such a terrible mistake. Threatened that if she ran, the whole settlement would come after us, and if something happened to me in the pursuit, well, that wasn't Felicity's fault."

I turn slowly on Felicity.

Her cheeks are bright red. "I didn't mean it like that. I was only trying to make Sidra listen to reason. I just wanted her to slow down and let me negotiate with my grandfather."

"All right," I say. "Felicity? Please join Petra in staying out of this. You've voiced your suspicions. That's enough. Baptiste? Your baby is fine. We didn't take her—we're trying to return her. I'm not sure who did take her. We found her with Ellen. And I'm very sorry to say, Ellen is dead."

Baptiste freezes, his color draining. "Dead?"

"Which is also not our doing," Dalton says. "Casey and I were out camping last week. She heard your baby crying and found her under the snow."

"Wh-what?" His eyes round. "Summer was—"

"She's fine," I say. "Ellen had her. She'd rescued her, and she was on the run, and someone killed her. She died clutching Summer to her, keeping her warm. She saved her."

"You both saved her," Petra says. "You're the one who found the baby before—" She stops, as if realizing Baptiste doesn't need that image. "Before anything happened."

"Thank you," Baptiste says. "I'm not sure how we can ever repay you, but we will. Thank you for finding her, and thank you for finding us. Ellen . . ." He slumps as the news of her death penetrates the relief at his daughter's survival. "She only wanted to help. She only *ever* wanted to help. I shouldn't have let her go after Summer. I knew it was dangerous, and we already owed her so much, and I should have said no. I was desperate, and now . . ."

"She's gone," Felicity says. "Falling apart isn't going to help you find Sidra. You're soft, Baptiste, too soft to—"

"Enough," Dalton says, the word harsh enough to make

Felicity give a start. "A woman is dead, Felicity. A woman who died helping your friends, and Baptiste is allowed a moment to feel bad about that. It isn't weakness. It's called being a fucking human being."

She flinches and then her face hardens, as if she wants to snap something back. She can't, though. The only comeback would be to accuse him of equal weakness, equal sentimentality. Whatever impression Dalton's made on her, it must not be that.

After a moment, she says, "You are right. I am sorry for this woman's death. I'm just concerned about Sidra."

"As am I," Baptiste says. "I don't want to fight over who is more concerned. We both are. Now, can we try to find her? Please?"

"Could you show us the spot where she disappeared?" I ask. "Our dog can track scents."

He frowns. Again, I'm looking for signs, this time of worry, of panic. I see only confusion and then surprise and then relief.

"Your dog?" He looks at Storm. "She's a hunting dog?"

"Just for people," I say. "Residents wander into the forest and disappear. She's trained to bring them back."

"Eric's the Rockton sheriff," Petra says. "Casey is his detective. Finding things is her job. Down south, finding killers was her job."

He doesn't hesitate at that. Again, he looks relieved. "So you'll find who killed Ellen?"

Am I certain that's relief? It certainly seems like it. Dalton is watching him with equal care. He's seen the gun. He's figured it out.

Is this not the gun that shot Ellen? Or was Sidra the person holding it, and Baptiste knows nothing about that? Or did Baptiste fire it mistaking Ellen for a hostile, maybe hoping to injure and question one about Summer?

So many possibilities. At this point, all I can say is that my gut tells me that if Baptiste is a killer, he's an accidental one, and Lane misunderstood the situation and is covering for him.

"Was Sidra taken here?" Dalton says, startling me from my thoughts as he looks around. "Someone camped here. I'm guessing that was you."

Baptiste frowns and follows Dalton's gaze to the campsite just beyond. He shakes his head. "No, this wasn't us."

"Not you last night?" Dalton says. "Or not you at all?"

"Not us at all. We have a permanent winter site closer to the mountain, with better shelter. This is someone's temporary camp." Baptiste walks into it and looks around.

"There's evidence that animals were slaughtered," I say. "A hunting camp?"

Dalton has followed Baptiste, and they're both poking around. After a few minutes, Dalton says, "Overnight camp. They killed their dinner, and maybe a little more to-go, but that's it."

"It isn't the wild people," Baptiste says. "We haven't seen anyone else in days." He turns to us. "What if it was a lone hunter who stole Sidra? There are a few of those around. There's a big man who calls himself Cypher. Sidra doesn't like him so we stay away. There's a younger man, Jacob, who we've traded with . . ."

He turns slowly to Dalton, who's bundled up, with a hat and hood, but now he takes a closer look and says, "Oh."

"Yeah, that'd be my brother."

"I . . . I've heard stories. Yes, all right. I don't mean to blame your brother for anything. I just thought, what if a man was hunting and saw Sidra . . ."

"Jacob's hunting far from here. Tyrone Cypher is in Rockton right now. But, yeah, I take your point. Some guy could have been passing through, saw Sidra, and waited for her to leave your shelter last night."

"More than one person stayed in this camp," I say. "I found multiple boot prints. One isn't much bigger than mine, which suggests a woman. That's why I thought it was your camp. A man and a woman . . ." I trail off.

"You thinking what I'm thinking?" Dalton says.

I nod.

Dalton sighs. "Fuck."

# THIRTY-NINE

Who do we think camped here? The couple I accidentally set on Baptiste and Sidra's trail.

No, let's be honest. The "accident" is that I hadn't meant to endanger this young couple, but that's because I'd been thinking abstractly. I offered Cherise an irresistible reward for finding Abby's parents. I just lacked the foresight, in that moment, to see "Abby's parents" as people who might be endangered by me setting a dangerous woman on that quest.

I'd realized my mistake the moment I made the offer, which is why we'd labored to make it ironclad, in hopes of protecting Abby's mother from Cherise's ruthlessness. Even if we'd rescinded it, though, Cherise would know how valuable this information was, and she'd search for Abby's mother in hopes of a reward. The only thing we could do was close off loopholes.

It wasn't enough.

Earlier, Felicity told me I was wrong for making the offer. She might not have said much more then. She does now. I take my lumps, even as Dalton and Petra come to my defense. Baptiste says he understands why I did it, and he's grateful that

I was so anxious to reunite Summer with her parents. He's cutting me slack, being kind, while I see the worry in his eyes.

In the end, all I can do is apologize, while Dalton insists that Sidra is in no actual danger.

"We were very, very clear on the stipulations of the deal," Dalton says. "We don't pay out until we see the baby's mother and confirm she hasn't been hurt. Yeah, Cherise is going to make Sidra spin us some bullshit story about how she went with Cherise voluntarily, but we know better. We'll get Sidra back, and tell Cherise where she can stick her deal."

"I would exercise more caution than that," Felicity says. "I understand the impulse. I also want to punish Cherise for what she did."

"But that's like punching a grizzly in the face," Baptiste says. "Even if the grizzly doesn't come after you, it's going to strike at the first human it sees."

Felicity nods. "She will find a way to punish Sidra and Baptiste for the loss of her reward."

The young settlers exchange a look, acknowledgment of shared ground.

"I agree," I say. "Ideally, we steal Sidra back from Cherise. If she figures it out and complains, we pay her off, as painful as that will be. And then we never, ever do business with her again."


We have two choices here. Return to where Cherise and Owen snatched Sidra or track the couple from here. Sidra and Baptiste's campsite is a kilometer away, and it seems likely that they brought Sidra back here before they broke camp. Dalton confirms that with the campfire. If they left last night, the coals would be cold by now. Also, it makes no sense to lie in wait for Sidra with all your gear on your back.

Tracking them from here makes the most sense, especially when we know they'll head for Rockton with their booty. There's no reason to do otherwise.

We split up, dividing our best trackers—Storm gets Petra and me, and Dalton takes Felicity and Baptiste. We head to the campsite first. If we had any doubt that Cherise and Owen are the couple who camped here, it disappears when Storm arrives. She's growling even before I ask her to snuffle the ground.

"When even dogs don't like you, that's a very bad sign," Petra says. I wait for her to make some comment on the fact that Storm likes *her* just fine, but Petra isn't so ham-handed. The implication dangles there, and she knows I'll see it.

I snort my response and ask Storm to follow Cherise and Owen's trail. She grumbles at that, a growling sulk that tells me she really doesn't want another encounter with the trader couple. I crouch in front of her and murmur reassurances, and she looks at me as if to say, *I hope you know what you're doing.* Then she sets out.

Our luck with using Storm as a tracking dog has been sporadic so far. Am I disappointed in that? Yes, I'll admit it. That's not her fault. While Newfoundlands are used in search-and-rescue, they aren't bloodhounds. Whatever Dalton's excuse for buying her, she really is a companion dog, and she's brilliant at that, an absolute joy in our lives. The fault may also be ours— we aren't dog trainers or trackers, and no amount of reading can fully overcome that. We've discussed sending her down south for professional training, and we might still do it. Yet she's still young, and when she can't find our quarry, it's not through lack of intelligence or commitment—it's the fault of challenging terrain.

Today, though, Storm proves that she's a perfectly fine tracker and the problem is that, too often, we've set her on the trail of people who know she'll come after them and use every trick for avoiding her. When it's someone who has no expectation of being tracked, finding them is puppy's play, and we have to hold her back from running along Cherise and Owen's trail. We get some dirty looks for that—clearly we should be able to keep up.

Finally I spot Owen, and I'm about to grab Storm's collar, realizing I lack an end-of-search signal. Another oversight on my part. Fortunately, she has no desire to get close to Owen, and she slows, glancing at me as if to say, *There he is. Can we go now?*

We cannot.

It's just Owen. He's sitting. Well, crouching actually, while performing a bodily function that Cherise obviously doesn't want to witness.

As Petra sneaks up on Owen's other side, he finishes his business, rising with his hands on his pants, pulling them up.

"Shit that stinks," a voice says, and Petra and I go still. It's Cherise. I can't see her, but it's clearly her voice.

"Yeah, it stinks *because* it's shit," Owen says. "Yours doesn't smell like roses, babe."

"Cover it up," she says.

He grumbles that this isn't their camp—they aren't sticking around—but he knocks snow over the steaming pile as he fastens his jeans.

Petra looks at me. I gesture for Storm to stay, and then I begin to circle around to where I'll be able to see Cherise. Petra stays ducked behind a bush.

After a few steps, I spot Cherise leaning against a tree. There's no sign of Sidra, but she must be nearby. I keep circling until I'm opposite the couple, and I can see everything around them. Trees and a few low bushes. Nothing big enough to hide Sidra.

Both Owen and Cherise are armed, but the rifles are slung across their backs. I glance around for Dalton, but his group is long gone.

I step out from my hiding spot. "Hey, guys."

They both spin on me. I raise my hands. Owen reaches for his rifle, but I say, "Uh-uh. You go for yours, and I go for mine, which is a lot more accessible."

Their gazes go to my open parka, my gun right there, ready to draw.

"Storm?" I say. "Come, girl."

She bounds from her hiding place. As she does, Petra appears five paces behind the couple, but they're busy watching the dog. Petra stops there, her gun out, and waits.

"We hear you've found the baby's mom," I say.

Cherise's expression doesn't change. Her partner, however, sneaks a look her way, one that tells me what I've already suspected.

"Let's trade now," I say. "You hand her over and collect your reward."

Cherise snorts. "Since you obviously don't have the goods we were promised, we're not handing her over. We'll meet you at Rockton."

"Sure, we can all go to Rockton. Together."

"We'll meet—"

"The only reason for you to argue is if you don't have the mother."

"Yes, we don't, all right. We know who she is. We're on her trail. But we still need to talk to her."

"Talk?" I say, brows rising. "Why not just grab her and save yourself the trouble?"

"Because someone put that into the terms of the damn

agreement," she says, scowling at me. "Did I misinterpret something? I sure as hell understood that we need to bring her to you of her own free will. Which, yes, complicates things and . . ." She looks from my gun to Storm and launches into a string of profanity.

"Yeah, they fucked you over, babe," Owen says.

She shoots a lethal glare at him and then swings it on me. "You did, didn't you? Set me on this girl's trail and then followed, waiting until I found my prey and then swooping in like a damn scavenger. I do all the work. You take the prize and then claim you owe me nothing." She steps forward. "That was a stupid move, girl. A really, really—"

"Stop right there," Petra says as Storm growls.

They both turn to see Petra, and I wince. Cherise hadn't gone for her gun. There was no reason for Petra to reveal herself.

"Yes, I brought backup," I say. "And she's going to lower her gun right now, having realized Cherise is justifiably angry with me and not actually about to attack."

Petra's expression says she doesn't appreciate taking orders from me. She still lowers the gun.

"If I did what you think, Cherise, you'd have every right to be pissed," I say. "I did not. I'm following a separate lead directly from Rockton. I'm sure if we'd been following you for the past three days, you'd know it. Now, do you have the baby's mother?"

Cherise throws up her hands and turns in a circle, as if to say, *Do you see her?*

"If we find that you kidnapped her—"

"Oh, for fuck's sake," Cherise snaps. "That's the kind of mistake this idiot would make."

She waves at Owen, who only protests with a halfhearted "Hey." When she looks at him, he flashes a grin and a shrug and says, "Fair enough. Never claimed to be the brains of the operation. You're with me for my pretty face. Not that I'm objecting. 'Cause you really like how I look, and I reap the benefits of your appreciation."

She rolls her eyes and then turns to me. "I understand the terms of our deal. I also understand that there is no way in hell I'd get away with kidnapping that girl. She'd tattle the moment my back was turned. Also, I'd have to kick the kid's ass for ratting me out, and if you think I'd enjoy that, then you and I have a fundamental misunderstanding of one another. I wouldn't mind if I had to, but I'm not going to do it for fun. I have other ways to spend my time. More productive ways."

"Like enjoying her husband's highly talented—" Owen begins.

"You done with the sales pitch?" Cherise says.

Owen's brows arch. "Sales pitch?"

"Casey doesn't want to fuck you. I know that comes as a tremendous shock, but I could write you a goddamned letter of recommendation, and it wouldn't change her mind. Now stop embarrassing yourself. The blonde seems tough enough for you. Maybe she'd like a romp."

"With him?" Petra says. "No thanks. However, if *you're* offering . . ."

Petra's trying to throw Cherise off balance, shock her. But Cherise only barks a laugh and says, "Not on the table, sugar. Not right now, anyway. I'm busy negotiating with your friend here." She turns to me. "I don't have the girl. I notice you aren't naming her. Neither am I. We're both covering our asses in case the other has mistakenly identified the target. I don't have her. I'm on her trail, though. I was given bad information on her exact whereabouts, but I spotted her this morning. Unfortunately, they were on the other side of the river, which isn't fully frozen, so I couldn't cross there and talk to them. I picked up the trail, and I thought we were getting close when my darling husband needed to take a shit."

"I had cramps."

"And now we're further delayed. Also, we're no longer the only ones tracking her. So here's my offer, Miss Casey. You can give me half the reward for finding her and setting you on the proper trail. Or we race to the finish line. But if we get to her first, I expect the full reward . . . or I *will* take her captive until I get it."

Petra balks, pointing out that we know who the target is and Cherise didn't "find" her. Yet Cherise did find out who Abby's mother is, independent of us, and unlike us, she knows where to pick up the trail. Also, as far as I'm concerned, if half the reward means Owen and Cherise fade into the forest without interfering, it's worth it. So I agree.

"You said *they*," I say. "She wasn't alone. You saw her with someone this morning?"

"Yep, her and her husband, out looking for their little one."

Petra's gaze cuts my way, but I pretend not to see it.

"So you saw this girl . . ."

"Sidra. Yes, I saw Sidra."

"And some guy . . ."

"*Her* guy. Baptiste. I saw Sidra and Baptiste across the river this morning, and I'd strongly suggest that you set your pup on their trail, because that sky says snow, and their trail isn't going to last."

# FORTY

Cherise shows us the trail, and I put Storm on it. The trail is a mess, and I can't help but wonder if we're being tricked. Whoever walked this way is following in the tracks left by a herd of caribou. The temperature is rising, and it's got to be above freezing, the sun beating down on a trail through relatively open land, meaning not only are the human prints almost lost among the caribou ones, but they're all melting into mush. And then it starts to snow, almost as if Cherise called for the skies to open and make it even more impossible to confirm her story.

"Here," she says, pointing at a clear footprint. "And before you say that's mine . . ." She puts her own foot beside it. Hers are about a size bigger. I don't trust Cherise, but she plays the long game, looking into the future and setting out her pieces for the moves that will ultimately benefit her rather than the ones that'll fill her pocket at this moment. It's not in her interests to trick us for one reward when she might be able to parlay this transaction into a long-term relationship.

They leave, and I set Storm on that print, the only one I'm relatively sure comes from Sidra. She snuffles around a bit. Once she's confident, she starts tracking.

"He lied," Petra says. "That son of a bitch Baptiste lied. I don't know how you bought his story, Casey. I'm sorry, but that was dead obvious. First his kid is kidnapped and then his wife? Not even by the same person? I'll tell you what happened. That hostile woman—Ellen—took Abby for good reason. Those two kids abandoned the baby or they were talking about it or they were just shitty parents. Ellen took Abby and ran. They caught up and shot her, and left their own baby to die in the forest."

I glance over at her. That's all I do. Heat rises in her face, and then her jaw sets. "Yes, I find it hard to believe any parent would do that, but as a cop, you know it happens. Even more likely, it was just him. My ex was the 'maternal' one in our relationship. Maternal in the traditional, ignorant sense that women are the 'real' parents, and the guys are just sperm donors and bottomless wallets. That's how men are raised. My ex grew up sneaking his sister's dolls to play with. If his parents caught him, they took them away, terrified it meant he was gay. That's what we do to little boys, and we do the opposite to little girls who *don't* want dolls. The result is that Mom usually *is* the maternal one, the protective one. How many family annihilators are women?"

"A few," I say. "But, yes, they're overwhelmingly men. Your point being, I presume, that you think Baptiste didn't want this baby. So he tried to get rid of her, shot Ellen, and is now leading us on a wild-goose chase after a fictional kidnapper."

"You saw his gun. Does it match the murder weapon?"

"Yes."

"Yet you still think the kid's telling the truth and Cherise is lying about seeing them together this morning?"

"No, I don't think Cherise is lying."

"Mistaken, then?"

"I'm not sure."

She grumbles at that. An idea is forming in my brain. It's been there since Cherise mentioned seeing Baptiste and Sidra across the river, and my gut screamed that she was wrong. Not lying. Just mistaken.

My brain demanded—and then supplied—an alternate explanation . . . and berated me for not asking more questions while I had Felicity and Baptiste here. Simple questions, easily answered, and yet I didn't ask, because they didn't seem germane to what was happening.

Baptiste or Felicity could tell me what I need to know. I also want to find Dalton to bounce this theory off him. He didn't hear our voices and come running while we were talking to Cherise. That bothers me, and I'm trying very hard not to freak out over it and shout for him. That would risk tipping off others in this forest. I must trust that Dalton is fine.

I could be wrong about Baptiste. If I am, then that may answer my "where are they?" question. My only consolation is that I haven't heard a shotgun blast. Which doesn't keep me from wishing we'd kept the damned weapon we'd taken from Baptiste.

After another half kilometer, I can't silence that fretting anymore. We might be hot on Sidra's trail, but we need to reunite with the others.

Petra agrees.

"I'll play signpost and mark the trail," she says. "You take the pup and go find Eric."

I set out with Storm. I've told her to find Dalton, and I'm hoping she'll catch his scent on the breeze. We walk through unbroken snow wherever possible, leaving bread crumbs back to Petra. It's less than ten minutes before Storm goes still. She sniffs the air. It's not Dalton. If it were, she'd veer that way without hesitation.

"Who is it, girl?"

Her body language is relaxed, meaning whoever it is doesn't worry her. Not Cherise and Owen then. It's a scent she recognizes, though, someone she has no strong feelings about either way. She glances at me, and there's question in that look. It suggests she's smelling another member of our party—Felicity or Baptiste—and while they aren't her target, perhaps I'm also looking for them?

"Good girl," I say. Then I tell her yes, please track the new scent. I'm not sure she'll understand my command, but she sets off at a lope.

I take out my gun. I must, in case this is Baptiste, and I am mistaken about him. We head into thick forest, and I slow Storm, only to get a look that says we're too close to the target to bother. Yet despite the thick forest, I don't see anyone.

Storm stops. She goes rigid and whines, anxiety strumming from her. I look around. There's no one here, no place for anyone to hide.

"What is it, girl?"

I follow her gaze. Just ahead, snow has been flattened. I see prints, multiple sets. That's when I spot the blood, drops of red sunk into the snow.

I race over.

There's blood. Definite blood, recently sprayed, droplets falling into fresh snow. Under my feet, the snow isn't just trampled—it's flat. Someone fell here. A struggle on the ground, a blow, blood flying.

Two sets of prints, coming from opposite directions. One significantly smaller than the other.

Felicity's prints. I recognize the imprint of fur around the edge. The other set is male. Not Dalton's boots. That's all I can tell. His prints would be instantly distinguishable from the tread-free ones. Felicity was here. Someone attacked her.

Or she attacked someone.

If it was Felicity attacking, though, she lost. I see the male prints leaving the flattened snow of the fight . . . and dragging something with him. Dragging Felicity.

I'm following that trail when Storm whines. Not the anxiety of smelling blood, though. This is excitement. Her nose goes up, and her entire body wriggles with the joy that can only mean one thing.

"Eric?" I say. "Do you smell Eric?"

She woofs, a deep adult-Newfoundland woof, even as her massive body puppy-gyrates with excitement.

"Good girl." I glance at the trail where someone dragged Felicity away. Is leaving it to go after Dalton the right move?

"Stop right there!" a voice shouts. Baptiste's voice, ringing through the forest . . . coming from the direction Storm is looking.

From Dalton's direction.

A shotgun blast, and I'm running, running as fast as I can. I hear Dalton's voice then. Thank God I hear Dalton's voice, even if it barely pierces the blood pounding in my ears. He's saying something I can't catch, his voice calm, and Baptiste shouts at him again, telling him to get back, get back right now, get away from her.

Her?

Felicity?

Sidra?

Either way, my gut drops. I've made a mistake. An unforgivable one. Cherise said she saw Baptiste with Sidra after Sidra was supposedly kidnapped. Petra jumped to the obvious conclusion—Baptiste was lying—but I'd wanted to believe otherwise. Yes, there's a selfish part of me that wants Abby's parents to be horrible people who do not deserve her, so I can keep her. But there's another part I only recognize now. The part that wants the best of all possible endings to this story by that little baby getting back to loving and capable parents. I want her to have good parents who love each other and love her and are beside themselves with panic at her disappearance.

That's the part that decided Baptiste isn't guilty. Not Baptiste and not Sidra. Neither of them killed Ellen. Neither of them got rid of their baby. Neither of them planned this fake kidnapping to get rid of us. They might be young and naive, but they are good and honest, and they deserve their little girl back. That is who I want them to be.

Then I hear Baptiste telling Dalton to "get away from her" and I realize I'm wrong.

As I work this through, I run. I don't stop running. Then I hear a woman's voice say, "Put the gun down, you son of a bitch," and I'm so caught up in my thoughts that I think it must be Sidra, talking to Dalton, and this means she is just as culpable—

No, not Sidra.

My mind replays the voice, and there is no question who I'm hearing, even before Petra says, "Lower that damned shotgun or I put a bullet through your lying-bastard head, boy."

I see Dalton now, just ahead. Others are with him, but they're only meaningless figures until I've found Dalton and confirmed he's on his feet, apparently unharmed.

"Petra, no," Dalton says. "Everyone just hold on."

I burst through the trees. The shotgun barrel turns on me.

Petra barks, "Don't you dare!" echoed by Dalton as he pulls his own gun, swinging it on Baptiste. Then we all freeze, guns pointing everywhere, and a voice says, "Stop, everyone please, stop."

It's a girl's voice, high and tight with fear. I follow it to a stranger, rising from the ground near Dalton as she claws off a gag. A girl no bigger than me, with long black curls. She staggers in front of Dalton, and Petra snaps, "Stop right there," but Sidra ignores her.

Sidra makes it to her husband, and he nearly drops the gun in his lunge to catch her. The muzzle is down, thankfully, and Petra doesn't fire as Baptiste grabs Sidra and the shotgun slides to the ground beside them.

"Put the gun down," Dalton says to Petra. "Everything's fine."

"Everything is not fine," she says. "These two tricked—"

"No one tricked anyone," Dalton says. "I found Sidra. I was freeing her when Baptiste showed up, and he misinterpreted. Sidra, did I kidnap you?"

She shakes her head. "He was helping me, Baptiste."

"Did Baptiste kidnap you?" I ask.

Her eyes round. "Of course not. I . . . I don't know who did it. Someone grabbed me at the camp and put something over my eyes."

"Then how do you know it wasn't Baptiste?" Petra asks.

Sidra's eyes flash. "I do not need to see my husband to know him. It was a man. I'm sure of that. He spoke to me, but his voice was distorted. We were walking but we kept stopping, and he'd tie me up. Then he'd leave and come back. He'd left me again when this man found me and said he was from Rockton and he was with you, Baptiste."

"He is," I say. "Your husband just panicked." I turn to Baptiste. "Have you ever lent Lane your shotgun?"

His face screws up, as if he's misheard.

"Lane from the Second—"

"Yes, I know Lane," he says impatiently. "He is my friend, and yes, I have loaned him our shotgun, but I don't understand—"

"That's the gun that was used to kill Ellen." I don't know that for certain, of course, but they'll never realize that. "Someone—"

"No!" Sidra says, and she wheels, and I think she's spinning on me to deny it, but instead, she faces the forest and shouts, "Lane!"

"That . . . That's . . ." Baptiste blinks, looking lost. "Lane wouldn't . . ." He trails off, unable to finish. Then he looks at me. "This gun? This gun was used . . ."

"To kill Ellen," Sidra says, and tears glisten in her eyes as she looks at me. "That's what you said, isn't it? Ellen is dead, and Lane killed her. Killed her and came for me. Killed her and stole . . . stole . . ."

She spins to face the forest again, and when she screams "Lane!" it's a raw and horrible sound, and the force of it buckles her knees. Baptiste catches her, his face still blank with shock. I see his face, and I see hers, and the missing piece falls into place.

Motivation.

Felicity said four kids from the two settlements hung out together. Tomas said Lane lost his best friend last year. That connection had clicked earlier. Lane knew Sidra and Baptiste, and Baptiste was his supposedly dead friend. I hadn't confirmed that because it seemed nothing more than a tragic collision of circumstance.

Lane knows Ellen. Lane also knows Baptiste and Sidra. A hostile steals their baby, and Ellen steals her back, and Lane sees her and shoots her because she's having an affair with his aunt. He has no idea she's clutching a baby under her parka. And the fact that that baby belongs to his old friends? Tragic, tragic coincidence.

That makes sense, right? And if the gun that murdered Ellen belongs to Baptiste, then that must mean Baptiste or Sidra actually shot her. The young couple have been trading their ʳame with Lane, who's been passing it off as his own arrow-

ᵗ kills. Then, when we accuse Lane of shooting Ellen with

that same gun, he realizes who actually did it and quickly spins a story to protect his friends.

That must be the answer, right?

Unless Cherise sees Sidra with a young man she presumes is Baptiste, while my gut says Baptiste *didn't* lie to us and his wife *is* missing. Who else could Cherise mistake for Baptiste? Another young dark-haired man of similar build.

Lane.

Before this moment, I could only guess at why Lane kidnapped Sidra. Maybe he confessed to her, and she hadn't forgiven him. Or maybe he took her hostage as a bargaining chip against his punishment for killing Ellen.

Neither scenario had satisfied me. Now, in Sidra's scream of rage and frustration, I hear the echoes of other women, and I see the answer.

"Lane . . ." Baptiste says, looking at me as he holds Sidra, who vibrates with fury. "You think Lane . . ."

"He confessed to killing Ellen," I say. "He didn't seem to know she was holding Summer when she died."

"H-holding . . ." Sidra says.

"Summer is safe," Baptiste says quickly. "This woman— Casey—found her, and she's fine. Ellen had rescued her and she—she died holding her, but they found Summer before— before anything could . . ."

"Lane murdered Ellen." Sidra stares at me. "While she was holding my baby. He left . . . he left her . . ."

"He didn't seem to know," I say.

Her face contorts in an inhuman snarl. "Oh, he knew. He knew." She turns and screams. "Lane! Show yourself, you coward! You want me so badly, come and face me!"

"Want . . ." Baptiste looks sick. "No . . . Yes, at first, yes . . . but he said he was over you. He said he was happy for us."

"He lied," Sidra spits, face contorting again. "He lied to you.

Not to me, though. Never to me. It didn't matter what I said. It didn't matter what I did."

"He . . . he kept . . . ?" Baptiste sways, face green. "He kept bothering you, and you never told me."

"He was your friend, and I thought he'd get over it. He would see the truth—that it was you, and it had always been you, and I never saw him as anything but a friend. I married you. I had your baby. He would understand soon. I kept telling myself he would finally understand. And he did not."

Baptiste goes still, processing. Then his face hardens, and he strides toward the forest. "Lane! Sidra's right. Show yourself! You have something to say to me, come out here and—"

A whistle. That's all I hear. An odd whistle, and then Baptiste falls back and Sidra screams. She runs to her husband as he staggers back, an arrow in his shoulder. Sidra knocks Baptiste to the ground as another arrow whistles past. She covers his body, protecting him, as we surround them, guns out, shouting for Lane.

The forest goes silent.

Dalton motions that he's heading in. I clamp down on the urge to stop him. Instead, I motion that I'll do the same, from the other side, and he gives me the same look, the one that resists saying no, don't go. Go or stay, though, we're in equal danger from an archer in the woods.

Dalton leaves first, as I call to Storm, loud enough to distract Lane if he's watching. I'm telling Storm to stay with Petra when Sidra shouts, "Lane!"

I look to see Sidra marching toward the forest, her arms spread wide. Petra is on the ground with Baptiste, checking his shoulder injury. Baptiste stares at Sidra and then tries to rise, but Petra holds him down.

"Sidra?" I say. "Don't—"

"Lane!" she shouts. "I do not love you. You could take me

captive, and I would only kill you the first chance I got. If I couldn't kill you, I would kill myself before I let you touch me. Is that clear? Do you understand? I will not be yours. I will never—"

"No!" I say. I hear her words, and I hear echoes of others, and I know what is coming, what is always coming in a situation like this.

I run for Sidra, but Petra is closer, and she knows the same thing I do. She's on her feet, launching herself at Sidra. That whistle sounds. That horrible whistle. Petra hits Sidra and sends her flying, and the arrow hits Petra in the chest. I'm already running at her, and I see it hit and her eyes round, mouth rounding, too, in surprise. Another arrow, this one hitting her in the shoulder, spinning her. She stumbles, and I catch her. I grab her, and her feet scuffle against the ground as she tries to stay upright.

"Cover!" I shout at Sidra and Baptiste. "Get to cover. Storm!"

Storm races to me as I half drag Petra. Baptiste says, "Here!" and I look to see him and Sidra ducking behind a deadfall off to our left. I manage to get Petra there. I glance at Baptiste, but he says, "I'm fine."

"He's not fine," Sidra says, voice quavering, "but his jacket is thick. He'll be all right."

Sidra helps me lay Petra down. Petra's fingers wrap around my arm, her face pale, eyes wide with impending shock.

"You're okay," I say. "Relax. Stay with us."

"Émilie," she says, and it takes me a moment to remember that that's her grandmother, one of the board members for Rockton. "The . . . the hostiles . . . Your . . . your theory."

"Tell Émilie my theory about the hostiles. Got it. But you can do it yourself. Just hold on."

We don't remove the arrows, not until we get a look at how deep they're in. I undo Petra's parka. While she hasn't been as lucky as Baptiste, the arrowheads haven't gone deeper than the head. One is in her shoulder, the other just above her heart. Serious, yes. Life-threatening, though? I hope not. I really, really hope not. I can't see well enough to be sure, not without removing the arrows.

"We need to snap off the shafts," I say. "If the shafts are off, we can get her out of that jacket and—"

"Eric," Petra whispers. "Go look after Eric. And get this guy. Stop him."

I hesitate, but Sidra shoulders me aside, taking over. "She's right. We'll leave the arrows in for now. Just find your sheriff and stop Lane." She meets my gaze. "Please stop Lane."

I nod, squeeze Petra's hand, and then take off.

# FORTY-ONE

From the arrow-fire, I know the direction to go. I do what we'd planned before Petra got shot—I sneak up in the other direction, presumably on Lane's opposite side. I hear Lane before I see him. He's breathing hard and fast, the sound pulling me easily through the woods, letting me approach alongside him, no danger of running smack into him. Not that I'm too worried about that. His weapon might be lethal, but he doesn't have an arrow nocked. I can see that as soon as I spot him. He's poised, bow in hand, his gaze riveted on the place where the others hide behind the deadfall.

He's waiting for movement. I don't know what he expects—someone to leap up like a jack-in-the-box? His heavy breathing tells me his adrenaline is pumping, blood pounding in his ears, rendering him deaf and blind to everything except what he wants to see.

Sidra.

He's waiting for Sidra.

He expects she'll leap up again to scream at him. Tell him that she'll never be his, and he will kill her for it. That is what men like him do. He's been raised to believe he has the right to a life partner, the right to the woman he chooses to fill that role, and if he can't have her, then by God, no one else will either. He'll kill Sidra and then himself. That is how this goes. It's how it always goes.

So Lane waits for his chance, and he doesn't hear me creep up on his left side. He hasn't seen the figure to his right either.

Dalton will have heard the commotion with Petra going down, and he'll have paused long enough to be sure we were safely under cover. Then he came here, where he'll wait to see what I do before he makes his move.

When I'm far enough behind Lane's peripheral vision, I lean out and catch Dalton's eye. He nods and motions a plan. Or I'm sure it's a plan, but we're forty feet apart in the forest, and it's not as if I see more than a few hand gestures. That's enough, though. I know what we should do, and it seems to coincide with what he's suggesting.

We both creep toward Lane from our respective positions, staying out of visual range and on either side of him. Then, without warning, Dalton steps forward, plowing through brush, winter-dry twigs crackling. Lane wheels on Dalton . . . and that's apparently my cue to swing behind him and cut off his escape route. I dart into place just as Lane looks over his shoulder to find me there, gun pointed at him, Dalton doing the same on his other side.

"If you reach for an arrow, we fire," I say. "You can run, but this time, we're close enough to catch you."

"Also close enough to shoot you," Dalton says. "Save ourselves the trouble of chasing."

"I'm fine with shooting," I say. "In fact, I'd say it might be our best option. Our only option, really. You stole a baby. You murdered Ellen. You hoped to murder the baby with her. Now you're trying to murder your best friend and the woman you supposedly love."

"Seems to me he doesn't know the meaning of that word," Dalton drawls.

Lane's face purples. "I'm the only one who *does* know the meaning of it. Baptiste doesn't. He's no friend of mine. Friends don't do that."

"Friends don't fall in love with the girl you like?" I say. "The girl who likes them back?"

"I *found* her," he says. "Not him. Me. I met Sidra and Felicity in the forest, hunting duck. I was their friend first, and then I brought Baptiste to meet them. I would get Sidra, and he'd get Felicity. He knew that. I found them first. So I was entitled to first pick."

"Yeah," Dalton says. "Like when you're hunting and you spot a herd of caribou. If you spot them first and bring your friend, you should get first shot, first pick of the herd. That's how it works, and if he shoots first, he's an asshole."

Lane straightens. "Yes. You understand."

"I understand if it's a herd of caribou," Dalton says. "But those were *girls*. Human beings. Not game animals. You can tell Baptiste you like Sidra, and if he's a decent friend, he won't make a play for her if there's a chance she feels the same about you. But that isn't how it went, was it?"

Lane shoots Dalton a look I can't see.

"Sidra fell for Baptiste," I say. "And he fell for her. He probably felt lousy about it, but from what I understand, you stood down. You told Baptiste it was fine . . . while you kept pursuing Sidra. She ran away with him, and you did what? Offered to help them? Bring their game to the Second Settlement in trade? Felicity backed off, but you stuck close in hopes of winning Sidra. Then along came a baby, and you couldn't allow that. You took Summer. Stole her."

"I had to," he snarls. "A winter baby? How could Baptiste do that to Sidra? It proved he didn't care about her. I did what needed to be done."

"Taking their baby and giving it to the hostiles?"

His jaw sets. "I gave it to a wild woman who wanted a child. I heard Ellen mention the woman, and I knew that was the answer. I left the baby where the woman went to get water each morning, and she took her. She was *happy* to take her. Then Ellen showed up and stole her back. I'd been out hunting with Baptiste's gun. As I headed home, I heard the baby, and I heard Ellen hushing her. I found them. I told Ellen to give me the baby, but she said no. She'd been hit on the head stealing her from the hostile woman, and she was confused. She ran, and I fired, and she kept running."

"So you let her go?" I say.

He doesn't answer.

"No, you didn't," I say. "You followed enough to see her lying down. She stopped to rest. Between the head injury and the shot, she was losing blood and confused, and she'd lain down to rest, and you left her there. You left her to die in the snow. You left the baby to die with her."

"I did it for her," he snarls. "For Sidra. To save her from *him*."

For fourteen years I have worried that someday, holding a gun in my hand, I will repeat the mistake I made with Blaine. Someone will say something, and the rage—the absolute rage I felt then—will rise again, and my gun will rise too, and I will pull the trigger.

For fourteen years, that possibility has terrified me.

And now, in this split second, it evaporates.

I feel that rage again, a blind wave of it washing over me. I see Ellen, lying in the snow, a woman who only wanted to help.

I see Ellen dead with Summer in her arms, and I think of how close that baby came to dying horribly in the snow, and all this time, I've told myself it was a mistake. It had to be, didn't it? No one would do that on purpose. Before me stands the boy who did it. On purpose. Murdered a kind and generous woman. Abandoned a baby to the elements. And for what? For a girl who never gave him a moment's encouragement. To murder her child, destroy her life, and then try to kill her if he couldn't have her?

Lane deserves my bullet more than Blaine Saratori ever did. He may even deserve it more than Val did. But I do not pull the trigger because I can control that impulse. The situation is under control, and we are in no immediate danger, and I cannot execute Lane for his crimes. That is not my place.

I know my place. I understand it, and I will never make that mistake again.

"Lane?" I say. "You are under arrest for the murder of Ellen and the attempted murder of Summer and Sidra and Baptiste. You will appear before a joint committee of the First and Second Settlements, who will determine your punishment—"

He runs at Dalton. I still don't fire. My finger moves to the trigger, and I shout at him to stop, but I don't need to shoot. Lane is a man with a bow in his hand, the arrows still in their quiver, and he's running at a law enforcement officer with a gun.

Dalton doesn't shoot either. When Lane draws near, he kicks, his foot connecting with a crack. The young man drops to one knee, and Dalton backs up, gun still aimed.

"Shoot me," Lane says.

"I'm not—" Dalton begins.

"You're going to have to. Because I won't stop. If you let me live, I'll never stop. I'll find a way to kill Baptiste, kill that baby, and if Sidra won't come with me, then I'll kill her, too.

She's mine. *Mine.* I will kill everyone who comes between me and her, and then I'll take her and—"

A figure rushes from the forest. It's a blur. That's all I see. A blur of motion, and I spin on it, my gun raised as it rushes Lane. The blur leaps on him, and only then do I see a face. A face not contorted in rage but ice-cold with it.

It's Felicity. Her hand flies up as I shout at her to get back, and as that hand rises, I see the blade in it. A blade already bloodstained, droplets flecking the snow.

The blade falls again, slamming into Lane's back, and I shout at her to stop, but I do not stop her.

I know my place, and it is not my place to stop her.

Only when she falls back, breathing hard, her hands clutching the bloody knife, does Dalton run over and pull her back. Lane falls face-first to the snow.

Felicity drops the knife and then wrenches from Dalton's grip. He lets her go. She walks over and drops to her knees beside Lane.

"You should have killed me while you had the chance," she says. "But that was always your mistake. You underestimated me. Underestimated Sidra. We made that mistake, too. We underestimated you." She leans down to his ear, her voice a hoarse whisper as she says, "Not this time. I did not underestimate you this time, Lane."

She stays there, at his side, until he breathes his last.

# FORTY-TWO

There's no time to process what has happened. No time to help Felicity process it, and I know from experience that will not happen immediately. She's done what she needed to do to protect her friend. Later, the doubts and second-guessing will come, and I don't know whether she'll let me help with that, but I will if I can.

Right now, our biggest concern is Petra. She has an arrow in her chest, and we are hours from Rockton. Dalton runs ahead to bring help and motorized transport. While he's gone, we fashion a stretcher for Petra. Storm pulls it, and Sidra and I help. While Baptiste and Felicity try to do their part, both are injured—Baptiste with a minor shoulder wound and Felicity with a head injury, inflicted when Lane found her in the forest. Their job is to walk behind the sled and make sure Petra stays awake and lucid.

We've been walking for almost two hours when I hear the whine of a snowmobile and the rumble of the ATV. Dalton cuts through brush on the snowmobile and then takes over the stretcher, guiding it through to where the ATV waits on a wider path.

Dalton sends me in the ATV with Sidra. I know why he picks her to go. He doesn't need to say it, but I know. After he sets Petra up for the ride, he stays behind with Anders to get the rest of the group to Rockton.

I drive the ATV as fast as I dare through the well-packed snow of the main trail. Sidra doesn't clutch the grab handles for dear life. She stares straight ahead, her face drawn, her mind already at our destination and what waits there.

I drive the ATV straight into town. April waits on the clinic stairs, Diana with her to help, several of the men ready to carry Petra inside. And as we pull to a halt, another figure appears from inside the clinic. Jen, holding a baby-size bundle to her chest.

Sidra is out of the ATV before it stops. She stumbles forward, tripping over her feet and nearly falling in her scramble to get to her baby. Jen descends the stairs and meets her, holding Summer out. Sidra doesn't take her. She wobbles there and then collapses to her knees, crying in relief, and Jen bends in front of her, letting Sidra take the baby there, kneeling in the snow.

I turn away from the scene and help the men with Petra.

It's morning. Early morning, not yet light. I'm beside Petra's bed in the clinic. She's stable. The arrow entered above her heart, piercing less than an inch. She's lost a lot of blood, and she'll need time to recover, but she's all right, sleeping soundly as I keep watch.

I've been here all night, not leaving the clinic since I arrived.

Hiding here? Yes, I have the self-awareness to admit that. April needed me, and I wanted to be here for Petra, but it also gave me the excuse not to face the joyous parent-and-child reunion.

I slept here, in this chair. In the night, I woke to find Dalton in a chair beside me, a blanket draped over us. When I wake again at six thirty, he's already gone, and I feel the regret of that, but I feel something else, too. Relief. I'm not ready to face him. I need time to process this and grieve on my own. And as soon as that thought comes, another follows it, a realization that has my cheeks flaming and my ass out of that chair in a heartbeat.

I check Petra. Then I hurry out to see Kenny walking past, and I ask him to step in and watch Petra for me.

"Actually, I was just coming for you," he says. "The kids are leaving soon, and they really want to see you first."

I hesitate, which is a shitty and selfish thing to do, and I am ashamed to admit it. I'm also snared between two sources of shame—the one that wants to flee any last moments with Summer and the one that needs to talk to Dalton.

"I should speak to Eric first," I say. "Is he around?"

"He's with the boy. Baptiste. They're talking, and Sidra wanted to bring the baby over to speak to you alone before they go."

I hesitate again, that childish impulse filling me, the impulse to lie and say I cannot see her. Nope, sorry, terribly, terribly busy. I squash it and say, "Of course. Send her over to the house, and let Eric know we're there."

"Before you go," he says. "The hot tub is ready. Where—?"

"Later," I say. "We'll talk later."

"But it's . . ."

His voice trails off as I hurry away.

---

As I walk through town, I hear carols and look over to see a group of people singing. I check my watch. Yep, it's seven in the morning. What the hell are people—? That's when I see the date on my watch.

December 21.

That's what Kenny meant. It's winter solstice. The biggest celebration of our year, and I could not feel less festive. I duck around the carolers and hurry to our house.

I'm opening our front door when Sidra appears. I hold it for her, and I smile, and I hope that smile looks every bit as genuine as she deserves. Because she *does* deserve it. This is her baby. She was, from what I can tell, a perfect mother, despite her youth. She's spent the ten days frantically trying to find her lost child. She confronted a killer to protect her family. And if there was any doubt about how much she loves Summer, it could not survive witnessing that heart-wrenching reunion scene last night.

So I smile for her, and it damned well better be a good one, or I will not forgive myself for my petty jealousy. I usher her in, and I'm about to apologize for the cold when I see that Dalton has laid the fire, in case I come back here. Thoughtful and considerate as always, which only twists the knife that reminds me I have not been the same to him these last few hours.

I start the kettle for coffee, mostly as busywork while she settles in with the baby.

Her baby. Not mine. Never mine.

"I can't thank you enough for what you did," she says. "Even saying thank you feels like such an understatement. But I don't know what else to say."

I'm not sure how to reply to that.

*It was nothing, really.*

*Any decent person would have done the same.*

*It was no trouble at all.*

Platitudes, and like her, I don't want to say them. They feel empty. So I only say, "You're welcome."

Then I turn, and she rises, holding out the baby, and I know she doesn't realize what that gesture means to me, how it is a knife in my gut. She is only being kind. So I must accept that kindness and accept Summer, and sink stiffly onto the chair, holding the baby and trying not to look down at her.

Summer fusses, and I tell myself she doesn't know I'm not looking at her, her eyes can't focus enough to find mine, but my gut calls me a coward, and I look down. Our eyes meet, and her lips purse, the way they do when she's considering whether to cry, and I'm almost hoping she will.

*Whoops, ha ha, guess she wants her mommy. Better take her back.*

Summer sucks her lips twice, as if considering. Then her nostrils flare, and it is as if she catches my scent, finally realizes it's me, and she snuggles down and my heart cracks. I feel it crack, and I feel the tears well, and I blink hard, clearing my throat.

"Have you given any thought to what Felicity offered last night?" I say. "Spending the winter with the First Settlement. I know you left because you didn't think they'd let you be with Baptiste, but you have a baby now. They won't separate your new family."

"Thank you, and yes, we're doing that. Only for the winter. We do want to be on our own. We could use help, though. Support and trade partners, and if either settlement will offer that, we'll take it."

"If you have any problems, come back here," I say. "I'm sure you'll be fine on your own once you're settled and the baby's a little older, but I'd strongly advise spending this winter in the settlement. Or here if they won't take you."

"And if they do take us . . ." She raises her eyes to mine, suddenly shy. "May we still visit?"

"Of course."

The door opens. Dalton and Baptiste enter, kicking snow off their boots. I hold Summer out to Sidra, but she motions for Baptiste to take her, teasing him when Summer fusses at his cold touch. I watch the three of them, and yes, my heart cracks a little more, but it swells, too. They are in love, with each other and with their baby, and no child can truly hope for more.

"Did you ask her?" Baptiste says to Sidra.

Sidra shakes her head and looks at me. "We . . . we named her Summer as a joke. Not a very good joke either. But we'd like, if it's all right with you, to change that. We'd like to call her Casey."

"I . . ." I swallow. "That . . . that's very kind. It isn't necessary, though, and I think she should have her own name. Summer is good." I force a too-bright smile. "And it'd be less confusing, when you come to visit. I am honored, though. Truly honored."

"Eric thought you'd say that," Baptiste says with a smile. "So Sidra and I have a backup plan. We heard you called her Abby here, after a young woman who died. May we keep calling her that?"

I glance at Dalton. He nods.

"Yes," I say. "That would be lovely. Thank you."

"We even have a toy our Abby brought to Rockton," Dalton says. "It's butt-ugly, but it meant a lot to her, and there's no family to give it back to. That and a necklace. You're welcome to take those. You can tell her about the girl she was named after."

Sidra's face glows. "Are you sure?"

"We're sure."

"That would be wonderful. Thank you."

———

Sidra, Baptiste, and Abby are gone. It doesn't matter that I never met Abbygail, the joy of handing over her toy and necklace will stay with me for a long time. They will be treasured, as they deserve to be. Giving her name to this baby is even more satisfying, not only to honor the girl who first carried it, but because, in an odd way, it helps me, as if something of the baby's visit here remains with her, even as she leaves.

Dalton and Storm walk with them for a bit. While they're gone, I hurry out to tell Kenny where I want the hot tub and ask if they can set it up later while I distract Dalton. I swing by the bakery and grab two dozen holiday cookies before they open their doors to the waiting line. I hand out the first dozen to those waiting, promise I'll see them all tonight at the big bonfire celebration. Then I go home.

The moment Dalton walks into the house, I say, "I am so sorry."

"For what?" he says as he walks into the living room, where I'm waiting with coffee and cookies.

"Being a complete and utter selfish bitch. I avoided you last night because I was dealing with Abby leaving. But I'm not the only one affected, and I ignored that. I made it all about me. It wasn't."

He sinks onto the sofa and tugs me down beside him. "I understood. And I think it was harder for you. You bonded with her. Me?" He tilts his head. "I'd have kept her. Happily kept her. But for me she was more of a . . ."

He purses his lips. "She was a glimpse of something else. A vision of a possibility I never really considered. Not just a baby, but a baby with you. A family that's more than you and me. After having Abby here, yeah, I can see that for us, and I think I want it. Except . . ."

He goes quiet, uncomfortably quiet, scratching at his beard. "Go on."

He sneaks a peek my way.

"Eric? Talk. Tell me what you're thinking. If what you want isn't what I want, we'll discuss that. I'd never hold it against you."

"I like the vision I saw," he says. "If Abby needed a father, I'd be that for her. But since she doesn't, I'm just . . . I'm in no hurry. I . . ." Another glance snuck my way. "I'm not sure I'm ready to share you just yet."

"And I am thrilled to hear that, because I'm not ready to share you either. As much as I loved seeing you with Abby, part of me wants you all to myself for a little longer."

He nods. It's not the decisive nod I expect, though, and I say, "There's more, isn't there?"

"Not about this. Yeah, I'd like a kid someday. But yeah, I want more time with just us. Seeing Sidra and Baptiste though . . ." A deep breath. "It brought back a lot of memories. They reminded me of my parents. Memories of them I didn't even think I still had. How they looked at each other, how they looked at Jacob. How they looked at . . ." Another scratch of his beard as he shrugs.

"How they looked at you."

He nods. "Those kids and that baby, they're a family, and I had that kind of family."

"A lot of hope," I say. "A lot of love."

His eyes glisten, and he blinks hard with a thick, "Yeah. I need to face that. Remember it. Deal with it." He looks at me. "Talk about it."

"I'm here whenever you're ready."

"I'm ready," he says. "Maybe not for a baby, but I'm ready for this."

"Then I'm ready to listen."

# Games Traitors Play

Also by Jon Stock

*The Riot Act*
*The Cardamom Club*
*Dead Spy Running*

# Games Traitors Play

## JON STOCK

Thomas Dunne Books
St. Martin's Press
New York

THOMAS DUNNE BOOKS.
An imprint of St. Martin's Press.

GAMES TRAITORS PLAY. Copyright © 2011 by Jon Stock. All rights reserved. Printed in the United States of America. For information, address St. Martin's Press, 175 Fifth Avenue, New York, N.Y. 10010.

www.thomasdunnebooks.com
www.stmartins.com

ISBN 978-0-312-64477-2

First published in Great Britain by Blue Door, an imprint of HarperCollins*Publishers*

First U.S. Edition: April 2012

10  9  8  7  6  5  4  3  2  1

*In memory of
my father Peter Stock*

'For while the treason I detest, the traitor still I love'

John Hoole

# 1

A hot afternoon in Marrakech, and the square was already full of people and promise. If the storyteller was aware of the crowd around him, he didn't show it. The old man sipped at his sweet mint tea and sat down on a plastic chair, first brushing something off it with his empty hand. Had he looked up, he would have seen men and women surge across the square like iron filings, drawn by the magnetism of his act. But he never raised his head, not until he was ready to begin his tale.

Daniel Marchant wondered if he prayed in these moments, or was just running a mental finger over the bookshelves, choosing his narrative. He had been watching this particular storyteller – or *halaka* – for a week now, convinced that he held the answer to a question that had occupied every waking hour and all of his dreams since he had arrived in Morocco three months earlier.

From his vantage point on the rooftop terrace of the Café Argana, Marchant was able to watch the half-dozen *halakas* who worked the northern end of Djemaâ el Fna square. None of the others drew a crowd like this one, with his cobalt-blue turban, untidy teeth and cheap pebble glasses that magnified his eyes. Locals came for the stories, tourists for the photos, unable to understand a word but swept along by the drama.

This *halaka* could tell a thousand and one different tales of dervishes and djinns, each one recounted as if, like Queen Scheherazade, his own life depended on it. Marchant had learned that storytelling had been in his Berber family for centuries, passed down from father to son. In his hands, the tradition was safe, despite the rival temptations of Egyptian television soap operas. And he knew just when to pause, leaving his story on a knife edge. Only when the money bowl had been passed around would he continue.

On a good day, he was even more of a draw than the Gnaoua musicians from the Sahara who somersaulted and swirled their way through the crowds down by the smoky food stalls. When he was talking, the square's snake charmers rested their cobras, fire-eaters paused for breath, even the travelling dentists put down their dentures and tools.

Marchant sat up in his chair, sensing that the time had almost come. He wasn't sure how the *halaka* judged when the crowd had reached critical mass. The man was a natural showman, milking the moment every afternoon when he finally lifted his sunbeaten face and surveyed his audience with a defiant stare. Marchant reached for his camera, focusing the lens on the top of the man's turban. The storyteller's head was still bent forward, concealing his face.

The lens was not the sort that could be bought in a camera shop, but anyone watching Marchant would not have suspected that it was many times more powerful than its innocuous length suggested. He appeared like just another tourist as he slid it through the ornate metal latticework of the restaurant railing and observed the scene below him. Except that a tourist might have taken a few photos, particularly when the *halaka* finally looked up to address his expectant crowd. But Marchant forgot he was watching through a camera, forgot his cover. He could see that the man in his lens was frightened.

Marchant had come to know the *halaka*'s assured mannerisms, the tricks of his trade. The street wisdom of yesterday had vanished, his stage presence replaced by fear. He should have been staring ahead, hypnotising his audience with a narrator's spell, but instead the man's eyes flitted to the back of the crowd, as if he were searching for someone. Pulling on the hem of his grey *djellaba,* the local head-to-toe garment, he rocked on his battered *baboush* slippers, shifting his weight from heel to toe. For perhaps the first time in his life, the storyteller appeared lost for words.

Marchant checked with his own eyes, as if the camera might be lying, and then looked again through the lens. He took some photos, cursing himself for his slackness, and scanned the back of the crowd. The man was here somewhere, he was sure of it, waiting to hear the *halaka*'s coded phrases that would send him off into the snow-tipped Atlas Mountains to the south of the city. And Marchant would follow, wherever the man went, however remote, knowing who the message was for.

For several weeks, Marchant had been convinced that someone was planning to make contact with Salim Dhar through the story-tellers of Marrakech. He had overheard something in the souks, a fleeting remark in amongst the chatter. Using the *halakas* was a primitive form of communication for the world's most wanted terrorist, but that was the point. Echelon, the West's intelligence-analysis network, was in meltdown, monitoring every email, phone call, text and Twitter for the faintest trace of Dhar. It had been ever since he had tried to assassinate the US President in Delhi the previous year. Every time the analysts at Fort Meade in Maryland thought they had found him, the information was relayed to the CIA's headquarters in Langley. Its drone strikes in Af-Pak, where most of the sightings were reported, were now running at thirty a month.

But Dhar was still free, on the run. And Marchant was certain that no amount of software would ever find him. Dhar was shunning technology, keeping one step ahead of the modern world by retreating into the old. Ancient oral traditions, such as the *halakas*, were beyond the range of the spy planes and stealth satellites that orbited the globe in ever more desperate circles.

It had worked for fugitives before. During the 1970s, when General Oufkir was Morocco's hardline interior minister, the *halakas* used code words to refer to him and alert the public to planned raids by his secret police. Snakes were more than serpents sliding through the narrative: they were warnings of time and place. It was a way of communicating without suspicion. Information could be passed anonymously, without one-to-one meetings: textbook tradecraft. And now the *halaka* was about to issue another message.

Marchant pushed his tea away, folded some *dirhams* under the silver pot, and went to the stairwell. He knew he didn't have long.

Down in the square, a man approached him from a narrow alley to one side of the café.

'Hashish? You want some hashish?'

Marchant managed a smile. His student cover must have been convincing. Officially, he was in Morocco for a PhD on Berber culture, and took his studies very seriously. His dirt-blond hair was cut short, and he was wearing a woollen *djellaba*.

'Thanks, no,' he said, walking on towards the crowd.

'Souk tour? Leather? Instruments? I show you Led Zeppelin photos. Mr Robert, he came to my friend's shop.'

Marchant ignored him and walked on. He could do without the attention. The tout was not giving up, though, trotting along beside him, pouring out a list of random words that he must have gleaned over the years, like a magpie, from visiting tourists.

'Which place are you from, Berber man? London? I know UK. Yorkshire pudding, 73 bus, Sheffield steel.'

But the tout was losing interest. He peeled away, calling half-heartedly after Marchant, 'M&S? A303?'

Marchant had almost joined the crowd now. He didn't want any trouble in future from this man, so he raised a hand in a friendly farewell, his back to him.

'Terrorist,' the tout said, loud enough for one or two people at the edge of the crowd to turn around. Marchant had been called a few things in Marrakech, but this was a first. The choice of that term of abuse was nothing more than an unfortunate coincidence, he told himself, but he scanned the square again. Most of the sellers had got to know him in the past few months, letting the diligent British student practise his Berber on them. This tout was new to the area. Marchant threw him another glance. He was now leading two female tourists into the medina, looking at their map. Was it a CIA cover? Did someone else share his suspicions of the *halaka*?

The Americans had kept an eye on Marchant when he had first arrived in Marrakech, but they had soon lost interest, believing that the British agent was barking up the wrong tree. Langley was sure that Salim Dhar wasn't in North Africa, but had headed north after attempting to assassinate the President, smuggling himself across the Kashmir border in a goods lorry. The trail had gone cold in Pakistan, as it so often did, and they assumed he was now in hiding on the north-west border with Afghanistan, along with many of America's other most wanteds.

Marchant joined the back of the crowd and listened, watching the people around him. They had already fallen under the spell of the *halaka*, who had regained his composure. As he listened to the story of Sindbad the sailor, Marchant wished his Berber was better. He was back lying on the floor of his childhood home in the Cotswolds. A recording of Sindbad was the first vinyl album his father had ever bought him. For weeks after playing it on the big old wooden-cased HMV player, Marchant had had nightmares about the Roc bird, terrified that the skies would darken with its enormous wings.

The *halaka* had paused. Marchant watched him closely, the droplets of sweat beading his brow. He had caught the eye of someone near the back of the crowd, holding his gaze for barely a second. Marchant had clocked the man earlier, a Berber, early twenties, calico skullcap. Marchant waited for the *halaka* to begin speaking again – of giant serpents and the Roc bird – and then glanced back at the man. But he was already gone, walking briskly across the square, trying not to break into a run.

# 2

The six US Marines had been travelling all night and most of the day, bound, gagged and blindfolded. But now the 4x4 had come to a stop, giving their bruised bodies a brief respite. The vehicle's suspension was shot through, and they had been driven over poor mountainous tracks. No one, though, was under any illusion about what lay ahead: if they had reached the end of their journey, they were close to the end of their lives.

They had expected to die the night before, when a group of Taleban insurgents had ambushed their radio reconnaissance unit on a notorious stretch of road near Gayan in Paktika, eastern Afghanistan. They should have been in Helmand with the rest of their Marine Expeditionary Force, but had been seconded to Paktika in a push to hunt down the local Pashtun warlord, Sirajuddin Haqqani. After a stand-off, waiting in vain for the air support they had called in, the Marines had stepped out from behind their disabled Hummer with their arms up, exhausted, expecting to be shot. But the Taleban had taken them prisoner. It was a high-risk strategy: the US response would be on an overwhelming scale. The AC-130 gunships, though, never showed, and the Taleban moved out quickly with their captives.

The rear and side doors of the 4x4 opened and two Taleban began to pull the Marines from the vehicle, grabbing the collars of their sweat-soaked fatigues. As their platoon commander, Lieutenant Randall Oaks knew he had to be strong, set an example for the others, but in truth he wished he had been shot the previous night. He thought of the videos of beheadings he had told himself not to watch before coming out to Afghanistan, the stories that had circulated in the camp when they had first flown in from North Carolina. It wasn't good to be a prisoner of the Taleban.

Oaks could tell through his blindfold that the daylight was dying. It was cooler, too, compared to Gayan, where they had been ambushed, and he had been aware of gaining height during the long drive. If they were being taken to the mountains, maybe they could hope to live for a few more days. They would become bargaining chips, a way to buy some advantage in a war that neither side was ever going to win. But now he sensed another agenda.

None of their Taleban captors said anything as they pushed the Marines along a track. Oaks could hear the others stumbling, like him, on the rocky terrain, but there was one noise that was different. The Taleban were dragging someone along, a Marine who was too weak to walk. Oaks knew it was Lance Corporal Troy Murray. They were a tight-knit unit, had been ever since they had arrived five months earlier, but Murray had stood out for all the wrong reasons from the start. It wasn't just the word 'INFIDEL' that he had had tattooed in big letters across his chest. He was physically the weakest and mentally a mess, unable to go out on patrol unless he had taken too many psychological meds. This was his fourth tour, and he should never have been sent.

One more month and they were due to return to Camp Lejeune. Their families' banners would soon be up on the fencing that ran along Route 24 outside the base, joining the mile upon mile of 'Missed you' and 'Welcome home' messages that had become a part of the North Carolina landscape. It was a public patchwork of loss, each banner telling a private story, of missed births, heartache, lonely nights, enforced chastity.

Oaks remembered the first time he saw them, returning from his inaugural tour of Iraq. Envious cheers had gone up on the bus when Murray, in happier days, had seen his: 'Get ready for a long de-briefing, stud muffin.' And then he had seen his own, written in bright purple felt-tip on a big bedsheet, near the main gate: 'Welcome Home Lieutenant Daddy. Just in time for the terrible twos.' He was a family man now.

In recent days, the platoon had begun to brag about what they would do when they got home. Visit the clubs in Wilmington: The Whiskey, The Rox; shoot the breeze on Onslow Beach, listen out for the bell of the man selling snowballs. But there was only one thing now on Oaks's list: to become a more loving husband, a less absent father. He would attend church every Sunday, every day if necessary. As an adult, he had never been religious, but in the past twenty-four hours he had prayed with a desperate intensity, trying in vain to remember the brief period in his childhood when he had fallen asleep in prayer, risen early to read the Bible at the kitchen table. Within the last hour, as his own elusive faith had slipped through his hands like desert sand, he had even attempted to address other people's gods, too, explaining, apologising, beseeching.

The group was being herded into what felt like a small farm outbuilding. The few outdoor sounds – faint wind, distant birdsong – were partly muffled, but not entirely. It was as if they were surrounded by walls, but were still outside. Above their heads, Oaks thought he could hear the sound of a canopy flapping. Before he could think any more about their location, he was pushed down to the dry floor, his back up against an uneven wall. The gag in his mouth was peeled up and a bottle of water put to his chafed lips. He drank deeply until the bottle was pulled away, his gag replaced. It was not as tight as it had been, though, and Oaks began at once to work his jaw, keeping it moving.

The removal of his sight had heightened his other senses. He knew there were two Taleban with them. One was administering the water, but what was the other doing? He listened above the delirious moaning of Murray, who sounded barely conscious. There was the click of a case and the sound of something metallic being placed high up on a wall, on a windowsill perhaps. Was it an Improvised Explosive Device, set to be triggered by their movement? There was silence again. The two Taleban were leaving them. There were more muffled moans from the men, sounds of primitive despair as they dug their boot heels deep into the mud.

Oaks heard the 4x4 start up outside. He was expecting some wheelspin, a triumphant circling of the prisoners before it roared off. But the vehicle just drove back down the track, as casually as his father's station wagon when he used to leave for work, until the sound of its engine was lost in the stillness of the night. That slowness terrified him. It was too calm, too rehearsed, indicative of a bigger plan.

Ten, maybe fifteen minutes later, his thoughts were interrupted by the sound of someone speaking Urdu, coming from close by. Oaks's tired brain struggled to work out what was happening, whether he was hallucinating. He tried to focus on the name the man had given when he first spoke. It hung in the air above them like a paper kite, nagging at Oaks's mind as it bobbed in the evening breeze: Salim.

# 3

This was the moment Omar Rashid had been trained for, but he had never actually expected it to happen, not to him. But there it was, an unambiguous flashing light on his console. He knew his life would never be the same again. He was just a junior analyst on the SIGINT graveyard shift, always had been, ever since he'd signed up to the National Security Agency at Fort Meade in Maryland. And that was exactly how he liked it. Success happened to the ambitious, to the hungry. Rashid was more than happy to draw his modest salary and listen through the night to the regional traffic, before heading home to his basement apartment in Baltimore. He enjoyed his work, but it wasn't loyalty to the NSA that drove him.

A few hours earlier, he had tuned in to a pro-Western Pakistani politician and his wife arguing on a phone in Lahore. Later, when the husband had returned to his home in a wealthy suburb, he had listened to them making love, too, thanks to a wire installed in the bedroom by the ISI, Pakistan's main intelligence agency. The ISI was unaware that its heavily encrypted surveillance frequencies had been breached, but Rashid didn't concern himself about that. Just as he tried not to dwell on the pleasure he derived from such interceptions, known as 'vinegar strokes' among the nightshift analysts. He had feigned indifference when he handed in his transcript to the line manager, but it was a gift, and he hoped she would enjoy it later. Didn't everyone at SIGINT City?

This, though, was different. The flashing light was an Echelon Level Five alert, triggered by a keyword integral to one of Fort Meade's biggest-ever manhunts. Rashid's able mind worked fast. Despite Echelon's best efforts, it was impossible for the West to monitor more than a fraction of the world's phone calls and emails in real time. Most of the daily 'take' was recorded and crunched later by NSA's data miners, who drilled down through the traffic, searching for suspicious patterns. They worked out in Utah, where a vast data silo had been built in the desert. Rashid was one of a handful of Urdu analysts who worked in the now. He cast his net each day on the Af-Pak waters and waited.

Real-time analysts knew where to listen, but the odds of catching anyone were still stacked against them. As a result, Rashid was left alone. Anything he could bring to the table was a bonus. But if this latest intercept was what the flashing light suggested it was, he would be fêted, hailed as a hero. His work would suddenly be the centre of attention. A manager would study his previous reports, discover a pattern, the unnaturally high number of bedroom intercepts. Someone would sniff the vinegar.

The keyword and a set of coordinates in North Waziristan were triggering alarms all over the system. Rashid adjusted his headphones. He was listening to one half of a mobile-phone conversation in Urdu: the other person must have been speaking on an encrypted handset. COMINT would track it down later, unpick its rudimentary ciphers. The voiceprint-recognition software had already kicked in, analysing the speaker's vocal cavities and articulator patterns: the interplay of lips, teeth, tongue. Rashid didn't need a computer to tell him whose voice it was. The whole of Fort Meade knew it. It had been played over the building's intercom in the months after the attempt on the President's life.

Photos of the would-be assassin were on every noticeboard, along with details of the bonus for any employee who helped bring about his capture.

In a few seconds, Rashid would have details of the mobile number's provenance and history. Occasionally, this yielded something, but ninety-nine times out of a hundred it was a clean pay-as-you-go phone, bought over the counter in a backstreet booth in Karachi. Rashid's supervisor arrived at his shoulder just as the screen started to blink.

'You got something for me, Omar?' she said, more in hope than expectation.

Rashid nodded at his computer, feeling his mouth go dry. Two lights were now flashing. The number had been used once before, in south India, days before the assassination attempt on the President in Delhi. It was the last time Salim Dhar had made a call on a mobile phone.

'Sweet holy mother of Jesus, you've been fishing,' the supervisor whispered, one hand on his shoulder. With the other, she picked up Rashid's phone, still staring at his screen. 'Get me James Spiro at Langley. Tell him it's a real-time Level Five.'

# 4

Marchant had nearly lost the man several times in the network of narrow lanes off Djemaâ el Fna. He appeared to be heading south, walking fast down the rue de Bab Agnaou, occasionally looking behind him, but only at junctions, where he could pass off the glances as normal behaviour. The man knew what he was doing. Marchant kept as much distance as he dared between them, but he was on his own. In normal circumstances, a surveillance team of six would be moving through the streets with him, ahead of and behind the target like an invisible cocoon, covering every possibility. Marchant had no such luxury.

He kept one eye out for a taxi as the street widened. It was a less popular part of town for foreigners, and he needed to work harder to blend in. Instead of shoe shops selling yellow *baboush* and stalls piled high with pyramids of dates and almonds, there were noisy industrial units, larger and less welcoming than the tourist-friendly workshops in the medina. Marchant would follow the man like-for-like. It helped the pursuer to think like his target, to try to anticipate his choices. If he had a car parked somewhere, Marchant would find a car. If he got onto a bicycle, Marchant would find a bicycle.

The man had stopped outside what seemed to be a small carpet factory. Marchant hung back in the shadow of an empty doorway, fifty yards down the street. He could hear the sound of looms weaving, shuttles shooting. Bundles of wool hung from an upstairs window, the rich cupreous dyes drying in the low sun. A woman came to the factory entrance. She chatted briefly with the man, looking up and down the street as she spoke, and pressed a key into his hand.

Without hesitating, the man walked around the corner, started up an old motorised bike and drove off slowly, blue smoke belching from the two-stroke engine. For a moment, Marchant wondered if it would be easier to pursue him on foot, but he checked himself: like-for-like. Despite being in a hurry, the man had specifically chosen low-key transport. He was trying not to draw attention to himself, which suggested he was worried about being followed or watched.

Marchant crossed the road to a row of parked mopeds. Marrakech was overrun with Mobylettes and other Parisian-style motorised bikes, a legacy of when Morocco was a French protect-orate. They weaved in and out of the tourists and shoppers in the souks, taking priority like the cows in the markets of old Delhi, which he used to visit on his ayah's shoulders as a child.

He glanced at the selection. There was an old blue Motobecane 50V Mobylette, top speed 30 mph, and a couple of more modern Peugeot Vogues. The Mobylette was slower, but it would be easier to start, and the man was already out of sight, the noise of his engine fading fast. It also held a certain appeal for Marchant. For years, the Mobylette was made under licence in India. A few months before his father finished his second posting in Delhi, the family had presented Chandar, their cook, with one, to replace his old Hero bicycle. Chandar used to maintain it lovingly, showing Marchant, then eight years old, how to start it, both of them laughing as Chandar pedalled furiously in his chef's whites until the engine coughed into life.

Marchant checked that the Mobylette's wheel forks weren't locked. Nothing he had done since his arrival in Marrakech had aroused any attention from the authorities. That was part of the deal, one of the conditions he had agreed with MI6 in return for being sent to Morocco and allowed to operate on his own. He hadn't wanted back-up or support. It was, after all, a very personal quest: family business, as his father would have called it. Marcus Fielding, the professorial Chief of MI6, had agreed, knowing that if anyone could find Salim Dhar, it was Marchant. But Fielding had warned him: no drinking, no brawls, no break-ins, nothing illegal. He had caused enough trouble already in his short career.

Marchant had kept his side of the bargain. For three months, he had stayed off the sauce, savouring life outside Legoland, MI6's headquarters in Vauxhall. The CIA had prevented him from leaving Britain in the aftermath of the assassination attempt, but after a frustrating year, Fielding had finally prevailed, much to Marchant's relief. London was no place for a field agent.

He had studied hard in Marrakech's libraries, researching the history of the Berbers and taking the opportunity to reread the Koran. It had been required reading during his time at Fort Monckton, MI6's training base on the end of the Gosport peninsula. But he read it now with renewed interest, searching for anything that might help him to understand Salim Dhar's world.

In the cool of the early mornings, he had gone running through the deserted medina. The first run had been the hardest, not because his body was out of shape, but because of the memories it brought back: the London Marathon, Leila, their time together. He had returned after two miles, in need of a stiff drink, but he managed to keep his promise to Fielding. After two weeks, he no longer missed the Scotch. In a Muslim country, abstinence was easier than he had feared it would be. And he realised that he no longer missed Leila. It felt as if life was starting anew.

In the year following Leila's death, he had been unable to go running. He had missed her every day, seen her face wherever he went in London. The coldness that had encased his heart since he arrived in Morocco had shocked him at first, but he knew it had to be if he was to survive in the Service. His trained eye had spotted one suicide bomber amongst 35,000 participants, but he had failed to identify the traitor running at his own side, the woman he had loved.

Now, though, he was about to cross a line, and for a moment he felt the buzz he'd been missing. It was hardly a big breach, but if someone reported a foreigner stealing a Mobylette, there was a small chance that the local police would become involved. A report might be filed. He would show up on the grid, however faintly, and he couldn't afford to do that. London would recall him. He would be back behind a desk in Legoland, analysing embellished CX reports from ambitious field agents, drinking too much at the Morpeth Arms after work. But he couldn't afford to lose his man.

He glanced up and down the street. No one was around. He sat on the Mobylette, which was still on its stand. He checked the fuel switch, then began pedalling, thinking of Chandar as he worked the choke and the compressor with his thumbs. The engine started up, and he rocked the bike forward, throttled back and set off down the road. It wasn't exactly a wheelspin start.

As the Mobylette struggled to reach 25 mph, the only thing on Marchant's mind was where the man could be heading on a motorised pedal bike. Marchant had assumed all along that if he was right about the *halaka*, the contact would carry his message south into the High Atlas mountains, to Asni and beyond to the Tizi'n'Test pass, where the Moroccan Islamic Combatant Group (GICM) was known to run remote training camps (it had others in the Rif mountains, too).

The GICM had its roots in the war against the former Soviet Union in Afghanistan, and had forged close ties with al Q'aeda, providing logistical support to operatives passing through Morocco. After 9/11, it had become more proactive, and a number of sleeper cells were activated. The synchronised bombings in Casablanca in 2003, which had killed forty-four people, bore all the hallmarks of GICM, and the leadership had helped with the recruitment of *jihadis* for the war in Iraq. Marchant was convinced, after three months in Marrakech, that the organisation was now shielding Salim Dhar in the mountains. But the smoking bike ahead of him would struggle to reach the edge of town, let alone make it up the steep climb to Asni.

# 5

Lieutenant Oaks had worked the wet gag loose enough to speak. It was still in his mouth, but the tension had gone and he was able to make himself heard.

'Everyone OK?' he asked, breathing heavily. He could tell from the grunted responses that the others had been propped against the wall on either side of him, two to the left, two to the right. Only one of them hadn't replied.

'Where's Murray?' Oaks asked. There was a faint reply from across the room. At least he was still alive. Outside, the noises of an Afghanistan night offered little comfort: the distant cries of a pack of wild dogs. The Urdu had stopped a few minutes earlier, and Oaks was now certain whose voice it had been.

'We don't have long,' he said, edging himself across the floor to what he hoped was the centre of the hut. Movement was difficult, painful. His legs were bound tight at the ankles, and his wrists had been shackled together high up behind his back, his arms bent awkwardly. No one moved, and he wondered if any of them had understood his distorted words.

'We've got to get into the centre, right here,' he continued, falling on his side. He lay there for a few seconds, his cheek on the mud floor. It smelt vaguely of animals, of the stables he had visited in West Virginia for a childhood birthday. They had minutes to live, and he only had one shot at saving them. 'Get your asses over here!' he shouted, his voice choking with the effort of trying to right himself. 'Jesus, guys, don't you get it?'

He heard the shuffle of fatigues across the floor. 'Is that you, Jimmy? Leroy? Bunch up tight, all of you.' Slowly, the Marines dragged themselves into the centre of the room, even Murray, who was the last to arrive, rolling himself over on the dry mud. He lay at Oaks's feet, listening to his leader, breathing irregularly.

'That voice,' Oaks said, composing himself, frustrated by his distorted words. He was sounding like the deaf boy in his class at high school. 'It was Salim Dhar's.' He worked his jaw again, trying to shake off the sodden gag. No one said anything. They still hadn't realised the implications. 'A UAV will be on its way, you understand that? A drone. The fucking Reaper's coming.'

Murray let out a louder moan. Oaks tried not to think about the two Hellfire missiles he had once seen being loaded under an MQ-1 Predator at Balad airbase in Iraq. The kill chain had been shortened since then. There was no longer the same delay. And the MQ-1 Predator had become the MQ-9 Reaper, a purpose-built hunter/killer with five-hundred-pound bombs as well as Hellfires.

America had learned its lessons after it had once seen Mullah Omar, the one-eyed leader of the Taleban, in the crosswires of an armed Predator. It was in October 2001, a few weeks after 9/11, and the CIA had wanted to fire at Omar's convoy of 4x4s, but the decision was referred upwards to top brass in the Pentagon, who consulted lawyers and withheld the order while Omar stopped to pray at a mosque. The moment passed, and the story, true or false, entered military folklore. Americans had been trying to make amends ever since, taking out hundreds of Taleban and al Q'aeda targets with pilotless drones, or UAVs, but Oaks knew that the military had never quite got over the Omar incident. Now the Taleban was taunting them again.

'We'll show up on the UAV's thermal imaging,' Oaks said. 'This lousy cowshed's just got a sheet for a roof.' He had little confidence in his plan, but he had to try something. He owed it to his daughter. 'Do exactly as I say, and pray to your God.'

# 6

Marchant knew as soon as the man pulled into the petrol station that he was going in for an upgrade. The bike had made it five miles out of Marrakech on the R203, across the dry plains south of the city, but it was now starting to struggle. His own Mobylette was suffering too, and the frosted mountains were looming, floating on the horizon in the evening light. But it wasn't the scenery that interested Marchant: it was the group of touring motorbikes that had stopped to refuel at the station. His mind was beginning to think like a thief's. He pulled up two hundred yards short of the garage, bought a bottle of mineral water from a roadside stall, and drank deeply, watching the dusty forecourt.

There were at least ten bikes, powerful tourers laden down with carriers covered in ferry stickers and English flags. Marchant knew from his three months in Marrakech that Morocco was a popular 'raid' for British bikers. He had seen them rumbling into town on their way to the Atlas Mountains, where the roads were good and the passes were among the highest in Africa.

The riders, bulked out in their padded leathers, had crowded around one bike. It was set apart from the others, next to a support Land Rover Defender. A man was lying on the ground beside the back wheel. The bike seemed to have a mechanical problem of some sort, and the group was deep in discussion, talking animatedly with two local guides. The other bikes were unattended. If the keys were in the ignition, it would be easy for the man to set off on one of them. But he drove past the bikes, past the petrol pumps, and parked his moped on the far side of the forecourt shop. He then walked around the back of the building, out of sight.

What was he doing? Marchant kept watching as he slipped the lid back onto the plastic bottle of water. Moments later, the man reappeared, helmeted and riding a powerful touring bike. As if making a token check for traffic, he looked back down the dusty road in Marchant's direction – was he taunting him? – and was gone, roaring off towards Asni and the mountains.

Marchant felt sick. He was about to lose his man. He also knew that he was right, that Salim Dhar was up there somewhere in the High Atlas. And that made his stomach tighten so much that he wanted to throw up. The only good thing was that none of the bikers had clocked the man as he had driven off. In Marchant's experience, bikers usually checked out each other's hardware, but they were too preoccupied with their own broken machine.

Marchant remounted his Mobylette and rode up to the garage. He switched the engine off before he turned into the forecourt, and freewheeled silently for the last twenty yards. He passed the first two bikes, checking the ignitions. Neither had a key. But the third, a BMW GS Adventure, did. Marchant parked up beyond it and glanced once in the direction of the group. It was then that he realised that the man on the ground was not trying to mend the bike. He was the focus of the group's attention, and he was lying very still. The bikers were too far away for Marchant to hear what they were saying, but he thought he heard someone mention a doctor.

Ignoring an instinctive urge to go over and help, Marchant switched quickly from his moped to the tourer, turned the ignition and felt the 1150cc engine rumble into life beneath him. Without looking up, he moved off the forecourt, joined the main road, and accelerated slowly away from the garage, heading for Mount Toubkal, the highest peak on the horizon.

# 7

James Spiro had not enjoyed his job with the CIA since he had been moved to Head of Clandestine, Europe. It was a promotion, and should have been rewarding, a few comfortable years in London before he returned to Virginia for greater things. But he hadn't counted on Salim Dhar proving so elusive. Ever since he had slipped through the net in India, Dhar had been Spiro's biggest headache. He would wake at night, sheets drenched in sweat, seeing his President take the bullet that had somehow missed him in Delhi. His in-tray was full of daily requests from the Pentagon, the White House, the media, all wanting to know where Dhar was and why he hadn't been eliminated. And in his darkest moments, he couldn't stop thinking of Leila, the woman who had died instead of the President, the woman he had slept with only hours before.

Spiro knew his career hung in the balance, which was why he was now back on home soil, coordinating the Agency's biggest manhunt since the search for Osama bin Laden after 9/11. There had been dozens of credible sightings of Dhar around the world, each one proving false, each one ratcheting up the pressure on Spiro to find him. The collateral damage from drone strikes hadn't helped his cause. The last one, in Pakistan, based on an ISI tip-off, had killed thirty civilians, mostly women and children.

And what were America's greatest allies doing to help? Diddly shit. London's relationship with Dhar was 'delicate', according to Marcus Fielding. Dubious, more like. Daniel Marchant, the one person who might be able to find Dhar, was on vacation in North Africa, if such a thing was possible, eating too much couscous in Marrakech. If it had been up to Spiro, Marchant would have been strapped back onto the waterboard, telling them all he knew about Dhar, rather than being allowed to wander around Morocco's souks as if nothing had happened.

Now, though, the end seemed finally in sight. It was always going to be only a matter of time until Dhar made a mistake.

'Run me those coordinates again,' he said to the operator next to him. He was standing in the 'cockpit', a hot and crowded trailer, also known as a mobile Ground Control Station, in a quiet corner of Creech US Air Force Base, Nevada. In front of him, two operatives were seated in high-backed chairs, each monitoring a bank of screens. One was a pilot with 42 Attack Squadron, a seasoned officer in his forties who used to fly F-16 fighter jets but was now directing MQ-9 Reapers, the most advanced hunter/killer drones in the world. The other was his sensor operator, a woman no older than twenty-five who controlled the Reaper's multi-spectral targeting suite.

Spiro had spent a lot of his time at Creech in recent weeks, too much for his liking. And he had eaten too many Taco Bells in Las Vegas, thirty-five miles south-east. Creech used to be a bare-bones facility, a rocky outpost in the desert, but now it resembled a building site. New hangars were going up all the time around the main airstrip, which had once been used for landing practice by pilots from the nearby Nellis Air Force Base. Spiro found it hard to believe that such a bleak, uninhabited place represented the future of aerial combat. But he guessed that was the point: the USAF's first squadron of Reapers was unmanned.

The pilot in front of him read out the coordinates. Dhar's voice had been traced to a remote location in North Waziristan, on the borders of Pakistan and Afghanistan. Fort Meade had done a good job for once. Someone had been listening in real time, and not just to Pakistani generals having sex. This was the big one, and there was a palpable sense of excitement in the cockpit, even from the base commander. He had stepped into the trailer when news spread across the base that Salim Dhar might be about to be taken down. It would be a big moment for the commander. His unit, 432 Air Expeditionary Wing, had stood up at Creech in 2007 to spearhead the global war on terror, and he needed a result. Spiro knew the commander blamed the CIA for the recent spate of bad publicity. The last strike in Pakistan had brought relations between the Agency and the USAF to a new low.

'I think we have our man,' Spiro said, turning to the commander.

'We need to do this by the book,' he replied. 'You know that.'

'Of course. And the book says we take Dhar out. We have an 80-per-cent confidence threshold.'

'Are there any legals?' the commander asked, turning to an officer next to him.

'Negative, sir. Potential for civilian collateral is zero. The building is remote, nearest population cluster five miles south. And this is a Level Five.'

'Colonel, we're locked onto the target,' the pilot said, turning to the sensor operator. 'Can you put thermal up on screen one?'

Spiro watched as blotches of bright colour appeared on the screen between the two seated operators. The surrounding screens were relaying live video streams from electro-optical and image-intensified night cameras mounted under the nose of the Reaper, and stills from a synthetic aperture radar. Spiro still hadn't quite got his head round the fact that these images were streaming live, give or take a one-to-two-second delay, from 30,000 feet above Afghanistan, 7,500 miles away.

'Fuse thermal with intensified,' the pilot said. The image on the main screen sharpened a little, but it was still no more than a series of yellow, red and purple shapes.

It was at this point that the young female analyst first began to worry about their target. She wasn't meant to be on duty now. The 24/7 rota they worked to had lost its shape in the previous few hours, and she should have been back in her room, getting some sleep and reading the bible before her next shift. (A lot of the analysts headed off to Vegas after work, but she found the contrast too great: one moment looking at magnified images of a destroyed Taleban target, the next shooting craps.) But the next analyst on duty had phoned in sick, and she had agreed to work on until cover showed up. That was two hours ago. She didn't like bending the rules. She tried to leave a quiet, disciplined life. All she could hope for was that the base commander didn't glance at the rota sheet on the wall behind them.

'Sir, we have multiple personnel in the target zone,' she said, looking closely at the screen. 'And what looks like a pack of wild dogs forty yards to the east.'

Night-time image analysis was a skill that not everyone on the base appreciated. The pilots did, but she resented the disdain with which the CIA officers appeared to view her profession. Spiro was the worst, but that was also because he kept trying to look down her blouse. He hadn't the first idea about the subtleties of either women or her job.

During the day, with clear visibility, it was easy enough to distinguish man from woman, cat from dog, even from 30,000 feet. The images were pin sharp. But at night you had to rely on the digitally enhanced imagery of the infra-red spectrum. Interpreting the ghostly monochrome of the mid-IR wavelengths required intuition and training to flesh out the shapes. You had to impose upon them known patterns of human behaviour. Two years earlier, she had averted a friendly-fire attack when she realised that the four targets on an Afghanistan hillside, thought to be insurgents, were doing press-ups. She had never seen the Taleban working out, and assumed, rightly, that they were US soldiers.

The shapes in front of her now, clustered together inside a hut on a mountainside in North Waziristan, were not normal, even allowing for the local atmospheric conditions, which were making the images less clear than she would have liked. She isolated the feed from the thermal infra-red camera, which detected heat emitted from objects, and then fused it again with the image-intensified images. She had seen Taleban leaders talking many times before, and they never stood so close. When they sat, they formed circles. These people had created something else: a glowing crucifix to warn off the Reaper.

# 8

Marchant pulled off the dusty track and parked the BMW behind a cluster of coarse bushes, out of sight. It was almost dark and he could see the headlights of a lorry coming down over the Tizi'n'Test pass in the far distance. He wished he had been able to steal a scrambler rather than a tourer, as the BMW had struggled with the rough terrain. They had left the main road, and followed an increasingly remote and bumpy track for the past half-hour, Marchant keeping at least a mile between them. The man he was pursuing had stopped here a few minutes earlier and parked his bike on the other side of the track, without bothering to hide it. He was in a hurry, and had already disappeared on foot, following a steep path that zigzagged up through windblown juniper-berry trees that clung to the hillside.

Marchant set off up the path, confident that he had left enough time between them not to be seen. He thought he was fit from his running and his abstemious life in Marrakech, but the mountains were soon sucking the thin air from his lungs. Occasionally, as he crested another false ridge, he saw his man in front of him, at least five hundred yards ahead, covering the ground with the ease of a mountain goat. Whenever he turned, Marchant pressed himself flat against the dry earth, feeling his chest rise and fall as he tried to keep his breathing quiet.

It was after forty minutes of climbing that he heard the first cries on the wind. The mountains around here were farmed by Berber goatherds, who called out to each other across the valleys as they followed their animals. Sometimes they sang bitter songs about arrogant Berbers who had travelled abroad and returned with enough money to build ugly modern houses on the hillside. But tonight they seemed to be singing of something else. Marchant struggled with the dialect, but he could pick up enough to detect the agitation and fear in their voices. Had his man come up here to give his coded message to the goatherds, who would pass it on from man to man across the mountains, until eventually it reached Dhar? It would be in keeping with the primitive means of communication used so far.

Marchant listened again to the Berbers' agitated calls as a goat stumbled out of the gloaming next to him and moved off down the hillside. Something had disturbed the peace of the mountains. The man he had been following had stopped now. His hands were cupped around his mouth and he was calling out into the dying light. The wind was in the wrong direction for Marchant to hear, but the man's body language said enough. He had sunk to his knees with exhaustion. Had he come with a warning? Was it that he was too late? Then he heard him cry out again. The swirling wind carried the sound down the hillside to Marchant. There was panic in his voice, and they weren't Berber words this time.

'*Nye strelai!*' he shouted. '*Nye strelai!*'

Moments later, a short burst of automatic gunfire rang out, echoing through the mountains, and the man slumped over. Marchant pressed himself closer to the earth, breathing hard, searching around for better cover, calculating where the shots had come from. He slid across to a bush, keeping his eyes on the horizon. And then he saw it, hovering up over the crest of the hill. *The Roc bird rose into the sky.*

He knew at once that it was Russian-built, an Mi-8, its distinctive profile silhouetted in the dusk light. It was white, but there were no UN markings. The shots had come from the machine-gun mounted beneath the cockpit. Marchant was dead if the pilot had seen him, but the helicopter turned, nose down, and rose into the star-studded sky, heading towards the Algerian border.

# 9

The doubt that had been sown in the young sensor operator's mind grew stronger with each passing second. She had tried to tell herself that she was just seeing things, that she was suffering from exhaustion, too many late nights reading God's word, but there was no escaping the yellow shape that the heat of the bodies had formed. Although the hut only had a canvas roof of some kind, it was impossible to tell precisely how many people there were inside, as the bodies were bunched so closely together – too close for Taleban.

'Sir, there's something abnormal about the target imagery,' she said, turning to her pilot.

'Would you care to elaborate?' Spiro said, before the pilot had time to reply.

The analyst paused, struggling to conceal her dislike of Spiro. 'They're too close together.'

'Perhaps they're praying. What's the local time anyhow? I'll put money on it being the Mecca hour. If we have no other objections, I say we shoot.'

Spiro directed his last comment at the base commander, who was on the phone to the Pentagon. Spiro knew the commander needed the break just as much as he did.

'We're green-lit,' the commander said, replacing the phone.

Spiro could tell he was concealing his excitement. He just had to make sure the USAF didn't get to take any credit.

'Then let's engage, people,' Spiro said, putting a hand on the pilot's shoulder. The pilot flinched, and Spiro withdrew it. He knew at once that it had been an inappropriate gesture. These pilots were under pressure, too. There was talk on the base of combat stress, despite their distance from the battlefield. Unlike a fighter pilot, who pulled away from the target after dropping his payload, the Reaper pilots stayed on site, watching the bloody aftermath in high magnification.

'Sir, given the subject is static, I'd appreciate a second opinion,' the pilot said, catching his colleague's eye. 'If she's not happy, neither am I.'

'Are you not happy?' Spiro asked the analyst. No one in the room missed his sarcasm. 'The Pentagon's happy, I'm happy, your commander here is goddamn cock-a-hoop. Salim Dhar, the world's most wanted terrorist, just spoke on a cell from the target zone, and you're not happy. As far as we know, nobody has gone in or out of that lousy shack apart from a pack of crazy Afghani dogs. This is paytime, honey. And we'll all get a share, don't you worry your tight little ass. I'll see to it personally.'

As Spiro's words hung in the air, a phone began to ring. The commander picked it up and listened for a few moments, nodding at the pilot. 'Could you stream it through now? I'd appreciate that. Channel nine.'

The pilot leaned forward and flicked a switch. Moments later, Salim Dhar's voice filled the stuffy room. It was only a few words, a short burst from someone who seemed to know the risk he was running by speaking on a cell phone, but no one was in any doubt. They had all heard his voice too many times in the last year, seen his face on too many posters.

'Fort Meade picked it up a few seconds ago,' the commander

said. 'Same coordinates, same cell, 100 per cent voiceprint match, confidence threshold now at 95 per cent. Gentlemen, ladies, I hope 432 Air Expeditionary Wing will be remembered for many things, but as of this moment, we'll be known for ever as the people who took down Salim Dhar. Engage the target.'

Lieutenant Oaks spent the last minutes of his life in frustration as much as fear. He had managed to corral everyone into the middle of the hut, including Murray, and persuaded them of the merits of his plan. The cross was as good as he could make it in the circumstances: four men lying in a line, hands still tied behind their backs, heads below the next man's shackled ankles, and then two lying perpendicular to them, one either side of Oaks, who was second in the upright. Even if it didn't show up as a cross, Oaks figured it would look pretty damn weird on a thermal-imaging screen.

But then, as they lay there, each praying to his own God, Salim Dhar was suddenly amongst them for a second time. It was only a few words, spoken on his cell phone, but it was enough to make Oaks realise what was happening. When he heard him, he screamed, hoping that his voice would be picked up by someone at Fort Meade, but he was too late. Dhar had stopped talking by the time he was railing at the sky.

He started to sob now, lying in the mud on his imaginary cross, the smell of urine filling the air. There was nothing left to do. For a moment he stopped, trying to hear the sound of the drone above the murmurings of his colleagues. A Reaper's turboprop engine at altitude purred like a buzzing insect – that's what they said, wasn't it? – but he heard nothing. Just the noise of the dogs, which whined and ran in all directions when the first Hellfire exploded deep in the Afghan mud beside him.

# 10

Marchant had to call London, tell them what he'd seen, but his mobile phone had no signal. Satisfied that the helicopter had been operating on its own, he broke cover and ran back down the path to the motorbike, stumbling and falling as he went. The mountains were quiet now, the Berber goatherds stunned into silence by whatever had just happened. He started up the engine and headed back down the track to the main road and on towards Marrakech.

He couldn't decide if it was safer to dump the bike and get back to his apartment before he called Fielding, or to ring as soon as he was in range. His mobile phone was encrypted, but the events he had just witnessed made him nervous of talking in the open. The sight of the man being shot had heightened his senses, stirred a primitive survival instinct.

He also felt an irrational sense of loss. He had never met the man, but they had been joined in some way, had listened to the same story in the square, ridden the same route out of town, first on Mobylettes then on more powerful machines. It could have been him in the line of fire. All he wanted to do now was get as far away as possible from the mountains, and the haunting Berber goatherds' calls that had warned of danger.

It was as he throttled back the engine that he began to rethink his plans. A line of single headlights had appeared a thousand yards ahead, coming up the straight road towards him, fanned across both lanes. He knew at once that it was the group of British bikers, one of whose machines he had stolen. Should he stop, try to explain? They had clearly seen him at the petrol station, and would immediately identify the bike as theirs. It was out of the question. He could never play his employer's card. It was a last resort, reserved for tight spots with foreign governments. He would have been allowed to tell his immediate family who he worked for, too, except that he didn't have any. Not any more. Not unless he counted Dhar.

His priority was to get a message to Fielding, tell him he had been right, that someone had taken Dhar away by helicopter. He was convinced that the *halaka* had relayed a message to Dhar, tried to warn him of a Roc bird rising into the sky. It would explain the recent increased level of chatter about Dhar in the souks. But had time run out? Had the warning come too late?

There was only one option. It had been a few years since he had ridden a motorbike at speed, but he had felt comfortable on the journey out of Marrakech. In his first months at Legoland in Vauxhall, working as a junior reports officer, a few of the new recruits used to take bikes out for test rides at lunchtime. There was a motorcycle dealer opposite the main entrance to Legoland, and the staff there were always obliging – one eye on a government contract, perhaps – without ever acknowledging which building Marchant and his colleagues left and entered each day. Marchant would sometimes play it up, hinting that he lived life in the international fast lane, when the truth of his head-office existence was much more mundane. That was one of the reasons he wanted to stay in Morocco.

He watched the needle move across the dial and adjusted his position in the saddle, wishing he was wearing a helmet. If he approached the bikers fast enough, he reckoned they wouldn't hold the line. Five hundred yards from them, he turned off his headlight and took the machine up to 90 mph, riding in darkness, his face cooling in the night wind. Not for the first time in his life, he felt liberated rather than scared as death drew near, sensing as he had done before in such moments that he was closer to those he had lost: his father, his brother.

Still the bikers were fanned across the road, no gaps between them. An image of the London Marathon came and went: the police roadblock, trying to find a way through. Then, as the needle nudged passed a hundred, a gap started to appear at one end of the line, in the opposite lane. He headed for it, feeling the surface change beneath him as he crossed the middle of the road. For a moment he thought he had lost control, but the BMW handled well and he accelerated again, touching 110 mph. Fifty yards from the line, all the bikes began to peel away, and then he was through them, the sound of their anger fading in his ears.

He liked the bike, but he didn't want to steal it. Turning the headlight back on, he glanced in the mirror and saw that no one had decided to give chase. A madman had clearly stolen their bike, and he would be dead quicker than they could catch him. When he looked ahead again, he saw the oncoming lorry's headlights, but there was no time to think. Instinctively, he swerved inside the vehicle and was almost thrown by the draft as it passed him, horn blaring in the darkness.

He moved back onto the correct side of the road. The petrol station where he had picked up the bike was shut, but he parked it there, flashing the headlight on and off once. A mile back up the road, one of the bikers broke away from the group and started to ride towards him. But Marchant was long gone by the time he had arrived, heading into the heart of Marrakech across rough ground, talking on his mobile to London.

# 11

Marcus Fielding, Chief of MI6, looked out of his fourth-floor window at the commuters walking home across Vauxhall Bridge beneath him. Two of them had stopped, jackets slung over their shoulders, to take in the evening sun as it set over a hot summer London. The Thames was out, the muddy shores busy with sand-pipers. On the far bank, below the Morpeth Arms, a woman weighed down with plastic bags was searching through the flotsam and jetsam.

Beside Legoland, one of the Yellow Duck amphibious vehicles that took tourists around London was parked up on the slipway, waiting while its captain briefed passengers on what to do if it sank. Sometimes, Fielding wished it would. Its proximity to Legoland had long made him uneasy, the guided tours attracting too much publicity, too many fingers pointing up in his direction. Still, Fielding couldn't deny that he had enjoyed the time he had taken the Duck with Daniel Marchant. They were happier days then, full of hope. Marchant had received a text while they were on board together, and the Morocco plan had been born. But that was over now.

Fielding was supposed to be going to the opera tonight, but he needed to wait for Marchant to ring in again from Marrakech. The call had come through earlier on Marchant's mobile, but the line had dropped, the encryption software unhappy with the integrity of the local network. He knew Marchant wouldn't make contact unless it was urgent, but it all seemed irrelevant now. He wondered how best to break the news about Salim Dhar to Marchant.

There was a chance, of course, that James Spiro was mistaken. He had been wrong before, most famously about Marchant's late father, Stephen, Fielding's predecessor as Chief of MI6. According to Spiro, Stephen and Daniel Marchant were both infidels, worshiping at the altar of a very different god to the rest of the West. Spiro had tried to bring down the entire house of Marchant, and MI6 by implication, until the son had cleared the father's name.

But the evidence coming out of North Waziristan suggested that this time Spiro was right. The CIA had finally nailed their man. Two intercepted phone calls, a red-hot handset last used in south India: it was hard to disagree with them. GCHQ was running its own tests on the voice, but the match was perfect, as Spiro had repeatedly told him a few minutes earlier on the video link.

There were few people Fielding despised more than Spiro. He should have been cleared out with the old guard when the new President was sworn in, hung out to dry with the attorneys who had sanctioned torture, but somehow he had survived, thanks to the President himself, of all people. The White House's attitude to the Agency had changed overnight after the assassination attempt in Delhi. Briefly a champion of noble values, it was now an admirer of muscle, and in particular of Spiro, who had taken all the credit for protecting his leader. The clenched fist had replaced the hand of friendship. Now, God help them all, there was no stopping him. Spiro's star was in the ascendant again. Not only were his enhanced methods back in fashion, but the CIA had been given permission to resume playing hardball with its allies.

Salim Dhar's elimination was a particularly sweet victory for Spiro. The Agency had never seen Dhar in the same way as the British, struggling to countenance the possibility that he might one day represent an opportunity rather than a threat. For them, Dhar was the problem, not a potential solution, a man who had come close to heaping the ultimate shame on them. From where Fielding stood, it was all deeply frustrating: the President had promised an era of more nuanced attitudes to intelligence, but it appeared to be over before it had begun.

Fielding turned away from the reinforced window and walked across to the cabinet behind his desk. The collection of books reflected his Arabist tastes, charting his career through the Gulf and North Africa. He envied Marchant his time in Morocco, operating on his own, without the bureaucracy of Legoland. It was how he had worked best when he was Marchant's age, drifting through the medinas, talking to the traders, listening, watching.

He took out a volume of *The Book of the Thousand Nights and a Night*, presented to him years ago by Muammar al-Gadaffi after he had helped to persuade the Libyan leader to abandon his nuclear ambitions. It was Sir Richard Francis Burton's ten-volume 1885 limited edition, for subscribers only, and he had never enquired too closely about its provenance. Fielding had been obliged to declare the gift to Whitehall, but it was his counter-intelligence colleagues across the Thames who were most interested, subjecting the volumes to weeks of unnecessary analysis.

The rivalry between the Services had bordered on war in those days, and Fielding had assumed that MI5 would do all it could to embarrass the Vicar, as he knew they called him. Gifts from foreign governments were a favourite cover for listening devices. No one had forgotten the electric samovar presented to the Queen at Balmoral by the Russian Knights aerobatics team, later suspected of being a mantelpiece transmitter, or the infinity bug hidden inside a wooden replica of the Great Seal of the United States, given by Russian schoolchildren to the US ambassador to Moscow at the end of the Second World War.

But the sweepers at Thames House found nothing, and resisted the temptation to insert something of their own. The volumes were reluctantly passed back over the river to Legoland. There was talk of donating them to the British Library, but the Vicar was eventually allowed to keep his unholy gift.

As he began to read about Shahryar and Scheherazade, there was a knock on the door and Ann Norman, his formidable personal assistant, appeared. She was wearing her usual red tights and intimidating frown, both of which had protected four Chiefs from Whitehall's meddling mandarins for more than twenty years.

'It's Daniel Marchant. Shall I put him through?'

'Line three.'

Fielding went over to his desk and sat down, placing the open book in front of him, next to the comms console that linked him to colleagues around the world as well as to his political masters. The book's presence made him feel more connected, less detached from Marchant's world. He let him talk for a while, about a *halaka*, and his trip out into the High Atlas. Fielding stopped him as he began to talk of helicopters.

'Daniel, I think you should know we've just had a call from Langley. NSA picked up a mobile intercept late this afternoon, from Salim Dhar in North Waziristan. One hundred per cent voice match.'

Marchant fell quiet, the hum of a Marrakech medina suddenly audible in the background.

'Have they killed him?'

'They think so. A UAV was in the area, eliminated the target within fifteen minutes of the intercept. I'm sorry.'

'Without even checking? Without talking to us?'

'The Americans aren't really in the mood right now for cooperating on Dhar. You know that.'

'But Dhar was here, I'm sure of it. In Morocco. Barely an hour ago, up near the Tizi'n'Test pass. The *halaka* spoke of a Roc bird.'

Fielding absently turned the pages of *The Arabian Nights*, hearing a younger version of himself in Marchant's voice. Fielding had been less hot-headed, but he rated Marchant more highly than anyone of his generation. A part of him wondered again if Spiro had made a mistake, but it was hard to dispute the CIA's evidence, at least those elements of it that they had pooled with Britain. The Joint Intelligence Committee was convening first thing in the morning, by which time Britain's own voice analysis from Cheltenham would be in. GCHQ was running tests through the night, but Fielding didn't expect a different result.

'And how do I present your evidence to the JIC tomorrow?' Fielding said, knowing it was an unfair question. Unlike police work, intelligence-gathering was seldom just about evidence, as he had explained to MI6's latest intake of IONEC graduates earlier that day. Agents had to be thorough but also counter-intuitive; 'Cutting the red wire when the manual said blue,' as one over-excited graduate had put it.

'Someone took him away. Whoever owns the helicopter has Dhar.'

'And who does own it?'

'It was white, UN, but no markings.'

'White?' Fielding's interest was pricked. He knew that the Mi-8 was used by the UN, knew too that the government in Sudan wasn't averse to flying unmarked white military aircraft to attack villages in Darfur.

'I was about to tell you that when you interrupted me.'

Fielding could hear Marchant's anger mounting. He had always preferred field agents who were passionate about the CX they filed to London. It made for better product.

'Suppose it was just an exercise,' he said, testing him.

'An exercise? They shot someone, the man I'd been following from Marrakech, the same man who'd been listening to the story-teller.' Marchant fell silent again. 'Remember when Dhar sent me the text, after Delhi?' he continued, trying to restore his Chief's belief.

Fielding stood up, his lower spine beginning to ache. It always played up when he was tired, and he suddenly felt world-weary, as if he had been asked to live his entire life over again, fight all his old Whitehall battles, relive the fears of raised threat levels, the waking moments in the middle of the night.

'Daniel, we've been over this many times,' he said, thinking back to their journey down the river. They had both thought the text was from Dhar. GCHQ was less sure.

'The words were taken from a song. *Leysh Nat'arak.*'

'And that text was one of the reasons I gave you time in Morocco. I would have let you go earlier if I could. You were no good to anyone in London. Langley thought otherwise. We all hoped that you'd find Dhar, that he'd make contact. But that's not going to happen now. I'm sorry. It's time to come home.'

'You really believe the Americans have killed him, don't you?'

Fielding hesitated, one hand on the small of his back. 'I'm not sure. But whatever happened in Morocco, I want you away from it. For your own sake. If someone was killed, and you saw it, we have a problem, and that wasn't part of the deal. I also sent you to Morocco to keep out of trouble.'

'*Yalla natsaalh ehna akhwaan.* That was the lyric. *Let's make good for we are brothers.*' Marchant paused. 'Dhar was out there, up in the mountains. I'm sure of it. And he wanted to come in. But someone took him, before he could.'

44

'Someone? Who, exactly?'

Marchant tried to ignore the scepticism that had returned to Fielding's voice. He had thought about this question on the way back to his apartment, wrestled with the possibilities, the implications, knowing how it would sound. But it was quite clear in his own mind, as clear as the Russian words he had heard on the mountainside: *Nye strelai. Don't shoot.*

'Moscow.'

# 12

Marchant swilled the Scotch around his mouth for a few seconds before swallowing it. He had hoped the alcohol would taste toxic, that his body would reject it in some violent way, but it was sweeter than he had ever remembered.

He was sitting under a palm tree in the courtyard of the Chesterfield Pub, a *bar anglais* at the Hotel Nassil on avenue Mohammed V. It was not a place he was particularly proud to be, but there was a limited choice of public venues serving alcohol in Marrakech. The Scotch was decent enough, though, and there were fewer tourists than he had feared. His only worry was if the group of British bikers had decided to turn back to Marrakech for the night and came here for a drink.

He had learned to trust his gut instinct since signing up with MI6, and at the moment it didn't feel as if Salim Dhar was dead. The Americans had claimed to have killed a number of terrorists with UAVs in recent years and later proved to have been wrong. Only time would tell if they were right about Dhar. It would be too risky to send in anyone on the ground to collect DNA. Later perhaps. For now, the CIA would look for other evidence, listen to the chatter, assess *jihadi* morale.

Marchant knew, though, that Fielding was right: his Morocco days were over. He had already booked himself onto the early-morning flight back to London. In India, when he was a child, his father had once told him to live in each country as if for ever, but always to be ready to leave at dawn. At the time, his father was a middle-ranking MI6 officer who had served in Moscow before Delhi. He was used to the threat of his diplomatic cover being blown, of tit-for-tat expulsions.

Marchant wasn't being expelled, but there had been an incident of some sort in the mountains and he had witnessed it. Whether anyone had seen him, he wasn't sure, but he knew MI6 couldn't afford for him to be caught up in another controversy, not after the events in India. And if he was right about Moscow's involvement, an international row might be imminent.

After finishing his Scotch he ordered another. He had swapped his *djellaba* for jeans and a collarless shirt before coming to the pub, and guessed the waiter had marked him down as just another drunken Western tourist, tanking up before a night at the clubs. So be it. He needed to cut a different figure from the one who had ridden out to Tizi a few hours earlier.

It was after an hour and too much Scotch that Marchant saw the dark-haired woman walk up to the bar. He recognised her at once as Lakshmi Meena, the local Operations Officer the CIA had sent to keep an eye on him when he had first arrived in Marrakech. London had briefed him about her. She was a beneficiary of the CIA's ongoing programme to recruit more people from what it called America's 'heritage communities', particularly those who spoke 'mission critical' languages. MI6 had always recruited linguists, unlike the CIA, which had been found wanting after 9/11. Even in its National Clandestine Service, only 30 per cent of CIA staff were fluent in a second language. Meena spoke Hindi, some Urdu and, most importantly, the Dravidian languages of southern India, which had been upgraded to critical in the ongoing hunt for Salim Dhar, whose parents were originally from Kerala.

Marchant had also been told that she was a breath of fresh air, one of the recent intake who had joined the Agency on the back of the new President's promises of change. He had yet to see any difference, at least in the CIA's attitude to him.

Meena was young, late twenties, dressed in jeans and a maroon Indian top with mirrorwork that caught the light around her neckline. Officially, she was in Morocco teaching English as a foreign language, working at the American Language Center up in Rabat. Marchant had to admit that she looked the part, one up from his own student cover. He wished he'd thought of it for himself.

Meena walked over to Marchant's table in the courtyard, checking her mobile phone before putting it away in her shoulder-bag. Marchant was momentarily wrongfooted by the direct approach. They had met face to face only once before, shortly after Marchant had arrived: a cold exchange in the foyer of a hotel.

'Do what you have to do,' Marchant had said, trying not to see Leila in Meena's limpid eyes, her dark olive skin. 'Just don't expect any answers from me.'

'You flatter yourself,' she had replied. 'We ask questions later, remember?'

It hadn't been the beginning of a beautiful friendship. He knew afterwards that he had played it too cool, that she was only doing her job, but he wasn't in the mood to mix with female field agents, particularly ones who reminded him of a woman who had betrayed him. Meena was taller, her manner more hardened, but there was unquestionably something of Leila in her: an attitude, sexual poise. And Marchant knew that any likeness was no coincidence, that it was a cruel joke by Spiro. Frustrated that he wasn't allowed to lock Marchant up and torture him again, Spiro had sent someone to remind him of his past. But Marchant

48

ignored the ploy, ignored Meena. For the following few weeks, they had played cat and mouse on the streets of Marrakech, before Meena had finally backed off to Rabat.

'Mind if I join you?' she asked, taking a seat.

'Go ahead,' Marchant said, concealing his surprise. A waiter was standing beside them. For a moment, he was back in a pub in Portsmouth, chatting up strangers as part of a training exercise. All new recruits at the Fort, MI6's training base in Gosport, were dispatched to the city's bars and pubs to chat up unsuspecting locals and solicit private information: bank-card details, National Insurance and passport numbers.

'Bourbon and Coke, thanks. Daniel?'

Marchant knew Meena was taking in the scene, measuring the milligrams of alcohol in Marchant's blood, whether his defences were down. The only consolation was that she wasn't the sort to flirt. He didn't think he could handle that right now. Leila had used her sexual charms shamelessly, in the office and in the field, but he sensed that Meena did things differently.

'A Scotch, thanks,' Marchant replied, nodding at the waiter.

'I thought you'd given all that up,' she said, fingering her Indian necklace. 'Gone native.'

'Celebrating. I didn't think you drank either.' He had read her files: vegetarian, non-drinker, decaffeinated coffee, herbal tea.

'Celebrating, too.'

Marchant thought her necklace was from south India, similar to one his mother had once worn. He raised his glass, trying to run his own check on himself, calculate the damage. A drinking session after three months' abstinence wasn't a good idea, but he was sober enough to extract some leverage from the situation, fool Meena into thinking he was drunker than he was. At least, that was the plan. His dulled brain could think of two reasons why she had stepped out of the shadows tonight. To say goodbye, having heard that Dhar was dead; or to find out if he knew anything about the helicopter in the mountains. He had a problem if it was the latter.

'You heard the news then,' she said, glancing around the bar before looking at Marchant, his already empty glass.

'I heard,' he said, thinking it could still be either.

'Mixed feelings, I guess.'

He sat back, relieved that she had come to talk about Dhar.

'To be honest, I don't really know what to say,' she continued, brushing some crumbs off the table. 'Langley's kind of over the moon, as you'd expect. But it's a little more complicated for you guys.'

'Is it? He tried to kill your President. Now you've killed him. End of story.'

'But, you know, the whole half-brother thing.' Meena leaned in towards Marchant. 'I realise you didn't exactly grow up together, but that could have been new territory, for all of us −'

'Why did you come here tonight?' Marchant was suddenly irritated by Meena's appearance on his last evening in Morocco, riled by how much she knew, her after-work pub manner. He had been about to leave, take one last walk around Djemaâ el Fna. Now he was in an English bar, having a drink with someone he had avoided for the past three months.

'I figured you'd be pulling out of town,' Meena said. 'Thought it would be civil to tie this whole thing off, say goodbye.'

Marchant allowed the awkwardness to linger for a few seconds, in case there was anything else to flush out. But there was nothing. The Americans thought they had killed Dhar, and he was happy to let them. Marchant wasn't sure if it was the alcohol or sudden empathy for a fellow field officer, but something made him change tack and end the awkwardness, drop his guard.

'Thanks,' he said, watching the waiter place their order on the table. 'You know, for coming. We should have had this drink three months ago.'

She wasn't so bad, he told himself. He was the one who had been stubborn, too angry with the way he had been treated by the Americans. Meena was younger than him, still believed that she was making a difference. And she could have made his life a lot more difficult.

'I wasn't really getting the right vibes,' she said, smiling, putting her hands up in mock defence. 'Hey, look, I don't blame you for not trusting us. Not at all.'

'I gave up trusting people when I signed up.'

'We're not all like Spiro,' Meena said, sitting back.

'I wasn't thinking of Spiro.' For a moment, Marchant wondered if she would take the bait, begin to talk of Leila, but she didn't, and he was shocked by his own disappointment.

'I don't know about you, but I joined the Agency in search of some light and shade. It's why I'm here in Morocco and not in some sweaty UAV trailer in Nevada. I can't pretend I'm sorry Dhar's dead, but I was open to other ways of winning this war.'

'I'm sure you were,' said Marchant. He looked again at Meena, wondering whether he could confide in her, open up, reveal what he had seen in the mountains. But he knew he couldn't. Despite the unexpected entente, they were working to different agendas.

'What made you choose the Agency anyway?' Marchant asked. 'You don't strike me as –'

'– the right colour?' She laughed.

'Christ no, I wasn't going to say that.'

'The right sex?' She laughed again, and then they both paused, her words hanging between them. Marchant thought he saw a sadness in her eyes, or maybe he was confused by his own nostalgia.

'My father wanted me to train as a doctor. Failing that, he

wanted me to marry one. I was studying medicine at Georgetown University, but then, after 9/11, everything changed.'

'Did you lose someone?'

'Not directly. Friends of friends, you know.'

'But it felt personal.'

'Yeah. And the CIA had always been a part of my life.'

'Really?'

'We grew up in Reston, Virginia, not far from Langley. My father used to talk so proudly of the Agency, said it was there to protect all Americans, including ones who had come from India. To prove it, we drove up there one day to take a look, when I was seventeen, maybe eighteen. There's a public sign on the main highway, next right for the George Bush Center for Intelligence. So we took the exit and drove up through the woods, Mom and Dad in the front, my younger brother and me in the back. We were nearly shot by the guards. I think they thought we were a family of suicide bombers.'

'What did they do?'

'Waved their machine-guns at us and shouted at us to leave. I thought they were going to shoot the tyres out.'

'And your father?'

'He was mortified. He couldn't understand why we hadn't been welcomed with open arms. He'd been naïve to go there, but I hated seeing him so upset.'

'And that's why you joined?'

'One reason. I wanted to prove to him – to me – that we're welcome in America. That the Agency is there to defend my family as much as anyone else's. When the Towers came down, they were suddenly looking to recruit from the subcontinent.'

'Why did it take you so long to sign up?'

'It took a new President.'

'And is it everything you hoped?'

'I'm seeing the world.'

'But not changing it.'

'I'm not sure tailing a renegade British agent on compassionate leave through the streets of Marrakech is quite what I had in mind.'

'You weren't very committed.' Marchant matched her smile, thinking back to the first time he had seen her, watching her from across Djemaâ el Fna before giving her the runaround.

'OK, so you lost me a couple of times in the medina. I salute your superior British tradecraft. But come on, Daniel' – she was leaning forward now, voice lowered – 'you didn't really think Dhar would show up in this place, did you? Maybe I missed him. Maybe he was that guy selling dentures in the main square, the one being photographed day and night by thousands of American tourists.'

'No, that wasn't him.'

Marchant thought back to the *halaka*. Again he wanted to confide in Meena, ask her opinion, but he knew he was drunk. He hadn't discussed Salim Dhar with anyone since he had arrived in Marrakech. The text he had received on the Thames had haunted him for the first few weeks. He had checked his phone repeatedly, in case Dhar made contact again, but he never had.

Marchant had begged Fielding to let him go to Morocco, but the Americans had insisted he stay in London. After a year of frustration and too much alcohol, he had finally arrived in Marrakech, expecting the trail to have gone cold. But as he settled into his sober new life, working the souks, listening to the story-tellers, he had begun to pick up chatter here and there that gave him hope he was still on the right track.

'Did you listen to any of those guys, the *halakas*?' Meena asked.

'One or two.' Meena's interest in the storyteller triggered a distant alarm, like a police siren a few streets away.

'Terrific tales, although some of the Berber street talk threw me.'

The alarm faded. Marchant was impressed by Meena's local knowledge. He hadn't given her enough credit, and chided himself for judging her too swiftly. Again, he wondered whether she had been a missed opportunity, someone he should have nurtured rather than avoided. But he knew why he had kept his distance.

'Where next for you, then? When I'm gone?' he asked.

Meena paused. Marchant thought that she too seemed to be weighing up how much to confide, thrown perhaps by how well they were getting on. Up until now, she had hidden behind her words, preferring to spar rather than open up. She sat back, glancing half-heartedly around the bar.

'I want out, if I'm honest. I thought I'd joined a different Agency, a new one working for a new President.'

'But you haven't.'

'No. I haven't.'

'Spiro?'

She paused again. 'For the record, he wanted me to make your life here not worth living.'

'But you chose not to.'

'What did you *do* to him?'

'We go back a bit. He thought my father was a traitor. Then he accused me.'

Meena stood up with his empty glass, ready to head to the bar. 'Must have been that terrorist brother of yours.'

The remark annoyed Marchant, cut through the fog of Scotch. It was a reminder of their differences, confirmation that a junior CIA officer had seen his file. He had hoped that his kinship would remain known only to a few people in Langley and Legoland, but he realised that was wishful thinking. Meena would have been fully briefed before arriving in Morocco, given the full, shocking picture.

He thought again about the text. *Let's make good for we are brothers.* The lyrics were by an Arabic singer, Natacha Atlas. Had Dhar known that she was one of Leila's favourite artists? Marchant was getting sentimental. He couldn't afford to dwell on Leila, not in his present state. And he couldn't afford to talk any more with Meena.

By the time she returned to the table with another Scotch, Marchant had gone.

# 13

Paul Myers wouldn't have bothered to listen to the audio one more time if it hadn't been for Daniel Marchant. He knew his old friend had spent the past three months in Marrakech largely because of him. His line manager at GCHQ had dismissed the theory that Dhar had texted Marchant from Morocco, but Myers had thought otherwise. Like Marchant, he didn't believe Dhar would hang around the Af-Pak region after the assassination attempt. It was too obvious, despite the mountainous terrain and the volatile political climate, both of which made it difficult for the West to search. He could never prove that Marchant's text had been sent by Dhar, but he had run his own checks on some dodgy proxy networks, and would gladly bet his (unused) gym membership that it had originated in Morocco. And if it was a coincidence that the lyric in the text was by a singer who shared her surname with a North African mountain range, he found it a reassuring one.

So it was guilt more than anything that made him put his headphones back on, adjust the fluorescent band at the base of his ponytail and play the US audio file again. He owed it to Marchant to prove that the Americans were wrong about Dhar. He sat back and yawned, scratching at his slack stomach through his fleece jacket as he looked around the empty office.

His desk, littered with chocolate-bar wrappers and filled-in sudokus from various broadsheet newspapers, was in the inner ring of the GCHQ complex, dubbed the Doughnut because of its circular shape. The Street, a glass-roofed circular corridor, ran around the entire building, separating the inner from the outer circles. Its purpose was to encourage separate departments to share their data. No one on the building's three floors was more than five minutes' walk from anyone else, and face-to-face meetings in softly furnished break-out areas were the way forward.

At least, that was the idea. In truth, people kept to themselves. Myers used the Street solely for walking to the Ritazza cafés and deli bars that dotted its orbital route. The workforce at GCHQ, with its mathematicians, cryptanalysts, linguists, librarians and IT engineers, was the most intelligent in the Civil Service, but it was also the most socially dysfunctional, steeped in a long tradition of strictly-need-to-know that dated back to Bletchley Park and its campus of separate huts. Myers wouldn't have had it any other way.

He looked out onto the secure landscaped gardens in the middle of the building, hidden below which was GCHQ's vast computer hall. It was down there, in the depths of the basement, that the mathematicians worked, and that the 'Cheltenham express', an electric train, shuttled back and forth day and night, carrying files along a track beneath the Street. To the right of Myers' window was a decked area, where people could walk out from the canteen. Beyond it was a large expanse of lawn that had been nicknamed 'the grassy knoll' and was meant for blue-sky meetings. Myers liked to sit there in the summer and take his lunch.

The garden was dark and empty now, its edges bathed in a pale, energy-efficient light spilling out from the offices around it. Myers used to work as an intelligence analyst in the Gulf Region, on the opposite side of the Doughnut, his desk looking out at one of the two pagodas that had been built in the garden for smokers, but he had asked for a transfer to the subcontinent after

Leila had died. He had carried a hopeless torch for her, and still hadn't come to terms with her betrayal, let alone her death. Listening to intercepts in Farsi had proved too painful.

The voice in the headphones was definitely Dhar's. His American colleagues had run every test there was, subjecting it to a level of spectrographic analysis that had even met with Myers' jaundiced approval. But what had caught his attention was the lack of data about the background noise. All ears had been tuned to the voice.

Myers listened to the Urdu, noting instinctively that it was a second, possibly third, language, but his eyes were on the computer screen in front of him and the digital sound waves that were rolling across it to the rhythm of Dhar's speech. When the Urdu stopped, Myers eased forward in his seat and scrutinised the data, watching the waves moving along the bottom of his screen until the segment ended. He moved the cursor back to where the Urdu had stopped and played the final part again, his tired eyes blinking. This time he magnified the wave imagery, boosting the background noise. At the end of the clip, he did the same again, except that he only replayed the final eighth of a second, slowing it down to a deep, haunting drawl.

After repeating the process several more times, he was listening to fragments of sound, microseconds inaudible to the human ear. And then he found it. Moving more quickly now, he copied and pasted the clip and dragged it across to an adjacent screen, where he had loaded his own spectrographic software, much to his IT supervisor's annoyance. He played the clip and sat back, taking off his headphones, cracking the joints of his sweaty fingers. The 'spectral waterfall' on the screen in front of him was beautiful, a series of rippling columns of colour; but the acoustic structure was one of intense pain. At the very end of the second call made by Salim Dhar, there was a sound that Myers had not expected to hear: the opening notes of a human scream.

# 14

Lakshmi Meena didn't know what to expect as her car pulled up short of the police cordon on the side of the mountain. She parked beside two army lorries and a Jeep and stepped out into the cool night, pulling a scarf over her head. The area beyond the cordon was swarming with uniformed men, one of whom Meena recognised as Dr Abdul Aziz, a senior intelligence officer from Rabat who had left a message on her cell phone half an hour earlier. She had been leaving the *bar anglais* at the time, wondering what she had said to so upset Marchant. She didn't like Aziz, disapproved of his methods, his unctuous manner, but he had been the first person on her list of people to meet when she had arrived in Morocco.

Two floodlights had been rigged up on stands, illuminating a patch of rugged terrain where a handful of personnel in forensic boilersuits were searching the ground. Meena talked to a policeman on the edge of the cordon, nodding in the direction of Aziz, who saw her and came over.

'I got your message,' she said.

'Lakshmi, our goddess of wealth,' Aziz said, smiling. 'Morocco needs your help.' He lit a local cigarette as he steered her away from the lights, his hand hovering above her shoulders.

Meena was always surprised by Aziz's displays of warmth and

charm, so at odds with his professional reputation. He had run a black site in Morocco in the aftermath of 9/11, interviewing a steady stream of America's enemy combatants on behalf of James Spiro, who had dubbed him the Dentist. It was before Meena's time in the Agency, but she knew enough about Aziz to show respect to a man whose interrogation techniques made the tooth-extractors in Djemaâ el Fna look humane. And Meena hated herself for it, the cheap expedience of her chosen profession.

'What happened here?' she asked. 'The Moroccan Islamic Combatant Group? Last I heard, you had them on the back foot.'

Aziz laughed. His teeth were a brilliant white. 'Since when did they fly Mi-8s?'

'Who said anything about helicopters?'

'The Berbers.' Aziz nodded to a group of goatherds sitting on the ground in a circle, smoking, *djellaba* hoods up.

'Oh really?'

'Our national airspace was violated tonight, and we'd like to know who by.'

'Forgive me, but isn't that what your air force is for?'

'The country's radar defences were knocked out. It was a sophisticated system. At least that's what your sales people told us when we bought it from America last year. Our Algerian brothers don't have the ability to do that.'

'Not many people do.'

'The Berbers are saying the helicopter was white.'

'Any markings?'

'None.'

Meena had been down in Darfur the previous year, and had seen the same trick pulled with a white Antonov used for a military raid. But the Sudanese government had gone one step further, painting it in UN markings.

She looked at Aziz, who was lost in thought, drawing hard on his cigarette. She remembered the cocktail party in Rabat when he had enquired about her health. A month earlier, she had checked in to hospital for a small operation, something she had kept from even her closest colleagues. Perhaps his question had been a coincidence, but it had disquieted her.

'Is that why you called me?'

'There's something else. An Englishman was seen heading up here this evening.'

Aziz handed Meena a grainy photograph taken from a CCTV camera. It was of the gas-station forecourt on the road out of Marrakech. Someone who could have been Daniel Marchant was in the foreground, arriving on a moped. The date and time was wrong, but otherwise Meena thought the image looked authentic. It was too much of a coincidence, an odd place to be heading on a bike. Marchant had gone off-piste, and Meena should have known about it. No wonder he had left the bar early. He hadn't been honest with her.

'Marchant's booked on the first flight to London tomorrow,' Aziz said.

'I know.' Meena looked at him. Neither of them wanted to say anything, but each knew the other was thinking the same. The only reason Marchant would have gone to the mountains was if it had something to do with Salim Dhar. And Dhar was meant to be dead.

'What do you think he was up to?' Aziz asked.

'I thought you were watching him.'

'Both our jobs might be on the line, Lakshmi. Please tell me if you want Marchant delayed.'

Aziz smiled, his teeth glinting in the beam of a passing flashlight.

# 15

Marchant stepped aside as a donkey cart was led past him by an old man, his face hidden by the pointed hood of his *djellaba*, his cart stacked high with crates of salted sardines. Marchant headed across the square to the food trestles and benches, where a few butane lamps were still burning, but the crowds and the cooks had long gone, the smoke cleared. The only people in the square now were a handful of beggars, some sweepers in front of the mosque and a woman taking dough to a communal oven in one of the souks.

It was not quite dawn and the High Atlas were barely visible, no more than a reddish smudge on the horizon. Marchant had been walking around the medina since he left the *bar anglais*, taking a last look at his old haunts, drinking strong coffee at his favourite cafés. Now, as he sat down on a bench in a pool of light, he felt ready to return to Britain. He was more confident of his past, clearer about his relationship with Dhar.

For almost all of his thirty years, Marchant had thought that he only had one brother, his twin, Sebastian, who had been killed in a car crash in Delhi when they were eight. Then, fifteen months ago, on the run and trying to clear his family name, he had met Salim Dhar under a hot south Indian sun and asked why his late father, Stephen Marchant, Chief of MI6, had once visited Dhar, a rising *jihadi,* at a black site outside Cochin. 'He was my father, too,' Dhar had said, changing Marchant's life for ever.

After the initial shock, the grief of a surviving twin had been replaced by the comfort of a stranger. Marchant was no longer alone in the world. He was less troubled by the discovery of a *jihadi* half-brother than by the thought of what might have been. There had been a bond when they met in India, an unspoken pact that came with kinship. They were both the same age, shared the same father.

Their lives, though, had run in wildly different directions, one graduating from Cambridge, the other from a training camp in Afghanistan. Marchant knew that Dhar would never spy for the US, but he might work for Britain. It was why Marchant had been so keen to travel to Morocco: to establish where his half-brother's loyalties lay, and then try to turn him. Dhar was not, after all, a regular *jihadi.* How could he be, with a British father who had risen to become Chief of MI6? Tonight, though, he had accepted that his plan had failed. Dhar had not come forward, as he had hoped, and agreed to work for the land of his father.

The butane lamp above Marchant flickered and died. Dawn was spreading fast across the city from the east, where the mountains were now bathed in warm, newborn sunlight. Marchant stood up, his aching brain holding on to two things: Dhar was still alive, and he could still be turned. But there was something else. Whether Dhar had chosen to leave Morocco without making contact, or someone had taken him, Marchant couldn't deny that he felt rejected. When it had come to it, Dhar's family calling hadn't been strong enough.

Perhaps that was why, as he left the square, he didn't at first see Lakshmi Meena standing in the doorway of the mosque, watching him with the same intensity as the hawk that had begun to circle high above the waking city. But then he spotted her, turned off into the medina and ran through its narrow alleys as fast as he could.

# 16

James Spiro took the call 35,000 feet above the Atlantic, sitting near the front of the Gulfstream V. He had a soft spot for the plane, which he had used regularly in the rendition years. The line wasn't good, but he knew immediately that it was Lakshmi Meena. He made a mental note not to call her babe.

'Lakshmi. What have you got for me?'

Meena explained about the unmarked white helicopter that had been seen in the mountains, then took a deep breath – another one – and told him about his old friend Dr Abdul Aziz, the Dentist, and what he had said about the GICM and their hideout in the Atlas mountains.

'Where are we running with this?' Spiro asked, cutting her short. 'I'm on the red-eye here.'

Meena sensed that their conversation would be over almost before it had started. Spiro was too full of Dhar's death to listen to a junior officer phoning in with a hunch. 'Aziz thinks Daniel Marchant was in the mountains,' she continued, feeling that she had nothing to lose. 'Stole a bike, took a ride up there at the same time the helicopter was seen.'

'Tell me you were with him.'

'I'd backed off, as instructed. The guy's done nothing but go jogging and read the Koran for three months.'

Spiro thought for a moment. Reluctantly, Langley had agreed with London to leave Marchant alone after Delhi, but he wasn't allowed to travel abroad. After a year, Spiro had acceded to Fielding's demands and let Marchant fly to Morocco. There was no doubt in Spiro's mind that the kid should have been locked up, just as his father should have been. The subsequent revelation that he was related to Salim Dhar only confirmed his worst fears. Now might be the time to take him out of the equation, particularly if everyone was distracted by news of Dhar's death. Besides, what the hell was his so-called vacation in Morocco all about? The Vicar had called it a sabbatical. As far as Spiro was concerned, if someone needed some R&R, they headed for Honolulu, not North Africa.

'Check him in for some root-canal work,' Spiro said. 'Aziz could do with the practice.'

'That would be a breach of existing protocol, sir,' Meena said.

'I think you misheard me, Lakshmi.'

'No, sir, I didn't.'

There was a pause, a calculation. Spiro knew she was right, but he wasn't going to let anyone ruin his visit to London, least of all Daniel Marchant. He cut her off.

It had been a good day in Washington, one of the best of his career. He had personally briefed the President about the drone strike on Salim Dhar. Although it was still too early to go public, the signs were good: no collateral for once, just a clean hit on the world's most wanted. It didn't get much sweeter. Now he was on his way to Fairford, and would shortly be making Marcus Fielding's life a misery, something he always enjoyed.

The CIA was already all over MI5, running its own large network of agents and informers in Britain. As Spiro had discussed with the President, a Pakistani entering the US from 'Londonistan' on a visa-waiver programme now represented the biggest threat to America. As a result, 25 per cent of the Agency's resources dedicated to preventing another 9/11 were being directed at Britain. MI5 wasn't up to the job, and the CIA had recruited half of Yorkshire in the past few years. Immigration security at all major British airports was being coordinated by the Agency, too. Now he was about to rub the Vicar's nose in it.

His phone rang again. This time he hesitated before answering it. His boss, the DCIA, only called him in the middle of the night if there was a problem.

# 17

It was two o'clock in the morning, and Marcus Fielding was still in his Legoland office, playing his flute: Telemann's Suite in A-Minor. It was something of a tradition in MI6. Colin McColl, one of his predecessors, had filled the night air at the old head office in Southwark with his playing. Fielding rarely drank, but tonight was an exception. A bottle of Château Musar from the Bekaa Valley stood on his desk, half empty. He knew Spiro had come to gloat in London and he was determined to deny him the pleasure.

He stood up, arched his stiff back and went over to Oleg, the Service's newest recruit, a two-year-old border terrier. Fielding had adopted him from Battersea Dogs' Home the previous month and named him after two great Russian servants of MI6. There had been a few raised eyebrows the first time he brought Oleg into Legoland, but he only accompanied the Chief to work when he had to stay late, like tonight. His driver had brought him across the Thames from his flat in Dolphin Square, Pimlico, walking him along the towpath before handing him over to security at a side gate.

Oleg had undoubtedly made life more tolerable, absorbed some of the stress. His presence broke up the neatness of Fielding's existence, which he was aware had become an obsession since his return from India. He had almost lost his job helping Daniel Marchant in Delhi. For a few dark days, the Americans had taken over the asylum. Legoland had been raided and he had been on the run, just like Marchant. He was too old for that game, too tired, which was why he had tried to restore some order to his life, a protection against the chaos of the raging world outside.

Tonight, though, that chaos threatened to return, and it had nothing to do with Oleg or the Lebanese wine. His mind had been racing ever since he had spoken with Marchant in Morocco. Normally, he would have dismissed his talk of Moscow as wild speculation from a field agent under pressure. But earlier in the day, a routine memo from MI5 had landed in his in-tray that made Marchant's words – *Nye strelai* – hang in the air long after the encrypted line from Marrakech had dropped.

Harriet Armstrong, Fielding's opposite number at Thames House, had come over the river to talk about it in person. She was no longer on crutches, but she still had a slight limp, the only legacy of her car crash in Delhi. One of her officers in D4, the counter-intelligence branch that monitored the Soviet Embassy in Kensington Palace Gardens, had intercepted a routine diplomatic communication. A man called Nikolai Ivanovich Primakov was about to be posted to London under cultural attaché cover. The young duty officer had run the normal checks, calling up Primakov's file from the library and cross-referring it with known SVR and GRU agents operating under diplomatic cover.

To the duty officer's surprise, he found that Primakov had once enjoyed a high-flying intelligence career, but his prospects had suffered when Boris Yeltsin set about disbanding the KGB in 1991. After a three-year stint in the private security business, protecting banks in Moscow, Primakov returned to the SVR, as the KGB's First Chief Directorate had become, where he continued to rise through the ranks until he suffered a series of sideways moves.

His imminent arrival in London was a promotion, prompting the duty officer to conclude in his daily report that it was significant.

At no point did he realise quite how significant it was, but behind the scenes his routine inquiry had triggered a flagged message to drop into Armstrong's in-box. As Director General of MI5, she was one of only a handful of people who knew that Primakov had once been MI6's most senior asset in the KGB and later the SVR, on a par with Penkovsky and Gordievsky.

Fielding and Armstrong were allies now, thick as Baghdad thieves, united in their resentment of America's growing influence in Whitehall. And Fielding sensed the makings of a mutually beneficial plan, a shoring up of defences against Spiro, something that might buy both their Services a little respect again after a torrid year.

He gave Oleg a scratch behind the ears and walked back to his desk. One of Primakov's restricted MI6 files from the 1980s, known as a 'no-trace' because any database search for it would yield nothing, lay in front of the framed photos of Fielding's favourite godchildren, Maya and Freddie. Beside it was a neat grid of Post-it notes he had been writing all evening.

The file was open on a page that showed a tourist-style photo of Primakov taken in Agra in 1980, standing in front of the Taj Mahal. Beside him was Stephen Marchant, smiling back at the camera. He had good reason to be happy, and not just because his wife had recently given birth to twins, Daniel and Sebastian. It was eight years before disaster would strike, when Sebastian was so cruelly taken from him. Stephen Marchant was already a rising star in MI6, but his recruitment of Primakov, then attached to the Soviet Embassy in Delhi, would propel him all the way to the top of the Service.

Primakov rose swiftly through the KGB, too, on his return to Moscow, specialising in counter-intelligence, much to the satisfaction

70

of Marchant and his MI6 superiors. But his relationship with the West was built on personal friendship. He would only agree to be handled by Stephen Marchant, which created problems for everyone. Not for the first time, Primakov began to arouse the suspicion of Moscow Centre, his career stalled and the RX eventually dried up. Primakov's posting to London marked a return to the fold. And Fielding sensed that it was in some way linked to whatever had happened in Morocco. Patterns again.

A line from the switchboard was flickering on Fielding's comms console. He had been about to look at another file on Primakov that not even Armstrong knew about. It told a very different story about his friendship with Marchant, but that would have to wait. He took the call, wondering who would be ringing him so late at night.

'I have a Paul Myers from GCHQ for you, sir,' the woman on reception said.

The last time he had spoken to Myers had also been in the middle of the night, when he had rung to talk about Leila. It was partly because of Myers that she had been exposed as a traitor, something that Fielding had never forgotten.

'I assume this is important,' Fielding began, sounding harsher than he meant. He liked Myers.

'Sorry for ringing so late, but I thought you should know,' Myers began. At least he wasn't drunk this time.

'Go on.'

'I've been working on the Salim Dhar intercept, in advance of the JIC meeting tomorrow.'

'And?'

'There was someone else in the farm building with him.'

'Quite a few people, I gather.' Perhaps Myers had been drinking after all.

'There's a voice at the end of the intercept, sort of screaming.'

Fielding instinctively peeled off a fresh Post-it note and began to write, trying to contain any implications within the boundaries of his neat hand.

' "Sort of" screaming? Either it was screaming or it wasn't.'

'I've been running it through filter analysis, comparing it with thousands of other screams. It's an American voice.'

Myers paused. The nib of Fielding's green-ink fountain pen hovered.

'There's something else. I ran a few spectrographic checks. There wasn't much to go on, but the voiceprint appears to match one of the US Marines who was taken by the Taleban.'

'Are you sure?' There had been a news blackout when six US Marines had been seized two days earlier, but the Americans had told a few of their closest allies, which still included Britain.

'Fort Meade patched over some voice profiles of the Marines to Cheltenham, told our Af-Pak desks to listen out for them. I think Salim Dhar might have been with them, maybe part of the team holding them hostage.'

There was a long silence. Oleg raised his head, as if sensing the missed beat.

'Sir?'

But Fielding had already hung up.

# 18

Spiro looked in the mirror and straightened his tie. The Joint Intelligence Committee was already assembling down the corridor, but there was still time. Entering and locking a cubicle behind him, he marshalled two lines of cocaine on the porcelain surface of the cistern, using his Whitehall security card. Then he stopped, held his breath. Someone had come into the room, humming. It sounded like Fielding. Did the Vicar know more than he did? Cheltenham would have picked up the *jihadi* website before Langley had shut it down.

Spiro waited for him to leave, listening to the crisp discipline of the Vicar's unhurried ablutions, the way he dispensed the soap with two short stabs, turned the taps, tore the paper towels. A man in control of his life, unhurried. Spiro envied him, but he knew that he too would have that feeling in a few seconds. When the Vicar was gone, he leaned over the powder, a rolled ten-dollar bill shaking in his hand. The next moment he was flushing the cistern, the tumbling water masking his snorts. Steady, he told himself. He had to hold it together.

Spiro unlocked the cubicle door and rinsed his hands, glancing again at himself in the smoked mirror. At moments like this he could take reassurance in his ageing face, find comfort in the lines of experience, each one a reminder of a hardship survived, one of life's obstacles overcome: brought up in Over-the-Rhine, then a rough quarter in downtown Cincinnati; an abusive father; the first Gulf War; his cheating wife; their disabled son and his desire to make the world a better place for him.

Few people saw him that way. The British had him down as an ex-Marine who had forgotten to leave his battle fatigues at the door, which was fine by him. He hadn't been hired to be nice. Christ, he hadn't been *born* to be nice. One of his first jobs at Langley had been to oversee the freelance deniables the Agency regularly hired to do its heavy lifting. They were all ex-military, like him, and they got along with him fine, respecting his distinguished career in the Marine Corps.

He knew, though, that he had been lucky to hold on to his job. The end of the rendition programme and the fall-out from the so-called 'torture memos' had led a number of staff to leave, sapping the morale of those left behind. Spiro had thought about jumping into the private sector before he was pushed, but he had stayed on, never doubting that his approach to intelligence would be in demand again in the future. He just hadn't figured it would be so soon. Salim Dhar was to thank for that. The jumped-up *jihadi*'s long-range shot at the President had changed everything, including Spiro's career prospects.

'Thank God, I didn't fire you,' the new DCIA, a moderate, had joked after promoting Spiro to head of the National Clandestine Service's European operations. 'The bad-ass guys are back in town.'

But his job now looked to be in doubt again. Dark clouds were rolling in from Afghanistan. The tone of the DCIA's voice on the phone in the Gulfstream V had reminded him of the consultant who had broken the news about their disabled child. Mom and baby were doing fine. They just needed to run some tests. Euphoria qualified.

According to the DCIA, a *jihadi* website was claiming that six and an interesting sideline in glamour photography. In short, Marchant saw it as a gift, his bonus from Legoland for a difficult year.

He checked the passport, his business card and the Billingham bag of cameras and lenses that he had kept in his flat, then caught a glimpse of himself in the driver's mirror and adjusted the sunglasses that were perched on the top of his head. McLennan's hair was slightly darker than his own, which was dirt-blond, but he had had no time to dye it. After spotting Meena, he had collected a small overnight bag from his flat and jumped in a taxi, ordered by a man he could trust in the medina.

Now, as the taxi drove down the highway to Agadir, Marchant thought back three months to when Fielding had called him into his office on the morning he had left for Marrakech. The Vicar had reminded him of his responsibilities, the need to keep his head down. They had both survived a challenging time together in India, and their relationship was close, at times almost like father and son. Fielding had risked his own career to support him, something Marchant would never forget. The ensuing year in London had not been easy for either of them. Confined to Legoland by the Americans, Marchant had drunk too much and caused trouble in the office. Fielding had grown tired of having to bail him out. They both knew that Marchant was the only person who could find Dhar, and he wasn't going to do it chained to a desk in London.

'The Americans have retreated, lifted the travel ban, but they insist that you remain a legitimate target for observation,' the Vicar had said, sipping at a glass of the sweet mint tea he had asked Otto, his Eastern European butler, to prepare for the two of them. 'We've protested, of course, but there's no movement.'

'And our rules of engagement, have they changed?'

'Despite everything that happened, to you, to me, to Harriet

Armstrong, America remains our closest ally,' Fielding said. 'Remember that. The appalling truth is that we can't live for long without them or the intel they share with us.' He paused. 'Langley is on record as having cleared you and your father of any wrong-doing. That counts for something. Salim Dhar is the enemy combatant here, not you. But we both know that your relation-ship with Dhar presents the CIA with a problem. If they ever cross the line again, hold you against your will, interrogate –'

'Waterboard,' Marchant interrupted.

'Yes, well – you may have to cross the line, too.'

'And the real reason for my presence in Marrakech remains deniable,' Marchant said.

'Utterly. As far as the Americans are concerned, you are in Morocco on sabbatical. Marrakech is a natural place for you, an Arabist, to sort your life out. HR have signed off on it, citing ill-health and low office morale. Given the disruption you've caused in Legoland over the past year, they are only too pleased to see the back of you.'

Marchant reckoned that the circumstances he found himself in now satisfied Fielding's conditions. Lakshmi Meena had crossed the line. The woman Langley had sent to keep an eye on him was suddenly on his case after weeks of inactivity. He might be wrong, of course, but it was odd that Meena had come back to watch him late in the night after their meeting at the *bar anglais*. The only explanation was that she must have heard about the heli-copter incident and Marchant's presence in the mountains. But who had seen him? He assumed it was a local informer. The CIA was closer to the Moroccan intelligence services than MI6, particu-larly after the courts in London had revealed details of torture at a Moroccan black site.

By the time he reached Agadir airport, Marchant was confident that nobody had followed him by road from Marrakech. His worry was that a reception committee might be waiting for him in the departures hall. If Meena meant business, she would be watching all the country's exits, particularly when Daniel Marchant didn't show up for his flight from Marrakech. But security at the airport was no more rigorous than usual.

After checking in one piece of luggage, Marchant was about to make his way to passport control when he heard a commotion behind him. He turned to see a man in shades being escorted into the departures hall by three policemen, an air stewardess and a posse of screaming middle-aged women. Behind them were half a dozen paparazzi, cameras flashing as they jostled for position.

'Who's the celeb?' Marchant asked the attractive woman behind the check-in desk.

'Hussein Farmi,' she said, a faint blush colouring her face.

Marchant nodded knowingly, but the woman wasn't convinced.

'Star of more than a hundred films,' she explained. '*Khali Balak Min Zouzou*? With Soad Hosny?'

'Of course.'

'He's one of the Middle East's most popular actors. And he has been married five times.' She stifled a giggle.

'I'd better get a few shots of him then,' Marchant said, nodding at the canvas bag slung over his shoulder. Without thinking, he pulled out a camera, snapped the check-in woman and gave her a wink as he walked off in pursuit of Farmi. Photographers could get away with murder, he thought.

# 20

Fielding couldn't remember such a tense meeting of the Joint Intelligence Committee. Even the ones that had been hastily called in the hours after 9/11 and 7/7 had been characterised by unity rather than discord. Everyone had been pulling together then. There were no divisions, no conflicting agendas. The Americans had needed Britain's help after 9/11, and the British had needed their help after 7/7.

This time the Cabinet Room in Downing Street was crackling with resentment and rivalry as Spiro addressed the London heads of the Canadian, Australian and New Zealand intelligence services, Harriet Armstrong, Director General of MI5, the head of GCHQ, accompanied by an awkward Paul Myers, a raft of faceless Whitehall mandarins, and the clammy-cheeked Sir David Chadwick, still chairman of the JIC despite the Americans' best efforts to unseat him in a cooked-up child-porn sting.

'I had hoped to bring better news to you all today,' Spiro said, studiously avoiding any eye contact with Fielding. 'As you know, we believe we have eliminated Salim Dhar in a Reaper strike in Afghanistan. We still maintain the target was destroyed, but there are rumours this morning that Dhar might have been with the six US Marines who were taken at the weekend by Taleban forces. In terms of potential collateral, that particular scenario couldn't be worse.'

Six US Marines struck Fielding as a result, compared to the normal quota of innocent women and children who were destroyed by drone strikes, but he kept his peace, preferring to make his point with a short dry cough. Spiro looked across at him for the first time.

'They are all fine soldiers. One of them, Lieutenant Randall Oaks, served alongside me in Iraq. As things stand right now, the picture is a little confused. A *jihadi* website posted images this morning of the strike zone, one of which I can show you now.'

He pressed at a remote in his hand and a grab from a website appeared on a flat screen behind Spiro. It showed a group of local Afghanis waving at the camera. One was holding a damaged Marine's helmet, its US markings just visible.

'NSA managed to crash the site by overloading the server, but it's fair to assume the images will soon appear elsewhere. We happen to believe they're fake, but clearly it's an unhelpful story. Right now, the President, whom I personally briefed yesterday, is holding back on an announcement about Dhar. He wants DNA, but that could be tricky, given the hostile location of the strike zone.'

Chadwick cleared his throat loudly enough for Spiro to pause. 'Just supposing Dhar is still alive, is he likely to address his followers, make a video to prove he's not dead?'

'First up, we don't believe Dhar's alive. Our position remains that he was killed in the Reaper strike. Personally, I also think the Marines story is a red herring, put out to distract attention from Dhar's death. No way would Salim Dhar, the world's most wanted terrorist, risk being with the Marines, knowing our ongoing military efforts to find and retrieve them. But if Dhar is still alive – and that's a mighty big if – it's not his style to show himself.'

'So should we be putting out rumours that he's dead?'

'Absolutely. Fort Meade's already posting to that effect in

*jihadi* chatrooms. We'd be grateful if Cheltenham coordinates the European side of things. I don't want a repeat of Rashid Rauf. His supporters were claiming he was alive and well within minutes of the Reaper strike. It's imperative we move quickly.'

Fielding caught Armstrong's eye. He wondered what she was feeling as she sat there, watching the humiliation of Spiro, a man she had once so foolishly admired. She glanced away and looked at Myers. The three of them had talked earlier about the audio evidence. The head of GCHQ was not happy – Cheltenham had better relations with the Americans than MI5 and MI6 – but Fielding had reassured him that he would take the heat.

Just as Spiro was about to speak again, Fielding began, his languid body language – long legs out to one side, head bent forward like a concert pianist's – at odds with the devastating intelligence he was about to pool.

'Some product crossed my desk this morning that I think should be shared.'

'That's very good of you,' Spiro said, managing a thin smile. Fielding savoured his rival's fluster, the nervousness that everyone in the room would have detected in the American's voice. 'Go ahead. After all, sharing product is what this meeting's all about, isn't it?'

'Your position, as I understand it, is that Dhar was not with the Marines at the time of the strike.'

'No, that's not my position. The Marines were not with Dhar when we eliminated him.'

Spiro's voice was wavering more now, a top-end tremolo that was music to Fielding's ears.

'Let's just suppose for a moment that we could prove that the Marines and Dhar were together when the Reaper struck.'

'I hope that this evidence, whatever it is, came in to your

possession after and not before we launched our attack. Because that would frickin' upset me if you weren't sharing intel.'

'I can understand that. For the record' – a nod at Chadwick, the chairman – 'we learned about it late last night.'

'And what exactly is this intel?'

'Paul?' Fielding turned to Myers, who was sitting next to him, looking more uncomfortable than usual. 'Paul Myers has been on attachment with us from Cheltenham' – a glance at the Chief of GCHQ, who turned away as if Fielding had just thrown up over him – 'and last night he ran some further tests on the Dhar audio intercept.'

Fielding looked again at Myers, who appeared too nervous to take up the story, biting at what was left of his nails.

'Some tests,' Spiro said, not trying to disguise his disdain. 'In addition to Fort Meade's thorough spectrographic analysis?'

'That's right. And he found a fragment of sound at the end of the second intercept that I think we should all hear.'

Myers stood up and walked over to an audio console beneath the main screen. He had suddenly grown in confidence, evidently more at ease with technology than people. After checking the levels, he half turned towards the room, instinctively crouching down at the height of the console when he saw all the faces.

'I was looking for something else when I found it,' he said, to no one in particular. 'Often the way.' A nervous laugh, immediately regretted. 'It's only a few milliseconds, but I've slowed it down so you can hear.' He pressed a button, and there was silence. Then a deep, distorted, drawn-out call, like a wounded animal's, filled the room.

'And what in God's name was that?' Spiro said, suddenly more confident. He had seen his enemy's best shot, and he could live with it. He stood up, as if to defend himself better, knuckles pressed into the oak table.

Myers stood up, too, and looked across at Fielding for guidance. Fielding nodded.

'It's a scream,' Myers began. 'An American scream.'

Fielding watched as the ensuing silence sapped Spiro of all his bravura, his large frame collapsing like a punctured tyre.

'An American scream,' Spiro managed to repeat, more as a statement than a question. Fielding had to give him credit. He was trying to put on a brave face.

'I've compared it with the audio IDs sent over by Fort Meade.' Myers paused, fiddling with his ponytail. 'It's a perfect match with one of the Marines.' He paused again. 'Lieutenant Randall Oaks.'

# 21

It was as Marchant was taking his seat in the departure lounge that he first sensed security at the airport had been raised a level. Two men in charcoal suits had appeared at the gate and were standing by the entrance to the airbridge that led down to the plane, a twin-turboprop ATR 42. Marchant knew that the aircraft was used by courier firms, but it also flew short-haul passenger flights.

The two men, badges on their jackets, scrutinised the group of people waiting for the flight, then glanced down the list of passengers with a member of the ground crew. One of the officers caught Marchant's eye, checked the list, and then looked at another passenger. They didn't appear to be interested in him, but he was on edge now, searching for anything that might suggest he was a target.

Earlier, after he had taken a few photos of Hussein Farmi and joked with the other photographers, he had passed through passport control without a problem. Not even a second glance at his photo. He hadn't been worried that the cobblers' work wouldn't be up to scratch; he was more concerned that Meena might have called in a favour, asked Moroccan intelligence to keep a lookout for him.

There were no more than twenty passengers in total, and they started to form an orderly line when their flight was finally called.

Marchant was about to get up from his seat when one of the suited men came over to him, smiling.

'Mr McLennan?'

'That's me,' Marchant said, keeping it upbeat. He followed up with what he hoped was a cheeky smile. 'Is there a problem?' He wouldn't have asked if he had been Daniel Marchant, but he felt Dirk McLennan was the sort of man who liked to put his cards on the table.

'Not at all. The flight is less than half full, and we are upgrading today. Please, follow me.'

'Great, sounds a blast,' Marchant said, assessing the risk. He was instinctively worried. The badge on the man's suit indicated that he worked for the local airline, but Marchant didn't believe it for a second. 'Terrific, in fact. But what about these good people here?' He glanced at the other passengers.

'I should say it is because you are a guest of our country and we have a long and honourable tradition of hospitality, but I would be lying.' He paused. Marchant thought for a moment about running, but he returned the man's steady gaze as a bead of sweat rolled down his back. 'We upgrade randomly from the passenger list, and providing the individual is what we call SFU – suitable for upgrade – we invite them to enjoy their flight in the comfort of business class. Come.'

Marchant shrugged at the other passengers and walked to the front of the queue, sprinkling apologies as he went. He showed his boarding card to a member of the airline crew and tried to flirt with her, but she was having none of it. He mustered a swagger as he walked down the airbridge towards the aircraft. It was tempting to look back, but he knew it would be inappropriate. Dirk McLennan was a chancer, and would be loving every minute of this. If only he felt the same. Something was very wrong, but how could he protest about an upgrade?

'Please, enjoy your flight, Mr McLennan,' the man said, ushering him on board the plane.

Marchant nodded at the two cabin crew who greeted him at the door. They steered him left into the small business-class area, where there were eight seats in total. He eased across to a window and sat down with his camera bag on his lap, his limbs heavy with adrenaline. Trying to control his breathing, he considered his options, but the sense of imminent danger was overwhelming. The plane would have been claustrophobic even if he hadn't felt out of control of the situation. The only exit point was the door he had just entered, and his last opportunity to escape was now. But how far would he get? The boarding gate, if he was lucky.

Again he ran through the situation in which he found himself: Lakshmi Meena was on his tail, turning up at dawn on the streets of Marrakech. Booking a flight as Daniel Marchant from the city's airport had given him a head start, but Meena had friends in the Moroccan intelligence service, and someone might have recognised him here at Agadir. No one had stopped him at passport control, but then he was given an upgrade. Perhaps he was overreacting, and Meena was just making sure he left town. It was too easy to see threats where none existed. But he knew he was right, particularly when another passenger was shown into business class and sat down in the seat beside him.

'Mind if I join you?' the man asked. He was Moroccan, and looked faintly familiar.

'Sure,' Marchant said, glancing at the empty seats on the other side of the aisle.

'You're a photographer?' he asked, nodding at Marchant's camera bag.

'For my sins,' Marchant said, struggling to stay in character. 'And you?'

'Me?' He paused. 'I'm a dentist.'

# 22

'There's something else,' Myers said, after Spiro had sat down. It was more of a slump, but Spiro somehow managed to make it look controlled. For a moment, Fielding wished he felt sorry for Spiro, a pang of pity. But there was nothing but cold contempt, the sort he normally reserved for Russians. 'Work for the Foreign Office if you want to be liked,' he had been told by the don who had tapped him up at Oxford. What Fielding didn't know was that another blow to Spiro's self-esteem, his career, his whole *raison d'être*, was about to come from Myers, who was still standing in front of the audio.

This time, Myers didn't look to Fielding for guidance. He was on his own now, score abandoned, improvising. 'Actually, I agree with the American analysis that Dhar would not risk being with the captured US Marines.'

Spiro seemed to take heart from this, and sat up to listen.

'I didn't at first, but I do now. Using this assumption as my starting point, I went back to the audio this morning and asked myself, in the light of the American scream, how it was possible for Salim Dhar and Lieutenant Oaks to be in the same place.'

'And?' Chadwick said, glancing at Spiro. Like Fielding, he was intrigued to see what this awkward analyst from Cheltenham was going to say next. Spiro was staring out of the window, lost in his own thoughts. The head of GCHQ didn't know where to look.

Myers picked nervously at the back of a front tooth and then stopped himself, as if being chided by a parent. 'The only explanation is that Dhar's voice was recorded.'

Spiro looked from the window to Myers, suddenly encouraged.

'Don't you think that scenario might just have been checked out by the NSA?'

'Of course. And I've looked into it, too. But the quality of the intercept is too poor to be able to establish if Dhar's voice is a recording. There's also no audio trace of a recorder activating before or after Dhar speaks.'

'So?'

'For once, the answer doesn't lie in technology.'

Fielding was enjoying this, watching Myers grow in confidence, trying to guess where it would lead. This was what intelligence work was all about: intuition.

'You're an analyst, right?' Spiro heckled. 'Stick to IT and leave the couch work to others.'

Myers ignored him, more out of dysfunctional shyness than defiance.

'Why did Lieutenant Oaks scream?' Myers asked, addressing the whole room now.

'Why?' Spiro echoed. 'He was about to be incinerated by a Hellfire missile, that's why.'

'About to be. Exactly. It's not my area, of course –'

'Too right.'

'– but my understanding of munitions is that such things are pretty instant. Like, no time to scream. Oaks had worked out what was going on. It was the second time Dhar had spoken. He wouldn't have known what was happening the first time he heard his voice. But when he spoke again, Oaks would have realised that there was nobody else in that hut apart from the six Marines. He was trying to give Fort Meade a message, tell them it was a mistake, that there was a tape recorder strapped to Dhar's phone. Just like this one.'

With uncharacteristic panache, Myers reached into his fleece pocket and pulled out a small mobile phone strapped with masking tape to an equally thin tape recorder. Myers was turning out to be a natural showman, Fielding thought, despite the phone catching awkwardly on his pocket. Next up, he'd be pulling rabbits from a hat, sawing Harriet Armstrong in half, performing the Indian rope trick. Armstrong would like that. She wasn't afraid to play to the gallery. At Cambridge, she had played the fairy godmother in a university production of *Cinderella*.

The two units were linked by a small audio lead, which might have looked like a detonator to an inexperienced eye. The room didn't exactly gasp – those present were too versed in the modern tools of terror to be surprised – but there was a shuffling of papers that Fielding had come to recognise over the years as civil servants' applause.

'As soon as Lieutenant Oaks heard the voice a second time,' Myers said, brandishing the phone, 'the penny dropped and he screamed, but it was too late. The phone had already disconnected. Except that it wasn't too late. We heard him, and we know Dhar's still alive.'

Spiro knew as soon as Myers had spoken that he was right. He thought back to the UAV trailer at Creech, to the sensor operator who had cast doubt on the target. For a moment, Spiro had imagined he had seen what looked like a crucifix, but the image was blurred and he had shut it out of his mind. Just as he had removed the operator's suspicions from his official report afterwards.

It took almost a minute for someone to speak after Myers

had shuffled back to his seat. Chadwick was the one who broke the silence, and his comments were addressed to Spiro.

'I think I speak for all of the British agencies when I say that we offer you our unconditional sympathy. It's at times like this that allies must pull together and help one other.'

Whitehall shorthand for *Thank Christ the mistake wasn't ours*, Fielding thought.

'That's good of you,' Spiro said quietly. America wasn't used to needing its allies. 'I must make some calls.'

Fielding thought that Spiro looked a genuinely broken man as he stood up to leave. But again there was no sympathy, just the thought of what could be leveraged from the situation.

'Before you go,' Chadwick said, 'I want you to know that there's no reason why our official position should change: Dhar is thought to have been killed, but it is believed, with great regret, that six US Marines whom he had taken were killed too. Adopting such a line carries a political risk, and the Prime Minister will make no official statement on the incident, but our experience of Dhar is that he's not the sort of *jihadi* who will turn up on a website telling the world he's alive and well. It suits him better that the world thinks he's dead. Clearly, we need to qualify any statement we make to give us sufficient slack if he does show up, but for the time being, Dhar is dead.'

# 23

'Please, have a rinse,' Abdul Aziz said.

Marchant sucked at the straw that was put to his bruised lips, swilled the liquid round his mouth and then spat out a mixture of blood and fragments of his lower right molar. Aziz held a kidney-shaped stainless-steel dish up to his mouth, resting it on his lower lip, and caught the debris.

The moment Aziz had introduced himself as a dentist, two men had appeared from behind the economy-class curtain. Aziz had stood up to let them through to Marchant, who had put up a fight, taking one of them out, but it was still two against one, although Aziz had held back, limiting himself to a gratuitous kick to Marchant's groin. Eventually, he was forced down into an aisle seat, his wrists bound to the armrests with plasticuffs and his legs secured to the footrest.

The two men left the plane before it took off, one helping the other, leaving only Aziz and a pilot on board. Lakshmi Meena never showed, but Marchant assumed she was the one who had set him up with Aziz. He regretted opening up to her in their chat the previous night, knew he should have listened to his instinct, not trusted anyone. The sole grain of comfort was his right hand. In the struggle to secure him to his seat, he had been cut in the soft flesh of his wrist. It wasn't a deep incision, but it was painful enough to give him hope, because it meant that somewhere there was a sharp edge.

Marchant had heard of Aziz, knew the enhanced techniques he had used on enemy combatants as they had passed through black sites in Morocco on their way to Guantanamo; but what was it with the polite small talk? Had he once trained as a real dentist? He'd be offering him an old copy of *Punch* next, something to read while he waited for his teeth to be extracted without anaesthetic. He wondered if Aziz knew about Marchant's long and painful relationship with dentists, or whether he just assumed that dentistry would always touch a raw nerve in his detainees.

'We don't have to do this, Daniel,' Aziz said, adjusting the settings on the steel brace that held Marchant's head in position. Marchant couldn't reply. His mouth had been wedged open with a metal clamp that tasted of linseed oil. He was also barely conscious. At least his business-class seat was upright. Up until now it had been fully reclined, reminding him of an actual dentist's chair, which was no doubt the point. Aziz's entire approach – the perverse offer of mouthwash, his authentic tools of the trade – seemed designed to remind him of the real thing. Except that there was no soothing classical music, no funny posters on the ceiling. Just the hum of the aircraft and a silence behind the curtain that confirmed Marchant's worst fears. He was the only passenger who had proceeded to boarding.

'All I need to know is what you saw in the mountains and if it had anything to do with Salim Dhar,' Aziz said. He was standing in the aisle, examining an ultrasonic scaler that was buzzing in his hand. The reverberating whine began to shake down memories from the walls of Marchant's skull.

'Unfortunately, this instrument is a bit faulty,' Aziz apologised, lowering the scaler into Marchant's mouth. 'I borrowed it from a horse vet who didn't seem to care so much about maintenance.

The problem is the sharp tip at the end – it isn't being cooled by water, so it becomes red hot. Normally, a dentist moves quickly from one tooth to the next to prevent overheating, but I am not a normal dentist.'

Marchant screamed as Aziz pressed down with the instrument, scorching into the soft pulp of his molar. The surrounding gum seemed to explode into flames, the heat spreading through his head, licking down into his neck and shoulders until it felt as if his whole upper body was being blowtorched.

'Please try to remember the mountains, Daniel. Because if what you saw did involve Salim Dhar and I didn't know about it, the Americans will remove my teeth after I've finished pulling yours.'

Aziz unfastened the clamp and put down the scaler. He then picked up a steel dental drill and tested it. More whining, as if the drill was suffering pain rather than about to inflict it.

'Tungsten carbide,' Aziz said, inspecting the drill's burr. 'You see, I'm meant to hear about everything that happens in Morocco, or as our friend James Spiro put it so politely, "every fucking fart from Fes to Safi". I know it's not fair, but that's the way it goes. The Americans, they expect a lot from us, and I would hate to let them down.'

'I didn't see anything unusual,' Marchant repeated, his voice thick with blood. He thought back to what he had said a few minutes earlier, knowing that if he repeated it verbatim, it would be a clear indication that he was lying. He remembered the instructor – army moustache, tight-fitting T-shirt – who had taught him at RAF St Mawgan in Cornwall, where all new MI6 recruits were sent for basic SERE (Survival, Evasion, Rescue and Escape) training. Small errors and variations were more convincing than perfect recall, which suggested a fake story that had been well rehearsed.

'It was my last night in Marrakech,' Marchant continued. 'I wanted to go up into the mountains one last time, so I borrowed a friend's motorbike, went for a ride.'

'Sometimes I think you British believe Moroccans are a genuinely inferior people,' Aziz said. Marchant braced himself for more pain. 'It's the only explanation for the way your courts of justice betray us. We interrogate terrorists on your behalf, in confidence, beyond your jurisdiction so nobody in your country breaks the law, then you release details of our work because of so-called freedom of information, and suddenly the whole world knows about it and treats us like pariahs. Never mind that it was your questions we were asking.'

'We objected to the publication of the information,' Marchant said. 'Unfortunately, the courts overruled us.'

Aziz laughed. 'What sort of secret service is it that gets pushed around by a judge?'

One that operates in a democracy, Marchant thought, but he held his swollen tongue.

'Tell me one thing, my friend: who is going to remember it was Britain's dirty work we were doing? No, all anyone remembers is that someone got tortured in Morocco. Happily, we're not in Moroccan airspace any more, so please answer my questions. Was Salim Dhar in the High Atlas?'

Marchant hesitated a moment too long. Aziz pulled his mouth open and inserted the clamp again, tightening it until his top and bottom jaw were so far apart that he thought his mouth would split at the corners. It was a repeat of what Aziz had done earlier, but he was angry now, curiosity replaced by irritation. Once again, Marchant couldn't talk, move his head or his jaw, but the sense of vulnerability was nothing compared to the next wave of pain that he knew was about to break over him.

'We have a choice, Daniel. Either you tell me what you saw, or I will have to remove the molar – it will be no good to you now.'

Marchant instinctively checked the bloodied tooth with his tongue, working it around the edge of the cavity. At the same moment, he flexed his right wrist, trying to find the sharp edge. He felt rough metal cut into his skin again. It was the lid of the ashtray in his armrest, flipped half open. Suddenly his predicament was bearable. He moved his wrist and felt the plastic of his cuffs rub against the edge of the ashtray. It would take time, but at least there was hope.

'All right, then. I think it's better we take it out,' Aziz said, just as turbulence rocked the plane enough for him to steady himself on Marchant's arm. He hadn't noticed Marchant working his right hand. 'I can see it's clearly causing you some discomfort.'

Again, Marchant wondered if Aziz had ever tried to go into dentistry. When it suited him, he had an excellent bedside manner, a soothing tone of authority that was utterly at odds with his work.

'Unfortunately, Morocco can be a very backward country at times, as tourists from Britain often remind us, and I'm afraid we have no anaesthetic with us today.'

Marchant thought for a moment that he saw genuine remorse pass across his face.

'But I do have these. Extraction forceps. The ones for molars have these beak-like ends, do you see?'

He didn't look at the steel pliers Aziz was holding up in front of him. They were in a medically sealed plastic bag, which seemed an unnecessary precaution in the circumstances. Aziz ripped it open and removed the pristine tool. Marchant guessed he had reached the point of Aziz's interrogation process that broke his victims. It used to be scalpel cuts to the genitals, but clearly things had moved on.

'First, though, we have a problem. Your molar is too big, even for these forceps. Maybe I got the wrong ones. Maybe they are for children's teeth. But it's OK. We have this.'

He put down the forceps and picked up the drill again, testing it one last time.

'Perhaps I will drill down through the molar, deep into the nerve, and split the tooth clean in two.'

Marchant could feel his legs shaking. His body was already in shock. He inhaled deeply, letting his diaphragm rise as high as it could, and breathed out slowly, trying to block the pain, focus on the only way out.

'It's funny, you know,' Aziz continued, resting the drill on Marchant's bottom lip. 'I was going to say "Open wide," the way they do, but I was forgetting.'

Fucking hilarious, Marchant thought, tasting the metal of the drill. His right wrist wasn't free yet, and he was beginning to wonder if it ever would be. The one thing he still had control over was his eyes. The point about torture, the SERE instructor had told him, was that the victim must feel totally out of control in order for it to be successful. He must not believe that he can influence anything in his immediate environment except through compliance.

When the CIA had waterboarded him in Poland, he had managed a soaked, defiant laugh, but he couldn't even muster that with his mouth levered open like Jonah's whale. He desperately wanted to shut his eyes, but he kept them open, fixing Aziz with a stare that momentarily unsettled his torturer as he began to drill.

# 24

'I'm sorry,' Myers said, cracking a knuckle so loudly it made Harriet Armstrong jump. The American, Australian and Canadian representatives had all left the Cabinet Room for the second half of the Joint Intelligence Committee, which was traditionally for UK agencies only. 'I know I should have briefed you all before, and I know it wasn't my business, but –'

'I think, in the light of your initial analysis, we can overlook the histrionics of the second act,' Fielding said, turning to Chadwick for formal approval.

'Of course, it was a significant breach of JIC protocol,' Chadwick said. 'But I agree, an exception can be made.'

'Does that unit actually work?' Armstrong asked, nodding at the handset in front of Myers. She was back to wearing her familiar severe suit jackets. Apart from her crocked knee, the only other visible legacy of her Indian adventure was a silver necklace, which had a hint of tribal art about it. She had also confided in Fielding that her mornings now began with half an hour of Vipassana yoga, something she wholly recommended as a way of getting through tedious meetings at the Home Office.

Myers picked up the handset.

'I tested it this morning. With the direct audio input between the two units, it sounds just like a phone call is being made.'

'So what now?' Chadwick said. 'Dhar is clearly not only alive, but several steps ahead of the Americans.'

'It might not have been Dhar's doing,' Armstrong said. 'All that was needed was a recording of his voice and his old SIM card, both of which could have easily been procured by Iran, his previous sponsors.'

'Our view remains that Dhar's too hot for Tehran,' Fielding said.

'So where is he?' Chadwick asked.

'Daniel Marchant is on his way back from Morocco,' Fielding replied.

'No surprise there. I don't think anyone seriously expected that avenue to yield anything, did we, Marcus?' Chadwick had been opposed to Marchant's trip to Morocco from the start, fearing that it would only aggravate Britain's already fragile relationship with America.

'I know you didn't,' Fielding said. He had never had much time for Chadwick, and often wondered if the Americans had been on to something when they had tried to frame him. 'As you all know, we had hoped Dhar would make contact with his half-brother, but he never did. However, something has come up in the last twenty-four hours which suggests that Marchant might have been right about Dhar seeking refuge in North Africa.'

The assembled chiefs looked up, but before Fielding could tell them about the unmarked helicopter in the Atlas mountains, there was a knock on the door and Ian Denton, now Fielding's Assistant Chief, put his lean face around the door.

'Marcus, sorry to interrupt, but I'm afraid Daniel Marchant's dropped off the grid.' Denton's voice, laced with a hint of a Hull accent, had become even more *sotto voce* since his promotion, Fielding thought, but he liked the fact that his trained ear was alone in hearing every word. It was almost as if Denton was speaking in a code known only to his Chief. 'He was meant to have boarded a flight from Marrakech this morning, but he flew out using his snap cover from Agadir.'

'And?' Fielding asked, wondering whether Spiro had already left the building. If Marchant had been taken, it could only be on the CIA's orders. They had done it once before, smuggling him out of Britain on a rendition flight to Poland. Spiro had given assurances that it would never happen again, but he had evidently hoped the death of Dhar would serve as a distraction.

'The local airline filed a false flightplan,' Denton said. 'All we know is that the plane has a very limited range.'

'Find Spiro and bring him back here. And if he complains, tell him we've decided to go public about Dhar.'

# 25

Marchant felt a new pulse of pain overload his nervous system as the drill began to work its way deep into his molar. He remembered the power surges they used to have in Delhi. Every room in the house would suddenly become unnaturally bright, then there would be the sound of popping lightbulbs, followed by the tinkle of glass. Bright lights were flashing across his vision now, and it felt as if synapses, rather than bulbs, were exploding in his brain, their sharp-edged debris falling across raw pathways.

He should have been unconscious, but Aziz would kill him if he passed out. Besides, the sustained eye contact had started to get to the Moroccan, breaking up his routine, causing his hands to shake. The turbulence didn't help either. Occasionally, the drill would slip away from the tooth and cut into Marchant's gum. He tried to focus on his teeth, their impregnability, the fact that they were the only body parts that survived intense fires. They were stronger than bones, weren't they? His molar wasn't going to split. It was too strong, too durable. He thought back to biology classes at school, labelled drawings of teeth: enamel, dentine, pulp, gum. Weren't strontium isotopes found in enamel?

Marchant was screaming now, deep guttural roars. Aziz covered Marchant's eyes with a scarf, but for some reason that interrupted his stride even more. Perhaps he needed to see his victim's eyes, open or shut. Would Meena have looked him in the eye if she were here? For a few brief moments, he had liked her at the *bar anglais*. He should have known better.

But amongst all the pain and anger, a crude plan had crystallised, forged from a visceral survival instinct. As far as Marchant could tell, the pilot had made no contact with Aziz since they had taken off. Marchant presumed he had been told by Meena to circle until he was ordered to land again. No questions, no reassuring chit-chat over the intercom. Which meant that it was just Aziz and him. When the clamp was in his mouth, Marchant was powerless, but Aziz would be removing it again in a moment to ask more questions. At least, he hoped he would. That had been the routine so far: questions, answers, clamp in, clamp out, more questions, more answers, clamp in . . . His only chance was at the point when the clamp was being unscrewed. Aziz was vulnerable then, leaning in close, inches from Marchant's face.

The plastic tie on his right wrist was still not broken, and it would take time before his hand was free. He also knew that he would need something to attack Aziz with. As he sat there strapped into a dentist's chair, only one course of action presented itself. The thought appalled him, but he was beyond caring now. Aziz was the one behaving like an animal. Marchant was simply responding in kind: a tooth for a tooth . . . It didn't get much more primitive, but Marchant had run out of options.

Aziz stepped away from him into the aisle and shook his head like a disappointed school teacher. He hadn't been able to get a clean run at the molar with his drill. He looked at Marchant for a moment, and then leaned across to unscrew the clamp in his mouth. His left hand was just above Marchant's open lips as his fingers loosened the screws on his right jaw. Marchant closed his eyes and inhaled deeply through his nose, trying to acquaint himself with the scent of Aziz's skin: the sweet musk of his aftershave. Then, as

Aziz lifted the clamp out of his jaw, Marchant opened his eyes and stared at his torturer, holding his gaze. It was enough to distract Aziz. Marchant's right hand broke free.

His arm flew upwards in a sweeping arc, clubbing the back of Aziz's head. Grabbing at his hair, Marchant pulled him down onto the brace that was holding his own head in position. Aziz grunted as his face crumpled against the steel frame. But the pain of the impact was nothing compared to the agony that started to shock-wave out from his right cheek. Marchant tried to put the taste of warm salt out of his mind as his front teeth closed, locking their two heads together.

With his right hand Marchant thrashed around for one of the tools on the fold-down table in front of him. He found one, and slashed at the tie holding his left hand, cutting his own wrist as he did so. Aziz's body made it hard to see what he was doing. When both hands were free, he held Aziz's head on either side as if he was kissing him, removed his teeth from the Moroccan's cheek and pulled him down hard into the steel frame again, bracing himself against the impact that shuddered through his spine. This time Aziz slumped to the floor in the aisle.

Marchant spat out whatever was in his mouth. It seemed to halt his rising nausea, so he spat again, and then again, purging his body of Aziz, expressing his disgust, at Aziz, at himself, at Meena. He knew that he was about to collapse. The adrenaline was draining away from his body like bath water, leaving his raw pain exposed. He unscrewed the steel head brace, then freed his legs. Next he lifted Aziz into the chair and secured his legs and arms, using the remains of the ties. He didn't bother with the brace, but he put the clamp in Aziz's bloodied mouth and jacked it open as far as it would go. At least he would be able to breathe.

# 26

Spiro was in no rush to call off the dogs, but he phoned Meena as he crossed Horse Guards Road and walked into St James's Park. He needed to take some air after the meeting.

'What do you mean you can't contact him?' he said, drawing hard on a cigarette as a gaggle of Japanese tourists cycled past him on hired bikes.

'He's with Aziz, as you ordered.'

'And where's Aziz?'

'Twenty-five thousand feet above the Mediterranean.'

'Christ, can't you get ATC to contact the pilot?'

There was a pause. Spiro knew it would take time. Meena had refused to contact Aziz earlier, but he guessed she would be more cooperative now that he was calling time on the dentist.

'Has something happened, sir?'

Spiro drew hard on his cigarette again, watching the flamingos. His hand was shaking.

'Dhar's not dead. He set us up, fooled Fort Meade, fooled fucking all of us, including six dead US Marines.'

He had been looking forward to disciplining Meena for her insubordination, but that would have to wait now. He was no longer in a position of strength. All he could ask of her was to clean up the mess.

'And you think Marchant knows where Dhar is?' she asked.

'Don't go dumb on me, Lakshmi. Of course not. But the British are holding all the cards right now, and if they find out Aziz is pulling Marchant's molars, we'll all have toothache. Get him off the plane, away from Aziz. And dump him somewhere nice, where he can recover. We might need him.'

He hung up just as Ian Denton appeared out of nowhere next to him. Spiro didn't know where to place Denton. The Vicar was easy: he was an upper-class, suspiciously unmarried academic with a bad back and too much sympathy for Arabia. Denton was more complicated. In theory, he should have been an ally: a grammar-school kid from Hull who had risen through the ranks because of hard graft and dirty tricks in the SovBloc, rather than old-school favours and fair play in London. But Spiro remained wary of him. There was something reptilian about Denton's body, lean and sinewy like a long-distance runner's. He also had an unnerving ability to be present in a room without appearing to have entered it. And that quiet voice.

'Daniel Marchant's missing,' Denton said, cutting straight to the chase.

'It's OK. He's fine. A little misunderstanding with our station in Rabat.'

'We had an agreement,' Denton said, surprising Spiro with the suddenness of his attack. Denton usually stayed in the long grass.

'Did we?'

'We go public about Dhar if anything happens to Marchant, is that clear?'

Spiro paused, looking at Denton, listening to his accent, its roughness softened by the quiet delivery. Denton's eyes were soulless, unblinking behind small oval glasses. It had been a smart move by Fielding to make him his deputy. Every Chief needed a troubleshooter, a hard man to sort out the messy stuff. Fielding liked to refer to Denton as his gallowglass. Spiro had played a similar role himself for the previous DCIA. But Denton was different, less muscular, more serpentine. Apparently, he had once saved Fielding's life in a tight spot in Yemen. Now it was payback time.

'Congratulations on your promotion, by the way. I never got the chance to say.'

Denton refused to rise to the bait. Instead, he just looked at him with his lifeless eyes.

'Marchant's doing fine, Ian,' Spiro continued, turning to head off into the park. 'The tooth fairy's watching over him.'

# 27

Lakshmi Meena took a deep breath before the member of the ground-crew staff opened the plane's heavy door. Her life seemed to be punctuated by deep-breath moments, she thought: informing her father that she wasn't going to pursue a career in medicine; telling Spiro that she wasn't prepared to sleep with him or with anyone else at Langley to further her career.

Now her lungs were full again, her chest tight. Did other people have to summon composure in the same way, make such a conscious choice to square up to the world each day? Her father, a structural engineer, had always stressed the importance of blending in, but when she looked at him now, designing bridges in Reston, West Virginia, she sometimes struggled to see anyone at all.

She bunched her right hand tightly around a silk handkerchief and nodded at the two ground crew. The three of them were standing at the top of a set of steps, bringing them even closer to the hot Moroccan sun. There was no shade on the runway, but at least the twin-turboprop had taxied to a quiet corner of Agadir airport, away from the restless tourists queuing to return home to Britain. Beyond the plane, a military ambulance stood waiting, two medics idling by its open doors, smoking and talking to an armed policeman and a couple of Aziz's intelligence colleagues.

One of the men put a hand up unnecessarily to keep the door open as Meena stepped into the plane. She had learned to command authority since joining the Agency, but it still felt like an act, not something that came naturally. She hoped Marchant hadn't suffered too much. Despite their differences, she liked him, envied his equanimity. He seemed to possess an inner calmness that she would never know. And although she had refused to help Spiro set Marchant up with Aziz, she knew she could have done more, protested formally to Langley.

It had also taken too long for her to be patched through to the pilot. As she had suspected, he had been given orders to circle for two hours and then return to Agadir. He had had no contact with Aziz during the flight. The cockpit door was locked, and Meena sensed that the pilot preferred it that way. It clearly wasn't the first time Aziz had taken a passenger on a tour of the Med.

Meena saw Aziz first, head back and to one side, his mouth wide open, as if he was singing grotesquely in his sleep. But there was no sound, and for a second she thought he was dead. She moved forward, trying to process the scene: the clamp in Aziz's mouth, the dark, congealed stain on his cheek, the faint rise and fall of his chest, the tools littered across the floor. Her orders were to get Marchant away from Aziz, but where the hell was he?

She glanced around at the two rows of seats in business class. Aziz was in an aisle seat, its upholstery stained and torn. The seats around were also flecked with blood, the crisp paper headrests ripped or missing. Then Meena saw him, slumped on the floor, his back against the open door of the lavatory, hands by his side. Marchant's eyes were open, but he was barely conscious. The bottom half of his face was badly bruised, his lips bloodied and swollen like slices of overripe peach.

'Daniel,' she said, putting the handkerchief to her mouth, as much to reassure herself about her own lips as to cut out the stale smell of burnt flesh, which was suddenly overpowering. She rushed over, but by the time she was kneeling down beside him, Marchant's eyes had closed.

# 28

Giuseppe Demuro was good at recognising guests. It was part of his job, one of the reasons they came back to his resort year after year. Guests liked to be remembered. Some of his colleagues kept notes on the high rollers, hoping that a personal aside on arrival – namechecking the children, asking after a relative – would secure a more generous tip. But Demuro was in no need of any props. He also had a unique manner, honed over the years into what he hoped was a self-respecting obsequiousness, somewhere between a butler and the boss. But it was his memory for faces that had helped him rise to become manager of one of the most luxurious resorts in Sardinia. It was also why he was in the employ of several of the world's intelligence agencies, who provided more reliable revenue streams than gratuities.

These organisations weren't after state secrets or sexual scandal. (A friend of his at a nearby resort made even more money by tipping off the newspapers whenever politicians came to stay with unsuitable companions, but that was beneath Demuro.) All they wanted to know about was unusual combinations of visitors: patterns. In recent years, the resort had become popular with Russians, from oligarchs who moored their yachts offshore to extended families who paid in cash, stayed mostly in their rooms (always sea-facing), lifted weights in the gym and consumed vast quantities of watermelon and cucumber. If an oligarch's holiday overlapped with a prominent politician's, Demuro would ring the relevant contact.

He liked working for the British the most. There was something glamorous – almost Italian – about the MI6 officers he had met, particularly the man they called the Vicar. He would have preferred working for a priest, of course, but he didn't complain, provided his monthly retainer was in euros.

Demuro had no hesitation, then, in dialling a secure London number after the young American woman checked in to a sea-facing room with a recuperating guest. It wasn't that he recognised her as CIA. Nor that she had a sick companion. The Americans had brought injured people before. It was the fact that a young Russian couple had arrived shortly after them, asking to be near the sea, too.

Normally, he would have greeted the couple in fluent Russian. The previous winter, in the off-season, he had been sent to study at a language school in St Petersburg for three months. There were now more Russian than Italian guests at the resort during July and August. But something made Demuro hold back, and speak in broken English. As he walked with the couple to their room, pointing out the tennis courts, pool and restaurant, he overheard a brief exchange between them. It was only a few Russian words, but when he repeated them on the phone, the Vicar hinted at a bonus and Demuro offered a quiet prayer of thanks.

# 29

Marchant awoke to the sound of a chipping noise. It took him a few seconds to realise that it wasn't coming from inside his mouth. He put his hand up to his jaw, which felt disfigured and swollen. His gums were throbbing, but the pain was less than it had been on the plane. Where was he? He was lying on white cotton sheets, in a whitewashed room. The ceiling was high and latticed with cream-coloured wooden beams. On one wall there was a large mirror, framed in pearl mosaic. A twenty-four-inch television screen perched on a chest of drawers, and fruit – peaches and apricots – had been left in a bowl in front of it. Beside his bed, on a writing table, there were several bottles of pills next to an orchid and some mineral water. He leaned across and picked up one of the bottles: it was amoxicillin, an antibiotic. The other was diamorphine.

He sat up with some effort. His neck muscles were sore and his head throbbed more when he moved. A net curtain had been drawn across an open window, its white shutters pushed partly open. The branches of a weeping fig stopped them from opening fully. Beyond its leaves, he could see pine trees against a brilliant blue sky. The sun was too bright for Britain, the birdsong too exuberant. As he listened to the chorus, a small bird hovered outside the window for a few moments and disappeared.

He reached over and examined the bottle of mineral water, reading its label: Frizzante – sparkling – and made by Smeraldina, a 'product of Sardinia'. Twisting open the metal cap, he drank deeply, resting the bottle gently on his swollen lips. His mind was still too muddled to think clearly. At least he was out of Morocco. It was only when he put the bottle down that he noticed a figure sitting outside on the terrace, beyond the double doors on the far side of the room. He couldn't see any more than their profile through the net curtains, which moved gently in the breeze. The doors were open a few inches, and the person must have heard him opening the bottle of water, because she stood up and put her head in the room.

'How you feeling?' It was Lakshmi Meena.

Marchant tried to speak, but his tongue failed to respond. Instead, he grunted and sank back into the deep pillows, closing his eyes. What sort of a question was that? He had that top-of-the-world feeling that usually followed a trip to a dentist with an aversion to using anaesthetic. Aziz should go into full-time prac-tice when he retired, set himself up in the square in Marrakech. Tourists would be queuing around the block for his gentle touch.

He heard Meena walk across the marble floor and draw up a cane chair beside the bed. He remembered that she worked directly for Spiro. Someone must have had a change of heart.

'I'm sorry, really. It shouldn't have happened. I should have done more, protested louder.'

Marchant wasn't going to make this any easier for her as he lay still, listening to the chipping noise that had started up again. He realised now that it was workmen, the rhythm of their hammers slowed by the day's heat. His brain had established some distance between the outside world and the inside of his skull, but the sound was still too familiar for comfort.

'They're fixing the path outside,' Meena continued, her manner

113

more businesslike than bedside. Marchant assumed that it was her way of dealing with the situation, which was fine by him. He didn't want her sympathy. 'One of the tiles was cracked, so they dug it up and are putting in a new one. Relax if you never made it to Jackson's Neverland, because it's right here, in Sardinia. No litter, no crime, sidewalks buffed up at night. I'm not kidding, I've smelt the floor polish.'

The less Marchant acknowledged Meena, the more she talked. He didn't have enough energy to interrupt, ask her to leave, tell her she was as bad as the rest of them, despite her protests.

'We flew in to Cagliari yesterday morning. You've been asleep ever since. The drugs aren't going to replace your molars, I'm afraid, but they should stop any infection spreading to the bone, brain and lungs, reduce the chance of systemic sepsis. And take the morphine in moderation, only when it's really hurting.'

He recalled that Meena had once trained to be a doctor. He opened his eyes, tracing the patterns in the plaster on the ceiling.

'We didn't get Salim Dhar.' Marchant looked across at Meena, who was standing now. 'Killed six of our own Marines instead. Spiro's butt's on the line, mine too. I don't know what you saw up in the mountains, but come to me, not him, if you ever want to talk. I might just listen.'

Meena turned away when Marchant caught her eye. She had found it difficult enough to look at him when he was sleeping, his bruised mouth distorted as if in accusation. Now that he was awake, she saw in his eyes everything that was wrong with the Agency, everything that was wrong with the decisions she had made in her life. This wasn't why she had signed up. She also saw something else, but buried the thought as soon as it surfaced.

The military ambulance had taken Aziz away from the airport, but not before two of his colleagues had threatened to inflict further injuries on Marchant. Meena had talked them out of it, pulling rank, acting the part, then arranged for another ambulance. They wouldn't allow him to travel in the military one. At the Hassan II Hospital, on route de Marrakech, a doctor had patched Marchant up and prescribed painkillers and antibiotics. He knew better than to ask how the British man had come to lose two teeth. He knew, too, that there could be consequences for helping him, but the American woman had given him a bulging envelope of *dirhams* as well as reassurances.

By the time Meena took Marchant out to the airport, a Gulfstream V had arrived to fly them to Sardinia, where the CIA had a discreet account with a luxury resort on the south of the island. It had the use of a villa away from the thoroughfare of restaurants and tennis courts. Senior officers checked themselves in for some R&R after tough tours of duty in the Gulf. NSA officers visiting the listening base in Cyprus also dropped by for a few days to clear their heads from intercepts. And there was always the possible bonus of picking something up from the Russians. Meena hadn't hesitated to book Marchant in. It was the least she could do. Besides, Spiro had told her to look after him and to send Langley the bill.

'London knows you're here,' she said, standing at the double doors now. 'You're on a flight back to Gatwick in a week. Relax, recover. It's on us.' She paused. 'I've got to go. Pacify the Moroccans. You nearly killed Aziz.' She paused again, fighting an urge to go over to him. 'You'll be safe here. And, you know, I'm sorry, truly. It was my fault. Should never have happened.'

Marchant stared at her blankly, then drifted back to sleep.

# 30

'I think someone should be with Marchant,' Denton said, wondering if Fielding had heard him. His Chief was standing at the window of his fourth-floor office, lost in thought, watching a pair of Chinooks fly up the Thames towards a setting sun. The Union flag outside the window was rippling in the evening breeze. Sometimes Fielding's apparent indifference to his own staff frightened Denton, but he told himself it was just his manner.

'Do we know what happened?' Fielding asked, turning around suddenly, as if trying to make up for his previous inattention.

'The Americans handed him over to Abdul Aziz. Marchant proved a difficult patient.'

'You think we should have protected him more, don't you?'

'I just –'

'Don't go soft on me, Ian. It doesn't suit you. Daniel Marchant knows how to look after himself. Besides, we had an agreement with Langley.'

'For what it was worth,' Denton said. He liked Marchant, and feared for his health if he was subjected to more trauma at the hands of the CIA.

'Spiro saw his chance. He thought the world would be looking the other way, watching the death of Salim Dhar on YouTube. Who's out in Morocco for them? Still Lakshmi Meena?'

'Yes.'

'Young enough to be my granddaughter.'

Except that you don't have one, Denton thought. No grandchildren at all, in fact. No children, wife or lover of any description. Just a dog called Oleg and an extended tribe of godchildren. There had been talk once of an elderly mother, somewhere on the south coast – Brighton, or was it Eastbourne? – but that was long ago. Denton used to have a wife. A shared love of jazz and canal boats had brought them together, the Service had driven them apart, as it eventually did with most of its married employees. She still worked as a librarian in the House of Commons, down the river, but they no longer saw each other. There were no children, just a few Miles Davis albums still to be returned. Perhaps Fielding's chosen path of apparent chastity was the only way to arrive at the top of MI6 without any baggage.

'She said the Agency was putting Marchant up for a few days – Sardinia – but she had to get back to Morocco,' Denton said.

'Send Hugo Prentice. Marchant helped him out in Poland. And he knew his father.'

Denton had never liked Prentice, but now wasn't the time to object. There would come a time, in his new role, when he could set the record straight, not just question Prentice's expenses, but his very worth. They had both worked the SovBloc beat, in very different styles, Denton's discretion in marked contrast to Prentice's public-school flamboyance. Both had done long spells in Poland. Everyone knew Prentice gambled, drank too much, but for as long as he continued to come up with good product, Fielding turned a blind eye. Denton knew a part of him envied Prentice. He was still out there in the field, where agents belonged, while he himself had chosen to climb Legoland's greasy pole.

He walked to the door, leaving Fielding in preoccupied silence. Not for the first time in his career, Denton felt that he had merely confirmed information already known to his Chief rather than told him something new. It was in such moments that he felt destined to be a deputy, one of life's permanent number twos. He glanced back at Fielding, pacing his spacious office, and closed the door with more force than was necessary.

Fielding didn't like to exclude Denton from anything, but sometimes it was unavoidable. The thoughts in his head were forming too fast to share even with his loyal deputy, the implications backing up like a restless queue. He went back to his desk, opened a drawer and removed a file on Nikolai Primakov.

# 31

The next time Marchant woke, it was to the sound of a Russian voice, talking on a mobile phone on the terrace outside his room. Marchant's Russian was rusty, but good enough to understand what was being said.

'Yes, he's here.' A woman's voice, not Meena's. 'Still sleeping.' He could see her outline through the net curtain, turning towards him, holding something in her hand, a photo perhaps. 'The American woman's gone, left yesterday . . . He's a little under the weather, but it's incredible, he looks just like his father.'

Marchant tried to rouse himself, but he couldn't even turn over. It was as if he was lying in thick treacle, the sort his father used to pour over sponge puddings on those rare occasions when they spent Christmas in Britain, at the family home in the Cotswolds. It was his father's only contribution in the kitchen. He stared at the lace curtain, billowing gently in the breeze, and tried to work out where he was, who the woman might be, why he didn't care. His mouth wasn't hurting any more, but he couldn't distinguish one part of his body from another. A numbness had cocooned him. *He looks just like his father* – the words floated around his medicated head until he drifted back to sleep again.

\*   \*   \*

'Marchant's got a babysitter,' Prentice said, grinding a cigarette into the dusty ground outside the roadside bar with his heel. The pine trees were shading him from the hot Sardinian sun, their roots pushing up through the dry soil, moulding it like a plasticine map of mountainous terrain. He had taken a walk out of the resort's gates and down to a collection of shops eight hundred yards along the straight main road. The only shop that was open was a deserted supermarket, where he had bought two bottles of chilled Prosecco, a packet of Marlboro cigarettes and too many Lotto tickets. Next door was a closed fishmongers and an empty bar, run by a woman in a short skirt whose red-lined eyes and swollen stomach suggested she drank more beer than she served.

'She's called Lakshmi Meena,' Fielding said, getting up from his desk in Legoland.

'Not unless she's dyed her fanny hair.'

Fielding knew Prentice was trying to shock him. He had a habit of being crude at inappropriate moments. Perhaps it was a reaction against his own proper background, or frustration at never having taken to the stage. Like so many agents Fielding knew, Prentice was a natural actor, the office joker who could mimic everyone in authority. (Fielding had once overheard Prentice's impression of his own voice: a combination of camp archbishop and repressed Eton housemaster.) Give or take a few venial sins, he was also one of the best agents he had in the field.

'Oh yes, and she's speaking Russian.' Prentice winked at a small boy who had appeared at the end of the bar, legs crossed, one hand in his mouth, the other tugging at his mother's nylon skirt. Prentice turned his back and walked away from the bar, cutting across the scrubland that lay between the shops and the main highway to Cagliari. He stepped carefully over the pine roots as he went. Despite the dust, his polished yard boots glistened in the high sun.

120

'Is she on her own?' Fielding asked, surprised at the speed of events in Sardinia.

'She checked in to a double room, near Marchant's. On the beach. Two sets of flipflops outside the door, couple of towels. Husband-and-wife cover.'

'But you haven't seen the husband yet?'

'I only reached here last night. What do you want me to do? Get him out of here? She's a swallow, sent to seduce him.'

'And Meena's definitely gone?'

'Checked out yesterday.'

'A little too hasty, no?'

'We met at the airport. She was embarrassed. Told me Marchant's room number, the medication he was on, then buggered off. Marchant's a sitting duck if the Russians want to compromise him.'

'They probably have already.'

# 32

The woman made no effort to cover herself as she stepped from the shower, walked across the bathroom and removed a towel from the radiator. She tilted her head, drying her blonde, shoulder-length hair as she looked over at the bed and smiled. Marchant wondered if she had been waiting for him to open his eyes. Her actions had a rehearsed choreography about them, more subtle than a porn star's but no less calculated.

He knew before she began to speak that it was the same woman who had been sitting on the terrace earlier, whenever that might have been. Bells were ringing so loudly in his head that he thought, for a moment, that they were the reason he had woken. He hoped that something visceral in his sleeping state had raised the alarm. An uninvited Russian woman in his hotel room was about as bad as it could get for an MI6 field agent, the sort of scenario they taught on day one at the Fort.

If the implications weren't so serious, his situation was almost funny. Textbook honeytrap, perfected in the 1960s, fell out of fashion after the Cold War, seemingly back with a vengeance. A British diplomat had recently been fired after he was filmed by the FSB with a couple of Russian tarts in a hotel room.

His head was clearer now, but he couldn't be sure how long he had been lying in bed. Several days, at least. Where was Lakshmi

Meena? Why had no one from London been to visit him? Hadn't she said that MI6 knew where he was? And what was a naked woman doing in his bathroom?

He propped himself up in bed and took in his surroundings, tried to order random memories. He was in Sardinia, brought here by Meena after the Americans had handed him over to Abdul Aziz. He touched his mouth again, which was less swollen. *He looks just like his father.*

'You've been sleeping for three days,' the woman said. Her English was good, but there was no disguising the Russian mother tongue that thickened her cadences. She was standing in the doorway now, between the bathroom and the bedroom. Her shoulders were broad, like a swimmer's, her breasts high and firm. Marchant estimated she was in her early thirties. Despite himself, he began to stir. Her pubic hair was tidy, trimmed rather than shaved, its soft brownness framed by tanned thighs.

'I tell you this because I know how much the British men like to be in control,' she smiled, glancing at the sheet covering Marchant. 'On top of things.'

For a moment, Marchant felt pity for her, the wooden lines spoken with all the conviction of a hard-up lap dancer. But something about the way she moved across the hotel room and picked up a hair dryer made Marchant's hands begin to sweat. And it wasn't because of any desire she might have roused. Despite the air of a performance, her manner had a lover's familiarity, an easiness born of intimacy. Instinctively, he felt about on the sheet next to him, trying to be discreet. It was damp.

'Please, put something on,' he said. More memories, scent, taste. 'A dressing gown, clothes, anything.'

'Clothes? It's 40 degrees outside and you want me to put something on? Relax. You're on holiday.' She was sitting now, one leg tucked under her, head tilted, hair dryer in hand.

'Where's Lakshmi Meena?'

'You ask too many questions. Please, try some of this.'

She picked up a plate piled high with watermelon and walked over to him, placing it beside the bed. Then she slid a piece into her mouth, holding it carefully between thumb and finger. A small trickle of juice escaped from her lips as she crushed the fruit. She gathered it in with her tongue, which lingered a moment longer than was necessary.

'Do you know why Russian men like watermelon so much?' she asked. Marchant had sat up now, careful to cover himself with a sheet.

'I need you to leave,' he said, strength returning to his voice, his body. More memories: Morocco, the mountains, *Nye strelai*. The woman might have some information on Dhar, but he wasn't in control. He needed time to think, rid his head of the drugs he must have been given with his morphine, work out how to play the hand in front of him, but she held all the cards. 'Ten minutes. Some time to wash, freshen up. Recharge.' He managed to garnish the last word with a twist of innuendo.

'Of course. I'll go to the beach. Join me in the restaurant when you're ready. I'm Nadia, by the way.'

He watched her walk over to a wardrobe and put on a black bikini. The bottom was decent enough at the front, but hardly covered her buttocks. Again, she knew she was being observed, which annoyed Marchant, who turned away when she catwalked towards the sliding glass doors. As she started to close them behind her, she leaned back into the room.

'Watermelon juice is a natural Viagra, at least that's what our men believe. Yes, it's sweet too, and we love sweet things in Russia, but this is not the main reason. Enjoy.'

She slid the door shut, the click of the catch cutting into Marchant's thoughts. Once he was sure she had gone, he lifted the receiver on the hotel phone, but the line was dead, as he expected. He stood up, unsteady on his feet, and went over to the wardrobe, where he had seen some of his clothes. His wallet was there, complete with some Moroccan *dirhams* and the 'litter' he had put in it for his photographer's cover (Dirk McLennan's business card, some studio receipts), but his phone was missing. He looked around the room. Had they slept together? He kept seeing them on the bed, caught in the reflection of the mosaic mirror. How could he have allowed himself to get into such a vulnerable situation?

After taking a shower, washing off any traces of what might have been, he put on a pair of shorts, a T-shirt, sunglasses and some flipflops that someone – Meena? Nadia? – must have bought from the resort shop for him. They all fitted well enough. He glanced in the mirror, put a hand to his bruised jaw, and stepped outside into the midday sun, watched discreetly by a gym-toned man lying on a sunbed outside the adjacent villa.

# 33

'I want you to hold back,' Fielding said, standing up to rub his lower back. No one had fixed the grandfather clock that stood against the far wall of his office. It had been built by Sir Mansfield Cumming, the first Chief, and had worked well enough until the Service's move from Southwark, since when it had kept stopping. Fielding meant to do something about it, but there was never enough time.

'It's too late anyway. She's all over him.' Prentice was back in the resort now, standing in some shade beside a rack of red bikes for hire. Behind him he could hear children playing football on an Astroturf pitch: German, English, Italian and Russian voices. He had taken a look earlier. The football facilities were provided by Chelsea, the club he'd followed since childhood, and there were huge posters of all the top players on the fencing around the ground.

'Has he met the man yet, or just the woman?'

'He's sharing a pizza with them both now. Down by the sea.'

'And no one's seen you?'

'Not yet.' Prentice glanced at a nearby CCTV camera, hidden in the bushes. He doubted the guests knew that every inch of the resort was being filmed, day and night, low and high season. The cameras were very discreet, he had to give them that. He had already checked out the control centre, behind the main reception building, where a bank of screens captured most things that went on at the resort. As far as he could tell, it was also from there that the master satellite TV signal was distributed to all the villas.

'Get him on your own after lunch and try to limit the damage.'

Prentice hung up, surprised by the Vicar's calmness.


'We want you to meet someone in London,' Nadia said. 'An old friend.'

'A friend of your family,' her partner, Valentin, added. He had joined them from the sunbed a couple of minutes after their arrival at the beachside restaurant. Marchant assumed that he had followed him from his room, in case he tried to leave the resort. But Marchant didn't have the strength to escape. Not yet. Valentin was tall, muscular, wearing a T-shirt as tight as his skin. Marchant was struck by his small, Prussian-blue eyes.

'I don't have any family,' Marchant replied.

He was sitting in the shade of their table's brightly coloured umbrella. It reminded him of the parasols that kept the *mahouts* cool when they were riding ceremonial elephants in India. The two Russians were in the sunshine. Valentin had just come back from a cigarette on the beach, ten yards away. The restaurant was open-air but there was still a no-smoking policy. Valentin turned the packet of Parliament cigarettes over and over on the table, looking out to sea. Then he looked straight at Marchant, his eyes even smaller.

'Our friend knew your father. He always speaks very highly of him, and would like to meet you. Talk about old times.'

'Which friend?' Marchant asked, his mind racing. The only Russian he could recall was someone his father had known in Delhi, but Marchant had been a child at the time, and the memories were distant. He knew there must have been many others, his father's illustrious career in MI6 being built on successes behind the Iron Curtain. Some he was aware of: the ones who had been blown and were dead now, executed by Moscow Centre after Aldrich Ames had exposed them. He would never know about the others who were still alive, still betraying their motherland, their files known only to a select few in Legoland.

'All we ask is that you meet him once,' Valentin said, ignoring Marchant's question. 'One meeting, nothing more. In London.'

Marchant wanted a name, someone to run past Fielding, who had known his father better than anyone, but they weren't playing. More important, he told himself, was the approach itself. The Russians' interest in him gave him hope that he could be right about Dhar, the mountains, the helicopter. And that thought banished any lingering effects of the medication, his brain suddenly as fresh as a forest after rain.

'He will attend an exhibition opening,' Valentin said, passing Marchant an embossed invitation card. 'In Cork Street. The artist is from the Caucasus, South Ossetia. He is very accomplished, but not as well known outside Russia as he should be. Picture number 14, a nude sketch, has been reserved with a half-dot on the price label. It's a very beautiful work. You may recognise the model.' He looked across at Nadia and smiled. 'Your contact will confirm the purchase on the night, towards the end of the evening. If it already has a full red dot beside it when you arrive, the meeting has been cancelled.'

Standard SVR tradecraft, Marchant thought. The plan was a little elaborate, but it implied intent. They meant business. A crowded place had been chosen, a venue where contact could be accidental, ambiguous, denied.

Marchant glanced around at the restaurant, trying to spot any watchers. It was one of his best skills as a field agent, the thing that had most impressed his instructors at the Fort. But this time he was struggling. More than half the diners were Russian. A senescent man with an eighteen-year-old escort in a short skirt; another, younger Russian businessman more interested in his BlackBerry than his gorgeous wife. She was wearing diamante jeans, listlessly following their young son as he tottered around the tables with a beach ball almost as big as him. Maybe Nadia and Valentin were operating on their own.

'And if he's not my kind of artist?' Marchant asked, knowing the answer. As far as they were concerned, he had already been compromised enough to guarantee his cooperation.

'Our friend will be very disappointed,' Valentin said.

'We all will,' Nadia added, smiling at him with a coyness that made Marchant's palms moisten again.

'You and your father, you both seem to share a dislike of America.'

'I wouldn't put words into my mouth,' Marchant said, touching his jaw. 'It's not a nice place to be at the moment.' Despite the bravura, Valentin's comment unsettled him. The Americans had long accused his father of disloyalty, eventually driving him from office.

'But they didn't treat you very well.'

'That wasn't the Americans.'

'Of course not. And they couldn't have cancelled your appointment with Dr Aziz.'

Marchant looked at him.

'Our friend is eager to see you again,' Valentin said. 'Your father once gave him a photo of all his children. He still treasures it.'

'All?'

'You, Sebastian . . .' Valentin paused, looking hard at Marchant, as if he hadn't finished.

'And?'

'And your father.'

Marchant didn't buy it. 'All his children' was an odd phrase for two sons, even allowing for some loss in translation. The Russians knew about Salim Dhar.

# 34

Fielding had told him he was coming. It was courtesy, but it was also a matter of security. Giles Cordingley lived at the top of Raginnis Hill, overlooking the Cornish fishing village of Mousehole, ten miles from Land's End, and visitors to his granite farmhouse were rare. He was too old for surprises. A security camera was positioned discreetly to the left of the high oak gates, and it took a while for them to swing open and let Fielding's Range Rover pass through into the gravel courtyard. His driver parked in front of an old stable block and took a look around, taking in other security cameras, the high walls that enclosed a forgotten orchard. Then he made a call on his mobile and returned to the car, leaving Fielding to approach the house on his own.

Cordingley had been Chief of MI6 in the 1990s, serving for three years before becoming master of an Oxford College and then retiring to Cornwall. He was the last of the Cold War Chiefs, the end of an era. Well into his sixties by the time he reached the top, he had enjoyed a long career that had begun with a role in Oleg Penkovsky's recruitment. He had managed the defection of Vladimir Kuzichkin when he was head of station in Tehran, overseen the handling of Oleg Gordievsky, and lost agents at the hands of Aldrich Ames. Most importantly, he was one of the few people who knew about Nikolai Primakov, having personally authorised his recruitment.

There was no answer when Fielding rang the doorbell and he eventually found Cordingley behind the house, tending to a row of beehives in what must have been the old vegetable garden. Fielding thought his face looked fleshier than he remembered, like pale putty, big heavy-rimmed glasses making it seem rounder, more vulnerable. Despite the dramatic clifftop setting, there was no sense of a man enjoying his retirement in the great outdoors, no ruddy, windblown cheeks or healthy complexion. He looked like a man unused to daylight. For a moment, Fielding wondered if he was ill, if that was why he had moved to Cornwall.

'Good of you to see me, Giles,' Fielding began, knowing that it would be futile to wait for him to stop tending his bees. Cordingley was wearing a protective veil but no gloves or suit. His hands looked feminine, unthreatening. Fielding assumed he had operated the main gates with the device that was hanging around his neck. His hospitality didn't seem to extend beyond allowing entry, and he hadn't bothered to come round and greet his visitor. It was a reminder that Cordingley's relationship with the Service was complicated, that he had left under a cloud of homophobia, been denied a KCMG, the usual gong for a Chief.

'Duty rather than goodness,' Cordingley said, putting a lid back on one of the hives. Fielding kept his distance, knowing that angry bees were all part of the welcome. The garden, he thought, looked tatty and tired. Only the hives were well tended. A gentle wind was blowing in off the sea far below. On the far side of the bay, St Michael's Mount rose out of the water like a fairytale castle. A brace of beam trawlers were returning home to nearby Newlyn under a high mackerel sky, their nets hung out on either side for a final trawl of the bay. If it wasn't for the *froideur* of his host, Fielding thought that the idyllic scene was almost heart-warming, reason enough for him to have dedicated his life to the Service.

Cordingley walked past him towards the back door of the house, a slow amble that still drew a cloud of bees in his slipstream. Fielding swatted one away as nonchalantly as he could. He felt a sharp pain on the back of his hand.

'They only sting when they sense fear,' Cordingley said, entering the house. He was almost eighty, but he hadn't missed Fielding's flinch.

# 35

Marchant knew that there was something wrong with his room twenty yards before he reached it. The sliding doors were open, and he could hear a couple inside, the unmistakeable soundtrack of sexual pleasure. At least, he could hear a woman; the man sounded more subdued, set upon. The Russian couple had told him to rest, agreed to meet for a drink before dinner, talking as if he had the liberty to do as he pleased. But he knew it was a pretence, that he had no freedom. They were already back at the villa next door, watching, waiting. Marchant wasn't a guest at the resort, he was a prisoner.

As he approached the sliding glass doors, he could see the blue flicker of a TV screen reflecting off his apartment's white walls. Had he got the wrong number? The layout of the sprawling resort, each house set back from the smooth-tiled paths that meandered through them, was confusing, but the number by his apartment matched the key in his hand.

He stepped into the small garden, careful not to touch the half-open iron gate, and edged towards the glass doors. He knew what was going on now, but he still kept his approach silent, in case he was wrong, in case there really were people in his room. But he knew there weren't. Not in the flesh.

He looked at the large TV screen for a second, distracted by the rhythmic movement of Nadia's taut buttocks, the winking recesses. Then he realised that it was his body beneath them, and felt sick. He stepped into the room and grabbed the remote, which was on the table beside a replenished bowl of watermelon. It was only as he turned away that he saw Hugo Prentice standing by the bathroom door, arms folded, watching the screen with a smirk on his fifty-something face.

'It's showing in my room, too,' Prentice said, careful to remain out of sight from the window. 'On a loop. Every room in the resort, nationwide release. It's the most exciting thing I've seen on an in-house hotel channel in years.'

'You took your time,' Marchant said, turning off the TV and dropping the remote onto the bed, which had been freshly made. 'Fielding send you by boat?'

'Take off your shirt and close the curtains. You're tired, remember? Sent to your room for a sleep.'

Marchant looked at Prentice for a moment, then pulled off his shirt, threw it on the bed and walked to the glass doors. Nadia was sitting outside her villa now, sunbathing topless, waiting to see how he would react to the video. She gave him a coy wave. He didn't wave back, but drew the thick curtains.

Prentice remained by the bathroom door as Marchant went over to the pedestal sink and splashed water on his face. He didn't want to dwell on the video, the fact that Prentice had just witnessed him having sex. Strangely, he found that more troubling than the implications for his career, the consequences of being compromised by a textbook honeytrap. Perhaps it was because Prentice had been a good friend of his father, who had perfected the knack during Marchant's teenage years of striding into the sitting room whenever he was watching a sex scene on television.

'It's OK, I looked away for the money shot,' Prentice said, trying to lighten the mood. 'Fielding sends big love and kisses.'

Marchant wasn't sure if he was pleased that London had sent Prentice. On balance, he thought he was. To look at, Prentice was smoothness personified, from the swept-back hair to the cut of his safari suit: old-school spy. Just the sort Marchant needed to help him out of the old-school fix he found himself in. Prentice had recently returned from a three-year tour of Poland, where he had helped Marchant escape from a black site, but he was too old for regular deskwork in Legoland, too much of a troublemaker for a management role. Human Resources had branded him a 'negative sneezer', spreading dissent rather than 'flu. Fielding had ignored the warning memos, as he usually did with anything sent from HR, and deployed him as a firefighter, ready to be dispatched to global trouble spots at the drop of a panama.

'They want me to meet someone,' Marchant said. 'A friend of my father's.'

'That narrows it down,' Prentice replied. 'Your old man was a popular Chief. Any other clues?'

'The meeting's in London.' He decided not to tell Prentice about the private view. In his current situation, it helped him to feel in control if he knew at least something that others around him didn't. 'I presume it's with one of theirs, given the need to persuade me,' Marchant continued, glancing at the television.

'Moscow still rules. Christ, it's a while since I've seen Eva Shirtov in action. Makes me feel almost nostalgic.'

'I need to sort it.' Marchant wasn't in the mood for flippancy. He was embarrassed.

'It's already taken care of.' Prentice walked over to the TV and ejected a disc from the player in the cabinet below it. 'Master copy,' he said, throwing it onto the bed next to the remote.

'I thought you said it was being broadcast around the resort.'

'That was their plan. I retrieved the disc while you were having lunch.'

Marchant felt a wave of relief, but he was also irritated. He hated being indebted to anyone.

'Aren't they going to notice?' He knew it was a pointless question, that Prentice would have tied off any loose ends. He had more experience of the Russians than anyone in the Service. Marchant remembered listening to him at the Fort, which he visited every year to address the new IONEC recruits. They had sat in rapt silence as he spoke of brush passes in Berlin, dangles, and how, as a young officer, he had played Sibelius's *Finlandia* on the car stereo to let a defecting KGB officer called Oleg Gordievsky, who was hidden in the boot, know that they had safely crossed into Finland. 'And you know what actually got us past the border guard? A nappy full of crap. My colleague's wife started to change her baby on the car boot when the guard asked to see inside. One whiff and he changed his mind.'

Sure enough, Prentice didn't reply to Marchant's question, letting its foolishness grow in the silence. Instead, he went to the window and peered through the curtain at the Russians' villa. Marchant joined him.

'When the Russians cross the line, you have to respond with interest,' Prentice said, watching as a suited man approached the villa with a posse of local Italian police behind him. 'Remind them where the line is. Otherwise it moves. They'll respect you more, too. They don't like weak enemies.'

'Who's that with the police?'

'Giuseppe Demuro, manager of the resort, old friend of the family. He received an anonymous tip-off half an hour ago that the occupants of villa 29 were trying to broadcast pornographic videos across the resort.'

'But we've got the disc.'

'I swapped it for a different one.'

Prentice turned and picked up the remote from the bed, then

clicked onto the resort's in-house channel. The footage was grainy, but it was possible to see an older man with a younger woman, lying on a bed. It was also possible to see that the man was the Prime Minister of Russia and the young woman wasn't his wife.

'The oligarch currently staying in the penthouse by the sea is a close friend of the Kremlin. He won't be amused. Come, we must go.'

# 36

'Nikolai Primakov was an unusual case,' Cordingley said, stopping at a disused coastguard hut to take in the view of the bay. 'Once in a lifetime.' They were walking west along the cliffs towards Lamorna. Cordingley was too old to go far now, but he had insisted that they should talk in the open, away from his house. His former hostility had passed, but there was no warmth, no offer of tea. 'The initial approach was made by Stephen,' he continued. 'Never forget that. He'd met Primakov a few times at cultural events in Delhi, liked him on a personal level, singled him out for company. He also sensed a deep unhappiness behind all the smiles.' Cordingley paused. 'Primakov wasn't the dangle, we dangled Stephen Marchant.'

'And you're still sure of that?' Fielding asked.

'More so than ever. And I think back over it often. Once Stephen had recruited him, Primakov's true value became apparent to us. Dynamite. K Branch, First Chief Directorate. You couldn't get better than that. And he knew much more than his rank should have allowed, particularly about KGB operations in Britain. The problem was, he kept talking about defecting, which would have been no good to us at all. To keep him useful, he needed to be promoted, not exfiltrated, so Stephen and I devised a plan for him, something to impress his superiors in Moscow Centre.'

'You let Stephen be recruited by Primakov.'

Another pause as they watched the seagulls circling below. 'It was actually Stephen's idea. Brilliant, even now. Moscow thought they'd turned a rising MI6 agent, giving Primakov an excuse to meet regularly with Stephen. There was just one problem: the intel we had to give Primakov to keep Stephen credible as a Soviet asset.'

They both knew what Cordingley meant by this, but neither wanted to speak about it. Not yet. The moment demanded a respectful pause, a lacuna. Instinctively, they looked around to see if anyone might be within earshot, then walked on. On one side the coast path was overshadowed by a steeply rising hillside of gorse, pricked with yellow flowers. On the other was the Atlantic, swelling over flat black rocks far beneath them. It would have been difficult for anyone to listen in on their conversation, except perhaps if they were on a well-equipped trawler, which both men knew was not beyond the realms of Russian tradecraft. But the last boat had now slipped past them towards Newlyn, and the bay was empty, the coast clear.

Cordingley spoke first. He had stopped again and was facing the Atlantic, his thin white hair teased by the sea breeze. 'We couldn't give Moscow chickenfeed. They would have been immediately suspicious. The decision to pass them high-grade American intel was never approved by anyone, never formally acknowledged. I assume it remained that way, even when the Yanks went after Stephen.'

'Cs' eyes only.'

Fielding thought back to his first week as Chief of MI6, the evening he had spent sifting through the files in the safe in his office. It contained the most classified documents in Legoland, unseen by anyone other than successive Chiefs. They were even more invisible than 'no trace' files, short, unaccountable documents that read like briefing notes from one head to the next, outlining the Service's deniable operations, the ones that had never crossed Whitehall desks. It had reminded Fielding of the day he had become head of his house at school, more than forty years earlier. A book was passed on from one head to the next, never seen by anyone else. It identified the troublemakers and bullies, in between tips on how to deal with the housemaster's drink problem.

'There's no doubt someone in Langley got enough of a sniff to distrust Stephen, but I'm confident that Primakov's still known only to the British.'

'So why have you come here today?'

'He's back.'

'In London?' It was the first time Cordingley had seemed surprised.

Fielding nodded. 'Next week. I need to know if we can still trust him.'

'Primakov only dealt with Stephen. Refused to be handled by anyone else. He must have been frightened when the Americans removed Stephen from office, and upset when he died. It's whether he's bitter that counts. For almost twenty years, we kept promising him a new life in the West.'

'I think Primakov's about to approach Stephen's son.'

# 37

Marchant and Prentice waited until the police had led the Russian couple away to reception before they stepped out of the villa. Giuseppe Demuro had sent a small golf buggy to pick them up, and the driver was waiting patiently in the shade, trying not to show any interest in the police activity. Discretion at all times, Giuseppe had told him. That was why, perhaps, he didn't spot the two suited men moving fast and silently along the tiled path that cut behind the villa, only their heads and chests visible above the privet hedge. But Marchant saw them, and wondered how they could be travelling so fast with their upper bodies remaining still. They weren't on bikes, their posture was too upright. Then he recognised one of them, and didn't care about the laws of physics any more. It was the man who had ushered him onto the plane at Agadir.

'We need to go,' Marchant said to Prentice, nodding towards the two men, who were closing in on them quickly. Marchant jumped onto the back of the buggy with Prentice, who had a small hold-all with him. Marchant had nothing other than his phone, which Prentice had managed to retrieve from the Russians' villa.

'Giuseppe's arranged a taxi, back entrance, where the staff live,' Prentice said, looking at the two men, who were now less than fifty yards away and arcing around towards them. 'Friends of yours?' He had fixed the Russians, but hadn't anticipated another threat.

'Let's move,' Marchant said to the driver, ignoring Prentice, taking control. 'Pronto.'

The driver sensed the urgency in Marchant's voice and accelerated away across the smooth tiles, glancing back at the two men, who were looking across the hedgerows, their speed still a mystery.

'They work for Abdul Aziz,' Marchant said, holding on to the side of the buggy as it rounded a corner. 'Gave me a free upgrade in Morocco.'

'And they appear to have perfected the art of low-level flying,' Prentice said. It was then that the path the Moroccans were on joined the main thoroughfare, revealing their means of transport. They were riding on Segway Personal Transporters, their big rubber wheels rippling across the tiles. Marchant had seen a member of the resort's staff passing the pizza restaurant on one during lunch, thinking at the time that it was travelling faster than normal. They were meant to have a top speed of 12.5 mph, but the two Moroccans were travelling at least twice as quickly as that, leaning on the T-bars to propel themselves forward. The resort's machines must have been customised, making them much quicker than Marchant and Prentice's electric-powered golf buggy. Marchant had heard that the police in Britain had made similar changes to their own fleet of Segways.

'Turn left up here, to the beach,' Marchant said. The Moroccans were thirty yards from them now, and closing. 'Pick me up in the car, further down the coast. I can outrun the Segways on sand.'

Before Prentice could say anything, Marchant had jumped off the buggy and was sprinting down to the beach, kicking off his flipflops. Prentice turned around just in time to see the two men passing him. Without pausing, he swung his hold-all up and out of the buggy, knocking the nearest Moroccan off his Segway. He hit his head hard on the tiles and rolled over. The other man stopped, pulling hard on the T-bar, looked down at his colleague and then across to the beach, down which Marchant was running away from them. For a sickening moment, Prentice thought the Moroccan was going to pull a gun on him, but he just cursed and accelerated off on his Segway, staying on the smooth path that ran parallel to the coast.

# 38

'The beauty of their relationship was that it was seemingly out in the open, beyond reproach,' Cordingley continued.

They were walking back to the farmhouse now, pursued by charcoal clouds tumbling in over Land's End. Cordingley had become increasingly animated as he recalled the past, almost breathless, and Fielding was starting to worry about his health. 'It was no secret that they were good friends. People expected to see them together at embassy parties, first nights at the theatre. Primakov reported back to Moscow Centre that Stephen had tried to recruit him and that he had refused. Stephen did exactly the same. At first, Moscow was suspicious of their closeness, even ordered him to stop seeing Stephen, but Primakov had always believed in friendship rather than blackmail as the best way to recruit someone, and for a while Moscow let him do things his way.'

'Did you ever doubt Stephen? Personally?'

'You knew him better than most. You were his protégé, his biggest fan.'

'I was. I still am. I was wondering where you stood.'

Fielding remembered how Cordingley had been the only Chief not to turn up at Stephen Marchant's funeral.

'If you're asking me whether Stephen sometimes passed on US

145

intel to the Russians a little too enthusiastically, with too much relish, then the answer is yes.'

'But that only made him more credible, reassured the Russians he was the genuine article.'

'Of course. Everyone knew Stephen was more wary of Langley than the rest of us, so we built on that for his cover story, turned a healthy scepticism of America into deep-rooted loathing. There were times, it's true, when I looked at the books and worried about the flow of information, the net balance of betrayal. We were getting the most extraordinary insight into KGB activities in the UK, but in return we were of course betraying our closest ally.'

'Would you run Primakov again?'

'Tomorrow. And if you're right and he's about to approach Stephen's son, then maybe there's a way. From what I've heard, Daniel shares many of his father's traits, not least a troubled relationship with our cousins across the pond.'

'I think it's fair to say that Daniel Marchant more or less ended the special relationship single-handedly.'

'The Russians will like what they see in him – a chip off the old Marchant block. But could you run the risk of giving them American intel again?'

Fielding paused. 'I think they're after something else this time.' He didn't want to mention Salim Dhar, the possibility that the Russians might have recruited him, too.

Cordingley was too seasoned to miss Fielding's reticence, knew he was holding something back. In his younger days he would have protested, but he didn't care any more. He was too old, too tired. Besides, they were at the house now, and he had done his duty.

'Just remember one thing, Marcus: Primakov had a cause, a genuine reason to betray his country. When his only child fell ill in Delhi, he asked Moscow if he could fly her to London. They refused. What was wrong with Russia's hospitals? She died on an overcrowded ward in Moscow. I don't think we ever upset Stephen that much, do you?'

Marchant didn't know how long he could keep running across the hot sand. The resort's private beach had already come to an end, and he was now amongst hordes of ordinary Sardinians on holiday: extended families gathered under umbrellas, toddlers paddling in the surf, teenage girls flirting, boys in shades keeping footballs in the air. Women of all ages were in bikinis, as if one-piece costumes were banned.

He glanced behind him to see if he was still being followed, and saw one of the Moroccans gliding along the path through the pine trees, set thirty yards back from the beach. He was momentarily hidden behind the wooden shacks serving espressos and ice cream, then he appeared again, looking across at him. If the man was armed, Marchant thought, he wouldn't attempt a shot while the beach was so crowded. And Aziz probably wanted to take him alive, book him in for a follow-up appointment.

He looked at the beach curving around the bay ahead of him. A fine spray hung above the surf in the late-afternoon sun. His body was no longer aching. The medication had cleared, and he felt the way he had on his morning runs through the souks of Marrakech, his body purged of alcohol, his mind disciplined by trips to the library. With each stride he felt stronger, dodging toddlers, jumping over towels. But he knew the real reason for the extra spring in his step, and it wasn't the glances from Italian women in shades. The Segway's electric battery was fading fast.

# 39

'You must forgive me if I seem a little underwhelmed by the prospect,' Fielding said, walking between the flowerbeds. Lakshmi Meena was at his side, glancing at the plants, reading labels: *Catharanthus roseus* (Madagascar Periwinkle), *Filipendula ulmaria* (Meadowsweet). 'This one here,' Fielding said, stopping in front of a bed, 'is *Hordeum vulgare*. Barley to you and me. It led to the synthesis of lignocaine.'

'A local anaesthetic,' Meena said.

'Correct.' Fielding walked on, leaving her to look at the plant. She drew level with him again, like a schoolchild catching up with her teacher.

Fielding stopped at the junction of two paths. He was tired after his journey back from Penzance the previous night, and had hoped the peaceful surroundings of the Chelsea Physic Garden would offer comfort and solace. He had become a member soon after joining the Service, but the garden had grown too popular in recent years to be of any use as a regular meeting place. In the past, he had used it when he met players from foreign intelligence agencies who wanted an encounter on neutral ground. Tonight, a warm July evening, the director had opened it especially for him. Half an hour on his own, the garden empty except for him and Meena, a chance to reacquaint himself with its pharmaceutical beds.

'Listen, we've hardly endeared ourselves over the past year or so, I'm the first to admit that,' Meena said. 'All I can say is that I think Daniel Marchant is a guy I can work with. And right now he's the only one who's gotten close to Dhar.'

Fielding turned to face her. He was struck again by how similar to Leila she looked in the soft evening sun. Perhaps that was why he had been wary of inviting her to Legoland. She brought back too many bad memories. They had all been fooled by Leila. So had the CIA, which had been out of favour with the British ever since it had renditioned Daniel Marchant.

The Agency had done little to improve its reputation in the subsequent year, wielding too much power in Whitehall. Marchant's treatment in Morocco at the hands of Aziz had tarnished its name even further. Now, following the very public death of six US Marines at the hands of a CIA Reaper, the Agency was a full-blown international pariah. Any trust that had started to come back between it and MI6 had turned to dust. But there had been something about Meena's call to his office earlier in the day that had made him agree to see her. A candidness that he feared he wouldn't be able to reciprocate.

'Do you think that Daniel was right about Dhar and the High Atlas?' Fielding asked.

'More right than we were about Af-Pak.'

'A shame that the Agency didn't let him travel earlier. Did you believe he was right when Spiro sent you to Marrakech?' Fielding knew it was an unfair question.

'Spiro was my superior. I did as he told me.'

'That's not what I've heard.'

Fielding had done some research since her call, walked down to the North American Controllerate and asked around. Meena had an impressive reputation for standing up to Spiro, which took courage, particularly for a woman. She had graduated from the

Farm with honours, impressing with her language skills but also her integrity, which must have been a novelty for the CIA examiners. In normal circumstances, her posting to Morocco would have been a sideways career move, but her brief was to keep an eye on Daniel Marchant, which reflected her importance.

Fielding had then spoken to his opposite number in Langley, the DCIA who had famously promised his President – and Britain – to end the bad old ways and then promptly promoted James Spiro to head of Clandestine, Europe. He had been phoning London repeatedly, presumably to try to patch things up, but Fielding had let him sweat. The last time he rang, Fielding had taken the call.

Spiro, the DCIA explained, had been suspended following the drone strike, and the Agency would be apologising formally for the treatment of Daniel Marchant in Morocco, even though it was at the hands of a foreign intelligence service over which the CIA had little control. 'And the British know all about that,' he had added caustically. (The British courts' decision to make public the torture of a detainee in Morocco hadn't played well in Langley.) As a gesture of goodwill, the Agency was transferring Lakshmi Meena to London and offering her services as a liaison officer.

'She represents the Agency's future, Marcus,' the DCIA had added. 'And this time she's above board.'

'Did you ever meet Leila?' Fielding asked Meena, sitting down on a bench in front of a bed of *Digitalis lanata*, a plant that he knew better as Dead Man's Bells.

'No, sir.' Meena glanced around briefly and then sat down beside him.

'She was a liaison officer for the Agency, too, only nobody ever bothered to tell us. We thought she was working for Six. In the end, it turned out she wasn't working for either of us.'

'But she saved our President's life.'

'Did she?' Fielding realised that Meena would not know about Leila's ties with Iran. That information was too classified. But had national loyalties really meant anything to Leila? Fielding couldn't deny that at the final reckoning in Delhi, she had stepped forward and taken a bullet meant for the US President.

'I appreciate that Leila's case was not straightforward,' Meena said. 'The Agency should have declared her to London as an asset. It was wrong, but those were different times. All I can say is that I'm not Leila.'

No, but you look like her, Fielding thought. Has anyone ever told you? That in a certain light, your hair falls over your eyes in a way that would have confused even your mothers.

'How did you get on with Daniel Marchant in Morocco?'

'Getting along might be stretching it. I don't blame him. I should have done more to stop Abdul Aziz.'

'Daniel's coming back to London today. Quite a toothache, I gather. With respect, can you give me one good reason why he would want to work with you?'

'Listen, we were wrong about Salim Dhar, and we've got six dead Marines to prove it. I don't know what happened in the High Atlas, but I think the DCIA now accepts that the only person who might be capable of finding Dhar is Daniel Marchant. And to that end, I'm here to help him, to help you.'

'I suppose we don't really see your arrival in London in terms of international aid. From where we stand, all the help would seem to be coming from our side. I'm not quite clear what you can give us in return.'

'I think our Delhi station has just found Dhar's mother.'

'Where?' Fielding struggled not to let his interest show. Dhar had always been very close to his mother, who had been identified by MI6's profilers as a possible weakness. Once it became clear that it was her son who had tried to assassinate the US President in Delhi, she had gone into hiding, unlike her husband, who had very publicly disowned his wife and son, and reiterated his love of all things American.

'They've traced her to a temple in south India. Madurai. Given your progress with Dhar and our own catastrophic failure, Langley would like it to be a joint operation. They're closing in on her now.'

# 40

Marchant walked through arrivals, instinctively checking for cameras, scanning the Heathrow crowds. Prentice was a few yards behind. He had insisted on staying with him after he had picked him up from the far end of the beach, three miles from the resort. He had driven him to Cagliari airport, sat next to him on the plane, made sure no one was offering upgrades. Fielding's orders. Prentice wasn't to leave him on his own until he was safely in his Pimlico flat. Marchant couldn't complain. He'd messed up in Morocco, failed to leave the country under snap cover.

Marchant spotted Monika a moment before she began waving in his direction. There was little that gave her away as the Polish intelligence officer who had helped him to flee Warsaw more than a year ago, sharing joints and her bed with him, all in the line of duty. The gipsy skirt had been replaced by a jacket and jeans, the braided hair disciplined by a tight bun, but she still had the same carefree gait. Marchant had been travelling under the name of David Marlowe at the time, and he knew that she wasn't really called Monika, but he would always remember her as that, the woman in the hippy hostel with a flower in her hair.

He was about to wave back, surprised by the sudden quickening of his pulse, but then he realised that she wasn't looking at him.

'Recognise her?' Prentice asked, coming up on Marchant's

shoulder with a grin. The next moment, Prentice and Monika were kissing each other across the barrier. Marchant couldn't believe it was jealousy that made him turn away. He and Monika had both been operating under cover stories when they had met in Poland. He had been on the run from the CIA, she was helping him escape: each living a lie, doing their job.

'Hello, Daniel,' Monika said, breaking away from Prentice to give him a kiss on both cheeks. He remembered her smell as their skin brushed, and he wondered for a second if it had been more than duty in Warsaw. 'I'm sorry about Leila,' she added more quietly.

'Do I still call you Monika?'

'Hey, why not?'

Because that's not your name, Marchant thought, but he kept silent. Her English was almost perfect, better than when they had met in Poland. And her smile was still too big, her full lips out of proportion with her petite body. She was no more than twenty-five, young enough to be Prentice's daughter. Marchant should have been pleased for him, an old family friend. But he wasn't. Something wasn't right.

'Did I tell you?' Prentice asked him when they were a few yards from the main exit. Monika had fallen behind a crowd of arrivals and was out of earshot.

'What's there to tell?' Marchant said, trying to play things down.

'That I'm sleeping with the enemy.'

'Were you in Warsaw?'

'You know me better than that.'

Marchant didn't miss the sarcasm. Relationships within MI6 weren't unusual, but they weren't encouraged, and they seldom ended happily. 'Don't poke the payroll' – it had been one of Prentice's first bits of advice to Marchant when he had arrived at Legoland. Seeing someone from another intelligence agency was more complicated, but clearly not impossible, particularly for an agent as experienced as Prentice.

'Last time I checked, Poland was an ally,' Marchant said.

'Let's just say it's easier now I'm back in London. Listen, sorry to be neckie, but can you get yourself to Pimlico on your own? It will buy me some time with the office. You know how it is. She's only over here for a few days.'

Monika was standing beside Prentice now, an arm through his, tugging him away. She was playing the sexually outgoing coquette, just as she had with him.

'Of course I bloody can.' Marchant had had enough of being chaperoned. And he needed a drink.

'Is everything OK?' Monika asked him. He searched her eyes, but he no longer knew what he was looking for, or why he even cared. Was this the real Monika? Screwing an old rake like Prentice? She had never once been herself with him in Poland, not even at the airport, when he hoped their masks might have finally slipped. For a moment, Marchant wondered if he would ever know anyone properly.

'Everything's fine,' he said. 'I never got the chance to thank you.'

And with that he lost himself in the crowds. He was happy to have left Prentice behind, but by the time he reached the escalator down to the Underground ticket hall he was aware that someone else was following him. When he reached the bottom, he looked at his watch and took the elevator back up again, scanning the faces of the people coming down. Most were looking ahead, but a tall man in a beaten leather jacket had his face turned away, taking too much interest in the electronic advertising posters. If it wasn't Valentin from Sardinia, he had a twin in London. Hit back hard, Prentice had said.

The thought of Valentin following him to Britain was irritating. Marchant had expected him to have been arrested at the resort in Sardinia and flown back to Russia in disgrace for exposing his leader's sexual preferences to the world, but here he was, about to follow him home to Pimlico.

Marchant turned and took the elevator back down again. The Russian was now at platform level, peeling off left to the westbound platform. Marchant just had time to clock his shoes: fashionably long with narrowed, flat toes. 'Look at the footwear,' his father had always told him. It was something he had never forgotten, whether it was colleagues in Legoland or targets in the field. Often it was the one thing that they failed to change when outfits were swapped, snap covers adopted in a hurry.

By the time Marchant had reached the bottom of the escalator, there was no sign of the Russian. He tried to turn left, but the crowds were almost spilling onto the tracks. He had lost him. He pushed his way to the platform edge. First, he looked left down the long line of people waiting for a train, then to the right. Twenty yards away, a pair of shoes was sticking out beyond everyone else's. He had found his man.

Marchant moved as quickly as he could through the crowds, feeling the warm wind of an approaching train on his face. Thirty seconds later, he was positioned behind the Russian. It was definitely Valentin. He must have decided to drop off his tail, suspecting that he had been spotted, and was now standing with his legs apart on the platform edge, trying to steady himself against the crush of people swarming in different directions.

A member of the station staff asked over the Tannoy for people to move to the far end of the platform. He was unable to disguise his concern. The station was overcrowding. Marchant glanced at the tourists around him, holding anxiously to their suitcases, and then looked again at Valentin, who was only inches away. His hairline was edged with a thin strip of pale skin, suggesting that he had had his hair cut between leaving Sardinia and arriving in London.

It would be very easy to make it look like an accident, Marchant thought as the train approached, sounding its horn. For a moment, he pictured Valentin rolling onto the live rail, looking back up at him. His father had seen a jumper once, said it was the rancid smoke that had shocked him the most. The image of Valentin's burnt body wasn't as unsettling as it should have been. Which friend of his father's did they want him to meet? And why did they talk about him in that familiar way? He realised now how angry he was, how humiliated he felt by the events in Sardinia. Uncle Hugo had been sent to rescue him. Christ, he wasn't a new recruit any more. He was thirty, with five years' experience under his belt, a promising career ahead of him.

A couple of seconds before the train reached the point where they were standing, Marchant looked over his shoulder. 'Hey, stop pushing,' he shouted, and grabbed Valentin's arms as if to steady himself. Then he shoved the Russian forward as hard as he could.

# 41

'Betrayal requires a great leap of faith,' Fielding said, looking out of the window of his office. Marchant was standing beside him, watching the Tate-to-Tate ferry head down the river, trying to understand what Fielding had just told him.

'You're sure it's Primakov who wants to see me?' he asked.

'Who else would it be? A good friend of your father suddenly turns up in London after years out in the cold. It's hard to imagine that they'd want you to meet anyone else.'

Marchant didn't reply. Before the approach in Sardinia, he had forgotten all about Primakov, but the mention of his name began to sharpen blurred memories. The Russian had been a regular visitor to their house in India, a short man always arriving laden down with gifts for the children, peering over the top of them. It was so long ago. There had been an Indian toy, a mechanical wind-up train that went round a tiny metal track. His mother had taken it away because of its jagged edges.

'There's something I need to show you,' Fielding continued. 'A document that you would never normally see, not unless you become Chief – an appointment that would first require North America to sink beneath the sea.'

The CIA hadn't stopped his father becoming Chief, Marchant thought, ignoring Fielding's attempt at humour. Instead, they had waited until he was in office before humiliating him. Fielding stepped out of the room and told Ann Norman and his private secretary that he didn't want to be disturbed, then closed the door and went over to his desk. But he didn't sit down. Instead, he turned to the big safe in the corner behind him.

'Give me a moment,' he said, and bent down in front of the combination lock. Marchant instinctively looked away, out of apparent politeness, then watched in the window reflection as Fielding punched in some numbers – 4-9-3-7 – into a digital display and turned a large, well-oiled dial beneath it. His brain processed the movements in reverse: one and a half turns clockwise, two complete opposite turns, a final quarter-turn clockwise. Everyone who had ever been in the Chief's office had wondered what secrets the safe held, which British Prime Ministers had been working for Moscow, which trade union leaders had been Russian plants.

'Let's sit over there,' Fielding said a moment later, like a don about to discuss a dissertation. In his hand he held a brown Whitehall A4 envelope. He gestured towards two sofas and a glass table at the far end of his office, below the grandfather clock that Marchant had yet to hear ticking. Before he sat down, he placed the envelope on the table and put both hands on the small of his back. 'The combination changes twice a day, by the way,' he said, stretching, 'should you ever think of opening it.'

'I'd expect nothing less,' Marchant said, trying to hide his embarrassment. He sat down on the edge of the sofa, watching Fielding unpick the quaint brown string that kept the envelope closed at one end. In addition to the normal security stamps on the front, Marchant saw another one, in faded green, that read 'For C's eyes only.'

'I don't need to stress the classified nature of what I am about to show you,' Fielding said.

'God's access?' Marchant asked. Fielding nodded. Product didn't come more secret.

'Your father was one of the most gifted officers of his or any other generation. We both know that. He recruited more valuable assets behind the Iron Curtain than anyone else. But the most prized of them all was Nikolai Primakov.'

'I remember him from Delhi. At least, I remember he used to bring us presents.' Marchant could also recall big smiles and warm laughter, but he couldn't trust his memory. Why hadn't there been the normal household caveats about Primakov, given that he was from a hostile country? After the family had left India for the final time, he had never seen the Russian again, although his father talked of him often.

'The two of them were well known on the South Asia circuit, celebrated sparring partners who were also close friends.'

'How did that work?'

'Such overt friendships were more common in the Cold War. Vasilenko and Jack Platt in Washington, Smith and Krasilnokov in Beirut.' Fielding paused. 'Only a handful of people know that Primakov eventually succumbed to your father's overtures and became one of ours. This is a brief summary of the case.'

He handed Marchant an A4 document that had been typed rather than printed out from a computer, an indication that it was an only copy. Marchant tried to hold it between his hands, but realised they were shaking, so he put the sheet of paper onto the glass table and read. It was a series of bullet points, explaining how his father had recruited Primakov in Delhi and how the Russian had returned to Moscow and eventually risen to become head of K Branch (counter-intelligence) in the KGB's First Chief Directorate. It made impressive reading, but something didn't stack up. Officers other than Chiefs would have been involved in the running of Primakov, heads of stations, Controllerates back in London.

'The version in front of you is for general reading,' Fielding said. 'It's the copy new Prime Ministers see when they come to office. This one is a bit more confidential. South of the river only.'

He slid another sheet of paper across the glass table. Marchant recognised his father's handwriting at once, the green ink faded but legible. He read fast, taking in as much as he could, trying to ignore his hands, which were still trembling. It soon became clear why no one other than fellow Chiefs had read the document. In it was an admission by his father that made Marchant swallow hard.

In order to keep the information flowing from Primakov, Stephen Marchant had let himself be recruited by the Russian. It was the highest stake an agent could play for. Marchant read on, and realised that his father had crossed the sacred line. To keep his enemy handlers happy, he had passed over classified Western documents to Moscow. As far as Marchant could tell, the CX seemed to have been about America, mainly Cuba. He could see nothing that might have directly damaged Britain. He hoped to God he was right.

'Is this why the CIA went after him?' he asked.

'Not unless I'm working for Langley.' Fielding smiled. 'No, the Americans never knew. No one knows. But it is why the Russians are going after the son. They've seen a pattern, a family gene. Some call it "the treachery inheritance". In their eyes, your father betrayed America. As for you, they look at the last year and conclude that the CIA is probably not your favourite intelligence agency either.'

Marchant felt a range of emotions, but in amongst them the thought of his father handing over US intel was strangely re-assuring. It made his own visceral distrust of the CIA seem more understandable.

'Cordingley? Has he seen it?' He was the only previous Chief who was still alive.

'Yes, but his issues were never with America.'

'Someone in Moscow might have told the Americans that an MI6 agent was betraying them.'

'There's always that chance. But not in this case. Moscow thought they had the crown jewels, and the operation would have been known only to a very few people. Your father went on to be Chief, after all.'

'But Primakov was working for us.'

'And we hope he will again.' Fielding paused. 'No one in Moscow Centre knows that he was once loyal to London. He's approaching you as a seasoned Russian intelligence officer with instructions to recruit an unhappy British agent with family form. And you must close your eyes and jump, let yourself be recruited by him.'

'Just like that?' Marchant liked to think of himself offering some resistance.

'See how he plays it. One or two senior people in the SVR still have reservations about Primakov's past, his relationship with your father. He knows that. They suspected your father might have been a worthless *podstava*, and will be quick to dismiss you as a dangle, too. Fight the rod a bit. As I said, betrayal requires faith. Don't expect the smallest sign that Primakov is one of ours. He'll give you nothing. When you meet him at the gallery in Cork Street, he'll be wired. Moscow Centre will be listening. And all you can do, deep down, beneath the cover, is hold on to what you believe to be true: that Nikolai Ivanovich Primakov once worked for your father, and is now hoping to work for you.'

'And what do we hand Moscow in return?'

Fielding paused. 'We give them Daniel Marchant, of course.'

Marchant looked at him and then turned away to the window, pressing his nails deep into his palms.

'No one other than me knows that we're encouraging Primakov to recruit you. As far as everyone else is concerned, you're trying to recruit him. It's important you understand that. Prentice, Armstrong, even Denton – they'll all think you're hoping to turn Primakov. No one must suspect the reverse is true.'

'And the Russians?' Not for the first time, Marchant was struck by the loneliness of being Chief, the solitude of the spymaster's lot, unable to trust anyone, even his own deputy.

'Moscow Centre must believe that you've been landed, not presented to them on a plate.'

Marchant nodded. It was unsettling to think that the Russians had believed for so long that his father was theirs.

'I'm sorry, you were right about the Russian-speaking Berbers,' Fielding continued. 'We're now certain that the SVR is protecting Dhar.'

Marchant had never doubted who had taken Salim Dhar from the High Atlas, but it was still reassuring to hear someone else spell it out.

'The approach in Sardinia confirmed it,' Fielding added. 'We know the SVR are not averse to using Islamic militants when it suits them. Roubles and rifles continue to flow freely into Iran and Syria. Moscow controls mosques in Russia that preach *jihad* against America.'

'And do the Russians know we're related?'

'It would seem so. We're back to the treachery inheritance again: the anti-American family gene. If you had to identify the one single thing that defines Dhar, it would be his hatred of the US. Moscow Centre is demonstrating an ambition we haven't seen from them for a very long time. If they're successful, they'll have two brothers on their payroll. One, the world's most wanted terrorist; the other, the Western intelligence officer charged with finding him. And they share a father who once worked for Moscow, too. A lethal combination, wouldn't you say? The house of Marchant could do a lot of damage.'

'Which is why they've recalled Primakov.'

'He's the only person in the world who could recruit both of you. He knew your father. Moscow Centre is still wary of Primakov, but they had no choice but to trust him, bring him back in from the cold.'

'And what do you expect Primakov to give us?'

'Advance warning, I hope, of whatever act of proxy terrorism the Russians and Dhar are planning. And given they're counting on your help, we must assume that this time Dhar's target will be mainland Britain.'

# 42

It was the incessant rain that Salim Dhar couldn't bear. He could put up with the canteen food, and the training, morning, noon and night. Even the lack of sunshine was something he felt he could get used to. But the interminable drizzle was like nothing he had ever experienced before. The rain of his childhood had been joyful, thick drops that drenched the dusty streets of Delhi within minutes. He had danced with friends in the downpours, celebrating the monsoon's long-awaited arrival, washing himself as the warm water cleansed the land all around. This rain penetrated the soul with its leaden persistence.

The surrounding countryside, deep in the Arkhangelsk oblast of northern Russia, offered little comfort from the misery of the weather: dense dark forests of pine and spruce as far as the eye could see. There was something about pine trees that he found particularly depressing, as if they had been sapped of the very will to live.

Dhar wondered if he would have been happier in the cold. It had been freezing at night in the mountains of Afghanistan, where he had gone after the attack in Delhi. But he had been there many times before, attending and then teaching at training camps, and his familiarity with the terrain seemed to reduce the chill. And winter was also over. It had been much warmer in Morocco's High Atlas. Mount Toubkal was still tipped with white when he had first arrived more than a year ago, but he had kept below the snowline, moving on every night, holding on to the latent warmth of the previous day, encouraged by the promise of morning.

There was no respite where he was now, no prospect of a break in the slate-grey skies. His veins felt like roof gutters, flowing with rainwater. The guards said it wasn't usually so wet. Early July could be beautiful. Some mornings, when he first woke up in his hangar, he wondered if he had travelled back fifty years and been sent to work at the nearby logging Gulag in the forests rather than to Kotlas air base. But as he rolled out his prayer mat on the concrete floor and heard the twin jet engines of a MiG-31 firing up in the damp dawn outside, he knew where he was and what lay ahead.

Kotlas, better known as Savatiya, was a small military airfield, headquarters of the 458th Interceptor Aviation Regiment. Security was already tight, but it had been discreetly increased around the perimeter fence to protect the airfield's anonymous guest. Dhar was being kept in a draughty hangar at the northern end of the 2.5-kilometre-long runway, close to a parking sector deep within a wooded enclosure. There was only one other building in the area, a smaller maintenance hut where he carried out most of his training. On the far side of the runway was an alert ramp where two MiG-31s were positioned on permanent standby. The base was also home to MiG-25s and, as one of his guards had told him, was the 'target of opportunity' that was destroyed by an American B52 bomber in Stanley Kubrick's film *Dr Strangelove*.

Dhar had been told that today would be different. Not the weather, which showed little sign of lifting, but the daily training: less theory. His personal routine, though, would remain unchanged. Self-discipline was how he had kept his life together, the only constant in his world. It was something that his mother had taught him from an early age, when they were living in the American Embassy compound in Chanakyapuri in Delhi, although in those days it had meant helping with her early-morning *pooja* rather than praying towards Mecca. He had been born Jaishanka Menon, a Hindu, but by the time he was eighteen he had converted to Islam and was reading the Koran in Arabic. At first, his conversion was about spiting the man he thought was his father, an infidel who had tyrannised his childhood with his demeaning obsession with all things American, but he had soon grown into his new life, first in Kashmir then in Afghanistan.

His guards knew not to disturb Dhar until he had finished his prayers and ablutions. Sometimes, as he lay awake at night, he heard the stamping of their feet outside, the strike of a match, the rubbing of thick gloves. He felt no sympathy for them. They were part of the FSB, the domestic arm of the former KGB, and had been instrumental in the slaughter of thousands of his Muslim brothers in Chechnya.

He knocked on the side door of the hangar and waited for the guards to unlock it from the outside. He moved his toes in his oversized flying boots, trying to force warmth into them. In winter, he had been told, there was a place in Siberia called Oymyakon where spit froze before it reached the ground, birds froze in mid-flight. He shivered, glad it was summer.

By the time the door was opened, Dhar had wrapped a scarf around his face so that only his eyes were visible, and then put on an old pair of mirrored sunglasses. Without even a glance, he walked past the two guards, who stepped back and followed him across the runway towards the training hut.

To his right, a jet fighter was being prepared in the secluded parking area surrounded by trees. Dhar knew at once what it was: a Sukhoi-25, rugged workhorse of the Soviet air force, the plane he had first seen in Afghanistan as a nineteen-year-old *jihadi*. That one had been a rusting wreck, a legacy of the Soviet invasion almost thirty years earlier. More than twenty had been brought down by Stinger missiles supplied to the Mujahadeen by the CIA. The pilot had been shot after he ejected, and the remains of the plane covered in camouflage netting, deceiving the Soviet search-and-rescue helicopters that had flown over later.

For years afterwards, Taleb children had sat and played in its titanium bathtub of a cockpit, until the wingless fuselage was eventually moved to a training camp. When Dhar had first set eyes on it, he too had sat at its controls, transfixed by the possibilities. It was eighteen months before 9/11. Planes and their potential role in the *jihadi* struggle had always fascinated him. One of the camp leaders had noticed his interest, and encouraged him to start playing flight-simulator games.

Gaming was widespread amongst *jihadis* at the time, a way to stave off boredom during the endless hours of concealment. (The only problem was the pirated software, which crashed continually.) There were a few consoles in Dhar's camp, run off car batteries, and there was talk of a real role for those who excelled at virtual flying.

Dhar had been one of the best, and he knew his planes. He looked again at the jet on the runway and saw that it was in fact an SU-25UB, similar to the model he had been flying on the simulator for the past week, except that it was a two-seater trainer. It must have flown in overnight, as there had been no plane there before. A mechanic was by the far wing, looking up at the underside. Dhar turned away when one of the guards gestured at him.

He felt a thrill ripple through his body as he looked ahead again. He pushed his gloved hand into his coat pocket and felt for the letter, which was still there, a little crumpled. But before he could pull it out and read it again, a voice was calling from the training hut in front of him.

'Today, I watch you fly the *Grach*, our little rook,' the man said, using the SU-25's Russian nickname. 'Then I must leave for London.' It was Nikolai Primakov.

# 43

Marchant had been surprised to get a call from Monika. She had wanted them to meet alone for a drink, and they were sitting now in the roof terrace restaurant at Tate Modern, after a whirl-wind tour of the galleries. He had thought her interest in art at the Polish guesthouse more than a year earlier had been purely cover, but like all good legends, it was based on fact. Her know-ledge was considerable.

'You know what Picasso once said?' she asked, sipping a glass of rosé. The London skyline was spread out below them, St Paul's immediately across the river. ' "Art is a lie that makes us realise truth." In our work, you and I lie every day, but somehow the truth gets lost along the way.'

'Were you lying in Warsaw?'

'Of course.'

'And there was no truth in what happened?'

She held his gaze as she put an olive to her full lips. Then she turned away.

'I lost my brother last month. He was with the Agencja Wywiadu, too. A more senior officer than me, always more professional. I tried to do a good job, make sure you had your freedom.'

'And you did.'

'I enjoyed being with you,' she said, keen to change the subject. 'You were very gentle.'

Marchant recalled the brief time they had spent together, making love, smoking joints, each playing out their legends: he the tie-dyed gap-year student, she the hippy hostel receptionist. He had thought about her often since then, her confident sexuality worn so close to her skin.

'But not as gentle as Hugo.'

She laughed, throaty and heartfelt, then lit a cigarette.

'You're not jealous, are you, Mr Englishman?'

Marchant looked away.

'You are.' She laughed again and prodded him in the ribs. 'Daniel.'

It wasn't what he had expected. For a moment, he wondered if he really was jealous. He had been with Monika for twenty-four hours in Poland, most of it spent in bed. But he knew it was something else – suspicion rather than jealousy – that made him keep probing.

'Of course I'm not jealous.'

Her smile faded. 'Hugo's been a good friend. Lifted my gloom.'

Marchant felt a pang of guilt. Prentice had helped him through difficult times, too, particularly when his father had died. He could be a generous colleague, a man who lived life for the moment and wanted others to share in his luck.

'I'm sorry about your brother.' Marchant sensed that Monika wanted to return to the subject, talk about him some more.

'He was shot by the SVR. Four of our agents have been killed in the past year. Another one was murdered last week.'

'All by the Russians?'

'We think so. Someone's betraying them. An entire network's been taken down. The WA's in turmoil, searching for a mole.'

'Is that why you're here in London?'

She paused. 'No. Hugo wanted to show me off to his friends.'

'I lost a brother once. He was called Sebastian. Sebbie. We were twins. He died when I was eight.'

'I'm sorry.' She rested a hand on Marchant's forearm. 'I had no idea.'

'He died in a car crash. His turn to sit in the front seat. We were living in Delhi at the time.'

'You must miss him. They say the bond of a twin is unbreakable.'

'Every day. I wish I could say it gets easier with time, but it doesn't. I'm sorry.'

They sat in silence for a while, her hand resting on his. For once there were no legends, no cover stories. Their grief was real, their own.

'I must go,' Monika said eventually, 'otherwise another Englishman will be getting jealous.'

She stood up from the table, gave Marchant a light kiss on the lips and was gone.

# 44

Prentice and Marchant were standing well back from the first-floor window of the Georgian townhouse, but they could see people walking up and down Savile Row beneath them in the summer-evening sun. Marchant hadn't been aware that the tailor's had a connection with the intelligence services, but it was an old arrangement brokered by Prentice, which made sense. He never bought his suits from anywhere else.

'The gallery will be crawling with SVR,' Prentice said. 'Armstrong's fixers tried to get a wire in there last night, but security's been like a convent's dormitory for the past three days.'

'So I'll be on my own,' Marchant said.

'I'll be wired, but it's too risky for you,' Prentice replied, glancing behind him. Two technicians with headphones were sitting at a table, fine-tuning a bank of audio units. 'The whole area will be flooded with jammers, but we must expect them to be able to communicate with each other. And to hear us, despite the best efforts of Five,' Prentice added, glancing again at the technicians. 'Primakov has been given the codename "Bacchus".'

Two minutes later, Marchant was turning into Cork Street. It was easy to see which gallery was hosting the opening. People were spilling onto the pavement outside the Redfern, glasses of wine in one hand, catalogues in the other. He checked the street – Harriet

Armstrong had provided a team of watchers at Fielding's request – and recognised an agent sitting at the wheel of a black cab with its light off, thirty yards down the road. He wasn't reassured. The Russians would not make contact if they saw he had company.

Inside the gallery, Marchant nudged through the crowds, declining a glass of wine. A tray of sushi canapés looked more tempting, but there was always a risk with the Russians that it might come with a side order of polonium-210. He headed downstairs, where there were fewer people. He was familiar with the gallery's layout, having studied the floor plans, but something told him that the artist would be lurking in the basement, and he wanted to see him. Sure enough, he was holding court with a couple of younger men, both of whom had notepads. Marchant assumed they were journalists, and tucked in behind them to hear what was being said.

The artist must have been in his seventies, short with a full but close-cropped head of dyed-black hair that had been wetted down in jagged edges. He was wearing a bright pink open-necked shirt and socks with sandals. His face was angular, chiselled like a rough-hewn bust, and he had a fidgety, eccentric manner, massaging the top of his head with both hands as he explained his art.

'This is one of my favourites,' he said in a thick Russian accent, gesturing towards an abstract nude, all spatchcocked limbs and vibrant colours. His hands moved back up to his head. 'Lots of cunt.'

Both journalists visibly flinched. Marchant glanced at the painting, the patch of cross-scratched charcoal. Even he was startled by the word, still hanging awkwardly in the air. Then everyone remembered that artists were meant to shock and the mood settled, more questions were asked. Besides, he was from South Ossetia, and might not even know what he had just said. Marchant doubted it. The old man's moist eyes were dancing.

Upstairs, Marchant looked at some paintings (more nudes, more scratching), making his way around in reverse order towards number 14. He recognised the nude model as Nadia and felt a flicker of unease, particularly as the naked figure next to her bore a striking resemblance to himself. He glanced around instinctively, wondering for a moment if someone might recognise him. The Russians sometimes had a warped sense of humour.

A half-sticker had been stuck next to the price, indicating that the picture had been reserved – and that his meeting with Primakov was still on. But he hadn't spotted anyone at the opening who matched the latest photos Fielding had shown him of the Russian. He looked around the crowded room again, and then he saw Valentin through the main window, smoking on the pavement outside.

Hidden by the surging crowds on the tube platform, Marchant had pulled Valentin back a moment after pushing him towards the oncoming train. He hadn't caught the Russian's curse, but he saw his blood-drained face as he turned around.

'So sorry,' Marchant had said. 'Everyone was pushing from behind.'

To his credit, Valentin had maintained his composure. 'In that case, I must thank you for saving my life.' There was no acknowledgement that they had met before, just the same shiftiness in the Russian's small blue eyes.

'London's a dangerous city,' Marchant had said as the train doors opened. 'I'll catch the next one. Less crowded.'

Valentin squeezed into the crowded carriage, and Marchant waved to him as the train pulled out, the Russian's pale face pressed close to the glass. A warning had been served. Next time, Marchant would push him under.

Valentin still seemed anxious now, glancing up and down Cork Street in expectation. Marchant wondered where Prentice was.

He had points to prove, and he wished he was operating on his own. Besides, Prentice had not been given the full picture about Primakov. According to Fielding, all he had been told was that the Russian had expressed an interest in making contact with Marchant. Primakov had known his father, and Marchant would use the meeting to sound him out for possible recruitment. Prentice knew nothing about Primakov's past role as a British asset.

Marchant looked across at the picture again, and was about to walk over and stand in front of it when he heard a commotion at the entrance. A loud group of Russians strode in: dyed-blonde women weighed down with make-up and designer labels, middle-aged businessmen in blue jeans and chalk-striped jackets. A few steps behind them was a short, overweight man in his late fifties whose gnomic smile and wine-flushed cheeks exuded bonhomie. He was dressed differently from the others. The cord jacket, open shirt and silk scarf suggested a man of culture rather than commerce. Primakov, no question.

Hugo Prentice slipped into the gallery a few moments after Primakov. A Russian waitress greeted him with an offer of wine. Instinctively, Prentice checked himself. He didn't drink on duty, but he needed to blend in, and there was only one glass of orange juice on offer. He took a red wine from the middle of the tray and smiled at the waitress.

'Za vashe zdorov'e,' he said, raising his glass and moving into the crowded room.

He recognised a couple of Primakov's babysitters, but the sight of Primakov in the flesh caught him off guard. Despite his experience, he struggled not to look at him twice. It was like seeing a reclusive celebrity come out of hiding for the first time in years. Prentice had read the files, watched film footage of him and studied various photos, but for some reason their paths had never crossed, which was unusual, given their respective Cold War careers.

He knew all about him, of course. Stephen Marchant used to talk to him of their public sparring, how he had tried in vain for many years to recruit the Russian. Everyone in Legoland had heard about his spats with Britain and America in the 1980s. Primakov seemed to love and despise the West in equal measure, teasing with his friendships, annoying his own superiors. And now he wanted to meet Daniel Marchant, the son of his oldest adversary, who was going to try where his father had failed.

'Bacchus has arrived,' Prentice said into his concealed lapel wire, moving towards the bar at the back of the gallery, where the crowds offered more cover.

Before Marchant could do anything, Primakov had placed both hands on his shoulders and was admiring him as if he was one of the canvases on the walls.

'It's so true, you look just like your father,' he beamed, standing in the middle of the gallery and making no effort at discretion. His accent was almost completely Westernised, more American than English, with only a hint of Russian. 'I can't believe it. Can you believe it?' He turned towards one of his babysitters, who shuffled awkwardly. 'This boy's father was my very dear friend,' Primakov said, 'and a lifelong enemy.'

The group's entrance had silenced the gallery. Still smiling, Primakov leaned in towards Marchant and kissed him on both cheeks before hugging him. Marchant caught the strong smell of garlic, and for a moment he was back in Delhi. Just before Primakov pulled back, he whispered into Marchant's ear. 'Goodman's, Maddox Street, ten minutes. I've a letter from your father. We'll take care of the Graham Greene joker.'

Marchant glanced across at Prentice standing by the bar, chatting up one of the waitresses, who topped up his glass as they flirted. He then turned to the group of Russians, who were now being introduced to the artist. *A letter from his father?* The room suddenly felt very hot as Marchant headed for the door. He had no time to warn Prentice. Not much inclination either.

Outside in the street, he hailed the parked taxi he had seen earlier. Its light came on as it drove towards him. Marchant met it halfway and climbed in.

'A friend of mine in there needs a cab, too,' he said, nodding at the gallery window. 'Now.'

'He's left the gallery,' Prentice said, walking down a side corridor and back into the main gallery.

'Get yourself out of there,' Fielding ordered, glancing at Armstrong. They were in his fourth-floor office in Legoland, watching a bank of CCTV screens relaying images from the West End. In one of them, a black taxi was making its way down Conduit Street.

'Repeat please,' Prentice said. His voice was being broadcast in the office, but it was barely audible, breaking up.

'Marchant's flagged a code red alert,' Armstrong said. She had never liked Prentice, but the message had been given to one of her officers, so she felt obliged to pass it on. 'You need to move now.'

Prentice hadn't heard Armstrong's words, but he caught her tone of anxiety just before his comms dropped. He had also noticed Valentin, the tall Russian from Sardinia, who had peeled away from the group around Primakov and was coming towards him, blocking his exit from the gallery.

'You caused me a lot of embarrassment with your little home movie,' Valentin said, his body language at odds with his thin smile. 'It was a fake, of course.'

'Of course. But a good one, no? An Oscar, surely, for best foreign film.'

'Our politicians don't like to be ridiculed.'

'And Her Majesty's agents don't like to be compromised.'

'The boy seemed to be enjoying himself. At least, that's what Nadia said. Where is he now? I thought I saw him earlier.'

'No idea. I must go, though. It's been a pleasure.'

But Prentice knew already that he was going nowhere. With a taut smile, Valentin took the glass of wine from him and handed it back to the waitress, just as the gallery began to spin and blur.

# 45

Marchant was shown by the female *maître d'* to a back room of Goodman's, separated from the main restaurant by a screen.

'A drink while you're waiting?' the woman asked, ushering him to a table that had been made up for two. She let her hand linger on his shoulder a moment longer than was appropriate. There were four other tables in the room, but they were empty. 'Nikolai will be here in a few minutes.'

'A whisky, thanks,' Marchant said. 'Malt.' He had drunk a glass of wine at the gallery once he had seen others being served from the same tray, but he had declined a top-up, despite the persuasive charms of the waitresses. He wouldn't drink his malt until he had heard what Primakov had to say.

The taxi from MI5 had dropped him off in Maddox Street, outside the restaurant, where the parked cars were a wealthy mix of Porsches and Bentleys. He needed to talk to Primakov on his own, but it was no bad thing if Armstrong's people knew where he was. He thought for a moment about Prentice. He had looked tired tonight, too old for street work.

Goodman's served American steaks, but it was owned by a Russian who ran a chain of similar restaurants in Moscow. To judge from the main room, at least half the clientèle was Russian too.

Marchant had seen few female diners when he was shown through to the back room.

He glanced at the starters on the menu – sweet herring with hot mustard – and listened to the subdued hubbub of conversation on the other side of the panel, which must have been more solid than it appeared.

Then suddenly Primakov was in the room, quieter now, taking a seat opposite him, leaning back to whisper something to the *maître d'*, who had reappeared with two crystal glasses of whisky. Marchant thought how at home he looked in a restaurant, his natural habitat. The waitress put the glasses down on the table then left the room, closing the sliding door firmly. They were alone.

'I presume you've had the "big talk" with the Vicar,' Primakov began, burying the corner of a linen napkin under his chins and spreading the rest out across his chest as if he was hanging out the washing. His breathing was thickened by a slight wheeze. 'Let MI6 believe what they want. Your father and I were very close, it is true – unnaturally so, I suppose. But I never once considered working for him. Please remember that.'

Marchant tried not to blink at the Russian's bold opening gambit. If Primakov was lying for the sake of Moscow Centre's ears, he was making a good job of it. For a split second, Marchant doubted everything – his father's judgement, his own, Fielding's. Maybe the Americans had been right to suspect the house of Marchant. Then he recalled the Vicar's words. *Betrayal requires faith. Don't expect the smallest sign that Primakov is one of ours. He'll give you nothing.* Marchant's immediate task, he told himself, was to be recruited by Primakov.

'So why do you want to see me?' Marchant asked. 'I don't really have the time or the desire to sit around discussing old times.'

'You share a family look, and the same taste in whisky.' Primakov took a sip from his glass, ignoring Marchant's insolence. 'Your father liked Bruichladdich, too. I ordered it in specially. It takes me back, just sitting here across the table from you. We shared many happinesses together, your father and me. They were good times.'

'Different times. The world's moved on.'

'Has it?' Primakov paused, raising a silver lighter to his cigarette.

Marchant wondered if his father might have been friends with the cultured Russian even if there hadn't been an ulterior motive. In Delhi, they had both enjoyed going to the theatre, visiting galleries, attending concerts, which had made meetings easier. And Primakov had an undoubted warmth about him: a camaraderie that drew people in with the promise of stories and wine, the stamina to see in the dawn.

'When we were both first posted to Delhi, we used to argue late into the night over local whisky – Bagpiper in those days – about the Great Game, what our countries were doing there. Your father was an admirer of William Moorcroft, an early-nineteenth-century East India Company official who was convinced Russia had designs on British India.'

Marchant knew the name well. 'He wanted to publish a book about Moorcroft,' he said. 'It was going to be his retirement project. Unfortunately, he found himself retired earlier than expected, and wasn't ready to write it.'

'No.' Primakov paused, lost in thought. 'Moorcroft was also dismissed earlier than he intended. He took it badly, felt betrayed by his own country, just like your father, but he continued on his great quest to buy horses in Bokhara. Turkomans. He was a vet by training. He tried to reach Bokhara through Chinese Turkestan, but was held up in Ladakh, where he discovered he had a rival.'

'A Russian?'

'Persian-Jewish, a trader called Aga Mehdi. But he impressed

181

our Tsar so much with his shawls that he was given an honorary Russian name, Mehkti Rafailov, and was sent to talk with Ranjit Singh, ruler of the Punjab kingdom, on behalf of Russia.'

'So Moorcroft was right.'

'Rafailov's orders were to open up trade routes, nothing more.'

'Of course.'

'What intrigued your father was the relationship between Moorcroft and Rafailov, who was due to arrive in Ladakh while Moorcroft was there. The British spy was keen to meet his Russian enemy, but Rafailov died in the Karakoram pass before he reached Ladakh.'

'So they never met.'

'No, but Moorcroft made sure that Rafailov's orphaned son was provided for and educated. He was an honourable man, respected his adversaries.'

'Maybe that's why my father wanted to write about him. He respected you.'

'And he had a son whom I promised to look after.' Primakov hesitated, but not long enough for Marchant to decide if he meant him or Salim Dhar. 'I'm sure there would have been a market for the book,' he continued. 'Maybe you should write it?'

'I don't think you came here tonight to offer me a publishing deal.'

Primakov sat back, looked around and finished his whisky. 'We are free to talk in here. The room was swept before we arrived. So tell me. How much did the Vicar explain to you? About your father?'


'Nothing,' Fielding said, removing his headphones. The live feed had deteriorated until he could hear little more than white noise. He had heard enough, though. Marchant was being swept out of his depth.

'The entire area's been jammed,' Armstrong said, putting one hand over her mobile. 'Our best people are on it.'

182

That was what worried Fielding, but he didn't say anything. He wished MI6 was running the show, but London was Armstrong's patch and he needed her support, particularly as his own man, Prentice, had uncharacteristically messed up.

'What about your officer in the restaurant?' he asked.

'Shown the door after his starter.'

Fielding turned away and looked out onto the river, glowing in the evening sun. The encrypted feed from the restaurant was being relayed to his office and to no one else, given the extreme sensitivity of Primakov's case. Armstrong was one of the few who knew that Primakov had once been a British asset, and Fielding trusted her. It was Marchant who was starting to worry him.

# 46

Marchant glanced at Primakov, trying to read his face for more. His nose was big, slightly hooked. It was a strange question to ask. *How much did the Vicar explain to you?* What did the Russian want him to say? *He told me everything, that you betrayed Mother Russia and worked for my father?* The room might have been purged of British bugs, but Moscow would be listening in on their conversation.

'He told me that there were doubts about my father's loyalty to the West. Fielding didn't personally believe them, but he said the Americans had harboured suspicions about my father for many years. But that was the nature of his job, the risk he took – when he agreed to run you.'

'Run me?' Primakov managed a dry, falsetto laugh, shifting in his seat as it dissolved into a wheezy cough. Somewhere in Moscow Centre, Marchant thought, an audio analyst would be adjusting his headphones, calling over a superior. Had he overplayed it?

'Fielding showed me some of the intelligence you supplied to him,' Marchant continued.

'It is true, we gave your father some product once in a while, to keep his superiors happy, but it was nothing important.'

'Chickenfeed?'

'Organic. Nice writing on the label, but overpriced.'

Primakov paused, as if to reassess the rules of their engagement. Marchant wondered again in the ensuing silence if he had said too much. Then the Russian leaned forward, his voice suddenly quieter, like a doctor with news of cancer. Marchant smelt the garlic again as he traced a delta of broken blood vessels across Primakov's cheeks.

'It was the least we could do, given the nature of the product your father was supplying us.' Primakov drew on his cigarette and sat back, watching Marchant, his barrel of a body turned sideways as he blew the smoke away into the middle of the room. 'I think you already knew, deep down.'

Now it was Marchant's turn to shift in his seat. Primakov's words weren't a surprise, but they still shocked him. Up until this moment, he had tried to convince himself that the knowledge of his father's betrayal of America could be kept inside Fielding's safe, confined to an A4 piece of paper covered with green ink. Hearing a third party confirm it brought it out into the open, made it tangible.

'You seem troubled,' Primakov said. 'Hurt, perhaps.' His voice was even softer now, almost tender in tone. 'Please understand why he never told you himself. It was not because he didn't trust you. He wanted you to come to it yourself, to reach your own, similar conclusions. And I don't think you are so far from the place that your father occupied.'

'No.' It was time to give Primakov some encouragement, to tire on the line, but Marchant was struggling to sound convincing. Too many thoughts were chasing through his mind. What if his father had been happy to give more than he received?

'Not everyone can boast of being waterboarded by the CIA, after all. And they accuse us of being animals. Understandably, you share a similar distrust of all things American, which is to be applauded. Apart from their grain-fed steaks from

185

Nebraska, of course, which your father loved, just as I do. Come, we must eat.'

Marchant laughed. It was detached, out-of-kilter laughter. Then he laughed again, like the last man standing at a late-night bar.

'What's so amusing?'

'I came here tonight with orders to sound you out for recruitment, but now here you are trying to recruit me.'

'I don't blame you for the confusion. Sometimes I find the Vicar's faith in his flock almost moving.'

Marchant looked hard at the Russian in the silence that followed. *Don't expect the smallest sign that Primakov is one of ours.* For the second time, as Primakov's words lingered in the twisting cigarette smoke, he wondered if the Russian was telling the truth and Fielding was wrong. *He'll give you nothing.* Perhaps there was nothing to give.

'I'm not trying to recruit you, Daniel. I just want you to meet someone. Another son who has discovered he has much in common with his father. Family business.'

Marchant paused. Had he fought hard enough against the rod?

'And if I don't want to meet him?' The words stuck in his throat. He realised how much he wanted to see Salim Dhar.

'Moscow will have no option but to go public on your father, expose him for the traitor he was. Your government would no doubt respond in kind, accusing me of treachery, but then we would tell the world about Salim Dhar, that his biological father was the former head of MI6. I think the world would make up its own mind, don't you?' He paused. 'Please, read this. It's a letter from Stephen, which I have kept with me until this day. I hope it will make things easier for you.'

Marchant looked at the folded letter before taking it, as much to steady his hand as wonder about its contents. He knew already that it was genuine, that the writing was his father's. He began to read, resting his hand on the edge of the table:

*My dear Daniel,*

*If you are reading this, it must mean that you have finally met Nikolai Ivanovich Primakov. I will not try to guess at what path led you to him, only to offer reassurance that I have trodden a similar one before you. You are old enough, of course, to make your own judgements in life, but in the case of Nikolai, I merely wish to assist you, because other influences will be in play. He is, first and foremost, a friend, and . . .*

# 47

'. . . *you can trust him as if he was a member of our family.*'

Salim Dhar rested the letter on his lap, tears stinging his eyes, and looked out of the cockpit at the slanting rain. It was only his second flight in the two-seater SU-25UB, but already he felt at home in the confined titanium-alloy space. It would take longer to adjust to the colossal G-forces that blurred his vision as the aircraft banked and climbed into the sky, but he was determined not to show any weakness.

Sergei, his Russian instructor, also known as the Bird, was sitting behind him, putting the plane through another roll, the Archangel countryside spinning around to settle above his head. There was something about Sergei that Dhar liked. He became a different person in the air, less lugubrious, as if all his worries had been left on the ground. And Sergei had plenty to worry about. According to Primakov, he had been one of Russia's best pilots until he had crashed a MiG-29 into the crowd at an air show, killing twenty-three people and ending his career. The crash still haunted him day and night.

'I don't trust him,' Sergei said over the intercom, spinning the jet back over and pulling into a steep climb.

'Who?' Dhar managed to say, his jaw heavy with G-force. He could feel himself being pressed down into his seat, the blood rushing to his legs and feet. In training, Sergei had taught him how to squeeze his abdominal muscles to prevent blood flowing to the lower body. He tried to squeeze, but his vision was already greying at the edges.

'Primakov,' Sergei said calmly.

'Why not?' Dhar harboured similar suspicions, but he was struggling to speak, unable to see anything now except blackness. He was close to losing consciousness as Sergei banked hard left.

'Just a feeling. Are you ready to fly?' According to the dials swimming in front of Dhar, the plane was levelling out at 15,000 feet.

'I'm ready,' Dhar said, his vision returning. Euphoria swept through him as he looked around, blood flowing freely to his brain. He had waited a long time for this moment. *Inshallah*, his new life was coming together. He could do this. What lay ahead suddenly seemed possible. More importantly, his past had shifted too, on a tectonic scale, giant plates of data slipping into place beneath the surface.

Primakov had left him twenty-four hours earlier, and in that time Dhar had read and reread the letter the Russian had given him, thinking back to the only time he had met his father, when he was being held prisoner at a black site facility in Kerala. *To Salim, the son I never knew.* South Indian *jihadis* were suspected of being behind a series of bomb attacks in Britain at the time, and Stephen Marchant, then Britain's head of MI6, had travelled all the way to Kerala to ask Dhar if he knew anything about the campaign. Dhar couldn't help him.

It was then, as the monsoon rain beat down outside, that Marchant had detonated a bomb of his own: Dhar was his own son.

'If it's any consolation, I loved your mother,' Marchant had continued, walking around Dhar's dank cell. A solitary lightbulb hung from the ceiling. 'I still do.'

Dhar had been too tired, tortured too many times, to feel anything at first. Instead, he just stared at the betel-nut juice stains that streaked down his cell walls. There was blood mixed in with the red marks; his own blood. Eventually, he looked up from the threadbare *charpoy* on which he was lying. Any anger he felt towards Marchant was tempered by relief that the man he had thought for so long was his father, a man he despised above all others, was no such thing. After a long pause, during which the rain outside increased to a deafening downpour, Dhar sat up with difficulty, and spoke.

'How did you meet her?' he asked, rubbing his bruised and swollen wrists together. They were shackled and chained to a steel ring on the wall.

'She worked as an ayah at the British High Commission when I was stationed in Delhi. 1980. She was there for a year, I think. Before she switched to the American Embassy.'

Dhar had cast his eyes down at the mention of America.

'She asked me never to make contact with her or with you again. I agreed, with reluctance, but I always provided for you both, sending money once a month.'

Dhar wondered why the British spymaster had broken his promise. He could have sent a colleague to interrogate him. The south Indian rendezvous was a risk in itself, but the news Marchant had brought was far more dangerous, more compromising – for both of them. Western spy chief fathers *jihadi*. Then, as Marchant had talked on into the monsoon night, peppering his conversation with anti-American asides, Dhar had begun to understand. His world, far from being fractured by the revelation, had in some way become more complete.

'The West is not as simple as your people sometimes like to think,' Marchant had said – the last words Dhar was ever to hear his father speak.

Now, here in his hands, 15,000 feet above the Archangel countryside, was written confirmation of what Dhar had barely dared to hope: a father who had the same enemies as him. If Primakov was to be believed, Stephen Marchant, Chief of MI6, had spent more than twenty years spying for the Russians, inspired by a mutual distrust of America.

'Your father was a true hero of Russia,' Primakov had said. 'It was an honour to work with him.'

Dhar knew it wasn't important, that, *inshallah*, he would answer to a higher calling, but it mattered. He was being asked to follow in his father's footsteps. And for a son who had never known paternal love, never been shown the way, the feeling of comfort was almost overwhelming.

He took one last look at the letter, then folded it into one of the clear plastic pockets of his flying suit. *I will not try to guess at what path led you to him, only to offer reassurance that I have trodden a similar one before you.*

'The *Grach* is yours,' Dhar heard Sergei say over the intercom. And for a brief moment, as his hands tightened on the stick and endless pine forests passed in a blur far beneath him, it felt as if life had a coherence that had so far evaded him.

# 48

'Call me if you need to talk,' Harriet Armstrong said, moving towards the door. Fielding nodded. He was grateful for Armstrong's support, but he needed time on his own. Inevitable cracks were beginning to show in their new-found friendship. Fielding had no choice but to keep her in the dark about some of the more sensitive aspects of the Dhar case, and she resented her exclusion. The encrypted audio file on his computer, procured by her officers, was for his ears only.

He didn't blame Armstrong, but he could never tell her that his real intention was for Daniel Marchant to be recruited by Primakov, or that his biggest concern was Marchant's seeming inability to play the traitor. Nor could he ever reveal the Faustian pact that Stephen Marchant had once signed with Primakov: the flow of American intel from London to Moscow in return for Russian product. He couldn't tell anyone.

Fielding waited for Armstrong to close the door before playing the audio file. Five's eavesdroppers had finally managed to get a live feed from the restaurant, but Daniel Marchant had already left. As soon as he heard it, Fielding recognised the voice: Vasilli Grushko, head of the SVR's London *rezidentura*. The Russian's cold tones still made his pulse quicken, even though he was familiar with it from countless intercepts. Perhaps it was because he hadn't heard the anger before. Grushko was reprimanding Primakov, and he could almost hear the sweat dripping from his brow.

'Give me one good reason why we should trust him,' Grushko said. He then used a word that Fielding had dreaded to hear in connection with Daniel Marchant: '*podstava*', a dangle. Grushko wasn't buying Daniel Marchant.

'His loyalties are no longer with the West,' Primakov protested. 'The apple never falls far from the tree. He is his father's son.'

'That's what worries me,' Grushko said. Fielding was well aware that Grushko was one of those SVR officers who believed that Stephen Marchant had been a *podstava*, too.

'What harm will it do if he meets Salim Dhar?' Primakov said. 'The Muslim has asked to see Marchant.'

'We already have someone in London who could help. Why can't you persuade Dhar to work with them?'

*We already have someone in London who could help.* Was Grushko bluffing, or had the SVR been on a recruitment drive? Fielding would run it by Ian Denton afterwards.

'Because I doubt that they can claim to be Salim Dhar's brother,' Primakov said.

'Half-brother.' Grushko paused. 'I am sorry, Nikolai, but I have not heard enough tonight to be persuaded that Daniel Marchant is no longer loyal to his country.'

'How much do you need? Here is a man who has been water-boarded by the CIA. And now he has been tortured in Morocco. If past experience is any guide, British intelligence must have been aware of what was happening to him. What more do you want?'

'So why does he keep returning to his job after being so poorly treated?'

'Because he wants to meet his brother, and he knows his best chance is with MI6.'

There was a pause, long enough for Fielding to wonder if the feed had dropped.

'Maybe you are right,' Grushko continued, his voice fainter now. 'I'm not so sure. It is clear that Marchant dislikes America with commendable passion, but that is not the same as being ready to break the bond with your own mother country.'

Fielding listened as Primakov showed his boss out, then took off his headphones and walked to his desk, mulling over what Grushko had said. Moscow Centre clearly didn't believe that Marchant was ripe for recruitment. He was too damn loyal. It was understandable, given the implications. Marchant was being asked to act as if his father had been a traitor, an accusation he had fought long and hard to disprove.

It would have been so much easier if Primakov had slipped up at the restaurant and given Marchant a sign, but the Russian had been too professional. Now Primakov's superiors were growing restless. Grushko wanted proof of Marchant's willingness to betray, evidence of his treachery inheritance. It was time to cut Marchant loose.

'Can you get me Lakshmi Meena on the line?' Fielding asked Ann Norman over the intercom. The American might be useful after all.

He then replayed Grushko's words for a second time. *We already have someone in London who could help.* Fielding moved to call Denton, but then he paused. If Moscow Centre really had penetrated Six, he knew what lay ahead. He had watched Stephen Marchant go through a similar molehunt when he had been Chief. There would be a top-down investigation. Morale in Legoland would plummet. Everyone would be under suspicion, especially people like Denton, whose reputation had been made in Russia. He couldn't tell anyone what Grushko had said, not yet.

# 49

Marchant walked up the iron steps, trying to get his bearings. Primakov had offered him a circuitous back exit from the restaurant, through the cellar into the basement of an adjoining wine bar, which he had gladly accepted. He wasn't in the mood for small talk in the back of a black cab with one of Armstrong's watchers. According to Primakov, Maddox Street was crawling with them, which had annoyed him. Fielding and Armstrong had promised him he would be left alone. One officer had even tried to get inside Goodman's, posing as a diner.

'It's the footwear that gives them away,' Primakov had joked. 'Only your policemen and MI5 wear such ridiculous rubber soles.' No wonder the Russian had got on so well with his father. Marchant resisted mentioning Valentin's tell-tale shoes.

He knew that Fielding would be expecting him back at Legoland for a debrief, but he needed to clear his head, walk the summer-evening pavements. He stepped out onto Pollen Street, a narrow, dog-legged lane that ran down between Maddox Street and Hanover Street. Opposite him was the Sunflower Café, closed for the day. He glanced right and then headed away towards Hanover Street, turning into the square. No one had seen him.

It was only as he was heading west down Brook Street that he became aware of a tail, and it didn't feel like MI5. At the junction with New Bond Street, he waited to cross the road, giving himself an opportunity to glance back down Brook Street. He spotted two of them, on either side of the road, a hundred yards away. The first man kept walking, head down, not letting Marchant get a look at his face. The second, further back, peeled away into a pub. Marchant guessed there would be at least two more. They didn't look Russian either. Or American.

He had two choices. Keep walking to see how good – and who – they were, or call in and get picked up by MI5. He opted for the former, and increased his pace, continuing west down Brook Street towards Grosvenor Square. The American Embassy was not his favourite building in London, but the armed policemen that guarded it night and day might unsettle whoever was following him. If his tail pursued him for two brisk circuits of the embassy building, there was a good chance that they would be stopped by the police on the third. But before he could give them the run-around, a car drew up next to him.

'You're a guy in a hurry.' It was Lakshmi Meena, sitting at the wheel of an Audi TT convertible. Its roof was down.

'Working off dinner,' Marchant said, continuing to walk.

'Fielding said I might find you around here. He wants us to talk.'

'Well, now you can tell him we have.'

Marchant stopped, glancing back down the road, scanning the pedestrians for signs, shoes. He could see four of them in total. They had broken cover, making no attempt to conceal themselves. Their body language was more lynch mob than watcher. Marchant recognised the one at the back from Sardinia. He opened the door of Meena's car and climbed in.

'Aziz is dead. Last night in the military hospital in Rabat,' Meena said, looking in the rear-view mirror as they drove off. 'Complications unrelated to his original injuries, but clearly he wouldn't have been in there if you hadn't ripped half his mouth off.'

'Are they lodging an official protest?'

'Not their style. They don't want to draw attention to what they did to you first.'

'On your orders.'

'Spiro's.'

'And you do whatever he says.'

Meena pulled up at a red light and glanced again in the mirror, her knuckles whitening on the steering wheel. 'Look, I'm sorry for what happened. Truly.'

Marchant felt the gap in his gum with his tongue, but decided not to say anything. 'Where are we going?'

'Your flat, then Heathrow.'

'Heathrow?'

'Fielding wants us to go to India. Our flight's tonight, and you need to pack.'

'Our flight? Not so fast. I'm not going anywhere until I've spoken to him.'

Marchant shifted in his seat. He hadn't been back to India since the US President's trip, Leila's death.

'Fielding's meeting us at Heathrow. He'll explain everything. How was Primakov, by the way?'

Marchant hesitated. A new arrival at the Russian Embassy in London would arouse even the doziest CIA desk officer, but her question still surprised him.

'The sous-chef at Goodman's is one of ours,' she continued by way of explanation. 'It's one of the most popular Russian restaurants in town. You showed up on our grid before you'd even ordered your herring with mustard. How can you eat that stuff?'

'You're not from Calcutta then?'

'Reston, Virginia, actually. Why?'

'Bengalis like their mustard.'

'I meant the fish.'

'They like that too. Primakov was fine. Fatter than I remember him. He was an old friend of my father.'

'Friend?'

'Sparring partner.' He paused. 'So who showed up first on your grid? Me or Primakov?'

Meena hesitated. 'OK, I'll admit, we don't have a great deal on Primakov. Cultural attaché, brought out of retirement, medium-ranking KGB officer before the fall.'

'But you have a bulging dossier on me. Says it all, doesn't it? So where in India are we heading?'

'The south, Tamil Nadu. Where my parents are from.'

'Great. Meet the in-laws time. A bit premature, isn't it? We haven't even slept together.'

Meena drove on in silence, glancing in the rear-view mirror.

'I'm sorry,' Marchant said, more quietly now. It had been a crass thing to say. Sometimes it was easy to forget Meena's Indian heritage. She talked like a ballsy, confident American, trading coarse comments with colleagues, but there was an inner dignity about her that he recognised as uniquely subcontinental.

'Actually, we're going to find your father's lover.'

He looked across at her for more.

'Our Chennai sub-station is closing in on Salim Dhar's mother. Fielding thought you should be there when we bring her in.'

# 50

Salim Dhar turned the navigation lights on as the canopy closed, and took a deep breath. Then, after running through the cockpit checks he had practised so often on his ancient PC, he leaned forward and flicked the switch to start the right engine. The RPM dial in front of him spooled up to 65 per cent, and the exhaust-gas temperature rose to 300 degrees. He did the same with the left engine, lowered one stage of flap and used his thumb to reset the trim to neutral.

For a moment, he was back in Afghanistan, sitting in the cockpit of the crashed SU-25. He remembered a solitary poppy pushing up through a broken dial. It was the first time in his adult life that he had been happy. The camaraderie at the training camp had made him realise how little friendship he had found until then. The darkest days of his childhood had been at the American school in Delhi, where his father had insisted on sending him. There were a few Indian pupils, sons of New Delhi's business elite, but he was not like them, nor was he like the diplomats' children, who made no effort to talk unless it was to taunt him – *Allah yel'an abo el amrikaan'ala elli'awez yet'alem henaak* (God damn the fathers of those Americans and whoever wants to study there!).

He turned the landing lights on, requested taxi clearance from the control tower, and again flicked the trim switch, setting it for take-off. Then he tested the wheelbrakes as he ran the throttle up to 70 then 80 per cent.

'Brakes holding, airbrake closed,' he said to himself as he felt for the switch on the side of the throttle. As jets went, the SU-25 wasn't a demanding plane to fly. Unlike its more recent successors, it didn't have a modern avionic suite, but it was a reliable ground-pounder, which was why it had been in Russia's air force for so long. According to Sergei, his instructor, the SU-25 could operate at very low speeds without 'flaming out'. Nor did it stall easily. 'It can take a real beating and still bring you home,' Sergei had said. But Dhar knew there would be no return flight.

After taxi-ing to the runway threshold and running through his pre-take-off checks, he waited for his clearance from control. At last it came. He took his position on the runway's centreline, gazing at the white ribbon that stretched away as far as he could see. Engaging the wheelbrakes, he ran the power up to 90 per cent and checked that all the gauges were still in the green. Then he released the brakes and applied full military power, watching the air speed build quickly to 260 kmh.

Something was wrong.

'Sometimes you need to add a little right rudder as you firewall the throttles,' Sergei had said, but Dhar remembered too late. His fingers fumbled to deploy the twin drogue chutes, but it was hopeless. There was too little tarmac left. 'Eject, eject!' said a voice in his head. But as he overcompensated for the yaw, the plane lurching right, left, right again, the right wingtip hit the ground, breaking off in a shower of sparks and fire. He thought of his mother, closed his eyes and prayed.

# 51

Fielding took the call in the back of his chauffeur-driven Range
Rover on the way to Heathrow. Cars didn't particularly interest
him, but he couldn't deny that he had been impressed with the
latest security upgrades to his official vehicle. Most of them were
to do with jamming opportunist electronic eavesdroppers, but
the car had also benefited from lessons learned in Afghanistan,
where IEDs had caused such havoc. Its floor was now protected
by hard steel armour blast plates, and the sides had been reinforced
with composite ballistic protection panels.

'Thank you for ringing back,' he said, trying to picture his
opposite number in America, his Langley office, the bland Virginia
countryside. Fielding's relationship with the DCIA had been at
rock bottom during the past year, but he knew that things had
to improve sooner or later. Much as it would like to, Britain
couldn't survive indefinitely without America's intel.

'What can I do for you, Marcus? No problems with Lakshmi
Meena, I hope?'

'No, she's fine.'

'Treat her as yours, Marcus. A shared asset. She's good.'

Better than the last one, you mean, Fielding thought, but he
said nothing. 'Thank you. She's briefed me fully about Dhar's
mother.'

'That's what she's there for. Keeping our allies in the loop.'

Like hell, Fielding thought. He looked out of the window at the grey scenery either side of the Westway: tatty tower blocks, car showrooms, digital clocks, vast hoardings. It was such a drab part of London, a depressing first impression of Britain for anyone driving in from the airport.

'How's Jim Spiro these days?' Fielding asked.

'I never knew you cared. He'll be touched, truly.'

'Is he still suspended?'

'To all intents and purposes. He's the subject of an ongoing internal inquiry, based largely on evidence provided by MI6.'

'I need to talk to him.'

# 52

Daniel Marchant moved quickly around his one-bedroom basement flat in Pimlico, removing a suitcase from underneath the bed that was already packed with three sets of clothes and a wash bag containing a razor, toothbrush and two passports. The cobblers had given him a new spare one after Morocco. He had asked for two, but they had talked about budgets and come back to him a few days later saying that the passport in Dirk McLennan's name, the snap cover he had used to get out of Morocco, had not been compromised.

Out of habit, he checked the issue date, making sure it was still valid, and then he saw an old Islamabad visa stamp on one of the pages. A trip to the Islamic Republic of Pakistan had been fine for Morocco, but it might cause problems in India. He cursed the cobblers and put the passport on his desk. He paused for a moment, looking at the photo of Leila that he had tried so often to throw out. She was smiling back at him, the bright lights of a carousel blurred behind her. He had taken the photo at the funfair in Gosport, across the water from the Fort, a few hours before they had slept together for the first time. The instructors had given them a rare day off after two weeks of intense training.

He knew it was a weakness to keep the photo, but something

about her expression made it impossible to get rid of it. For a few heady months, he had thought it was love in her eyes. It was still hard to accept that he had been deceived. Wasn't it his job to be vigilant while deceiving others? Perhaps he kept the photo as a reminder, a warning.

'I guess you still miss her, right?' He turned to see Lakshmi Meena standing in the doorway. She had dropped him off outside on Denbigh Street. He put the photo back on the desk, annoyed that he hadn't heard her walk down the iron steps to his flat. Leila could still make him drop his guard, even now.

'Have you ever had to sleep with someone as part of the job?' he asked, unnecessarily adjusting the photo frame on his desk.

'Spiro once tried it on. Said it was all part of the promotion process.' She could still recall the approach: first month at Langley, fresh from the Farm. Spiro liked to call all the new female recruits into his office for a friendly one-to-one.

'I don't mean with our side.'

'I know we're not always the good guys, but we're not the enemy.'

'Leila wasn't just working for you. Read the files.'

'I tried. Hey, way beyond my security clearance. All I know is that she saved our President's life.'

'That's one way of looking at it.'

'And another way?'

'She betrayed me.' Spiro had used similar words when she played him back an audio recording of his advances. A colleague had tipped her off, and she had gone into his office wired, claiming later that she was testing out new equipment and had forgotten to turn it off. It had been a colossal career risk, but Spiro had never bothered her again. If anything, he respected her more.

'And you can't forgive her that?' she asked.

'Not yet.'

'Is that why you won't trust anyone?'

'Anyone?'

'Women.'

'It was a calculated act of betrayal.'

And now, like King Shahryar's virgin wives, we all stand accused, Meena thought, but she didn't have time to say anything. They heard a car slow down on the road above them. Marchant glanced up through the basement window at the pavement.

'Where did you park?' he asked.

'Around the corner, Lupus Street. I drove round the block twice first. No tail.'

'Come, quickly,' Marchant said, locking the front door to the flat, where Meena was standing, and going through to the bedroom. A pair of french windows looked out onto a small patio garden. He opened them and ushered her outside, glancing back at the front of the flat. Someone was coming down the metal stairs. How had they got his home address? He went into the small adjoining bathroom, turned on the light and the shower and returned to the bedroom. Then he took the key from the inside of the french windows, joined Meena on the patio and locked them from the outside.

'Spiro's orders again?' he asked.

'No,' Meena said. 'The Moroccans are upset Aziz is dead. Very upset.'

Marchant walked across to the back wall, which was about twelve feet high and covered in a wooden lattice for climbers he had never planted. In the corner, there was a rockery. Soon after he had bought the flat, he had built up the rocks at the back to help him climb up the wall, should he ever need to. He had cemented in three bricks above the highest rock, at eighteen-inch intervals up the wall, that stuck out by half a brick and acted as steps, but he had never got round to trying them.

'Up there, quick,' he said, pointing at the corner as if it was the obvious way out of the garden. When Meena reached the top of the wall, she looked back down at him.

'You forgot to build any steps on the other side,' she said before jumping. He heard a groan as she landed in the mews below. Then he followed her, glancing back at his flat as he reached the top of the wall. Two men had broken in, and one of them was looking at the passport he'd left on his desk. The other was moving towards the bathroom, gesturing to his colleague. For a moment, Marchant wanted to go back inside and confront them, show them his broken teeth, knock out theirs, but he resisted.

As he jumped from the top of the wall, a car turned into the quiet mews, driving too fast for a resident. Marchant got to his feet and rushed at its sweeping headlights, ignoring a shooting pain in his ankle. He knew he had to move fast. Without hesitating, he opened the driver's door and grabbed the driver, pulling him out onto the road. He was aware of Meena doing the same on the other side. It was only as he pinned the man up against the wall, holding him by his throat, that he realised it was one of Armstrong's watchers.

He held the man for a moment, then released him.

'They're Five,' Marchant called across to Meena, who had wrestled the passenger to the ground and was holding both his arms behind his back. He made a mental note that she was no slouch when it came to unarmed combat. Marchant's man dropped to his knees, one hand massaging his throat.

'Christ,' he said, out of breath. 'Armstrong sent us.'

'I'm sorry. I thought –' But he suddenly felt too tired to finish.

'Two men are in Daniel's flat,' Meena said, taking over, reluctantly releasing her man. She made no apology for the mistake. 'Moroccan intelligence.'

206

'That's why we're here,' the other man said, getting up off the road. 'They showed up on the grid this evening.'

A bit late, Marchant thought, recalling the trouble he'd had earlier in Grosvenor Square.

'Delay them, will you?' he said. 'We need to get to the airport.'

# 53

Salim Dhar sat back and stared at the screen, watching his plane spin in a sickening cartwheel of flames.

'You forgot to add some right rudder,' Sergei said, coming over to the simulator with a cigarette hanging limply from the corner of his mouth. He was tall and loose-limbed, wearing a flying suit and holding a helmet in one hand. His face was awkward and angular, almost avian in its features. Dhar assumed that was why comrades called him the Bird.

After the air-show crash, Sergei had been stripped of his wings, tried and sent to prison, where he would have remained for the rest of his life if it hadn't been for the unusual summons to train up a surly Muslim for an SVR black op. He knew enough not to ask any questions, that he was expendable if he played up. 'They will shoot me after I have served my purpose,' he had once said, only half jokingly, to Dhar.

The daily training sessions took place in an airless hut across from the hangar where Dhar was living at Kotlas airbase. Dhar didn't know where the Bird roosted at night. They didn't do small talk. No one else was in the hut, and there were two armed guards positioned outside the door.

'How will you ever learn to deploy your missiles if you're always crashing on take-off?' Sergei continued. 'We've one week left and you've only got the *Grach* airborne twice.'

Dhar sat in silence, his hands resting on his legs. He tried to filter out the instructor's tone of voice and focus on the content. He was right. Just then a jet roared low over the hut, mocking Dhar with its menacing ease.

'Let's do it again,' Dhar said calmly. 'In formation this time.'

Sergei looked at him for a moment and smiled.

'OK,' he replied, tossing away his cigarette as he walked over to the other simulator. 'So the Bird is your wingman.'

# 54

The lights were off in St George's Chapel, but Marchant could make out the tall figure of Marcus Fielding sitting quietly at the back of the airless room, in front of the font. It was Heathrow's only chapel, built into the basement like a vaulted crypt. Marchant had found it quickly. Its location between Terminals 1 and 3 was well signposted. He was sure he had been here before, a long time ago, coming from or going to India. His father had sat outside with him in the memorial garden, where he could picture a large wooden cross. It must have been not long after the death of his twin brother, Sebastian.

Fielding didn't look up as he entered the room, and for a moment Marchant wondered if the Vicar was praying. His eyes were closed. Marchant hesitated by the door, looking at a plaque that commemorated the crew of Pan Am Flight 103, who had died 31,000 feet above Lockerbie. Then he walked over and sat down on the brown padded seat next to Fielding. Still the Vicar said nothing, his eyes closed behind his rimless glasses. Finally, he spoke.

'Did he give you anything?'

'Nothing. He told me he'd passed information to my father, low-grade product, but that it was the least he could do in return for the quality of RX my father was giving to the Russians.'

Fielding's face creased into a smile as he opened his eyes.

'And did you begin to doubt him?'

'Who? My father?'

'Yes.'

Marchant didn't say anything. Instead, he tried to read the words on another plaque, by the font, which had been put up by Dr Jim Swire, whose daughter had died over Lockerbie, too.

'Moscow was all ears,' Fielding said. 'I told you he'd give you nothing.'

'Were you able to listen?'

'I heard enough to be worried.'

'About Primakov?'

'About you. Perhaps it was asking too much. No one likes to hear his own father being branded a traitor.'

Marchant bridled at the implied criticism. Did Fielding think he wasn't up to the job? 'Can I ask you something?'

'Please.'

'Did you ever doubt him?'

Fielding paused, long enough for Marchant to look up, for more thoughts to ferment.

'Your father always talked about this country as an island, our sceptred isle. It wasn't shared democratic values with America that made him go to work in the morning. It was the mist rising from fields at dawn in the Cotswolds.'

'I take it that's a "no", then.'

Fielding didn't answer, closing his eyes instead. For a moment, Marchant wondered if he hadn't heard. He hated it when Fielding did this. The ensuing silence unnerved him enough to keep talking, just as Fielding intended. It was how he got people to reveal more than they wanted to.

'I still thought Primakov might give me something – a look in his eye, a scribbled note on a napkin, the smallest hint that we both knew. But nothing. Just a letter.'

Fielding opened his eyes. 'From whom?'

'My father. It told me to trust Primakov as if he was family.'

'Well, there's your sign. If you trust your father, then you must trust Primakov, too.'

'And if I don't trust Primakov? If I don't believe he's one of ours?'

*Then you must accept that your father was a traitor.* It didn't bear thinking about. Fielding clearly thought the same, as he chose to ignore Marchant's question.

'Did Primakov mention Dhar?' Fielding asked.

'He wants me to meet him.'

'That's good. But you mustn't appear too keen. Not yet.'

'Which is why you're sending me to India with Lakshmi Meena, the delightful dental assistant.' Fielding had met Meena in the chapel before Marchant. She was now waiting in departures.

'Our new Leila. At least this time we know she's working for the CIA.'

'And for anyone else?'

'She's different, Daniel. You can trust her.'

'Thanks for the advice.' The Vicar as agony aunt, Marchant thought. God help us all.

'I want Dhar's mother brought back to the UK. It won't be straightforward. The Russians have got wind of her too, and will try to bring her in.'

'What about the Americans?'

'I've spoken to the DCIA. Provided we pool everything, he's happy for her to be brought here for questioning, given their recent track record with Dhar. But they want Meena to run the operation. That's the deal.'

'Is that wise?'

'They won't try anything with you on board. They need you.'

'That didn't stop them in the past.'

212

'That was before they killed six of their own Marines in a drone strike. The truth is, it's too dangerous for us. We can't jeopardise London's relationship with Delhi. An unauthorised flight into Indian airspace is a risk the Americans can afford to take. We can't.'

Fielding stood up and walked towards the door, stopping to read the names of the Pan-Am crew. Marchant followed him.

'Tell me, Daniel, do you think Salim Dhar still wants to make contact with you?' Fielding asked.

'Yes, I do.'

'Why?'

It was a question Marchant had been wrestling with ever since Dhar had failed to make contact in Morocco. In the early days, he had genuinely believed that Dhar might be turned, persuaded to work for Britain, the country his real father had served. But now he was less sure.

'Why does Dhar want to see me? Because we're lonely half-brothers? I doubt it. I think he wants to meet up because he believes I'm a traitor, just as he believes our father was.'

'At the moment it's more a case of hope than belief. Primakov will have told Dhar exactly what he told you about your father: that he was a Soviet mole at war with the West. And he will also have told Dhar about your treatment by the CIA, your growing disaffection with the West. Dhar sees you as a potential ally, which is a good start.'

'Is it?'

'Primakov can only do so much. He can bring two brothers together with tales of their father's treachery, but it's up to you to persuade Dhar that you're a traitor too.'

And if you don't, Fielding thought, Dhar will kill you. But he said nothing as he walked out of the chapel into the harsh neon lighting of the airport.

# 55

The Hotel Supreme was not Madurai's finest, but their room did apparently have a view of the temples, which was what Marchant and Meena had asked for when they checked in unannounced at the wood-panelled reception desk. Too many staff were standing around, some in dark suits behind the desk, others in baggy brown bellboy uniforms waiting by the lift, hands behind their backs. Guests seemed to be a mixture of businessmen and Indian tourists. Meena had made an advance booking at another place across town, but switching hotels reduced the chance of their room being bugged.

'The view is there, but it is only partial,' the manager explained, at the same time indicating to two staff to carry their suitcases to the lift. He picked a brass key off a row of hooks behind him and handed it to Marchant.

'Meaning?' Meena asked, raising her eyebrows at Marchant.

'They are painting the temples at this time. You will see.' The manager wobbled his head from side to side, smiling like a child with a secret.

'But we've come a long way to be here. A view of them at sunrise would be nice,' Meena said, sticking to her legend. As she had explained to passport control at the airport, she and Marchant were a couple. They were visiting India for a traditional wedding in a village near Karaikudi, about eighty miles east of Madurai, where one of Meena's distant cousins was marrying an accountant from Chennai. First, they were doing some sightseeing in Madurai, where the main tourist attraction was the Sri Meenakshi temple, with its brightly painted towers, or *gopurams*, and ornate carvings.

As soon as they looked out of the window of their top-floor room, the view of the temple became clear. At least, the manager's explanation did. As he had promised, it was possible to see the tallest *gopuram* from the room's balcony, if you leaned over the side of the crumbling wall. But every inch of it was covered with scaffolding and organic sheeting made out of matted palm fronds. From a distance, it looked like a giant *papier-mâché* structure.

'I think that's what he meant by partial,' Marchant said. Meena was walking around the double bed, checking the light switches and wall hangings for audio devices.

'I was hoping for twin beds,' she said.

'We're married, remember?'

'I know. I'll sleep over there, on the sofa.'

'It's OK. I will.'

There was silence for a few seconds as Marchant watched her go through her suitcase. She was wearing white trousers and a cream-coloured shirt with long sleeves. On the plane, she had been in tight jeans, but she had changed in the lavatory, explaining about temple etiquette. Marchant had reminded her that he used to live in India, promising he wouldn't wear shorts and a T-shirt, however hot it was.

'Thanks for not making all this any harder than it is already,' she said quietly, her back to him as they stood on either side of the bed. 'Blame my strict upbringing.'

Ever since they had boarded their flight to Chennai in London, Marchant had done only the bare minimum that was required for them to appear as a couple. In his experience, intelligence officers the world over usually took husband-and-wife cover as an opportunity to flirt with colleagues, a brief and unconditional escape that often led to more, but he could see how much Meena struggled with it. She seemed troubled, not her usual sparring, confident self. Her sexual poise had disappeared. She hadn't spent long with Fielding on her own, but whatever the Vicar said had left her even quieter. Marchant suspected he had laid down a few ground rules, reminded her about Leila.

'Come on. Let's go and be ignorant Western tourists together,' Marchant offered, trying to lighten the mood.

Meena seemed to rally at the thought of the task that lay ahead of them. She found the map she had been looking for in her suitcase and spread it out on the glass coffee table in front of the windows.

'We think Dhar's mother is working in the centre of the temple complex, near the main shrine to Shiva,' she said, pointing at the map. 'We've got two of our people inside, posing as temple staff, and two more outside.'

'Indian origin?'

Meena gave him a sarcastic smile. 'Yeah. It kind of helps them to blend in.'

'I didn't know Langley was so enlightened.'

'We're getting there. And there's someone from our Chennai sub-station – OK, white guy, redneck – who's hanging around Madurai as a tourist. Have you been inside a temple like this before?'

'Not since my gap year.'

'Believe me, it's one big crazy city in there. Shops, animals, ponds, people, food. Worship is just a part of it.'

'Did you used to come here when you were younger?'

'As a little girl, yes. We moved to the States when I was seven.

I grew up near Karaikudai, where we're meant to be going for my cousin's wedding.'

'So this was your local big temple.'

'I guess so. I don't remember a lot about it. Just that it was very full-on inside. Let's go,' she said, hooking her arm through Marchant's and heading for the door.

# 56

Salim Dhar looked at the photo of Daniel Marchant on his wall as another jet took off outside. Kotlas airbase was busy today, more activity than usual. He was meant to be flying with Sergei, but they had been grounded on account of the increased air traffic. More classroom theory, more work on the simulator.

He tried to think back to the time he had met Marchant in India. The Britisher's appearance had been different then, a crude cover identity. His hair had been shorter, his clothes more dishevelled, like those worn by the Westerners he had seen and despised in Goa. He reached out for the photo, gently prised it from the wall, and studied it more closely. According to Primakov, it had been taken by a young SVR agent from the top of a number 36 bus in London. Marchant was in a suit, looking through the window of a motorcycle showroom, across the road from MI6's headquarters in Vauxhall.

Dhar had never been to London, but he felt he knew the city well. Although he had studied at the American school in Delhi, his education had been heavily influenced by Britain. He didn't know why at the time, but his mother used to bring home books about London, talk to him about the country in a way that he realised now expressed a heartfelt affection. She had only been employed briefly at the British High Commission in Delhi, before he was born, but she had loved the place and its values. Dhar remembered playing Monopoly with her under a lazy fan, wondering at the names on the board: Old Kent Road; The Angel, Islington; Marylebone Station.

He had thought about the game again when the London Underground was attacked on 7 July 2005: Liverpool Street, King's Cross. For some reason, his mother had always liked to buy up the stations.

'Mama, but the maximum rent is only £200,' he used to tease her.

'I know,' his mother had said, smiling, with a knowing tilt of the head. 'But there are four stations, and only two or three of everything else.'

Dhar was in Afghanistan at the time of the London attack, fighting American troops, but he hadn't joined in the cheering when news reached his camp of the bombings.

'Why do you not salute our brothers in Britain, Salim?' the commander of the camp had asked.

Dhar had walked off. Such methods had never been his style. His approach had always been to target the West's troops and political leaders rather than its people. It was why he preferred to operate alone whenever he could, outside al Q'aeda's indiscriminate umbrella. But he knew it was something else, too. In his mind, it was his mother's world that the 7/7 bombers had desecrated; a board-game fantasy, but still her world. It was only later that he had understood why: it was his father's, too.

It would have been easy for Dhar to dismiss Marchant's bond of half-brotherhood as worthless. In his childhood he had had countless 'cousin brothers', distant relatives who played up family connections whenever it was convenient. It was acutely comprom-ising, too, for a *jihadi* to be related to a Western spy Chief. But now that Dhar understood his father's loyalties, he knew that he had to see Marchant again. The Britisher had been a potential ally when they had met in India. He was a man on the run from the CIA, but who had returned to a job at the infidel's castle on the shores of the Thames, ignoring his coded text to join him in Morocco. Now, according to Primakov, he was finally ready to betray his country, to follow in their father's footsteps.

Dhar pinned the photo of Marchant back on the wall. He knew there was another in London who could help him, but he had insisted to the Russians that it should be Marchant, telling them that the mission was off if it was anyone else. It wasn't ideology. It was curiosity. There were too many questions he wanted to ask him. How had he coped with being waterboarded by the Americans? Who was the beautiful woman in Delhi he had shot instead of the President, the woman whose *meenakshi* eyes had haunted him ever since? And, most of all, what was their father like, the man who had hoodwinked the West for so long?

# 57

There was a queue of people waiting to enter the Meenakshi temple by the east gate. A female police officer checked the women, frisking their saris with a lollipop-shaped metal detector, while a male officer did the same with the men. No one was wearing any shoes, not even the police. Marchant and Meena had left theirs around the corner at a stall with thousands of others, not expecting to see them again.

Marchant approached the policeman and stood with his arms out and legs apart. Security seemed to be tight today, he sensed – thorough rather than a gesture – and he wondered if the temple was on a heightened state of alert. It wouldn't have anything to do with Salim Dhar's mother, but it might make things more difficult when they lifted her. They had already had to abandon their plan of using their wires in the temple, as they would have been picked up by the police detectors.

He smiled at the policeman once he was done and walked on, waiting for Meena at the bottom of the stone steps. He couldn't be certain, but he thought he detected a slight hostility towards her from the female officer, who glanced over at him as she frisked her. Meena had daubed her hair parting with vermilion, a sign of marriage, but she couldn't do much about the colour of Marchant's skin. Perhaps mixed-race marriages didn't play well in Madurai.

'Sometimes I remember why we left this country,' Meena said as she joined him. They walked down a colourful colonnade of pillars, leaving the sunlight behind them. Marchant thought he heard the sound of hesitant *slokas* being recited in a distant class-room. In front of them he could make out the profile of an elephant, its head almost touching the ornate roof, from which carved lions looked down. A queue of worshippers was waiting to be blessed by the animal. In return for a banana, bought from the elephant's *mahout*, it would raise its trunk and touch their heads.

Before they had entered the temple complex, the CIA officer from Chennai had given Meena an update, in between shooting a tourist video of devotees queuing up to smash coconuts before entering the temple.

'It's kind of quaint, isn't it?' he had said. 'Signifies leaving one's identity behind.'

Marchant wasn't sure if the American was playing his legend or being himself. He showed them a video he had shot earlier of a Russian behaving erratically outside the east entrance. Marchant recognised the tall figure as Valentin.

They walked further inside the temple complex, the light fading until all Marchant could see were pillared halls and corridors disappearing off into the darkness in all directions. In every corner there seemed to be small shrines to Hindu deities, like tiny puppet theatres, the gods visible deep within dark recesses, their bright colours lit by flickering oil candles. Stone sculptures of animals with lions' bodies and elephants' heads reared out of the shadows. A man wearing only a *lunghi* around his waist was lying prostrate, hands in prayer above his head, in front of a statue of Ganesh. They stepped around him and walked on, passing briefly through a courtyard where three camels were tethered. All around them, Hindu prayers were being chanted over a loudspeaker system, the priests' voices distorting at full volume.

'I told you it's another world,' Meena said, stopping beside a pillar encrusted with what seemed like centuries of crumbling red turmeric powder and candle wax. 'This is Lakshmi, my goddess,' she added, looking at an idol of a benign woman with four arms. Its surface was also streaked with yellows and reds, and weathered by generations of worship. 'The goddess of wealth and fortune, courage and wisdom.'

'And beauty,' Marchant added, looking at the lotus flower the goddess was sitting on. He thought back to the Lotus Temple in Delhi, where Leila had been killed. Her lips had still been warm as she had lain lifeless in his arms, her hair sticky with blood. He watched Meena daub some red on her forehead and bow in front of the statue. For a moment, she seemed genuinely at peace. Then she turned to a man standing behind a trestle table beside the idol. On it were tumbling garlands of white jasmine, coconuts and pyramids of turmeric. She gave him a few rupees and picked up a garland. At the same time, they exchanged a few words, too quietly for Marchant or anyone else to hear. Then she placed the fragrant flowers around Lakshmi's neck, turned back to the table and dabbed her finger in the turmeric.

'Come on, Indian boy,' she said, smudging a *tilak* on Marchant's forehead and walking on. 'She's here.'

A moment later, she pulled him back from the main thoroughfare, just as a white cow came running out of the shadows, draped in a gold-embroidered cloak and accompanied by two breathless temple priests. The tips of the cow's horns had been painted red and green, and two drums had been strapped to its back, one on either side. The priests, chests bare and glistening with oil, were beating the drums, accompanied by the jangling silver bells that swung from the cow's neck.

After the cow had gone, Marchant and Meena headed towards Shiva's shrine, walking through a thriving market of brightly lit shops selling souvenirs and incense that hung heavily in the air. Further on, they passed the Golden Lotus Pond, a bathing pool on the stepped sides of which pilgrims and worshippers washed and chatted. Marchant was alert now, his senses heightened, on the lookout for other agencies. Because Meena was leading the operation to find Dhar's mother, he had been momentarily entranced by the temple's sights and sounds, let them carry him back to his childhood in Delhi.

Their plan was a simple one. If Meena's colleagues were right, Dhar's mother, Shushma, was selling devotional candles in the hall outside the Shrine of Lord Sundareswarar, Shiva himself. She had been there for the past two days, making the small clay pots at night and filling them with *ghee*, or clarified butter, and wicks during the day. The CIA had not wanted to alert the Indian authorities to her whereabouts, preferring to interview her in the West, so Meena could not call on local police support. And the temple surrounds made it impossible to seize her against her will, even if she was sedated. Instead, the operation would be low-key and discreet, not words Langley was familiar with; but this was Meena's job, and she had insisted on it.

Marchant would strike up a conversation with Shushma in his rusty Hindi, explaining who he was and that she was in danger. Better to come with him back to Britain, where waterboarding was still off the menu, than be seized by the CIA. After he had walked her out of the temple complex, they would drive her to a disused airfield east of Madurai where Meena had arranged for a plane to take her to the UK.

It was a risk, but there weren't many options. Legoland's profilers had given Marchant a brief psychological assessment of Shushma, which he'd read on the plane. Their conclusion was that she was on her own, abandoned by her husband and wanted by the authorities, and that the thought of being protected by

Daniel Marchant, son of the man whom she had once loved and who had financially supported her, would prove sufficiently comforting for her to cooperate.

Marchant wasn't so sure as he passed a small statue of Hanuman the monkey god – covered in *ghee* and worn smooth with endless touching – and then turned into the hall that led to Shiva's shrine. Ahead of him was an imposing icon of Nandi, Shiva's bull. As a non-Hindu, this was as far as he was allowed to go. Several foreign tourists had entered the hall at the same time as him, one of them peering into the shrine to try to get a glimpse of the holy *shivalingam* that lay within. Out of the corner of his eye he spotted another foreigner moving away in the darkness, disappearing beyond a statue that he recognised as Nataraja, Shiva as lord of the dance. His father had always kept a small bronze one beside his bed.

Marchant looked again at where the foreigner had been standing, and saw that Meena had clocked him too. She nodded in the direction of the shrine entrance and then moved towards Nataraja. The deal was that he would focus on Shushma while she dealt with any outside interest. He joined a queue of people waiting to collect their *ghee* candles and enter the shrine. It wasn't easy in the darkness, but he caught a glimpse of the woman who was handing out the candles to the devotees. She had shaved her head and was wearing a threadbare *kurta*. Outside the temple complex she could have been mistaken for a beggar.

As he drew near to the front of the queue, Marchant glanced behind him, but he couldn't see Meena. He was on his own, just how he preferred it. As far as he could tell, the people around him needn't give him any cause for alarm. His only worry was the priest up ahead at the shrine entrance. The chatty couple in front had travelled from Bangalore, and the extended family immediately behind him were from Chennai. Both had expressed their friendly concern that he wouldn't be permitted to enter the shrine for *darshan*.

'The priests, they are very strict about this sort of thing, you know,' the man from Bangalore had said. But Marchant had reassured them, explaining that he was just there for the atmosphere. In the darkness, he had calculated that he wouldn't be turned away before he reached Shushma.

Suddenly he was at the front of the queue, standing before her. They exchanged eye contact, and he could already see surprise in Shushma's eyes, which was just what he wanted. She glanced across at the priest, who was wearing a white *lunghi* bordered with green and gold, and a sacred thread slung diagonally across his bare chest. He was too busy with a big party of devotees to have noticed a foreigner apparently trying to talk his way into the shrine.

'Sorry, Hindus only,' Shushma said, in surprisingly good English. He remembered that she had worked at the British High Commission for a year. He studied her for a moment, tracing her features, thinking that his father had once looked into the same big eyes. She was undeniably beautiful. Marchant's mother had never been a big influence in his life. If she had, he imagined he would feel some hostility towards the woman who had slept with his father and was standing before him now. Instead, he felt only warmth. And pity. Her small features had a filigree fragility about them.

'You need to come with me, now,' he said quietly. 'Your life is in danger.' Shushma dropped the candle she was holding. The yellow *ghee* spread out across the table. 'Don't be alarmed, please. I'm here to help you. Look at me.'

She fumbled with the spilt candle and slowly raised her eyes.

'Who are you?' she asked. Was there a flicker of recognition? Marchant detected a growing restlessness in the queue behind him.

'I'm not with the police,' he said quietly. 'I'm Daniel, Stephen Marchant's son.'

226

# 58

Meena moved quickly back through the hall, following the foreigner at a safe distance. He looked Russian to her. Something about his manner, the tan socks on his shoeless feet. When he passed the Golden Lotus Pond, he broke into the open and pulled out a mobile phone. Meena dropped back and did the same, calling her CIA colleague who was still stationed outside the east gate.

'We're bringing her out in five,' she said.

'Your taxi's waiting,' he replied.

'And we've got company,' she added.

She hung up and rang her colleague at the Lakshmi idol. The signal was faint, but he heard enough to make his way quickly towards the Golden Lotus Pond, picking up another colleague, who was posing as a market-stall seller, along the way. They knew what to do. Delay the Russian for as long as possible, accuse him of taking photos without a camera ticket. Anything. Just play up the paperwork, Meena had told them.

'How can I trust you?' Shushma asked, glancing around her again, but Marchant sensed that she already believed he was who he said he was.

'My father used to keep a Nataraja on his bedside table in Delhi,' he said. She looked at the icon across the hall, and then back at Marchant. It was a gamble. He didn't know where his father and Shushma had made love, where they had conceived Dhar, but there was a chance it had been in his parents' bedroom in Delhi.

Shushma stared at him, this time tracing his features, recognising in them the man she had once loved.

'I have been in danger most of my life.'

'The Americans want to ask you some questions. We'd rather you talk to us, in London.'

'I don't know where my son is,' she said. 'If that's what you want.'

'I'm sure you have no idea. But the Americans won't believe you. Trust me, I know. Please, we have to go. The east entrance.'

Shushma paused for a moment and then went over to talk to another female temple worker, who was lifting candles out of boxes in the shadows. After a brief exchange, the woman came up to the table and began to hand out candles to the devotees who had grown increasingly agitated in the queue. Shushma said something to her in Hindi, touched her forearm and then made her way out of the hall, followed a few yards behind by Marchant.

# 59

Marchant saw Meena up ahead and drew alongside Shushma, who was walking swiftly, her small feet barely lifting off the ground.

'This is Lakshmi, she's with us,' he told her as Meena approached. 'You can trust her.'

Meena stopped, expecting them to slow up. But Shushma kept moving, head down, as if she was trying to shut out the world, an approach to life that Marchant reckoned didn't look too out of place in a temple.

'A car's waiting for us outside,' Meena said, catching up with them. She turned to Marchant with raised eyebrows. Hadn't she expected him to close the deal, to appear with Shushma?

'She's American,' Shushma said quietly, still walking fast.

'Don't worry,' Marchant said. 'We're going to London. I promise.'

'Please, relax,' Meena said, speaking in fluent Hindi and slipping an arm through Shushma's. For a moment, she resisted, but after glancing at Marchant, who managed a smile, she let Meena's arm stay interlocked with hers. 'We're here to help you,' Meena added.

Satisfied that Shushma was in safe hands, Marchant looked back down the crowded colonnade. Again he thought he saw someone slipping away, disappearing behind the pillars. He was certain it was Valentin.

'I thought your people were taking care of the Russian,' he said.

'They were. Why?'

'He's behind us. I'll catch you up.'

'Daniel, we need to get her out,' Meena said, a sudden urgency in her voice.

'You don't know this man. Get her into the car. I'll find you.'

Before Meena could protest further, Marchant had peeled away and was heading back down the colonnade. He knew it wasn't part of the plan – Meena was meant to neutralise any threats – but Valentin wasn't going away. He should have pushed him under the train.

# 60

The tall Russian was moving fast through the devotees now, walking towards the Hall of a Thousand Pillars in the west corner of the complex. It was one of the temple's main tourist attractions, a sixteenth-century architectural marvel, according to Meena. She had talked about it on the flight, explaining with a smile that there were in fact only 985 pillars. It reminded Marchant of a round of golf his father had told him he once played at the Bolgatty Palace in Kochi harbour, southern India: nine holes, but only six tees.

Marchant hung back behind a pillar to watch Valentin, trying to establish what he was doing. The Russian showed a ticket and entered the hall, glancing in his direction before he disappeared out of sight. Marchant was confident that he hadn't been seen. Was he meeting someone? Hoping to draw him away from the others? Marchant knew he should have stayed with Meena and Shushma, but it wasn't tradecraft that was driving him now. The Russians – Valentin, Primakov – were too closely associated in his mind with something he never wanted to accept. They represented all that he despised about himself, about his father: the potential in everyone to betray.

He paid for a ticket and entered. Ahead of him was a low-ceilinged hall supported by row upon row of carved pillars. It was about to close for the day and was almost deserted, but there was no sign of Valentin. He walked forward, keeping close to the pillars and looking down the lines as they stretched away from him. He thought he saw a movement to his right, in the far corner, and headed towards it. But by the time he reached it there was no one there.

Then he spotted him, at the end of another row of pillars. The hall was also a gallery, and Valentin seemed to be studying a glass display cabinet of some kind. Marchant moved quickly, his bare feet silent on the cold floor. He stopped behind a pillar, four feet from Valentin, who still had his back to him. Marchant watched for a moment, wondering whether to strike from behind or get him to turn first. It seemed less cowardly. But then Valentin glanced at his watch and looked around, making up Marchant's mind for him.

He hit out hard and instantly, knocking the Russian to the ground. *His father was no traitor.* Without hesitating, Marchant fell on him and struck again and again, ignoring the voices, Valentin's, his own, others'.

'Stop, please,' someone was repeating behind him.

Marchant stood up, wiping his mouth, and backed away from Valentin, who lay bloodied and unconscious on the floor. It had felt good, too good.

# 61

The sun was setting, but it was still bright outside compared to the gloom they had left behind in the temple complex. Meena was surprised by Marchant's behaviour. He had been disciplined in Marrakech, which had impressed her. She was also concerned about her two colleagues inside the temple. They were meant to have delayed the Russian, kept him away from the exits. She knew mobile reception was patchy inside the complex, but neither was answering his phone.

Cars weren't allowed up to the east gate, so Meena had agreed to bring Shushma to the end of the closed-off street immediately opposite the entrance. It was a walk of about two hundred yards. She glanced up and down the road. A parked car had already caught her eye. Someone was sitting in the driver's seat, but she couldn't see their face. There was no time to collect her shoes.

She kept walking, her arm still linked through Shushma's. The older woman had remained silent since Marchant had left them. Meena thought again about her conversation with Fielding at Heathrow. She trusted him, but it didn't make what was about to happen any easier, particularly after her chat with Marchant at his London flat. King Shahryar would continue to distrust his wives.

At the end of the road, beyond a barrier, a white Ambassador had pulled up. Meena and Shushma climbed into the back. Meena glanced again at the car down the street.

'Where's your British friend?' the driver asked, dropping his tourist manner.

'We must leave without him. Let's go, *challo*.' Shushma looked up and felt Meena's arm tighten around her own.

# 62

Marchant brushed off the member of the temple staff who was attempting to hold him. He glanced down at the Russian. His eyes were closed and swollen, but he was trying to open them. Marchant turned and fled the hall, pushing away another temple worker who had heard the disturbance.

He thought he was heading straight for the east exit, but found himself in an open courtyard. A group of elderly priests, naked to the waist, were sitting on the ground in a circle, talking quietly as they ate food from stainless-steel tiffin boxes. One of them – bushy grey chest hair, forehead streaked with vermilion – was speaking on a mobile phone. He glanced up at Marchant and then looked away. Marchant asked one of the other priests for directions to the east gate and then set off again, walking fast.

He knew the authorities would soon be looking for him, and his heart sank as he turned the corner and saw a group of four policemen running down the corridor. But something about their manner made him hold his nerve. They hadn't reacted when he came into view, and were now turning off the main corridor. He glanced after them and saw a crowd gathered around the edge of the Golden Lotus Pond. Two bodies were lying still on the stone floor, surrounded by devotees. Marchant couldn't be sure, but one of them looked like the CIA officer Meena had met at the Lakshmi idol. Clearly, Valentin had been busy.

It took him longer to get out of the labyrinthine temple than he had intended, so he wasn't surprised when he didn't see Meena or a car in the street outside. He looked up and down the road and then walked over to the barrier, where Meena had arranged for them to be picked up by her redneck tourist friend. No one was about. He went to retrieve his footwear, watching the man take his ticket and turn to a row of hundreds of shoes. A moment later, he was holding two pairs, his and Meena's. He hesitated and then took both, slipping into his own and walking away with Meena's in his hand.

Meena had had no time to collect her shoes. Someone other than Valentin must have been outside. He glanced up and down the street, looking for a taxi, and then his mobile phone rang.

'It's me. Sorry,' Meena said. 'Where are you?'

'Waiting for you to pick me up outside the temple, as agreed.'

'We had to go. Head for the airfield. Call me when you get near.'

She had briefed him earlier. The airfield was near Karaikudi, outside a small village called Kanadukathan, and had fallen into disrepair. In the Second World War, the Allies had used it as a base for Flying Fortresses targeting Malaya and Singapore. It was also the place where Meena's legend was meant to be heading for her family wedding. She was thorough, Marchant couldn't fault her on that.

Half an hour later, he was out of Madurai and heading east through remote countryside in a taxi with a dodgy horn. To begin with, he had assumed that his driver was simply more eager than usual in his use of it, knowing that in India the horn was like a friendly nod of the head, but it was definitely broken, staying jammed on for ten seconds every time he deployed it.

'Sir, I will manage it, don't worry.' The driver grinned in the rear-view mirror.

Not using the horn would be a good start, Marchant thought,

but he knew that would be impossible. He tried to cut out the noise and take in the scenery. The reddish earth was barren and unfarmed, flat and dotted with sparse bushes. In the distance, he could see an outcrop of rock that had had its top sliced off. Earlier, he had passed rainbow-painted trucks carrying quarried rocks back to Madurai.

'Sir, are you knowing about the tourism business?' the driver asked, in between sustained blasts of the horn, which was beginning to grow hoarse. 'I have a good friend –'

'No, I'm afraid not,' Marchant interrupted.

'Cement sector?'

'No. Can we go a bit quicker? Faster?' It was not something he had ever thought he would ask on Indian roads, but he was worried that Meena hadn't rung again. He had tried to call but her phone was switched off.

'No problem. Isuzu engine.'

The taxi might have had Japanese technology under the bonnet, but its Indian suspension had long since gone. Marchant found the discomfort oddly reassuring, taking him back to his childhood, driving out of Delhi on a Friday night, the bright lights of the lorries roaring past, waking up at a remote Rajasthani fort. Then he thought of Sebbie and felt a ball tighten in his stomach. It shocked him how much he still missed his twin brother. He stared out of the window at the scenes of rural-roadside life: a woman shaking the coals out of her iron, a threshing machine, schoolchildren cycling home on oversized bikes, their long legs languid in the heat.

'Sir, am I boring you?' the taxi driver asked, his face in the mirror now long with concern.

'Not at all. I'm sorry,' Marchant said, feeling guilty. 'Please, tell me about the cement sector.'

# 63

Meena's car turned off the dusty road into what at first looked like scrubland. The area was completely flat, covered in green bushes. Peacocks were strutting about, picking at the dry ground, the green sheen of their feathers glinting in the dying light of the day. She knew the airfield was disused, but she had expected a little more infrastructure. In the distance there were a few low buildings, derelict and overgrown. The control tower had long since been demolished. Towards the far perimeter, near a group of trees, a team of local women were loading long logs into stacks and covering them with tarpaulins. Beside the piles of wood someone had laid out cow dung to dry.

Meena left Shushma in the car and walked out into the open expanse. Beneath the vegetation the ground was concrete, but it had broken up over the years, and she wondered if a plane would still be able to land there. As she walked out across the wide expanse, she could see where the main runway had been. It was in better condition than the rest of the airfield's surface. She had been told that a local flying club had been campaigning for years for it to be reopened, and it looked as if volunteers had cleared away some of the vegetation.

She glanced at her watch and stared up into the dusk sky. There was no sign of a plane. If it didn't come before nightfall, the operation would be abandoned. A night-time landing was out of the question without any airport lights. She didn't know whether Delhi was onside or not about the flight, but that wasn't her problem. She looked again at her watch. A part of her hoped that Marchant would turn up after they had gone, but she owed him an explanation. She turned on her phone and dialled.

'Where are you?' she asked.

'Ten minutes away,' Marchant said. 'I've been trying to call.'

'There's a change of plan.'

'What sort of change?'

'I'll explain when you get here.'

She hung up and walked over towards the car, fighting back a tear.

Marchant saw the plane coming in low over the scrubland. He was still two minutes away, and urged his driver to hurry up. Events were spiralling out of his control. Meena's tone worried him. Nobody was being straight with anyone. He cursed himself again for going after Valentin, but he had felt better for it.

Marchant asked the driver to drop him off at the edge of the airfield. He ran across the broken surface, watching the plane turn slowly on the old runway, scattering peacocks. It was a Gulfstream V, the CIA's preferred choice for renditions after 9/11, the plane Spiro had used to fly him out of Britain the previous year. It had taken him to an old Russian airfield outside Syzmany in northern Poland, where they had waterboarded him. He shut out the thought as he approached Meena. Shushma was standing beside her, their arms too close.

'Glad you made it,' Meena said, glancing at the plane, which had now drawn up a few feet behind them. The noise of the jet engines made it necessary to speak loudly to be heard. Shushma was not happy, staring at the ground, trying to cut out the world again, or just in shock.

'Are you?' Marchant asked.

'It was your call to go after the Russian,' Meena said. 'The operation was compromised. I had no choice.'

'And if I hadn't?'

'There was another Russian on our tail, but we lost him. I know how to look after myself, Dan.'

'And her, I see,' he said, nodding at Shushma's wrist. It was joined to Meena's with handcuffs. 'Comforting.'

'They're a precaution.'

'I gave my word we'd take care of her, not treat her as an enemy combatant.'

They both heard the noise of the plane's door opening behind them. Meena turned around to look, and then faced Marchant again.

'Daniel, I told you, there's been a change.'

He detected something dancing in her eyes, but he couldn't be certain what it was any more: loyalty and deceit had begun to look the same in recent months. Then he glanced up at the open door behind her and saw James Spiro filling the frame, a gun in his hand.

'We need to get out of this hellhole,' he drawled.

'I'm sorry,' Meena whispered, still looking at Marchant.

'You knew?' Marchant said, glancing at Spiro again, trying to process the implications.

'Ask Fielding,' she replied, turning towards the plane. Shushma followed, pulled along by her wrist. Then she stopped and faced Marchant. For a moment, he thought she was going to say something, but instead she spat in his face and walked on.

'Fielding?' Marchant said, wiping the saliva off his cheek. He couldn't blame her.

'Send my love to the Vicar,' Spiro called out. 'And hey, thanks. We couldn't have got our hands on this piece of brown shit without you.'

Marchant wanted to run at the plane, pull Spiro down onto the Indian dirt, but there was nothing he could do, not while the American was armed. He thought about Fielding, who had sanctioned the change of plan without telling him, and wanted to drag him into the dirt too. Dhar's mother was meant to be flown back to the UK. Now she was heading to Bagram, or worse, with Spiro. A deal had been done. He knew he should never have believed in Meena, but this had been brokered far above her head. She was irrelevant. Why would his own Chief let Salim Dhar's mother – the only lead the West had – fall into Spiro's heavy hands? It didn't make any sense.

He watched helplessly as the plane taxied down the decrepit runway, shimmering in the heat as peacocks ran in all directions. It turned and then accelerated, lifting up into the evening sky. As it passed him, he picked up a rock and hurled it at the fuselage. On the far side of the airfield, the female workers were watching too, one of them transfixed by the mad *ghora*, a load of logs still balanced on her head. Marchant started to walk back towards his car, kicking at the dust, thinking fast what he could do, who he should ring. Fielding wouldn't take his call, but he wanted to challenge him, make sure his anger was logged by the duty officer in Legoland.

He started to dial London, and then stopped. Up ahead, a black car turned off the dusty road and drove towards him, bumping across the concrete. Marchant stood back as it drew up beside him, a darkened rear window lowering.

'Your American friends were in a hurry to leave,' a voice said. It was Nikolai Primakov.

# 64

Monika had always been relaxed about sex, ever since her first encounter, as a sixteen-year-old, with an English tutor who was five years her senior. It was something that came easily to her, which was a relief, as she was struggling at the time with other areas of her life. Her mother, a teacher, was desperate for her to achieve academic success and study at the University of Warsaw. Her father, a lecturer, had died when she was younger. She was bright, top of her class in languages, but she had no siblings, and life at home as a teenager with her mother could be claustrophobic, until she discovered sex and the freedom it gave her.

But she hadn't enjoyed sleeping with Hugo Prentice, who was lying next to her now. It wasn't his habit of smoking before they made love – she wasn't averse to kicking things off with a joint. And she wasn't upset that she was doing it for work rather than pleasure. She knew when she signed up to the AW that her job would occasionally require it, and in this case there had been a redeeming motive. What had cast a shadow over the sex was an encrypted text message that had come through from General Borowski. She had ignored her phone beside the bed, even though the unique alert tone indicated that it was her boss in Warsaw.

'Work can wait,' she had said, easing herself on top of him.

It hadn't been easy – Borowski only made contact when it was serious – but she didn't want to arouse Prentice's suspicions.

Now that he was asleep, she peeled away from his heavy limbs and dressed. Watching him all the time, she went to his bathroom, where evidence of Prentice's single life was everywhere. The small room wasn't unhygienic, but it wasn't clean either. The old iron bath had greenish stains where the brass taps dripped, and the sink hadn't been cleaned after his morning ablutions. A wooden-handled shaving brush lay between the taps, still covered in lather, and the lid hadn't been put back on a pot of hair-styling wax.

But none of this bothered her. It was his London pad, and he had been living in Warsaw for the past two years. What worried her was Borowski. She looked at the text again and then replied with a blank message, the agreed protocol. Moving fast, she removed the back of her phone and took out the SIM card, replacing it with another she kept in her purse. It had never been used before. She looked in again on Prentice as the phone rebooted, peering through a gap in the bathroom door. He seemed to stir, scratching himself before going back to sleep. Seconds later, a new message had appeared on the screen.

Monika stared at the words, barely able to believe what she was reading. Then she bent double over the lavatory and threw up.

# 65

'Tell me something,' Primakov said. 'What ever made you think you could trust them? After all they've done to you?'

'I put my faith in the Vicar,' Marchant said.

'A mistake your father never made.'

They were driving back towards Madurai in Primakov's car. A thick glass partition divided them from the front, where a Russian driver sat without expression. It was evident that he couldn't hear their conversation. Marchant wasn't surprised that Primakov had turned up at the airport. More worrying was his lack of concern that Dhar's mother was now in US custody. Marchant had told him the whole story: Fielding's assurances about Lakshmi Meena, how the CIA had agreed for Shushma to be taken to the UK. Primakov had been particularly interested in Fielding's role, asking Marchant to repeat exactly what he had said. Marchant had been happy to tell him. He no longer knew where his own loyalties lay, let alone Primakov's.

'Did you know that she was working at the temple?' Marchant asked.

'Of course.'

'Why didn't you do more to stop the Americans from taking her?'

'Like you, we had heard she was bound for Britain. I was also a little under strength. Valentin is in the Apollo hospital.'

Marchant didn't believe him. Moscow could have drawn on more resources to stop Shushma's departure. But for some reason they hadn't.

'Her son won't be happy,' Marchant said, trying to steer the conversation towards Dhar. The only thing he knew for certain was that he needed to see him, discuss their father man to man, brother to brother. Primakov had avoided referring directly to Dhar before, but it would be hard not to now.

'It will confirm his worst fears about the West,' Primakov said.

And then Marchant began to see things more clearly. Primakov hadn't flown to Madurai to prevent Shushma's exfiltration: he wanted to be sure that she was taken. It was the one act that could be guaranteed to get under Dhar's skin. Whatever the Russians had planned for him, it suited them if Dhar's blood was up.

'A son will do anything for his mother,' Marchant offered.

'Rage is important. It can persuade others to take you seriously. People who had their doubts.'

For the first time, Primakov looked at Marchant with something approaching knowingness in his moist eyes. Was it a sign at last? A part of Marchant no longer believed Fielding's reassurances about Primakov's loyalty to London. The Russian wouldn't give him anything because there was nothing to give. His brief was simply to keep the *jihadi* fires stoked in Dhar's belly, and to persuade Marchant to help his half-brother. There was no hidden agenda, no resurrection of old family ties, no belated clemency for his father. But somewhere inside him, Marchant still hoped he was wrong.

'Are you angry, too?' Primakov asked.

'Wouldn't you be? I promised Shushma I'd look after her, only to see her renditioned in front of me by James fucking Spiro.'

Even as Marchant spat out the expletive, a sickening feeling had started to spread: a realisation that he had been manipulated, that actions he thought were his own had actually been controlled by others. *Rage is important. It can persuade others to take you seriously. People who had their doubts.* He was the one raging now, against Fielding, Meena, Spiro, the West. And it would be music to Moscow's ears.

He closed his eyes. Christ, Fielding could be a cold bastard.

# 66

Even Marcus Fielding, working late, was surprised by the swiftness of Moscow Centre's response. GCHQ's sub-station at Bude in Cornwall had intercepted a call from Primakov to Vasilli Grushko, the London *Rezident*, within half an hour of Lakshmi Meena's departure from a remote airfield outside Madurai. Fielding played the recording again. Primakov spoke first, then Grushko.

*'He has been humiliated, which is always a good moment to strike.'*

*'And by his own side. Fielding is more heartless than I gave him credit for.'*

*'I can only assume that he wanted to win favour with Langley. By giving them Salim Dhar's mother, MI6 has gone some way to restoring a relationship they cannot live without for ever.'*

*'Where is Marchant now?'*

*'I dropped him off at a village. There was a wedding. He wanted some time on his own.'*

*'And has he agreed to help us?'*

*'Of course.'*

*'Then there is no time to waste. He must meet Dhar.'*

Fielding sat back, poured himself a glass of Lebanese wine and turned on a Bach cantata. It was a rare moment of triumph. Oleg, asleep in the corner, looked up briefly, sensing the change in mood.

There was no longer any talk of dangles, no equivocation in Grushko's voice. Fielding's only headache was Marchant. It hadn't been an easy decision to call on Spiro's services, let alone Lakshmi Meena's, but it was the only way to provoke Marchant. He wouldn't want to talk to his Chief, not for a while, which was why he had sent Prentice to pick him up from the airport, take him out for a meal in town, suck some venom from his wounded pride.

Fielding had told Prentice only the bare essentials of the operation to lift Dhar's mother. He wouldn't have expected to be given any detail. Need-to-know was a way of life for both of them. Prentice was unaware of Marchant's ongoing attempt to be recruited by Primakov, given that it was linked to the Russian's highly classified past. All he knew was that there had been a change of plan in Madurai, and that Marchant would be upset.

'We had to screw him,' Fielding had explained. 'You know how it is.'

Marchant would be astute enough to work out what had happened, why Fielding had been forced to intervene, pull the strings, but he would still be angry. He could let off steam with Prentice, have a moan about means and ends and Machiavellian bosses.

After he had calmed down, Fielding would have one last talk with him. Then he would be on his own, free to go off the rails, not turn up for work, drink too much. Marchant had form when it came to falling apart. In the months before he had left for Marrakech he had been a mess. And the Russians would lap it up, reassured that he was ready to be turned. Only then would it be time for him to meet Dhar. He owed it to Marchant to prepare him properly, let him genuinely feel what it was like to hate the West. Dhar would detect a false note at a thousand yards.

It was as he poured himself a second glass of wine that another encrypted audio file from GCHQ dropped into his inbox.

# 67

Marchant had asked Primakov to drop him off in the centre of Kanadukathan, about ten minutes from the airfield. It was a small village, and Marchant would have described it as poor if it hadn't been for the vast deserted mansions that dominated the dusty lanes. Meena had talked about them in Madurai. They were the ancestral homes of the Chettiars, a once-wealthy community of money-lenders, merchants and jewellery dealers who had fallen on hard times since the end of the Raj. Used now for storing dowry gifts, the mansions only came alive for family weddings, when the Chettiar diaspora would descend from around the world and fill the pillared courtyards with music and laughter.

Marchant strolled around the village square. The ground was covered in a confetti of paper and cardboard, the remains of exploded firecrackers. He could hear a wedding party in the distance, and wondered if one of Meena's cousins really was getting married. He had seen the celebrations from a distance on the way out to the airfield. It didn't matter either way, but he wanted to know. The world of lies and legends had lost its appeal after the scene with Spiro, and he needed to be reassured by something tangible, real.

He thought again about what had happened with Dhar's mother. It was clearer now, painfully clear. Fielding hadn't trusted him to betray, didn't think he had it in him to persuade the Russians of his treachery. So he had given Marchant a helping hand, asked Spiro to humiliate him in front of Primakov. The American wouldn't have needed much persuading.

'Are you angry enough to meet your brother?' Primakov had asked as he stepped out of the car. Did the Russian suspect what game Fielding was playing? That Marchant's rage had been conceived five thousand miles away in Legoland?

'I'd like to see him, yes,' Marchant had said.

'And he'd like to see you. But first I want you to do something for me. For Russia. Then we will get you out of Britain.'

Marchant walked around the corner towards the mansion where the wedding was taking place. A crowd had spilled out onto the road beneath loops of bunting that had been strung between tangled telegraph poles. Two women were walking towards him, arm in arm, their bright carmine saris illuminating the dusk. The one on the left reminded him of Meena, the same lambent eyes, the subtle sashay of hips. A stray pie dog lingered in the shadows.

'Can you help me?' Marchant asked her, ignoring the field agent's normal caveats. He was drawing attention to himself in a place where he was already a curiosity.

'We'll try,' she said, masking a giggle with her hand.

'I had a friend who was meant to be here today.' He nodded at the house behind them. 'Over from the States. Lakshmi Meena. You don't happen to know her, do you?'

'Sure. She's my friend's cousin. It's such a shame. Lakshmi was meant to be here, but she got held up in Madurai.'

'Thank you,' Marchant said. He felt stronger already, as if the world had been veering off its axis and was now spinning true again. He realised, as he walked on, how much he wanted to believe in Meena, believe that she wasn't another Leila. He was no longer sure he could face a life of trusting no one. Meena was beautiful, there was no point denying it, but it was his sympathy rather than his love that she kept asking of him. She had claimed that she had tried to stop Aziz in Morocco, then admitted that she could have done more. The appearance of Spiro at the airfield appeared to have pained her, but she had still boarded the flight.

He stopped, and turned back to the square, where he had seen a taxi waiting, and thought about Primakov's request. He was certain it was a test. If he was caught, the consequences would be serious. Should he run it past Fielding? Or was he now expected to play the traitor's game alone?

# 68

Monika had always thought she would be able to do it herself, that she owed it to her brother, but she couldn't. She hoped he would understand. She had the money in cash, £20,000 withdrawn from an emergency AW fund in London that was meant to be used for bribing disillusioned SVR agents.

As she stood outside a snooker hall in Haringey, north London, waiting for her contact to arrive, she wondered if she had any energy left to hide her tracks, to invent a cover story for the money. To begin with, she had resigned herself to being caught. She had imagined standing over him, waiting calmly for the police to arrive, but she couldn't do that either. Her survival instincts, honed in the field, were too strong. So she had contracted out her revenge instead.

She was spoilt for choice in London, but had settled on a Turkish gang with a proven record and an obsession with forensics. They had never been caught, and they asked for more when she told them the West End venue.

'It's very public.'

'Good. I want everyone to know.'

General Borowski would certainly know, but at least this way there was a chance of protecting herself afterwards, providing the political will was there. She was in his hands now.

# 69

Dhar listened in silence as Primakov told him about his mother's rendition. He knew that anger was a weakness, but it took all of his strength to remain calm and listen. The only outward sign of distress was a twitch in his lower left eyelid.

'This Spiro is the bane of many brothers' lives,' Dhar said. He was sitting upright, his hands flat on the table in front of him, on either side of a glass of water. They were talking in the hangar at Kotlas. Outside, it was raining again, rattling the metal roof.

'He was the one who waterboarded Daniel Marchant.'

Dhar tried not to think where the Americans would take his mother, how she would cope.

Reaching for the glass of water, he watched Primakov walk over to the window and look outside. Sergei was right. There was something about the Russian – other than the mix of cologne and garlic – that made Dhar wary. But he had no option but to work with him. He had come straight from seeing Marchant in India.

'If it's any consolation, your British half-brother is distraught,' Primakov said, turning back to face him. 'He gave your mother his personal word that she would be taken to London. If Spiro hadn't been armed, Marchant would have killed him.'

'He is ready to help us, then?' Dhar asked, happy to move the conversation away from his mother.

'Marchant could forgive the West once. But now, following your mother's rendition, he is struggling to call Britain his home.'

Dhar flinched again at the mention of his mother. He closed his eyes, trying to calm the twitch, control the body with the mind.

'We need to be sure,' he said, raising a reluctant hand to steady his eyelid. It was too much. 'Rendition' and 'mother' were words he never wanted to hear together again. 'After all that happened to Marchant before, he still went back to work for the infidel.'

'He wants to meet you. I have told him everything about your father, how I recruited him in Delhi, his twenty years of service to Moscow.'

'How did he react?'

'Like you, I think he suspected already. There was relief in his eyes. Let us see. He must pass one final test before he joins us.'

# 70

'I thought I should drive to Heathrow, pick Daniel up,' Ian Denton said, standing in front of Marcus Fielding's desk. Fielding was lying on the floor behind it, partly out of sight, trying to relax after another back spasm. 'He must be pretty cut up after what happened in Madurai.'

'It's OK,' Fielding said. 'I've just sent Prentice. With orders to get Marchant drunk. Look out for him when he's back in the office, though. He'll have no desire to talk to me.'

Fielding was touched by Denton's concern. Despite his cold-blooded demeanour, he had a warm heart. And he had always taken an interest in Marchant's welfare.

'Of course.' Denton paused. 'Is everything all right with Daniel?'

'As much as it ever is with him,' Fielding said. He wanted to confide more in his deputy, but he couldn't. Denton's own deep suspicion of the Americans had brought him close to Marchant in recent months, but Fielding knew that the plan to help Marchant defect must remain known only to himself.

'I'll leave it to Prentice, then,' Denton said. 'And look forward to signing off his exorbitant expenses.'

Fielding sometimes wished his deputy would unbutton a little, let things go, but he could never remember an occasion when Denton had got drunk. After he had left, Fielding unzipped the second encrypted audio file from GCHQ and listened, reading the covering note from his opposite number at Cheltenham. Grushko again, this time talking to an unnamed colleague in Moscow Centre. It had been recorded a few hours earlier.

*'I still have my doubts.'*

*'About Marchant?'*

*'About everyone. Marchant, Comrade Primakov.'*

*'The Muslim is keen to see his brother.'*

*'I just think we should use him.'*

*'Argo?'*

*'That's what he's there for, isn't it? Moments like these.'*

*'It's a risk. Warsaw is on to him.'*

*'They get on well. Marchant will confide in Argo if he's genuinely upset. He should try to meet him at the airport when he arrives back in Britain.'*

The recording ended suddenly. 'Argo' was an unusual choice, nostalgic. It was the codename the KGB had assigned to Ernest Hemingway in the 1940s. Fielding tried to linger on the historical detail, delay the realisation, the rising nausea, but it was impossible. In one awful moment, he had traced the line of succession, identified the inheritor. He reached for the phone, too heavy in his hand, and dialled General Borowski, head of Agencja Wywiadu, Poland's foreign intelligence agency, at his home on the outskirts of Warsaw.

# 71

'Come on, Daniel. That's what we do. We use people.'

Marchant hadn't been pleased to see Prentice waiting for him at arrivals. It was a sight that was starting to annoy him, particularly as this time Prentice explained that he had been sent as a peace envoy by Fielding. But he was an old family friend, someone he had always found it easy to confide in. His offer of alcohol was welcome, too. Marchant had been drinking on the plane, and was happy to keep going. A bender loomed. Prentice had driven him into central London, and they were now sitting at an outside table at Bentley's Oyster Bar in Swallow Street, off Piccadilly. It was one of Prentice's favourite restaurants.

'Are you using Monika?' Marchant asked, a smile softening the question's harsh undercurrent. Something about their relationship was still bugging him, and he was sure it wasn't jealousy.

'You've got a thing for her, haven't you?' Prentice washed an oyster down with a deep draft of Guinness. 'I can see why. She's a great lay.'

'I'm sorry, Marcus, we should have informed you of our suspicions.'

Usually, Fielding's conversations with General Borowski were upbeat. He was an old-school spy who liked to be taken to the

Traveller's Club for a sharpener whenever he came to London. Now, as they talked, Fielding felt only numbness. There was always the chance in his line of work that the man sitting at the next desk was praying to a different god, but it had still come as an almighty shock. Was this how the happily married felt when they discovered their partner had been cheating all along?

'How long have you known?' Fielding asked, trying not to think back, recalibrate the past, reassess the future.

'We never knew exactly, but the worry has been there for several months. At first, we thought it was someone else.'

'Who?'

'Come on, Marcus. You know there's little point in our game of causing offence unnecessarily. We have the right man now. That's all that matters.'

'And you're confident the codename matches?'

'We picked up "Argo" in an intercept last month.'

Fielding closed his eyes. For the first time in years, he felt he wanted to weep. 'You really should have pooled it. The damage could be irreducible. Ongoing operations jeopardised, entire networks blown.'

'I'm sorry, truly.' Borowski paused. 'There's something else. We put someone onto him as soon as he became our main suspect. Monika is one of our best agents – you may remember she helped Daniel Marchant earlier last year – but I'm worried. Argo has not only betrayed our country, he has caused the death of several colleagues, most recently her brother. She's taken it very personally.'

Marchant ordered another Guinness, his smile now slack with alcohol. Prentice liked to provoke him, and the only response was to join battle.

'I'm surprised you can still eat seafood, after what happened with the sushi at the gallery,' Marchant said.

'It wasn't the food, it was the wine,' Prentice replied.

'And there was I thinking you had a strong head. One glass of red and you were arse over tit.' Marchant paused, thinking back to the evening at the Cork Street gallery. He hadn't seen Prentice since he had collapsed in the corner. It had been unlike him. 'Monika was good to me in Poland, that's all. I wouldn't want her to get hurt.'

'She's a big girl, Dan.'

'Maybe she's using you.'

Prentice looked at Marchant for a moment, his gaze cutting through their drunken banter. Marchant was in no doubt that one of them was using the other. He just wasn't sure why.

'I'm a father figure. She lost hers when she was young. We're in the same business, we lie and cheat for the same noble causes.' Prentice shucked another oyster open with a knife. 'Where's the harm?'

CCTV cameras never pointed exactly where you wanted them, but Fielding could see enough from the intercepted live relay in his office to know that both men were drunk, relaxed, laughing. It couldn't be worse. The reason he had sent Prentice was to re-assure Marchant, give him an opportunity to whinge about MI6 and its methods. And that was exactly what the two of them appeared to be doing. He could only blame himself. They were good friends, even closer after Prentice had rescued Marchant from the CIA's waterboarders in Poland.

Fielding had to move fast. Moscow would be listening to their man, live-streaming every word. It was essential that Marchant played the right music, said nothing that undermined the genuine anger he had displayed in Madurai. If he revealed that it had been fabricated in order to convince the Russians, they would never go near him again. As far as Moscow was concerned, Marchant was ready to defect, not comparing drunken notes with a colleague about an unscrupulous boss. Fielding reached for his mobile phone.

'Talking of lying,' Marchant continued, 'you've known Fielding a lot longer than me. Has he ever double-crossed you?'

'First, he's using you, now it's double-crossing,' Prentice said. 'What mortal sin did our Vicar actually commit?'

Marchant knew Prentice had been told the basics about his trip to India, that he was there to bring back Salim Dhar's mother, but it was still an unusual question to ask another officer. Both of them were steeped in MI6's strict culture of compartmentalisation, Prentice more than anyone. He was one of MI6's longest serving field men, an old friend of his father's and one of Fielding's allies. He should have known better. Marchant decided to keep things general.

'Fielding told me I was to bring the target home, but that was never the plan. She was always heading further west.'

'And our cousins couldn't have renditioned her without your help?'

'That's about it.'

'A premier-league stitch-up. But it's unlike Fielding. Lakshmi Meena?'

'Way over her head.' Marchant suddenly felt protective. He was sure it hadn't been her plan. 'Spiro.'

'What an arsehole. You don't seem too cut up about it all. Fielding said you'd be out the door.'

'Did he?'

Marchant tried to gauge where the conversation was heading, what he could reveal. He wanted to confide in Prentice, confess to him that he had failed to play the traitor. But he knew he couldn't. Prentice had been told nothing of Primakov's past, or of Marchant's efforts to be recruited by him. There was something else bothering him too, a distant nagging that he had learned not to ignore.

'Let's face it,' Prentice continued. 'It wouldn't be the first time you were on the outside.'

But Marchant wasn't listening any more. His phone had buzzed in his pocket, and he glanced at the text. It was from Fielding, and it consisted of only one word: 'Resign.'

He put the phone away and looked at Prentice, smirking. 'Lakshmi Meena. She wants to buy me a peace drink too.'

'Will you accept?'

'I'm not sure.' Marchant sat back, trying to look relaxed as he glanced around the bar. *Resign*. He assumed Moscow must be listening. 'You know, perhaps Fielding's right. I'm finished with all this. I've had enough. I hear what you say, but I'm not prepared to be a part of what happened in India. I gave Dhar's mother my word, for what it's worth. Now Spiro will kill her.'

A moment later, an Italian motorbike was beside their table on the pavement. Marchant had heard its accelerating engine, but assumed it was heading up Piccadilly, not coming down Swallow Street behind him. The next few seconds seemed to slow down, but he knew afterwards that they had passed with the speed of a professional job. There were two people on the bike, both wearing black leathers and helmets with tinted glass. The one on the pillion raised a silenced, long-barrelled revolver and fired twice at Prentice before the bike roared away, narrowly missing a group of pedestrians walking up from Piccadilly.

Marchant had instinctively turned his back as the shots were fired, lifting his legs and arms to protect himself. When he looked up, he saw a woman standing ten feet away, a hand to her mouth.

After what seemed an eternity, she began to scream, a terrible, almost inhuman cry. He turned to look at Prentice, slumped in the metal chair opposite him, his eyes more startled than pained. He had been shot twice in the forehead, two neat entrance wounds beginning to weep thick red tears.

# 72

'It's a bloody mess,' Fielding said, walking through the graveyard of the small Norman church at Coombe Manor. 'Officially, we're mourning the passing of one of the Service's finest officers. Unofficially, we're burying a traitor.'

Marchant looked out on the idyllic English setting, down the valley across fields dusted with poppies. It was the sort of pastoral scene his father had loved: rolling hills dotted with small pubs where eighteenth-century cartoons hung on deep red walls and cool slate floors offered respite from the somnolent heat of summer. At the far end of the valley the land rose steeply to Coombe Gibbet, where a group of cyclists was silhouetted against the blue skyline.

The secluded setting was on the borders of west Berkshire, in a green pocket of Albion that was thick with retired ambassadors and politicians. Many of them had turned out today, their dark suits jarring in the July sunshine as they gathered around the grave. Prentice's younger brother, who worked in the City and lived in the hamlet, had helped to carry the coffin, which was now being lowered into the ground.

'The Polish evidence is strong?' Marchant asked as the two of them dropped back from the main group.

'Incontrovertible. It's just a pity she took matters into her own hands. A debrief would have been helpful.'

Fielding nodded at a small gathering of people under the trees, at the far end of the graveyard. Monika was flanked by two bulky men in suits, one of whom was handcuffed to her. Marchant hadn't seen her inside the church, and assumed that she had just arrived. He would talk to her later, when his own feelings had settled. Prentice was dead, unable to justify himself, explain why he had crossed the divide. He couldn't forgive Monika for that, for ending the treachery but not the confusion. She had denied them all an answer, a taste of the forbidden fruits of defection.

He caught up with Fielding, who was heading over towards Ian Denton, a lean presence in the shade. Marchant knew that the deputy's attendance at the funeral was purely for appearances' sake. Most people assumed he had only turned up to make sure Prentice was dead. Denton had been sympathetic to Marchant, though, acknowledging that he had lost a close friend.

It was more complicated for Fielding. The news of Prentice's betrayal had aged him. Late nights at the Foreign Office defending his officers had left him gaunt and withdrawn. It wasn't just the security implications, it was the personal humiliation. Everyone knew that in Prentice he had finally found someone he could trust. He had dropped his guard. The D-Notice committee had done what it could to limit the media fallout, while Fielding had called in personal favours with security correspondents, but there was little disguising that the Service was reeling. A High Court injunction was out of the question, as national security was not at risk. Just MI6's reputation. I/OPS had set to work planting exaggerated press stories of Prentice's gambling habits, but the damage had been done.

'The one mercy is that Warsaw's not going public,' Fielding said. 'They can't afford to. Hiring gangland hitmen isn't part of the AW's charter. Hugo was in debt. He liked to gamble, owed bad people money. End of story.'

Marchant knew that Prentice had often rolled the dice. Even in death, his cover story was based on truth.

'Were our own networks compromised?'

'We're still checking. Did you manage to tell Prentice that you were resigning?'

Marchant thought back again to the restaurant, a scene his mind was keen to erase. He had relived the details too many times already for the police and MI6's own counter-intelligence officers: the unusual Benelli TNT motorbike, the silence before the screams, as if no one could quite believe what they had seen.

'It was the last thing I said before he was shot.'

'Then there's hope that the Russians still believe in you.'

'You're sure they were listening?'

'Moscow asked Argo to sound you out when you arrived back at the airport. And I bloody sent him.' Fielding shook his head and walked on. 'I'm sorry about Madurai and Spiro, but for a time they had their doubts.'

'And now they don't?'

'Let's hope not.'

'Where is she now? The mother.'

Fielding paused before answering. 'You tell me.'

Marchant stared at him and then turned away. He knew what he was meant to say. 'Bagram.'

The very name made him flinch. The airbase's notorious theatre internment facility was not for the faint-hearted. Up to five hundred enemy combatants could be housed there at any one time. Marchant was sure Shushma was safe, in a secure location somewhere in Britain, not at Bagram, but Fielding wasn't prepared to break the spell, not yet. It was a reminder of what lay ahead, the mindset he needed to adopt if he was to convince Salim Dhar of his treachery.

'And still with Spiro,' Fielding added. 'Don't resign just yet.

You'll be of more use to them in the Service. Dissemble, rebel, fall apart. Remember how you felt in India, how you feel now. They'll be watching.'

Marchant deeply resented the way he was being handled, but no doubt that was the point. It wasn't the time to challenge the Vicar about tactics, his lack of faith in him.

'They've asked me to do something,' Marchant said. 'A final test before they exfiltrate me.'

'Then make sure you pass it. I can't help any more. You're on your own now.'

Fielding was about to move to join the main group in the churchyard, but he hesitated, knowing there was something else that Marchant wanted to ask. They both knew what it was. The wider implications of Prentice's treachery stretched like poison ivy back into the Service's past as well as out across Europe's network of agents.

'Hugo was like family,' Marchant said, watching a red kite wheel in the sky above the church. He felt his eyes begin to moisten, and turned away from the bright sun. 'My father trusted him.' *Trusted a traitor. If Prentice could betray his country, then so could my father, his oldest friend.*

'I know. Use it. Embrace your worst fears. They may be the only thing to keep you alive when you meet Dhar.'

# 73

Primakov's test had sounded relatively straightforward at the time. He had asked Marchant to knock out Britain's early-warning radar system on the north-west coast for two minutes. Within that narrow window, two MiG-35 Russian fighters would penetrate British airspace, travelling just below the speed of sound until they were over land. Then they would turn around and head back towards Russia, leaving Britain's airspace before the radar was up and running again.

After Marchant had made some discreet enquiries, the reality seemed much more complex. The radar network was overseen by the Air Surveillance and Control Systems Force Command (ASACS) at RAF Boulmer in Alnwick, which was stood up in 2006 in belated response to the terrorist threats highlighted by 9/11. The Control and Reporting Centre, located in a reinforced bunker at ASACS, monitored the airspace around the UK, and was responsible for providing tactical control of the Tornado F3 and Typhoon F2 jets that were scrambled whenever the skies over Britain were violated.

The planes were part of the RAF's Quick Reaction Alert Force, and were based at Leuchars (covering the north) and Coningsby (the south). They had been particularly busy in recent years, shadowing the increasing number of Russian bombers that flew into the UK's Air Defence Identification Zone, a sensitive area just outside Britain's airspace.

There was only one man who could help Marchant, and he was sitting opposite him now in a corner of the Beehive pub in Montpelier, Cheltenham. Paul Myers liked his beer. He liked talking about Leila, too. Marchant gave him both, endless pints of Battledown Premium and stories of Leila in her early days at the Fort, and despised himself for it. Despite her betrayal, Myers had never managed to get over her, or dismiss the fantasy that she had once fancied him.

'She used to talk about you often,' Marchant said. Myers was clumsy enough when he was sober, but he looked even more vulnerable and awkward when he was drunk. Perhaps it was because he liked to remove his thick glasses after a few beers, exposing his clammy face to the world.

'Did she really? That's great. What did she say?'

'That you were a good listener.'

'They always say that. Particularly when they're pouring their hearts out about other men.'

'And if she hadn't met me, then maybe . . . '

'Honestly?'

'Be careful what you wish for. You'd be the one feeling betrayed now.'

'I do anyway. She betrayed us all, Dan.'

Had she? Marchant was always less sure when he was drunk. Alcohol could be very forgiving. For the first round, he had tried to sip at his beer, let Myers do the boozing, but it was no good. He had been drinking heavily ever since Prentice had been killed. There was no need to lay it on for the Russians, who were meant to be watching him for signs of disaffection. Besides, pretending to get drunk was not a skill he possessed. The KGB had become famous for it during the Cold War. His father had once told him a story about the *Rezident* in Calcutta, who appeared to get lashed on vodka with his contacts, trading on Russia's reputation for hard drinking, then be spotted sober as a judge half an hour later. Barely a drop had passed his lips.

'Listen, bit of a turf war going on at the moment,' Marchant said, anxious to change the subject. 'I need your help.'

'New government, new rules. Fire away.'

Marchant knew that relations between Fielding and his opposite number at GCHQ, where Myers worked, had not been great in recent weeks, ever since Myers had pulled his rabbit out of the hat at the Joint Intelligence Committee. GCHQ was much more friendly with the Americans than MI6, and it had felt embarrassed by Myers's role in Spiro's humiliation. Myers was still meant to be on secondment to MI6, but had been ordered home.

'We need to put the wind up the National Security Council. The coalition has been throwing its weight around.'

'We?'

'Fielding. Armstrong. Listen, a couple of Russian fighters will be tipping their wings off the Outer Hebrides next Tuesday. Usual operation. Into our Air Defence Identification Zone, fly along the borders of UK airspace for a while. Only this time we want them to get a bit closer. Smell the whisky.'

'Nice one,' Myers said, his eyes lighting up. 'MiG-29s?' Marchant knew that he liked his planes, and thought the idea might tickle him. Myers was an active member of a remote-control flying club in Cheltenham.

'35s.'

Myers let out a loud whistle of approval, as if a naked blonde had just walked past. He had no self-awareness, Marchant thought, looking around the pub.

'No one's going to get hurt,' he continued, 'just a few politicians' noses put out of joint. Any ideas how we do it?'

'Build a massive wind turbine off Saxa Vord.'

'Why?'

'They're degrading our air-defence capabilities. It's quite a worry. Apparently, they create a confused and cluttered radar picture. Too much noise. Above, behind, around the turbines – you're invisible.'

Myers lived and breathed this stuff, Marchant thought.

'I'm not sure we've got time for that.'

'They're upgrading the system soon, anyway. No, what you need to do is take out a couple of remote radar heads. Saxa Vord, Benbecula, maybe Buchan. Depends where they're flying in.'

'We can't really "take out" anything. This is meant to be low-key, deniable. I was thinking of a cyber attack, untraceable.'

'The radar housing's reinforced anyway.'

Marchant tried not to be impatient, but Myers had an annoying habit of suggesting seemingly credible options, only to point out their flaws.

'Thinking about it, your best option is to target the Tactical Data Links, either the communication system between the radar heads and the Control and Report Centre at Alnwick, or between Alnwick and the Combined Air Operations Centre at High Wycombe.'

'Which would you suggest?'

'The second one. The inter-site networks are fully encrypted, but they still use an old 1950s NATO point-to-point system called Link 1 for sending the RAP from Alnwick to High Wycombe.'

'The RAP?'

Myers always seemed puzzled when others didn't understand what he was talking about, which was most of the time. And he used more bloody acronyms than the military, Marchant thought. 'Recognised Air Picture. It's a real-time 3D digital display, based on primary and secondary radar traces, showing what's in the skies over Britain and evaluating contacts against specific threat parameters.'

'And this vital part of our national defence is transmitted using sixty-year-old technology?'

'The Americans have been trying to get NATO to upgrade it for years. Link 1 does the job. It's a digital data link, but it's not crypto-secure. As it hasn't been encrypted, it would technically be possible to corrupt the air-surveillance data before it reached High Wycombe.'

'So the order to scramble the Typhoons might never be issued.'

'In theory, yes. At least, the order could be delayed. Only High Wycombe can send up the jets, and they like to have the full picture.'

'Could you do it? Get into Link 1 and delay the message to High Wycombe? The Russians will be out of there in two minutes. We don't need long.'

# 74

Salim Dhar pulled back the stick and put the SU-25 into an unrestricted climb. He felt in control, stomach tensed, ready to absorb the G-forces. For the first time, he had taken off on his own, without any help from Sergei, who was in the instructor's seat behind him. He wasn't one to lavish praise, but even the Bird had been impressed. The speed with which everything happened would still take some getting used to, but Sergei had drilled into him the constant need to think ahead.

All that remained now was for Dhar to release his ordnance onto the firing range that lay 20,000 feet below. According to Sergei, only the best jet pilots were able to fly solo and drop bombs accurately at the same time. It required precision flying and a rare ability to focus on specific parameters – height, speed and pitch – in order to get inside the 'basket'. The SU-25 had eleven hardpoints that could carry a total of almost 10,000 pounds of explosive. There were two rails for air-to-air missiles, and the capacity for a range of cluster and laser-guided bombs, two of which his plane had been loaded with before take-off.

Dhar felt for the weapon-select switch. It was on the stick, along with the trim, trigger and sight marker slew controls. Laser engage was on the throttle, along with the airbrake, radio and flaps control. He was finally beginning to know his way around the cockpit. From the moment he had first sat in it, he knew that the plane's myriad dials and switches represented order, not chaos, that each one served a specific purpose. He liked that. All his life he had been guided by the desire to impose discipline on himself and on the world around him. It was his mother who had taught him the importance of daily routine: prayers, ablutions, exercise, meditation.

Sergei had worked hard with him on the simulated targeting system for the laser-guided bombs, or LGBs, and he felt confident as he reduced power to level off at 25,000 feet and settled back. For the next few minutes, until they reached the target zone, the plane would fly with minimal input from him.

He was less happy with Primakov. It was never going to be an easy relationship with the SVR. In return for his protection, Dhar had agreed to strike at a target in Britain that was mutually important to him and to the Russians. It wasn't a martyr operation, but it was beginning to feel like one. There wasn't enough detail about his exit strategy. In Delhi, his escape route had been planned meticulously, from the waiting rickshaw to the goods carrier that took him over the Pakistan border.

Whenever he raised his concerns with Primakov, the Russian reminded him of the risks Moscow was taking by shielding him. Without the SVR's help, he would be dead. It was hard to disagree. The global scale of the CIA's manhunt had taken Dhar by surprise. It had also upset him. Drone strikes were killing hundreds of brothers. Using six kidnapped Marines as a decoy had bought him time, and the taste of revenge, but he knew he had been close to being caught on several occasions. Primakov reassured him that the SVR would help after the attack, but the truth was that he would be on his own again, on the run.

'Do you know what your final combat payload will be?' Sergei asked over the intercom as they approached the target zone. Dhar moved the gunsight onto a column of rusting tanks.

'A pair of Vympel R-73s,' he replied. He was sure that he would be able to deploy Russia's most advanced air-to-air missiles after endless sessions on the simulator. Besides, if all went to plan, the enemy would be unarmed and unprepared. And he would only need one of them.

'Watch your trim on the approach. What about LGBs?'

They will kill you after this is over, Dhar thought, easing the stick to the left, so there was no harm in telling him. But for the moment he said nothing.

'Engage the target now,' Sergei ordered, frustrated by Dhar's reticence.

Dhar released the bombs. The aircraft seemed to jump before, climbing, he rolled away to the left.

'Two thousand-pound laser-guided bombs,' he finally said, almost to himself. 'One of them is a radiological dispersal device.'

Sergei didn't say anything for a few seconds, as if he was allowing time for both of them to acknowledge the implications of what had just been said. 'That's a lot of collateral.'

Dhar couldn't disagree. A thousand-pound radioactive dirty bomb would cause widespread panic, fear and chaos. There would also be multiple civilian casualties. Not at first, but when the caesium-137 began to interact with human muscle tissue, the radiation dose would substantially increase the risk of cancer. If decontamination proved difficult, entire areas would have to be abandoned for years, if not decades, as the wind and rain spread the radioactive dust into the soil and the water supply. Were the British people innocent? He would have said yes a year ago. But something had changed since the discovery of his father's allegiance to Russia. Britain and its people were no longer off limits.

Dhar looked down at a rising plume of smoke below him, and thought again about what lay ahead.

'Target destroyed,' Sergei said. 'And no collateral.'

# 75

Myers had taken every possible precaution when he phoned Fielding. The GPS chip in his SIM card had been disabled, making its location harder to trace. It also incorporated triangulation scramble technology, first seen by GCHQ's technicians in a handset seized in Peshawar's Qissa Khwani Bazaar. By altering the broadcast power, it confused network operators about the handset's proximity to base-station masts.

He didn't want anyone to know that he was phoning MI6, least of all Marchant, who he felt he was betraying by making the call. It wasn't that he doubted Marchant's story. He knew there was an unspoken pact amongst the intelligence services whenever a new government arrived. Chiefs would stick together, wary of their new political masters as they established themselves. But his request to embarrass the National Security Council by allowing Britain's airspace to be breached made Myers uneasy. Marchant was on the warpath, which meant fat arses like his own had to be covered.

Myers looked around his untidy bedroom in Cheltenham as he waited to be connected: an empty pizza box on his unmade bed, dirty clothes on the floor, a half-built remote-control plane on top of an open wardrobe, and the bank of computer screens. He knew that some of what was on the hard drives should have stayed within the circular confines of the Doughnut, but at least he hadn't left his office laptop on a train. At the last count, thirty-five had been lost by GCHQ staff.

Myers justified his own software breaches on the grounds that he liked to work late, often through the night. And 99 per cent of the work he did on his home network was in the interests of the taxpayer and national security. Just not this particular request. He switched the phone to the other hand while he wiped the sweat off his palm. He never liked calling Fielding.

'This is starting to become a habit,' Fielding said. 'I trust the line is secure.'

'Untraceable. I'm sorry to ring you again, but I thought you should know.' Slow down, he told himself.

'Know what?'

'Daniel Marchant came to see me yesterday. He's asked me to do something, said it was your –'

Myers looked at the phone. Fielding had cut him off.

# 76

'I was performing a manoeuvre we call the "Pugachev cobra". The nose comes up like a snake and the plane almost stops in mid-air.' Sergei put down his glass and lifted his hand from flat up to ninety degrees, as if a venomous head was rearing. 'It is a Russian speciality, useful in combat, too. Hard to see coming. Pull a cobra, your attacker overshoots and suddenly you're on their six o'clock. My instructor at aviation school, Viktor Georgievich Pugachev, was the first. For many years, we were doing this in SU-27s, much to the embarrassment of our American friends. They can do it now in an F-22, but in other Western jets this manoeuvre is not possible.'

'And it went wrong?' Dhar asked, sipping at a mug of warm water. They were sitting in the hangar at Kotlas, the regular guards standing outside. The Bird had burst into song, talking more than he had ever done before. Vodka had loosened his tongue; or perhaps he had finally accepted that he was a man condemned to die. Apart from the alcohol, Dhar was enjoying his company. He had grown fond of Sergei in the past few weeks, liked the fact that his respect had to be earned. Their conversation tonight seemed to be a reward.

'Terribly wrong. We Russians like to push it to the limit at air shows. Give the people some value for their money for a change.

I was attempting the hardest, a flat cobra – it is easier in a climb – and I was entering too fast. I passed out for a few seconds – almost 15G. In order to perform the manoeuvre, first we must disable the angle-of-attack limiter, to allow the nose to pitch upwards. But this also disables the G-Force limiter. When I regained consciousness, it was too late. I tried to turn away from the crowd, but –'

Sergei stopped and blinked.

'And twenty-three people died?'

'Including seven children. I was sentenced to fifteen years, so was my co-pilot and two of the air show's officials.' Sergei paused. 'I don't understand your beliefs, and I don't expect you to understand mine. All I know is that you are at war, fighting your global *jihad*, and Russia has many enemies in the world. Sometimes our battles are the same. It's not worth my life to know any more. My orders are to train you for an operation that might help to restore the world order. But please, if you can spare the lives of twenty-three civilians, then do it. For me, for the Bird.'

# 77

Marchant didn't know how many twitchers would make the journey to the Isle of Lewis, but he knew that a Steller's eider was an extremely rare visitor to the Hebrides. The sea duck bred in eastern Siberia and Alaska, and had only been spotted a few times in Britain in recent years. A solitary drake had stayed off South Uist from 1972 to 1984, while another loner had summered at roughly the same time in Orkney. There would be some twitchers who would not make the journey, wary that it might be another hoax. In 2009, a golfer claimed to have spotted one in Anglesey, prompting a rush to Wales, but it turned out that the photo posted on the Internet was a reverse image of a bird that had been snapped in Finland.

Myers had been understandably nervous about interfering with the RAF's Tactical Data Links, but he had been far more excited about hacking into a birdwatching website and sending out a false alert. Earlier that day, thousands of twitchers and birders had received messages on their mobile phones and pagers telling them that a Steller's eider had been spotted off the coast near Stornoway and was 'showing well'.

All Marchant had to do now was monitor the blogs and chat-rooms. He had left Legoland early, and was sitting in an Internet café near Victoria Station, waiting for the first comments to be posted. The photos would follow, uploaded by twitchers who had spotted a very different flying visitor from Russia. At least, that was the plan.

By Marchant's calculation, the two MiG-35s would be entering the UK's Air Defence Identification Zone in thirty seconds. The Remote Radar Heads at Benbecula and Saxa Vord would already have picked them up, and the Norwegian air force would have tracked and shadowed their progress across the North Sea, alerting NATO allies along their projected flightpath. The order to scramble Typhoons from RAF Leuchars would only be given when the planes entered Britain's ADIZ – and if the Recognised Air Picture ever reached Air Command at High Wycombe, something that Marchant hoped Myers was about to prevent.

He looked at his watch again, and then his mobile rang. It was Myers, unbearably nervous, calling from an unknown mobile number.

'It's done,' he said. 'You've got two minutes.'

# 78

Thirty thousand feet above a roiling sea, two MiG-35s turned sharply to the south, their cockpits winking in the evening sun. As they began their descent towards the waves far below, both pilots knew that they were taking an unprecedented gamble, but they had been assured their presence would not attract the usual RAF escort. So far they had been left alone, apart from requests for identification from commercial air-traffic control on the 'guard' frequency, which they routinely ignored, a brief visit from two Norwegian F-16s, and a mid-air rendezvous with an Ilyushin IL-78 refuelling tanker.

At 1,500 feet they levelled out and took another, far graver risk. Within the next five seconds they would be entering Britain's national air space, where they could be legitimately shot down. They set a course for Stornoway on the Isle of Lewis, twelve nautical miles away. Then, after wishing each other luck, both pilots hit their afterburners and accelerated to Mach 1.

In Alnwick, on the other side of the country, the Aerospace Battle Manager on duty at RAF Boulmer froze as he watched the two primary traces on his radar. The Russians were ten miles off the north-west coast, and closing. He had already rung through to Air Command at High Wycombe when the planes first entered the UK's ADIZ, picked up by the radar head at Benbecula off North Uist, but his was a lone voice. The Russians weren't showing up on Air Command's real-time Recognised Air Picture for the sector. On his word, High Wycombe had brought two Typhoon crews at RAF Leuchars to cockpit readiness, but they were reluctant to scramble them until they had more concrete data.

'The skies above the Outer Hebrides are showing clear,' his opposite number had insisted.

Clear? He smacked the side of his radar screen in frustration. What the hell was going on? A terrorist strike? Two pilots trying to defect? It didn't make any sense. He was used to long-range Russian bombers – most recently a TU160 Blackjack – keeping him busy on their eleven-hour flights around the Arctic. Usually, they would head for the North Pole and then hang a left just outside the Scandie's ADIZ radar coverage and head down between Greenland and Iceland, skirting Britain's ADIZ.

Both sides knew the game. The Russian pilots liked to test the range of Britain's radars at Saxa Vord, Benbecula and Buchan, waiting for a response, which would often be intentionally delayed to confuse them. Moscow was also keen to measure the Quick Reaction Alert Force's response, and the RAF was happy for the practice, shaving a few seconds off every time. There was no real animosity. (On one infamous occasion, an RAF pilot had held up a Page 3 girl in the cockpit, prompting his Russian counterpart to moon from a window of his bomber in response.)

But this time was different.

# 79

'Any sight of the Sibe?' a birder in a bobble hat asked no one in particular. The men, more than fifty of them, and a handful of women, were standing in the evening light on a cliff in Stornoway, looking down across Broad Bay, where a group of seabirds were riding on the water. Some of the birders were using digiscopes mounted on tripods, others were looking through telescopes. All had binoculars – Zeiss, Swarovksi, Leica, Opticron. Marchant had given a precise grid reference of where the bird had last been seen, knowing that the modern twitcher's armoury also included hand-held GPS units.

'Not a squawk,' someone else said. 'Time to dip out. They're all common eiders.'

'And no sign of the stringer who phoned in the sighting.'

'I saw someone earlier with a nine iron.'

'The closest we're going to get to a Steller is in the pub. Anyone coming?'

'Hold on,' an older man said, adjusting his binoculars.

'What are you seeing?'

'Christ. To the right of the big rock, two o'clock.'

As one, the group of birders raised their magnified gazes out to sea.

'What the –'

Three seconds later, the two MiG-35s swept in low over their heads, forcing the group to duck and cover their ears. A couple of them remained upright, taking photos as the planes disappeared into the distance.

'No sign of any Steller's eiders, but we've just been buzzed by another Sibe – a brace of MiG-35s!! Beautiful-looking birds, particularly in supersonic flight. Take a butcher's at the photos below if you don't believe me.'

Marchant read the chatroom message, smiled and sat back, glancing around the Internet café in Victoria. On his walk over from Vauxhall he had been aware of a tail, possibly two, but he had no desire to shake them off. He thought at first that they were Russian, but then began to think they were American: the dispatch cyclist, the woman at the back of the 436 bendy bus, a tourist taking photos on the north towpath. Either way, they were too thorough to be Moroccan, and it would have taken hours to lose them. Besides, their presence was reassuring, evidence he was attracting attention, arousing suspicion.

He wasn't sure if it was the Bombardier he had drunk at the Morpeth Arms on the way, or a sense of professional satisfaction, but he felt a wave of happiness pass through him as he stared at the photograph on the computer screen. It was a good one, visual proof that he had done what had been asked of him. He was tempted to intervene, but he knew that he should let the web take its own viral course. The pilots would already have reported back, and Primakov would be relieved that he had passed his final test.

Then he thought again about the doubters in Moscow. According to Fielding, Primakov's superiors would be analysing his every move. If they had been listening in on his last fateful meeting with Prentice, they would know he was about to resign. But had they heard? And was that enough? An MI6 agent on the eve of defection would be keen to embarrass the Service as much as possible. Marchant didn't know how or when Primakov intended to exfiltrate him, just that it would happen quickly. Primakov had promised a heads-up if he could manage it. Marchant realised how impatient he had become, how keen he was to meet with Dhar, talk about their father. The waiting game had gone on long enough.

He sat forward, copied the image of the MiGs and attached it to an email. Then he sent it to as many news desks as he could remember from his brief stint with I/OPS, writing 'MiG-35s over Scotland' in the subject box. He wasn't as careful as he would normally be on the Internet, but that was the point. He wanted to force Primakov's hand, get himself out of the country as soon as possible. Dhar wouldn't wait for him for ever.

After he was done, he glanced at his watch. Lakshmi had asked him on a date. The invitation bore all the hallmarks of a trap, but he had to go. He hadn't seen her since the Madurai débâcle. He just hoped nobody would get hurt.

# 80

Fielding stood at the window of his office and looked towards Westminster. A tugboat was towing a string of refuse barges downriver. He knew it was a gamble, but he couldn't afford anyone to suspect that Marchant's actions, whatever he was up to, had been sanctioned by him. If the Russians detected Fielding's touch on the tiller, however light, they would never let Marchant meet Dhar. And that remained the most important thing. Fielding was convinced that only Marchant could stop the *jihad* that was soon to be unleashed on Britain.

He had wanted to talk to Myers more, discover what he had been asked to do, just as he had wanted to ask Marchant about the test that Primakov had set him. But he couldn't. He didn't trust himself. If Marchant or Myers had told him, he feared a part of him would have demanded action: a visceral response honed over thirty-five years of public duty. That was what he did, why he had signed up. There was also the very real possibility that there might be other Hugo Prentices in the Service, listening in, reporting back to Moscow.

Instead, he had put his faith in Marchant, trusted him to defect responsibly and in isolation. He wasn't sure why he trusted anyone any more. He had relied on Prentice too much since Stephen Marchant's departure and death. In some ways, his old friend had been a hopeless choice of ally. Prentice had never been interested in fighting Foreign Office battles or playing Legoland politics. But it was what he represented that had appealed to Fielding: an old-fashioned field man who had repeatedly turned down promotion in favour of gathering intelligence. Prentice had been immune to legal guidelines on human rights, tedious departmental circulars on personal-development needs, blue-sky meetings and resource planning. Mistresses had appealed more than marriage, rented digs more than mortgages. He had just wanted to get on with his job. Nothing more, nothing less. Except that it hadn't been as simple as that.

'Ian for you,' Ann Norman said over the intercom.

The next moment, Ian Denton was standing in the middle of Fielding's office, looking a new man.

'Good news and bad news,' his deputy said, louder than usual. 'All our old SovBloc networks appear to be intact. Out of some perverse sense of loyalty, Prentice only seems to have burned Polish agents.'

Everyone knew that Denton had never liked Prentice.

'He did it for the money, Ian, not to skewer us,' he said, unsure why he was defending Prentice. But Denton's triumphant tone was irritating. He preferred his deputy when he was bitter and quiet.

'Does that make it any better?'

'Less personal. The bad news?' Fielding knew it would be Marchant. His line manager had filed a formal complaint about him earlier in the day, citing poor hours and a disruptive attitude. HR had added a note on his file asking if Marchant was drinking again. All was going to plan.

'We're getting word of a major security incident in the Outer Hebrides. The JIC is being convened, and we're being blamed. Oh yes, and Spiro's back.'

# 81

'Your brother has excelled himself,' Primakov said, walking around the bare hangar at Kotlas that had been Dhar's home for the past month. 'Do you not want for any more comforts?'

'I have all that I need,' Dhar said dispassionately. He was sitting at a bare wooden table, a copy of the Koran open in front of him. The austerity made Primakov crave a drink, a nip of whisky, but he had learned not to offend Dhar on the few occasions they had been alone together.

'He has proved that it is too easy to penetrate British airspace. You will have no problems.'

'Won't they be more alert now?'

'If Marchant can knock out the system once, it can be done again.'

'When is he arriving?'

'We will lift him tonight. The Americans are closing in on him.'

'And you are sure?'

'Sure?'

'About Daniel Marchant.'

Sometimes, Primakov found Dhar's stare too chilling. He looked away, out of the window, steeling himself, then turned back to face him, hands clutched tightly behind his back.

'Your brother is ready.'

# 82

In normal circumstances, Fielding would have objected to the presence of James Spiro at the Joint Intelligence Committee table, but their relationship was now one of delicate expedience. Spiro had been useful in Madurai, unknowingly helping to build up Marchant's credentials for defection. In return, Fielding had agreed with the DCIA to drop British opposition to Spiro's rehabilitation. He had been suspended from his position as head of Clandestine, Europe, but was now back at his desk at the US Embassy in Grosvenor Square.

Everyone knew Spiro had messed up over the drone strike, but the truth was that the CIA needed people like him, and they didn't have anyone to replace him with. What Spiro didn't know, as he addressed the meeting in tones of barely disguised vindication, was that he was still dancing to Fielding's tune.

'I'm sorry to do this to you again, Marcus, but Daniel Marchant has got a lot of questions to answer.' Fielding had to admire Spiro's resilience. A few weeks earlier, he had been sitting at the same spot at the table, his career in tatters, listening to Paul Myers humiliate him.

'Are you saying that Marchant in some way facilitated the breach of airspace?' the chairman of the JIC, Sir David Chadwick, said, looking across at Fielding.

' "Facilitated" is one way of putting it,' said Spiro. 'It wouldn't surprise me if he was standing on the shores of Stornoway with a couple of paddles and a fluorescent jacket, instructing the MiGs where to taxi.'

A chuckle rippled through Sir David's jowls, then he checked himself when he realised that no one else was laughing. He was an odious chairman, Fielding thought, obsequious in the extreme, always looking to see where the real power lay. Not so long ago, Spiro had been trying to frame him in a child-porn sting. Now he was cosying up to the Americans again.

'These are serious allegations,' Fielding said. 'Sorry to sound so old-school, but do we have any evidence?'

'I appreciate that this is the last thing you need, after the Prentice affair,' Spiro said, hoping to pile on the public embarrassment. Although he owed his own rehabilitation to Fielding, he couldn't resist the moment. There was too much history between the two of them, their respective organisations. 'One Soviet mole could be construed as careless. But two . . .'

'The evidence, please,' Sir David said, convincing no one with his attempt at neutrality.

'Where do we start?' Spiro asked, shuffling some papers and photos in front of him. 'The covert meeting with Nikolai Primakov in central London?' He waved a couple of photos in the air, one of Marchant entering Goodman's restaurant, the other of Primakov.

' "Covert" might be pushing it,' Fielding said. 'I seem to remember the dinner – sanctioned by me – took place at a well-known Russian restaurant in the middle of Mayfair. We were listening.'

'So were we,' said Spiro, 'until the Russians jammed the entire area. Must have been quite an important meeting. Then we have Madurai, south India. After we took Dhar's mother off your hands,

Marchant hitched a ride back into town with – guess who? – one Nikolai Primakov.'

He waved another surveillance photo in the air. 'I'm not sure I want to ask why Marchant's meetings with Primakov, former director of K Branch, KGB and now high-ranking member of the SVR, were sanctioned by MI6, so let's not go into that here. It kind of brings back bad memories when you discover Primakov had been good friends with Marchant's father. Of more interest to today's meeting is what Marchant was doing in an Internet café yesterday – after knocking off work early and dropping in for a warm beer or three at his favourite pub – forwarding photos of the MIG-35s to various national newspapers.'

Another sheaf of documents was waved in the air, this time press cuttings, as a murmur went around the room. Fielding was conscious that all eyes were on him now, but he had read the cuts in the car into work, smiled at the quotes from the twitchers. He was a bit of a birder himself, when he had the time, although these days he was reduced to spotting oystercatchers on the bank of the Thames below his office window.

'He used an anonymous Gmail account,' continued Spiro, 'but our people at Fort Meade narrowed the IP address down to three Internet cafés in Victoria. They needn't have bothered. All emails leaving that particular café go out with marketing headers and footers – unless you switch them off, which Marchant failed to do. I don't know how much evidence you need, Marcus, but we have photos of him entering the café five minutes before the anonymous emails were sent out.'

Fielding didn't reply. Instead, he was thinking of Marchant, the intentional trail he was leaving. Primakov must be close to exfiltrating him. According to the UK Border Agency, the Russian had left on a flight to Moscow earlier in the day, which Fielding took as a good sign. Marchant had been smart to attract the attention of the Americans: it was the easiest way to reassure Moscow Centre that it had the right man, that he was ready to defect, keen to meet Dhar. But it was a risk if the Americans got to him first. He hoped Marchant had his timing right.

'Marcus?'

'Let's bring him in,' Fielding said. He had no choice. He must be seen to be hard on Marchant.

'I kinda hoped you'd say that,' said Spiro. 'He's with Lakshmi Meena as we speak. Having yet another drink. She's ready when we are. I just thought that, you know, in the interests of resetting our special relationship, I should inform you first.'

Spiro looked around the table. His eye was caught by Harriet Armstrong.

'Would you like us to handle Marchant?' she asked. Fielding turned away. It was an unusual offer, a blatant challenge to MI6 that had all the hallmarks of their old turf wars. She was also reaching out to Spiro, a man she had once admired before she had fallen out of love with America. Fielding knew that she had felt increasingly sidelined by Six, but he was still surprised by the move.

'That's kind of you, Harriet,' Spiro said. 'And unexpected. I appreciate it. But I think, if it's OK with the assembled, this has now been upgraded to a NATO Air Policing Area 1 issue. And as such, we'd like to take care of it.'

# 83

Marchant knew his defences would drop if he had any more alcohol. Meena was looking more beautiful than he could remember, wearing the same embroidered Indian *salwar* that she had worn in Madurai. Her body language then had been diffident, hard to read. Tonight she was radiant, the mirrorwork on her neckline reflecting the candlelight, lightening her whole demeanour. He just wished they were meeting in different circumstances, where they could be true to themselves rather than to their employers' agendas. The last time he had felt like this was when he had said goodbye to Monika at the Frederick Chopin airport in Warsaw, hoping that she would step out of her cover and into his life.

'My mother used to read me a new tale every night,' Meena was saying as they sat at the small bar in Andrew Edmunds, a restaurant in Lexington Street. Her mask was slipping too. Marchant stuck to his script, trying to stay sober behind the miasma of Scotch. Soon they would be moving from the bar to the cramped dining area, where the lines of sight were less good. In his current position he had a clear view of the main entrance and the door to the kitchen. Tonight he needed to see everyone who came in or out.

'After each story, I would ask if Scheherazade had done enough, if King Shahryar would spare her,' Meena continued. 'I was more worried about her dying than anything else. And each time, the King let her live for another night. I was so relieved.'

'And this all took place in Reston? In between trips to the mall?'

Marchant had eaten a meal in Reston once, as part of a visit to the CIA's headquarters down the road, in the days before the Agency had become too suspicious to allow him on campus. All he could remember was the piazza at the Reston Town Center, an open-air mall that had boasted Chipotle, Potbelly Sandwich Works and Clyde's, where he had been taken for lunch by a gym-buffed field agent who swore by its steaks. It was strange to think of Meena living in such a sterile suburb in Virginia.

'Our home was a little corner of India. At least, my bedroom was. Wall hangings, incense, my own *pooja* cupboard. Mom didn't want me to forget.'

Marchant signalled to the barman for another drink.

'I don't want to sound like your mom, but haven't you had enough?'

She was right. Marchant was at the very edge of what he could consume and still be able to react quickly when it happened. There were only a few more hours, maybe less, of playing the drunk. A coded text from Primakov had told him it would be sometime tonight. It wouldn't be pretty. The American presence had made sure of that. He looked again around the small, candlelit room, scanning the punters. Someone had followed him to the restaurant, but he was confident that they were still outside.

'I don't blame you for Madurai,' he said. 'You had your orders.'

'That didn't make it any easier.'

He wanted to ask if Shushma was OK, but he knew he couldn't. It was better that he could still entertain the possibility that she was with Spiro. The thought of her in CIA custody, the genuine anger the thought stirred, was central to his imminent defection. It might even save his life when he finally met Dhar.

'I'm going away,' he said quietly. 'I've had enough.'

'Of me?'

Marchant managed a smirk. 'Of the West.'

'Was that why you helped to give the MiG breach so much publicity?'

He struggled to conceal his surprise.

'I don't know what you're talking about.'

'Dan, we met here tonight because I've got orders to bring you in.'

'Spiro's?'

'With the Vicar's blessing.'

Marchant paused, weighing up the situation. He was pushing it to the limit, and hoped that Primakov would move soon. Meena knew how to look after herself, but he was still concerned for her. And for the first time he felt that she was being straight with him. He wished he could reciprocate, but he knew that he couldn't, not yet.

'Are you going to ask me to come quietly?' he asked.

'No. I'm not going to do anything.'

'Nothing?'

'I just want you to tell me what's really going on.'

'You know I can't do that.'

'If you did, then maybe I'd know how best to help you.'

Marchant studied her eyes, calculating the implications. She was speaking too freely to be wired, which made him believe her. 'You really mean that, don't you?'

'I want to do one worthwhile thing while I'm still with the Agency, and I'm not sure bringing in a drunken MI6 agent with a penchant for rare Russian seabirds is what I had in mind.'

'The Steller's eider breeds in Alaska, too, you know.'

'Spiro's fallen for it, hasn't he?' Meena said, turning the wine-glass in her hand. 'He's seen you go off the rails, but he's forgotten to ask why. Well, I know what makes a British MI6 agent try to be recruited by the Russians. Because he knows they have someone he desperately wants to meet. Fielding knows it too, which is why he asked Spiro and me to take Dhar's mother away. You hated the West for that, didn't you? And it made the Russians love you even more. That helicopter in Morocco – I know now that it was Russian. You were right all along. Tell me what I need to do, Dan. You're the only person who can stop Dhar.'

Marchant hesitated before speaking. 'How many people have you got outside?'

'Two vehicles, six people.'

'Do you know any of them?'

'Some, yes.'

'Good friends of yours?'

'Decent colleagues.'

'Walk out into the street and tell them I'm leaving in five. Then go home. All of you.'

'Why?'

'Because I don't want anyone to get hurt.'

But he already knew it was too late. He heard the car before he saw it, a black Audi pulling up outside. Two men wearing balaclavas got out from the back and ran into the restaurant while a third stood by the front passenger door, a handgun aimed into the dark street.

'Don't touch her!' Marchant shouted, as several diners screamed. The men grabbed him by both arms and frogmarched him out of the restaurant, barking orders at each other and at the diners, and waving a gun at Meena. The men were Russian, and it wasn't subtle, just as he had predicted. A moment later, the shooting started. The third man fired down Lexington Street towards Shaftesbury Avenue, where a black SUV had stopped at a diagonal, blocking the road. As Marchant was bundled into the back of the car, he looked back at the restaurant. The front window had been shot out, and the noise of the screaming diners was sickening. There was no sign of Meena.

# 84

'It just makes us look like such a bunch of bloody fools,' Harriet Armstrong said, declining Fielding's offer of a chair in his office. 'I've got Counter Terrorism Command demanding answers, and Jim Spiro can barely speak.'

A quiet American, Fielding thought. He almost felt sorry for Armstrong, but her recent *rapprochement* with Spiro had extinguished any sympathy he might have had for her situation. Besides, there was very little he could say to mollify her. MI5 *was* a bunch of fools.

'Much as I'd like to say that this was Marchant's work, the facts are these,' he said, steepling his fingers under his chin and sitting back. 'One of my agents has been seized on the streets of London by what we think were officers of the SVR –'

'Come on, we *know* they were.'

'– and I have urged the Prime Minister to protest in the strongest terms to the Russian Ambassador. Meanwhile, Six's stations around the world are on heightened alert, and I hope that the same can be said for Britain's ports, railways and airfields.'

'What's going on here, Marcus? Primakov was once one of ours.'

'A fact that only a very few people are privy to.' The last thing he needed was Armstrong spilling state secrets to Spiro.

'I thought Marchant was being sent to see if Primakov could be ours again.'

'He was. But I should remind you that certain senior figures in the SVR – Vasilli Grushko, for example – were opposed to Primakov's London posting from the start. They didn't completely trust him. It's no coincidence that Primakov left the country in a hurry this morning, and my guess is that seizing Marchant is the SVR's consolation prize. Marchant will be interrogated about Primakov, who will no doubt shortly be charged with betraying the motherland.'

Armstrong looked at him, weighing up what he said. She wasn't convinced.

'You don't appear to be too concerned that one of your officers has just been taken by a hostile country.'

'It's not the first time, and I doubt it will be the last.'

'America is not our enemy,' Armstrong said, walking to the door.

'It was when you and I were in India, fighting for what we believed in. Why are we suddenly being nice to Spiro again?'

Armstrong paused by the door. 'Because we've got no option, have we?'

Fielding knew she was right. Britain needed America. 'I'll let you know as soon as we hear word of Marchant,' he said. 'We're doing everything we can to find him.'

He watched her leave. As with the best lies, there was a strong element of truth in what he had told her. Grushko had long had his doubts about Primakov, but he must have overcome them to sanction the operation in Soho. Such a brazen act on the streets of London could not have gone ahead without the consent of the SVR's local *Rezident*. Which meant that Marchant was in. He had passed all the tests, and would soon be with Salim Dhar. Fielding just hoped that Dhar would believe in him too.

# 85

An alert officer at UK Passport Control at Heathrow had picked up Primakov's hurried exit, but they had failed to spot Vasilli Grushko, who had also left Britain earlier in the day, travelling with false documents on a flight to Moscow. He was now standing in the hangar at Kotlas with Primakov and Marchant.

'Welcome to Russia,' Grushko said, looking out at the rain on the runway. He was a short, wiry man with rimless glasses and sallow skin, in stark contrast to Primakov's rubicund presence. 'Is it your first time?' There was no warmth in his voice, nothing excessive about him at all, just a cold matter-of-factness that made Marchant wary.

'Officially or unofficially?' Marchant replied. His head was hurting from the alcohol of the night before, and the journey in an Illyushin cargo plane from Heathrow to Moscow, which he had spent curled up in a container. He had then been flown by an Antonov military transporter to Kotlas.

'You must be tired after your flight,' Primakov suggested, filling the awkward silence. 'If it's any consolation, my Aeroflot flight was no more comfortable. Your brother is out flying at the moment. Sleep now, and you will be ready to meet him.'

'Just one thing,' Marchant said. 'Was the American woman hurt? In the restaurant?'

'I am surprised by your concern,' Primakov said, glancing at Grushko, his superior, who remained impassive.

'She will shortly be leaving the Agency,' Marchant added. 'Disillusioned, like me.'

'She is in hospital, a gunshot wound to the arm,' Grushko said. 'Our men were authorised to kill her if necessary, but she did not resist, and for some reason you asked for her to be spared.'

'But she'll be OK?' Marchant asked, thinking back to the chaotic scene, his shout to protect Meena.

'She's fine,' Primakov said. 'She should be grateful for the injury. Her superiors are already a little surprised that she did not do more to stop you being taken. We will leave you now. You did well with the MiGs. Your brother was impressed. We all were.'

Primakov turned to Grushko, hoping for some supportive words, but none came.

'Do not step outside,' Grushko warned. 'The guards have orders to shoot.'

Marchant had passed two armed guards standing by the side entrance to the hangar when he had arrived. After Grushko and Primakov had gone, he looked around the empty space. Some camouflage nets had been hung on one wall, otherwise there was little to soften the oppressive concrete surfaces. So this was where the world's most wanted terrorist had been hiding, in a draughty hangar, surrounded by rain-soaked woodlands in a remote corner of a Russian military airfield in the Arkhangelsk oblast.

He turned away from the large doors, and saw a curtained-off area at the far end of the building. He assumed it was where Dhar lived. A mattress and some bedding had been put in the opposite corner for Marchant, along with a towel, a bar of unwrapped soap and a change of clothes. It wasn't exactly a defecting hero's welcome.

After washing in a bucket of lukewarm water that had been

left by the side entrance, Marchant looked again at Dhar's corner. Checking the door, he walked over and pulled back the curtain. There was a mattress and bedding on the floor, with a small wooden cargo crate beside it for a bedside table. A copy of the Koran lay shut, a letter inside it acting as a bookmark.

He recognised the handwriting at once. Glancing at the door again, he picked up the Koran and slid the letter out. The paper was creased, and looked well read. It was from his father, written in the same hand and in exactly the same words as the one Primakov had given to him. For a moment, he wondered if it was a forgery, but he was sure it was his father's hand.

*To Salim, the son I never knew*

*If you are reading this, it must mean that you have finally met Nikolai Ivanovich Primakov. I will not try to guess at what path led you to him, only to offer reassurance that I have trodden a similar one before you. You are old enough, of course, to make your own judgements in life, but in the case of Nikolai, I merely wish to assist you, because other influences will be in play. He is, first and foremost, a friend, and you can trust him as if he was a member of our family.*

He put the letter back in the Koran, which he placed back on the crate. In front of him, pinned to an old pilots' briefing board on the wall, were several photos. One was of a group of *jihadis* at a training camp, possibly in Kashmir. Another was of a young Salim Dhar sitting in what looked like the cockpit of a crashed Russian jet. The background scenery suggested it was in Afghanistan. Then he saw a photo of himself, taken with a long lens. He was outside Legoland, on the street opposite the main entrance, peering into the window of the motorbike showroom that he used to frequent in his lunch breaks.

'I used to ride an old Honda in Afghanistan,' a voice said behind him. Marchant spun round to see a man standing by the curtain, wearing a flying suit and holding a helmet in one hand. It was Salim Dhar.

# 86

Myers had drunk one too many Battledown Premiums at the Beehive and was struggling to slot the key into the lock of his Montepelier flat in Cheltenham. It was sometimes stiff, but tonight he wondered if he had got the wrong door. He looked up at the front windows to reassure himself, and then tried again. The door opened and he fell into the hall, gathering up the post that was on the doormat: the latest issue of *Fly RC*, a magazine for remote-control plane enthusiasts, and a takeaway pizza flier.

At the back of his addled mind he wondered if the lock was stiff because it had been tampered with, but he dismissed the thought. He had become paranoid since carrying out Daniel Marchant's request, seeing people on street corners, lurking behind curtains. As far as he could tell, no one had managed to establish a cause for the temporary delay in the Recognised Air Picture data at RAF Boulmer, let alone follow it out of the Tactical Data networks to Cheltenham. He had covered his tracks carefully, and he couldn't deny that the result had been spectacular. Whatever Marchant was up to, he was doing it with style. A pair of MiG-35s over bloody Scotland!

He tore open the magazine as he stumbled into the kitchen, idly flicking through the pages. A sport-scale park flyer of the Russian jet would be entertaining down at the recreation ground, but he couldn't find one listed. It might also attract unnecessary attention to himself, given the furore over the breach of airspace. Relations had plummeted between London and the Kremlin in the twenty-four hours since the incident. They weren't helped by the subsequent kidnapping of an MI6 officer on the streets of Soho.

For a moment, when he first heard the news at work, Myers had thought it might be Marchant, but his old friend was too streetwise to be picked up by the SVR in central London. He didn't dare ring him to check. Myers was nervous about making any calls after his brief chat with Fielding. Besides, Marchant was clearly up to something big, and he didn't want to be further implicated. He had already done too much.

After taking a leak that seemed to last for ever – he almost fell asleep as he stood swaying at the bowl – Myers headed for his bedroom. He knew he should drink some water, but he wanted to check his emails, maybe surf a few porn sites before crashing. He always kept the door to his bedroom locked because of the computers inside, but as he fumbled for the key fob in his pocket, he saw that the door was ajar. The sobering effect was instant. His brain cleared as an adrenaline rush ripped through his body, making his legs feel so heavy that they almost buckled.

He stood there for a few seconds, listening for a noise, pressing his heels into the carpet to stop his legs shaking, but there was only silence, broken by the noise of a solitary car passing outside. He took a deep breath, pushed open the door, and walked in.

'Don't say a word,' a voice said from the darkness. A moment later, Myers felt the cold metal of a barrel against the racing pulse in his temple.

# 87

'I became too fond of this in Morocco,' Dhar said, pouring out two glasses of mint tea. 'It is my one other luxury.' He had already offered Marchant some dried apricots from a paper bag on the floor between them. He was sitting cross-legged, his posture upright. He had changed out of his flying suit and was now wearing a long white *dishdasha* of the sort that Marchant had seen in Marrakech and a matching *kufi* skullcap. His austere appearance was reflected in the formality of their conversation. There was a stiffness to proceedings that was making Marchant tense. He was also struggling to sit comfortably on the ground. His crossed legs were cramping up, forcing him to rock forwards. He knew it made him look nervous.

'How long were you in Morocco for?' Marchant asked, taking the hot glass by the rim. 'Did you go there straight after Delhi?' He was hoping to slip into small talk, but knew at once that it was the wrong question to ask a man on the run.

'Please,' Dhar said. 'Let us talk first of family. My journey is of no concern. All that matters is that we are once again reunited.'

Dhar had hugged him when they first met in southern India. This time there had been no such warmth. Marchant had been caught snooping around his possessions, which didn't help, but there was also a different tension in the air: a pressing sense of expectation. Fielding had warned him that he would be killed if Dhar suspected anything. *Embrace your worst fears. They may be the only thing to keep you alive when you meet Dhar.*

'Dad wrote me a similar letter,' Marchant said, nodding at the Koran on the crate.

'Dad,' Dhar repeated, mocking the word. 'Father. Papa. Pop.' He reached forward and took another apricot. 'All those years I never knew him, never knew he was waging the same wars against the *kuffar*. It must be harder for you. Coming to the crusade so late. In some ways, I am closer to him than you ever were, even though I met him only once.'

Marchant could feel himself bridling inside, but he remembered why he was here, why Dhar had wanted to see him. They were the sons of a traitor, united in family treachery.

'It's true,' Marchant said. 'The man I thought I knew was someone else.'

'And it wasn't a shock? Primakov said you were relieved.'

'It was like finding the missing piece of a jigsaw. After the way I was treated by the Americans –'

'The waterboarding.'

'Yeah, after being nearly drowned at a CIA black site in Poland, I was beginning to wonder, you know, about our great Western values. When Primakov told me about Dad, my life began to make sense.'

'Brother, come here,' Dhar said, beckoning Marchant to stand. Both men rose, and hugged each other long and hard. Marchant was expecting it to feel awkward, but it wasn't. He hadn't been embraced by his own flesh and blood since his father had died. And as he held Dhar, breathing in the faint aroma of apricots, he wondered if this was what it would have been like to hug Sebastian if he had survived into adulthood. He had told Dhar all about his twin when they had met before, explained how his death had cast such a long shadow over his life, but, for the first time in years, Marchant no longer felt like an only child. When they let go of each other, both men's eyes were moist.

'My life made sense, too,' Dhar said. 'Can you imagine how hard it was for me when I first discovered that my father was the head of an infidel intelligence agency?'

Dhar managed a laugh in between wiping his eyes with the sleeve of his *dishdasha*. Marchant smiled, too, as they sat back down on the floor. It was a rare moment in a spy's life. Marchant had crossed over, immersed himself in a role like a seasoned actor, forgotten that he was playing a part. But no sooner had the spell been cast than it was broken. All the old fears came tumbling down around him again. Why had he found it so easy to celebrate his father's treachery?

'After he had been to see me in Kerala, the clouds began to clear,' Dhar continued. 'At first, I was confused by the visit, some of the things he said, but when I met Primakov and he told me everything – the nature of the American intelligence our blessed father had once passed to Moscow – it was like being reborn.'

'I'm sorry about your mother,' Marchant said, trying to steer the conversation onto safer territory. He had been genuinely angry about what had happened in Madurai, regardless if it had been fabricated by Fielding, and knew he could talk about it with conviction. He wasn't sure how much longer he could listen to Dhar extolling their father's treason.

'I'm sorry too. This man Spiro . . .'

'I promised your mother I would look after her. I feel I failed her, and you.'

'*Inshallah*, the time will come when such things will not happen again.'

'The deal was that we would bring her back to Britain, keep her away from the Americans. I gave her my personal undertaking that she would be safe. I can never forgive myself for what happened. I let her down, Salim. She trusted me, against her better judgement. I persuaded –'

'Enough.' Dhar held up a hand, as if he was halting traffic. Had Marchant pushed it too far? Dhar was angry, his equanimity disturbed by talk of his mother. He moved his raised hand to his eye as he turned to look out of the window.

'Do you trust Primakov?' Dhar asked, changing the subject.

'I don't know him well, but I respect our father's judgement. You read the letter. "Trust him as if he was a member of our family." '

'Grushko, the Russian who came today, has his doubts.'

'Grushko doesn't trust anyone. I think he even doubts me.'

Dhar turned to look at him with an intensity that Marchant had never seen in anyone before. In a certain light, his brown Indian irises shone as black as onyx.

'So do I.'

'I don't blame you. It doesn't look that convincing on paper, does it? MI6 agent bonds with *jihadi* half-brother.' Marchant was keen to lighten the mood, but Dhar wasn't smiling.

'What I am struggling to understand is why you returned to your old job in London. After all that had happened. The water-boarding in Poland, the way the Americans treated our father. How could you continue to be a part of that?'

'Because I wanted to meet you again. Remaining in MI6 was the only way. I wanted to come sooner, but the Americans wouldn't allow it.'

'The Americans,' Dhar repeated, smirking. 'You could have travelled on your own.'

'I thought I'd be more useful to you if I still had a job with MI6.'

'Such a Western way of looking at things. The job more

important than the person. You're family. You got my text? *Yalla natsaalh ehna akhwaan. Let's make good for we are brothers.* It was sent more than a year ago.'

'I got it. It was impossible to come sooner without losing my job. I couldn't have helped you – arranged for the MiGs to fly over Scotland – if I was on the outside, on the run again.'

'Tell me one thing. Your return to MI6, after Delhi, was before you discovered our father had been working for the Russians.'

Dhar's probing was beginning to worry Marchant. He was right. He had gone back to his desk in Legoland with his head held high, proud of his father's innocence rather than celebrating his guilt.

'There was a time when I believed in Britain, I can't deny that. Just as there was a time when our father believed in his country too. But the doubts were growing when I returned to MI6. About what I was doing, why I was doing it. I'm sure you've sometimes questioned what you do too.'

Dhar didn't respond.

'And those doubts became something stronger when Primakov showed up in London with the letter,' Marchant continued.

'We are blessed to have had such a brave father.'

Dhar smiled, and Marchant thought he was through the worst of it. But he wasn't.

'There is only one problem. Grushko is convinced that Primakov is lying.'

Dhar leaned over to his bed and took a pistol from under the pillow. He brushed the handle with his sleeve, then cocked it with the assurance of someone familiar with firearms. 'And if Primakov is not telling the truth, then neither are you.'

# 88

'How did you know I was involved?' Myers asked, sitting at the bank of computers. There had been two Russians waiting for him in his bedroom, one tall, the second one shorter with rimless glasses. The tall one had frisked him, while the other did the talking, although he wasn't one for idle chatter. It took Myers a few minutes to be sure of his identity. It was Vasilli Grushko, London *Rezident* of the SVR. He had seen his photograph at work, intercepted occasional calls.

'We have been following your friend Daniel Marchant for some time now,' Grushko said.

'Was it him who was taken? In London?'

Myers tried to prevent his left leg from shaking, but it was impossible. Instead, he bounced it up and down as if the movement was voluntary. At least they had stopped pointing the gun at his head. After frisking him, the weapons had been put away, but Myers was still all over the place, too many possible scenarios unfolding in his mind. The computers had already been turned on when he entered the bedroom. Had they hacked into GCHQ using his passwords? If they knew about his role with the MiGs, who had they told? Who else knew? He was just glad that he had gone to the bathroom when he first arrived, otherwise he would be pissing himself now.

'Your concern is almost touching. He is fine. Unharmed.'

'What do you want from me?'

'He came to see you. At the Beehive pub near here. Marchant chose the location well, because it was busy, but we think you were talking about the MiGs. Now that we have discovered you bring your work home' – Grushko nodded towards the bank of computers – 'we know for certain that it was you who helped him.'

'What do you want from me? Please. There was no harm. Nobody died. It was good publicity for Russia, your air force. Bloody lousy for ours. Air defences like a sieve.'

'It is quite simple. We want you to help him again.'

# 89

Dhar held the cocked gun to Primakov's head. The Russian had entered the hangar full of his usual bonhomie, and had not seen him standing behind the door. Dhar closed it and pushed Primakov into the middle of the building, where Marchant was standing beside a wooden chair, holding a rope in his hand. Marchant felt like a guilty executioner. It was as if Dhar had put their own relationship on hold while he sorted out Primakov. He had asked Marchant to help him interrogate the Russian, a process that Marchant assumed he himself would be subjected to later.

'Salim, this is unexpected,' Primakov said, nodding at Marchant, who looked away. Whatever else Primakov was, he was dignified, and the next few minutes would be demeaning. Marchant felt a mix of shame and nausea. After Dhar had shown him the gun, they had both slept, but Marchant's sleep had been fitful. He had woken at dawn full of dread, envying Dhar, who was praying calmly on a mat in the middle of the hangar.

'Is it really?' Dhar asked. 'Grushko says you have been under suspicion for many years.'

'A small price to pay for knowing your father so well. May I sit down?'

Dhar kicked the wooden chair towards Primakov, the scraping sound echoing in the hangar. The SU-25 jet that Dhar had flown the day before had been wheeled in through the main entrance overnight, and was now parked at the end of the hangar, the doors closed behind it. Marchant had noted that it was a two-seater, used for training. Apart from the plane, resting up like a vast squatting insect, the hangar was empty.

Dhar nodded at Marchant, who grabbed Primakov's arms and bound his hands tightly behind his back. He tried to do it painlessly, but he was aware of Dhar's eyes on him. Primakov's breathing had become heavier, rasping like a Siberian miner's. Marchant could smell the cologne, mixed now with the strong scent of sweat. If Primakov was going to give him a sign, something to reassure him about his father, it would have to be soon. Time was running out for all of them.

'Grushko is on his way back to Britain,' Dhar said as Marchant finished tying Primakov's wrists to the back of the chair. 'He would rather you were dead, but I wanted to ask a few questions first.'

'About your father?' Primakov was working hard to keep his voice steady, but it was fraying with fear.

'Grushko does not believe that you recruited Stephen Marchant.'

'What does he believe?'

'He accuses my father, our blessed father' – a glance up at Marchant, who remained behind Primakov, to one side – 'of having recruited you. I don't want to believe Grushko, but he is a meticulous man. He has been going through old KGB archives, file by file. Our father gave you intelligence about the Americans, it is true, but Grushko says that with hindsight much of this information was not as important as it seemed at the time.'

Marchant closed his eyes. It was the first time he had heard anyone on the Russian side question his father's worth as a double agent. But any relief he felt was short-lived. If Dhar decided that his father was not a traitor after all, he would come to the same conclusion about him, too. It was down to Primakov now, balanced on a high wire. He had to reassure two sons about their father, one hoping to hear of his loyalty, the other of his treachery.

'Comrade Grushko will find whatever he wants to find in the archive to support his case,' Primakov said, treading carefully. 'The files are endless, and so is his jealousy. Your father was a priceless signing. At the time, I was fêted by the Director of the KGB, hailed as a hero. Within months, I was awarded the Order of Lenin. I could do no wrong. I admit that on some occasions the intelligence was gold, at others it was dust. But I knew your father better than many – and all I can say is that he detested America to the day he died. Whether that makes him or me guilty of treason, I leave to others.'

Marchant looked down at Primakov. His chest was heaving, his voice beginning to crack under the strain. One wrong word and Marchant's cover would be blown, but he still needed something.

'Salim, Daniel' – a cock of the head towards Marchant – 'I don't know why you have suddenly decided to listen to Comrade Grushko, but before you give him too much time, there is something you should both know.' A pause as he gathered himself. More rasping. 'My instructions were quite clear: I was asked to bring you two together. A rising *jihadi* and an ambitious MI6 officer. Now that I have done my job, I may rest peacefully.'

'And whose instructions were they?' Dhar asked, walking up to Primakov. Marchant could hear his suspicion, his mounting anger. Primakov was wobbling on the wire. This was the moment, the sign Marchant had been waiting for.

Primakov paused. 'Your father's. He had witnessed the birth of Islamic terror, watched it grow in strength, knew that one day it would pose the greatest threat of all – to everyone: Britain, America, Russia.'

With no warning, Dhar whipped the pistol across Primakov's face.

'You are lying!' he shouted. Marchant had never heard him raise his voice before. 'It was Moscow Centre that asked you to bring us together.'

A trickle of blood was dripping from Primakov's mouth.

'So it was Moscow Centre,' he said finally, with the air of a condemned man. 'But at my suggestion, and your father's wish.'

'A lying *kuffar*,' Dhar muttered, walking over to the window.

'Salim, your father had always followed your progress from the other side of the world, but when there was a chance to meet you in person, he took it, knowing there might be some common ground between you.' Primakov was talking with difficulty, his cut lips bleeding, distorting his words. 'And of course he had another son, Daniel, carving out a career in intelligence in the West, despite the best efforts of the CIA. There was some common ground there, too, between all three of you. On the last occasion I saw him, your father made me promise to bring the two of you together when the time was right. He said you would both know what to do. That time has now come.'

Dhar walked past Primakov and stood with his face inches from Marchant's. The smell of apricots was strong and sour now.

'Do you want to, or shall I?' he asked, holding out the gun. 'We cannot let him continue to insult our father in this way.'

Marchant's heart was racing. He knew it was a test, one final challenge. If Dhar suspected Primakov, he suspected him too, but for the moment it appeared that Dhar wanted to believe in his father, his half-brother – his family.

'I saw something in our father's eye when I met him,' Dhar continued, now looking down at Primakov. 'And do you know what it was? Approval. Anything to stop the American crusade: MI6 officers passing US secrets to Moscow, *jihadists* shooting the President in the name of Allah. And now that he has gone, it is left to you and me.'

He turned back to Marchant, who hesitated for a moment, looking at the gun that was still in Dhar's outstretched hand. Suddenly he saw Dhar as a child, desperately seeking a father's endorsement, something he had never been given in his childhood. If his real father hadn't been a traitor to the West, Dhar would be left with nothing. Dhar had to believe in his father's treachery, dismiss Primakov's talk of another agenda. In his mind, Moscow Centre had brought Dhar and Marchant together for one simple reason: they were both their father's sons.

Marchant listened to the sound of Primakov's wheezing, the loudest noise in the hangar. The Russian had finally told him the truth, knowing that he would pay for it with his life. He had avoided any admission that he was working for the British – that would have implicated Marchant, too. Instead, he had told Marchant that his father had wanted him to meet Dhar, explore their common ground. That was enough. And Marchant knew now exactly what he had to do.

'Let me,' he said, taking the gun.

# 90

'I shouldn't be here, but I wanted to thank you in person,' Fielding said, standing at the foot of Lakshmi Meena's hospital bed. One arm was heavily bandaged and she had bruising below her left eye, but she seemed in reasonable spirits.

'For what?'

'For letting them take Daniel. It must have gone against everything you were taught at the Farm. I brought you these.'

He waved the bunch of full-headed Ecuadorian roses he was holding, and put them on the windowsill. He had also brought a box of honey mangoes from Pakistan.

'Thank you. I wasn't armed. There were at least four of them. In the circumstances, I had no choice but to protect myself. Have a seat.'

She gestured at a chair, but Fielding remained standing.

'Is that what you told Spiro?' he asked.

'It took a while for him to accept that they weren't your people.'

'We haven't had to resort to kidnapping our own officers on the streets of London. Not yet.'

'I don't suppose you're going to tell me what Dan's up to.'

He hesitated. 'All I can say is that you were right to trust him. I'm sorry about your arm.'

'You're asking a lot of him. To stop Salim Dhar on his own.'

Fielding glanced towards the door at the mention of Dhar's name. Through the frosted glass panel, he could see the profile of an armed policeman standing guard outside. He wanted to tell Meena that Marchant's orders weren't just to stop Dhar, but to turn him as well, but he couldn't. The stakes were too high. If Marchant could persuade Dhar to work for the West, it was not something Britain would ever be able to share with any of its allies, least of all America, whose President Dhar had come so close to killing.

'No one else can,' Fielding said, moving towards the door. 'It's family business.'

# 91

'Please place a flower on my daughter's grave,' Primakov whispered, leaning forward, his whole body shaking now. 'And may your father forgive you.'

Marchant wanted to look away as he fired. It took all his strength to pull the trigger, leaving him with no will to watch. But he knew Dhar was scrutinising his every move. Primakov's head lurched forward as if in a final drunken bow, and then he fell to the floor.

As the sound of the single shot faded in the echoing spaces of the hangar, Marchant prayed for the first time in years. He tried to tell himself that Primakov would have been executed by Grushko or Dhar if it hadn't been by him, but it didn't make it any easier. He had never killed anyone in cold blood before. Primakov deserved better. He had been one of his father's oldest friends, a courageous man who had carried out his wishes to the last. He hoped to God his death was worth it.

Dhar looked on impassively, then took the gun from Marchant without a word and walked over to his living area.

'Our father told us to trust him as if he was family,' Marchant called after him, feeling the need to explain himself as he tried not to stare at Primakov's slumped figure. A pool of blood had formed around his disfigured head, dust floating on its surface like a fine skein of flotsam.

'He made an error of judgement,' Dhar said. 'Primakov had other interests.'

'Like stopping the global *jihad*?' Marchant asked, regaining some of his composure. He needed to reassure himself that Dhar had moved on, no longer suspected him. 'He must have known you wouldn't like what he said.'

'Primakov was working to his own agenda. There are many within the SVR who are at war with Islam. He was trying to turn you against me, suggesting that our father had somehow sent you here from beyond the grave to halt my work.'

'Was he anti-Russian, too?' Marchant asked, thinking that was exactly what their father had done. His question was a risk, but he needed to know what Dhar thought.

Dhar fixed Marchant with his eyes, now shining blacker than ever. 'No. I do not believe Primakov was a British agent, if that's what you are asking. Grushko was simply trying to frame him. As Primakov said, there were people in Moscow Centre who were jealous of him when he recruited our father. His signing was quite a coup.'

Marchant couldn't ask for more. Dhar not only still believed that Primakov was working for Moscow, he was also sure that their father had been too. Primakov had chosen his words carefully. Thanks to him, Marchant was now safe, free from suspicion. He looked again at Primakov's body, remembering his final wish.

It was the first time Marchant had heard that Primakov had a daughter. He would make enquiries when all of this was over, find out where she was buried and put flowers on her grave. It was the least he could do. *And may your father forgive you.*

'Now I must prepare to fly,' Dhar said.

'Where are you going?' Marchant asked as casually as he could, glancing at the aircraft at the end of the hangar. From the moment Primakov had requested him to help with the MiG-35s' incursion,

Marchant had assumed that Dhar's plans involved an airborne attack of some sort. All he had to do now was persuade him to take him along.

'To the land of our father,' Dhar said, patting him on his shoulder.

'Then let me come with you,' Marchant said instinctively. It was the only chance he had of stopping Dhar. 'We still have so much to discuss. And I know the country well.' He managed a light laugh. 'I could show you the sights.'

Dhar paused for a moment, smiling to himself as he seemed to consider Marchant's offer. There was something Dhar wasn't telling him that made Marchant think that he had a chance. 'That is true. And it is a long flight. Have you flown in a jet before?'

'Only a Provost. But I have a strong stomach.' Marchant was thinking fast now, improvising. The last time they had met, Dhar had abandoned him on a hillside in south India when he left to shoot the US President. Marchant wasn't going to let him get away again. He had to be in the cockpit with him, find out what the target was, get a message to Fielding.

'You know they won't allow another Russian jet to enter UK airspace,' Marchant continued. 'I might be able to help, talk to traffic control. It could buy us a crucial few minutes before we're shot down.'

'Grushko has already taken care of that. He's with your friend Myers in Cheltenham now.'

# 92

'As far as we know, the facts are these,' Harriet Armstrong said, addressing a meeting of COBRA in the government's underground Crisis Management Centre. MI5, MI6, GCHQ, the Joint Intelligence Group, the Joint Terrorism Analysis Centre, the Defence Intelligence Staff and Special Branch were all represented by their heads, a measure of the gathering's importance (number twos or threes were usually sent). The Prime Minister was chairing the meeting, flanked by the Home Secretary and the Foreign Secretary. The Chief of Defence Staff was also in attendance, along with the Chief of the Air Staff.

'There are a number of possible domestic targets over the coming forty-eight hours, which we'll come to in a moment. In the meantime, Cheltenham' – a nod to GCHQ's director, sitting on Armstrong's left – 'has picked up a raised level of chatter, but I think Marcus will be able to enlighten us further on Dhar's possible intentions.'

The handover was brusque rather than warm. At an earlier meeting in Armstrong's office, Fielding had persuaded her not to go into any details about Marchant's attempt to recruit Nikolai Primakov. She had agreed, but it was clear she still resented Fielding for excluding her from other operational details.

'Thank you, Harriet,' Fielding said. 'I'll keep this short. We

323

believe Dhar was taken from Morocco last month by the Russians, who have offered him protection in return for a shared stake in a state-sponsored act of proxy terrorism. What that act is, we're not sure, but it appears that Dhar has put aside a previous reluctance to strike against UK targets.'

'What about Daniel Marchant's kidnapping by the SVR?' asked the head of JTAC, looking across at Armstrong for support. 'I assume there's a connection.'

'We're not certain it was the SVR,' Fielding interjected.

All eyes turned to Armstrong, who paused before answering, keeping her own eyes down as she shuffled some papers. A Russian operation on the streets of London was her beat. 'Preliminary reports have established that the kidnappers were Russian, but we can't be sure they were SVR. D Branch is still working on it.'

Surprised by her support, Fielding tried to acknowledge Armstrong, but she didn't look up. He had expected her to confirm the SVR's involvement, make life more difficult for him.

'In answer to your question,' Fielding said, 'Marchant, one of our most gifted field officers, has been on Salim Dhar's trail for a number of months. After the terrorist attack on the London Marathon, he wanted to travel to Morocco, where he had good reason to believe that Dhar was in hiding, possibly being shielded by the Moroccan Islamic Combatant Group in the Atlas Mountains. Unfortunately, the Americans insisted that he stayed in Britain. It was a deeply frustrating time for all of us. After a year, we got our way and dispatched him to Marrakech. He was closing in on Dhar when he was exfiltrated by the Russians in an unmarked Mi-8 helicopter. He returned to London and was establishing Dhar's location through an SVR contact when he himself was seized.'

'What are the Russians saying?' the director of GCHQ asked.

'They're denying everything,' the Foreign Secretary replied, glancing at the Prime Minister. 'But it seems that Dhar had become too hot for Tehran, and Moscow took him on. We've protested formally about Marchant's disappearance and enquired through back channels about Dhar.'

'Just as the Russians denied that two of their MiG-35s were over Scotland,' the Prime Minister said. The incursion had made his coalition and its armed forces the laughing stock of NATO, giving him no option but to accept his Defence Secretary's resignation. The MiGs had turned around and were halfway across the North Sea before the Typhoons were even airborne.

'We're working on the assumption that the violation of UK airspace is in some way connected with Dhar,' Fielding continued. He knew it for a fact, of course, but he could never reveal that Marchant, one of his own agents, had facilitated the incursion in order to meet Dhar. Or that Paul Myers at GCHQ had also been involved. The breach had been put down to a cyber attack by Moscow, one of many in recent months.

'Which is why this weekend's RIAT, the Royal International Air Tattoo at Fairford, is top of our list,' Armstrong said. 'We've also got a Test match at Lord's against Pakistan, which could be a target, given Dhar's connections, and WOMAD, the world music festival in Wiltshire, which is less of a security worry, although I gather there was a bit of a disturbance in the Qawwali tent last year.'

The faint murmur of laughter released some of the tension in the room. Armstrong enjoyed being centre stage, Fielding thought. Not everyone appreciated her stabs at humour, or her Johnsonian memos on poor grammar. In another life, she would have been headmistress of a public school. The subcontinent had knocked some of the pomposity out of her manner, but not quite enough.

'The good news is that Fairford is already a secure site,' she continued, 'with a perimeter fence protected by the Americans.'

'The bad news?' the Prime Minister asked. Armstrong looked across at the director of the Defence Intelligence Staff.

'Washington is using the air show to showboat a big arms deal with Tbilisi,' he said, taking over from Armstrong. 'They're currently equipping the Georgian air force with C130 cargo planes to replace their ageing fleet of Antonovs. The US has also agreed to lease them F-16 fighter jets to replace their SU-25s, most of which were shot down by the Russians in the 2008 South Ossetia war.'

'An arms deal that Moscow is obviously far from happy about,' the Foreign Secretary said.

'Given the MiG débâcle, shouldn't we have our Typhoons and Tornados airborne all weekend?' the Prime Minister asked. 'Over Lord's, Gloucestershire and Wiltshire?'

'If only that were possible,' the Chief of the Defence Staff said.

'How long's the show?' the PM continued, ignoring the jibe. The RAF was locked in acrimonious discussions with the coalition about cuts to Britain's fighter-jet capability.

'Seven and a half hours of flying time.'

'Do what you can,' the PM said, looking at his watch.

'The US base commander at Fairford is an old friend,' the Chief of the Defence Staff said. 'I'll speak to him. Personally, I think it's highly unlikely the Russians would try anything, particularly on a weekend when there's so much hardware on the runway. The F-22 Raptor will be in town. The violation of our airspace, while deeply regrettable, was a one-off, a distraction. A Test match against Pakistan at the home of cricket is a far more probable target.'

'I agree,' Ian Denton said. There was a newfound confidence in his voice that surprised Fielding, who was sitting next to him. 'RIAT's the largest military air show in Europe. It's an American-run base, and security is always very tight. The Test at Lord's strikes me as a more likely target.'

326

Denton might be right – perhaps the MiGs were just a distraction – but Fielding doubted it. He'd been weighing up the possible options ever since Armstrong had alerted him to the air show. Marchant had been asked to help with the MiGs, an involvement that nobody else around the COBRA table knew about. Now he had been taken to join Dhar, wherever he was. In Fairford, with its American hosts and Georgian guests, Dhar and the Russians had found a mutual target.

# 93

'You are only carrying two Vympel and two LGBs, so we've loaded you up with four 1,500-litre drop tanks, two under each wing,' Sergei said over the r/t to Dhar, who was in the rear cockpit of the SU-25, where the instructor normally sat. It was raised a little, giving him a good view of Marchant, who was strapped into the seat ahead, listening in on the conversation. The avionics and weapons suites were identical in both cockpits – full dual control – but Sergei had disabled them in the front.

Marchant had met Sergei only briefly. Dhar spoke warmly of him, but the Russian had shunned eye contact as he had inspected the plane's undercarriage in the hangar. Afterwards, when he handed Marchant an ill-fitting flying suit and helmet, he had again avoided his gaze. There was a haunted look about him, Marchant had thought.

'Distance to target is 2,875 kilometres,' Dhar said, reading from a sheet of waypoints in the clear-panel leg pocket of his flying suit. 'And the *Grach* has a ferry range of approximately 2,500 kilometres. "Do the math," as our American idiots like to say.'

'The extra fuel and a good tailwind should get you there,' said Sergei.

*Should?* Marchant could have done without the mordant banter. He closed his eyes and tried to picture what lay ahead. Dhar had finally agreed to let him fly with him. Marchant wasn't sure if it was a reflection of how much he trusted or distrusted him. Either way, it had bought him precious time in which to work out what to do.

'We can be martyrs together,' Dhar had joked, making no mention of a return journey.

Earlier, Dhar had revealed their route – north into the Barents Sea, south-west down the coast of Norway into the North Sea, and then west into UK airspace – but there had been no talk of the target. Whatever it was, timing was evidently crucial. Dhar had checked and double-checked windspeeds on the journey, going through the waypoint ETAs several times with Sergei.

Marchant had already clocked the two missiles on the wings' hard points. Air-to-air suggested that Dhar expected airborne company, but why not a full complement? And now Sergei had mentioned two laser-guided bombs for a ground target. It was a tailor-made suite of weapons. But for what?

Marchant glanced around the cramped cockpit at the array of dials. The Jet Provost he had once flown in had been privately owned by an ex-RAF friend of his father. Taking off from Kemble airfield, near the family home in Tarlton in the Cotswolds, had felt like rising into the sky on rails: surprisingly smooth and steady. He suspected the SU-25 would be a rougher ride.

As the plane began to roll forward, Marchant peered through the mist at the godforsaken scenery. Dhar had taxied to the far end of the main runway. A light drizzle was falling. All Marchant could see was pine trees. The control tower was a long way off, barely visible in the murky distance. Halfway down the runway on the right were two MiG-29s. He guessed that they must be on permanent standby, like the Typhoons at RAF Leuchars and Coningsby that would be scrambled if Dhar showed up on the radar. Then he noticed the armed guards, dotted about on the periphery of the trees, out of sight of any US reconnaissance satellites. He had only spotted the two guards outside the hangar door before. Security had been ramped up for their departure.

Marchant thought again about Primakov, the sharp intake of breath just before he fired, as if the Russian was bracing himself. After the shooting, Dhar had not wanted to talk, preferring instead to spend time on his own behind the curtain. Marchant assumed that he was praying, not for the Russian's soul but for a successful *jihad*. As far as Marchant could tell, no one else seemed to be running the show or telling Dhar what to do. He was very much his own man, ignoring the guards and talking only with Sergei before climbing into the cockpit. There was a quiet confidence about Dhar, a self-assurance that gave him an air of authority.

'Comrade Marchant?' It was Sergei's voice on the r/t.

'Yes?' Marchant said, taken by surprise.

'Talk to comrade Dhar about collateral. He will understand.'

Marchant was about to ask for an explanation, but Sergei had already signed off.

'Did you get any of that?' he asked Dhar over the intercom.

'We can talk more later. Our flying time is more than three hours. Now we must prepare for take-off.'

# 94

Paul Myers had given up trying to make conversation with the Russians. They had sat motionless in his room throughout the night, waking him with a prod at first light. He had stumbled out of bed, forgetting that his hands were still tied, and they had accompanied him to the bathroom, where he managed his ablutions with difficulty.

It was only when they sat him down in front of the computers that he persuaded them to untie his wrists. If it had been a working day, he would have been missed by now, as he liked to work the early shifts at GCHQ in the summer, getting in at 7 a.m., sometimes earlier. It gave him longer in the park afterwards to fly his model planes. But today was a Saturday, and no one would miss him. He had made a loose arrangement to meet a couple of colleagues in the pub in the evening, but otherwise his diary was free, as it was most of the time.

The Russians wanted him to do exactly what he had done for Marchant: delay High Wycombe's real-time Recognised Air Picture feed. He had already told them that it would be hard to repeat the trick, but the Ministry of Defence's IT experts, many of whom he knew, had yet to trace the source or cause of the Link 1 breach.

Of more concern to Myers was what Marchant and Fielding would want him to do. Marchant was clearly party to the planned second violation of UK airspace. Would he want Myers to help him, or to stop him? His instinct told him to let the Russians run with it, whatever they were planning.

Nursing a hangover, he logged in to his GCHQ account and prepared once again to tamper with the Tactical Data Links that were meant to keep the skies above Britain safe.

'All I need is a start time,' he said, looking at his watch. 'I can't delay the RAP for long. A few minutes at most.'

'This time we need a little longer,' Grushko said.

# 95

The morning had dawned bright and clear in the Cotswolds, and the ground staff at RAF Fairford were already busy laying out the tables and chairs in the private enclosure towards the eastern end of the runway. It was a big day for the base, and General Glen Rogers, head of the United States Air Forces in Europe, was taking his run around the airfield early, before the VIPs began to arrive. The USAF would shortly be pulling out of Fairford, leaving it as a standby facility that could be reactivated at short notice for the use of B-2 Spirit stealth bombers and U2s.

All the usual merchandise stands were present. Jogging at a steady pace, Rogers passed the Breitling Owners' Club, a dogtag stamping stall for wannabe GIs, and a stand that would later be selling Vulcan memorabilia. Now that was a plane he wished he had flown. This weekend, though, was all about modern military hardware, and in particular the global export market for the F-16 Fighting Falcon, one of America's finest fourth-generation jet fighters, otherwise known as the Viper.

The delegation from Georgia had spent the night on the base, drinking too much of their own Kakhetian wine in the officers' mess, but he couldn't blame them. Today marked the official beginning of a new era for the Georgian air force. Six F-16Ds had already been delivered to Alekseevka Military Airbase, but the deal between Washington and Tbilisi would be formally signed off in the private enclosure. To mark the occasion, the F-22 Raptor, a plane that was strictly not for export, would make its debut at Fairford with a breathtaking display of fifth-generation manoeuvrability.

Rogers used to fly jets himself in the mid-1980s, briefly serving with the Thunderbirds F-16 display team, and he was particularly looking forward to the Raptor show. Today's pilot, Major Max Brandon, would demonstrate its vast air superiority over an old Russian SU-25 'Frogfoot', the current mainstay of Georgia's air force, in a mock-up of a Cold War dogfight that promised to be one of the highlights of the weekend.

The only blot on the Gloucestershire landscape was the arrival of Jim Spiro, the CIA's Head of Clandestine Europe. He had turned up in the middle of the dinner with the Georgians, wanting an urgent talk about a perceived security threat that was making the Brits jumpy. (Fairford always made the Brits nervous. A few years earlier, a B52 had flown in low over the runway as part of the display, only for the pilot to be told by ATC that he had got the wrong airfield. So much for precision bombing.) Rogers had not met Spiro before, and he hoped their paths would never cross again. Marines had that sort of effect on him, particularly ex ones who had featured in the infamous CIA torture memos.

If the Agency had its way, the contract with the Georgians would be signed in a reinforced bunker five hundred feet underground, and there would be no Royal International Air Tattoo at all. He had told Spiro to relax and enjoy the day, reminding him that it did much to reinforce the special relationship between Britain and America. That was the problem with the spooks – they saw threats everywhere.

# 96

Fielding had agreed with Armstrong that it was too much of a security risk for both of them to travel to Fairford, so she had stayed behind in London to liaise with COBRA, which was now sitting around the clock. The air show remained the most likely target, and Fielding needed to be there, even though he knew it could be dangerous. He also wanted to get out of London, away from the endless meetings, and clear his head. Ian Denton had offered to mind the shop in his absence – a little too keenly, Fielding thought afterwards.

Just outside the airfield's perimeter fence, he asked his Special Branch driver to pull into a lay-by, where several plane-spotters had parked up in camper vans, ready to watch the display without paying. Marchant had Fielding's personal number, and he still hoped that he might call him, give him some warning, however late, of Dhar's murderous intentions.

If the threat was airborne, it would involve a repeat of the earlier breach of British airspace. Had Marchant asked Myers to help him out a second time? So far, Fielding had resisted talking to him about Marchant's earlier request. The risk of being monitored by the Russians was too high. He assumed Myers must have hacked into Britain's early-warning radar network, allowing the MiG-35s to fly over Scotland unchallenged. Now he needed to know for sure if Myers was involved again. He dialled his mobile number.

Twenty miles away in Cheltenham, Myers watched his handset vibrate on the desk next to the keyboard. He looked at his Russian minders.

'Answer it,' Grushko said, waving his gun at him. 'And let us listen.'

Myers picked up the handset and switched it to speaker phone. The number was unknown, and he assumed it was someone from GCHQ. Colleagues often called him at the weekend with technical queries. He would remind them about GCHQ's internal IT support unit, and then do what he could to help.

'Paul Myers,' he said, as casually as possible.

Fielding detected the tension in his voice at once.

'It's Marcus Fielding. Is everything OK?'

'Fine, all fine,' Myers said, swapping the phone to his other hand and glancing at Grushko. Fielding always made his palms sweat. The added presence of the Russians was almost too much.

'Is it convenient to talk?' Fielding asked. Grushko nodded. 'I wanted to ask you about –'

'Could you hold on a moment?' Myers pressed the privacy button and turned to Grushko. 'He's going to suspect something. I'm sorry, I'm trying to act normally but this guy always makes me nervous. And he just knows when someone's lying. It's his job.'

'Then keep it brief. Does the Chief of MI6 ring you often?'

'Yes, no, I mean . . . I was seconded to Six for a few months, I worked directly for him.'

'He is an important man,' Grushko said, waving his gun at the handset. 'Talk to him.'

'Sorry,' Myers said, speaking to Fielding again. 'There was someone at the door.'

'Are you at home?' Fielding asked. He had expected him to be at work. If he was about to help the Russians again, he would be preparing to do it now. He sounded even more nervous than usual, under duress. Fielding couldn't risk asking what Marchant had requested him to do, but he still needed to give his call some purpose, a reason for Myers to be rung by a security Chief, in case he was being monitored.

'Yeah, got the weekend off.'

'I wanted to ask you about Daniel Marchant.'

Myers glanced up at Grushko, who leaned in towards him, listening intently.

'Dan? Is there any news? Was he definitely the one who was taken in London?'

'Yes. I was wondering when you saw him last, if he'd discussed anything out of the ordinary with you.'

'Is he OK?'

'We don't know. How did he seem when you last met him?'

Myers thought back to the pub, when Marchant had asked him about the MiGs. He glanced up at Grushko, who shook his head. Why did Fielding suddenly want to know? Last time they spoke he had hung up on him.

'Fine. I don't remember anything unusual. We drank too much beer and talked a lot about Leila.'

'We're working on the theory that he might have defected rather than been taken.'

'Defected? Dan?' Myers had never been good with people, but one thing in life he was certain of was Daniel Marchant's loyalty. He was about to say as much to Fielding when he saw that Grushko had sat back and was more relaxed. Myers had no idea what game Fielding was playing, but he did know when to keep his mouth shut.

'I'm afraid so,' Fielding replied. 'Listen, if you do remember anything, give me a call, will you?'

'Sure.'

In the lay-by outside Fairford, Fielding put down his phone. His rash impulse to find out more had nearly jeopardised everything. Myers was evidently about to repeat whatever he had done before for the Russians, and it sounded as if he was being babysat. If they were listening, he hoped he had said enough to confirm Marchant's defection story.

Myers placed the phone back on his desk. 'I can't believe it,' he said, as if to himself. 'Daniel Marchant defecting?'

'Is it really such a big leap for him to make?' Grushko asked. 'I am only surprised that he did not come across earlier, given the way he has been treated.'

Myers checked himself. He wanted to clear Marchant's name, tell the Russians how much his friend loved his country, but he had to shut up. Whatever was going on, Fielding and Marchant were in it together, and he didn't want to do or say anything that might compromise them. Marchant's defection had to be a cover story, otherwise Myers might as well pack his bags and emigrate.

'We have ten minutes before they reach the edge of the UK's Air Defence Identification Zone,' Grushko said, looking at his watch. 'Are you ready?'

# 97

The American Raptor took off before the Russian SU-25, accelerating down the runway to the thumping soundtrack of 'I Don't Want to Stop', by Ozzy Osbourne. It lifted off the ground and flew past the private enclosure at twenty feet, before pulling up into a vertical climb that had the crowds gasping. A pugnacious American had taken over the commentary box, his wild WWF style of delivery in stark contrast to the clipped tones of the ex-RAF pilot who had introduced the earlier aircraft.

'Ladies and gentlemen, I present the most feared combat aircraft in the world, the fifth-generation F-22 Raptor,' the commentator said, rolling out the Rs. 'This awesome aircraft enjoys superiority in every conceivable dogfight scenario. It has no rivals. There is no battlefield that the Raptor cannot dominate. There is no battlefield that the Raptor *will* not dominate. Designed without compromise to sweep our skies of all threats, keeping the peace through strength.'

The Georgian delegation had been joined by a posse of US military top brass and senior executives from the global arms industry. Acting against the CIA's advice, the US Secretary of Defense had also flown in to join the celebrations. Not everyone was pleased to see him, as he had halted future production of the $155-million Raptor, but his presence was a sign of the strategic importance of the Georgian deal.

After the Raptor came the SU-25, taking off without a sound-track and eliciting barely disguised disdain from the American commentator.

'Ladies and gentleman, a plane from another era, a mudfighter from the past, a relic of the Cold War, the SU-25, known without affection in the West as the Frogfoot. In a moment, the two planes will pass from left to right along the display line, where the quantum difference in technology will be plain for all to see.'

'Frogfoot One, time for your farewell tour,' Major Bandon, the American pilot, announced over the r/t as both planes banked at the far end of the runway.

'Copy that, Raptor One,' the young Georgian pilot replied, peeling away. The plan was to put the Raptor through its paces, while the SU-25 took a sanctioned tour of southern Britain before returning for the mock dogfight. 'Good luck.'

'Thank you, Frogfoot. Only sorry you won't be here to see the fun and games.'

'Doing anything special while I'm away? To please our generals?'

'A few tail slides, paddle turns and muscle climbs, the usual. Maybe a power loop or two. If you take your time, I might even pull a Pugachev cobra at the finish. There's been too much talk in your neck of the woods that we Americans can't get it up.'

'Dream on, Raptor One. Out.'

'And go to hell,' the American said to himself as he watched the SU-25 head off to the east. He knew the pilot was from Georgia, one of America's new allies, but the plane was Russian, and old habits died hard.

# 98

Marchant no longer thought that he had a strong stomach. He had been sick shortly after take-off, when Dhar over-corrected a sudden lurch to the right and put the plane into a 3-G turn. For a painful few seconds, in which he had nearly blacked out, he had wondered if they might not get further than Finland, but he was starting to relax as they flew low and fast over the North Sea towards the east coast of Britain. It was the speed of their progress that he found the most disorientating. At first, it had felt as if he was being dragged along behind the aircraft, like a waterskier. Dhar had told him to look far ahead, to anticipate. Marchant was impressed by how much Sergei must have taught him. He was flying well, untroubled by the G-forces. His only concern appeared to be their ETA.

'You're a natural,' Marchant said over the intercom.

'Another two weeks of training and you wouldn't have been sick, but there was not enough time,' Dhar replied.

'What's the big rush?' Marchant asked. Dhar had synchronised watches before they left, and had regularly asked him to call out the minutes and seconds.

'There is an important air show today. At a place called Fairford. It only happens once a year. I don't think they would have delayed it while I improved my flying skills.'

'Are we topping the bill?' Marchant asked, calculating the implications. He knew the air show well, having been taken there by his father when he was a child. Red Arrows and Airfix models, candyfloss and Concorde. Fairford held less happy memories, too. It was where he had flown from with a hood over his head and shackles on his feet, when the Americans had renditioned him to a black site in Poland. But his first thought now was of the number of people on the ground. Tens of thousands of potential casualties.

'That's one way of putting it.'

'Sergei mentioned collateral.'

'I know.'

'What did he mean?'

There was a long pause. Marchant adjusted his helmet and oxygen mask, thinking that contact had perhaps been lost.

'One of our LGBs is a dirty bomb.'

Marchant felt sick. It was only a few feet away from him. He thought of the contamination on the ground, the years of cleaning up. A thousand-pound dirty bomb exploding in the middle of a packed crowd would kill hundreds, but many more would fall ill afterwards from radiation sickness. And no terrorist had ever deployed one before. It had become the Holy Grail, not so much for the number of people it killed as for its propaganda value. The problem was its difficulty to assemble, unless you could tap into the caesium resources of a country like Russia.

'And Sergei didn't approve?'

Another silence.

'My mother loved Britain. For a long while I never knew why. Now I know her loyalties were misplaced. Our father's heart beat for another country. One day I will tell her. Despite Iraq, despite Afghanistan, I never hated Britain in the same way that I detest America. Perhaps I was blind, but it gave shelter to many brothers. Now it has become a legitimate target.'

342

'Its people or its politicians?'

Dhar said nothing. Marchant wished he could see his face, gauge his mood from his eyes. It was hard to tell from his voice alone, particularly over the plane's intercom, but something had shifted. Hairline cracks were appearing. Should Marchant tell him now about their father and Primakov? He instinctively glanced around the cockpit, above and to the sides, checking for threats. Marchant felt vulnerable with his back to Dhar, but there was nothing his half-brother could do except listen. He couldn't kill Marchant, physically throw him out of the plane, unless he could operate both ejector seats.

'Vasilli Grushko was right to be suspicious of Primakov,' Marchant said over the intercom, taking the risk. He would tell it to him straight, give the bare facts. 'What he found in the KGB archives was true. Primakov used to work for MI6. Our father signed him up in Delhi more than thirty years ago. In order for him to recruit Primakov, our father let himself be recruited by the Russians. It was a risk, and once or twice he handed over more than he should have, more than Primakov was giving to London. But he never once betrayed Britain. All the intel was about America.'

There was another long silence. Again Marchant began to think the intercom was faulty, and adjusted his helmet. He felt so defence-less with his back to Dhar.

'How do you know this?' Dhar eventually said, almost in a whisper.

'I've seen the file. Moscow Centre thought it had the Chief of MI6 on its books, when in fact Primakov was working for us. He was, right up until the moment he died.'

Marchant closed his eyes, imagining Dhar's face behind him. He had to keep it together, not let Primakov's death choke him up.

'Until the moment you shot him,' Dhar said.

'I'm my father's son, Salim. I've never stopped working for MI6, or believing in Britain. My defection was hollow, nothing more than an elaborate charade, a way of meeting you, my brother.'

'Is there no truth in your Western life? Is everything lies?' The aircraft rocked in a pocket of turbulence.

'Our father disliked America. There was nothing false about that. If the CIA had ever found out what he was telling the Russians about them, he would have been arrested and tried for treason, if they didn't torture him to death first. I dislike America too. I mistrust its military foreign policy, its corporate and cultural power, its fundamental values, the way it's started to define what it means to be human. But our father loved Britain with a passion, just as I do. Your mother wasn't misguided. She was right. And she isn't in the hands of the CIA. She's safe, in Britain. I give you my word, just as I gave it to her.'

Marchant was bluffing now, but he was confident that Shushma hadn't been with Spiro for long in Madurai, that it had just been a ruse by Fielding to get him into the right mental place. And Lakshmi wouldn't have allowed any harm to come to Shushma, he was sure of that. Despite everything, he realised how much he had come to trust her.

'So you lied to me about my mother too,' Dhar said.

'I had no choice. Unlike you. What is our exact target? Why the dirty bomb, the air-to-air missiles?'

'Do you know why I agreed to bring you along today?'

'Tell me.'

'Because I discovered that Fairford is close to Tarlton, where our father lived, where you grew up with your other brother. I wanted you to show me the village as we flew over, point out the house. It is 18.5 kilometres due west of the airfield.'

Marchant was taken aback by the way Dhar's mind worked. Everything was thought out, had a reason. For a moment, his task seemed hopeless, but he had to turn around the *jihadi* juggernaut.

'I can still show you. Tarlton's a beautiful place. We used to play in the orchard, Sebbie and me, throw apples into the long grass behind our father's back, pretend the rustling sound was approaching tigers. He was always fooled – at least, he said he was. Do you know what his wishes were? Why he asked Primakov to bring you and me together? He wanted you to work for MI6. He didn't expect you to change your views on America – he shared many of them himself, as I do. It's what unites all three of us. He just hoped to explore some common ground. Find out what each side wants from the other. We need a back channel into the global *jihad*, just as you need one with the West. It's what our father most wanted, Salim.'

After another long pause, Dhar eventually spoke. 'I'll be of no use to anybody if I don't go through with this today. The *jihadi* who almost shot the US President, who almost –'

'Almost what? Tell me the precise target.'

But before Dhar could speak, a deafening noise above the cockpit made Marchant duck. He turned around and saw a jet fighter disappearing into the distance.

'What the hell was that?' Marchant asked.

'Another SU-25. From the Georgian air force. And only thirty seconds late. *Inshallah*, our time has come.'

# 99

The Aerospace Battle Manager on duty at RAF Boulmer had been tracking the solitary Russian jet for some time now, ever since the Finns and Noggies had flagged up a warning. It was heading from the north-east directly towards the UK's ADIZ at 600 mph, and was running out of time to alter course. In a few minutes it would be flying over the Humber estuary. Of equal interest was another trace heading towards the coast in exactly the opposite direction. He had run a check on its assigned squawk transponder code, and it appeared to be an authorised aircraft flying out of the Royal International Air Tattoo at Fairford. It was north of its permitted flyzone, but what concerned him more was that it was on a near-collision course with the incoming jet.

He had been off-duty when his colleague had cocked up over the MiG-35s, but everyone at RAF Boulmer had been dragged over the coals afterwards. So he didn't hesitate to call up Air Command at High Wycombe and recommend that two Typhoons be scrambled from RAF Coningsby to intercept, identify and report. Their reaction made him break out into a cold sweat. There were no incoming or outgoing military jets showing up on Air Command's Recognised Air Picture for the region.

\*     \*     \*

The crowd at Fairford was loving the Raptor display, particularly in the main hospitality marquee, where the Georgian delegation was now drunk on the spectacle as well as their wine. Each manoeuvre was accompanied by a thumping soundtrack: 'Saturday Night's All Right for Fighting', by Nickelback, for the high-speed pass; 'Come Back Around', by Feeder, for the J-turn.

'Major Brandon will now utilise the awesome vector thrust of the twin engines to literally rip the aircraft through the vertical and back to a level flight,' the commentator continued. 'Ladies and gentlemen, I give you the power loop.'

The mood was no less ebullient in the static display behind the Georgians. A child in a pram wearing big red headphones arched his back and clapped with joy as the plane made another fly-by in a weapons-bay pass. An American crew in their flying suits was perched on the wings of a Lancer B1 Bomber that had flown in overnight from Texas. They were enjoying the sunshine, heads rocking to the music as they admired their compatriot's performance.

'Supercruise speed?' one of them asked.

'1.7,' another replied, shielding his eyes from the sun as he tracked the plane into the distance. 'He's yanking and banking the hell out of it today.'

The commentator came over the loudspeaker system again as the Raptor turned sharply at the western end of the runway.

'The pilot will be experiencing something approaching 9G as this fine fifth-generation fighter sweeps through a flat 360,' he said. 'On his return to the display line, Major Brandon will perform a slow high-alpha pass at 120 knots, then hit the afterburner and accelerate into a near-vertical climb to 10,000 feet in a manoeuvre we proudly call the "muscle climb". After that he will be rejoined by the SU-25 Frogfoot, which should be heading back towards the airfield from the east any time now – providing it hasn't run out of gas.'

\* \* \*

Fielding rang through to Armstrong as he watched the Raptor climb vertically into the sky at the end of the runway. He remembered seeing the Vulcan do something similar in the 1970s.

'Can you hear me? It's Marcus. Any news?' Armstrong was sitting at the COBRA table in the underground crisis-management centre, monitoring developments.

'Air Command has just given the order to scramble two Typhoons from Coningsby,' she said. 'There's been a similar systems error with the Recognised Air Picture. They're not taking any chances this time. It seems a rogue Russian jet is heading your way fast.'

'It's Dhar,' Fielding said quietly.

'A ground sighting in the Midlands suggests it's a two-seater.'

'Dhar and Daniel Marchant.'

'I hope to God you know what you're doing, Marcus. The Typhoons have orders to shoot it down.'

The Aerospace Battle Manager at RAF Boulmer was relieved that the two Typhoons had been scrambled, but he was still dealing with the most stressful day of his professional life. The Russian jet was now deep inside British airspace, flying fast and low towards southern England, but what had happened to the outgoing Georgian aircraft? It seemed to have vanished moments after it had passed the Russian one, just off the coast. What was more, the incoming Russian jet was broadcasting exactly the same transponder squawk code as the one that had disappeared off his screens.

He put an emergency call through to the coastguard, informing them that a plane had gone down ten miles off the coast of Grimsby, and then he rang Air Command again.

Major Brandon glanced down at the crowds as he flew over them in a dedication pass. After banking, he looked across the airfield towards the east. Frogfoot One had enjoyed its farewell tour of the British countryside and would shortly be rejoining the air show for the finale, a dogfight that would leave no one in any doubt about the superiority of the Raptor. He didn't really know why the Georgian pilot was bothering to show up again for a humiliating few minutes. It was just a shame that he was only carrying dummy weapons today. Two clicks over the r/t alerted him to someone else on frequency, and he saw a familiar shape closing from the east at his altitude.

'Welcome back, Frogfoot One. You've missed quite a party. Give me thirty more seconds before I'm on your six o'clock. I'm about to pull that Pugachev cobra we were talking about. One final treat to keep your generals sweet.'

Dhar heard the American, but chose to remain silent, just giving two more taps on the PTT switch to signal his assent. He was confident that everyone – the crowds, air-traffic control and the American pilot – would assume that his aircraft was the same one that had left the air show twenty minutes earlier. After all, SU-25s weren't a common sight over the Cotswolds. To look at, it was identical – except that the weapons slung beneath its wings were not dummies. A few moments ago, he had held a brief conversation with the control tower at RAF Fairford. The exchange had passed without suspicion, their warm welcome back confirming that the switch of squawk codes had been successful. Dhar had never met the brave Georgian pilot who had been recruited by the SVR. All he knew was that he had orders to ditch his plane and eject after passing him over the North Sea.

'Frogfoot One, do you copy me?' The American said. 'I'm proceeding east to west along the display line, with all due respect to Viktor Pugachev. Watch and learn, Frogfoot.'

Dhar could see the Raptor in the far distance now, rearing its nose as it seemed to almost stall, exposing its underbelly. He flicked the weapons select switch on the stick, just as he had done countless times on the simulator with Sergei. Only this time it was for real. The Vympel under his left wing was a heat-seeking air-to-air missile that travelled at two and a half times the speed of sound. It was packed with a 7.25-kilogram warhead and had a maximum range of twenty-nine kilometres. Dhar was less than two kilometres away now, and closing. Minimum engagement range was three hundred metres. He looked across at the American aircraft, using his helmet-mounted sighting system to designate the target. And then he fired.

Marchant thought they had been hit when the missile scorched away from under the plane's left wing. Then he realised what was going on.

'Jesus, Salim, what are you doing?'

'Exploring the common ground.'

# 100

At first, the crowd assumed that the missile streaking across the sky was all part of the spectacular show, and a cheer went up. Major Brandon was less ecstatic. His heart missed a beat when an alarm in his cockpit warned that an incoming missile had locked on to the infra-red heat of his F-22's exhaust. His first thought was that the aircraft's flat vector nozzles were meant to disguise the heat. His second thought, honed in hours of training, was to deploy his Chemring flares, but he wasn't carrying any because their use had been banned by the air show's organisers. The last thought he ever had was that he was a sitting duck, nose stuck in the air and travelling at a hundred knots.

'Frogfoot One?' he said, a moment before the missile found its target, embedding itself deep within the left engine and then tearing it apart.

Dhar took the plane on a long sweeping arc away from the airfield, glancing down to his right at the plume of smoke rising from the runway.

'Now we drop our first bomb.'

'Salim, we've got to stop this!' Marchant shouted. 'We're going to be shot down any minute. Every fighter in southern Britain will have been scrambled.'

'Frogfoot One, please identify yourself,' a voice from the control tower demanded on the military emergency frequency. Dhar flicked off the radio. He could see the flames of the Raptor now, the wreckage on the runway, as he continued to bank around to the east. He thought of Sergei, the photos he had shown him of his own crash, the carnage as his MiG had skidded through the crowds, carving families apart. The Raptor had broken up over the runway, causing little collateral damage. But Dhar knew that what he was about to do now would not be so precise. The hospitality marquees were to the left of the runway, just before the control tower. The American military had assembled *en masse* in the largest tent, entertaining their Georgian counterparts. Enemies didn't get more legitimate.

'Tell me the target,' Marchant said, desperate to engage Dhar. The aircraft had levelled out now, and was about to begin a low approach from the east.

'The Georgian government is converting their country into a Christian one, turning their back on our Muslim brothers to appease America.'

'Are they here? The Georgians?'

'In the marquee next to the control tower. Here to buy F-16s from the Americans.'

So that was why they had flown to Fairford. There was a logic to Dhar, a rationale, however dark, that demanded Marchant's respect, if not his understanding. He knew that neither the SVR nor Georgia's Muslim population was keen on the country's realignment with America. Had Dhar done enough already in the eyes of other *jihadis* to cool the relationship? Marchant looked down through the canopy. The SU-25's cockpit visibility was not great, but he could make out a row of stalls, packed with people, immediately behind the hospitality marquees.

'Don't do it, Salim. It's too crowded. Too many innocent lives will be lost.'

Marchant knew he had to keep talking, try to sow seeds of doubt. Despite his self-assurance, Dhar would be questioning his own actions. Marchant had read enough intelligence reports from Guantanamo. Even the hardest *jihadis* deliberated about the legitimacy of targets, wrestled with how to determine the innocent.

'The dirty bomb is not for now,' Dhar said, flicking the weapons select switch on the stick. He opted for the conventional LGB and locked onto the marquee with his gunsight, letting the Klyon laser range-finder retain the target as he approached. Then he closed his eyes and thought again about his father. Deep down, below the layers of prayer and wishful thinking, he knew that Marchant had spoken the truth. It had been too much to hope for the Chief of MI6 to betray the West. At least, in his father's anti-American stance, there had been some evidence of their shared blood. Stephen Marchant would have approved of the swaggering Raptor's destruction, the silencing of the hysterical commentator and the incessant rock music.

'This is not what our father would have wanted,' Marchant said, scanning the skies. 'You've made your point, given America a bloody nose, screwed the arms deal. Now let's get out of here.'

Dhar was determined to release the bomb as the plane flew fast along the display line. He had rehearsed it so many times on the simulator in Kotlas and above the ranges of Archangel with Sergei. *Please, if you can spare the lives of twenty-three civilians, then do it. For me, for the Bird.* Innocent lives would be lost, but the military target was legitimate. Generals, Georgian and American, chests blooming with medal ribbons, plotting their next assault on the Muslim world.

But as he looked down at the marquee, his mind surging with thoughts of Sergei, his father, Daniel, he pulled up at the last moment into a steep climb, the G-forces pushing him back into his seat as if in reprimand for the destruction he had been about to unleash.

'If I am to retain any credibility,' Dhar said quietly, as he levelled out at one thousand feet and turned towards the north-west, 'I must go through with my final target.'

# 101

Fielding had watched with horror from the lay-by as the Raptor was engulfed in a fireball and fell from the sky. His thoughts were with the pilot, but he was also trying to calculate the damage to Britain's relationship with America should it ever be known that Daniel Marchant, a serving MI6 officer, was with Salim Dhar in the cockpit of the other jet, as he now suspected was the case.

He had to redo those calculations as he saw the SU-25 turn and begin a second approach. If Dhar attacked the marquee where the American Secretary of Defense was holding court with the Georgians, Fielding knew his career was over. But as the aircraft drew close to its target, he began to sense that his faith in Daniel Marchant had not been misplaced. Dhar was leaving it very late to strike at the marquee. Had Marchant talked him out of it?

His phone rang as the aircraft passed low over the control tower and pulled into a steep climb. It was Harriet Armstrong.

'Is it true? Dhar's just taken out an American fighter jet?'

'It's true.'

'And Marchant's with him?'

'Yes, he is.'

'Jesus, Marcus, what the hell do I tell COBRA? And the Americans?'

'Tell them that Marchant's just saved the life of the US Secretary of Defense, as well as a tent full of American and Georgian top brass.'

He hung up as he watched the SU-25 disappear into the distance, wondering why Dhar was now heading north-west towards Cheltenham.

The Russians had left Paul Myers shortly after he had begun to corrupt the Recognised Air Picture. He didn't know how many jets would attempt to violate the UK's airspace while its defences were compromised, or what their mission was. All he knew was that Daniel Marchant was involved in some way.

'I suggest you keep the window open for as long as you can,' Grushko had said, just before he departed with his colleague. 'Unless you want your friend Daniel Marchant to be shot out of the sky.'

Myers was suspicious that they weren't remaining with him. It was true that he didn't want to do anything that might put Marchant in more danger than he was in already. Again he tried to think what Marchant would want, and decided to interfere with the Recognised Air Picture for as long as he could. But the Russians had been in an unseemly hurry to leave.

'Have you lived in Cheltenham long?' Grushko had asked just before he left.

'Ten years, maybe longer.'

'It's strange. The poorer parts remind me of Chernobyl, where I grew up. Before the accident, of course.'

After twenty minutes of delaying and corrupting the RAP, Myers had left his flat and driven to work. He wasn't due in until Monday, but the experience of being held hostage in his own home had left him feeling shaken and vulnerable. He also needed a change of scene after being cooped up in his airless bedroom for twelve hours. GCHQ was bright and airy and, as the director often reminded staff, one of the most secure work environments in the country. He would walk the Street, buy some food and sit out on the grassy knoll in the sunny central enclosure. Then he would ring Fielding back and tell him what had happened, although he suspected that the Vicar already knew.

'Just so you know,' Armstrong said, back on the phone to Fielding, who had ordered his driver to head at speed for Cheltenham, 'there are now six jets closing in on Dhar with orders to shoot him down. I've stressed to the Chief of Defence Staff that an officer of MI6 is also on board, but he has been deemed expendable. In your absence, Ian Denton has signed off on it. I'm sorry.'

'I'd be grateful if you could pass on my objections to COBRA,' Fielding said. Denton's decision surprised him. His deputy should have rung him first. 'Salim Dhar doesn't do things by halves. He didn't try to assassinate the American Ambassador in Delhi, he pointed his rifle at the President. He thinks big. Before we take out the jet, it's worth considering the payload it might be carrying. There's a chance Dhar's armed with a nuclear weapon, or possibly a dirty bomb, which would rather spoil the Gloucestershire countryside if we shoot him down. The Russians are behind this, remember. The difficulty of sourcing radioactive isotopes isn't a factor here.'

'Are you saying we should just hold fire and watch while a state-sponsored terrorist flies around Britain attacking targets at will?'

'Of course I'm bloody not. But we need to establish contact with Marchant first, before we risk triggering a major nuclear incident.'

# 102

'There it is,' Marchant said, looking down at the circular silver roof of GCHQ, shimmering like an urban crop circle on the outskirts of Cheltenham. Its grassy centre was surrounded by the ring of the main building and, further out, radials of parked cars. The town was to the east, and the M5 to the west. It had taken two minutes to fly the twenty miles from Fairford. For a moment, Marchant thought the building would make an excellent substitute for Wimbledon's Centre Court.

'So this is the place that has led the global hunt for me and many of my brothers,' Dhar said. 'It is smaller than I thought.'

Marchant was thinking fast now, measuring opportunities against risks. His priority was to persuade Dhar not to drop a dirty bomb on a densely populated area. But it was also evident that Dhar was willing to consider working for MI6. This was a hope that Marchant had held onto ever since he had first met Dhar in India more than a year ago, when he had found out they were half-brothers. It was why he had travelled to Morocco, chased leads into the High Atlas, flown to Madurai and faked his defection to Russia. And it was why Nikolai Primakov had died in a draughty hangar in Kotlas. He owed it to his father's old friend to turn Dhar.

The risks of running him would be considerable, not least the problem of London's relationship with Washington, which would want his head more than ever after the attack at Fairford. Dhar would never stop waging his war against America. If he did choose to share information with Britain, spare the land of his father from the full wrath of his *jihad*, the rest of the world must never know.

But would Dhar's stock have risen after taking out the US Air Force's pride and joy at an air show? It was brave and spectacular, in a *Top Gun* sort of way, but not exactly another 9/11. If Dhar was to be an effective British asset, he would have to do more. Which was why Marchant was desperately trying to think through the implications of an attack on GCHQ.

A dirty bomb dropped into the middle of the doughnut would partially disable the facility for months, if not years, and would be a massive propaganda victory for *jihadis* everywhere. Air filters and life-support systems in the underground computer halls were designed to ensure that basic services continued in the event of a surface nuclear attack, but the disruption to the offices above ground would still be considerable. Caesium was particularly difficult to clean off metal surfaces such as the building's aluminium roof.

Then there was the population of Cheltenham to consider. It was too late to evacuate the town, even if it was possible. The panic as people fled after an attack would cause chaos as well as deaths; and then there would be those who died later from radiation-induced cancer.

'A conventional thousand-pound bomb would do it,' Marchant said. It seemed that it had been Dhar's plan to drop the standard LGB on Fairford and the dirty bomb on Cheltenham: one for the SVR, one for himself, both sides happy. Marchant had talked him out of the first; now he had to do the same with GCHQ.

'Do what?'

'Give you front-page headlines around the world and destroy much of the building.'

'But I hate this place, and the people who work there,' Dhar said, banking the plane around to the south. 'They are the foot-soldiers of Echelon. Do you know how it feels to be hunted day and night, searching the skies for satellites and drones, not knowing if you can breathe at night for fear of being heard?'

'You tricked them easily enough about your location in North Waziristan,' Marchant said. He was surprised to hear Dhar namecheck Echelon, the Western computer network that sorted and analysed captured signals traffic. The hunted had finally found the hunter.

'That was the fools at Fort Meade. They are easier to shake off. The people down there have been on my tail for years. I will never have a better opportunity.'

'We'll be shot out of the sky any second now, trust me. But if they know we've got a dirty bomb on board, they might just think twice before firing.' Marchant paused. 'Drop the conventional bomb on GCHQ.'

Dhar seemed to hesitate, long enough to give Marchant encouragement. It was so frustrating to be sitting in front of him and not face-to-face. A conventional bomb was the lesser of two evils. Marchant knew that the GCHQ building had been built to withstand a plane crashing into its roof. The glass was bombproof, too. With a bit of luck, a thousand pounds of explosive dropped into the central garden would cause only minimal damage. Again, it was about finding common ground.

Dhar would get his headlines, and it might buy them some time to escape, although the SVR's exit strategy did not inspire confidence. The plan was to head south-west after Cheltenham and eject in the Bristol Channel, where Dhar would be picked up by a Russian-manned trawler. Marchant would have to make his own way in the water.

'I need to use the radio, tell traffic control we're carrying a dirty bomb,' Marchant said, but he was interrupted by an alarm signal in both cockpits. The aircraft's internal and external fuel tanks were almost empty. 'And I need to ring my friend at GCHQ, get everyone to move away from the windows.'

'No warnings.'

Before Marchant could argue, Dhar had banked again and was flying straight towards the building.

'I need to call traffic control,' Marchant insisted.

'Afterwards,' Dhar said, as he locked his gunsight onto the grassy heart of GCHQ.

# 103

Paul Myers heard the jet overhead, and thought its engine sounded different from the Typhoons and Tornados that were a regular sight in the skies above Gloucestershire. He glanced up as he walked past the smokers' pagoda and headed back into the main building, but the sky was bright and he couldn't see anything. Besides, he was still hungry, and he needed to buy something else to eat from Ritazza.

A moment later, he was lifted up and thrown through the open door with enormous force. His crumpled body landed in a heap on the smooth tiles of the Street as the sound of broken glass cascaded behind him and thoughts of Chernobyl faded from his mind.

Marchant didn't know until later whether the bomb dropped on GCHQ was conventional or radioactive. Events moved fast after Dhar banked the aircraft towards the Bristol Channel. Amid the noise of the fuel alarm, Marchant persuaded him to switch the r/t back on, and a warning came over the emergency military frequency almost immediately that their aircraft was about to be shot down.

'We have a dirty bomb on board!' Marchant barked back in reply, looking around frantically as he tried to spot the RAF jets that he assumed must be approaching. He hoped to God he was right. Even if Dhar had already released it, the threat might save their lives. 'Repeat, we are carrying a thousand-pound radioactive dispersal device.'

The pilots of the two Typhoons closing in on the SU-25 from the west heard Marchant's words. Surprised by the English accent, they referred upwards to Air Command for confirmation that they had permission to destroy the aircraft. They added that the SU-25 was losing speed and altitude, and appeared to be about to ditch in the Bristol Channel. After a brief pause, during which Air Command consulted COBRA, the order came back to hold fire. Marcus Fielding had finally managed to get through to the Chief of the Defence Staff.

In the event, there was no need for the Typhoons to deploy their missiles. Dhar had been battling to keep the aircraft airborne, and it had now become a lost cause. He had managed to reach the Bristol Channel, but they were a mile short of the planned rendezvous with the Russian trawler.

'Prepare to eject,' Dhar said calmly. Marchant realised that his ejection seat was controlled by Dhar. He could have removed him from the plane at any time. It gave him hope that Cheltenham had been spared too.

'I promise I'll take care of your mother,' Marchant said, as he closed his eyes and braced himself.

# 104

'Are you telling me that Daniel Marchant should be regarded as a hero?' Jim Spiro said incredulously, looking around the table. The Joint Intelligence Committee was at full strength, with senior intelligence officials from Canada, Australia, New Zealand, Britain and America in attendance.

'Salim Dhar was on a mission to Britain to destroy three targets,' Fielding began. 'The F-22 Raptor because it was a symbol of American military might; the delegation of Georgian and US military personnel as a thank-you to the Russians for protecting him; and GCHQ as part of his own personal crusade.'

'And he achieved two of the three,' said Spiro. 'Remind me why exactly we should be thanking Marchant?' He nodded towards the director of GCHQ on his left. 'I'm not sure Cheltenham will be putting a photo of him in their hall of fame. If any halls are still standing.'

Fielding had hoped he could let Spiro down gently, as relations with America had to continue, but it was hard to resist giving him a bumpy landing.

'We believe Dhar was carrying two air-to-air missiles, and two thousand-pound laser-guided bombs. One of them was packed with radioactive caesium-137. I don't need to remind anyone here of the devastation that would have been caused by a dirty bomb dropped either on the crowd at Fairford or on a town the size of Cheltenham. I've just come back from a debriefing with Marchant, and he confirmed that it was always Dhar's intention to drop the dirty bomb on GCHQ – a personal *bête noire* of his. As we all know, the thousand-pound bomb that struck the building was, thankfully, a conventional one, and there was only minimal structural damage and one life lost.'

'How can we be sure the bomb he didn't drop was dirty?' Spiro asked.

'Royal Navy divers have found wreckage of the SU-25 in the Bristol Channel, and are in the process of stabilising the unexploded ordnance. They've confirmed the presence of caesium-137. We're lucky it wasn't detonated by the impact of the crash.'

'So why did Dhar bother to drop anything?' the director of GCHQ asked. 'He'd clearly had a change of heart.'

'Marchant talked him out of the dirty option, but failed to persuade him to abandon the whole idea,' Fielding replied. He had to be careful what he said at this point. It was fair to say that Marchant might have been able to prevent the conventional attack too, but had been mindful of Dhar's *jihadi* credentials. A discredited Dhar would have been of no use to anyone. Nobody in the room, not even Harriet Armstrong, knew that Dhar had finally been turned, and had the potential to be the biggest asset MI6 had ever run.

'So what you're saying is that Dhar only achieved one of his original three targets,' Armstrong said, seemingly supportive.

'Correct. And for that we must thank Daniel Marchant.'

'It's all very well you guys patting each other on the back,' Spiro said. 'I've got to explain to Washington why the most advanced jet fighter ever built was taken out by a lousy lump of old Russian hardware, flown by the world's most-wanted *jihadi* and a rogue MI6 agent.'

'You can tell them that if it hadn't been for the presence of an MI6 agent in the cockpit – and, for the record, Daniel Marchant is no rogue – the damage would have been incalculably worse.'

'There's only one thing that's going to make my President happy, and that's the scalp of Salim Dhar. Are we any closer to knowing how he disappeared?'

'The helicopter that found Marchant reported nobody else in the water. The entire area continues to be searched as we speak, but so far it's as if Dhar never existed.'

Fielding was lying, of course. He had no choice. According to Marchant's debrief, the SVR had arranged for a trawler to be in the area. It had taken it a few minutes to find Dhar, as the plane had fallen short of the agreed ejection zone, but by the time the search-and-rescue helicopter had arrived, Dhar was on the trawler and heading out towards the Irish Sea.

# 105

Marchant still had a sore back from the Zvezda ejection seat, but otherwise he felt fine as he waited in one of the debriefing rooms for Fielding to return for a second visit. At Marchant's request, the helicopter had taken him to the Fort, MI6's training facility at Gosport, after picking him up from the Bristol Channel. The pilot had initially objected, but it was eventually agreed after some calls had been put through to Whitehall. Marchant had been given a physical check-up, then allowed to rest in one of the old rooms overlooking the sea, where he had studied as a new recruit with Leila.

As Marchant had explained to Fielding, he had thought Dhar was dead when he first spotted him in the water, a hundred yards away. He had released himself from his parachute and swum over to him, dreading what he might find. A dead Dhar suited America, but not Britain. But Dhar was fine, if a little groggy. Marchant had doubted whether the trawler would show up, but a forty-foot vessel registered to St Ives was soon approaching from the south-west.

'For a few moments, I thought I was going to drown,' Dhar had said.

'I know the feeling,' Marchant had replied. When he had first hit the sea and water had filled his nostrils, memories of being waterboarded had come flooding back.

'You know I cannot take you with me,' Dhar said.

'I'm not sure I'm invited,' Marchant replied, glancing at the approaching trawler. They were both shivering, speaking slowly as they trod water. 'Thanks, by the way.'

'For what?'

'For letting me come along. And for not destroying Cheltenham. Will the Russians be happy to see you?'

'No. Georgia's drunken generals will still try to impress America. But it is time for me to move on. Islam is sometimes useful to Russia, but mostly it is a threat.'

'And you never did get to see Tarlton.'

'Next time, perhaps.'

'How will you make contact? The storytellers of Marrakech?'

Dhar smiled at Marchant. 'You know me too well. My taxi is here.'

Marchant swam away as the trawler drew near. He wanted to be at a safe distance in case the SVR had already concluded that he wasn't such a committed defector after all.

'Our father, he would have approved,' Marchant called out, hoping that Dhar could still hear him. 'Family business.'

Now, as he heard someone approaching the debriefing room at Gosport, Marchant was certain that he had turned Dhar. Last time, after India, he had hoped in vain.

It was Fielding who knocked and appeared in the doorway.

'I've brought someone along to see you,' he said, slipping away as Lakshmi Meena entered the room.

'Is your arm OK?' Marchant asked as they embraced. Her wrist was in plaster, and her hug was not quite as warm as his.

'I'm fine. How about you? I went by your flat, brought you some clean clothes.'

'Thanks. Was the door open?' They both smiled. Then she kissed him gently on the lips.

'I found this, too. It had been delivered. I thought it might be important. The rest of your post was just bills.'

She held up a padded envelope, addressed to him in unfamiliar handwriting. Marchant looked at it, then put it on a table to one side.

'How's Spiro?'

'Mad at me for not preventing your so-called defection.'

'Even though I stopped him killing your Defense Secretary and his generals?'

'You still took down a $155-million Raptor. The media lapped that up.'

'I hope they're keeping me out of it.'

'It's been agreed by London and Washington to airbrush you from the story. It was getting kind of hard to explain.'

'But it was a two-seater plane.'

'The media are reporting a bold strike at the West by Salim Dhar and a *jihadi* brother.'

'Half right, at least about the brother.'

'You did well to stop him. I don't suppose you have any idea where he is now?'

'Is that you asking, or Spiro?'

'Most of the Western world.'

Marchant hoped that one day he would be able to tell her that Dhar had been turned, that Britain now had an asset at the heart of the global *jihad*.

'Is his mother safe? Shushma?' At least he could talk to Lakshmi about her.

'She's fine. Spiro handed her over to MI6 when we landed back at Brize Norton. That was always the deal with Fielding. He wants a word with you on his own, by the way. I'll get him.'

'Will you stay after that? Please?'

'Is a graduate of the Farm allowed to stay at the Fort?'

'I'm sure it could be arranged, in the interests of a special relationship.'

Two minutes later, Fielding and Marchant had stepped outside the debriefing room, leaving Lakshmi on her own, and were walking along the perimeter fence that overlooked the sea. A warm wind blew in off the water, lifting strands of Fielding's thinning hair. It was greyer than Marchant remembered.

'You did well,' Fielding said. 'It was a tough call to make about GCHQ, but the right one. Dhar's value has soared on the international *jihadi* markets. The chatrooms were ecstatic after his attempt on the President's life in Delhi. This time they're beside themselves. They never thought someone could strike at the heart of Western intelligence.'

'I gather there were some casualties.'

'I wanted to talk to you about that. While the government's been playing down the damage, our stations abroad are exaggerating it to the foreign media. Well-placed sources are talking about cover-ups, crucial computer networks down for months, morale at GCHQ at an all-time low.'

'And the truth?'

'One death, thirty injuries. Minimal structural damage. But I'm afraid Paul Myers took quite a hit.'

'Is he OK?'

'Conscious, a little confused. He should make a full recovery. He'd been in the central garden, but he was hungry, and was on his way back inside to get something to eat when the bomb struck.'

'Saved by a doughnut.'

They both laughed and walked on, watching the wind whip off the tops of the waves.

'And you're confident that Dhar is ours?' Fielding eventually asked.

'This time I am. We found some common ground.'

'Coastguard located a drifting trawler just off the coast, by the way. Three dead Russians on board, no sign of Dhar.'

Marchant thought back to the sight of Dhar bobbing in the water. Even then, half drowned and semi-conscious, he had been full of confidence.

'If this proves successful, we have your father to thank,' Fielding continued. 'You know we couldn't have done it without him. A long time ago, he realised where the world was heading, and saw in his two sons a possible solution.'

'The old man made some mistakes along the way.'

'Did he?'

'Trusting Hugo Prentice.'

'We all did that.'

'The silly thing is, I miss Hugo, despite everything he did.'

'*For while the treason I detest, the traitor still I love.* Lakshmi's waiting for you. Enjoy your evening. I have a meeting back in London with Denton. If I was a more suspicious man, I might think he was after my job.'

# 106

Marchant couldn't sleep that night. It wasn't that the Fort's beds were more uncomfortable than he had remembered, or because he was sharing his with Lakshmi. They had made love after dinner in the room in a way that had restored his faith in women. In some ways it had been cathartic to sleep with Lakshmi in the place where he had first done so with Leila, the woman who had so wholly deceived him.

Lakshmi had told him stories of her childhood, and he had opened up about his father and Sebastian in a way he hadn't done for years. The only person he didn't talk about was Dhar.

Now, as he lay there listening to the sea wind rattling the Fort's old leaded windows, his hand on Lakshmi's sleeping thigh, he remembered the package she had brought from his flat. He slipped out of bed, careful not to wake her, and unwrapped it by the moonlight of the window.

His hands turned cold when he saw what was inside. It was the sketch of the nude that had been for sale in Cork Street, number 14, the one that had been used as a signal by Nikolai Primakov. Someone had stuck half a red sticker onto the corner of the glass, like the one that had once denoted that it was under offer and that the meeting with Primakov was on.

Marchant glanced across at Lakshmi, then turned the picture over.

There was some writing on the back giving the gallery details, the price and the artist. He inspected it more closely, and saw that the brown adhesive tape had been slit open and resealed down one side. He reached across for a knife from their dinner, the remains of which had not been cleared from the room, and cut the backing open. Inside was a letter. He slid it out and read.

*By the time you read this I will be drinking Bruichladdich and eating grain-fed Nebraskan steak at the great Goodman's in the sky. I suspect there will be no other way to bring you and Salim together. Have no regrets. I don't. Your father was a good man who had faith in both of his remaining sons to do the right thing. He had faith in me too, and I hope I have had the courage to repay it. He saw the future, and in his sons he saw a way forward, an opportunity to stop the conflict. It is up to you now.*

*What I have to tell you today, as I prepare to leave London for the last time to meet you at Kotlas, is something that I wanted to say in person, but the risks were always too high when we met in London. Moscow Centre has an MI6 asset who helped the SVR expose and eliminate a network of agents in Poland. His codename was Argo, a nostalgic name in the SVR, as it was once used for Ernest Hemingway.*

*The Polish thought that Argo was Hugo Prentice, a very good friend of your father, and I believe a close confidant of yours. He was shot dead on the orders of the AW, or at least of one of its agents. Hugo Prentice was not Argo.*

*That mistake was a tragedy, destroying his reputation and damaging your father's. The real Argo is Ian Denton, deputy Chief of MI6. The SVR asked Denton to meet you at the airport on your return from India, but Fielding, by chance, had already sent Prentice. Go carefully. Denton's treachery is destined to extend much further than Poland.*

Marchant put the letter down. His first thought was to ring Fielding, but there was no knowing if the line was secure. He went over to the door and checked that it was locked. Then he walked to the window and glanced around. It was a full harvest moon, and its reflection stretched out across the water from the horizon. No one was about, and he knew the Fort was secure, but old instincts had kicked in. If Denton was working for Moscow, then no one was safe from the Russians, least of all him. He had tricked the SVR into a false defection, and sabotaged Dhar's Russian-sponsored attack on the Georgian generals.

He put the letter back in its hiding place behind the nude sketch, and climbed into bed. Suddenly he felt exhausted, more tired than he had felt for years. Lakshmi was stirring. Marchant lay there, thinking of Prentice and Primakov, friends of his father, both of them now dead. Then he turned and hugged Lakshmi, linking a leg over hers.

'Is everything OK?' she whispered, half asleep.

But he didn't answer. He didn't want to lie any more, not to her. Instead, he held her head gently between both hands and kissed her warm lips. Eventually, after they had made love again, he sat up in bed.

'There's something I need to tell you,' he said, thinking of Dhar, the burden of running him on his own. He could tell her now. She wasn't like Leila. Hadn't Fielding said she could be trusted? Then he thought of Denton, the threat he presented. He could tell her about him, too, confide his fears. He wasn't sure he could cope with the loneliness of deceit any more, the isolation of espionage. He craved companionship, the truth of honest love.

'What is it?' Lakshmi asked. Marchant paused, looking at her lying naked in the moonlight. Then he spoke.

'There was once a king called Shahryar, whose wife was unfaithful to him. He executed her, and from then on he believed that all women were the same, until finally he met a virgin called Scheherazade, who told a thousand and one stories to save her own life.'

'And did he trust her?'

'He did.'

Lakshmi looked at Marchant for a moment, her eyes moistening. 'Was that all you wanted to tell me?'

'That's all.'

# ACKNOWLEDGEMENTS

Many thanks to my panel of pilots, Steve Allan, Peter Shellswell, Peter Goodman, Jerry Milsom and Mike Wright. To Andy Tailby for sharing his knowledge of UAVs. To Rob and Mags Hunter, Marilyn Heilman and David Stevenson, who read early proofs. To Jane Bayley at Naturally Morocco and Said Ahmoume, who drove me over the Tizi'n'Test pass in the Atlas mountains, where this story began. To Giuseppe Zara in Sardinia. To Johnnie and all the staff at Visalam in Chettinad, south India. To Mike Strefford for his insights into mobile-phone security. To Ollie Madden and Kevin McCormick at Warner Brothers, and Steve Gaghan. To Sylvie Rabineau at Rabineau Wachter Sanford & Harris. To my agent, Claire Paterson, and Rebecca Folland, Kirsty Gordon and Tim Glister at Janklow & Nesbit. To Patrick Janson-Smith and Laura Deacon at Blue Door, and to my editor, Robert Lacey and Andy Armitage.

I am also grateful to Andrew Stock, Andrea Stock, Stewart and Dinah McLennan, Giles and Karen Whittell, Christina Lamb, Nick Wilkinson, Rob Fern, Justin Morshead, Ann Scott, C. Sujit Chandrakumar, Neil Taylor, Wendy Lewis, Charlotte Doherty, Jessica Kelly, Len Heath, Hayley, Sheri, Andrew and Deki at Karmi Farm, the three Saras and Susan, Chandar Bahadur, and Abdou id Salah. There are other people who have helped with this book but wish to remain anonymous. They know who they are and that I am indebted to them.

Finally, a big thank you to my children, Felix, Maya and Jago, and most of all to Hilary, my wife and muse. أَنت قدري.